BISON
BOOKS

Swords from The Sea

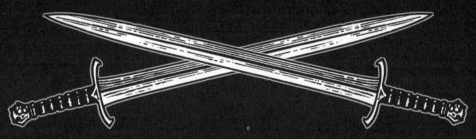

Harold Lamb

Edited by Howard Andrew Jones
Introduction by S. M. Stirling

UNIVERSITY OF NEBRASKA PRESS
LINCOLN AND LONDON

Library of Congress Cataloging-in-Publication Data

Lamb, Harold, 1892–1962.
Swords from the sea / Harold Lamb; edited by Howard Andrew Jones;
introduction by S. M. Stirling.
p. cm.
Includes bibliographical references.
ISBN 978-0-8032-2036-2 (pbk. : alk. paper)
I. Title.
PS3523.A4235S947 2010
813'.52—dc22
2009036423
Set in Trump Medieval.
Designed by R. W. Boeche & Kimberly Essman.

Contents

Foreword

This volume of Harold Lamb stories collects his historical magazine tales of seafarers, wanderers, marines, and Vikings. There are even some Cossacks here because there wasn't room for them in the final volume of Lamb's Cossack collections. Truth be told, they would have been an odd fit, as the Cossacks themselves are secondary characters to John Paul Jones, commander of Catherine the Great's navy, and the political double-dealing that proves more treacherous to Jones than the enemies on the water in two short novels of naval action upon the Crimean.

Here too is the exciting tale of a doomed search for the northeast passage by an English expedition, challenged by both the elements and a traitor in their ranks, and Lamb's last long historical, a compelling novel of the American expedition against the Barbary pirates. "The Drub-Devil March" shows that Lamb could well have kept spinning historical yarns of the quality from his *Adventure* days, if he'd had the time or inclination.

I became a Lamb fan by stages. I enjoyed his Hannibal biography so much in high school that I sought out more by him, hoping that *The Curved Saber* would contain more tales of the great Carthaginian (I didn't have a clue then that sabers weren't remotely Carthaginian). It proved instead to be a collection of Khlit the Cossack stories, which I read and loved. I didn't discover for many more years that there was a sequel volume, or that *White Falcon* featured many of the same characters, or, later still, that there were dozens of other Harold Lamb historicals that had never been collected. I was naive enough to assume that if a story hadn't been collected it must not be as good, a notion quickly dispelled when I purchased Dr. John Drury Clark's Harold Lamb *Adventure* collection from his widow. These stories were just as good—and some of them were better—than those already between book covers.

I enjoyed myself so thoroughly with those Lamb tales that I went looking for more. The earlier fiction from the more obscure pulps proved disappointing, as I've discussed elsewhere. But the first tale I read in *Collier's* impressed me mightily, a 5,000-word adventure of a Cossack, an allegedly haunted tower, a lovely princess, and a scheming noble . . . all in all, pretty grand stuff. I thought I'd found another treasure trove until I read the next *Collier's* story, which was a pretty similar tale with different stage dressing. So too was the next, and the next, and the next . . .

Maybe that's how the *Collier's* editors wanted things. Perhaps they didn't think their readers would care for historical adventure unless it was a romance. Maybe Lamb's own outlook had changed and he wanted to write stories with dependably happy endings. *Collier's*, *Pictorial Review*, and the *Saturday Evening Post* published him regularly, and all of his work began to read the same. Not everything was formula, though—from this period came "Lionheart" and "Protection," both found in *Swords from the West* (Bison Books, 2009), powerful pieces with romance as a driving theme but simply head and shoulders above the others, and one of my very favorite Lamb shorts, the moving "Devil's Song," found in *Swords of the Steppes* (Bison Books, 2007). On reading these it becomes clear that Lamb could still surprise with those characteristic twists and turns, and I can't help wondering if the change in tone was the fault of editors who were saying, "We'll take these, but try not to be so bleak next time—can you give us more *happy* endings?" How else then to explain away forgettable fare like "The Lady and the Pirate" and several others included here only in the interest of completeness?

Every good critic knows that you should judge a body of work by its most outstanding successes first. Lamb had many more successes than most writers, and it must be said that when viewed singly, most of these later stories *are* fine writing. Even if the endings are reminiscent of each other, the path to that conclusion varies. It must be remembered, too, that they originally appeared in magazines over a span of years; they were never intended to be read one after the other. Like Lord Dunsany's tales of Jorkens or Seabury Quinn's Jules de Grandin stories, they are better when they're not read back to back.

Aside from the aforementioned, my favorites from this period are Lamb's seven Viking yarns. Lamb always presents the Viking mind-set ably and gets a lot of play out of the honorable barbarian facing off against civilized schemers. His Vikings may be uneducated in the ways of civilization, but they're no fools, and they're stout warriors with flashes of grim humor.

Lamb's ability to slide into the viewpoint of other cultures seems almost effortless. Having been schooled in rationality ourselves, we sometimes forget how cultures in other times viewed the workings of the world around them. Thus, in "Elf Woman" the Icelander Rang believes without question that there is a god slumbering in his volcano, and in "Forward!" the Cossack Ivak realizes, not with surprise but with understanding, why the men he chances upon react in astonishment to his reappearance, for they had assumed him dead. Their natural conclusion isn't that he has survived his wounds and come galloping after them:

> By their bearing they were outlaws of the band, and their jaws dropped when they saw my face. Afterward I remembered that they must have thought me dead, and when the big black rushed on them in the eye of the rising sun they believed a bloody specter had come up out of Father Dnieper to settle their hash.

Magic and the supernatural are woven throughout the belief systems of these cultures; through the eyes of Lamb's characters, commonplace events can take on supernatural significance—the sight, for instance, in "Wolf Meat," of a man on skis who seems to his observer to be flying across the face of the snow. Showing us magical thinking in this way is a technique Lamb used sparingly but well throughout his historicals, and it is a technique seldom applied by other writers.

This collection concludes with Lamb's first printed story for the magazine that published his very best historical fiction, *Adventure*. "His Excellency the Vulture" might be simpler work than some of the other material included here, but it was a leap forward for Lamb, and contains what would soon become his trademarks: clever plotting, driving action, and wily lead characters. The appendix contains an added treat. In addition to the usual letters is an essay by *Adventure* editor Arthur Sullivan Hoffman that provides a fascinating behind-the-scenes look at Lamb's drafting practices and the challenges he faced in writing and publishing.

For those in search of other Lamb stories, I hope it hardly needs to be pointed out that there are eight Bison Books collections brimming with Harold Lamb's work, and three novels of Sir Hugh and the sword of Roland (*Durandal*, *The Sea of Ravens*, and *Rusudan*) from Donald M. Grant. But if you're still wanting more Harold Lamb adventure stories, *Omar Khayyam* and *Nur-Mahal* are historical novels even though they're often located in the biography section of your local library. There may yet be some stirring historical work in other pulp magazines from Lamb's early days; Jan Van Heinegen and other fans still search diligently. And lest we forget, there is a whole shelf full of histories and biographies that brought Lamb fame and recognition.

It is almost criminal that the work of such an accomplished writer has been neglected for so long, and I am grateful that Bison Books stepped forward to give this fiction the treatment it warranted. Now that all of these tales are so readily accessible, I hope it is time at last for Lamb to be recognized as a master of adventure and for his fiction to take its place upon the shelves beside Dumas and Stevenson and Lamb's contemporary, Sabatini. We Americans have waited too long to acknowledge the worth of adventure fiction and even now look askance at it more regularly than we value it. We should be proud that men like Jack London and Robert E. Howard and Harold Lamb lived and worked here and spun new fables for us.

Any educated person can write, but storytelling is a gift that must be honed and crafted. Harold Lamb had that gift, and he practiced his skill until his prose shone with a high gloss. He took his readers to new lands through the eyes of fascinating characters, and he told wonderful tales with a precision and a depth of knowledge and understanding that only a small number of writers can match. Few if any have surpassed him in his chosen field, and none has ever matched his particular voice. We should treasure these stories and his skill in telling them, but, more particularly, we should read and savor them.

Enjoy!

Acknowledgments

I would like to thank Bill Prather of Thacher School for his continued support. This volume would not have been possible without the aid of Bruce Nordstrom, who long ago provided me with Lamb's *Collier's* texts as well as his *Saturday Evening Post* and *Pictorial Review* stories and the text of "The Drub-Devil March"; Alfred Lybeck, who provided *Camp-Fire* letters and additional information; and Brian Taves for the essay written by Arthur Sullivan Hoffman. I also would like to express my appreciation for the advice of Victor Dreger, Jan van Heinegen, James Pfundstein, and Kevin Cook, gentlemen and scholars all. Lastly, I wish again to thank my father, the late Victor Jones, who helped me locate various *Adventure* magazines; and Dr. John Drury Clark, whose lovingly preserved collection of Lamb stories is the chief source of 75 percent of my *Adventure* manuscripts.

Introduction

S. M. STIRLING

One thing we tend to forget about the pulps was how *many* of them there were, and how much was written for them. The science-fiction and fantasy segments and the superhero pulps remain freshest in memory, because they were at the root of traditions that have continued and flourished ever since; and the Western, if not in such condition, is not forgotten. But in fact, the adventure pulps contained *dozens* of distinct subgenres: Western, Oriental, Detective, South Seas, any number of historical types such as the pirate story or the tale of the Crusades. And miscegenation in plenty—tales of detectives having adventures in Chinatown, for example, or of super-science set among Tibetan mahatmas (the last a specialty of Talbot Mundy, a contemporary of Lamb's), or psychic Chinese detectives involving "spicy" tales of white slavery.

Harold Lamb specialized in Oriental/historical adventures—for a number of reasons, starting with the exceedingly rare one that he was a genuine historian of the Orient, the author of well-regarded biographies of Genghis Khan and other figures, and of a redaction of the autobiography of Babur, the first Moghul emperor of India and descendant of Tamerlane. Together with a grasp of history and character far above the average of the tribe, Lamb had a driving narrative focus and a talent for depicting action as vigorous as any, even Robert E. Howard's. But he wasn't limited to stories of Cossacks and Mongols, well known though his efforts in those fields are.

The stories in this collection are largely crossover; pirates-plus-something-else, for example. We have Vikings on the Golden Horn in Constantinople . . . which really happened, by the way. Vikings actually ruled Russia for some time—the very word *Russ* originally meant *northman*—and some of their raiders actually sailed down the Volga, took ship on the Caspian, and pillaged Persia! The Byzantines were so impressed by Viking fighting abilities that they recruited a special "ax-bearing Guard," also known as the Varangians, which for centuries came mostly from the Viking countries.

We also have a story of Renaissance England—in the obscure reign of Edward VI, Elizabeth's little-remembered half brother. It's a rousing story of proto-buccaneers and obscure northerners in the terrible lands beyond the White Sea, but it also illustrates how Lamb actually *knew* history, not just the high points that other writers instinctively reached for. Not for him the well-known exploits of the Elizabethan sea-dogs; instead he sets his story a generation earlier, when the English made their first tentative steps to break the hold the Iberian peoples had on the routes to the world beyond Europe.

Lamb also had a taste and talent for centering his fiction upon the unusual hero. For one thing, he generally avoided the noblemen who populated so much of historical fiction—and often enough the sweet noblewomen. He was more likely to take a battered middle-aged Scot or a Venetian flower girl as his companion—or to match John Paul Jones with a Cossack and set them on the Black Sea!

Another notable feature of Lamb's adventure stories is that they are much more like an actual adventure than most—that is, they're full of discomfort, misery, and danger. The end never feels predestined; they have a sense of brooding *risk* that's unusual. When the Barbary pirates swarm in, you feel the terror that caused the hill-towns all around the Mediterranean to be sited high up for the sake of defense, not aesthetics.

I've said that Lamb wrote historical fiction; but in a way, all his fiction was historical in another sense: he had a deep awareness of the depth of time. A tale of a "modern" American soldier in Turkey—set in the 1950s, and so growing historical to us!—draws parallels with the same city in the age of Justinian and Belisarius, fourteen hundred years before. The Cathedral of Holy Wisdom plays a role in it, and the gallery above the nave. Just as an aside, there's runic graffiti scratched there, from when the Byzantine emperor's Varangian bodyguards waited out the ceremonies by scratching "Yngvi Was Here" in the marble! The sheer otherness of the past is there, and also the constants—love, hate, the intrigues and treachery of the powerful, whether emperors or Viking kings or Hansa merchants, and the rarity of honor and trust.

With Harold Lamb, the whole bright tapestry of the past is open to you. There's never been a better guide!

Longsword

When they brought Irene before the Caesar, he looked at her in silence. He wanted to be rid of her forever.

But Irene's hair gleamed like pallid gold; her eyes reminded him of green sea water. Her slight young body held itself erect before him. She was utterly still, in her wayward pride. The Caesar wished that she were not so lovely. People would remember her, if she disappeared.

The Caesar, John Dukas, supreme commander of the armed hosts of the Byzantine Empire, was quite capable of making people vanish into thin air. He had at his command certain obscure assassins, Asiatic slave dealers, and eminent physicians. Not long ago he had executed in public Mikhail Comnenus, the father of Irene Comnena, who had in his veins the blood of the Emperor, and had rebelled against the Emperor, who was the cousin of John Dukas.

Irene, the only child of the dead rebel, remained to be disposed of. Otherwise she would in all probability bear children of her own, who would nourish the death of their grandfather in their minds. The Emperor himself had ordered that she should be made away with, but he had not indicated how this was to be done.

"What would you like, Irene Comnena?" he asked gently. "To be sent to the house of a friend? What friend?"

The girl did not answer. She was afraid that this Caesar who sat in a chair shaped like a throne and who wore a blue mantle almost the hue of the imperial purple intended to trick her with words. Besides, she had no real friends in Constantinople.

"You must have a protector, Irene."

She shook her head. The only thing she wanted was to be sent back to the palace on the Pontus shore where the Judas trees were in bloom and the funny fishermen sang as they dragged the nets in. But they had told her that the estates of her father belonged to the Emperor now. She was really very frightened, and pressed her fingers tightly into her palms. She did not want the protection of this quiet bronzed man with the oiled hair.

The Caesar reflected that even black slaves can be bribed to tell their secrets, and the deep waters had been known to yield up weighted bodies. The Emperor did not wish the body of this girl to be found, and if it were found, he, the Caesar, might have to take the blame.

The Caesar and the Emperor were cousins, and they hated, each one the other, like cousins. At times the Caesar wondered if that gaunt figure in pearlsewn cloth-of-gold did not possess the art of reading another's mind—even while he brooded everlastingly over books and jewels and legends of mad saints.

"Let me go away," the girl whispered.

"I will find someone," the Caesar assented, "to take you away."

When the slaves led her back to the tapestried room that was her prison, she had no longer need to appear proud. She crouched down on the window seat, sobbing convulsively, because she was alone and she had no one she dared confide in any longer.

John Dukas considered how he might find someone who could carry her beyond the borders of the empire without attracting attention. This would not be easily done, for the nobility of Constantinople was an inbred society, a few families all related more or less to the Emperor, tracing their descent back to Constantine and imperial Rome. For some seven hundred years these few families had preserved themselves and their amusements behind the triple wall of Constantinople, while barbarians overran the ruins of western Rome. Huns and Bulgars and Turks had not conquered them.

The aristocracy of the city hired other barbarians to defend them, and their greatest dread was boredom. During the seven centuries they had achieved mastery in intrigue and enlightenment in subtle vice, quite certain that beyond the circle of their intelligence lay only the darkness of Chaos.

The women especially treasured their secrets of refinement; for their bodies they had the sheer silks and the perfumes and cosmetics of all Asia. The galleys of Venice brought them rare glasses and silverware; the carpets of Tabriz and Kashan covered their floors, and at the end of their whispering galleries they could hear the gossip of the unchanging city.

These aristocrats knew Irene Comnena as a self-contained girl who preferred the country house on the Pontus to her city palace and their society; most of them knew her by sight. So John Dukas must needs smuggle her into oblivion without attracting attention. Byzantine society winked at assassination, but it never forgave bungling.

"What is that?" the Caesar asked, staring at something within the rim of the Golden Horn.

A secretary came to the window, standing respectfully behind him. Below them extended the imperial gardens, and—beyond a guarded wall—the jetties crowded with galleys and trading vessels. In a private anchorage lay the Caesar's barge, gilded and carpeted and canopied, with space for forty rowers. Upon this barge he was accustomed to journey up the Bosporus or to cross over to Chalcedon—even to take pleasure trips out to the islands. But he was looking at a strange craft coming in past the guard-ships.

It was smaller than a galley. It had a prow that reared up into a wooden dragon head much the worse for wear. Battered shields were ranged along the rail above the oars.

"Your Illustriousness," the secretary explained, "it is a dragon ship from the far northern sea."

The Caesar had never seen such a craft in Constantinople. "From what land?" he asked.

"May it please your high Excellence, from the end of all land—what is called the ultimate Thule."

John Dukas nodded as if satisfied. "Bring me a report," he said, "of its master, and its probable length of stay—" for the first time he glanced at the secretary—"Theophile."

Now the dragon ship lay in the bight of the Golden Horn. A gangboard stretched from its foredeck to a stone jetty. On the afterdeck its master sat, gazing at the lofty towers and the mighty domes of such a city as he had never seen in his days before now.

Brian was his name—Brian Longsword, a sea rover and a great manslayer by reason of his strength in weapon-play. Wide shoulders he had, behind an arching chest; he had such legs that he could leap his own height into the air, and with his fingers he could pull nails from a plank. But he was handsome and gentle until something angered him overmuch. He had a youthful beard curling around his chin, and he had mild gray eyes.

"It is a good hamlet," he said, "for spoiling."

Beside him squatted an old Viking of more fell than flesh. A far-wandering man he was—Fiddle Skal they called him—and he had many tales at his tongue's end of the wonders he had seen. "Rather," he grunted, "would yonder dwellers spoil thee, Brian."

The tall rover gazed down affectionately at the gray steel blade that lay upon his knee. He was polishing with a sheepskin the long sword that had won him his name. "Oh, I would bid them take their weapons," said he, "and many of them would be raven's meat before that happened."

Fiddle Skal grunted again. He had been in Constantinople, which the Vikings knew as Micklegarth, before.

"These men—" he waved a crooked hand at the crowded waterfront—"do not stand their ground with weapons. Nay, they have other ways of plucking gold and gear from the likes of us. But they have grand horse racing, whatever."

"I would like well," observed Brian Longsword after a while, "to see that."

So they went ashore, the Viking sea rover and his foredeck man. They walked with a clumsy rolling gait, yet many heads turned after Brian, who had put on a red cloak. At the first booth where carved ivory trinkets were displayed he stopped to stare admiringly.

"Come away, man," urged Fiddle Skal, who was impatient to get off to the Hippodrome to watch the chariot racing.

Just then a Greek peddler edged up with one thing in his hand, holding it so Brian could not help but see it—a round miniature painting no larger than a man's hand, with a frame of gold and pearls. A dainty woman's head the size of his thumb looked up at Brian.

"Does your Lordship wish to buy a slave—such a slave?" The man asked in fair Norman French, which the Vikings understood well enough.

The hair of the head was pale gold, and the eyes met Brian's no matter how he turned the miniature. He had never seen anything like it before.

"Her portrait," the Greek whispered.

Meanwhile Fiddle Skal had peered around Brian's arm. "Put it down," he urged. "'Tis a Greek trick. One like that is not for the likes of you."

Brian thought this would be true. Still, he gave it back reluctantly and followed slowly after the hurrying Skal. The eyes of the miniature still seemed to be beseeching him.

So he stopped readily enough when that same Greek bobbed up at his elbow again, out of the crowd.

"This way your Lordship," the fellow whispered. "Up this alley—come."

Brian looked over the heads of the chattering throng. By now Fiddle Skal was almost out of sight hurrying toward his horse racing. The tall seafarer wanted above all things to set eyes on the woman of the miniature. There could be no harm in that, he thought, and he might find Skal later. But the truth was that whatever Brian had in his mind to do, he did that, no matter what might be in his path.

Following the Greek, he made his way through a kind of garden, into a gate where lounging spearmen inspected him curiously and a softly stepping person with a staff appeared, to whisper to the Greek. Again the big Viking followed patiently through dim corridors, up winding stairs into a tapestried room.

There he stopped, motionless. By the window the woman of the miniature lay, curled among cushions. She was twisting her heavy hair with slim, white fingers, and she looked up at him, startled. Brian felt the hot blood rush into his cheeks. It seemed to him that here was an elf-maid, come among mortals.

When she spoke, her voice was like the chiming of a golden chain. Not a word did he understand. He had seen the girl, though, and that was enough. He would have liked to pick her up in his arms and bear her off to the ship. But it seemed she must be bought.

After avid questioning by the Greek, and—through the Greek—by the man with the staff, Theophile by name, it turned out that the woman's price was two hundred and ten gold byzants. That, strangely enough, was the exact number of coins Brian had confessed that he had in his wallet. So he handed his wallet to the fellow, who began to argue fiercely with the bearded Greek. They did not count the money before the woman, and Brian moved toward her shyly.

"Thy name?" His deep tones rumbled through the room.

She only looked at him strangely, as if puzzled, and turned suddenly away to the window.

"Her name is Irene," the Greek was whispering, "and now she is shy—you understand? Consider, my lord. Now she is a slave, but once she was the daughter of a magister militum—of—of an earl, you understand." He addressed the girl respectfully, and she answered briefly. "She asks an hour or so to gather her belongings together. At the hour of the vesper bell she will be brought down to your ship."

Still talking, he edged Brian from the room and into the corridors. At the garden gate he said farewell hurriedly, to hasten after the man with the staff who had retained the purse.

Veiled women looked quickly into Brian's flushed face as he strode down toward the waterfront. He thought of nothing but the living thing that was Irene, who would, soon, belong to him.

Halfway down the market street, however, he had an idea. Here, in a booth at his side was a carpet somewhat like the luxurious carpet in Irene's room. He motioned to a bowing shopman to roll it up and carry it after him. He did not know anything about haggling. But after that he looked to right and left. When a thing caught his fancy he had it carried forth and strode on, with a growing procession of merchants' boys at his heels. The last purchase he made was a couch with a brocade covering.

When he reached the dragon ship he went to his sea chest and ransacked it for gold rings and bits of silver. When he had a handful of these he distributed them among the bearers.

Only a few of his stalwarts had remained to guard the ship; the rest were amusing themselves on shore. These few he set to work swabbing down the half-cabin under the afterdeck. He made them wash down the sidewalls that looked of a sudden bare and inhospitable.

He moved his sea chest and sleeping skins to one side and spread the new carpet over the rough planking. The couch he arranged on the other side, with an ebony chest, cushions, and gilt candelabra. The linen cloths with pictures of strange birds—meant to cover the walls—he did not meddle with. Such as that was woman's work. But he did have his men rig up a length of tapestry to screen the newly adorned cabin from the open waist of the ship.

It was after dark when Fiddle Skal pushed through the tapestry and blinked in astonishment. "What wine," he growled, "did they pour out for you, to turn your mind to this peacock's nest?"

Brian admitted it was for a woman.

"What manner of woman would set foot on a dragon ship?"

"One that I bought."

Fiddle Skal's jaw dropped open, and he remained speechless for a moment. "You—the warfarer—bought a woman? Where is she, then?"

"After the vesper bell she will be brought down to the boat."

The foredeck man pondered and his beard twitched in a grin. "That is to be seen. Did you buy her in the slave market?"

When Brian described the garden and the lion-guarded portal, Skal burst into a roar of laughter. "May the dogs bite the Greeks! That was the Sacred Palace. It must be that the imperial slaves have shown you some dancing girl. And for that you gave them all your gold!"

And he struck his hands together. "A princess, no doubt, she was—for two hundred byzants—"

He stopped, amazed. A seaman came under the hanging to say that armed men in uniform had come to the gangboard. Skal went to the rail, to peer into the darkness.

These men carried no torches. But he saw a white-veiled figure emerge from a litter and come down the gangboard. Behind her followed a black slave in the red cloak of the palace guard, and he carried on his shoulder a box.

The Vikings stared in silence as if spirits had appeared among them. The guards and slaves departed with the empty litter, and Brian stepped toward the veiled girl, who was now alone. Fiddle Skal heard her speak slowly, as if the Norman tongue were strange to her. "My lord, you are he that will take me to my home. But what manner of ship is this?"

Fierce joy surged through Brian's body. Irene had come. She was here on his boat—she was his. When he tried to speak his throat closed and he could not utter words, although he was laughing softly from sheer exultation. Beckoning her to the afterdeck, he clumsily drew back the tapestry hanging so she could see her new quarters. And she cried out in dismay. The common bazaar hangings and the glaring rug appeared to be a stage set to deceive her. Theophile had sworn to her on holy relics, and she had hoped—although she had not quite believed—she would be sent back unharmed to her summer home on the sea. Theophile and the Greek trinket seller had shown this great Viking to her that afternoon and assured her that he had been commissioned by the Caesar to bear her thither in his ship. And she had thought that the Viking's gray eyes were honest. So she had hoped. But this cabin—a pagan Tatar would have provided better quarters for a slave.

"Let me go!" she whispered.

Slowly Brian shook his head. He would never do that.

It seemed clear, now, to the girl: the Caesar had sent her to this strange ship with the dragon's head to be slain at sea.

"Is—is it thy will," she whispered again, "that I should find my death here?"

Brian could only shake his head. "That," he growled at last, "will never happen while I can hold a weapon."

She let the veil fall from her face and looked into his eyes to read the soul behind them. And in that moment she knew more of Brian than he knew of himself. A flush of blood darkened her cheeks and she spoke shyly, "Then why did they bring me here?"

"First tell me," he bade her, "who thou art."

So it happened that she told him of the capture of Comnenus and the slaying of him, when the Caesar's ax-men hewed her father into five pieces under the eyes of the mob in the Hippodrome. And then of her imprisonment in the Sacred Palace, when the slave girls whispered one day that she might be spared, and the next day that the Caesar would poison her food—until that afternoon when Theophile had ushered Brian into her room.

The Viking listened without moving. At the end he nodded, because he had thought it all over carefully and he knew now what was to be done.

"It is clear to me," he said, "that they are mighty liars. Now, sleep."

Sitting on his chest with the sword on his knee, he kept watch while the tired girl stretched out on the couch. At first she pulled the mantle over her head and cried a little. Then the slapping of the wavelets against the hull and the swaying of the curtain made her drowsy. Not until the last candle had guttered out did the Viking rise and go forth to the deck.

There a shaggy shape croaked at his elbow. "The messmates are saying that harm will come out of taking that mighty dame on the ship."

"I will take her, and I will keep her."

Fiddle Skal sighed. "That is to be seen."

The last thing John Dukas expected was a visit from the master of the dragon ship. He was seated at his noon meal on a terrace overlooking the sea when his chamberlain announced that the Viking demanded admittance. It pleased the Caesar's humor to see him, although Dukas instructed Theophile to have in four stalwarts of the Varangian Guard to stand behind the table. These mercenaries were the Emperor's personal guard, but the Caesar cultivated them against the day when he might feel himself strong enough to seize the imperial palace and the throne of Constantinople. There was a proverb that he who ruled the army would someday rule the empire.

The Caesar looked up indulgently while he selected a bunch of grapes and dipped them into wine. "What says the barbarian?" he asked Theophile.

Brian had his shield on his arm, an iron cap on his head. He gazed about him in wonder, and, obviously, he did not know how to prostrate himself fittingly.

"Your Illustriousness," explained the secretary, "he hath a grievance."

It seemed to the Caesar amusing that a sea rover who had just been given a fair girl should come with a grievance.

"And what is it?" he asked.

"He says your Illustriousness hath dealt churlishly by his bride. He says that the woman who will be his bride was held in captivity here like a slave . . . For that reason he comes to challenge your Illustriousness to combat with weapons, ahorse or afoot, on sea or land, with sword or spear or ax."

John Dukas selected a grape, rather regretting that the four Varangian swordsmen should be within hearing. He himself was skilled in handling weapons; he judged himself a match for the slow-moving seafarer who had been mad enough to defy him, but he had no intention of settling a quarrel in this fashion. "Ask him," he responded, "by what right he claims a bride in Constantinople."

Everyone in the room heard Brian's answer. "By two hundred and ten byzants paid down."

With lifted brows the Caesar glanced at Theophile, who fingered his staff uneasily. Then, gently, he shook his dark head. "Tell him a Caesar of the empire does not cross words with a warfarer."

"I am Brian," the Viking said slowly, "Sigurd's son, Earl of Drontheim at the land's end, and I hold myself equal in blood to any man so faint of heart that he will war against a girl. Tell the beardless one so."

This baiting John Dukas had found amusing. He contemplated the earl of a thatched village at the land's end who meant to marry Irene. This dull man was waiting patiently, unmoved as the timbers of his storm-battered dragon ship. And in this patience John Dukas found something disturbing.

He had not, it seemed, managed to make Irene disappear without notice. It might be better if she did not join herself to such an outspoken earl.

"Seize him," he ordered his Varangians. "Disarm him."

Not a man moved to obey. Those four mercenaries from the Norse lands had seen the gold ring of a chieftain of their folk; they had heard the broad accents of the north. In their scarlet cloaks and gilded helmets they stood motionless.

Theophile and the slaves cast down their eyes, trembling. Only John Dukas found amusement in the situation.

In another moment, he thought, they might salute the barbarian. A feckless breed, touchy about points of honor, yet dense of brain. So—they served the Byzantine princes for hire. To Brian aloud, he said, "So be it. I will meet this earl on the morrow, when he comes ashore again, and I am armed. Until then, bid him go without harm."

Brian considered, and nodded. "Tell this lordling to arm himself well." And he strode from the hall between the silent guards.

When the Caesar and Theophile were alone, the secretary wiped the sweat covertly from his cheeks. But John Dukas was little concerned about the byzants that had found their way into his wallet. Instead, he reflected that it was necessary now to dispose of this sea-roving earl. After which he could confidently expect that the Viking crew would dispose of the troublesome Irene in their own fashion.

"Theophile," he said, "I do not wish another such conversation with your barbarian. You will go to Phocas and bid him place his spies on the jetty by that dragon ship. He shall observe the movements of the barbarians, and when this Brian, son of Sigurd, comes ashore again, Phocas's men shall set upon him in the market street. They can pick a quarrel with him, and knife him in the back. Then, Theophile, you might reward Phocas with some of your ill-gotten byzants. Do you understand?"

"Your Magnanimity," cried the secretary, "it shall be done."

"I hope so," smiled the Caesar. "This evening I go to the Asia shore to take command of the army encamped there. But I shall hear the gossip of the town. And if there is more bungling, Theophile, you shall be given red gloves to wear."

The secretary looked down at his hands, at the skin upon his hands. When the Caesar smiled, he was quite capable of ordering the skin stripped from the fingers of one who had displeased him.

As for the Caesar, he had many other things to think about that afternoon. The sun telegraph was winking a message to him from the dark hills of the Asia shore, across the blue waters of the Marmora. Officers from distant points waited to talk with him, apart from listeners. Once, indeed, a bearded man in a striped robe appeared like an ominous djinn, at his elbow. The bearded one, the Bokharian spy, prostrated himself before the Caesar and whispered tidings.

"May the star of good fortune never fail your Magnificence. I come at command of Phocas, who serves your—"

"What says he?"

"The barbarians of the ship thou knowest sent men to the market for grain and oil and dried fish. Phocas himself, waiting in a fishing skiff, listened to their talk. He heard the voice of the woman thou knowest in the cabin of the ship. Ai! He heard her voice many times, and she urged the master of the ship to go away from the city in his boat."

"And what said he?"

The oriental spy glanced up shrewdly to judge if his message pleased or not. "Phocas thinks he will not go. Ai—he spoke angrily with the woman, swearing that he had a duel to fight."

With a gesture the Caesar dismissed his spy. If he knew the mind of Sigurd's son, the Viking would never turn his prow away from a combat. But when late that afternoon—when the sun had gone down behind the Golden Horn and lanterns were appearing like sparks in the darkening alleys—he looked out over the waterfront, he noticed that the dragon ship was moving out from its berth. It was turning toward the sea.

At the same time a cortege was proceeding from the Sacred Palace toward the great basilica, the gaunt Emperor was walking in his cloth-of-gold to the place of prayer.

The Caesar liked to overlook the city at this hour of candle-lighting, when the round domes merged into the blue haze, and the sea wall faded against the dark water. It would not be long, he fancied, before he would walk, clad in gold, at the head of his court while the singers intoned hymns of praise. He was thinking then of the four Varangians who had disobeyed his spoken order. Perhaps his cousin the Emperor suspected him—so the Varangians had dared defy him, hoping that he might be struck down by that barbarian.

If so, John Dukas reasoned, he should lose no time in joining his army. By degrees he could move his cataphracts, his mailed cavalry, across the strait, into the city. The Caesar could act swiftly without seeming to hurry. By full starlight he was at his barge, sitting the saddle of his white charger, with a dozen nobles and officers armed at his side. Beneath the tossing flames of torches his Bulgarian archers, twoscore strong, manned the waist of the great barge. (Dukas had chosen no Varangians to go with him this night.)

The barge captain struck a chant and the slaves on their benches heaved at their oars. With a fanfare of trumpets and a waving of torches the barge moved out of the harbor toward the distant shore. The Caesar was aware that with the plumes swaying upon the goldplated helmets, and the purple cloaks of his nobles fluttering in the night breeze, it made a fine sight for the crowds on the shore.

A half-hour and he would be at the head of his army on the Asia side. Then the captain of the slaves cried a warning, and the oars hung motionless. John Dukas heard the thresh of other oars. A shape appeared on the bow.

A wooden dragon head, crudely carved, with its tongue sticking out, loomed above the rail of his barge. The two craft drifted together. Wood crunched against wood. The barge captain shouted furiously, but the deep voice of Brian, Sigurd's son, cut through his complaining.

"I see well that you have come armed for weapon-play, lordling."

It was all absurd, the Caesar thought. That clumsy dragon head that should have been well on its way into the Marmora under the starlight by now. Those twoscore wild figures leaping from the rail of the Viking's ship to the foredeck of his barge—so swiftly that the Bulgarian archers had no time to string and raise their weapons. Absurd, the way the unarmed slaves slid under the rowers' benches or dropped into the water to cling to the oars.

"Shield wall—shield wall!" cried a grotesque bearded man. Roaring their glee, the Vikings pressed into double ranks, shield overlapping shield, stretching from rail to rail of the barge. The shield wall, topped by iron helms, moved forward swiftly over the benches.

The Bulgarians took to their axes, and hewed at it. Steel clanged against iron, as the long swords flicked out among the axes. Several of the Bulgarian mercenaries leaped into the water, and more were trodden down by the Vikings. Blood flecked their arms and heads, but when a man went down the warrior behind him stepped forward to his place.

John Dukas looked to right and left. Far off shone the lights of Constantinople; no vessels except fishing craft were afloat in the darkness. Over his head, hugging the long wooden neck of the dragon, he made out the slender figure of a girl.

"Stand fast!" John Dukas cried at his men. "Stand—for aid is coming."

Leaning down he snatched a spear from an officer. Rising in his stir-rups he hurled it fair at Brian, in the center of the shield wall. The Viking swayed his head aside and the spear went by.

Brian had changed. His eyes were shining. He sang as his sword whirled. The muscles rippled along his bare arm. Here, in the weapon-play, he tasted his joy.

John Dukas flung himself from the saddle of the white horse—for the trembling charger was useless in a boat. In the boat he must fight, for in armor he could not swim through the water. With his nobles he rushed forward.

"Now," cried Brian, "there is little between us, Caesar."

Absurd that John Dukas should be fighting sword in hand, under the last of the guttering torches, under the dragon's head and the eyes of the girl he had put there to make an end of her.

But Brian thrust the boss of his shield into the face of a Byzantine cap-tain; he drove the pommel of his sword into the jaw of another. "Make way," he said between his teeth, and came at Dukas.

The Caesar slashed wide at his head, and Brian's iron cap clanged off, leaving blood flowing down. The Viking's sword crashed full upon the Caesar's unlifted shield, cracking it and driving it back on his arm. And Dukas felt sick, at the power that numbed his arm and drove the links of his mail into his chest. Raising his sword again, he was only in time to parry a second terrible blow that beat down his blade and wrenched his right arm from wrist to shoulder.

He staggered, his crippled arms flapping at his side. A voice was scream-ing in his ears, and it was his own voice. His jaws snapped together and fell apart, while the Viking's sword was sweeping toward him a third time out of the air.

John Dukas's body lay on the boards of the deck, the knees moving slowly. Apart from it, still fast in the goldplated helmet with the Caesar's crest, lay his head. Above it the Vikings were stripping gear and jewels from the nobles who had thrown down their arms at his fall.

"Well, it cannot be said that he was a great man with his weapons."

Brian leaned on his long sword, staring down at the body, puzzled. It had been a brave encounter, he thought—that of the two boats on the water. But this Caesar had brought with him too many niddering fighters to the duel, and after all he had fallen as easily as a common man.

He had fallen and the duel was over. "Back to your benches, lads!" cried the Viking. "Out oars and away!"

When the oars churned the water white under the star-gleam, he stood by the steering sweep, watching for pursuit. No sail followed. Slowly the lights of the great city merged and dwindled astern. Fiddle Skal was singing to the laboring messmates of the sword that wrought a lordling's doom. But Brian wondered why the sea was without hue and cry after them.

In his mind he recalled that afternoon, when he had seen again the two men that sold him Irene. The bearded Greek peddler had been fishing in a skiff; but Theophile had brought a message to the ship. Theophile, that confidential man with the staff, had said that Dukas would fight the duel that evening, coming out in his barge to meet the dragon ship midway between the city and the Asia shore after the first starlight. Theophile had whispered it, showing fleetingly a signet ring in his hand. And now Brian wondered.

He washed the blood from his head and went down into the cabin where Irene was sitting, with a curtain cloth on her knee. The place looked bright now and not at all like a wolf's throat. She held out her hands to him. "You are brave, my lord."

It pleased him, but still he did not forget the doubt in his mind. "I am thinking," he explained, "that Dukas the Caesar did not relish that duel of ours. It may be that he did not seek it. Yet that man of his, Theophile, showed me his signet ring."

Irene sewed a stitch or two. "It was not his. I saw it." She sighed and thought for a moment. "The ring was the Emperor's. Aye, Theophile must have been his spy."

Brian could make little of this. "Then why, after that, didst thou pray me to sail away?"

"Because—" she lifted her eyes suddenly to him—"I was afraid for thee. Do not think now of that which is past, and I will not." She took his face between her hands and smiled unsteadily. In her heart she had said farewell to the sunlit palace by the Judas trees. "Wilt thou take me to that land where the lotus eaters are, and no one remembers aught?"

"Aye—if it will make thee glad, my lovely one."

"So glad," she said softly, "so glad."

Wolf Meat

Out of the mist the dragon's head appeared. Then came its body, long and low and lined with shields. From the mist it wallowed toward the shore. It turned into a narrow bay, long oars moving slowly like fins at its side.

So, upon a winter's noon when the snow lay deep under the firs, the dragon ship came into Thord's bay. The first to see it was a young girl, walking upon the outer wall of Thord's hall.

Bright quick eyes she had, and she knew well the like of ships. An instant she stared with a swift-drawn breath, and then was flying down the stone steps, her tawny hair twisting about her slender throat. Into the great hall she burst.

"My father, a Viking ship has put into the shore." And she stamped her foot. "Make haste!"

Sir Thord, a broad, mild man, reached behind his chair for his weapons. In other days he had fought off raids of the Vikings who came in their long boats from the northern sea. But of late he liked better to trade with them. Times were hard and he had few men to follow him when he went warfaring out of the manor.

Another man got to his feet. A champion he was, tall and dark, with a shield of arms embroidered on his long robe. He had fur at his wrists and throat, this Valgard—for he was the king's warden of the coast who gathered in tithes and hung up miscreants. Few could match him ahorse or afoot, with sword or ax or spear. A man of mark—a fine huntsman, and rich. He laughed across the table at the excited girl.

"God send," said he, "that this seafarer be the Red Elf. I have looked long for him."

The girl, Astrid, had heard much talk of the Red Elf, who was the most elusive of the Vikings. Men said that he sailed all the seas, in any weather. He followed war like a raven, and he wooed the kiss of the young storm maidens adorned with seaweed. Some said that devils flew behind his sail, beating air into it with their wings. All agreed that he had the gift of foresight—he could see that which was to be. And a drunken Scot swore that he had seen the Red Elf land and flit over the snow more swiftly than a running horse. A hard man to lay hand on, this Red Elf who haunted the seas.

"What luck," muttered Valgard, while his squire laced his mail habergeon upon his shoulders, "that this Viking ship should put in while I am guesting here."

"Luck!" echoed old Thord, drinking from his goblet. The hall was full of the stalwart, well-armed liegemen of the warden. Two score and ten of them. They would be a match for a Viking crew. The warden had looked twice at Astrid, and had lingered here, after the storm that brought him to seek a haven had passed on.

Valgard said no word about the maid, but he lingered, and Thord bethought him that it might come to a match between them. A good thing it would be, too—if the proud Valgard should ask Astrid for his bride. Thord no longer had gold or silver in big chests. The fishing had been bad, and he could not pay the tithes the warden demanded. Aye, by chance and misfortune the wolf of poverty sniffed loud at Thord's door.

Two fishermen came running in with word from the shore.

"My lord," said they, "a Viking ship is at anchor by the rocks. Yea, 'twas harried i' the storm and seeketh meat and fresh water. Yonder seafarers will be after peace, and not war."

Thord looked up. "Will they trade?"

"Yea, my lord, that they will do. They have rich trove from other lands and they will trade this day for meat and drink, which they lack."

Valgard lifted his shield, smiling. "If 'tis the Red Elf himself, we must beware. He hath more tricks in him than a fox.

"Now I will tell you what to do. Send word to the rovers by these churls—" he nodded at the fishermen—"that you will keep the peace and in an hour you will come to the landing with cattle, wine kegs, and grain. You will do this, but I will go with my liegemen into the wood beside the landing. When the Viking chief comes ashore I will sally out and make him captive. Then will we have some of his men and his trove that he brings ashore. And the devils left in the ship can do naught but row away."

Thord got to his feet uncertainly. He thought that the Vikings might be wolves; still, if they pledged a peace they would hold to it. But before he could speak Astrid was at his side, holding high her small head.

"Sir Warden," she cried, "this ship has come into my father's land, not yours. What do we know of this Red Elf—surely it may be another!"

"Hush, child—" began Thord.

"Why," she demanded, "do you not go, Sir Warden, with your armed liegemen and guard my father openly at his trading, so that no harm may come of this landfall?"

Valgard smiled, his eyes upon hers. "I will not have it said that I stood by with sword in sheath while the Red Elf fed and got away. We know not for certain it is he, but who else would come out of the sea at this time?"

The girl looked up at her father. "Will you do this?"

"Aye," said Thord heavily, and bade the fishermen take back the message of peace to the ship. He could not do without Valgard's help—and his wild girl had angered Valgard. She said no more, but when she would have slipped from the room, the warden laid hand upon her arm. At once she freed herself and sprang away through the door.

"Forgive her, my lord," muttered Thord uneasily. "I have spoiled the girl, I fear—"

"Nay, she is a beauty and knows it not." Valgard wondered why the image of this maid should be burned into his brain. She was willful, and untaught—a shabby little brat queening it in this dark, cracked hall. But the flash of her eyes, the soft gleam of her hair haunted his thoughts. What if she should be clad in brocaded silk with pearls twined around that slim throat? What if her hair were shaken loose upon her shoulders, and color brought into the pale cheeks?

So Valgard mused, until it was time for him to set out with his men to the ambush in the wood by the landing. It would take him some time to work his way quietly around, through the trees.

Astrid was before him. In soft boots and flying cloak she flitted over the drifted paths. The firs, sighing under the wind, drowned the slight sound of her feet, until she came out in a clearing within sight of the shore. And then she stopped, frightened, hands pressed against her heart.

The man in the clearing had been amusing himself tossing pine cones at squirrels. Before he heard her, he sighted her figure moving toward him—and he turned, snatching up a long spear from the snow and poising it. Astrid thought to see it flying toward her. But he lowered it, looking from right to left. He came swiftly toward her.

He had fiery red hair, cut short of his shoulders. Over his left arm hung a bossed shield with gold gleaming, and a long scarlet mantle. Gaunt and brown was the face from which his blue eyes glanced warily. But when he stood leaning upon the spear shaft before her, his eyes smiled.

A thought came to her. "Are you the Red Elf?" she asked, breathlessly.

He had the arm ring of a chieftain, and silver shone on his belt. Although he did no more than look at her, she felt afraid. "My name," he said slowly, "is Karli. But what are you?"

"Go back to your ship," she whispered. "Go back quickly, and away. One is coming in secret through this wood, and he will deal badly by you and he hath fifty swordsmen to back him."

The Viking did not move. "Is it so?" he asked. "Yet just now the people of the manor sent a pledge of peace."

"I will not have my father foresworn and mocked by men. 'Tis the king's warden who comes by stealth, seeking to take the Red Elf, who hath a rare good price on his head, and is beside a playmate of fiends—"

Dismayed she stopped, wondering tardily whether this red-haired Karli might not be the Red Elf himself. She had looked for an old and crafty man, while this Viking was young and aimless enough to sport with the squirrels. Yet his spear had almost sped into her breast.

"Sit down," he said quietly, laying his mantle upon a rock, "so that we may talk. You must be Sir Thord's daughter?"

"'Tis so, and 'tis the truth I have told you. Go—call in your men and make away from the shore, or they will hang you."

"Listen," quoth Karli the Viking.

Anxiously she strained her ears, bearing a distant roar. "A heavy sea beats on the headlands," she explained.

"Aye, and we have come out of it well with our lives, into the shelter of your bay. For a day and the half of a day we have tasted no food. Now my men are eating snow. Think you they will put out again unfed?"

She noticed then that his leather jacket was stained, his hands cracked and bleeding. Had the dragon ship been out in that two weeks' storm? "What will you do then?" she asked.

"Talk a bit," he said gravely. "My neck, it is safe enough now that I have such a hostage."

For a moment she did not grasp his meaning, and he began to speak of the Red Elf. "So the landsmen call him. Now the truth is, that he is son of the slain Earl of the Norsemen, and the price has been put upon his head by his foes, who would like well to send the son to the sire. So this Red Elf and messmates hie them far over the sea—aye to the Emperor at Constantinople, and the dukes of Sicily. They are warfaring elsewhere to save their skins, and—"

"Stop! Are you a churl to hold me captive, when I came to warn you?"

Karli's blue eyes gazed at her impassively. For all his ready words, she could not guess at his thoughts,

"Hold you fast I will," he said. He reached out his hand to hold her loosened hair, and she did not see that his powerful fingers trembled, so amazed was she at his words.

Swift as a startled deer she sprang to her feet and away from him. Valgard said rightly that Astrid did not know her own beauty. Standing there with hair untied and indignant, she had, Karli thought, the bearing of a storm maiden. He knew she was a girl who had never been humbled by man's hand.

"You would like," she cried again fiercely, "to lead me into your ship, to hold hostage to save your life from the warden's swords."

He rose to his feet and his ruddy face went white.

"Use you as a shield I would not," he said gravely, "for it is in my mind to take you as a bride from Sir Thord."

She gasped. "And—and what think you he would answer?"

"I am not skilled in this matter of wooing," muttered Karli uneasily, "but perhaps he will give you up without too much regret."

Astrid's gray eyes twinkled and she laughed low. "You are not a wooer at all but a great fool. Now you cannot keep me as a hostage—see, I am out of your reach."

"You will not fly so fast I cannot overtake you."

Challenged, the girl turned and ran fleetly toward the trees. She heard metal clash behind her and glanced over her shoulder to see if Karli had fallen. Instead, he had come upon her with two long leaps. He caught the girl up in his arms, his shield beneath her knees, his free arm pinning hers behind her back. His strength astonished and dismayed her. Then his head bent and he kissed her eyes and lips.

Gently he set her down. "Tell me your name," he said.

"Astrid."

"Now, you see, Astrid, that I free you of my own will. It shall not be said of the Red Elf that he took his wife by force without a fair and proper wooing."

Blood rushed through her heart, heating her cheeks and singing in her ears. Then a new thing came into her bewildered head. The Red Elf had the gift of foresight. Was he looking now into the unseen? Fear came upon her again, and she ran back into the trees. Once she stopped and looked back. After all, he had let her go. He was leaning on his long-spear, his eyes following her. She went on, vanishing into the dark pines.

Karli walked slowly down to the shore. He had forgotten his scarlet mantle that lay upon the rock. At his coming a dozen stalwart Vikings looked up inquiringly.

"Back to the ship," he said, passing them.

He went on, to the flat rock of the landing, and over the long plank, stepping past the shields on the ship's rail. He went to his quarters on the high stern, curtained in with leather sheets. Rolling aside his sleeping furs, he lifted a plank beneath them, reaching down into a compartment where chests of iron and sandalwood were stored with rolls of cloth-of-gold, brocades, and silk. He took out a carved casket that held ropes of softly gleaming pearls, with emerald necklets. They would bring color to Astrid's beauty.

After a moment he said, "Bring out the carpets, and hang out the gold lanterns. I mean to bring a bride to the ship this night."

The Vikings exchanged glances, surprised and amused. Some of them clashed their shields, thinking that they would be led to a landfall and a spoiling of the manor house in the distance beyond the trees. Karli heard the sound.

"'Bide ye! No man may set foot out of the ship until I give the bidding. We have made a peace with the manor folk."

"Karli," growled one, "when will we have food to set between our teeth?"

"Tonight, messmates," he laughed, "we will feast in Sir Thord's hall, or we will not eat at all. There is a warden sitting in yonder wood with fifty swords behind him. So if ye set foot ashore they will cut you down, and say afterward that you came raiding. But for my head they would get a price."

It was late afternoon before groups of men appeared on the road to the landing that ran beside the wood. These brought neither cattle nor barrels

with them. Instead they carried arms of sorts, and a few wore mail. A broad
figure with a gray beard strode before them, bearing sword and shield.

"This is not good, Karli," spoke up one of the crew, "for these landsmen bring iron to us instead of meat."

"Keep to the ship," said the Red Elf, "and the iron will not harm ye.
That should be Thord with his henchmen—not the warden's band."

"What is in your mind to do?"

"I will try my luck, for there is no other way."

Karli went back over the plank with his shield and spear, and the small
casket that held his bride-gift tied to his belt. But he carried also a pair of
lengths of wood, seasoned ash, each as broad as his hand and each curved
over gracefully at one end. When he had climbed out of the rocks he laid
these skis down in the smooth snow and bound his feet in the leather
thongs at the middle of each. He did this swiftly, for the Norsemen all
used skis from childhood. On the other hand, the people of this coast did
not know the use of them.

Slowly Karli went forward, planting each ski with a short step, since
he was climbing the slope toward the oncoming landsmen. "A greeting
to you, Sir Thord," he said.

"May the Devil burn you and all yours, Viking," responded the lord
of the manor.

Panting, Thord stood there with his hand on his sword, and the red
faces of his men glared behind him.

"Sir Thord," he said, "I will do you no ill, and I am after keeping the
peace. But where are the cattle and wine you would bring?"

"By God," cried the old man, "is it not enough that you have taken my
daughter—that you ask for meat and wine also?"

Karli smiled. "Astrid is not upon the ship, nor have I carried her any
whither."

"She is on the ship. This fisherman here saw you snatch her up i' the
wood, and ran with the word to me. Another saw you bear her over the ship's
rail. And now yield her up to me, you spawn of Satan's penthouse!"

"Is this your peace?" asked Karli without anger. "Now, listen. Where
is the lying knave who said he saw me carrying Astrid to the dragon
craft?"

"He is not here. He is—" Sir Thord swallowed hard—"one of the warden's liegemen."

"Well, find him and fetch him. And since you must e'en go to the am-

bush in the wood, look well at the tracks there in the snow. For yonder are
my tracks, coming and going. A stone's throw within the trees you will
see where Astrid came to speak with me—she who hath more of honor
than the lord her father and his messmate the Lord Warden. You will see
where she went back to the manor."

Without a word Sir Thord went off into the wood. He was gone a long time
and he came back trailing Karli's forgotten mantle in the snow. He came
alone and stood there, pulling at his beard.

"No one," he said, "is in the wood any more. They have gone, every
soul of them, upon the forest road."

"The girl, Astrid?"

"Aye, else she would be with me."

Karli looked keenly at the dazed man and saw that he spoke the truth.
Then Karli turned his mind back to what had happened in that wood. He
thought of Astrid running back to her house, and coming upon the horsemen. She might have told the warden what had passed between her and
the Red Elf, or she might not. But he had kept her there, and presently
a man of his had been sent to say to Thord the lie that his daughter had
been carried to the ship. So the warden had not meant Thord to see his
daughter again.

Even while he pondered, a woman came down from the manor, saying
that some of the warden's men had hastened back to the house and loaded
all Valgard's gear upon the packhorses, and had departed an hour since.

Twilight fell upon them with a darkening fall of snow. The people
crowded about, whispering and waiting to hear what the Viking would
say. Thord had sent for his horse, which was led up, saddled.

"How many more have ye?" Karli asked. "Swift-paced horses?"

"No other than this," Thord admitted, ashamed. He held his life as little against his daughter, and he meant to ride after the warden.

"Well," said Karli, "it seems that we twain must go upon this search
alone. But do you ride fast, old man, for I have need of you."

Thord, his foot in the stirrup, stared at the dim form of the Viking.
"What! Your boat cannot follow the inland road, and this quarrel is not
yours."

"It is not to my mind," the Viking responded, "to leave my bride in an
another man's arms for long. Show me the road."

Although Thord galloped headlong, following the tracks along the road, the Viking kept beside him. The horse plunged down slopes, slipping and pulling itself together. The Viking whirled from side to side to break the speed of the descent. Over fallen trees the horse leaped, and the man leaped beside him.

Night had fallen, but the snow had ceased and the air grew clear. Thord could no longer make out the tracks of the riders. Karli, however, went on without faltering. The forest thinned out around them, and they saw ahead of them at one side two red eyes of light.

Cautiously they went ahead. They saw that the lights were fires. Valgard and his men had turned off the road to halt for the night. They did not look for pursuit so far from the sea, and they had gone down a steep slope, across clear ground to a cluster of pine trees. So they were a hundred paces from the road—some of the men cutting up a dead tree, others taking the saddles from the horses. Valgard's servants were rigging up a shelter out of boughs and tent cloths, between the two great fires.

Valgard was sitting on a log. He still had on his steel cap and mail and he held a wine cup on his knee, while he gave orders to his men. Within the shelter beside him the girl Astrid crouched upon a mantle. Her face was white but she did not weep.

All this Thord and Karli saw clearly, in the red glow of the fires.

"Men say," Thord whispered to the Viking, "that you have the gift of foresight. Can you see what will come out of this?"

"Faith, no," Karli laughed, leaning on his spear.

Anxiously Thord peered at him. After all, this seafarer was young and heedless. He had only human strength in him.

"Hail them, Sir Thord," he said, "and summon this Valgard to give up Astrid, if he will not have manslaughter at this place."

Throwing back his head, the old lord shouted: "Ho, Valgard! I am Thord and now I call upon you to release my daughter to come to me. 'Tis an ill deed you have done, to lay hand upon the maid of the house that sheltered you."

In the moment of surprised silence Valgard stood up, his hand on his sword, peering up into the night. But he could not see the two of them. Yet in that moment—for he was a shrewd man—he had guessed that Thord, escaping from the Vikings, must have followed alone on the solitary charger of the manor.

"Good or ill," he shouted back, "'tis not for you to say, old man. You are

the messmate of the Red Elf and his outlaws—aye, you have given them food
and shelter, despite me—and now must I hold your maid a hostage."

Some of the men-at-arms laughed, and Thord ground his teeth.

"That is a black lie, Valgard. Will you give up the girl?"

"She is here. Come you down, and take her."

Suddenly Astrid's clear voice rang out: "Nay, Father—for they—"

Turning swiftly, Valgard dealt her a heavy blow on the mouth, and she
fell back. Thord saw then that her ankles were bound together, so that
she could not move upon her feet. "May God requite you for that blow,"
he roared, and jerked at the rein of his horse.

But Karli's hand held the rein and forced the beast back to the road.
"Bide here, old man. Sure it is weary of life you are this day." Then his deep
voice bailed the camp: "You need not shout so loud, Valgard, for the Red
Elf hears. Now you must make ready and take your weapons and summon
your men, for the Red Elf will be coming down with his arms."

Valgard's manner changed on the instant. He called his men from the
horses; they snatched up weapons, and at his bidding ranged themselves
in a long half-circle before the fires—two or three paces between the men.
A half-dozen archers advanced steadily beyond the half-circle toward the
slope. Valgard fitted his shield on his arm, drew his sword, and stood beside the shelter.

All this Karli watched attentively. Except for his eyes he did not move
at all, until he began to clear the snow from his skis by sliding them back
and forth.

Then he leaned forward a little, half crouched. He slid one foot forward
and was over the edge of the slope. In a second he was speeding down the
wide track made by the horses—faster and faster. He reached the archers,
who had barely glimpsed him. One threw a shield in front of him with a
warning shout, and he leaped over it.

Out of the night he shot into the half-circle of the men-at-arms. Erect,
he sped between two of them. An ax swept at him wildly and he crouched
on his skis to let it clear his head.

Faster than a bird on the wing, with the great spear gripped before him,
he bore down on Valgard.

No time for Valgard to leap aside. Throwing his shield before him, the
warden struck blindly at the spear with his sword. No swordsmanship
could turn that spear with such weight behind it. The blade clattered off

the wood—the spear's point crashed through the shield, smashed through the body armor, and came out red between Valgard's shoulder blades.

But Valgard's body had been cast back through the tent shelter, and Karli was whirling on the snow beside it.

The Viking gripped the ground, drew his skis under him, and reached out his free arm. He caught Astrid by the waist, threw her over his shoulder. With an effort he stood erect, shouting at the dazed watchers.

"The Red Elf has taken his bride away. 'Tis ill to follow!" And he slid one foot before him, gliding out of the light among the trees, in a wide circle that would take him back to the road through the darkness.

Few realized what had happened until he was passing from sight. Javelins were flung, and some of the warden's henchmen started to run after, through the deep snow. But he was lost to sight, and they stopped at the edge of the firelight. Some cried out to saddle the horses, but no one did so.

They were looking at the dead body. Of what avail to follow a man who could fly through the night like that, and strike such a blow? They crossed themselves and shook their heads. And afterward they told in the towns a tale of how they had seen the Red Elf swoop down out of the night sky, riding on his hoofs, with the wings of a fiend beating behind him and fire coming out of his head.

In his arms Karli carried the girl home. And at dawn Karli and his Vikings were still breaking their long fast, while the lights glowed in the hall and a great fire roared from the hearth. The maids of the place hastened from table to table carrying pitchers of ale, and the men made a song when they heard how Karli came down with his spear on the warden's men. Old Thord thumped the board, for good red wine had been carried in without stint and his mind had grown a little mixed. He was proud to have an earl's son sitting in honor beside him on the high seat, and he thought that the days of the manor would be lively now.

As for Astrid, she had put on her best red garment—although she knew, now that she had seen the silks and brocades in one of Karli's open chests, that her dress was shabby indeed. The other maids looked at her in a new way, and she held her head high. At the same time she was half frightened. For Karli said no more of his suit before these people—in fact he said nothing at all. With flushed cheeks he looked down at his hands. The Red Elf had grown fearful. And Astrid ever listened for his voice.

Until suddenly he rose from his place and caught her hand. He led her apart from the others, and took a casket from his belt. From it he drew ropes of pearls, and hung them, with quivering fingers, about her throat in a clumsy tangle. Then he thrust great silver arm-bands set with shining emeralds upon her wrists, so that he hurt her. Still he had naught to say, but he put his arm about her and kissed her.

At the tables the Vikings laughed deep.

"Astrid," he whispered, "I am crestfallen and fearful, for I know not how to set about wooing you."

She straightened the pearls upon her throat, and looked up at him gently.

"I know little of such things," she said, "but it seems to me that you manage well enough as it is."

The Snow Driver

Chapter I

The Man-at-Arms

Upon a fair day in May, in token of the honor due them for long and valorous service in Flanders, a small group of men were chosen to mount guard at the pavilion of His Majesty King Edward the Sixth of England. They were armigers or esquires-at-arms, and the youngest of their company was placed at the entrance of the pavilion nearest the person of the king.

The name of this armiger was Ralph Thorne. He was selected for this post because, of these survivors of a gallant company, he had done the most in battle.

"Because, sire," explained the politic Dudley, Duke of Stratford, "he has never failed in the execution of a command. Because, being distant from the court and the eye of his sovereign, he has yet performed deeds of hardihood, suffering thereby sore scathe and wounds."

This tribute, lightly rendered by my lord duke, was remembered by him in latter years. Verily he had good reason to regret his words and his selection of a sentinel.

For there befell in that hour and in that day of the year 1553 a strange event. And here is the tale of it, justly set down, giving every man his due, and no man more; for it is not the task of the chronicler to praise and dispraise, but to make manifest the truth.

Master Thorne walked his post, after receiving signs and orders from my lord, the aforesaid Duke of Stratford. The armiger was not by much the elder of the boy king who lay within the pavilion on a couch covered with a deerskin. He wore the armor of the guards—cuirass and morion—and carried a harquebus on one shoulder.

A slow match in his other hand was kept alight by swinging gently back and forth. Walking slowly from one pole of the entrance to the other, he did not look within. And the grievously sick Edward took no more notice of the sentinel than of the ancient hag who crouched at the head of his divan, shredding herbs in her bony fingers.

Thorne's first hour of duty had not passed before a cannon roared from the river below the marquee. He had seen the flash before he heard it, and glanced keenly at four ships that were abreast the royal standard.

The court had removed that day from London town to the meadows of Greenwich on the lower Thames. Edward's pavilion was pitched nearest the shore. Across the stream was anchored a galleon that flew from its poop an ensign bearing the triangular cross of Spain.

This ship had entered the river some time since, and the nobles in attendance on Edward remarked that it fired no salute when the king's standard was raised. This omission was set down to the absence of the captain or neglect or more probably to the intolerant pride of the Spaniards.

But the cannon had been fired from one of three vessels coming down the Thames. Ignorant as he was at that time of ships, Thorne saw only that they were merchant craft, stoutly built, no more than half the tonnage of the Spaniard. As they passed between him and the galleon he noticed that the mainmast of the leader came no higher than the Spaniard's mizzen.

The ship that had fired the salute bore an admiral's colors and devices painted on the after-castle, also on the wooden shields that lined the rail. From the green and white coloring, and the Cross of St. George on the banner, he knew that they were English.

"Are they come at last?" cried Edward from within. Raising himself on an elbow, he added eagerly, "I pray you of your courtesy Sir Squire, tell me what ships go out with the tide."

Turning about, Thorne lowered the muzzle of his harquebus to the earth and knelt.

"Three tall and goodly vessels, may it please your majesty, having the Tudor colors."

"'Tis Sir Hugh's admiral ship," amended the duke, who had come to the entrance to look out, "and the two consorts."

The boy on the couch tried in vain to catch a glimpse of the river, and sank back with a sigh. Under his transparent skin blue veins showed. Then a sudden attack of coughing sent a flush even to his forehead. The duke, who was the only noble in attendance, hastened to the old woman and took a cup from her hand, pressing it upon his royal patient.

"Nay, Dudley, nay—" Edward coughed—"I am better without these drafts. So, doth Sir Hugh truly fare forth into the sea?"

"Sir Hugh Willoughby—" the chamberlain bowed—"and Master Richard Chancellor have weighed anchor. You will remember, sire," he ran on officiously, "that they are resolved to seek a passage to Cathay and the new world, America. They will lay their course to the northeast, endeavoring to sail beyond the Christian shores, through the Ice Sea and so south to Cathay."

"Faith, my lord duke," smiled the king, "the Spaniards and Portugals have left us nowhither else to sail. The Pope at Rome hath divided the known world between them."*

A fanfare of trumpets at the shore acknowledged the salute, and Edward lifted his head impatiently.

"Am I not to see them? I warrant you, 'tis a brave sight. Sir Squire, thou'rt stout and stalwart; can'st bear our poor body from this tent?"

"That can I," cried the armiger quickly, and would have laid aside his harquebus, but hesitated.

Edward was ever quick to read the thoughts of those who were near him. He studied the sentinel attentively, taking notice of the wide shoulders, the thews of neck and wrists, dwelling a second on the freckled, sunburned cheeks, still lean from convalescence.

Thorne was no more than eighteen, the king sixteen. Yet in the poise of the head, in the quick gray eyes of the squire-at-arms was manifest the surge of life and health.

"Your thoughts run to grave matters, good youth," Edward said at once. "You are charged to keep your post and weapon. Nay, lay it aside, at my bidding."

Thorne bowed and placed his firelock against the pavilion wall. Then, advancing to the couch, he put an arm under Edward's knees and shoulders and lifted him easily. The slight form of the sick boy in its black velvet cassock seemed no weightier than straw.

At the entrance the king urged him to go forward a few paces so that he could look up and down the river.

---

*In the end of the fifteenth century the Pope decided the conflicting claims of the two monarchs in question by totaling 180 degrees of longitude to each.

"Look, Dudley," Edward cried, "the Spaniard overtops Sir Hugh's ship."

"But yonder craft from Seville," the noble pointed out, "is a galleon fashioned for war. The ships that bear the colors of your majesty were built for the merchant adventures."

"Then, Dudley," cried the boy, "they were stanchly built of seasoned and honest oak."

"True. In the time of your majesty's illustrious grandsire and good King Harry, your father—whom may God save and assoil—no three ships could be got together, but one would be Venetian and one Dutch."

He turned to wave back angrily the throng of soldiery and attendants that had presumed to draw near the pavilion, hoping for a word or a look from the sick boy who was beloved by kitchen knave and noble of the realm alike. Strict orders had been issued by Stratford and those who had the care of the king's person that no one should approach within arrow flight. For this reason the picked guards had been stationed.

But Edward's eyes were on the passing ships wistfully. Here were men faring from the known seas into the unknown. Here were ships built and furnished and manned in England, going forth to discover a new route to the Indies, to bring to England some part of the trade with Cathay and the new world that had swelled the power of Spain and Portugal.*

He watched the burly shipmen in their blue tabards, laboring at the oars of the boats that were towing the vessels. When they became aware of the king they roared out a cheer and pulled the harder. Others climbed up the shrouds to stare and wave a greeting, and a tall man on the poop of the last ship doffed his cap and bowed low.

"Now, by St. Martin," exclaimed Edward, "I should know that gray-beard."

"Sire, your eyes are as keen as your memory is unfailing," responded Stratford after a moment's hesitation. "That venerable ship's captain is the notable navigant and cosmographer—"

"Sebastian Cabot, the Venetian. I know him well, Dudley. And my memory of which you prate tells me his age is fourfold my own. Yet is he strong and hale enough to—"

---

*De Gama, Albuquerque, Cortez, and Magellan were opening up the gold and spice routes for rival princes. In this dawn of the age of discovery it was still believed that America lay near to Cathay. Cathay (China) had not been reached, and was thought to be the heart of the Indies.

The boy's lips quivered and were silent. Thorne the armiger turned his head to gaze at a falcon hovering over the rushes on the far bank of the river, so that he might not behold his sovereign's distress.

"Sire?"

The duke bent closer, and pursed his thin lips.

"Master Cabot or Cabota," he added, "is indeed past his prime. 'Tis a mere courtesy that he stands on yonder deck. For-by he is governor of the Mystery and Company of Merchants-Adventurers, for the discovery of places and dominions unknown, he sails with the ships as far as the haven of Orfordnesse on the Suffolk coast. There Cabot leaves them. He is too aged to attempt the voyage into the Ice Sea. Ha, Sirrah Squire, bear your royal burden into the pavilion from which you should never have advanced. He is ailing!"

Edward was coughing, flecks of blood showing on his pallid lips. His eyes closed and he lay voiceless a moment on the couch. When he spoke it was in so low a whisper that nobleman and armiger both bent lower to catch the words—Thorne expecting that the king might have some command for him.

"Nay, Dudley. Of what avail to guard the body when life itself is leaving me?" With an effort he opened his eyes and made shift to smile. "My lungs are in consumption, the priests say. Good youth, we trust we have not wearied you. Edward will never again rise from his bed."

Both the listeners started. Thorne had heard frequently of the feebleness of the boy, although he had not looked to find him so wasted away. To hear that Edward expected to die was a shock. Few men were victors in the long battle with the white plague. Stratford took no pains to conceal his anger that the sentinel should have heard the words of the king.

"To your post!" he whispered, drawing the youth back from the couch, where Edward was wracked by another fit of coughing. "Keep your ears to yourself, or the provost's knife will e'en trim them to a proper size. Ha—your weapon has been taken."

The harquebus was not where Thorne had placed it, nor was it to be seen in the pavilion. He searched the tent with his eyes, and flushed hotly, realizing that he had allowed someone to steal his firelock while on duty.

He was more than a little puzzled as to how it had been done. The officers of the household and some soldiers had pressed to the entrance of the marquee when he carried Edward forth, but he had noticed no one step within. Perforce, he had not been able to watch the weapon while he stood outside.

Stratford, he knew, had not taken the harquebus. The hag by the bedside sat as before, fumbling with her herbs. Her wrinkled face, brown and dry as a withered apple, was empty of all expression. Certainly the firelock was not concealed under her kirtle.

"So you would make the Gypsy the butt of your carelessness?" grunted the duke. "Have you aught to say, before I make a charge to your officers that you have suffered your arms to be taken from you while on duty?"

"I say this."

Thorne drew the sword that hung from its sling at his hip and took his station at the entrance.

"My lord, if any man seeks to cross my post unbidden he shall taste steel instead of lead."

"*Humph!* The young cock can crow. What more?"

The gray eyes of the youngster narrowed and he kept silence. Although the fault had not been his, he could make no explanation. Stratford, an experienced soldier and a martinet, had no reason to make a charge against him. The duke, however, was irritated by the appointment of the Flanders veterans over his own yeomen and the officers of the household.

"What more?" he repeated sharply.

The second question required an answer, and a bleak look overspread the countenance of the armiger, drawing sharp lines about eyes and chin.

"My lord of Stratford, the command of his majesty was heard by your lordship. He bade me put down my weapon and carry him forth."

"Ha! Master Thorne, you have yet to serve your apprenticeship as a bearer-of-arms at court. To gratify the whim of a boy you made naught of your orders. You were placed here not to act a playmate or to seek royal favor, but to guard the life of your prince. What if you had been attacked by yonder canaille? Body of me!"

This time Thorne kept silent. The nobleman's blame was unjust, but there was enough truth in it to make the armiger realize that his offense would be held unpardonable if Stratford chose to press a charge against him. True, he might appeal to the king, who was honorary captain of the guards.

But Edward lay passive on his couch, forgetful of sentinel or nobleman.

Stratford paced the pavilion, hands thrust into his sword-belt, and came to a stop by Thorne. Seeing that Edward was asleep, he said in a whisper:

"When you are relieved, go to your quarters. Abide there without speaking to anybody of what you have seen or heard in this place. A soldier on duty," he added brusquely, "may not give out what has come under his eye on his post. Can you do that?"

It was long after the armiger had left with his companions of the guard, but without his firelock, that the Gypsy drew from beneath the couch where it had been hidden by the deerskin the harquebus that she had stolen.

Unseen by Stratford and unnoticed by the new sentinel, she slipped the short weapon under her ragged mantle and slouched from the pavilion. She had stolen as naturally as a crow picks up something that catches its eye.

The superstition of high noblemen had invoked her to try to save the life of a dying ruler with her simples, and shrewder than they who had called her forth, she fled with what she could snatch before Edward should die.

Meanwhile the three ships had passed out of sight down the Thames, and out of the minds of the courtiers who talked of changes that were to come, and fortunes to be made and lost. But Edward still dwelt upon the glimpse he had had of the voyagers.

Chapter II
The Signior d'Alaber

My Lord of Stratford sat late at table the evening he summoned Ralph Thorne to his quarters and looked long upon the flagon, both Rhenish and Burgundy. He had a hard, gray head for drink. It helped him make decisions, a vexatious necessity of late.

In a long chamber gown he sat at his ease, a pair of barnacles on his nose and a book printed in the new manner from black letters on his knees. My lord had excellent eyesight and did not need the spectacles; and, although he was not scholar enough to read the book, he firmly believed that it was a mistake to be found doing nothing.

"Master Thorne," he greeted the armiger, "there is a saying—*Quis custodiat ipsos custodies?* Who shall watch the watchmen themselves?"

He put aside the volume and cleared his throat.

"I have been at some pains to learn who you are."

Thorne bowed acknowledgment in silence. He had no patron at court, and the duke was powerful. He had entered upon his duties in the guards with high hopes. In the camps over the sea the name and character of the boy king had aroused the loyalty of the lads who were beginning their military service in the petty wars of the lowlands, and they had waited anxiously for the time when they could appear at their own court.

Now, lacking anyone to take his part and with Edward unapproachable, a word from Stratford could disgrace him or restore him to honest service.

"Your father, sirrah, is Master Robert Thorne, who once rendered yeoman aid to his country by bringing out of Spain a *mappamundi** faithfully drawn. He is known as the Cosmographer, and he dwells on the coast at Orfordnesse."

Again the squire bowed assent.

"You have a reputation. 'Tis said you use a sword like a fiend out of ——, which is to say with skill but little forethought. You have been in more broils than any dozen of your fellows. Once, I hear, you presumed to go forth alone in the guise of a wherryman. So habited, you ventured rashly to row armed men across a river within the hostile camp."

"My lord, we had need of information."

"So it was said. But you forgot your part of a spy and fought a knight of the Burgundian party in the skiff. The matter ended with your placing the Burgundian adrift, fully armed as he was, a nosegay in his hands and candles lighted at his head. In this guise he was discovered by his friends, who buried the body."

"'Twas fairly fought between us, my lord, in the boat. He had the worst. It would have been foul shame to throw an honorable foeman into the water."

The man at the table paused to snuff the candles that stood on either hand and to glance curiously at the youth, his visitor. To draw steel on an adversary in full armor in a small skiff was a thing seldom done, and Thorne had not despoiled the body.

"Stap my vitals!" he laughed. "You have a queer head on you. Now thank Sts. Matthew and Mark and your patron of that fellowship that it has pleased Edward to stand your friend."

Thorne flushed with pleasure and strode forward to the table.

"Grant me but the chance to serve the king's majesty!"

---

*Map of the world.

"*Humph!* As a spy you are not worth your salt. But the king is minded to send you upon a mission."

He glanced upward fleetingly and saw only eagerness in the boy's clear eyes.

"You have learned to handle your sword, but not to handle men. You will want seasoning. The king is pleased to lay command upon you to journey to Orfordnesse and there await the setting out of Sir Hugh's fleet. Do aught that within you lies to aid Sir Hugh in his venture. Your prince hath the matter much at heart.

"Take a horse from my stables, and here—" Stratford signed to one of his servitors who stood by the buffet—"is a small purse for your needs."

Thorne, who had not one silver piece to jingle against another, accepted the gift with a bow.

Stratford hesitated, then rose and came around the table.

"Hark in your ear, young sir. The Spaniards who hold the sea would be well pleased to spoil this venture of Sir Hugh's. Watch your fellow travelers well upon the road and keep your sword loosened in scabbard. Be silent as to this mission, and hasten not back, but return at leisure with Master Cabot. Greet your father well for me."

"A good night to you, my lord. And accept the thanks of the Thornes."

Stratford smiled.

"Body o' me! 'Tis said the Thornes are more generous with blows than thanks. A good night, young sir."

He waited until the armiger had left the room, then went to the door and, closing it, shot home the bolt himself. Idly he turned the hourglass in which the sands had run out.

"Another hour brings other guests. Well, 'tis an easy road to a boy's heart to promise him danger i' the wind. Paul—" he nodded at the servant—"have in D'Alaber and his cozening friend. And," he added under his breath, "may your sainted namesake grant that young Thorne's wit be dull as his sword point is sharp."

The two men who entered the cabinet of my lord Duke of Stratford were dressed in the height of fashion, and one, who wore a doublet of green silk, who bore in his left hand a high-crowned and plumed hat, bowed with all the grace of an accomplished courtier, his cloak draped over the end of a long Spanish rapier. He had the small features of a woman, utterly devoid of color.

"Ah, signior," exclaimed Stratford as soon as the door closed upon

Paul, "you are behind your time. I have been awaiting your ship this se'nnight."

"From the secrecy with which I am received," responded the young D'Alaber in excellent English, "it would seem that I am before my time."

And, turning his back rudely on his host, he walked up to a long Venetian mirror, fingering the ruff at his throat.

"Is the Fox in London, my lord?" he demanded, turning sharply on Stratford, his sleepy eyes downcast yet missing no shade of expression in the nobleman.

"Renard has taken coach to Orfordnesse."

"And why?"

"Signior," said Stratford slowly, and more respectfully than the younger man of lesser rank had addressed him, "who knows? Perhaps the Fox prefers not to be in London when—if—"

"Edward dies," amended the Spaniard coolly.

The duke started and glanced uneasily at the closed door. Then he poured out with his own hand a measure of Burgundy into a gold goblet on the table. This he offered to D'Alaber, who glanced at it quizzically and waited until he was certain that his host would drink from the same flagon.

"To the happy alliance between our two peoples!" cried Stratford, gulping down his wine. "Nay, do you fancy the goblet, D'Alaber? Then, I pray you, keep the thing."

The Spaniard turned it in his fingers indifferently and handed it to the other man, who made less ado about thrusting it into the breast of his robe, first weighing it in his great fist covetously.

He wore the dull damask of a merchant, yet his sword with its inlaid hilt was costly. He stood utterly still—and few men do that—looking down from his looming height on the two noblemen as if he were the solitary spectator of a rare play.

And, in reality, he was attending upon a discussion only too common in these eventful days, wherein the fate of England rested in the balance. While Cornelius Durforth and D'Alaber sat on either hand, Stratford talked feverishly, giving the Spaniard the tidings of what was passing in the court, and at the same time justifying himself.

Edward was dying. Stratford and certain other officers of the royal household had contrived to keep this secret until now. And secrecy they must have to gain time to raise their liegemen on land and sea and discover who was of their party.

Stratford and the Papists of the kingdom supported Lady Mary, the elder sister of the king. She was daughter of Catharine of Aragon, the first wife of the late king, Henry the Eighth.

Others of the Protestant nobles favored the Lady Jane Grey, or the young Princess Elizabeth. But Elizabeth had inherited her father's love of hawking and the chase and carelessness of affairs of state. Meanwhile, Parliament, ignorant of the true condition of the king, did nothing. A few weeks, and the Papist nobles near London would have enough swords to cut down all opposition to Lady Mary.

"And the king?" D'Alaber asked thoughtfully. "No one suspects his evil case?"

"No one," nodded the duke, "save—"

"Ah. It was your part, my lord duke, to draw a veil around his sinking."

The Spaniard spoke courteously, but his words were like dagger pricks.

"A chuckle-headed squire—a niddering—a nobody overheard Edward make lament that his time was drawing to an end."

"And you?"

"I sent the youth on a bootless errand to Orfordnesse, saying that it was Edward's will. Nay, he will not set foot in London again till all is over."

"And there you blundered, my lord. Only one physic will keep a tongue from wagging. His name and time of setting forth?"

"The lad is Master Thorne of Orfordnesse. On the morrow at dawn he hies him hence."

"Then—" D'Alaber tapped a lean finger on the hilt of his poniard and glanced at Durforth, whose eyes, so dark that they appeared to be without expression, were fixed on him reflectively—"we must try phlebotomy, a trifle of blood letting. And now, messers, I deliver me of my charge."

Unfastening one of the laces of his doublet, he drew out two papers folded and sealed with the royal signet of Spain. These he handed to Durforth, who looked at the seal and thrust them into his wallet. Stratford seemed afire with curiosity as to the nature of these papers, but D'Alaber vouchsafed him no satisfaction. Durforth, however, spoke up, twisting powerful fingers in his black beard.

"My lord duke, you are now one of us; you must run with the hounds now, not with the hare. In your presence I have received from his august majesty, Charles, Emperor of Spain, a letter of commission. The other missive I understand to be a matter of state to be delivered when the voyage hath achieved its end."

The duke filled his goblet moodily, chafing inwardly at the insolence of the Spaniard. He could not do without their aid, but he found that their countryman Renard, advisor to Princess Mary, was taking the leadership from him. Stratford knew there was in England at that time a man who was called the Fox by those who had dealings with him; who had caused to be slain secretly some of the nobles who opposed Mary. And he suspected that this Fox was Renard the philosopher.

Stratford knew that another conspiracy was in the wind. Durforth, who had in past years been a merchant of Flanders and the North Sea, had been seen in company with Renard. Durforth, alone of the navigators, knew the coast of Norway. So he had been chosen by the council of Cabot's merchant-adventurers to go with Sir Hugh Willoughby as master of one of the three ships.

Of traffic and discoveries my lord of Stratford recked little. He wondered fleetingly why D'Alaber and Renard set such importance on the voyage of Sir Hugh. He had spoken truly to Ralph Thorne when he declared that the Spaniards would like to make an end of Sir Hugh and his ships. And why were they giving letters to Durforth to bear upon this voyage?

Aloud he said to the merchant—

"Your dallying here hath aroused no suspicion?"

"Not a jot," responded Durforth with his usual bluntness, "thanks to gaffer Cabot. The old cockatrice was afire to sail with Sir Hugh as far as Orfordnesse. So I yielded my place to him and will strike across the country to that haven with D'Alaber."

"Who will return to London," put in Stratford meaningly, "in the train of Princess—shall we say, Queen Mary?"

D'Alaber's dark eyes lighted with some amusement.

"*Señores, porque se tardo tanto*—why this beating about the bush? Nay, it shall be Mary future wife of Philip of Spain, King of England."

"What?" cried the nobleman, the blood rushing to his brow. "Now by my soul and honor, that will never be. Your emperor's dark-faced brat will not be King of England!"

"Mary," made answer D'Alaber, heedless of the other's surprise and wrath, "is ill favored and shrewish. She hath overpassed thirty years and dotes on Philip, who is yet willing to have her for his bride. I see no hindrance to the match."

"But the men of England—Parliament—"

"Will not take kindly at first to a nobler monarch than the Tudor lineage can show. But Mary will have her way, and you of the court have gone too far to draw back, unless you would care to make your excuses to the Fox."

"'Tis the fable of Master Aesop come true," grunted Durforth, who cared little about matters of state, so he was permitted to trade as he listed. "The gentry who were weary of King Log called for King Stork and had sorrow thereby."

"*Por estas honradas barbas!*" cried D'Alaber, drawing himself up in his first flash of temper. "You rovers* and cloth peddlers have no wit to see where power lies. Philip will be monarch of Spain before many years."

He swept his hand about the bare rush-floored chamber of his host.

"Instead of on this filth, you will walk on the carpets of Araby, and these foul walls will be covered with the silks of Cathay. Your table will bear its spices, which now it lacks. For—" his eloquent voice rang with the arrogance of one schooled in a militant and conquering court—"you will be allied to the master of Christiandom, to Charles, Emperor of the Romans, King of Spain, Germany, and the Two Sicilies. Lord of Jerusalem and Hungary, Archduke of Austria, and Duke of Burgundy and Brabant, Earl of Flanders, and—"

One finger, bearing rings set with flawless blue diamonds, tapped the table before the stricken nobleman.

"—and sole monarch of the New World, with all its riches."

His words, sinking into the spirit of my lord of Stratford, left the man silent, sucking in his thin lips. D'Alaber, who had dealt with defeated noblemen before now, glanced at him as a physician might study a patient in convalescence and took Durforth's arm.

"Sir, I leave you to the meditations of prudence and I count upon your pledged aid. Send post to Orfordnesse if Edward nears the end, and so—fare you well."

But Stratford was voiceless, beholding in the eyes of his imagination

---

*The Spaniards and Portuguese were supreme on the high seas in this age and called shipmasters of all other nations rovers.

the chains that were to be put upon him, no less binding for that they were of gold.

D'Alaber shrugged and whispered to Durforth.

"Our islander hath served his turn, but for you señor we have a worthy commission."

"And a mort of danger."

"Ah, true. Have you put upon your ship the globe prepared by us?"

"That I have, and a fine piece it is, bearing a *mappamundi* of all the known world."

"Use it. You know the course you are to sail, and what is to befall in the Ice Sea?"

Durforth nodded and smiled.

"'Twill be a merry company gathered at our setting forth. Nay, how will you keep this lad of Edward's from spying upon us? Had you forgotten him?"

Passing by the long mirror, D'Alaber paused to adjust the clasp of his cloak. "Memory is a good servant but a poor mistress. 'Tis my part to remember this unfortunate youth, yours to forget him. Study your part, Durforth, and *remember* that many an actor hath fallen foul of the pit by mistaking his cue."

Chapter III
A Hawk Is Slain

Ralph Thorne had been born, his comrades said, with a lucky hood on his head. Which was indeed only another way of saying that the boy managed to accomplish what he set out to do. His father, a merchant, was too wrapped up in the mystery of cosmography to thrive at barter and trade. The goods of the Thornes and then the ships and finally the manor in Suffolk had gone into the hands of those who had sharper wits.

Left to his own devices by a father who pored over globe and chart, for years young Thorne kept apart from other boys, who, after the fashion of children, made mock of him for his father's oddities, calling him the brat of the "Mad Cosmographer." He trained hawks, built bird houses in the oaks behind the Orfordnesse cottage, and ran with his dogs when the nights were clear.

Something of woodcraft he learned; he could keep still by a stream for half a day to watch the deer that came down to drink; he could bring down a charging boar with a spear; he could follow the trace of a stag and read, when the snow was on the ground, the stories told by the tracks.

Robert Thorne, after the way of parents, bade him follow the new pursuit of gentlemen, that of mariner adventurer. It irked the cosmographer that his son cared little for his maps and naught for his talk of ships and unknown seas, and bitter words passed between them.

But when a kinsman of his mother, wounded in a northern feud, abode at the cottage until his hurt mended and taught Ralph how to use a sword, the boy went to court with his relative and became an armiger, a squire-at-arms.

There he became devoted to swordplay, but remained what his early years had made him—a boy silent and grave beyond his years, with few friends and his full share of quarrels, because of a passionate temper, the heritage of the northern Thornes.

Having lacked parents and comrades and patrons, he liked best to be left to himself, but there was in him a burning loyalty to those who won his esteem.

And now, on a misty morning, he rode from the stables of the Stratfords in high spirits, though his eyes and lips were somber. He had been given a charge by his king.

To do what lies in me to aid Sir Hugh," he repeated under his breath, "to win to Cathay. For his majesty hath this venture much at heart."

That this was a large command did not trouble him; a youth of eighteen is nothing loath to tilt against windmills or seek, in his thoughts, the stronghold of legendary Prester John. And it often happens that good comes of high thoughts.

At the gate opening upon the northern highway he trotted into a group of men-at-arms who carried halberds though they did not seem to be on duty. They were lean and dark-skinned; they wore finely wrought and polished armor, with thigh pieces and crested morions, inlaid with silver and gold. Thorne knew them for Spaniards.

One of them rose and took his rein as he would have passed.

"Hold, young sir. Thy name?"

Except for the light sword at his hip and the old-style leathern buckler strapped over his back, the squire was unarmed. On one wrist was a hawking gantlet; his favorite gerfalcon perched on it, and a velvet wallet bearing food for the bird was slung over the other shoulder.

"Stand back, knave," he made prompt answer in Spanish. "Loose my rein and curb your tongue to respect. Whose men are you?"

The one who had spoken did as he was bidden, though sullenly. Thorne wondered how Spaniards came to be posted as a guard.

"Signior, I kiss your hands," grinned the leader, "and would have of you your name. We are ordered to deliver a letter to a certain caballero who will pass through here."

"I am Ralph Thorne. Is your missive for me?"

The halberdier looked at his mates and then at the pavilions. "Ride on, signior," he responded. "Nay, go free, for all of us."

Thorne, without a backward glance, struck into the highway and left the last of the hedge taverns of Greenwich behind. The mist pressed about the fields on either hand, shrouding the oaks that lined the road, and to rid himself of the morning chill he put his horse into a brisk trot. After a little he looked up from adjusting the hood tighter about the hawk, and listened.

Then he reined to one side and half turned his beast so that he could see the road behind him, winding at the same time his cloak over his left arm. Another horse was coming up swiftly through the mist, and he had no wish to be stripped and perhaps knocked on the head by thieves.

Seeing that the newcomer was a Spanish gentleman, mounted on a fine Arab, he was about to take up his reins again, when the stranger spurred his beast so close that Thorne's horse tossed its head and edged back, while the other shied.

"Now out upon thee for a mannerless lout!" D'Alaber exclaimed. "To block the road against thy betters!"

Thorne glanced at him swiftly, seeing under a plumed velvet hat a face small and white with intent eyes.

"Nay, Sir Stranger," he laughed, "the shoe is upon the other foot. For a man who cannot manage such a mettled beast as that of yours is mannerless, indeed."

The other smiled indifferently.

"A pox on thy clownish merriment. Here's to requite thee for thy wit, my witless jester!"

So saying he drew the long rapier at his hip and, bending forward suddenly, ran the blade through the falcon that, blinded by its hood, perched on the young squire's wrist. The hawk screamed and fell the length of its chain, its wings threshing. Thorne stared down at his stricken pet, and the blood drained from his face.

"If you were Renard himself," he cried, "you should suffer for this."

Whipping out his rapier, he shortened his rein and kneed his horse toward the other, who awaited his coming with the same indifferent smile.

This smile stirred Thorne to recklessness; sheer anger made the tears come into his eyes and he attacked incautiously. A thrust of the long rapier through the cloak on his left arm brought him to his senses in time to parry the point that might otherwise have passed into his side.

D'Alaber was a man of moods. His retainers at the highway gate could have disposed of the troublesome armiger without risk to himself, but he wished it otherwise. He might have shot Thorne with one of the pistols at his belt, yet he chose to rouse the boy and then to spit him with a certain trick of the sword that he fancied.

The mist hid them from observers, and he could not dally because other riders might come up.

So he engaged Thorne's blade, parried a hinge at his throat and whirled his point. But when his arm went out, the armiger had caught his blade and turned it aside.

"A pretty conceit," muttered the squire, "clumsily executed."

He warded a second riposte, and reined his horse nearer. "You should blindfold me, as well as the hawk."

Now D'Alaber prided himself on his swordsmanship, which was more than good, and the gibe rankled. It was Thorne's trick to talk when steel was out or lead was flying, and the Spaniard's pride was touched. He had the better horse and determined to end matters at once.

He saw his chance when Thorne's beast shied. The dying hawk had fluttered into the road and startled the horses, but D'Alaber's was under control at once. He plunged in his spurs and leaned forward. The two rapiers flashed and sang together, and the Arab swerved away. D'Alaber dropped his weapon and clutched the mane of his horse.

"*Por Dios!*" he cried faintly.

Thorne dismounted swiftly and came to his side, helping him to the ground, where the Spaniard lay moaning, one fist pressed under his heart. His breath came jerkily and his eyes stared up into Thorne's. By an effort of will be opened his lips.

"Tell Master Durforth," he whispered, "on the road a league toward Harwich—tell him D'Alaber is down. The Fox must know. Will you do this?"

Thorne was silent a moment.

"Aye, that I will."

The Spaniard continued to stare at him, and even after the dark eyes held no life in them they seemed to smolder with vindictive rage. Thorne drew the body to one side of the road and tied the Arab's reins to a branch. This done, he mounted again and rode on with furrowed forehead.

"It likes me not," he mused. "The don was a fellow of Renard's and 'tis ill meddling with such. He set upon me with full intent, and there were none to see it. If I am charged with his taking off—"

He was riding on the king's business and did not mean to be delayed. But a pledge to a dying man must be kept, and he wanted a glance at this Master Durforth.

"My lord of Stratford did say that the Spaniards wished us evil, and here is one full of it already, and requited therefore, poor knave. He meant to ride, it would appear, with Durforth, and I must keep his rendezvous for him."

Some moments later he spurred out of the mist at a crossroads where several men had dismounted, evidently to wait for someone.

"Is Master Durforth in this company?" he called out, reining in.

"Aye, so."

A tall man in a fur-trimmed mantle looked up from his seat under a sign post.

"A Spaniard did put it upon me to tell you his sorry case. He lies by the hedge, a league toward Greenwich, and his horse is tethered there. It was his wish that a certain Renard should know of it. And so—keep you better company, my master."

Without waiting, Thorne spurred on and, when the mist closed around the forms of the astonished watchers, bent low in the saddle. A second later a pistol roared behind him and a ball whipped close to his hat. For a while he heard hoofbeats coming after him, then they dwindled as the unseen riders perceived the folly of pursuit in the heavy fog.

Not until the sun broke through the mist and he could see the road ahead and behind did he allow his horse a breathing spell. Then he jogged on toward Orfordnesse, sorely puzzled.

Chapter IV
The Mad Cosmographer

It is ever the way of crowds to mock what they cannot understand. And the good folk of Orfordnesse were in no wise different from other crowds: children thumbed their noses at old Master Thorne; young men sharpened their tongues with witticisms at his expense at the White Hart tavern; the elders shook their heads, saying that no good could come of such doings as his, and there was talk of putting him in the pillory. The very dogs of the haven barked at his threadbare heels when he limped to the ale house.

So that now old Master Thorne rarely showed himself in the village, subsisting no one knew just how, but laboring of nights, as the gleam of a candle in the casement showed. Honest men, it was well known, did not work in the hours of darkness.

So they called him the Mad Cosmographer.

He had gathered in the cottage the fruits of years of wandering, of talks with outland shipmen, of studying mariners' journals and the manuscripts of Oxford. He had brought charts from Paris, and once he had been forced to flee from Spain when he managed to copy fairly the world-map of Ptolemy the Astrologer.

For in Venice and Genoa and Seville the secrets of navigation were jealously guarded; the charts of hidalgos errant were the property of the state, and knowledge of the deviation of the compass, and the use of the cross-staff for observation of the sun were kept from other nations.

But Master Thorne labored of nights comparing charts and drawing the coasts of the Western Ocean and the vague Pacific that was supposed to be no more than a wide strait lying between New Spain and Cathay.

"For, my masters," he said in the White Hart tavern, "how may our shipmen and navigants set forth an' they have not true charts of the outer seas? I have seen the wealth of the new worlds swell the coffers of the dons, and great fleets of caravellas come in from the gold coasts and spiceries. What share have we in this trade?

"The notable navigant, Messer John Cabot, did draw a true and fair *mappamundi*; where is it to be seen now? Where is the good Cabot? Both have met foul play."*

To this the folk of the village made response with many a wink and covert nudge.

"Take care, Master Thorne. Thou be'st grown so great in opinion, the hidalgos may prick 'ee. Thou may'st drink a bitter browst of thine own brewing."

---

*John Cabot's maps perished with him. There was a dearth of charts in England at this time, except for the Sebastian Cabot "Mappe Munde" of 1544.

Master Thorne always faced his tormentors defiantly, stick in hand, his high quavering voice cutting through all other talk as a boatswain's whistle pierces the rattle of gear.

"Our fortune lies beyond the known seas and we men of England have no heart to seek it."

"What boots it," they made answer, "if cargoes of silk and oil and balm come to us from Cathay, out of the Levant in Venetian bottoms? We have enough of our own, God be praised."

They fared well enough to their thinking with the coast fisheries and the occasional run into Antwerp or Venice. Only the Hollanders and the Spaniards built the tall vessels that could venture beyond the edge of the known world. And they were soon weary of Thorne's warnings and urgings that someone must set out on the longer voyages.

"We hold no traffic wi' the seas of darkness, nor the pagan folk," they said.

"Aye," one added, "'tis true beyond peradventure that mariners who sail over the edge of the known seas enter into the realm and dominion of the Evil One."

"Art mad, Gaffer Thorne," gibed a tippler. "Art plaguish wi' thy tongue as thy wildling boy Ralph wi' his sword—he that swashes bucklers and ruffles it among the squires of dames in London town."

"A foul lie," cried the old man, drawing his weather-stained cloak about him and grasping his stick as if it were the hilt of a sword.

It irked his pride that Ralph had never sought for service on the king's ships, and the wits of Orfordnesse knew it.

"Ralph at least is oversea."

"Nay, Gaffer Thorne, he's opzee—seas over. He's drunk as a lord."

"I warrant—" another gibe cut through the shout of laughter that went up at this sally—"the Mad Cosmographer hath come to learn if his lad be master of one of the three tall ships that be standing in past the sand spits."

In this moment, when Sir Hugh Willoughby's three ships had been sighted and many of the folk of Orfordnesse had gathered at the White Hart, Ralph Thorne dismounted from a sweat-darkened horse in the courtyard and entered the taproom, pausing for a moment on the threshold when he heard the words of the last speakers.

He was recognized, although not at once, because he had been a gawky boy in tatters when he left the village some years before. Now his wide gray eyes swept the room tranquilly. The Orfordnesse folk stared at his Spanish boots of good leather, his embroidered baldric and slender rapier, shaped after the new fashion.

They saw a man who could keep his temper at need and his own counsel at will, who walked with a purpose and evidently rode hither with one, since his horse was winded and bore no saddle bags.

"My masters," he said, "I greet you well. My service, sir, to you."

He bowed to his father, who had been peering at him uncertainly.

"Fulke," he added to the innkeeper who came up rubbing his hands, aglow with curiosity, "a stable knave to tend my horse and do you draw me a mug of the opzee* beer that, by reason of being strong and heady, sits but ill upon a loose tongue."

And he smiled gravely on the assembled company.

"Why lad—Ralph!"

The wrinkled eyes of the old merchant-adventurer gleamed joyfully; then he drew into himself with a kind of cautious dignity. Making room beside him on the bench, he stole a glance ever and anon at his son's dusty hip boots and excellent weapons.

"Ha, Spanish leather! And one of those Roman toys. Give me a good, broad tuck now, and I would break you that steel spit you call a sword."

"Fulke," commanded Thorne when that worthy came up with the beer, "do you fetch this company somewhat to drink. Meseems they are but dull and silent."

So indeed the men of Orfordnesse had fallen, and all their eyes were for the young squire and their ears for his words.

"Ah," quoth the landlord glumly, "and who's to pay the reckoning?"

From the purse Stratford had given him Thorne pulled a gold piece and spun it on the table top.

"So you may know it sound and full weight," he assured Fulke.

"Ralph," whispered the cosmographer, "you've been serving the king's majesty. Perhaps you've been on a tall ship of war, eh?"

"Not I."

"Then it may have happened, you've surely an appointment as ship's captain."

---

*This upsea or "opzee" Dutch beer seems to have originated the phrase "seas-over" or "half seas over."

Thorne shook his head.

"Not even for a row-galley?"

"Faith, nor a cockboat." He glanced down at his father quizzically. "Nay, you cannot make me out a personage; no more than an armiger."

"An arms-bearer. An esquire-at-arms. *Pfaugh*, it hath an outlandish ring. And I—"

He broke off as he was about to tell Ralph of the persecution he had endured. Grimly he closed his lips, reflecting that it was ever the way of the Thornes to choose their own path in the world, to keep their own counsel and ask favors of no one.

"I did think that you were a follower of the worshipful Master Cornelius Durforth, who is a ship's captain upon Sir Hugh Willoughby's fleet. Aye, he was pleased to make mention of your name, asking if you had come to Orfordnesse."

"Where abides Durforth?"

"In the manor house, with my lord Renard who is new come from London."

Thorne emptied his mug and looked into it thoughtfully. Durforth must have changed horses several times during the three days' ride from London to reach Orfordnesse ahead of him. He had not known until then that D'Alaber's companion was one of Sir Hugh's gentlemen, and captain of a ship.

"Where did you speak with Durforth?" he asked.

"At the cottage." The old cosmographer lifted his head and nodded proudly. "Aye, he had heard of my poor work. Master Durforth is a skilled navigant. He spared some praise for my charts of the northern seas, and did ask my aid in a vexatious problem."

"In what?"

Master Thorne blinked shrewdly and lifted a warning finger.

"Nay, Ralph, you were loutish indeed to think the secrets of cosmography are to be blabbed in a pothouse."

Ralph had some knowledge of his father's stubbornness.

"Then must I talk with you this night."

"Nay, the reverend Master Cabot hath sent word that he will visit me, upon the evening Sir Hugh makes his landfall, or perhaps it was the next morning. My memory—ah!"

A boy had run in crying that the ships had come to anchor and boats were putting off. Straightway the throng in the tavern dwindled as the Orfordnesse folk went out to stare at the vessels and their crews.

"Enough!" cried Master Thorne, hobbling to his feet and seizing his stick. "We have tarried too long. Come, Ralph, we must greet these worshipful gentlemen; aye, and talk with them concerning the course they will sail and the charts. Now I wonder what charts they would have? What, will you not come?"

He stamped off, forgetting everything else in his eagerness, leaving Ralph smiling at his father's familiar eccentricity.

But, once he had the taproom to himself, the smile vanished and he stared into space with a furrowed brow.

Durforth was in Orfordnesse. Surely the man had been bound hither when he left London with D'Alaber. And the Fox himself was lying at the manor house nearby. Durforth had spoken with Renard.

"Fulke," he called to the landlord, who was leaving the room, "how many followers hath lord Renard in his train?"

"A round score of lusty fellows, who have turned out the stables to make place for their nags," responded the innkeeper sullenly.

Stables! Thorne recalled the guard posted at Stratford's gate, and the attack upon himself that followed. He had spoken to no one of his mission, yet Durforth had known that he was riding to Orfordnesse. Stratford must have told the ship's captain, or possibly D'Alaber. But why?

"Fulke," he called the landlord back again, "here is a fair purse of gold crowns. I fear me 'tis attained with Spanish treachery and so will have none of it. Will you take it?"

He tossed the embroidered sack on the sand that lay underfoot and the tavern keeper caught it up, hefting it in his fist. Then, with a glance around to see that no one was looking, he edged over to the armiger and bent down his hairy face.

"Hark 'ee, Master Ralph, what's the lay? What's i' the wind? I can do a pretty trick for him as is free-handed. Is it a matter of trepanning, or a wench—"

"'Od's life, Fulke, you have a belly that refuses naught. I'm over fanciful as to such tools. Now get you gone and let me think."

Scratching his head and with more than one backward glance, the innkeeper obeyed, and presently bethought him that Ralph was the son of the Mad Cosmographer and so might reasonably be expected to share his sire's lunacy. And after the events of that night Fulke was certain of it, though he never showed the purse to prove his point.

Meanwhile, head clasped between his clenched fists, the armiger was considering how he was going to warn Sir Hugh—whom he had never seen—of a danger that confronted the knight and his ships.

Renard would never have come to Orfordnesse unless high stakes were on the table. Evidently a blow was to be struck at Sir Hugh. But how? The Spaniard's retainers were too few to risk a fight; moreover even the Fox would not dare do that as yet.

Thorne was morally certain that Durforth was an agent of the Spaniard's party. In that brief moment in the mist he had read guilt in the other's startled face. Certainly Durforth had not scrupled to use a pistol on him. Moreover this same ship's captain had by ill chance—he cursed his father's dotage and pride—seen the maps in the Thorne cottage. Renard would be interested in those.

To go to Sir Hugh with the tale? What proof had he to offer? It would be his word against Durforth's, and the matter of D'Alaber's death might be charged against him. That would not serve.

After a while he took up his sword. Here was no matter for words. Two attempts had been made on his life, and he intended to make the third move. He would go among the voyagers, listen to what was said and, if he still suspected Durforth, would pick a quarrel with the man and leave the issue to the swords.

Chapter V
Cathay

The sun was low when Master Cabot landed with his companions. The bent figure clad in dark velvets was unmistakable; the forked white beard had not its like in England. With Sir Hugh, a tall man, florid of face, Cabot drove off to the manor house, leaving Richard Chancellor, master of the *Edward*, and Durforth of the smallest vessel, the *Confidentia*, to sup at the tavern.

This was by reason that three of the mariners on the ships had fallen ill and must be put ashore.

Chancellor, a young gentleman, simply clad in gray broadcloth, without a hat on his tawny curls, made plea to the Orfordnesse loiterers to embark in the stead of the sick shipment; but no one volunteered.

Thorne waited until Chancellor, Durforth, and his father had taken their seats at the long table in the public room, then seated himself at the far end where they could not see him for the Orfordnesse merchants that crowded to places between. And, while he did full justice to Fulke's mutton and pastry, he listened to the talk, which was all of the voyage.

"'Tis clear," observed old Master Thorne, "that a northwest passage to Cathay does not exist—at least where we hoped to find it. The Spaniard, Balboa, has sighted the ocean that lies beyond America. Yet no passage by water hath opened out."

"So," demanded a merchant, "Sir Hugh ventures to seek it in the northeast?"

"Master Cabot," put in Durforth with a slight smile, "doth believe that the open sea extends north of the Easterling* coast to Cathay."

The men of Orfordnesse stared at him in amazement. At rare intervals they had seen the small, single-masted vessels of the Easterlings driven on the coast by a tempest, or come to trade cod and whale oil. These dwarfs—for the men from the edge of the known world were no taller than an Englishman's armpit—were dressed always in fish skins and pelts of beasts.

It was said of them that they possessed the power of sorcery, of putting a blight on cattle, of carrying off maidens unresisting, by the lure of their slant eyes. They could foretell the future, and in their own country they rode from place to place on the back of wild deer, called reindeer.

Between this land of the Easterlings and the pole lay the stretch of water called the Ice Sea. But to sail up, beyond the edge of the known world, into this Ice Sea to seek Cathay!

A red-bearded merchant, who had once been blown up to the Shetlands, smiled knowingly.

"Nay, my lords, you embark upon a fantasy! For a hundred and fifty leagues the coast of Norway is a desert land. And know that off this coast there lies a mighty indraught or whirlpool of waters."

"Malestrand," assented another.

"So men call it. The currents of all the seas do tend to Malestrand, and there are engulfed with a fearful roaring and rack, whirling down to the depths."

"'Tis said," put in the tavern keeper, who had lent his ear to the talk, "that whales, feeling themselves drawn toward this whirlpool, do cry out most piteously. Aye, as ever was!"

---

*Easterlings—Lapps, Finns, and Tatars.

"And ships," nodded the red-beard, "be lost that touch on Malestrand, for-by they're spewed out again as bare timbers and planks. From this central in-draft o' the seas the tides have their being."

To these warnings Master Thorne harkened with small patience, but Durforth, ever smiling and crumbling bread into his empty glass, seemed to be weighing the effect of the tales on his companions.

"So," he observed at last, "I take it the merchants of Orfordnesse have no will to risk goods on this venture?"

One by one they shook their heads, some swearing with a great oath that here was no mere risk but the certainty of loss. He of the red beard, their spokesman, explained matters.

"For that," he cried triumphantly, "the Easterlings are able to summon tempests out of the heavens and floes of ice taller than ships to close the channels. Aye, and a more marvelous thing, to arrest the sun in its natural course, so that it hung ever above the rim of the world and there was no night."

Now for the first time Richard Chancellor spoke quietly.

"The sun will bide where it will, my masters. Our governor, Messer Cabot, doth relate that off the Labrador of America the days are of twenty hours and the night is brighter than in this part of the earth. Storms and ice we may meet and will deal with them, God willing."

At this the aged Master Thorne blazed out eagerly:

"Well spoken! Sir, in my time I have made shift to draw a true card of the world and, to my thinking, open water extends from Norway to the mighty empire of Cathay."

Laughter and muttered pleasantries greeted the Mad Cosmographer, but Chancellor glanced at him with interest, and made courteous answer, slowly as was his habit.

"By experience, Master Thorne, we may come at the truth. By my reckoning, if a northeast passage exists, 'twill shorten the voyage to Cathay by two thousand leagues. So—"

He laid the dagger, with which he had been cutting slices off the leg of mutton, at the top of his plate and touched the pommel.

"Here, or below here lies Cathay, and the island of Zipangu where all silk comes from." He ran his finger from the point to the end of the hilt. "Thus may we voyage from England to Cathay by the northeast passage—if one is to be found."

Then, moving his finger from the point of the dagger, around the plate, he added:

"In this way do the ships of the emperor and the Portingals go to their spicery at the far Indies. As you see, the distance is more than twice as great."

Master Thorne cried approval and lifted his glass, calling upon all present to drink the health of the seafarers, the navigants. The merchants of Orfordnesse responded with an ill grace, and Chancellor, who was a blunt man, eyed them in angry curiosity.

"Your greatest peril," Thorne remarked, "lies in the cold. Passing the seventh clime, the cold is so great few can suffer it."

"We will do what men may," said Chancellor, who was the pilot-major.

"By your leave," put in Durforth, rousing up suddenly, "I hold it folly to go on."

"And why?"

Chancellor frowned as if an old point of debate had arisen.

"Master Thorne hath the right of it; the lands at the pole are uninhabitable."

"Nay," the cosmographer corrected him, "I said you must guard against the cold. Our fathers held that the lands under the Equinoctial* Line were full of an unendurable heat, yet hath experience proven them both fair and pleasant. There is no land uninhabitable, no sea innavigable!"

Durforth emptied the crumbs from his glass with a gesture of irritation.

"Words! As advisor of the council, I say, Chancellor, that we must bide another season. 'Tis now hard upon midsummer, so greatly have we been delayed. 'Twill be the season of autumnal storms when we pass north of Norway. If you and Sir Hugh—who knoweth little of the seas—will not wait another year, at least send to the court and learn the wishes of his majesty."

Now, hearing this, Ralph Thorne pushed aside his plate and stood up, waiting until he caught Durforth's eye. The ship's captain started slightly and his jaw set, so that his pointed black beard seemed to jut forward.

"It is known to me," observed the armiger when silence fell, "that his majesty doth pray for the success of this venture. And any man who puts

---

*The Equator.

an impediment in the way of this voyage is a traitor, no less. Who saith otherwise, lies."

"I will venture where any man dare set foot," cried Cornelius Durforth and beat upon the table with his knotted fist.

No one, seeing the muscles set in his sun-tanned face, doubted that he was capable of making good his words.

"Do not spill the wine," put in Ralph Thorne, his hand on his glass. "And do not bring in question again the wishes of the king, which you should know as well as I."

Durforth frowned at the youth and went on without heeding him.

"Ill luck dogs us this season. The ships had the wind over the hawse standing down the Thames, and three of our mariners be taken sick. These be portents. Turn back, say I."

Again he smote the table until the jugs and glasses leaped and clattered.

"I pray you," said the armiger softly, "do not spill the wine."

"Still your springald's tongue when elders speak!" cried his father angrily.

"Will you bide for word from the king?" Durforth demanded of the pilot-major.

"Sir Hugh will not, nor will I hang back. If it is not God's will we win to Cathay this season, we may yet find new lands and Christian princes to offer us haven."

The ship's master, fingering the gold chain at his throat, shrugged, and the silence that fell upon them was broken by Ralph Thorne.

"Do not spill the wine again, sir."

Anger glowed in Durforth's dark eyes.

"Your loutish words, sir, hint at the manner of your birth. Was it in a ditch, or perhaps a gutter that you first looked upon the world?"

The youth from the court raised his glass in his fingers and tossed its contents into the face of the shipmaster who sat across the table from him.

"Nay, my lord, this should be evidence that I have not learned manners from the Fox."

Durforth gained his feet, and, wiping the liquid from his cheeks, found no words to reply. His hand groped for his sword hilt and he whipped the blade clear, kicking back the chair upon which he had sat. The armiger drew his rapier and placed it point to pommel, against the quivering weapon of the older man.

"Art' content, Master? Our swords be of a length."

"By the eyes of ——, would you stand against me, Thorne?"

"Aye, so, unless," the youth made response gravely, "you are pleased to confess to this company the manner in which you learned my name."

Fleetingly Durforth glanced from the cosmographer to his son, and Master Thorne answered the unspoken question.

"Lad," his old voice quavered with anxiety, "what is this?"

Then, beholding the settled purpose, stern in the youth's face, he flew into a rage at the unforeseen quarrel.

"Better you had died in the gutter, than thus to affront honorable gentlemen. Nay, you are no son of mine."

"'Tis the cosmographer's whelp!" cried an Orfordnesse man. "Have him to the dogs!"

But Durforth swore a great oath and announced that however the villain had been whelped, he would put him into earth before an hour had passed, and summoned Chancellor to act as his second.

"'Tis clear, my lord," cried the armiger, "that you have profited from the teaching of Master Fox. Nay, I have no second, so must perform the office myself—not for the first time. Beside the inn is a fair meadow, and the evening light is good."

Now at the second mention of the Fox, Chancellor looked thoughtfully at the youth, as if he would ask a question. But, meeting with no sign of understanding, he turned away, palpably puzzled. The surgeon from the fleet was at the tavern and accompanied them to the clear stretch of grass that Ralph Thorne pointed out.

The red-bearded merchant was selected to give the word that would set the two men against each other. Ralph stripped himself to his shirt and stood for a moment to let the breeze cool his forehead.

Chancellor and the surgeon were arguing with Durforth in lowered voices, seeking to have the quarrel patched up before harm was done, pointing out that Thorne was scarce a man grown, but Durforth would have none of them.

And Thorne, listening to the break and wash of the swell on the beach where he had played many a time not so long since, now had eyes only for the stalwart figure that loomed in its white shirt over against the trees.

"Begin, gentlemen," quoth the red-beard.

Durforth stepped toward his antagonist, his point advanced, the dagger in his left hand gripped at his hip. The armiger took time to salute him, smiling, and this seemed to anger the shipmaster, who lunged and sprang in, his dagger flashing.

Engaging and parrying the sword, Thorne stepped aside from the dagger thrust, half turning as he did so. For a moment the two blades slithered together as the swordsmen felt each other out. Durforth was in no mood for this and leaped in, grunting, for his antagonist had turned his sword aside and avoided the dagger thrust again.

This time the armiger stepped clear, lowering his point. "Guard yourself better, Durforth, or I will spoil you."

He had not used his poniard yet, but as Durforth thrust powerfully, he locked sword hilts, and stabbed at the man's heart. Durforth was quick to see the dagger flash, and his own poniard went at Thorne's throat.

There was no parrying and no avoiding the double cuts. But Durforth swayed to the right as he struck, so that the armiger's dagger missed his heart, ripping through his side instead. And Durforth's poniard, instead of entering the youth's throat, grated against the collarbone and caught in the shoulder muscles.

They drew their daggers clear, and Thorne, feeling his left arm grow numb, let his own fall to the grass.

"A cool head, I vow," muttered the surgeon, calling Chancellor's attention to this. "He may not strike a good blow with his left, and so presses the tall fellow with his sword. Ha!"

Durforth, feeling the blood drain from his wound, had advanced to the attack again, his dark eyes venomous. But Thorne's rapier coiled over his blade and forced him to give ground. Back and back he went, to the side of the field where they had entered. All his skill was bent to the task of guarding his life, for he was given no further chance to use the poniard.

"A moment ago," quoth the surgeon critically, "the lad would have exchanged his throat for a blow, but now—a rare sword, he. Give you odds, sir, black beard."

It fell out otherwise. Figures appeared in the dusk, running from the tavern, voices cried out and the ringing of steel ceased. Two gentlemen who came upon the scene had struck up the weapons of the antagonists, and between them stood a form there was no mistaking.

"In the king's name, have done!"

Master Cabot's thin voice was rife with anxiety. He breathed hard, having come in haste when he heard at the inn of the duel that was to be fought. With him were others in a green livery, and one especially, who, attired in all the splendor of costly sables and seal skin with a massy chain of gold around his throat, kept in the center of the newcomers as by right and stared about him thoughtfully, pinching his lip between thumb and forefinger.

Durforth dashed the sweat from his eyes and flung down his weapons, calling upon the surgeon to bind his hurt, but Thorne confronted Cabot sword in hand, quivering with anger.

"Sir, by what right do you come between us?"

The old navigator leaned on his stick composedly.

"Tush, lad, is the voyage to Cathay not a greater thing than thy wild-fire temper? I cannot have Master Durforth spoiled for the venture. Nay he knoweth, above all others, the proper course to round Norway. Amend thy quarreling and cry quits."

"Never!" broke in Thorne.

Cabot fingered his long beard, frowning.

"Thy father came to me at the manor house, and did ask that the duel be stopped, for like the loyal Englishman he is, he hath the success of the venture at heart."

"Nay, your Durforth hath earned his death."

"How?"

Thorne opened his lips to reply, but beholding the new arrival who stood apart among the men in livery, he kept silence while the company in the meadow scanned him curiously.

"I may not say, at this moment."

Hearing this, Durforth, who had been bending over the bandage on his side, smiled and sheathed the sword that the surgeon handed him.

"You are discreet—a trifle late, my young hotspur."

"Here is a riddle," murmured Sebastian Cabot. "A youth who proclaims a just quarrel and a man grown who admits of none. Stay! Knowest thou this springald, Master Durforth?"

"Not I. His face is strange to me."

"Perhaps, gentlemen," observed a level voice, "I can rede ye this riddle."

"Aye, we may well profit by thy wisdom, Renard," assented Cabot. "And so shall I be twice thy debtor, since thou hast been at the pains to come from London hither with a coach for my conveyance from the coast."

Chapter VI
Master Cabot Speaks

The man addressed as Renard answered the navigator's courtesy with a bow. He had the assurance of one who makes himself at home in all company, yet the manner of one born in a high station. Carrying his head a little aslant, what with his beaked nose and his fur necklet he did somewhat resemble the fox that his name signified.

"This youth, my masters," he went on, "is known to me and others as a follower of a certain person of the court. It is in my mind that his patron desired the death of your ship captain, and so dispatched this Thorne upon his mission of mortality. 'Tis said others have fallen by his blade in the duello."

His words were tinged with a foreign accent, and he seemed to find in them food for a jest. At any rate he smiled, his thin face saturnine in the dusk.

"Who sent you?" demanded Chancellor the outspoken.

"The king," responded Thorne as bluntly, "by my lord of Stratford."

"Ah," observed Master Renard, "a moment ago you did not deny that Durforth had not the honor of your acquaintance."

The armiger looked at him silently, bending the slender steel between his fingers, paying no attention to the gash in his shoulder.

"And as you do not deny it now," the newcomer pointed out, "'tis passing strange that you should name Durforth a traitor. Nay, is a man a traitor because he spills wine in a hedge tavern? Or—and you are a soldado, a bearer of arms—do you hold him doomed because he resents a slight?"

Still Thorne was silent, alert as if he faced a new antagonist whose speech was no less deadly than the tall man's steel.

"Lacking other evidence," Renard concluded, "it must appear that you picked a quarrel with Master Durforth, who is embarking upon the king's business. Did anyone lay such command upon you?"

Thorne perceived at once the shrewdness in this questioning. Renard must have heard from Durforth of the death of D'Alaber. Nothing was more certain than that the Spaniard desired vengeance for the death of his follower. And Renard had several gentlemen in attendance, with a score of men-at-arms within call.

To make known that Edward was dying and the Papists all but in power might give excuse for a general drawing of weapons in which Chancellor and Sir Hugh, who had no men at their backs, would be slain.

"'Tis a hanging matter you have embarked upon," resumed Renard lightly, "but—"

"No 'buts' my lord!" The armiger laughed. "Either I am a murderer, dealing death for so much silver in hand, or I am a gentleman affronted in his cups. If the second, my quarrel is my own affair and you are cursedly inquisitive; if the first, why summon up the bailiffs to hale me into jail, there to await the king's justice."

"The lad stands upon his rights," assented Chancellor gruffly. "Durforth miscalled him in the tavern. Let him go."

Cabot had been questioning the surgeon, and now turned, palpably relieved.

"Aye, no harm has been done to either. The hurts are slight. Come, my masters, a glass of wine. The ships sail before dawn with the tide."

"I pray you," put in Renard, "come up with me to the manor house, where we shall fare better."

He spoke briefly to two of his men, and Thorne, who watched them in the deepening dusk, saw them move off toward the tavern and the waiting coach. With a stifled exclamation he strode forward, coming between Chancellor and the old navigator. "Master Cabot, do you know with whom you drink?"

"Surely," smiled the navigator, "with the Lord Renard, preceptor of the Princess Mary Tudor."

"And a Spaniard who is no mean cosmographer—who hath no love for us of England."

Sebastian Cabot was old, and loved quiet better than angry words; moreover he was governor of the Mystery and Company of Merchants-Adventurers of London, newly formed. He had labored greatly to outfit and man the three ships, and the last thing he desired was a quarrel with the powerful envoys from Spain at the court.

He rested his hand on the arm that Chancellor held out, and made answer not so much to Thorne as to the others who listened in astonishment to the charge of the young armiger.

"Nay, we would have lacked many things in this venture, had not my Lord Renard given us aid, in weighty advice. He hath been diligent in our council for which we are beholden to him."

By now they had come to the street where Renard's lackeys with lighted torches awaited them, with the merchants of Orfordnesse and those who had come from the ships. These bowed respectfully to the old navigator,

who, leaning upon the arm of the pilot, looked around in benign satisfaction.

"Gentlemen, it is seemly that we should bid farewell to these navigants in such a pleasant hour."

The vague unrest that had clouded his lined features at Thorne's accusation disappeared; his eyes brightened and his voice rang out with something
of the assurance of other days when he had stood on his own poop.

"Let no factions arise in your company, my masters; if you differ in
opinion, submit the question to the council of officers of the captain-
general, Sir Hugh. Remember, when you reach the new lands, to take pre-
cautions against attack.

"The natives you will see, perchance, have no knowledge of Christians
or their ships. If you take one of the savages on your ships, entreat him in
friendly wise, give him food and apparel, and set him safely ashore.

"When you go ashore, leave mariners to guard the pinnace and venture
not to any city of the pagans save in numbers sufficient for your protection and with swords and firelocks in hand. If a storm arises, agree upon
a meeting place where your ships may join together if you are parted."

Then, turning to the people of Orfordnesse, he lifted his hand.

"And you, sirs, who keep to your own coast, bethink ye that these navigants go of their own will into the perils of the sea, and the uncertain-
ties of pagan lands. We hazard a little money upon Fortune, they risk their
lives. For those who, by God's will, are not to return to this coast, whose
sepulcher shall be the sea or pagan earth, let us offer our prayers."

He bent his head, and the folk of Orfordnesse, amazed at his gentle
words, followed his example in silence, harkening to the spluttering of
the torches, the mild rustle of the wind in the foliage, and the sighing and
muttering of the distant breakers. Perhaps it was the first time they had
ever prayed for men who were yet living.

Thorne waited until the last of the gentry had gone off in the coaches of
the manor house, attended by linkmen. Then he allowed the innkeeper,
who had a liking for gossip, to wash out the cut in his shoulder and wrap
wet cloths around it. Which being done, he called for his horse.

"Alack, Master Ralph, thou'lt not ride, wi' thy shoulder hacked and
bloodied."

Master Ralph, pacing the yard betwixt pump and threshold, offering
no response, the fellow tried another tack.

"The gentry be mortal angered at ye, angered as ever was! Thou'lt not be for London town, where the worshipful lords would set thy body on a gibbet. Or it may be a wrack, or e'en fire and the stake."

Abruptly—so quickly that the worthy keeper of the White Hart quivered in the ample region of his stomach—the armiger stopped his walk, close beside him.

"Where is the nag?"

The other muttered something about the horse being foundered and his men all beside themselves, what with the king's gentlemen and the Spanish lord.

Thorne took up the lanthorn which Fulke had fetched with him.

"Nay, I'll wait upon myself." And, glancing back a moment later, he was amused to see his stout host legging it around the tavern.

Reflecting that he had gained, overnight, a reputation for violence, he sought the stables and halted to peer within the carriage house at the line of stalls in the rear. The horses were stamping and restless but he could not see any stable knaves.

Thoughtfully he set the lanthorn down between his feet. The delay in bringing his horse out, the uneasiness of the beasts in the stalls, the alarm of the tavern keeper, all this bred in Thorne an undefinable suspicion.

He was at some pains to make certain by listening and watching the shadows in the stable that no retainers of the Spaniard were awaiting him here.

He was alone in the stable, but not at ease in his mind. Instinct urged him to turn and run through the door, or at least to look around. Instead, the armiger unbuckled the clasp that held his cloak at the throat. Still grasping the loosened ends he stepped forward, over the lanthorn, and let the long riding cloak fall. So it covered the light, and the stable was in darkness that same second.

Thorne stepped to one side, his soft leather boots making no sound on the trodden earth, and laughed aloud. From one of the windows behind the carriages a pistol had blazed and roared, filling the place with smoke and setting the horses frantic.

"A popper is no weapon for the dark, my masters," he cried. "Come in, with your cutters. The door is open."

As he spoke he shifted position again, drawing his rapier and considering how to get himself out of this trap with a whole skin. With his injured arm extended to the full in front of him, and his sword drawn back

ready for a thrust, he moved toward the entrance, through utter blackness. At once his groping fingers touched something that moved and
started at his touch.

His rapier went out, and was turned aside by an iron corselet. In the
same second a pistol went off under his chin, the ball thudding into wood
behind him. The explosion sent a myriad sparks dancing across his sight,
and the powder stung his cheek. Swinging his blade over his shoulder he
struck with the pommel, feeling it smash against a man's head.

A heavy morion clattered on the ground and his assailant staggered back.
Coughing and gasping from the powder fumes, Thorne leaped through the
door and ran across the inn yard. A cart shaft tripped him, and he stifled
a groan as his injured shoulder struck a heap of manure.

Before he could get to his knees he heard men run past him. Others, who
had found the lanthorn, were searching the stable. He lay where he was
until the first of his pursuers had gained the highroad. Then he crawled
around the wagon and between an evil-smelling ordure to the hedge that
he knew formed the fence around the field wherein he had fought Durforth an hour ago.

Following this he reached a thicket and paused to brush himself off and
listen. Horses were being taken from the stable and saddled, and riders
were pounding away on the road. Men were shouting at the tavern—questions to which muffled answers were flung back.

Someone cried out that thieves were at the horses, and a lieutenant of
my lord Renard's harquebusiers swore in two languages that the thieves
had got away.

"You are clever, you who serve the Fox," Thorne mused. "But your master will give no thanks for this night's bungling after he was at pains to
draw away the other gentlemen and leave you a clear field."

Old acquaintance with the White Hart and the village served him well
now, for, avoiding the highroad, he walked down a path that led to a spring
and from thence to a homestead.

Crossing the fields, he headed up Orfordnesse Hill, and so came presently to the cottage of his father.

Lifting the latch, he stepped into the utter darkness of a room. As he was
swinging shut the door, a rush-bottomed chair creaked and a voice addressed him.

"So, sirrah, your lust for blood is still insatiate? Have you come to add your father to the number of unfortunates that have fallen to your sword? Or do I now behold you in the role of a simple thief? Nay, I know your step."

The armiger closed the door gently and felt his way around the table to an empty chair. Master Thorne, he judged, sat alone within arm's reach. Since the fire on the hearth was cold and the candles all unlighted, he knew that the old cosmographer was grieving over the events of the last few hours.

The familiar smell of the room, of leather and musty parchments, stirred in him the memory of other evenings when he had sat at ease by a roaring fire while Master Thorne talked of ships and strange lands and ever of the sea.

"Sir," he said, "I must be gone within the hour with certain garments of mine. Do you propose to give me away to Renard's retainers?"

"I hand over no man in my house. But how will you win free? The soldiery is upon the road and the village is being searched. I met a company of riders who did maintain that you had set upon and foully slain two of their number in a tavern brawl."

Warning his father not to make a light, Thorne felt his way up the narrow stair to his room under the roof, the room that Master Thorne had promised should be kept for him against the time of his return.

And everything was as he had left it. Opening a clothes chest, he drew out a soiled woolen doublet, and hose and light buskins that had served for hunting in other days. Going down with his possessions, he stumbled and uttered an exclamation of pain when his shoulder struck against the stair post.

"Art hurt, lad?"

"Gashed a trifle. 'Twill not keep me from the business of ridding the earth of him who did it, the rogue Durforth."

"Wert ever a wildling, Ralph. I—I had told my people in Orfordnesse that they would see you upon the deck of a king's ship. But now—"

The anxiety that had been in his voice fell cold, and he kept silence while the youth changed to the old garments. It caused Ralph no little ado and pain to ease the stiffened doublet over his shoulder, and he favored his hurt by keeping on the good linen shirt that he had worn to Orfordnesse—a circumstance that he had reason to regret afterward.

Meanwhile Master Thorne had been cogitating, and, while his son wrapped up the blood-stained riding attire into a bundle, delivered himself of his thoughts:

"You may not return to the village; the folk in the manor house would turn you off, if they did not clap you into jail; the highway is closed by my lord Renard's men. So, are you for the woods, where the outlaws and half-plucked gallows birds lurk? Have you a horse?"

"Where I am going no horse may serve."

The armiger felt his way out of the cottage and returned presently without his bundle, explaining briefly that he had hidden it in a hay rick.

"So that the men of the Fox will not come upon it when they search this place, as they will. My sword—" he hesitated, reluctantly—"nay, do you keep it, an' you will—"

"But—"

"The blade is cleaned. Hang it in scabbard on the wall and put dust upon it. 'Twill bring no shame upon the house," he added.

"——'s light, fool! Wilt have need of sword; aye and firelocks i' the forest?"

"The Fox would put such a price on my head that your runagate rogues of the woods 'd have me out of there in a trice. Nay, all roads are closed but one. I'm for the ships."

Master Thorne leaned forward, striving to catch sight of his son's face in the gloom.

"Not Sir Hugh's ships?"

"Aye, Sir Hugh's ships. When do they sail?"

"With the morning tide, lad. The officers go out to their vessels at midnight. But, Ralph, how will you join their company? They need no more gentlemen adventurers and, faith, Master Cabot would not have such a roisterer as you."

"Nor would Durforth, that is certain. But I have a plan; nay, it must keep, for time presses. Renard's men may pay us a visit within the hour. So, harken to what hath befallen me, for you must bear these tidings to London."

Slowly, that the old man might understand everything, and in few words that he might remember, Thorne related all that had taken place at Greenwich.

Chapter VII
The Turn of the Tide

Master Thorne was old, and the old live in their memories; these are real, and the events of the passing days were no more than the spume cast up by waters, to vanish with another day. Master Thorne, sitting in the darkness by his son, could not grasp the changes that he heard as words.

"Edward dying? Now by the good St. Dunstan, that is an ill thing, for the lad was the miracle of our day, being learned and gentle. Aye, I mind him well. Surely, Ralph, you have made much out of little. In the days of good King Harry—"

"These are other days," the armiger reminded him patiently.

"Alack, you have sent one Spanish noble to his long home, and mayhap others. So great a lord as Renard will harry you from the kingdom, lad. These be hard tidings, hard tidings. But you must abide in the cottage, Ralph, and I will betake me to London. They will have a welcome for Robert Thorne. His grace of Northumberland and Sir John will hear me out and bear a petition to the king."

"No, father, the twain great lords are dead long since, and the fortunes of the Thornes are low."

"So you say, Ralph, and so it is." The cosmographer sighed profoundly. "'Tis cold of nights, and no one to sit by the fire."

"We have tasks to perform, sir, and may not sit at ease. Can you not understand? Renard is chancellor in all but name, now that Mary is to be chosen queen. Faith, we may have Philip coming out of Spain to woo her with a fleet of galleons."*

"A Spanish king!" breathed Master Thorne, a little aroused. "Nay then I must fare to court—did you not say it, Ralph?—with my charts and present them to Edward, my completed work, the magnum opus."

"Do so," cried his son, "and relate my story as you have heard it. Nay, hold! You said Durforth came here to solve a certain riddle of navigation. What was it?"

Here Master Thorne was on familiar ground, his memory stanch and quick.

"This Durforth, it comes to me now, is a Burgundian, and a man who loves the bawbees. He has an itch for gold in his fingers, and my lord Renard hath paid out to him some round sums. Aye, I mind he bought a pin-

---

*A year after Sir Hugh set out, Philip of Spain came into the Thames escorted by a hundred ships, to marry Mary. There ensued the short and calamitous reign known as that of "Bloody Mary," when the queen to satisfy her husband caused to be put to death the innocent Lady Jane Grey and her husband. Elizabeth, though imprisoned, was spared—a circumstance that the Spaniards had reason to regret later.

nace with a dragon figurehead, to sail around like a lord in the northern seas. He did bespeak my aid in charting a course."

Master Thorne pondered a moment.

"The man is bold and a skilled navigant. He has coasted the shores of Norway to the north point where begins the Ice Sea. From there, the course he had in mind ran thus:

"From the Wardhouse a hundred and twenty leagues to the arm of the inland sea, south by east. A hundred leagues across the sea to the Town of Wooden Walls. From there the road lieth due south."

The armiger pondered this and shook his head. "It hath the seeming of a cipher of words."

"'Tis no cipher but plain speech."

"How, then?"

"Why the Wardhouse or Guardhouse lieth—so I have heard, for no Christian voyager hath set foot upon it—at the north point. 'Tis there in a tower or castle the Easterlings keep watch and ward upon the Ice Sea. Aye, and the Laps and reindeer folk."

"And what is the sea?"

"Aye, lad, there's the rub. South and east of the Wardhouse there standeth no sea upon my charts. Nor did Durforth know of any."

"He spoke of a town and a road. Surely here is a journey over land. Whither?"

"Why, you should steer north of east from the Wardhouse, if there is a passage open to Cathay. But, turning south and east, you would e'en come to the limbo between Christian lands and Cathay."

"And what is that?"

Master Thorne smiled unseen, and stifled a chuckle.

"Why, lad, do you seek the mysteries of cosmography? Some do say the elf king rules this region; others, a Christian king, Ivan the Terrible, rules over Easterlings, Tartarians, and Muscovites."

"What more?"

"'Tis related that this monarch hath a great treasure of gold and silver, but that is hearsay."

Thorne, sitting by the dark hearth, head in his hands, could make little of this. He sensed, rather than understood, a scheme afoot to betray Sir Hugh. Durforth, who was to lead the fleet around Norway, had another course in his mind, had counted so much upon it that he risked going to see the cosmographer and his charts.

Yet, even while he pondered, he was conscious that his father was moving about cheerfully; he heard a tankard clink and something gurgle into it.

"Ralph," quoth his father, "be the times what they may, I drink to your seafaring, with the good Sir Hugh. 'Tis a proud day and a glad day."

A cup was thrust into the armiger's hand and he tasted spiced wine.

"To your journey, sir," he said blithely. "Seek out the lady Elizabeth and her gentlemen, for she at least is stanch. But go swiftly hence. Tarry not the dawn, for each hour brings its peril. Fare ye well!"

They clasped hands at the door for the first time in many years. Master Thorne took his son's rapier and watched until Ralph had passed into the shadows across the highway. After listening a while, the old man kindled a fire in the hearth and fell to furbishing and polishing the weapon in his hands.

He was tired and bewildered by the swift passage of events and turned to his unfailing consolation, his maps and manuscripts of voyages. Lighting the candles on the table he settled down to pore over them; and lost all account of time.

Dawn had marked the treetops and a fresh wind set the candle flames to flicker when he looked up at last, having been the past moment conscious of horses trotting along the road. The door had been thrown open and two men stood within it watching him.

One, a slender fellow in a broad plumed hat, Thorne did not know. The other was my lord Renard, attired for traveling, who pinched his chin between thumb and forefinger while his glance strayed from the sword and the two cups beside it on the table to the old man's charts and from them to Master Thorne.

"You keep late hours, sir," he observed, advancing and taking the weapon in his hand.

"Come to the fire, my lord," muttered the cosmographer. "'Tis a fair cold night."

"A cold night to bide awake," nodded the envoy. "You are alone, too, I perceive. Yet I am informed that your son passed this way, going to London."

He raised his voice as if he had asked a question, his eyes full on the Englishman. Master Thorne, who was no adept at falsehood, held his peace, wondering what had occasioned this visit from such a notable. He did not think my lord Renard would hunt his son in person; indeed, the behavior of the envoy was far from alarming.

Master Thorne wished now that he had thought to conceal the sword, but his visitor seemed to attach no importance to it.

"I thought, my master," went on Renard slowly, "that you had no son."

"Nay, we had a way of quarreling," spoke up the cosmographer frankly, "but Ralph is a good lad."

His eyes, too, dwelt on the gleaming sword with more than a little pride.

The sallow face of the nobleman was impassive, but he raised his heavy brows and bent over the table to scan the charts and papers spread thereon. And now he frowned, picking up first one sheet, then another. Evidently he was able to judge of their contents, for a muttered exclamation escaped his lips when he examined the chart of the northern seas.

"Ah, you have skill in cosmography, 'tis clear. I seem to remember that you learned your craft in Spain in Seville."

"That is true," assented Master Thorne readily, pleased at the compliment in spite of his distrust of the strangers.

"Such knowledge is priceless in these days of discovery," pursued my lord Renard amiably. "Perhaps it had been better for you if it were not. The merchants of Orfordnesse do not value you justly, but I—"

As idly as if he were casting dust from his fingers, he tossed the sheets he held into the fire, first handing the rapier to the gentleman who attended him. As the sword left his grasp he spoke swiftly under his breath and the other nodded understanding.

Master Thorne gave a great cry when he saw the flames catch at his precious maps. He ran around the table and plucked one of the smoldering sheets from the hearth.

As he did so, the gentleman who attended my lord Renard stepped forward and ran the rapier through the old man's body, withdrawing the blade in the same second and wiping it clean on his handkerchief, which he then tossed upon the floor.

Master Thorne made no further outcry. Swaying on his knees, he fell forward, his head dropping among the crackling logs. Stung by this fresh agony, he moaned and drew himself back rolling over on the hearth, the smoking paper still clutched in the hands that were pressed against his breast.

In spite of the odor of scorched flesh and singed hair my lord Renard would not leave the room until he had seen the last of the maps burned upon the hearth. Then he removed the lace handkerchief that he held against his nose.

"Here, D'Ayllon, lieth a prophet who had no honor in his own country. Leave the stripling's sword by the carcass of the sire. Now—" he considered the tableau attentively—"the yokels of this coast may cudgel their brains, and no harm to us."

D'Ayllon nodded indifferently.

"Still, signior, the son is living and may cause us to be harmed. And that Maestro Cabota—"

"*Pfaugh!* Cabota dodders to his grave, and the stripling we will silence in London."

Master Thorne's body was found within the hour by Cabot, who came to pay his call, and the Orfordnesse folk wagged their tongues apace. They agreed that the cosmographer, being a man of dark belief and uncertain religion, had come to a fitting end. The Thornes were ever a wild lot.

Some held that Ralph had slain his father, by reason of the rapier seen beside the body, and the complete disappearance of the armiger who had come up from London. Although town and countryside were searched by the bailiffs, no trace of young Thorne was to be had.

Certain men who had gone down before midnight to the shore to watch the setting out of Sir Hugh and Richard Chancellor, and had been talking to the shipmen waiting by the boats drawn up on the strand, remembered that a strange youth had approached them, walking unsteadily and to all appearances drunk. Assuredly he must have been drunk, since he offered to join the shipmen to go upon the voyage to Cathay.

He was a well set-up lad they saw in the faint light, and the shipmen called him a lad of spirit. His soiled leather doublet and his features were smeared with blood—this struck them afterward—and he spoke thickly.

A burly man from the ships, with limbs like an ox and brass rings in his ears, hauled the volunteer into one of the boats, and there he collapsed on the thwarts, perhaps from loss of blood, perhaps from the drink in him.

The other boat keepers argued that such a man would do them little good; but the boatswain with the earrings swore in a way that made the Orfordnesse folk stare that the *Edward* was short three wights and he would make a hand of the young yokel.

Chapter VIII
Peter Discourses

A fortnight later Sir Hugh Willoughby's ships had left the coast of England far to the south, and with favorable winds were passing along Norway. Luck was with them, for in a region where storms and mists were expected they were able to keep in company. Every evening a cresset was kindled on the poop of the admiral ship, the *Bona Esperanza*, to mark its position during darkness, and every morning the two consorts would run up while the admiral ship lay to. Hails were exchanged, the number of sick reported to Sir Hugh, the course set for the day, and a rendezvous appointed in case of separation by a storm.

This was the hour when the watch below came on deck, to harken to the daily fanfare of trumpets, and to muster for morning prayers at the image of Our Lady.

"For-by," observed Peter Palmer, boatswain of the *Edward*, "Sir Hugh be a man for discipline, aloft and alow. 'E's sailed under the king's colors many a time, and a rare, fine gen'leman 'e be. Brave as ever was. Though 'e's no hand for pilot work or laying a course."

And the boatswain spoke with the voice of authority, having voyaged to the far seas, to Malabar and Zipangu in Portuguese ships. He approved strongly of Richard Chancellor, the master of the *Edward*.

"Blast my liver, but 'e's a proper man, steady and determined-like. 'E reads to us lads out of the Bible itself, and 'monishes us like a minister of God. 'My bullies,' says 'e, 'forasmuch as all who sail the sea be standing on and off the port of the Almighty, we should stand by in readiness to face our Maker. So,' says 'e, 'let me hear no blaspheming, nor ribaldry, nor ungodly talk upon this ship.'

"And a fine thing it be," he concluded, "to have along of us a reverend gentleman as can grapple the —— himself. Now, —— me if it a'nt!"

Peter Palmer knew his own mind, and was quite ready to speak it upon all occasions. He was built on the lines of the *Edward* herself, broad and solid of timber. Although he must have weighed close to two hundred and fifty pounds he could move about as quickly as the cabin boy.

His freckled face was a mirror of good nature, belied by the hard gleam of blue eyes that were always restless.

He took Thorne under his wing from the first, after the armiger had lain ill—what with fever from his wound and the tossing of the high-pooped merchant craft—for the first few days.

The ruddy boatswain brought him the half of a fresh-cooked cod as soon as he was able to eat, and plumped himself down in the berth across from his victim, chewing his thumb in silence until Thorne had finished the cod and the nuggin of wine that came with it.

"Captain's orders—fresh fish and wine for the hands that be taken sick. And why? Because the salt pork is corrupt, and the beer is vinegarish. Aye, as ever was. Likewise, the wine casks are not stanch, so the half of it hath leaked out."

"Hm."

Thorne passed a hand ruefully over the bristle of beard on his chin and throat.

"Some of the merchants are all for turning back," added Peter, "but Sir Hugh's not the man for that. Hark 'e, my master. What game might ye be a playing-of? Thou'rt no more a lout than I be."

"What, then?"

"Why, by token of that white shirt, thou'rt gen'leman born. Come now, what's the Jay, a gen'leman born passing hisself off for a yeoman? Ah, that were a good song."

Grinning, even while his shrewd eyes dwelt on Thorne, the boatswain began in a very hearty voice:

> *"I saw three ships come sailing in,*
> *On Christmas day, on Christmas day.*
> *I saw three ships come sailing in,*
> *On Christmas day in the marning."*

Chuckling he slapped his thigh, and cocked his great head to one side.

"Ralph, lad, that were well sung!" And added in his stentorian whisper:

"In the dark ye fooled me. But now, ye talks like a gen'leman, drinks like a lord, and eats dainty as a prince. Why come off to the ships, Ralph, lad?"

"Have you forgotten," asked Thorne, "that I was fuddled—seas-over?"

Peter scratched his head over the black hood that he wore ever about his massive shoulders and sconce.

"Why, no, Ralph, no. But ye sniggled me as to being a yokel. Y'are a gen'leman born. I say and so it is. Now mightn't ye be a sniggling of me as to being fuddled. Supposing, now, ye was sober? Eh? We had sore need of mariners, so I took off the first likely lad that showed in the offing. But supposing ye was sober; why ever did ye go for to be took off?"

He glanced around the narrow forecastle, lighted after a fashion by two small ports and reeking of the bilge. Smoke from the galley—the wind being over the stern—clouded it, and the odor of grease and burned meat vied with the stench of soiled garments.

"This fo'csle a'nt suited to a gen'leman's disposition now. But y' are content to lie abed here. Most 'mazing content ye be, Ralph.

"So I says to myself, 'Peter, this young un's lying alow for a good and sufficient reason.' And what might that reason be? 'Peter,' says I, 'in all likelihood he does not wish to show his mug on deck for a while.' Until when? 'Why, Peter,' says I, 'until the coast of England lies well astern.'"

The blue-eyed boatswain was not far wrong in his surmise, though Thorne's lean face told him little.

"I'm not a chap to ax questions," he went on, "and it's all one to me whether ye put a knife to the innards of another gen'leman, or summat else. Let bygones be bygones."

He held out a hairy fist and Ralph took it. Peter Palmer was the only man on the *Edward* who knew the manner of his taking off, and so long as the boatswain kept his counsel, no talk would arise to come to the ears of Master Chancellor. Ralph himself determined to keep both his identity and his mission secret for a while, until he could look around and get his bearings.

At first he had been disappointed to discover that he was not on Durforth's ship. Now he was glad of it.

On Durforth's vessel, the *Confidentia*, which was much smaller than the *Edward*, he did not think he could have escaped notice. And, if Durforth had knowledge of him in his present situation, the easiest fate he could expect would be to be cast into the bilboes.

Peter saw to it that he was provided with a heavy robe from the merchants' stores to fend off the cold, and a small slop chest, with needle and thread, a knife, and a wrapping of frieze to sleep in, proceedings that aroused the curiosity of the shipmen who berthed in the forecastle and had experienced no such tender mercies from the boatswain. Until one day Peter haled the landsman into the depths of the ship.

Here he was turned over to a being who answered to the name of Jacks and was the ship's cook. His duties were to tend the galley fire, fetch the victuals to the mariner's mess on the main deck, to wash plates, swab out the galley, and in general to do whatever Jacks was minded he should.

"Ho, a landsman!" grunted the cook.

"Ah," nodded Peter, "a landsman as is a fancy hand with dirk or fist. A man as has put better men than you, Jacks, where only the —— could find them. So speak him civil and keep your hand off him, or we'll have a new cook and fare better by the same token."

"Fare better!"

Jacks was blind in one eye and the other was askew in his head, giving him a limited range of vision, but a baneful stare when his feelings were aroused, as now.

"You sons o' bilge puncheons 'ud like pickles with your beer, and rum every time you spit, I'm thinking. Half the stores were rotting in the salt barrels when they were stowed."

"So ye say—" Peter winked at the armiger—"but I say it's enough and more to spoil the beer to have it under hatches along of you, Jacks."

He took Ralph aside for a word of advice.

"Bide here for a time. Y'are a landsman, mind, and Master Dickon and his bullies will stand for no favorites. Be a swabber for a while, then we'll make shift to have ye out of the orlop. By then thy natural mother, Ralph, 'ud not know ye for her son."

This proved to be true. For days Ralph labored in the dark hold, at duties that turned his stomach even more than the pitching of the *Edward*. Once, watched by the saturnine eye of Jacks, he tried to wash head and hands in a bucket of salt water and surveyed the result ruefully. Soot and smoke coated the grease that clung to his skin.

Once on the spar deck, during evening prayer when all hands except Jacks were mustered in the waist, Chancellor met him face to face and half frowned as if something about the landsman struck him as familiar.

But at that moment a hail came from the masthead.

"Sail ho!"

That day they had entered a belt of fog, and though the shore was scarce a league distant they could see it not. They were lying-to, upon command of Sir Hugh, near a village from which Chancellor had been able to procure a boatload of fowls, to eke out his scanty stock of meat. Ralph could smell the hay that the people on shore had been cutting and the fresh, strong odor of pine trees.

But by degrees, as he watched the curtain of mist from the windward rail, he became aware of another odor, less pleasing.

Out of the mist a black vessel took shape—a long pinnace with two masts, only the foresail being set. It moved down the wind sluggishly, and he heard Chancellor mutter that it had the seeming of a pirate craft. Ralph wondered why such a small boat should venture to attack the *Edward*.

Chancellor sprang into the shrouds and bellowed through cupped hands:

"Stand off, or you will foul us. Keep to our lee, or take a shot!"

He repeated the warning in Dutch, but the pinnace kept its course. The master gunner, with some of the hands, climbed briskly to the foredeck of the *Edward* and whipped the tarpaulin from one of the calivers, while others ran below for shot and powder and Peter came up from the galley with a slow match that he had kindled at Jacks's fire.

The weather-beaten faces of the men about Ralph brightened at prospect of a fight. They were a rugged lot; many of them had sailed with Chancellor before and Peter dubbed them "tarry-Johns." Yet the master gave no order to issue swords and pikes to the crew.

His hail had not been answered, and before long all on the *Edward* saw the reason. The pinnace slid nearer, and veered away uncertainly. A man was visible now at the wheel, and another was perched under the bowsprit on the crudely carved dragon that served for figurehead.

Another pair hung from the yard on the foremast, and two others from the main yard.

They hung by the necks and turned slowly as the yards swung with a dry creaking. A puff of wind bore the pinnace almost under the *Edward*'s counter and Ralph saw that the helmsman was as dead as the others, bound to the tiller. So, too, the sailor on the figurehead remained immovable, lashed to his place, his head sunk on his chest.

The rank smell of decay was stronger on the air. And then the black pinnace glided out of sight in the mist, vanishing without guidance from living hand and bearing with it that strange crew of inanimate beings.

With its disappearance the spirits of the men on the *Edward* revived perceptibly, some saying that it must have been a plague ship, or a craft from Danemarke that had been taken by pirates.

"Be that as it may," muttered Peter, "it bodes no good to us. Those chaps had been strung up for many a day by the looks of them, and still it keeps the sea."

"You are wide of the mark," put in another, who had made the voyage to Iceland. "Yon's the handiwork o' the Easterlings."

"What's them?" asked a young sailor, who was listening with all his ears.

"Why, the little people as keeps watch and ward upon the Ice Sea. East-erlings they be. They've set their hands to that pinnace."

"Save us!"

"Aye," nodded the old hand, "here we be up beyond the *Circulus Articus*."

"By what token?"

"By this token, bullies all. 'Tis now nine o'clock, and yet the light holds. Come on watch at three bells and the light will be upon us anew."

"Aye," assented Peter moodily. "The hours o' darkness be dimin-ishing. But the powers o' darkness be a-growing and a-girding and a-coming about us."

As if to bear out the truth of his remark, the wind turned contrary and held the ships back. They seldom saw the sun now, except as a ball of silver hung in the mist. As the Iceland-farer prophesied, the nights grew shorter instead of longer as the season advanced.

Hard bitten and callous as were the hands of the *Edward*, they were su-perstitious to a man, and the visit of the black pinnace had set them on the lookout for more omens. The very day they changed course from north to east, having rounded the North Cape, one of the men on Sir Hugh's ship reported that he had seen a mermaid in the half-light of late evening.

He swore that the white body of a woman had appeared under the stern, a woman whose long hair was like seaweed, and who beckoned and smiled at him, before diving into the depths again. When she dipped out of sight he beheld clearly the scales of a fish and a great tail that whipped the water.

Both Peter and the Iceland-farer were agreed that the sight of the mer-maid presaged death on board the *Bona Esperanza*. They recalled other occasions when shipmen who had been beckoned by women swimming upon the waters had fallen overboard in a storm.

The burly boatswain kept a careful rein on his own unruly tongue thereafter. Ralph he relieved from duty in the galley and made boatswain's mate, saying that the lad had done his work well and could help him upon the deck.

So the armiger enjoyed a good wash in fresh water, and persuaded the quartermasters to give him a new, clean leather jacket and hooded frieze shirt as a protection against the growing cold. The sailors believed that they were about to enter the Ice Sea, because they saw several whales, and noticed that Chancellor took his noon observation with more care than usual.

More than once Ralph caught sight of Durforth, when the little *Confidentia* drew abreast of them—the tall figure, clad in a robe of foxskins trimmed with ermine was unmistakable. He could even see the broad chain of gold the man always wore.

It was the day they saw the whales, the last of many upon which the circle of the sun was visible through the mist, that Durforth hailed the *Edward*. He had just completed his noon observation and held the backstaff in his hand.

Ralph, busy in the waist of the ship, caught a few words.

"Seventy degrees of latitude—the first of August, and soon the ice—Wardhouse."

Every hand of the watch on deck cocked an ear to hear Chancellor's reply, which came at once.

"It stands not with honor to turn back."

"We lack victuals to winter in the Ice Sea—a barren coast."

Chancellor's ruddy face darkened with anger, whether at Durforth's words or because the master of the *Confidentia* had spoken within hearing of the crew Ralph did not know.

"Sir Hugh is general of this fleet. And we are for Cathay, not the Wardhouse."

Peter nudged the young landsman in the side with force enough to crack a rib.

"There's Master Dickon for ye! Aye, but he did not see the mermaid. Nor does he sour his throat with the beer in our butts."

Ralph glanced at the mariner curiously.

"Would you run from a woman, Peter?"

"Aye, younker, that would I. Signs and portents are sent for our understanding. Whatever befalls, some chap on the *Bona Esperanza* is doomed."

The big boatswain glanced at him sidewise and shook his head soberly.

"Lad, I be fair 'mazed at 'e. Thou'lt say next there is no black magic as well as white; aye, no powers of numbers or planets."

"It seems to me," quoth the armiger, "that a man stands or falls by his own deeds. I have come upon no spell that a sword would not sever."

Peter's great jaw fell open and he stared, round of eye.

"Now, —— take 'e, I mean, Our Lady save us! Lad, lad! I'll not gainsay the potency of Our Lady—" he nodded at the image on the mast—"but here we be on the Ice Sea; so Master Durforth did maintain, and who else should reck as well?

"Now Satan hath dominions of his own, and if this be one of them, why hold hard, lad, and do not miscall the powers o' darkness. Especially—" he nudged his friend violently in the ribs—"*especially* if ye have the blood of another gen'leman on your soul."

"If we are truly entering the Ice Sea," responded Thorne, "I must speak with Master Dickon, at once. Do you see to it, Peter."

To his surprise the boatswain rolled off without objection or question, and the armiger braced himself for the task of accusing Durforth on his unsupported word. By now he knew it was no light matter so to bring in question the master of a ship—this knowledge had impelled him to hold his peace, until he could win the confidence of Chancellor. But the pilot-major seemed to avoid Thorne.

However, Thorne walked toward the poop rail, having fully decided to go to Chancellor and tell him his own side of the story.

Chapter IX
The Rendezvous

Chancellor was seated in the narrow stern cabin by the table on which lay astrolabe and backstaff. Powerful hands clasped behind his curly head, he nodded as the landsman entered.

"You asked for a word with me, my lad?"

"Yes, Master Dickon. And I pray that you will hear me to the end, for this is a matter that I may no longer keep to myself."

Gripping the deck beam overhead, to steady himself against the roll of the ship, Thorne began his tale.

"I am Ralph Thorne, son of him called the Cosmographer, and I fought Master Durforth at Orfordnesse in your presence."

The master of the *Edward* showed no surprise at this, but as the youth went on to unfold all that had taken place in London, he fell serious and his eyes never left the speaker's face.

"It is ill doing," he made response in his slow fashion, "to lay a charge against a man without proof, on hearsay and suspicion."

"That is true, Master Dickon. But so is my tale."

"According to your story, you came secretly to the ship. Since then you have lain hidden. How am I to take your word against that of a gentleman?"

Thorne felt his cheeks grow hot as he leaned forward, checking a harsh retort with an effort.

"Sir, my presence here should be a surety of my mission, which is to serve the king."

"Was the murder of the honest gentleman your father included in this mission?"

"My father? Nay, he is alive and hearty."

Something in the face of the older man choked the words in his throat.

"My father—what of him?"

"Within an hour of our embarking Master Robert Thorne was slain with your sword in his cottage, and all his maps were burned on the hearth."

As the youth made no response, Chancellor added slowly:

"The truth of this is established by Master Cabot, who, after bidding us farewell on the shore, went to your father's cottage to have speech with him. Finding him as I have said, Master Cabot returned to the shore and came out to us in a skiff, to ask if any upon the ships had knowledge of the deed or of my lord Renard."

"What of Renard?" asked Ralph through set teeth.

"He was to have escorted the venerable pilot back to London, but, missing him in the village, apparently went on alone."

Ralph bent his head a moment, touching with his hand the rude drawing on the table, so unlike the delicate tracery of his father's charts.

It came into his mind that the Cosmographer would never, now, behold him returning with the king's navigants, and the certainty that Master Thorne was no longer living filled him with a longing to have lived otherwise. With his own sword!

"Sir," he cried, "I do hold it ill of you that you should have thought me guilty of my father's murder. One thing I must ask of you—nay, two. A sword and to be put aboard the *Confidentia* where Durforth is."

"Not so."

Chancellor rose, stooping to avoid the deck beams overhead, and held out his hand.

"I did no more than test you with words. A man may lie with his tongue, yet his eyes must e'en bear witness of his honesty. Your eyes are honest. 'Tis so I judge a man."

"Your friends," assented the armiger, "do say that you are just, Master Chancellor. I have found you so."

The big pilot shook his tawny head as if impatient of a burden that was not to his liking.

"In these treacherous days when poison is in the very air of England, I may not easily know who is friend and who is unfriend. Before this I had other evidence that approved your innocence."

"How?"

"A ship's master is more careful than you reck. When Peter rowed me out that night, I questioned him of the new hand that he had trepanned."

Chancellor smiled, and when he did so his weatherbeaten face glowed with a kindly light.

"Peter's a rare rogue—cheats the gallows with every breath; yet is he loyal to those he serves. None so long before you appeared upon the shore he wandered off to the ale house to wet his throat. There he heard the tumult raised by my lord Renard's fellows when they sought to put an end to you.

"Peter hath the Spanish gab and heard something of their secret talk. I examined you straitly while you lay unconscious, and knew you for Robert Thorne's son."

"Yet told me naught of his fate!"

"It is not easy to relate such news, my lad. You lay ill. Moreover," the pilot added quietly, "I will not join in fellowship with other men if they be not open with me. I bade Peter put you to test, the which he did after a fashion of his own."

He motioned Thorne to a seat beside him in the stern casement and put his hand on the youth's shoulder.

"It was not in my mind to deal hardly by you. 'Twas best you should lie hidden, lest Durforth come to know of you and demand your punishment of Sir Hugh, who holds him in much esteem."

"And what, Master Dickon," cried the armiger, "is your thought of Durforth? I will face him and accuse him of abetting my father's murder—which was by Renard's hand I will swear."

"Master Durforth was on his ship when it took place."

"It is true that the pair of them slew my father," insisted Thorne from set lips, "and I shall take vengeance for that black deed."

"But Durforth we may not accuse. Others might have caused the moldering victuals to be put in the holds. Durforth is a skilled navigator, and hath on the *Confidentia* a rare globe showing the passage we must follow."

"What of the course he laid down, to the inland sea?"

"Faith," smiled the pilot, "I would give half my share in this venture to know the truth of that. He hath made no mention of it in council. 'Tis a riddle that will someday resolve itself.

"My lad, I will enroll you among the gentlemen adventurers. You will be the fourth upon this ship. We will observe closely Durforth's actions, and know whether he be honest man or rogue. On the morrow the council meets in the cabin of Sir Hugh and I will ask Durforth of this inland sea and Town of Wooden Walls."

Chancellor was a man slow of decision but one who would not draw back once he had made up his mind. Seeing this, Thorne shook his head, yet would not gainsay the plan of an older and wiser man. He thought that the master of the *Confidentia* was too shrewd for Chancellor's questioning, and in this he was right.

But it fell out not as they had planned. The mist thinned away steadily though the nearby shore was still hidden. They could hear the surf breaking on the rocks, and the cries of rooks and gulls. Once the lookout of the *Edward* sighted a skiff with one man in it—a dwarf whose fishskin garments glittered with spray.

He pulled out to stare at the *Edward*, which was making little way in the heavy cross seas. And then, with a glance to windward he bared pointed teeth in a soundless laugh and pulled away for the shore.

The three ships bore in, and presently sighted the cliffs of a headland. But the wind, which had been rising steadily, grew to a full gale, twisting and buffeting the little vessels until Sir Hugh made signal to put about and gain sea room, entrance into the bay being impossible.

A lowering sky seemed to press the very masts of the *Edward*, and through the sweeping cloud wrack Ralph caught a glimpse of the silver circle of the sun, low over the land. He noticed that the cries of the birds had ceased, and that the mariners were taking in all but the main- and foresails.

Obeying a second signal from the admiral-ship, Chancellor, whose vessel was the handiest of the three, ran within hail of Willoughby on the lee side. The shout of the captain-general came to them faintly over the thud and hiss of the waters and the whining of rigging.

"The rendezvous is Wardhouse. A' ——'s name, Dick, stand by me."

The next moment the dim light was eclipsed as if a lamp in the sky had been put out; a blast heeled the *Edward*, splitting the main course. As far as Thorne could see the horizon was a void, laced with the white of flying foam.

Out of the blackness the white crests of waves roared at him, crashed on the bow, filling the air with spume, and raced aft to merge into the boiling wake. He propped himself against the bulwarks and hooked one arm around a backstay, bending his head to snatch a breath of air.

He did not dare to stir from this post of vantage, but the able shipmen he could see laboring at the jeers, where the mainyard with its shreds of sail was being lowered away and secured. Ever and anon he heard Chancellor's shout—no louder than a whisper—and the answering pipe of Peter's whistle.

For a while he watched the stern lantern of the *Bona Esperanza* pitching in the murk ahead of them. Sir Hugh was carrying more sail than Chancellor, and drifted farther to leeward, so that presently the point of light winked out. Ralph, awed by the racing seas, kept the deck, full of wonder and interest, and half believing that the ship would break into pieces the next moment.

So it happened that some hours later—he judged it to be the mid hours of the short night—he heard a startled cry from the foredeck.

"Ice on the weather bow!"

From the topgallant poop behind him came the hoarse bellow of Burroughs, the master.

"Helm hard a-weather! Veer out the foresheet to wear ship!"

For a moment the *Edward* seemed to hang back and Thorne loosened his hold to peer over the side. He could see no ice, nothing save a vague blur of white where the seas were breaking. Then the ship brought-to on the other tack with a lurch and he lost his balance, rolling into the lee scuppers.

A rush of water drenched him, and he struggled to his knees, coughing and shivering, when a powerful hand caught him under the shoulder and drew him erect. He made out the great bulk and the reeking leather garments of the boatswain.

"Gunner," Chancellor's clear voice rang out, "fire me a caliver to leeward."

The wind all at once seemed to Thorne to grow bitter and chill as in mid-winter. He waited until one of the small guns of the forecastle flashed and roared.

"Are we doomed, Peter?" he cried. "Is our time run out?"

The boatswain, who had been peering over the bulwark, roared with laughter.

"'Tis the younker! Nay Master Ralph, thou'lt live yet to be hung. This is no more than a fairish blow, a goodish blow, ye might say. The caliver was fired to warn the others of the ice, if so be they are within sight or hearing, which I doubt."

The *Edward* rode out the storm and headed back to the coast without sighting either of the consorts. Chancellor thereupon set about finding the Wardhouse. He picked up the two headlands from which they had been driven by the gale and ran east for a day along a coast that was brown and bare of trees, with snow lying on the heights.

This snow, the Iceland mariner maintained, never melted, a thing that seemed beyond belief to the other shipmen. But they saw nothing of any habitation, much less a town.

They did sight a clump of islands lying several miles offshore, and Chancellor decided to put out and land upon one of them. The *Edward* was in sore need of both wood and water.

The island they selected was overgrown with stunted firs and birches on the higher ground, and a rocky pinnacle offered a good lookout. Burroughs had noted a likely cove for anchorage where he thought they would find fresh water.

The work was not at an end when those on the ship saw the boat put out without the casks, and half the men. Peter, coming over the side, reported to Chancellor that a man sent to the height had seen a dwelling near the center of the island, where the forests hid it from view from the sea.

"What manner of dwelling?"

"A great house it be, with wall and tower."

"Then it is the Wardhouse. For this is the northernmost point of land, and must lie along the seventieth degree of latitude. Aye," Chancellor added thoughtfully, "no other ships from our part of the world have ventured as far as this."

He ordered Robert Stanton, master gunner, a dour man, except in liquor, with two gentleman, Thorne, and a half-dozen hands to make ready to accompany him to the shore. The gentlemen donned corselets and girded on their swords, taking also hand guns, while the mariners were content with pikes and cutlasses. Leaving the ship in charge of Burroughs, they went off in the pinnace.

On the gravel of the beach they noticed marks where other boats had been drawn up—fishing craft or ketches, the Icelander said. And Stanton hit upon a beaten path that led in the direction of the house. It bore the signs of frequent use, but no heel marks were visible. And it took them up through the pines, past gullies where snow lay in deep patches, to a clearing where only ferns and a kind of flowering moss grew.

A stout log palisade stood in the center of the open space, and a thatched roof and the bole of a rude stone tower were to be seen above it. Chancellor, bidding his men look to their arms, went up to the gate and thrust it open.

"Christians have been here before us by token of yonder grave and the cross above it," one of the gentlemen observed, and they went on with more assurance to the door.

It opened as readily as the gate.

"Ho, within! Have you no welcome for wayfarers?"

The cry went unanswered, and the house was found to be deserted, though signs of occupancy were not wanting. In the hall were stacked bales and fardels of traders' goods, broadcloth, kerseys, and raisins, and round pewter. A book of reckoning bearing the name of one John Andrews, of Cairness, lay upon the bundle.

This book disclosed no more than lists of barter, by which Chancellor made out that the cloth and pewter had been exchanged in the past for such things as furs, tallow, and fish. It did mention that these shipments had been made to and from the Wardhouse.

"So a Scotsman, Andrews, hath been before us hither at the Wardhouse," he observed, more surprised than chagrined at the discovery. "A bold trafficker, by all that's marvelous!"

"Why, this Andrews had his lady with him," remarked the gunner, who had been exploring the tower. "At least divers skirts and cloaks and other gear lie up aloft."

By the size and number of the cooking pots that were hung, neatly polished, by the hearth, a fair-sized company had dwelt in the house not long since. Chancellor ordered a search of the island, and posted another man in the lookout on the peak.

By evening they were sure that the island was inhabited by no more than foxes and squirrels and a host of sea birds that circled, screaming, about the invaders. So the ship was left with Master Burroughs and a half dozen, and the main company repaired to the palisades, glad enough to set foot ashore again and gathered around the great fires.

The trader's stores Chancellor would not touch, saying that they belonged to another.

For six days they rested at the Wardhouse, keeping watch for Sir Hugh's two vessels, but sighting nothing except several icebergs that drifted near the island, and on the sixth day a large pack to the north. Chancellor went to the lookout to study this and called a council that evening.

"'Tis now seven days that we abode at the tryst," he said slowly, "and before now Sir Hugh should have put in appearance. Wherefore, I deem that something has befallen him, to make him change his plans, and it is my wish to go on alone. What say you, my masters?"

Burroughs and the two merchants agreed with him, and one of the gentlemen adventurers added a word.

"Please you, Master Dickon, we grieve sorely that misfortune hath been the lot of the two goodly ships and our companions. But, for the reason of the love we bear you, we will fare on with right good cheer."

"Sir Hugh and his men are worthy of better fortune, I must needs say. I have reason to think—" he hesitated—"a traitor hath led them elsewhere. I know not whither. But each day the cold increaseth, and if we do not venture forth, the passage will be closed to us by ice."

At this the Icelander moved forward from the outer circle to where Chancellor sat on a stool close to the fire. Knuckling his forehead, he asked leave to speak.

"Save ye, my master, and if so be ye will let me have my say—"

"Say what you will," put in the pilot, to encourage him, for the man was ill at ease.

"Thankee, Master Dickon, thankee! If we weigh with a southeast sun* we will come before long upon the great ice pack, which we may not pass around. Then we must make a landfall and endure the winter as best we may. Saving your respect, the winter in this sea is perilous. Now, God be praised, we have a fair harbor here at this place, and the good Sir Hugh may join us if we abide here."

---

*Sail east.

"Honestly spoken," nodded the pilot. "And to my mind we go into danger, the greater since Sir Hugh hath left us. But, my masters, I hold it dishonorable to avoid a great attempt for fear of danger."

"Aye," cried the others. "'Tis so we think, Master Dickon."

Thorne, who had been frowning into the fire, looked up quickly.

"By your leave, sir, it is in my mind that we should leave a man in the Wardhouse."

Chancellor looked a silent question.

"Sir Hugh," explained the armiger, "knoweth not that a traitor is in his company. If so be the captain-general should come to this island after we have sailed, who is to tell him? And how is he to know the course we follow?"

"Ha! We could leave a written message."

"A writing, so please you, might fall into other hands. 'Tis clear that folk do come to this Wardhouse. And, by the same token, we hit on this rendezvous only by chance. A man left here could signal to Sir Hugh from the peak, if the sails were sighted."

This aspect of the situation had not struck the pilot, who was readier for action than planning.

"That is true," he nodded, "but even so, I will not order one of my shipmen to bide alone on this island in peril of his life."

"Nay, Master Dickon," Thorne smiled, "I will stay here. For, look you, I am of no use upon a ship. None knoweth so well as I the warning that should come to Sir Hugh's ears. As for peril, I would face a thousand Laps and all their sorcery rather than another storm like the last. Nay, indeed here is scant peril, for if you come not to death, you will return hither to search for me."

"Aye, that we will." It was Chancellor's turn to smile. "Lad, I fear me you are disposed to have the blood out of Durforth, will-he, nill-he!"

"Aye, that I will," responded Thorne so promptly that the others stared and laughed, knowing for their part little of his suspicions or his desire to avenge his father.

"Then let it be so. But I will not leave you alone." Chancellor turned to the ring of faces that glowed ruddy in the firelight. "My masters, you have heard the talk between us. It is expedient that we man the Wardhouse. This youth maintains that the lesser peril is his, but I think otherwise. I'll order no man of mine to abide with him, yet such is my desire."

When no one spoke up, he glanced at the young adventurer who had first assented to going on.

"Nicholas Newborrow, what say you?"

"I say this, in all due respect." Newborrow flushed, and fingered the clasp of his cloak. "I dare what any man dare, but in this unknown part of the world we face no human foes. Whither passed Sir Hugh? What of the good men and true he had with him? Whence came this grave?"

He pointed through the gray vista of the enclosure to the rough wooden cross.

"Whither fared the humans who were in this Wardhouse none so long before our coming? We saw no boat put off from the island."

"It is idle," quoth Chancellor, thrusting out his long chin—for he liked not Newborrow's words or their effect on the listeners—"to wonder upon that which we have not seen."

"We have seen, my master, this place where night cometh not at all, but a continual light shining upon a huge and mighty sea. Fare on with you I will, but here I abide not. This is an evil place."

"So that is your mind. What of the others?"

A brief silence fell, and after a moment Peter Palmer thrust aside the shipmen in front of him and greeted his leader. His round face was knotted with uneasiness.

"A plague on them that hangs in stays when there's work to be done. I'll bide with the younker. If so be my time's run out, here is Christian soil and sepulcher."

He pointed to the grave and its cross.

"I can ill spare you, boatswain." Chancellor thought it over with palpable concern. "Still, you and Thorne are mates, and that is good. Stay then, and God keep you."

To the armiger he added:

"My course I cannot give you, save that we sail east from here, and—I fear me—must winter on the Ice Sea. So, if you follow, watch the shore for the ship and huts. Master Burroughs, see to it that Thorne has weapons and victuals enough for two men for a twelvemonth. We hoist our sails at the third running out of the glass."

Chapter X
Peter Interprets an Omen

"And now," quoth Peter, closing one eye and laying a finger along his massive nose, "we be our own masters, ye being captain and I mate, as it were. In a year from now we'll be living at our ease, a-riding in coaches and a-swearing hearty at our own serving knaves, like gen'lemen to the manor born."

They were then sitting at their ease in the Wardhouse hall, which seemed bare and gloomy despite a roaring fire, since the departure of Chancellor and his company.

"You sang another tune, Peter," responded Thorne with amusement, "two days agone."

For two days the boatswain had worked like a Trojan, carrying up from the shore the gear and arms left them by Burroughs—a serviceable harquebus with three barrels, a hand gun for Thorne, who now wore a sword. Peter had his own cutlass, and had gleaned from the *Edward* a small keg of powder, and a cutty ax.

They had a cask of brandy in addition to a butt of the familiar and detested beer, which, nevertheless Peter preferred to water, salt fish in plenty and a little beef, with a liberal allowance of biscuit and cheese and olive oil.

All this they had stowed in the hall. They had taken turns climbing the peak to keep watch on the sea and cutting firewood, which Thorne stacked inside the palisade.

"Well," ruminated the boatswain, drawing himself a mug of brandy, "that was afore Master Dickon cut us adrift. When we sailed along of him I obeyed orders and kept my tongue between my teeth. But all the while I had tidings of that which will make us rich as lords."

"On this island?"

"The —— take this island! Nay, here's the lay, Master Ralph. Gold and silver to be had for the picking up. Or else to be traded for—a knife or piece of pewter, look ye, for a fair pound of red gold."

Thorne hitched nearer the blaze, for the chill of the place touched his back with invisible, icy fingers.

"We are a long way from Cathay," he yawned.

"'Tis not Cathay."

Peter took a sip of the brandy and licked his thick lips.

"I've sailed the seas I have, with the Portingals. And evil shipmen they be, but full o' knowledge and tidings of the unknown world. At Fermagosta I first heard tell of this gold. Then at the Texel, when the Dutch merchants had looked too long on the cup. By reason of what I heard, I shipped along of Master Dickon."

He drained the mug and tossed it over his shoulder.

"Here's the tale. Both the Spaniards and Hollanders talk of a certain prince whose dominions lie between Christiandom and Cathay. A long way it is to this prince, and now the Polanders and other pagans and the Easterlings be at war, one with another. So the way by land is closed. The name this prince bears is Ivan."

Expectantly, he paused, seeing that his companion was giving close heed to his words.

"Ivan," he repeated. "And in the Texel ale shop 'twas said that Ivan's land o' gold and silver lieth south by southeast from this Wardhouse."

"Southeast!" The armiger sat up abruptly. "Why, so lieth the course given Durforth by my lord Renard. How distant is this land of—of gold?"

"A mooh's journey."

"Not so far. Durforth's reckoning—"

After considering the matter, Thorne related to his companion all that he knew of Renard and his agent. And the boatswain's prompt reply surprised him.

"Sweet doxies and dells! It fits like a merlyn-spike in a man's fist. Look ye! The Spaniards may not adventure to Prince Ivan by land, so one is sent by sea. For the Spaniards are not wont to endure peril without reason. Wherefore, you and I will set forth this day week, to seek the land of gold."

"Set forth? How?"

"Why in a week we may build us a fair raft of dried wood, secured with rope and pegs of wood. We'll take the gear and victuals and the firelocks. 'Tis no more than two leagues to the main. Sweet lad, we'll trade with the pagans of this outlandish prince and make our fortunes."

His red-veined eyes gleaming cheerfully, he rolled to his feet and filled two mugs at the brandy cask. One of these he held out to Thorne, who was sunk in a brown study by the fire.

"What, bully lad! Here's luck. May good Saint Dunstan guard us from the Horned One!"

Under his breath he added, remembering that he stood, perhaps, on unhallowed ground—

"May the —— deal with us in kindly wise."

"With what would you trade, Peter?"

The big shipman jerked a thumb over his shoulder at the bales of goods that had been found with the book of one John Andrews. Placing his finger against his nose again, he tossed off his brandy and heaved a pleasant sigh.

"With yon."

"Softly, my shipmate! That is not ours for the taking. And how would you add goods to gear, and carry the same overland?"

Peter's face fell and he scratched his head. His imagination ran no farther than reaching the coast with all the spoil.

"Welladay, one thing at a time, Master Ralph. Belike, fortune will aid us one way or another."

"It will not, for the reason that I will abide on this island, having pledged my word."

"Now, the plague take ye for a dolt," muttered the boatswain earnestly. "If Sir Hugh come not he lieth at the bottom of yonder sea. Or else treachery hath been brewed against us and Master Dickon."

But argue as he would, and he did right soulfully, Peter could not budge Thorne from his decision a whit. He ended by swearing up and down that he would go in search of the promised land alone. But the next day he showed no signs of readiness to set out; in fact felt sulky and sat in the house hunched over the fire.

Thorne did not appear to notice his ill behavior, but labored at the wood until he judged it midday; then he bade Peter briefly to take a turn on the lookout.

With an ill grace and much grumbling the boatswain obeyed, and set out for the "masthead," as he termed it. But within an hour he hove into sight again, much more rapidly than he had departed. He was panting from the depths of his lungs and stumbling over the rocky ground.

"Stand by, Master Ralph!" he bellowed hoarsely. "Look aloft. The sweet Mary aid us—look aloft!"

Thorne put down his ax and glanced at the hill, then at the fringe of firs and the misty gloom of the rock gullies.

"The sky," croaked Peter, staggering through the gate of the stockade, "yonder to windward."

Thinking that his companion had glimpsed a sail or had been beset by enemies of some kind, the armiger surveyed the horizon eagerly. And presently, having beheld what Peter had seen, he frowned. Arching high over their heads, a rainbow stood against a cloudbank in the sky. But this rainbow was inverted, glowing with a myriad colors where it circled almost to the tree tips, and fading into nothingness where its ends merged with the clouds. He had never seen its like before.

Being unable to account for this phenomenon, he held his peace while the shipman struggled to regain his breath.

"Master Ralph, I have seen the Southern Cross over a ship's mast; I have seen the eye of the Big Bear; but never a rainbow capsized. 'Tis an omen—daddle me else."

"'Tis a rainbow, no more."

Peter eyed the youngster with dark triumph.

"Master Ralph, the mariners o' the *Esperanza* saw a mermaid come up out of the waters. Aye, an omen, that, as ever was. And where be they now?"

Seeing that his companion was no whit cast down by this comparison, Peter went on stubbornly.

"And now our time is come. What d'ye think on it?"

"Think? That you have guzzled the brandy overmuch."

"Now, shiver my soul else, that is ill said. Look you here, Master Know-All: When I came down from the masthead yonder, the very beasties of the wood were up and about. Aye, they know when an ill wind is to ward. Wolves and bears, they were a-capering and a-rushing all about me, through the trees."

"There are no wolves, nor bears on this island."

"I laid my deadlights on them. They were hiding, crafty-like, a-slipping and a—"

"Nonsense—"

"On two legs, Master Ralph. A-peering at me they were."

Thorne was puzzled by Peter's statement, stoutly reiterated when he questioned the boatswain anew that he had seen bears on the path to the lookout. He reflected that Sir Hugh's men had made only a casual examination of the island, and such animals might have remained unseen in the patches of woods.

Bear's meat would add splendidly to their larder, and he decided to try his hand at hunting.

Taking up the crossbow with its winder and a few shafts—this weapon being both handier and more accurate than the harquebus—he left the palisade.

A heavy mist was blowing in, and the chill of it struck through his light cloak. It swept like smoke athwart the line of the forest, rendering him for the moment subject to the illusion that the pines and the rock gullies were moving past him while he was standing still.

Under the mesh of the wood the fog did not penetrate, and he walked hard and fast to stir up his circulation. The gale whined overhead, and the piping of curlews and croaking of gulls filled the space with tumult.

The wood opened out in time, and he passed through a labyrinth of scrub oak, all bent in one direction by the winds of countless years. Until now he had not known that he had come a full two leagues to the other end of the island. But for the moment he paid no attention to his surroundings.

High and clear and yet faintly a voice was to be heard, a human voice, dwarfed by the note of the wind. It reached him in snatches, and he could not be certain of its direction until he reflected that it must come down the wind.

As he rounded a mass of rocks, coated with moss, he heard it clearly and stopped in his tracks. The voice was a woman's, and she was singing an old ballad:

> "As I was walking all alane
> I heard twa corbies making a mane;
> The tane unto the t'other did say,
> 'Where sall we gang and dine to-day?'
>
> —In behint yon auld fail dyke
> I wot there lies a new-slain knight;
> And naebody kens, that he lies there,
> But his hawk, his hound, and lady fair."

A woman's voice was the last thing he had expected to hear, and Thorne paused to wind his crossbow and fit a shaft in the slot. Where a woman was, in this island of the Ice Sea, men must be, and it behooved him to draw near with care.

He pushed between two boulders and looked out into a mist-shrouded glen. On the far side, in some high bracken and fern he made out the form of a deer, with its antlered head pointed fairly in his direction. Surprise and excitement brought his crossbow to his shoulder. He pressed the trigger when the stag moved—the eagerness of the hunter strong upon him. The shaft sped and the deer vanished, not bounding away, but sinking, as it seemed to him, into the ground.

> "Many a one for him make mane,
> But none sall ken where he is gane;
> O'er his white bones, when they are bare,
> The wind sall blaw for evermair."

The voice stopped on an unfinished note and there fell the familiar silence with its monotone of the gale overhead. Thorne ran forward, and sought eagerly in the ferns for the prey that he thought he had slain.

He found nothing, neither deer nor shaft. Nor, indeed, any sign of the singer, though he hunted through the broken ground until he came out on the shore and saw the line of surf an angry white under the leaden gray of the mists.

"Are you friend or foe?" he called and, after waiting a moment, "I'll harm you not."

But the only response was the impatient and mocking calling of the birds.

Taking his way home, his eye fell on a shaft half buried in the ground, and he took it up believing it was the bolt he had shot. It proved, however, to be an arrow, such as he had never seen before. It was a small shaft, feathered with black crows' feathers and bearing two small iron heads. After inspecting it, he thrust it into his belt and charged his crossbow anew.

For a while he quested along the ridges, until, the mist thickening, he knew his search vain and turned to the Wardhouse.

When he told Peter all that had taken place on the shore, the boatswain nodded indifferently.

"Aye, it were a pixie or a wood troll, or mayhap a Robin Goodfellow. Faint and clear it sung, say ye? Why, it were anhungered. Ye should have left it a bit of a sup."

"But I saw naught, Peter."

"And why should ye, Master Ralph? 'Tis sartain and sure that pixies dwell in cromlechs, which is to say hollow mounds, beneath the sod. Where rocks stand, like a circle, with linden trees, keep your weather eye out for trolls and such-like."

Thorne was far from satisfied with this. Had a ship come to the island? If so, where was it anchored? Were there natives, pagan folk, about the Wardhouse, and were they invisible? He could have sworn there were no deer on the island, which was too small for a herd; yet he had seen one.

Chapter XI
The Sea Maiden

A touch on his arm awakened him from the deep sleep of early morning. The hall was visible in the half-light that never quite left the island. Somewhere he heard Peter snoring comfortably.

The woman who stood by his couch, whose hand had touched his arm, held her finger on her lips. She was no taller than one of the great bales of goods beside her, and she was swathed from head to foot in a heavy sea cloak. Only two braids of hair of the brightest red gold were visible.

"You may not abide in this place," she said softly. "You must get you gone from here."

Her eyes, he noticed, were dark and they glowed with excitement. Her age he could not guess, but manner and voice were youthful, and the voice was that of the singer of the day before.

"Why?" he asked briefly, watching her face.

It was characteristic of the armiger that he showed no surprise at her presence. She was here, and in due time he would know all about that.

"The Easterlings are angered, lad. They will not endure you more."

"Why are they angry?"

"You shot a shaft at one; besides, you hold the Wardhouse and they would have it for my comfort. What seek you here?"

Thorne rose to his feet, and she stepped back as if to ward him off.

"Nay, sir, touch me not, for that would be your death."

"Here are threats and warnings," quoth the armiger impatiently, "but no sense. Mistress, I have loosed me no shaft at any pagan, nor have I a mind to harm you. Come, we will build the fire anew and you shall rede me this riddle."

He turned to call Peter to go for more wood, but again the girl in the sea cloak checked him in his purpose.

"Nay, let the lout sleep. The Easterlings have no love for him and they would slay him out of hand if he came near me."

"Now by my faith," growled the youth, "this is ill hearing. If any man lifts hand against Peter I will put my sword through him."

The girl smiled at this, yet there was anxiety in her eyes, which traveled beyond Thorne to the far corners of the hall. And he, following her gaze, became aware of shapes that stood without the narrow windows—of heads, covered with the fur of animals, and, once, of a form that resembled a deer with spreading antlers.

These, he knew, were men wearing bear and deer skins, but men so stunted that they stood no higher than his shoulder. And each one, with bow and arrows ready in hand, stirred restlessly as if ill at ease. Fear or uneasiness in savages and animals he knew to be a portent of danger. And his sword and pistols would avail little against their arrows.

It had been Peter's watch, and, judging by his snores, these folk of the island had taken possession of the palisade with small trouble. So reflecting, he brought wood himself, laid twigs on the embers of the hearth. When flames crackled and gripped the logs his gray eyes turned to the girl questioningly.

"And now, the tale, child," he said calmly, stretching his hands to the blaze.

She had seen that he was aware of her followers, and she glanced at him with fleeting curiosity, one hand smoothing back hair from her forehead. The fire tinted her thin checks with color and made her fair indeed. Yet she was unconscious of this charm of hair and eyes and voice.

"If I tell what you would know," she whispered not to awaken Peter, "will you pledge me your word that you and the churl will leave the island so soon as may be?"

Thorne considered this and shook his head.

"I may not do that, for I have sworn an oath to abide here."

"Ah, that would avail you naught, for you would lie under the sod with a cross upon your grave."

"Like the other?"

Thorne nodded at the palisade.

In a flash he saw that he had hurt the girl; her eyes glistened with tears and she bent her head, looking into the fire, her hands clasped on her breast.

"Peace, I pray you, sir. That is my father's grave. He was not slain by Easterlings, but by pirates who have e'er now made atonement for their ill deed."

When he still kept silent, she saw fit to tell him her name.

She was Joan Andrews, daughter of Andrews the trader. He was Scotland born, and had come in recent years to the Wardhouse by way of the Orkneys and the Norway coast, impelled to this course by sight of gold among the natives. This season he had taken Joan on the trip for the first time, and had met with misfortune, being followed to the Wardhouse by a pinnace with a dragon figurehead, manned by lawless Burgundians.

These had attacked the trader, killed him, and loaded his goods on their vessel which was anchored in the harbor. Andrews's cutter they had sunk a short distance from the island. But Joan had escaped from the Wardhouse after the death of her father, choosing to fly to some few

Laps who had come to the island to trade rather than to trust to the mercies of the pirates.

The Easterlings, she explained, had a mound dwelling at the other end of the island, a hollowed-out knoll which was entered by a tunnel hidden from sight in the rocks.

The pirates might easily have escaped in their boat, but, unaware of the presence of the Easterlings, scattered over the island to search for the missing girl, and so fell victim to the arrows of the savages. The goods of the trader Andrews were brought back to the Wardhouse for safe keeping, until a large sailing skiff could be fetched to convey them to the mainland.

Before this vessel arrived, the English ship came into the harbor, and the Easterlings hid themselves with the maiden in their underground dwelling. They watched the *Edward* sail off and were astonished to find two men left on the island. These they had decided to kill, believing them kin to the pirates.

Joan Andrews had seen Thorne the day before, and by his bearing and voice thought him English and of gentle blood. She had begged the Laps as best she could with signs and her few words of their speech to hold their hands until she could speak with the men in the Wardhouse.

Thorne considered her story and went to the heart of the matter with a word.

"Do these Easterlings cherish you, Mistress Joan?"

"My father ever dealt with them fairly, for such was his way. They have been kind to me. Aye, they be not evil-minded, though foul of feature. But command them I may not, for they be changeful and timid as the wild creatures in whose skins they clothe themselves."

"Faith—" Thorne smiled ruefully—"they appear to be Christians in one respect. They hang their foes to the yardarm as readily as any shipmaster."

Joan shook her head.

"'Tis their way of burial. They leave their dead fastened to the branches of trees, fully clad, with weapons bound to them. So they made shift to do with the thieves of the pinnace, before they towed the vessel out and set her adrift."

Through Thorne's brain passed the thought that this was not the method of burial Peter would prefer. It was clear to him that Peter and himself stood near to the edge of a grave, of whatever nature it might prove to be. Yet his curiosity was all for the maiden and the fate in store for her.

"What plan have you, child?" he asked. "How will you contrive to leave the Ice Sea and return to your home?"

She seemed surprised that he took thought of her.

"Why—the skiff may put in at the Wardhouse before the ice floes gird us in."

But she added, less cheerfully—

"I have no kindred awaiting me."

The armiger was not minded to dally over the situation.

"Who is the chief of these folk? Have him in, and let him speak his mind. If it is his intention to compass my death, I will e'en take him with me to the nether world." Placing his back against the fireplace, he waited until the girl, after a moment's hesitation, called softly.

"*Tuon, hulde na.*"

And after a moment there appeared in the doorway the same Lap who had rowed out to the *Edward*. Tuon's stocky shoulders were covered by a wolf skin, and the empty muzzle of the beast leered at them over the broad, greased-coated muzzle of the savage whose yellow, pointed teeth resembled the fangs of the wolf.

Even his hands were covered with fur mittens, and Thorne reflected that these Laps must have been the beasts that Peter glimpsed on the lookout height. He suspected that beside the warmth of the furs, they availed themselves of these strange garments to hunt down other animals, remembering the Lap that, dressed in a deer's skin and antlers, he had taken for a stag the day before.

Tuon walked forward warily, peering about him as if entering a cage.

"Put down your weapons, sir."

Joan pointed at Thorne's pistol and sword.

"Nay, I'll yield me to no savage. Let him take the weapons, an' he will."

Tuon sidled closer, several of his companions following him into the hall. Thorne was aware of a strong animal scent, of foul flesh and sweating hair. His gorge rose and he clapped hand to the hilt of his sword, having no mind to be made prisoner by such as they. Joan's dark eyes widened in alarm, and Tuon, sensing the rising excitement of the Christians, became uneasy.

At this instant Peter awoke. He sat up, stared at the strange beings who were moving toward Thorne in the vague light of the hall, saw the slender girl in the sea cloak, the fire ruddy on her tawny hair, peered at Thorne who stood as if turned to stone.

Springing up, he drew a blanket over his head and rushed toward Joan Andrews before Thorne could speak. Arriving, as he judged, before her, his eyes being swathed in the cloth, he fell on his knees.

"A' ——'s mercy, if thou be'st troll or Ellequeen, spare an honest shipman. Thou'st put my mate under a spell, so that he speaks not nor moves an eye. Have mercy on a sorry wight that never harmed hair of thy head."

The spectacle of the giant seaman muffled in a blanket aroused the interest of the Laps. It was clear to them that he intended no violence to the maiden they had taken into their protection; in fact, they must have suspected that he was performing some ritual.

No arrow was loosed at him, and when he withdrew the blanket cautiously he found Thorne smiling at him broadly, and Joan Andrews broke into a rippling laugh at sight of his red and foolish countenance.

Laughter is a key that unlocks many a black mood. The Laps had mirth in them, and Tuon grinned fearsomely. And this served to change Peter's mood in a twinkling. He cast down his blanket with an oath and spread his stocky legs, clasping his great fists.

"So ye would bait Peter Palmer? Put up your fibbers and I'll best the lot of ye scurvy dogs."

"Let be!" cried Thorne. "Here is no troll maiden, but a child out of the Scot's land."

In spite of this assurance Peter regarded Joan Andrews with misgivings while the others strove to talk with Tuon; and to the end of his time on the island gave her a wide berth. He never forgot that she had influence over the Laps, and by a process of reasoning all his own, was convinced that she must be a troll maiden out of the sea in human form.

Meanwhile Joan made a bargain with Tuon. The Laps were to have possession of the trade goods, all Thorne's stores and weapons except his sword. She was to be allowed to live in the tower, and the two Englishmen in the hall, and they were not to be harmed.

Thorne was not pleased, for it amounted to a surrender, but the girl pointed out that he was giving no more than the Laps would take in any case, and, besides, his only follower had assuredly yielded himself without any terms at all to her mercy.

"This island is theirs," she added practically. "'Tis true the Wardhouse was built by other hands long dead—perhaps by the Norsemen. But Tuon's men hold that it is theirs. They ask why you have come hither, if not to plunder or avenge the death of the pirates."

So Thorne explained the voyage and its purpose, and she shook her head gravely.

"I fear me for your comrades. There lies no passage to the eastward. My father often said that it is closed with ice that never opens. So the Easterlings told him."

For a space Thorne thought that this might bring about Chancellor's return, until he recalled the stubborn courage of the pilot-major and his settled determination to find new lands. There might be no northeast passage to Cathay, but Chancellor would press on as long as strength remained to him and his men.

Chapter XII
Snow

The days passed, and Thorne went more often to the lookout because it irked him to sit in the Wardhouse, where he felt that the very food he shared was taken from her bounty.

Moreover she had warned him earnestly not to venture abroad without her, and this went sorely against his pride. And there came a day when the hoarfrost was white on the ground. Snow fell that night, driving the Easterlings into the Wardhouse. Their hunger sharpened by the bitter wind, the savages fell upon Thorne's store of victuals. Only half warming the meat and fish at the fire, they gorged until their bodies swelled.

Thorne went out to the hill as soon as the snow ceased, after cautioning Peter against quarreling with Tuon and his men.

The aspect of the island was changed; the sun was invisible behind clouds and the gray light seemed to arise from the white ground under his feet. In spite of the brisk walk he was shivering when he reached the rocky height and searched the sea with his eyes.

No sail was to be seen and, peering to the eastward, he saw ice floes in the course taken by the *Edward*. This made it certain that Chancellor would not return to the islands until next season.

No animals were astir, and Thorne, who was not given to imagination, could not rid himself of the belief that invisible and malignant forces were closing in upon the island; elementals, his father had termed them.

Thrusting his numbed hands into his belt, he was setting himself to

consider means by which they could live through the winter, when a clear
voice hailed him cheerily.

"Ho, Master Thorne, you have disobeyed orders again. I' faith, you have
led me a merry chase!"

The girl was climbing swiftly to the lookout, clad in a new manner, her
small feet snug in deerskin boots, her slim body wrapped in a fox-fur tunic, and a felt hood drawn over her head. It was the first time he had seen
a woman without a skirt that came clear to the ground, but Joan Andrews
was careless of her unwonted dress.

"Why, the lad is in a pet." She glanced searchingly at his drawn face.
"The frost will harden in you, if you go not abroad in warmer garments
than those. La, sir, such things may do well enough in London town, but
not upon the Ice Sea. I will beg furs of good Tuon and sew ye a proper
mantle."

"You need not, and—I am not angry, child."

"Child, quoth'a! You are a large lout for your age, Master Thorne, but
you are not old enough to call me child. Nay, I think you very young."

So saying she beckoned him to a spot where the wind was warded by
a great rock and, when he came reluctantly, sat close to afford him the
warmth of her furs.

"Peter says that you were a gentleman at court. Is it true?"

Thorne found the girl difficult to understand; her gaze, as searching
and guileless as a child's, was more disconcerting than the eyes, the bright
and calculating eyes, of the ladies in waiting, for whom he had had a boy-
ish awe.

"I can break me a lance in the tournaments, and keep the saddle of a
horse," he admitted. "I can train a goshawk for hare or wild fowl."

"What else?"

"I have killed several in fair fight with sword and dagger."

"Any lout can do as much, if luck be with him. What else?"

"Why, I can put a shaft from a crossbow through the ribs of a running
hart at a hundred paces."

Mistress Joan smiled behind the fur collar of her jacket. She had seen
Thorne fail to do just that not so long ago, but she did not remind him of
it. Instead her mood changed swiftly.

"Now, sirrah, tell me this: Was it courteous in you to run off and leave
me beleaguered by the drunken Easterlings? They are near mad, with the
spirits they have taken."

"Are they so?"

Thorne frowned, thinking too late of the brandy and beer. Tuon and his men had seemed little inclined to try these strange drinks, but now apparently they had done so, and the result was not pleasant to contemplate.

The fault being his, he was loath to admit it.

"I knew it not, Mistress Joan. 'Swounds, I grew weary of your following. A man may not think aright with a vixen's tongue going like a bell clapper at his ear."

The corners of her lips drew down, and she moved a little farther away.

"So my father used to say, when things went ill. Nay, Master Thorne, I followed you because I feared for—" she hesitated with an upward glance that judged his mood shrewdly—"I feared to be left by myself in the company of the Easterlings, and I am lonely, by times."

"In that case," assented young Master Thorne gravely, "you may walk with me as often as you are minded, aye, and talk also."

Around the corner of the rock, Peter, the boatswain, hove in sight, his head bent against the wind.

"Stand by, Master Ralph," he muttered hoarsely, "stand by to go about. Luck sets our way."

Thorne motioned to the shipman to join them, saying that they owed their lives to Mistress Joan and it would be ill repayment of her courtesy to talk apart.

At this Peter pursed his lips and was heard to growl that there was no knowing whether the maid was friend or unfriend, and for his part he would liefer keep his distance from one who ran about with Easterlings and dressed like a lad—a mortal sin to his thinking.

"The beer is gone," he vouchsafed darkly, "ah, and the brandy. 'Twill be a dry winter for us."

"Gone?" cried Joan Andrews. "Then the Laps have guzzled it."

"As ever was. They drained the casks and now lie about the house like fish out o' water. Fuddled!"

He winked at Thorne and contorted his face in the effort to convey some hidden meaning unperceived by the girl.

"Scuppers awash! They screamed and danced and fit among themselves. You could stow them in the fire and they would not stir—all *twenty* of them."

And he touched his dirk on the side away from Joan, beckoning with his head to his companion.

"Stir a leg, Master Ralph. Blast my eyes but here's luck a-playing our game, and—"

He lifted a huge hand to his lips and mouthed in Thorne's ears: "Has the wench put a spell on ye? We can be masters in this island before the sand runs from the glass again."

Thorne looked at him silently. He and Joan had not been gone from the house an hour, and in that time twenty savages had downed two half barrels of brandy and beer. They were not accustomed to such liquor, and he wondered whether they would ever stand upon their feet again. Here, as Peter said, was a chance to make sure they would not. And yet he had made a truce with these same savages.

"Mistress Joan," he observed, "the boatswain here has a mind to rid us of the Easterlings while they lie befuddled. What say you? Are you for us, or for them!"

The girl lifted her head impatiently.

"You are both fools—faith, I know not which is the greater. Peter, have not the Laps eaten up the main part of your victuals?"

"Aye, mistress—" Peter was civil enough to Joan's face—"that they have. And they have e'en drunk up my beer."

"Now if you kill them, how are we three to get us food to live through the winter?"

Peter started to reply, and scratched his head.

"How will we live in any case?"

"With bows and snares and nets that they make, these savages will get us small game and fish. If you had slain them you would starve before another seventh day."

To this Peter had no answer, but waxed surly for being reproved in his folly.

He had hastened to Thorne after watching from the tower stairs until the Laps were past heeding his doings, and he had expected that the armiger would fall in at once with his plan. Now he stared at his young companion distrustfully.

Thorne's mind seemed to be elsewhere. His eyes narrowed and his lips close drawn, he was staring at a wrack of clouds out to windward. Peter shook his head moodily, marking the high color in the lad's checks, the splendid poise of the curly head.

Aye, the boy was rarely favored, being more than handsome, and this was why the maiden, who must be a sea troll in man form, had laid her spell on him. She wanted to have him for her own.

Belike, thought Peter, she would suck the life from Master Ralph or else beguile him into the waters and swim down to the sea's bottom, she who had taken a dead man's name, who sat each day in the evening hour by a grave, who had a man's wisdom and a witch's craft.

"Peter," said Thorne, and his words came in an altered voice, so that the girl glanced at him fleetingly, "this is what we will do. Fetch me my arbalest from the Wardhouse, with pistols for yourself. Look yonder!"

The boatswain knitted shaggy brows and presently made out what the armiger had been looking at. A boat was heading into the harbor. He sprang to his feet to shout joyfully, when he paused uneasily. This was no full rigged ship, but a longboat that tossed on the swell, moving sluggishly under a lug sail.

"'Tis the sailing skiff that Tuon sent for," cried Joan.

"It will be ours before Tuon is on his feet again," said Thorne.

The lugger—if the long, ramshackle skiff could be called that—staggered slowly through the crosscurrents at the mouth of the cove and was coaxed to the shore, where three men sprang out, to tug it up on the sand. A fourth Easterling, who seemed to stand no higher than Joan's chin, loosened the sheets and left the leather sail to flap as it would.

Then, without more ado, they started up the path to the Wardhouse and were confronted by Thorne and Peter with the crossbow ready wound and a brace of loaded pistols.

"Avast, my bullies!" roared the shipman. "Bring to and show your colors, or swallow lead the wrong way."

And he brandished a long pistol, motioning with the other hand for them to remain where they were. His aspect and voice had a startling effect on the savages; three of them dropped the light spears they carried and raced away; the fourth, the smallest of the lot, fell to his knees behind a hummock of grass.

Before Peter could sight his pistol, the little Easterling had strung his bow and loosed an arrow that flicked past Thorne's throat. The armiger pulled the trigger of his arbalest, but the bolt flew high, so closely did the miniature warrior hug the earth.

"Hull him, shipmate!" bellowed Peter. "Down between wind and wat—ugh!"

A second arrow from the native's bow struck Peter fairly under the ribs with a resounding thud, driving the breath from his lungs. Instead of penetrating, the missile hung loosely from his stout leather jerkin. Peter, being suspicious of the Easterlings, had prudently donned a steel corselet under his jerkin and mantle.

Pulling out the arrow, he tossed it away, and was sighting anew with the pistol when Thorne cried to him to hold hard. The Easterling champion had stood up, in round-eyed amazement, and was drawing near them, fascinated by the sight of men who were invulnerable to his shafts. As a sign of submission he unstrung his bow, and laid it at Thorne's feet, with a curious glance at the cumbersome crossbow.

Unlike the other Easterlings he wore tunic and trousers of gray squirrel skins, neatly sewed together with gut and ornamented at knees and neck with squirrel tails.

Joan Andrews, coming up, called him Kyrger, and said that he was a Samoyed tribesman, a young hunter who brought very good pelts to her father at times. The sight of the girl seemed to reassure Kyrger, who made no effort to escape; instead he took to following Thorne around.

Peter rolled off to inspect the lugger, and returned with mingled hope and disgust written upon his broad countenance, to report that she smelled like a Portugal's bilge, and was open from tiller to prow, some buff being stretched across the gunwales at either end. She seemed stout enough, he added.

But Joan, who had been questioning the hunter, cried out that Kyrger had sighted two ships several days before the lugger put off from the coast. The Samoyed had followed the vessels for a while, never having seen ships of such size in his life.

"That would be the *Esperanza* and the *Confidentia*, Sir Hugh's vessels," observed Thorne. "Ask him where they were sighted."

Kyrger pointed to the eastward.

"How were they headed?"

The Samoyed indicated the same direction, and Thorne was puzzled. Sir Hugh had not put in to the Wardhouse but had gone on, apparently three or four days after Chancellor. The three vessels might be expected to join company again. At all events, Sir Hugh would not come to the Wardhouse now. But why had he not appeared at the rendezvous?

"Ask him if he has ever been far along the coast to the east," he said at length.

Kyrger held up all the fingers of both hands, and nodded his head emphatically.

"He means either ten days' travel or ten kills of game," Joan explained. "It might be a hundred leagues."

"In ten days?" broke in Peter, who scented deceit. "'Tis not to be believed."

"They ride behind reindeer when the snow is on the ground," Joan assured him. "They go very swiftly. And Kyrger says what I have told you, my masters. The ice hath closed the sea a hundred leagues from here."

Thorne considered this, and saw that there was no reason why they should remain on the island. He could be of more assistance to Chancellor by seeking him out; besides, he now had the maid on his hands, and had found in Kyrger a guide who might be invaluable to the voyagers.

"Then will we follow the ships," he said slowly, "and, in God's mercy, may come up with them. And you, Mistress Joan, will come with me to the fellowship of Christians again."

He watched the Samoyed and believed that the Easterling had no ill feeling toward them. What went on in the mind of the little hunter was a mystery; but it was certain that the man had attached himself to them.

Kyrger assented to their plan without comment. He seemed more interested in Thorne's crossbow, which he was allowed to examine while Peter returned to the Wardhouse for a sack of biscuits and cheese and their few personal belongings, the girl accompanying him, to bid the grave inside the palisade a last farewell.

Seeing that Kyrger had not been slain, the other Samoyeds put in appearance and squatted down a bowshot away, and were induced to go to the lugger when the others returned, Peter lamenting the fact that Andrews's trade goods must be left behind. There was no room in the boat for the bales and the seven of them.

The wind was favorable, and in a few hours the island group was lost to sight, Peter guiding the lugger toward the shore that soon loomed over their heads. They coasted for a while until Kyrger called out that his camp lay inland from where they were.

By nightfall they were sitting around a fire, in a clump of firs, thawing out their chilled limbs while the hunter roasted wild fowl on a spit over the flames, and the two Samoyeds crouched at the edge of the circle of light, watching the actions of the white-skinned strangers, afraid to come nearer.

Afterward, Joan slept soundly in Kyrger's diminutive tent of heavy felt stretched over a frame of small birch poles, while Thorne and Peter took turns at mounting guard by the fire, both in good spirits at being again upon the mainland. The hours passed, and the light did not grow stronger.

Instead, the surface of the snow, broken by the dark patches of bare earth under the trees, seemed to glow with a radiance of its own. Not a breath of air stirred; the tips of the firs hung lifeless. It was as if a curtain had been drawn over the sun.

Joan awakened, and they prepared food in silence, and before they had done Thorne uttered an exclamation, pointing out to sea. During the night, the Samoyeds, aroused by something unperceived by the Englishmen, had gone down to the shore and launched the lugger. Now it could be seen half-way out to the blur of the islands, tossing on a restless swell.

Clearly there was wind out here and overhead a shrill whining was to be heard from a vast height. Peter cocked his head and listened attentively, becoming more and more uneasy without being able to put his foreboding in words; but Kyrger, who had come up with a pair of reindeer, cast one glance at the white-capped swell and fell to work taking down the tent.

He threw away the birch frame and cut heavy stakes from the pile of firewood. These he drove into the ground in a circle about the edge of the felt, which he clewed down, using twisted strands of hemp.

"Aye, aye, shipmate," cried Peter, bearing a hand at the task as soon as he saw what the hunter wanted done. "Here's all taut and snug. But what's the lay?"

Working swiftly and moving about silently in his fur footsacks, Kyrger pounded in all the stakes but two until, save at that one point, his circular felt was tamped down to the ground.

Then, with broad leather thongs, he bound up his supply of dried meat, with the belongings of his companions, and lashed the bundle fast in the crotch of a big fir. The bag of biscuit and cheese he thrust under the felt.

"'Tis little he will suffer us to take with us when we set out," grumbled the boatswain.

"Nay, I think he intends to bide here," said Thorne. "Look at the harts."

The reindeer were behaving strangely. They were short-legged gray beasts with heavy hair and longer antlers than the men had ever seen before. As soon as Kyrger had turned them loose they had gone to a hollow

between the trees and stretched out on the ground, their muzzles pointing toward the sea.

The hunter trotted past Thorne, his arms filled with moss that he had
grubbed up from bare patches of earth. This moss he piled under the nostrils of the beasts. He ran off and reappeared with three fur robes, one
having a buff lining. This he gave to Peter, sharing one of the others with
Thorne.

His own he wrapped around him quickly, covering his head completely,
and, walking to the hollow where the reindeer lay, stretched himself at
full length close to one of the beasts. Springing up and throwing off his
robe, he motioned to Peter to follow his example.

"Kyrger says," Joan explained, "that we must wrap our heads in the
coverings and lie down with our heads toward the sea. A *khylden* is coming out of the Ice Sea."

"What is that?" Thorne asked.

"A snow driver. I do not know what it is. Kyrger says we must do as his
reindeer." The hunter spoke to her again, and she added, "You and I are to
creep under the felt—'twill not hold Peter's bulk."

"A snow driver? Faith, man or beast or elemental, let it come," growled
Peter. "Who fears a storm on the mainland? I'll not lie battened under
hatches."

He went back to the fire and sat down, while Thorne went to see if
the skiff was still visible. By now it must have reached the harbor at the
Wardhouse, and before long Tuon and his men would be returning, he
reflected.

But Tuon and his men did not come that day. The sky overhead darkened to a black pall; only along the edges of the horizon a half-light played,
like fen fires or phosphorescence at sea. The shrill and invisible voice in
the heights deepened to a howl that was almost human, punctuated by
the roaring of the surf.

Thorne noticed that the trees of the grove were moving unsteadily;
he heard a human voice calling him plaintively, and at once the sound
was snatched away by a mighty droning in the air. The ranks of firs bent
back and quivered, as a ship heels over before a sudden blast and labors
in righting herself.

And then he felt for the first time the breath of the Ice Sea, the touch
of the snow driver.

In that instant cold struck through him as if he had been utterly naked.

He was driven from the knoll on which he stood, and pushed toward the camp. Without volition of his own he began to run, and heard his name called. He turned toward the sound, and saw Kyrger kneeling at the edge of the felt, beckoning him.

Thorne crawled under the covering, and found that his fur robe had been pushed in ahead of him. Joan was there beside him, invisible in the darkness, her man's sea cloak drawn over her.

"Roll up in your coverall," she cautioned him. "Kyrger says that we must keep warm, else we never shall be warm again."

He both heard and felt the Samoyed driving home the two stakes that had been left loose. He was lying on a dry bed of pine needles, and even as he wriggled into his furs he was conscious that these were being driven against his face with something that stung his skin like tiny specks of hot iron.

Covering his head, he lay still a while until the chill had left him, listening to the whining of the wind that came in great gusts, wondering how Peter and Kyrger were faring.

At length, being minded to find out, he crept from his furs and pushed up the flap of the tent enough to thrust his head and shoulders out. And he almost cried aloud in astonishment. Snow, a fine, dry snow, was whirling about him, driving into eyes and ears, and making it difficult to breathe. This was not like the snowstorms that he had known, where flakes fell heavily into a moist mass underfoot.

This was the breath of the snow driver, tinged with the cold of outer space, more malignant and pitiless than human enemies. Thorne knew now the meaning of *khylden*, knew too that it would be utterly useless for him to try to stir outside their covering.

He crept back, shivering, and felt the girl draw nearer him for warmth.

Chapter XIII
The Gate in the Sky

For nearly three days the snow driver raged, and then there fell a calm. The whole of the earth was blanketed in white and only the dense clump of firs showed the spot where four human beings slept, two feet beneath the surface of the snow.

The reindeer were the first to sense the passing of the storm, and staggered up, tossing their heads and going off at once to paw at the drifts with their cleft hoofs in search of the moss that was their winter food.

The movement aroused Kyrger, who bobbed up and shook himself like a dog. Picking up a fallen branch, he went to where Joan and Thorne were buried, feeling around with his feet until he found the spot.

Here he hesitated a moment, his eyes traveling to the bundle of gear secured in the tree. This was to him incalculable treasure, and, above the other things he coveted the crossbow which sent a shaft twice as far as his bow.

It came into his mind that if he let the outlanders sleep on they would die and the weapon would be his as well as the other things. In fact he wondered whether the other three were not dead already.

Then the Samoyed began to thrust snow away with his branch. The same instinct that had led him to safeguard the lives of the helpless three now called to him to rouse them. Kyrger had accepted Thorne as his master. He looked upon the armiger as a young lord, in much the same way that Thorne cherished the memory of Edward, his king.

He hauled up the felt and satisfied himself that Thorne still breathed; about the maiden he was more doubtful. He examined the biscuits and saw that they had eaten something. Then he set to work rubbing snow on the man's face and hands until the blue tinge faded from the skin and Thorne opened his eyes, grimacing with pain, and incapable of movement until the hunter had rubbed his limbs.

"Mistress Joan?" he croaked, and rose to his knees, swaying dizzily as the blood began to circulate through his veins again.

He drew back the hood from the girl's face and felt for the pulse in her throat. He could feel nothing through the numbness of his fingers.

"Fire," he muttered. "We must have a fire."

Helped by Kyrger, he plowed his way to the bundle in the tree and took from it a powder horn and steel and flint. Then, cutting off a length of the Samoyed's loosely woven rope, he untwisted the hemp strands. Gathering a double handful of dead twigs from the firs, he went back to the spot kept clear of snow by the felt and his own body.

Building a small mound of twigs and pine needles, he poured a little powder from the horn and fell to striking the steel against the flint stone. Presently a spark flew into the powder grains and flared up, eating into the dead twigs and the hemp strands.

Kyrger, who had watched with interest, now brought larger twigs and coaxed the tiny flame into a crackling blaze. To this branches were added until the fire glowed warmly. The heat only served to quicken the girl's heavy breathing, until Thorne chafed her wrists and throat with snow.

After a while her eyes flickered, and she sighed. A kind of smile touched her lips, bringing the semblance of life back into her again. He himself ached in every joint and his vision played queer tricks. He fancied that the whole sky over the sea was on fire.

Kyrger had anticipated his need and brought frozen meat, which he placed on rocks in the fire. A savory odor spread into the air, and, as if roused by this summons, Peter Palmer dragged himself out of his white mausoleum and crouched down by the fire.

Thorne noticed with weary surprise that the stout boatswain was weeping. Tears trickled down his hollow cheeks, but he said no word. He kept his eyes fixed on the meat until Thorne had forced a piece between the girl's teeth and induced her to chew and swallow it.

When Joan would eat no more the three men fell on the meat and divided what remained between them. Then Peter tightened his belt and looked around him slowly.

"I said truth," he grunted at length. "This maiden was a sea troll; the land is not her place. By black arts she hath fetched us to the very portal of —— which is plainly to be seen over yonder."

Thorne looked over his shoulder and rubbed his eyes. What he had taken for a fantasy was still visible.

A light cloud arched over the northern horizon, and from this cloud fiery streamers stretched to the zenith. Up and down these streamers passed a radiance, now purple, now yellow, but always flickering up to an immense height where it vanished in a kind of mist.

As Thorne watched, the radiance vanished, to reappear almost instantly in a different form. Gigantic, glowing pillars seemed now to rise from the dark horizon to the regions of outer space. This glow palpitated and grew stronger until his eyes ached. The pillars were columns of fire, towering over their heads, but giving out no heat.

Then the fiery portals, which had so wrought upon Peter's fancy, vanished and the elusive streamers sprang into being again.

"I have sailed the seas of the earth," said the shipman solemnly, "and I have seen the water rise up into pillars that reached to the sky. I've clapped my deadlights on the serpent that the Good Book names Leviathan, daddle me else. I've seen fishes fly through the air, off Madagascar, it were. But yonder gate in the sky is the gate of Satan's dominions."

Having relieved his mind of this augury, he fell into a troubled sleep. Somewhere in the lurid darkness a tree trunk cracked sharply, and Thorne heard far inland the howling of a wolf pack, coursing the hard snow on the heels of the storm. Hunched close to the fire that warmed them into life, he wondered what the morrow might bring.

The armiger admitted to Joan that they must have heavier garments, if they were to enter the unknown world to the east. The girl labored with Kyrger in sewing rude coats out of the furs for the two men to wear. For thread she had the supple gut preserved by the Samoyed, and for needle a bit of whalebone rubbed into the desired shape.

Meanwhile Kyrger got out what appeared to be a pair of great wooden skates, nearly two ells long and as wide as the palm of his hand, with strips of reindeer skin fixed to the underside.

Thus shod and carrying a long staff, he could glide over the surface of the snow beside the sled on which the girl rode. Thorne and Peter ran or walked in the hard track made by the cloven hoofs of the beasts and the run of the sled.

It was necessary to carry on the sled powder, tinder, and pine branches enough to kindle a fire at a moment's notice. Only in this way could they ward off the attacks of the lean, gray wolves, larger than any the voyagers had seen before.

It was after they had beaten off a pack of these wolves and were pushing forward warily that Thorne halted and pointed down at some large tracks that ran across the slot of the sled.

"I pray you, Mistress Joan," he said, "tell the Samoyed we must have good fresh meat, ere ever we can reach the ships. Here are bear's tracks, and we will hunt down the beast."

But when the maiden translated his speech to Kyrger, the Easterling shook his head and uttered one word decisively.

"Kyrger says," she explained, "that this is ermecin—the strongest. 'Tis thus they name the white bear of the Ice Sea."

"Nevertheless we will seek it out."

The small Samoyed appeared to be troubled. Ermecin, he declared, could not be brought down by his arrows. Nor would the pistols of the outlanders serve to stop the rush of this beast. Moreover the white bear was sacred to a neighboring tribe, the Ostiaks.

Thorne was determined to get good meat for the girl, and took his crossbow from the sled, winding it with care and setting a bolt in the slot. Joan insisted on going with him, saying that she had a dread of being left alone. Peter was put in charge of the reindeer and the three set out toward the shore.

The tracks were fresh, and Kyrger followed them easily, though reluctantly enough. They descended a gully and came out on the shore, sighting the bear before long, among a nest of rocks.

It scented or saw them at the same time and raised its head on a swaying, sinuous neck. Thorne saw that its head was small and its body greater than that of any bear he had set eyes upon. Moreover, being white tinged with yellow, it blended with the snow behind it.

It did not seem to fear them because it made no effort to move away when they approached within bowshot.

"Bid Kyrger loose his shafts," said Thorne briefly. "For he can shoot several, and I but one."

The Samoyed shook his head, reluctantly, yet obediently fitted an arrow to the string and bent his short bow. The missile whipped through the air and struck the white bear in the flank, but did not penetrate half its length. The brute swung toward them instantly, its head weaving from side to side.

A second arrow pierced its shoulder, and it swept through the snow, moving with unexpected speed, so that Kyrger's third shot merely glanced along its ribs.

The hunter cast down his bow and drew his knife, the breath hissing between his teeth, while Thorne planted his feet and sighted the crossbow, sending a bolt into the bear's throat.

The beast plunged forward, and gained its feet slowly, blood streaming from its open jaws. Then it fell on its side, not a dozen paces from them.

Kyrger shouted, wild with excitement. He pointed admiringly at Thorne's weapon and ran to the bear, chanting something loudly. To Thorne's surprise Joan smiled, although her lips were bloodless. She had not stirred or spoken during the charge of the great beast.

"He is saying," she laughed, "that the spirit of the bear must not be angered at us. He is telling the spirit that we did not slay it, nay, a wicked Ostiak sped the bolt. And when the bear's spirit seeks blood revenge in another body it must follow the tribe of Ostiaks."

"What are they?"

"My father said they dwell more to the east. They are cruel people, who slay strangers. They are the dogsled people, more warlike than the reindeer-sled Samoyeds."

Leaving Kyrger to skin the animal, they returned to the camp, where Peter had kindled a fire and Thorne took the shipman aside.

"Many days have passed since we bade Master Chancellor farewell. By my reckoning this should be close to Christmas, if indeed it is not that very day."

"Noël!"

Peter glanced up at the flickering arc of the northern lights, and at the gray sweep of the shore with its fringe of ice floes.

"That is ill said, younker, for it puts me in mind of the honest Yule log, aye, and the boar's head, and a pudding with brandy afire. And here us be on Christmas eve, where the very angels would fear to raise a chant, and the good Christ—"

"He would not fear to venture here."

Thorne wrinkled his brows in thought.

Peter regarded his companion in some surprise, for he had not noticed that Thorne was given to prayer or meditation.

"'Tis of Mistress Joan I am thinking," went on the armiger. "Her spirit lags, and if we do not show her some care she will not endure in this life. Now, she is ever mindful of prayer and such-like. How if we hold the Yule-tide as best we may?"

"Aye, but how?"

"Why, we can cut us a proper tree and make shift to trim it. Then may we sing a round of carols."

Peter rubbed his chin, and eyed his friend sidewise.

"Fairly said, if we had e'en a nuggin of brandy or a sprig of holly-wood. But carols—harumpf! Do you sing the words, Master Ralph, and I'll carry the melody, blast me else! A fine voice have I for melody, but as for words—now that's a craft of another rig."

Nevertheless, he got his hatchet from the sled and disappeared into the twilight, while Thorne aided Kyrger in preparing the steaks the Samoyed had brought up with the bearskin. By the time the meal was ready, and Joan seated on the sled, he returned, carrying a small fir which he set erect in the snow a little distance from the fire and proceeded, with an air of mysterious importance, to set icicles in the branches.

Then he placed the last of the biscuits in Kyrger's solitary pewter dish and drew from his girdle a small leather flask.

"I filled it at the Wardhouse," he said defensively when he caught Thorne's eye on him. "Aye, 'twas cherished 'gainst sore need. 'Tis the last bilge of the brandy."

With that he took a splinter of wood from the fire and touched the pewter plate with flame. Blue fire sprang up about the biscuits, and Kyrger, who had been watching with growing interest, hid his face in his arm.

It was obvious to the Samoyed that these outlanders were making shaman magic, a magic that involved the cutting of a pine tree and burning what appeared to be water on a common pewter plate.

Peter raised the dish on high and his dumpy face split into a grin.

"Fair greeting to ye Mistress Joan. My service to ye, lady, on this eve of evenings, this merry Yuletide."

"Is it truly so?" The dark eyes of the maiden grew somber. "Nay, you have taken all our biscuits, and burnt up your brandy."

"No matter." Peter waved a huge hand grandly. "I know where more is to be had. Aye, we will have no more troubles to ward. Now—" he laid the burning dish at her feet and cleared his throat—"a bit of chantry, to ease this down the ways:

> *"The boar's head in hand bring I,*
> *With garlands gay and rosemary;*
> *I pray you all sing merrily—*

"To be sure," he broke off apologetically, "we do lack summat of a boar's head, and garlands. We must e'en make shift without the rosemary, but Master Ralph and I will pipe up a song, having, as it were, a pretty face—a fair, sweet face, I say—whereby to lay our course."

He puffed out his cheeks and made his bow, and Thorne, who had been no little surprised at his high spirits and hearty manner, saw that the girl had smiled. So he went to stand by the fire and lifted his fine voice against the leaden silence of the night.

> *"Forth they went and glad they were;*
> *Going, they did sing,*
> *With mirth and solace they made good cheer,*
> *For joy of that new tiding."*

His voice, which had been hoarse, now rang out clearly:

> *"Neither in halls, nor yet in bowers,*
> *Born would He not be,*
> *Neither in castles, nor yet in towers*
> *That seemly were to see;*

> *But at His Father's will,*
> *Betwixt an ox and an ass,*
> *Jesu this king born He was;*
> *Heaven he bring us till!"*

Peter nodded approval, beating time with a finger as if he was a criterion of good music. His rasping roar joined in the chorus, while he kept an eye on the maiden:

> *"Forth they went and glad they were;*
> *Going, they did sing—*
> *Noël!"*

"And now," quoth the shipman, "God lack, the maid is weeping. She is a-leak at the eyes."

So, in truth, Joan was crying, her hands pressed to her cheeks. The two men surveyed her doubtfully, rather taken aback at the result of their holiday spirit. Peter made bold to lay his hand on her shoulder.

"What cheer, mistress? Sets the wind foul or fair?"

She glanced up, her face flushed and a smile twitching her lips.

"Nay, I am a simpleton, good Peter. The ballad minded me of Christmas Eve long since when we had candles in the casements of the cottages of Cairness, and the children sang sweet carols. Nay, my tears were not—not of grief. I do give you thanks for your entertainment, good Peter."

The boatswain drew back as if satisfied and motioned Thorne to one side.

"Does 'ee love the lass, Master Ralph?"

"Why not? Certainly, she is a fair companion and a brave soul."

"Ah." Peter nodded sagely. "Y'are a dullard with words, but still, with an observant eye. In a manner o' speaking, ye keep a sharp lookout, Master Ralph. But not so sharp as Peter Palmer," and he made mysterious motions with brows and lips. "I have good tidings for ye, younker. The maid is an honest maid, and no sea troll."

Thorne laughed.

"And why, Peter?"

"By reason of the holy words of the Christian song. When it was sung, she did not vanish, she did not slip cable and leave us. If she had been a witch, now, or a troll, she would not be here. So I say, if ye love the lass, why cherish her and ye will have no harm by it."

"I am indebted to your wisdom, Peter, and to your—observant eye."

"Y'are so," assented the shipman. "For I was about to tell the lass my tidings. While I was on yonder headland seeking the Yule fir I saw the ships. Aye, Sir Hugh's ship and the *Confidentia*, lying in the ice of a bay. Come morrow, we'll be with our mates."

Kyrger, squatting by the fire, waited solemnly for the end of this ritual of the outlanders. He wondered if they had been paying reverence to the *quoren vairgin*, the Reindeer Spirit.

Perhaps, he thought, like himself they had been paying their respects to the elder souls, the spirits of their dead companions, which were quite visible in the sky.

Purple and fiery red, these elder souls flamed on the broad gate of the sky. Kyrger knew well that the northern lights were the souls of the dead, rushing from earth to the zenith in their wild, merry dance.

Never had he seen the gate in the sky so broad, the flames so bright.

Chapter XIV
Thorne Meets Sir Hugh

The little *Confidentia* lay stranded in a chaos of jutting ice fragments and rocks. A few cables' lengths farther out the admiral-ship rode at anchor, although so girdled with ice that it was wedged fast.

They were in a shallow bay, where the wind, sweeping in from the open sea, had driven ice floes into a solid pack. The shores were treeless.

Under the wind gusts the waist curtains, that had been put up to shelter the crews, shivered, and the long pennant of Sir Hugh's ship whipped around the mast. From the solid ice near the *Confidentia* a trail ran through the snow to disappear over the distant hillocks.

Thorne and Peter shouted joyfully and Kyrger clucked on his reindeer until they entered this trail and reached the shore. Without waiting for a hail or a sight of their shipmates, the two men crossed the frozen surface of the bay, climbing between the rocks, and reached the ship's ladder.

Peter was first under the waistcloth and Thorne found him standing by the bole of the mainmast, staring aft. The helmsman of the *Confidentia* faced them, on his knees, one arm crooked around the tiller. He had a ragged red cap cocked over one ear.

"God's mercy," whispered the boatswain, "look at his skin!"

The seaman's whole face was purple, his lips, drawn back from the teeth, were no longer visible. Peter climbed the poop ladder and bent over the man; then he touched the fellow's arm.

"Stiff as a merlyn-spike," he muttered. Thorne had gone to the door

on the quarterdeck and thrust it open, his pulse quickening. For this was
Durforth's ship.

In the dim light from the narrow ports the great cabin seemed deserted
and he wondered if the officers were on shore.

Presently he stooped down and touched a misshapen form on the deck
planking, a human body so bundled up in cloaks and blankets that it was
hardly to be recognized. It was bent up in a knot as if gripped by intoler-
able agony.

With his hand on the man's shoulder he tried to turn him over, and was
forced to pull with all his strength. The body did turn over, but the bent
legs came up into the air without altering their position.

"That would be Dick Ingram, master's mate," said Peter behind him
in a strained voice, "his carcass, poor ——."

Thorne released his hold and the coiled-up body fell over on its side
again with a muffled thump.

"Save us!" cried the boatswain, his eyes starting from his head. "I've
seen the workings of dropsy and scurvy and such, but here is a black
plague. The black death itself hath fallen upon this ship."

"Nay," said Thorne slowly, "these twain are frozen."

"Aye, they are now. But how did they *die*? Let us go for'ard."

They searched the forecastle in vain, and descended from the hold to
the galley, which was nearly in darkness. But Peter stumbled over another
body, and fumbled around on his hands and knees, breathing heavily.

"Here be a mort o' dead men," he grunted. "What cheer, mates, who
has a word for Peter Palmer that's come a weary way to have speech with
ye? Who is living?"

Their ears strained, they listened for a space, then Peter gave a yell of
fear, and, thrusting Thorne aside, sprang up the ladder. On the spar deck
he wrenched down the waist curtain, staring out at the *Bona Esperanza*.
His broad red face was streaming perspiration, as he cupped his hands and
sent a quavering hail over the ice.

"Ahoy, the *Esperanza*! Nick Anthony, where be ye? Ho, Allen! Master
Davison—Garge Blage—"

When no response came from the admiral-ship, Peter choked and the
blood drained from his face. Wagging his massive head from side to side
he began to walk unsteadily toward the ladder.

"Feared I be, Master Ralph. Feared and boding—let be; by all the saints,
let me go."

"Then go," assented Thorne, "and bid Kyrger make camp beyond sight of the ships. I will seek out Sir Hugh and his company."

An hour later Thorne stood alone in the roundhouse of the *Bona Esperanza*, his brows knit in thought, his eyes heavy with grief. Alone he was, assuredly, except for the wide-winged gulls that circled over the masts, swerving away when the tip of the pennant flapped. Yet was the *Esperanza* fully manned, the stern cabins occupied. The cook was in his galley, curled up on the cold stove, Sir Hugh seated at his table by the stern casements.

Crew and officers were dead. Cadavers leered at the armiger from deck planks or berths, the eyes standing open as if gazing upon some devastating horror. All the faces were tinged with the same bluish cast. All the bodies were wrapped in odds and ends of garments, tabards and cloaks over all.

Some, apparently, had died while crawling to the lower portions of the ship; others, chiefly the merchant-adventurers, in their berths.

Thorne fought down a rising fear that impelled him to run after Peter and escape from this assemblage of the unspeaking dead. He had seen on the captain-general's table two folded pamphlets and judged that Sir Hugh had written therein. This message must be read.

With an effort, he made his way into the passage and so to the main cabin, which was nearly dark, the ports being boarded over. And at once the skin of his head grew cold, a cry trembled in his throat. Before him and below him in the gloom two red eyes were fastened upon him.

He knew that they were eyes because they moved, and he was aware of a faint hissing. Before he could take a grip on himself, or reach for a weapon, the tiny fires glowed brighter. There was a scampering of little feet and something darted past him.

Turning swiftly he saw an ermine, a white creature kin to the weasel, void of fear and relentless as a ferret on the scent of prey.

"What a chucklehead I am," he cried aloud, "to be frightened by a ferret."

But his own voice, ringing hollow in the chill of the pent-in ship, did not serve to reassure him. Passing into the presence of the dead leader, he forced himself to take up the papers under the open eyes of tall Sir Hugh.

He saw that both pamphlets were inscribed on the outside. One, marked

The will and testament of Sir Hugh Willoughbie, Knight, he laid down again.

The other he made out to be a short journal of the voyage. This he pored through slowly, for he was fairly skilled at reading, weighing everything in his mind, as was his habit.

Sir Hugh had been driven far out of his course by the storm that had separated the ships, and had picked up the *Confidentia* when the weather cleared. They put back, but failed to fall in with the Wardhouse.

> We sounded and had 160 fadomes whereby we thought to be farre from land and perceived that the land lay not as the Globe made mention.

For a month they cruised in the Ice Sea, finding the coast barren, and, putting into this haven assailed by

> very evil weather, as frost, snow and hail, as though it had been the dead of winter. We thought it best to winter there. Wherefore we sent out three men Southsouthwest, to search if they could find people, who went three days journey but could find none: after that we sent other three Westward four days journey, which also returned without finding any people. Then sent we three men Southeast three days journey, who in like sort returned without finding of people or any similitude of habitation.

At this point, on the eighteenth day of September, the journal of Sir Hugh Willoughby ended.*

Thorne read over the line "the land lay not as the Globe made mention" to be sure that he was not mistaken. No, the words were clear and honest in their meaning.

Why had Durforth, who was in company with Sir Hugh, failed to pick up the Wardhouse? He knew its bearing. Why did the journal end, as it were, in the middle of a day, and that day long before the death of the captain-general?

---

*No explanation has been reached as to why Sir Hugh's journal ceased some three months before his death. By the date of the other paper, his will, found by him, it appears that the knight was living in December 1554. One other fact has escaped the attention of his chroniclers. On the outside of his journal was scribbled a memorandum: "Our shippe being at anker in the harborough called Sterfier in the Island Losoote—" an island on the west coast of Norway, several hundred miles from the Arzina River in Lapland where Sir Hugh and his men perished. Evidently, his globe misled him from the first.

Now Thorne wished that his father, the Cosmographer, could have been at his side to answer these riddles. He was no navigator. But the thought came to him that his father would have gone to Durforth's cabin to look at the globe which had failed Sir Hugh. Durforth must have led the ships away from the Wardhouse to separate them from Chancellor.

Then the agent of Spain had put the ships upon the coast in a desolate region, swept by the winds that came off the pack ice. And, perhaps Sir Hugh had come to suspect Durforth, perhaps the journal had recorded his suspicions after this day in September and Durforth had removed the pages after the death of his commander.

That Durforth was still alive Thorne believed firmly, after he returned to the *Confidentia* and searched the master's cabin. Durforth's body was not to be seen. And, upon the table he found a candle burning, a mass of wax with a wick stuck in it, the whole floating in water in a tin basin. This was the only kind of candle Sir Hugh would permit to be lighted in the cabins, owing to the danger of fire. It might have been burning for two or three days.

And the fresh tracks from the ship to the shore had been made after the last storm. One man, possibly more, had left the ship within the last days. Thorne picked up the candle and looked at the globe. He had some skill at chart reading—having watched many a time the Cosmographer drawing the outlines of the earth—and he knew that this was a complete *mappamundi*. Both hemispheres and the northern and southern seas were traced on the great copper ball very clearly.

And he saw, running due east, from the island of the Wardhouse, a long body of water, a strait that extended to the mark of "Cathay." But the natives said no such passage existed, and the journal of Sir Hugh bore them out.

Durforth's globe was false. It had been drawn to mislead Sir Hugh, even as Renard's agent had been sent to put an end to the voyage. This had been done, and the lives of two hundred men snuffed out like so many candle flames.

Thorne lifted his head, hearing, in the utter silence of the ship, a foot-fall in the main cabin. It was as light and elusive as an animal's, yet he was certain that it drew closer to the door by which he was standing.

Drawing his sword and taking the mitten off his right hand, he put out the candle with a sweep of the blade. Waiting until his eyes were ac-customed to the gloom, he lifted the latch with his left hand and opened the door with a thrust of his foot. The half-light of the outer cabin disclosed Kyrger.

"Ostiaks," murmured the hunter, and glanced expectantly at the white man.

Kyrger was as restless as one of his own reindeer in a pen. When he moved it was as if his feet slipped over thin ice. He kept one eye on the deck beams within inches of his skull. In all his life he had not stood within four walls, certainly never in the maw of a giant's ship such as this. One that went forward *against* the wind.

"Faith, here's a coil," thought the armiger. "I'd best go with him to see what's in the wind."

But Kyrger did not wish this. Motioning for Thorne to watch, he began the pantomime which all primitive races understand. First he impersonated the voyagers, sitting around the fire. Then he jumped up and grasped at his bow, sending an imaginary arrow at an enemy.

By degrees Thorne understood that Ostiak tribesmen had attacked the camp; they had bound Joan and Peter and the reindeer. They had chased Kyrger nearly to the bay.

A very few of the Samoyed's words Thorne had picked up in the last months.

"*Sinym ka-i-unam?*" he asked quickly. "Has the little sister gone to the regions below?"

By shaking his head Kyrger signified that Joan was still alive. So was Peter, thanks to the mail jerkin the shipman wore.

Looking through a crack in one of the boarded-up ports, Thorne saw that the hunter had been telling the truth. On the shore a group of natives were descending toward the ice with two sledges drawn by dogs. Thorne counted eleven of them, armed with long spears and clubs.

He cast a glance aloft. The battle nettings that might have been slung from the quarterdeck rail to the forecastle, to keep out boarders, were not to be seen. Turning into the roundhouse, he looked at the racks where harquebuses and crossbows should have been stacked about the butt of the mizzen. None were there, and he found time to reflect that Durforth must have taken them from the ship.

But his eye fell upon a weapon more potent than any firelock, a murderer.

Bolted to a pivot on the quarterdeck rail was one of the light cannon that could be trained at will upon any part of the waist or foredeck. Signing to Kyrger to watch the approaching Ostiaks, he dived below, searching until he found an open keg of powder in the hold.

Dipping up a good quantity in his cap, he climbed the after companion to the roundhouse, which served as the armory. Here he filled a small sack with bullets, nails, and scraps of iron. Here, too, he found flint and steel and a slow match.

Back at the gun again he rammed home the loose powder, stuffed in wadding and his shot. Then he primed the touch hole and drew Kyrger back with him to the far angle of the roundhouse where they could not be seen by the natives climbing up the starboard ladder.

It did not take long to strike a spark that ignited the long fuse in his hand. Nursing the slow match, he waited, listening to the chattering talk of the Ostiaks and smiling at the sudden silence that fell when the first of them saw the dead helmsman.

Then he walked out to the quarterdeck rail. Nine pairs of small, bleared eyes fastened on him instantly and a spear whirred through the air, striking the chest of his fur jacket. The heavy skin and the leather jerkin under it broke the bone point of the spear, which did no more than shake him.

For a second he looked down into flat, swollen faces, fringed by ragged and greasy hair. About each neck was coiled a string of something whitish, the entrails of deer, he discovered a moment later, which served the Ostiaks for food as well as ornament. Then he trained the gun and touched it off as two more spears flashed by his head.

Kyrger bounded his own height from the deck when the murderer roared. Coughing, as the dense powder fumes swirled back, the Samoyed saw that three of the nine Ostiaks who had come over the rail were stretched on the deck and that two others were limping around in the smoke, yelling with pain.

Never before had Kyrger heard a gun go off, and he was struck with the awfulness of his leader's magic. Perceiving that he himself was without hurt, he plucked up heart and glided to the side bulwark, from which point of vantage he shot one of the natives who had remained on the ice, before they recovered from their astonishment.

Meanwhile Thorne had descended to the waist, sword in hand. Four of the Ostiaks snarled at him, and rushed through the eddying smoke. They had thrown their spears and wielded knives or clubs, and Thorne ran the first one through the body before they realized the length of his sword.

Then a thin man came forward, armed with the shank-bone of some animal. He wore a woman's leather skirt and his long black hair hung to his shoulders, over a kind of crude armor—so Thorne judged it to be. A multitude of iron images were suspended on cords slung from neck and waist. These images were of dogs and sheep and birds, crudely wrought, but covering his emaciated body completely.

Thorne remembered that this leader of the Ostiaks had been in the very path of the cannon's discharge, but had come through unharmed.

"So you are for your long home, my iron rogue," he gibed, for it was his way to talk when steel was out.

He stepped forward and thrust at the Ostiak's side. But his blade seemed to pass through air, or the loose tunic of the strange man, who screamed at him and struck with the bone club.

Thorne would have been brained if he had not ducked instinctively, the club smashing down on his shoulder blade.

He recovered for a second thrust, but the old native glided away from him, and disappeared under the waistcloth. The armiger sought for him along the rail, but saw him presently running over the ice.

Turning quickly, he was just in time to ward the knife of an Ostiak who had crept up from behind. Slashing at the throat of this newest antagonist, he sprang after the man of the iron apron, seeing that the few surviving tribesmen were fleeing in as many different directions.

"Shoot him!" he cried to Kyrger, who had been watching the annihilation of the remaining foemen with interest.

Believing that Thorne was aided by supernatural powers, it had not occurred to the Samoyed to join in the melee. Now he shook his head.

"Shaman menkva," he grunted. "A wizard and a devil."

It would have been quite useless to send an arrow after a wizard, Kyrger knew. Had not his friend and the wizard tried to slay each other and failed? How then could Kyrger be expected to slay the shaman?

Thorne swore under his breath and started in pursuit of the Ostiak. The lanky shaman seemed to float over ice ridges and rocks, his long hair flying out behind, his iron tunic rattling. Gaining the shore, he shrieked at his dogs and set to work to tie the second team by a leather thong to the first sled.

When this was done he hopped into the rear sled, cracked his whip, and glided off as the beasts dug their claws into the trail and strained at the traces. The sleds picked up speed and presently whirled out of sight in a smother of snow, the shaman peering back at his pursuer, his pointed teeth gleaming between writhing lips.

Thinking of Joan and Peter bound in the camp, Thorne settled down grimly to the trail. His heavy boots made clumsy going on the hard surface, and the cries of the wizard and the snapping of the whip drew farther away from him.

Kyrger had lingered on the *Confidentia* to visit each of the wounded Ostiaks, and when he dropped from the ladder of Durforth's ill-fated ship, had added to her crew of dead men.

Chapter XV
Darkness

By the fire that Kyrger had built, Thorne found Peter stretched like a stout log in the snow, his arms bound to his side, and a blue bruise swelling in his tangle of red hair. He was still breathing, and Thorne dragged him into the Samoyed's sledge, covering him up with the skin of the white bear to keep him from freezing to death. Joan was gone; so were the dogs and their master, and the reindeer. After a little Kyrger appeared and took in the scene with a comprehensive glance.

As best he could, Thorne explained to the attentive hunter that they must follow the dogsleds. All other matters must wait until he had set Joan free from the creature in the leather apron.

"*Sinym—sinym thusind,*" muttered Kyrger, nodding assent, for he saw that the outlander was very angry. "Young sister—the pursuit of blood atonement."

He lifted his head and called shrilly, and Thorne saw the two reindeer appear from the nearest thicket, munching at the branches as they came. They had been driven off by the shaman or had run away from the dogs. Thorne learned thereafter that dogs and reindeer were as hostile as the two tribes that were served by each animal.

Kyrger lost no time in putting the reindeer into the leather traces, tying the guiding thong attached to their off horns to the hand bar of the sledge. Then he beckoned Thorne, who discovered that the savage had picked up a pair of the wooden skates dropped by one of the Ostiaks. They were shorter than the Samoyed's and heavier, and Kyrger bound them firmly to Thorne's boots.

Then he led the outlander to the rear of the sledge and made him put his hands on the waist-high bar at the back.

"Thus," he murmured to himself, "we will go as swiftly as the white pigeon flying before the wind. Be quiet my master! Let your spirit be strong when we meet new enemies who dwell where winged things cannot enter and things with bones cannot pass. *Kai*—it will be a long journey, O Thunderer, O Leaner-Against-the-Wind."

He glided off and picked up the two staffs, which, pointed and bearing sizeable crosspieces a foot from the point, enabled him to push himself along rapidly where the snow surface was level, as if he were poling a light canoe through shallows.

Alone, he would never have started after the wizard, who could make the long journey to the hall of Erlik in the spirit world of the cold, underground region, or invoke ermecin the white bear.

But after the fight on the bark, Kyrger had immense confidence in Thorne. He believed that the armiger as well as the shaman was possessed by a spirit, whether the reindeer, the gull, the bear, or the eagle, he did not know. How else had he scattered eleven Ostiaks?

He went ahead of the deer, running at times, but oftener thrusting himself onward a dozen paces with the staffs. Faster he went and faster, squatting on his haunches when the head of a slope was reached and flashing down with the speed of a flying thing.

The reindeer struck into their loose-limbed trot that covered distance amazingly. Thorne for a while had all he could do to hang on and keep his feet. Once the toe of his skis caught in a fallen branch and he was thrown heavily. But he soon learned how to lift himself over obstacles and to keep his feet together.

The gray obscurity of the day merged into the flickering radiance of night with its attendant fires in the northern sky. Kyrger looked like a winged gnome, speeding over the slot in the snow; Peter was no more than a motionless bulk under the fur pelt. Thorne could not stop and make camp for the shipman's sake. Joan, somewhere ahead of them, was flying through this wilderness of unmarked snow.

The reindeer no longer seemed to him to be running. They flew through the air, their whitish bodies invisible in the smother of powdered snow, their black-muzzled heads laid back so that the horns rested along their shoulders.

How long they raced through the night he did not know. They were sliding down a winding gully where a few stunted larches thrust up through the drifts, when Kyrger whirled to a halt and strung his bow. His arrow sped and struck something invisible to Thorne. But the hunter pushed himself to where it lay and brought back a long white hare.

With his knife he stripped the skin off its back and offered it to the outlander. There was no time to stop to make a fire, even if wood had been at hand. The ache of hunger was strong enough for him to suck some of the blood from the hare; but then he handed it back to Kyrger, who ate the raw flesh, still steaming hot, without a qualm.

Meanwhile Thorne satisfied himself that Peter was breathing. From the gully they descended to the level surface of a frozen lake, down which the trail of the dogsleds ran. Here the reindeer, refreshed by the brief halt, made fast time and Thorne peered ahead for a sight of the Ostiak.

For hours they followed the windings of the lake, which grew steadily narrower. Trees appeared on either hand and soon they were moving between the solid walls of a forest of spruce and fir. When the strip of water was no more than a stream, Kyrger slowed down and halted his reindeer, which had been running the last few miles with tongues lolling out.

Coming to Thorne's side, the Samoyed pointed above the trees ahead of them and to the right, and after a moment the armiger made out what his companion had seen, a wavering line of smoke rising against the gray sky.

For the first time Kyrger turned aside from the trail, leading his deer into a grove of spruce where they were sheltered from the wind. Then he took up the crossbow that he had placed in the sledge, and the two advanced through the timber in the direction of the smoke, the hunter circling to keep away from the stream.

They heard voices, distinct in the thin air, and crawled warily to the summit of a ridge. Here they crouched, motionless. Below them within stone's throw were three large dog sledges and a half-dozen Ostiaks. Seated on a log beside the embers of a fire, Master Cornelius Durforth and Joan Andrews were talking. Squatting on a white horse skin near his two dog teams was the wizard they had pursued from the Ice Sea.

Joan had been freed of her bonds by Durforth, who sent the shaman away from the maiden, and prepared food for her, with hot, spiced wine. Refreshed, she gazed curiously at the man who sat by her in his coat of black foxskin with an ermine collar. Joan knew the value of such things.

She saw, too, that the powerful fingers of his left hand played with the links of a gold chain at his throat; that his strong teeth glimmered through

the tangle of his jutting beard. His brown eyes, utterly without expression, moved restlessly as if instinct made him uneasy. A sudden foreboding
gripped Joan, who was as sensitive as a child, and fear burned in her veins
more fiercely than when the shaman had thrown her into his sled.

She had seen that gold chain before, and the face that reminded her of
a wolf. Too few events had come into the life of the daughter of John Andrews that she should forget one of them. Two years before at Yuletide,
when the candles were lighted in the windows of Cairness—a ship driving into the haven for refuge—a stranger sitting in the tavern, listening
to the tales of John Andrews of gold to be found by one who could pass
south of the Ice Sea.

"Oh," she cried, "you are the master of the black pinnace!"

Cornelius Durforth did not take his eyes from the fire.

"I have had many ships to my command."

"The black pinnace with the dragon's head, which was manned by
Burgundians."

"Ah. Then you—" he looked at her—"would be John Andrews's
daughter."

"Aye, so. And so was my father slain by your churls."

"How?"

"Your pinnace entered the haven of Wardhouse—" Joan faltered, but
passionate anger, long pent up, was rife in her—"and your knaves looted
it over the body of John Andrews, who once gave you shelter."

"Did they so? By the Three Dead Men of Cologne, they were not my
knaves. The boat once carried my flag and was made a prize by pirates
out of Danemarke."

His lips drew back in a soundless laugh.

"They paid in good coin for their frolic; I saw the boat with their bodies hanging like ripe fruit, drifting down the coast."

His words carried conviction, but the girl drew back from his face.

"Who are you?" she barely whispered.

"Cornelius Durforth, the Burgundian. What, wench, have you never
heard of the merchant of Ghent?"

Her mind flitted among questions. What was Durforth doing on the
Ice Sea? How had he escaped alone from the stricken ships of the English?
Why had the Ostiak brought her to him?

He thrust out his hand to take her chin and study her face.

"Nay, wench, you wear your heart upon your sleeve. You are fair as a golden eaglet, but, on my faith, only a hooded falcon may sit on perch at its master's table. Weigh well your answer to this question: Do you trust me? Are you friend or unfriend?"

Whereat she sighed and dropped her gaze to the chain of gold about his neck.

"Good my master, who am I to stand against your will? Take me with you out of this forest to Christian folk, and I will thank you on my knees. But let us set out at once!"

In silence Durforth considered her, until a flush mantled her cheeks and his beard bristled in a wide smile.

"So! I am no wizard like Shatong the shaman—" he nodded at the Ostiak who was tapping on a drum between his knees, upon a white horsehide—"yet can I read your mind. You fear me, you have no faith in me. A witless boy follows the track of your sled through the wilderness, and it is your thought that if he rushes in upon us here he will be slain, which, indeed is most true.

"Under a cloak of meekness you would have us set out so that he will see our following and learn caution, which is a thing he never will learn. In another hour or so your armiger will be wolf meat."

She drew away from the man, hands pressed against her cheeks.

"Would you slay him shamefully in this pagan land?"

"That will I, and he would do no less for me. By the eyes of —— you should know no land is wide enough to hold us twain. He serves his king, who is shent—aye, who lieth under sod ere now. Hath a man allegiance to the dead?"

"Aye, so," the girl responded promptly.

"Then is he a traitor. For—and here is a merry matter—the lord prince who laid command upon me to voyage hither is now your squire's lord."

"That may not be," she cried passionately, "I think you are liegeman to Satan, prince of darkness."

"Some do call him that. And, by the Three Dead Men, if Mephistophele were anointed monarch on this earth, he would not lack for followers, being both sagacious, courteous, and untainted by remorse. Yet I serve Philip, son of the Emperor Charles, the mightiest lord in Christendom. And this same Philip will sit presently upon the throne of England."

While he spoke he had been studying the maiden, marking the tawny hair held back by the hood, the slight, firm lips, and the pulse that beat in a white throat. Such beauty would command its price, and Durforth knew the very barons who would lighten their purses of a hundred gold crowns to possess her.

Yet he was embarked upon a delicate mission, and it was necessary that her tongue should be silent as to what she had seen on the Ice Sea, and what she would presently behold. He considered permitting Shatong to cut out her tongue; but she might be able to write.

Women, he knew, were like hawks. Tamed and hooded, fed and wing-clipped, they would be content under the hand of a master for a while—until he could be paid his price for the maiden. To tame her, she must first learn to fear him.

Unclasping his cloak, he took from the breast of his doublet two papers, folded and sealed. These he held near the fire, for the light was dim under the trees, so that she could see the imperial signet on the seals. When he saw that she had recognized it, he put the letters back very carefully in a silk pouch attached to the end of his gold chain.

"These letters missive," he said, "are from Charles of Spain to Ivan the Terrible, emperor of Muscovy, and they are my charge."

"Sir Hugh's letters—"

Durforth's head went back and he laughed from an open throat, a roaring laugh that reached to the ears of Thorne and the hunter who crouched behind the ridge, waiting until darkness could cover their approach to the fire. Yet they heard not the words of the agent of Philip.

"Death of my life, wench, Sir Hugh's letters are ashes long since. Sir Hugh, gallant fool! Sir Hugh, lack-wit leader! Why, he ventured blindly into the Ice Sea. He sailed in circles when he lost company with Chancellor, and he proposed to winter in an open bay without fuel or food."

Shivering, she looked up at him, and he took a savage pleasure in heightening the horror in her eyes.

"*I* had ventured to the northern coast before this, and had talked with the Easterlings. *I* knew the peril of the *khylden* and the cold that stiffens a man's sinews and soul. So I baled me from the fleet, to the southeast where the tribe of Ostiaks had their dwelling. Before we could return to the ships the storms had snuffed out the Englishmen.

"My pinnace had fallen foul of the Laps, and the lads that manned it were drying i' the wind. I had sent it to the Wardhouse so that I might sail in it to the inland sea, and thither into Muscovy. But it fell out otherwise.

"So was I set afoot. And by mischance that murdering wight Thorne, who hath crossed my path twice before now, was journeying along the coast. My Ostiaks sighted your fire on Christmas night, and I sent Shatong with ten others to the ships to greet your comrades while I conveyed the goods I had taken from the *Confidentia* hither and awaited the coming of the savages."

Again he laughed, for Durforth could enjoy a jest.

"Body of —— Thorne played in luck there. The Ostiaks had never heard a gun roar. But Shatong is a match for your wildling squire. Aye, that long-haired imp is a familiar of the powers of darkness."

"God grant," cried Joan, "that Master Chancellor meets with you."

"If you wish the pilot well, pray otherwise," responded Durforth grimly. "I know where he must lie, if he lives, and it should go hard but I bring the Easterling pack upon his back."

Into Joan's whirling thoughts came memories of childhood tales, of werewolves that took the form and semblance of men by day and turned to beasts at nightfall, of beasts that ran to join the unhallowed company of the witches' sabbath.

"How did you gain this power over the savages?" she whispered, fearful of hearing what was in her mind.

Durforth's face seemed to change, and the fire in his brown eyes died down.

"Power?" He waxed thoughtful. "Why, I can speak with them. Power springs always from wealth, because it feeds the desire of men. I promised Shatong riches incalculable if he would guard me with his men to the Town of Wooden Walls, which is the door to Russia, or Muscovy. I promised to show him the mystery of gunpowder."

He was gazing at her now, narrowly.

"My hold on them is slight. Remember that. And now say if you will cast your lot with me?"

"I will not. For-by you have said that you sent the pinnace that wrought evil to my father."

Durforth shook his head slowly.

"Here is irony. 'Tis true the men and the ship were mine, but I did order them to conduct themselves straitly and do no harm, for fear of a broil with the English rovers. They fell a-plundering."

It amused him that he, who had been forced to lie without cessation, should not gain credit for the one truth.

"I see," he added, "you will have none of me. May the foul fiend take you, slut, didst think an empire is built out of billing and cooing and tying of breast-knots? Shatong, then, shall have you."

Glancing into her stricken face, he moved impatiently.

"My pretty vixen, I put no value on your beauty, nor does Shatong. He will e'en have a use for you."

Durforth laughed again in amusement at her obvious signs of fear.

Now as he beckoned to the shaman who had been peering at them and at the ridges about the camp, through the tangle of his long hair, Durforth's eyes began to glow. His tongue touched his lips and a certain eagerness was apparent as he signed for the Ostiak to lead away the maiden.

"*Khada ulan obokhod*," the wizard muttered. "The dead souls that dwell in the mountains and high places have spoken to me. They say the man who is your enemy is near this place. I can bring him to the fire."

Durforth looked at the old savage curiously. He was more than a little superstitious, and he had seen the shaman do unaccountable things.

"Before the last of the light is gone, I will bring him." Shatong's thin hand closed on Joan's arm. "But I must take the maiden for this work."

The man nodded, and Shatong led Joan to a stone on the other side of the fire, and went to his horsehide. Striking on the drum slowly he began a song, the copper bells and the iron trinkets on his leather apron keeping a rude sort of time.

Chapter XVI
The Snow Bear

Kyrger, flat on his belly in the snow, wriggled uneasily. They had been too far away for Thorne to hear what was said between the two outlanders, but Shatong's shrill voice was distinct enough in the thin air. Kyrger knew that the shaman was trying to draw Thorne to the Ostiaks, although the white man was clearly waiting for darkness before he made any move.

More logs were thrown on the fire, and as dusk fell the figure of the shaman was covered with a ruddy tinge. On one knee he bent over the drum, chanting his discordant song. Then he rose to his toes and spread out his arms, moving toward Durforth.

Kyrger knew by this that the *kam*, the spirit of the wizard, had become separated from his body and was flying through the air. Shatong, therefore, meant to journey to the cold underground region where Erlik ruled the spirit world.

"The dead souls say," chanted the wizard, "I must cut myself. I will cut myself with your knife."

Durforth handed the savage his dirk and Shatong crept nearer the girl. Thorne rose to his knees, taking the crossbow from Kyrger, but uttered a stifled exclamation of astonishment. Shatong had thrust the weapon under his own gaunt ribs. Or so it seemed. His two hands gripped the hilt, and blood ran down upon his apron. The blade of the dirk had disappeared.

Presently the shaman drew it forth, stained with blood, and screamed. Joan hid her face in her hands.

Durforth, chin on hand, seemed unmoved; but his eyes were intent. Meanwhile Shatong took up his journey to the presence of Erlik. He went through the motions of leaping over mountains and staggering through the sands of a desert; then he walked forward gingerly, swaying from side to side.

Kyrger knew that the spirit of the wizard was moving over the single hair that bridges the abyss between the land of the living and the abode of the dead souls.

He watched Shatong cringe back as if at the gate of Erlik's domain—heard the snarling chorus of welcome from the dogs of the underworld—saw Shatong driven back by a gust of wind, then approach fearfully the seat of Erlik, represented by the fire.

The chorus of animal cries grew louder, though Shatong's lips did not move. Invisible wings beat overhead, and Kyrger's skin grew cold. He knew what would follow.

Shatong lifted his hands to his lips as if drinking the welcoming cup, and fell down in a huddle on the trampled snow. His dark skin glistened with sweat. At this moment his kam was listening to the words of Erlik.

He bounded to his feet and pointed toward the trees where Thorne and Kyrger were hidden.

"Winged creatures cannot fly hither; things with bones cannot come; how have you made your way to my abode?"

Staggering, he laid his hand on his chest.

"I have ridden far, my strength fails; I have faced great terrors, and I am hungry."

So saying, he advanced on Joan, who drew back, half faint with fear. Grasping the fur surcoat at her throat, he jerked it away and bared a white shoulder with his claw. His teeth snapped and his lips writhed as he drew nearer the girl's arm.

Kyrger sat up on his haunches with a grunt of dismay. Shatong, he saw, had prevailed, because now, without any effort to draw back, his companion, the white man, was running toward his enemies.

Thorne at first had taken up the crossbow; but the wavering firelight and the numbness in his fingers made the risk too great for a shot. Moreover, to kill Shatong would not free Joan. As he plodded forward through the snow she saw him and cried out clearly:

"Get you hence, Master Ralph. They lie in wait for you."

At this the shaman released her and turned to his men, saying something in a low voice. To Durforth he added triumphantly:

"*Lili khel mkholas*—my soul looked into the hiding place of this enemy. My soul summoned him forth from the hiding place."

Durforth, who did not know that the sharp eyes of the wizard had picked out the armiger on the ridge, was more than a little startled. Whether or not Shatong had planned his ritual of the drum and the spirit visit to hearten himself or to bring the outlander forth would be difficult to say.

Because his limbs were stiff with cold Thorne moved slowly, and Durforth at first did not recognize the gaunt figure in the wolfskin hood and jacket. And the newcomer, instead of putting hand to sword or approaching Joan, went to the fire and stretched out his hands, first taking the mittens off, to warm them at the blaze.

"I give you greetings, Master Durforth," he said quietly.

The voice and the smile that accompanied it banished the last doubt in the mind of Philip's agent.

"Slay me this man," he said to Shatong, after a long breath of hesitation. "I will give the price of five deerskins to the one who takes his life with the first arrow," he added when the shaman made no response.

But Shatong was squatting again on his white horsehide mumbling to himself. And the six natives had eyes only for the wizard. If Thorne had rushed at them, or shouted or drawn his weapon they would have stretched him in the snow at once. Meanwhile Shatong had arrived at a decision; his slits of eyes glimmered at the white men and he gabbled at Durforth.

"I am very weary with the long journey to the Erlik-hall. My ears are filled with the beating of spreading wings. Lo, one of the wings veils the moon; the other hides the sun. I have flown with the mother of eagles over Yaik. I cannot hear your words, outlander."

Placing his hand before his eyes he turned his back on Durforth, who repeated his order to the others, increasing the bounty he offered for the visitor's life. But the Ostiaks continued to gaze at him with wooden features, and he understood that they would do nothing for the moment. Shatong, after throwing wood on the fire to make it brighter, would do nothing at all.

He had been watching the strange white man. He saw that Thorne's motions were assured and purposeful. Shatong had felt the other's sword rasp his ribs, and the skin of his face still stung from the powder that had belched from the cannon.

This young outlander might cause a second explosion at any moment, he reasoned. Evidently the other's kam, his tutelary deity, was powerful and unfriendly to Shatong's kam. Durforth's power, too, was doubtful. So Shatong waited to see what would happen.

"These be men of power. No hoofed beast can protect itself against them, creatures with claws flee away. There is a *thusind*, a pursuit of blood between them. Let us see what they will accomplish."

Durforth rose and advanced to the fire with hand outstretched.

"'Od's life, Master Thorne, I greet you well! In this pagan land we cannot afford to nourish our late quarrel. We must abet one another. So, let us cry a truce."

He had no means of knowing that the armiger had caught the gist of his command to Shatong, and he thought to silence Joan with a warning glance. This had quite another effect on the girl.

"Do not put faith in him," she said instantly, "for he will not keep faith with you."

Thorne motioned her to be silent.

"Yield ye," he said to Durforth. "Throw down your weapons if you are bent on life."

The man in the foxskins still held out his hand, but he was thinking. And Philip had not chosen an agent for a dull wit.

Durforth said slowly:

"Bethink you, Master Thorne, Edward hath breathed his last by now. The odds are, Mary is queen, and so is England joined to Spain. What will it profit you to meddle with me?"

"Because we are here in the hands of savages I offer you a fair surrender. We have this maid to bear to safety, and you know the way. Yield and I will do what in me lies to bring you to England. For the rest, I care not. Yield your sword or draw it."

"You are bold, young sir, and foolhardy." He paused. "Why do you press this quarrel when it mars both our fortunes?"

"Because," quoth the armiger, "I have looked upon the bodies of a hundred honest men, marred by your treachery. Come—"

Durforth started and looked beyond him at the shadows of the forest, open mouthed. Thorne, noticing the quick dread in the other's face, turned to see what had caused it. In the thicket he perceived that something moved, something white and massive. Then he sprang to one side.

In the second when he had taken his gaze from the merchant, Durforth had stooped to pick up from the snow the dagger left there by the shaman. No sooner had his fingers closed upon it than he lunged at Thorne's back. The sudden movement in so big a man had aroused the armiger, who stepped wide of the thrust, drawing his sword as he did so.

"Ha, stand to your guard, rogue. No one will come between us this time."

Durforth recovered his balance and his composure at once. He had acted before he thought; the blood-stained knife had caught his eyes as Thorne turned away. Taking off his surcoat, he stood in doublet and boots, smiling a little. In drawing his sword he whipped it through a salute.

"A pity, my hotspur, that you gave your allegiance to the wrong prince. Had you cast your lot with Mary and Spain we twain might have gone far."

While Joan sat upon her log, her eyes glued to the flicker of the two rapiers that gleamed ruddy in the firelight, the Ostiaks followed with absorbing interest the struggle between the two outlanders.

In the treacherous footing of the trodden snow they moved warily. Durforth, who had the dirk in his left hand, sought to come to close quarters; failing that, he circled to get the fire at his back and drive Thorne out into the deeper snow. Red light played up and down the bright blades, and the slithering click of steel punctuated the quick breathing of the men.

Shatong saw that Durforth's face had changed; it had darkened, the beard jutting out, the forehead creased. The lips were drawn back, and Shatong saw in this face the likeness of a wolf. So, he reasoned, the taller outlander served the wolf spirit.

The other, whose yellow mane gleamed in the firelight, who fought with closed lips, he fancied served the *quoren vairgin*, the reindeer spirit. And it was well known that the wolf-clan was powerful enough to tear to pieces a member of the reindeer clan. And, certainly, the clan of ermecin, the great white bear, would prevail over either. So Shatong reasoned, while he crawled around the fire to watch the struggle of the white men.

Durforth pressed the attack now, following thrust with thrust. Both men, the shaman thought, were tiring, and Thorne was staggering. It was clear to the Ostiak that Durforth's kam was the stronger, and he began to breathe quickly in anticipation of the end.

He saw Thorne stumble in a drift over a fallen tree and go down on one knee. Durforth sprang in, cutting down his adversary's blade, and struck with the knife. Thorne had not tried to rise, but gathered his strength and lunged as Durforth came down on him.

Shatong saw a point of steel through Durforth's back; saw the big man rise to his toes and fall forward, soundlessly, into the drift.

Freeing his blade, Thorne turned about in time to face the rush of the Ostiaks led by Shatong. The shaman had not expected to see Durforth go down, but now he knew that the other outlander must be exhausted. The three sled loads of goods from the ships would be his in another moment.

Something whirred past the shaman and thudded into the back of the foremost Ostiak. It was a crossbow bolt and it knocked the man from his feet. The others turned to stare at the forest and yelled in shrill and astonished fear.

Two figures were advancing on them from the trees, Kyrger running in advance, fitting an arrow to his small bow. Behind him, grasping the crossbow that he had picked up when the Samoyed let it fall, was Peter. Peter with the skin of the polar bear wrapped around him, the muzzle over his head, his face almost invisible between the gaping jaws.

Some hours since, the shipman had awakened from the stupor into which he had fallen after the blow on the head dealt him by Shatong. His heavy leather cap and stout skull had brought him off none the worse except for a mighty bruise over one ear. Kyrger had roused him by thrusting the end of the crossbow into his ribs.

By frantic signs the Samoyed had made it clear to Peter that trouble was brewing near at hand, and the shipman had lumbered off without delaying to rid himself of the bearskin. Heaving into sight of the fire, he was in time to see Durforth go down and the Ostiaks rise from their haunches and rush at Thorne.

"Stand to quarters, lad!" he bellowed. "Lay them by the board!"

Shrewd Shatong saw what effect this apparition of the burly man in the white fell had upon his followers. They had not known that another out-lander was present, so intent had they been upon the duel. And the skin of the white bear filled them with superstitious dread.

"Ermecin!" they cried.

No Ostiak had ever slain a white bear. And while they hung back, gripped alike by fear and the bloodlust, Shatong ran at Peter from the side, swinging his club.

Out of the corner of his eyes the shipman saw him, and swung the crossbow down and outward in a powerful hand. The steel bow and the iron-tipped head struck the shaman on the temple.

Without a cry Shatong's body dropped upon the earth, seeming to shrink into its grotesque garb of leather and jangling iron, its long hair covering the shattered skull and the gap where his eyes had been.

A shout from Kyrger, who had beheld what was in his estimation a mira-cle, brought home to the Ostiaks the fact that they were dealing with men, not spirits. One of the eight sent an arrow through the little hunter.

Others swarmed upon Peter, screaming and stabbing. It was Thorne's sword that checked their rush. The armiger, thrusting and warding, strengthened by the brief rest, put down two of his assailants, and drove another back on the huddle around Peter.

In this hand-to-hand struggle the Easterlings could not use their bows; but Peter, dropping the crossbow, used his fists. He knocked one man headlong, and Thorne, bruised by a thrown club, ran another through the heart. The deadly play of the rapier was more than the rest could stom-ach and they fled beyond the circle of firelight, vanishing into the gloom under the trees.

"Faith," muttered Peter, glancing around, "we were sore beset, but we cleared the deck. Where lie the ships?"

He was astonished past belief when he understood that they were twenty leagues from the coast and Sir Hugh's vessels.

While Peter and Joan washed Kyrger's hurt and made him comfortable on some cloths from the goods on the sleds, Thorne put more wood on the fire and—when Joan told him all that had passed between her and Dur-forth—took the letters from the pouch of the Burgundian. Carefully he read them through after breaking the seals, and when he had done, placed them in his belt.

"In these missives," he said to the expectant girl, "lieth the true way to Cathay."

"Is it far?" she wondered. "Could we adventure there?"

He smiled at her wish.

"Nay, Joan. There is no passage by sea; but the way by land hath been discovered already by the Muscovites. The silks and spices, aye, the ivory and carpets of Cathay and the Indies are borne each year through Tatary to the emperor of the Muscovites, Ivan, called the 'Terrible,' and entitled in these missives emperor of Astrakhan and lord of the forests and the Sibir Desert."

"Now marry and amen!" cried Peter, who had come up and had been fingering Durforth's chain longingly. "Here is that same lord Ivan or John of the land of gold and silver. The dons were wiser than we. What more, lad?"

"Why, simply this: The Spaniards desired Ivan to make a compact with them, so that the trade of the Indies could be borne overland, which is shorter by much than the sea route to the Indies, to them. They would have the great Emperor Ivan know that they are masters of all Christendom, save England, which will soon be under their hand."

"Then," cried Joan angrily, "we must bear these missives to the lords of England, and rouse them to their peril."

"Faith, Joan—" the armiger laughed outright—"are you Puss-in-Boots, to girdle the earth, east or west? We will do what we can, but if we are to live we must gain the borders of Muscovy."

"What says the other missive?" pressed the boatswain, who had great faith in letters.

"Cornelius Durforth, the Burgundian, was a trusted councilor of Spain." He glanced down thoughtfully at the body of his enemy: "Peter, 'tis my thought that the Fox is dead."

"How?" quoth the shipman, scratching his head. "Meseems we left my lord Renard on his feet."

"It is evident," said Thorne, "that Renard was Durforth's man. And Durforth was Philip's spy called by us the Fox. While we watched Renard, the Fox came and went. D'Alaber served him and came against me while Durforth waited. When there is a killing to be managed, 'tis the servant who handles the knife while the lord waits the result."

"Your father!" cried Joan and fell silent.

"Aye, Durforth desired his end, and Renard saw that it was done. The spy's work in Burgundy was finished long since; his task in England done, and but for one thing he would have gained to the court of Ivan."

"Your sword, it was," said Joan proudly.

"Nay, greed. Durforth was petty in craving gold. He stopped to snatch it where he could. He went back to plunder the ships when Sir Hugh and his brave company died."

Peter put his hands behind him and looked away from the Burgundian's sword hilt and gold chain.

"The black rogue!"

"Nay—" Thorne shook his head—"rogue he may have been, but brave he was. Now that he is sped it is not honorable in us to miscall him."

Chapter XVII
The Inland Sea

It is written in the chronicles of that reign how the armiger and the shipman, knowing not whither they should take their course, turned southeast as Durforth's route had been planned.

So it was said of them that the hand of Durforth, which had been ever against them, living, now guided them out of the *tayga*, the dense forest of the Easterlings. They drove the dogsleds, loaded with trade goods, and Joan made shift to drive Kyrger's reindeer and the sledge on which the wounded Samoyed lay. They took their course from the stars.

And so they left the fires in the sky behind them and came out on a snow plain without track or tree or village. Still Thorne pressed south and east. He would not change his course for any direction that seemed likelier, and because of this they passed through a girdle of hills and found themselves on the shore of a sea that stretched to the horizon.

Its waters were a clear green, unlike the dull gray of the Ice Sea, and for this reason Thorne said they could not be the same.

And following this coast they came to men spearing seals among the ice cakes. Some of these men were Muscovites, but in their number was Master Stanton, gunner of the *Edward*, who greeted them with a glad outcry.

And from this same Master Stanton they learned what was afterward set down in the chronicle, that when Richard Chancellor parted from the Wardhouse, he held on his course toward the unknown region of the world, aided by the continual light.

Coming to the mouth of what seemed a great bay, he entered and sailed many a league to the south without seeing land again. But they came upon a fishing boat manned by barbarians who were filled with amazement at the great size of his ship.

He entreating them courteously, they made report in the villages of the Muscovites of the arrival of a strange nation of a singular gentleness. Master Chancellor was conducted to a town built on a fair harbor, within wooden walls,* and was told that this was the bay of St. Nicholas and the sea was the White Sea, which ran far into the dominions of the great prince Ivan.

Master Chancellor departed to seek this prince at his court in Moscow, leaving the *Edward* at anchor in charge of Burroughs. And so began the trade of Muscovy with the outer world, for it was a land rich in gold and silver and furs. As for Thorne the armiger and Joan Andrews, they fared to the court of Ivan the Terrible and what there befell them is set down in the chronicles for all to see.

But when Kyrger's wound healed he harnessed up his reindeer and journeyed back to the Ice Sea. It was more than he could endure to live within walls, and in the beginning of spring he reached the Wardhouse where Tuon and his Laps had taken up their quarters to watch the possessions of Joan Andrews and to wait whatever would take place.

Kyrger the hunter spread under their eyes the skin of ermecin, the white bear, and squatted down on it, taking full heed of the astonishment of the Laps.

"*O nym tungit,*" he murmured, "O my tent companions, since I turned my face from the north star many new fires have taken their place in the gate in the sky. Many men have gone to greet Yulden to whom the three stairways lead."

He pointed to the skin.

"With an arrow my master slew this one. And with the bow that sent the arrow Shatong the shaman was struck down. The spirit that dwells in my master is very powerful. It is not the Reindeer-Being; it is not kin to the bear or the wolf or the eagle."

The listeners held up their hands in bewilderment.

"O, my brothers harken, for this is a very great magic and a thing beyond belief. My master hurries through the forest, looking neither to right nor to left; when he is in trouble he makes a magic with water that

---

*Archangel.

burned, and ice put upon a tree; he went against his enemies and the blood feud is atoned.

"In the Town of Wooden Walls he claimed the *sinym*—the young maiden—for his bride, although there were many warriors of her race who cast their eyes upon her.

"The spirit that dwells in him is that of the *khylden*. He has run with the snow driver. So in all things it is better, O my friends, to follow him than to stand against him."

Flower Girl

A black night it was. Mist hanging over the canals, hiding the stars. Damp breath from the lagoons, creeping along the stone walls of Venice—blind walls without eyes of light.

Through the darkness Donald Ban made his way, listening to the warning cry of an unseen boatman, peering at the red blur of a lantern swaying over the black surface of the water. An ungodly night, he thought, shifting his kit to his other shoulder. And a strange city, with canals where the streets should be, and blind walls in the stead of honest doorways.

In all Venice he knew no living soul, having come off a ship that evening with his great sword at his hip, his buckler on his back, and his garments and gear slung over his shoulder in a red velvet *caftan* that he had taken from a slain Egyptian *mameluk*. For Donald Ban was home from the wars in the East—finding his way home from the crusades after six years of service.

A dark Scot he was, with candid gray eyes and few words. A brown beard curled on his long chin, and a baron's mantle hung from his wide shoulders. Women looked at him invitingly, but he went his own way as a rule, having found these outland girls even more troublesome than the lasses of the Clan Arran.

In a leather wallet, slung securely from his belt under the mantle, he carried his gleanings of the last six years—a few gold *dinars* and *byzants*, mixed with silver coins and a jewel or two. For the present he was in search of a decent lodging for the night where the people spoke good Norman-French and the wine had body to it.

He was having trouble finding such a place. Other men pattered by unseen, their footfalls echoing between the walls—they knew their way about. When he accosted a Venetian the other laid hand to knife, scowl-

ing, and slipped away; if he spoke to a group in the Norman-French of the
armies, they answered in a mocking gabble that sounded like Latin.

"'Tis no priest's Latin, I'm thinking, nor the dog lingo of the Catalan
lads. 'Tis fair uncouth."

He had no desire to go back to the stinking deck of the galley, off the
riva dei Schliaovni, and by now he doubted if he could retrace his steps
to the waterfront. He was standing irresolute on a narrow bridge when
two men brushed past him, following a servant with a torch. They were
wrapped in cloaks and seemed to be in excellent spirits. Donald Ban fell
in behind to take advantage of the light, reasoning that the two gentlemen might well lead him to a wine shop and food.

Instead they passed under an arch and came out in a small square where
the great door of a church rose against the darkness. Beside this door a candle flickered under a wall shrine, and beneath the shrine stood a flower
girl, resting her basket against her hip. When the two gentlemen passed
with their torch she turned her head aside, but she looked up at Donald
Ban. Beneath the shawl he caught a glimpse of quick, dark eyes and young
lips, and he noticed that she was shivering with the cold.

"Seigneur," she cried, "for God's love buy a flower of me!"

The good Norman-French words brought him to a stop, and he peered
into the eyes under the hood. This was no hour for a fair young thing to
be hawking in the street.

"Aye," he muttered, "a flower."

Beyond the sea Donald Ban had fallen in with the soft-skinned Syrian
girls, and the women of Cairo, who smelled of musk and paint, but not for
long years had a slender lass looked up at him with shy eyes and spoken
Christian speech. He thought she might be French, adrift like himself in
this misty city of gabblers and quarrelers. So instead of taking coppers
from the pocket in his mantle, he loosed his wallet to find a silver coin.

"But which one do you wish?" She smiled, thinking that he had such
somber eyes, and that she had not beheld the like of him among the young
lords of Venice.

He had put down his bundle and was fumbling in the wallet. "Two will
I have," he decided. "Aye, yonder red—"

With the words, a thief struck at him. The Scot saw the flash of a knife
passing under his hands. A jerk at his wrists, a cry from the girl, and the
robber leaped back into the mist, escaping a sweep of Donald's long arm.

With him he bore off the wallet. Donald sprang after him—saw his shape vanish into the maw of an alley.

At the alley mouth the Scot turned back reluctantly, knowing that a chase into darkness would earn him no more than a knife between the ribs. The thief had his purse, and Donald had not so much as a silver shilling upon him now to pay for bed or bite.

At the shrine light he found two men standing by his bundle, confronting the girl, and recognized the pair whose torch he had followed hither. One, a sallow youth clad in black velvet, spoke to him in Italian and then in French.

"Eh, Seigneur, the alley birds have flown away with your wallet, but we caught this little dove for you before she could escape into the church."

The girl shrank back against the wall, clutching her basket. "By Our Lady, I swear I know naught of it."

"Par Dex, you swear prettily." The youth in black thrust the shawl from her head and surveyed her idly. "Vettore, here is a rare, sweet handful. I am minded to carry her off to judgment."

The man called Vettore—an older fellow with a scar upon one cheek—laughed and said something under his breath, holding fast the while to the girl's wrist. She stared up at them like a wild thing at the feet of hunters. And Donald, looking from one to the other, made up his mind.

"Nay, let be," he said. "I'm thinking she had no hand i' this stealing."

"And I," the young Italian responded, "think otherwise. I pray thee, Messer Stranger, stand aside. I am Paulo Bragora of the Ca' Doria."

"I said let be, and I shall hold to my word. Neither hurt nor harm hath come to me from this maid, Signor Paulo—so loose her."

"Rather will I send thee to meddle with Satan."

Bragora's hand caught at his sword hilt, and Donald drew his round shield over his head, upon his left arm.

Before the swords could be drawn, Vettore clutched his companion's shoulder and whispered urgently, and as he listened the youth's expression changed.

"You are new come to the city?" he asked. "An Englishman, 'tis like?"

"A Scot," Donald corrected him, "of the Clan Arran that followed the Bruce."

"Eh, well. You are a man to stand your ground, I see well. And what need that we should bare steel for a girl of the night?"

"Then loose her."

With a smile at the Scot's stubbornness, Bragora signed to Vettore to release the girl, and she vanished after one swift birdlike glance up at Donald Ban.

"You are overtrusting, Signor Donal'," Bragora observed, affable again. "Behold, you are robbed by a cutpurse and deserted by this wench. If we cannot restore your purse, perhaps we may find you another. We were looking, Vettore and I, for a bold wight who will not step back at sight of a sword—a bold fellow, see you, who is yet a gentleman. Will you talk with us?"

It seemed to Donald Ban that he had those qualifications. He must have food and a bed, and to get them he might as well serve one man as another.

"Oh, aye," he said, picking up his bundle, "I'll parley wi' ye."

Bragora escorted him around the church through an alley that gave upon a private court. Here he unlocked a narrow, iron-bound door that seemed to be part of a dark wall. Holding the smoldering butt of the torch high, he led the way down a corridor to a leather curtain, where he paused to speak in rapid Italian.

"Good," he explained. "The Signor Zorzi, my honorable uncle, will greet you."

The chamber behind the curtain was lighted only by a great charcoal brazier. An older man sat huddled close to it, his long fingers playing upon the lions' heads that formed the arms of his chair. He did not look up when Donald entered, but as the Scot surveyed the room—the barred embrasure that served for a window and the weapons hung upon the wall—he felt that the old Italian studied him covertly.

"Ah, Signor," Zorzi remarked in broken French, "my nephew Paulo he relate to me that you serve me, perhaps, this night. Is it so?"

Donald looked at the younger Bragora expectantly.

"It is," Paulo vouchsafed, "that you should carry a letter. Now listen to the reason. We of the Bragora family are not men of warfare, yet in Venice we have enemies. They are powerful—even the names in the Golden Book of nobility are not above their reach. You do not understand? Eh—enough that we are afraid. I say it without shame. I know a dagger slits the hide of a Bragora as quickly as that of a boatman. I am not a fool.

"Now my uncle has written a letter of warning to a friend. It must go this night to the Ca' Cornaro, that is to say the castle of the Cornaro family, which lies distant a half hour by water—an island in the lagoon beyond Canareggio."

He picked up the hourglass with the tally stick that kept count of the hours. "See, the third hour is half ended, and the letter must go very soon. If I carried it, or a servant, we would be watched—followed. But no one in Venice except that flower wench knows your face. No one at all saw you enter this house. I do not hide the danger from you, but I believe you will reach the Ca' Cornaro with a whole hide. When you have handed in the letter at the door, wait for the package they will give you, and bring it to this house at once."

"And what then?" Donald asked.

"Eh, we will then weigh out and put into your hands two silver pounds. After that you are a free man. We trust you to keep your tongue between your teeth."

Donald considered. It seemed clear enough. If he brought back the package they expected, the Bragoras would know that he had delivered the letter. If he did not he would have no pay.

"Well," he responded, "I will do it. Much talk have I heard of brigands and the like. But I have yet to see one who will stand up to an honest sword."

"*Par Dex*," Zorzi muttered, "you may see even that, Signor. Know you the *bravi* of our city? Or the *Signor del Notte*, the Lord of the Night, who rules the boatmen and cutpurses and hath his spies even i' the great council—"

At an exclamation from Paulo he fell silent. Then he drew out a letter, tied and sealed. "You will take this?"

Donald nodded.

"There is a condition. The letter explains itself to the Cornaro people, our friends. Do not speak my name or my nephew's, or tell any soul of this house. Do you swear, Signor?"

The Scot grunted impatiently, disliking oaths, which were needless if men kept faith, and worthless otherwise. "Aye—aye."

Thrusting the letter through his belt, he followed Bragora to the postern door, where the Venetian handed him two silver shillings to pay a boatman, explaining that any man on the canals would know the Ca' Cornaro, and advising Donald to retrace his way past the church to the canal beyond before hailing a skiff.

Then the Scot heard the door close behind him and heavy bolts click home. It occurred to him as he turned away that he knew nothing of the face of this house, which might be one of the palaces on the outer canal. He could find his way back to the door, however, and that would suffice.

As for his mission, he had no liking for either Paulo or Zorzi Bragora, and he wondered why they chose to pay two silver pounds to the bearer of a missive that any beggar could take for a shilling—although perhaps a beggar could not be trusted.

"Signeur Donal'—wait!"

The whisper came, soft as the lapping of water against stones, out of the darkness. He had passed the shrine, and was walking along the edge of the canal looking for a boat. Donald wondered who could know his name and face, and he turned, setting his back against a wall. Presently he made out a slender figure no higher than his shoulder, with a dark object held against its hip. The flower girl—she must have listened to the talk between him and Bragora when they left the church square. "Nay," he muttered, "is not one stealing enough for thee this night?"

"I did not!" the girl whispered indignantly. "Ah, I thought in truth you knew that. Seigneur Donal', please—I had only seven *piccoli* all day, and I waited, praying to Our Lady, and you came—the flowers would have wilted by morning."

"And now you have a blind mother or a grandsire who starves; but I have no more money."

"I have no one at all, and I am not hungry because I bought bread with three of the *piccoli*, and ate it while I waited for you."

She came so close to him that her shawl touched his shield. "Ah, my lord, you must listen just a little. You went with Bragora, and he never does good work. He is a spy."

"Faith, meseems he lacks not company."

Peering up at him, she tried to read his face—no easy matter at any time. "Are you going forth upon this business of Bragora's?"

When Donald said nothing she whispered anxiously.

"My lord, I feared you would. I heard the one with the scar say to him, 'By the blood'—it was a terrible word he spoke—'here is the man for your hand, my Paulo, and he hath no more wit than a blind ass!'"

The Scot grinned, and then rubbed his beard thoughtfully. Well, he had no such wit as these Venetians, but at least he would not be trapped by a girl's tongue. Why should she take thought for him unless she wished to learn his business?

"They send you to strike a dirty blow," she nodded gravely, "so that their own hands may be hidden. Do not go."

When he tried to thrust her aside she clung to his arm, and he could feel the rapid throbbing of her heart.

"My lord, you are not the sort of these braves. Listen to Marie—the one with the scar takes tribute from the beggars of San Marco, and Bragora dogs ladies at night. Once they stole a child from a contessa and demanded gold for it. May good Saint Michael let his anger fall on them! Please, Seigneur Donal'—"

Dark eyes fluttered under the shadow of the hood, and a wisp of hair brushed his cheek. She would not let go his arm, and under her touch the blood warmed in his veins as if with wine. He pressed his lips to the tangle of hair, and then swiftly kissed the warm mouth so near his own. And now the girl Marie had naught to say. She looked up at him, dimly seen as some vagrant elf of darkness.

"So, it is much better," she observed calmly. "You come with me, and forget Bragora's business."

"Nay, little Marie," the Scot objected. "Bide a bit, and I will find thee tomorrow."

No doubt, he thought, she was a girl of the streets, but she had a way with her.

"Not tomorrow. Now—you must come away now."

Donald shook his head. Strange that she should have waited for him at the square.

"Then give me a little silver," she demanded.

So that was it. Donald felt cautiously in his belt to make sure that the letter and the two shillings were safe. He did not mean to be robbed twice, not he.

"Get thee gone, Marie," he grumbled.

"Please!"

At that moment a skiff came drifting along the edge of the canal, and Donald hailed the boatman, who stopped abreast him.

"I will show you the way," Marie ventured eagerly. "And I will be quiet, not troubling you at all."

"Ye'll bide here," said Donald grimly. He stepped into the skiff, thrusting it from the shore. When he had seated himself in the stern he saw her standing on the stone embankment, her basket in her arms, her head turned toward him anxiously. Then she laughed like an excited child.

His boatman was gabbling, waving his arms, to ask where to go. Donald rubbed his chin thoughtfully. Someone had been lying to him—either the two Bragoras or the flower girl. Still, he had promised to carry the letter, and there could be no harm in that. A bargain was a bargain, and Donald needed those two silver pounds.

"Ca' Cornaro," he told the boatman, who nodded, gestured at the canal ahead of them, and stood up to the long oar. They lurched forward under the light of a bridge. Donald felt again to make certain his letter was secure, at first carelessly, then anxiously. The letter with its seals was there under his belt, but one of the two shillings had vanished.

"Now why did she do that?" he wondered. Marie must have taken it in that last moment—the Scot had never lost coins so heedlessly before coming to Venice—yet why did she take only one coin?

The boatman weighed his oar and turned to listen, saying something that Donald could not grasp. After pointing behind them and shrugging his shoulders, the man leaned against the oar again, and they entered the darkness of a lagoon.

In the mist of the lagoon nothing could be seen. Once Donald thought that he heard the *clug-cluck* of an oar laboring over the water, but no other boat approached. Guided apparently by a sixth sense of direction, his own skiff pierced the fog until the blur of lights appeared, and it drifted in, by mooring stakes, to a stone landing.

The Ca' Cornaro was a square marble palazzo rising sheer from the water except for the small landing before the door. The embrasures of the lower floor were barred by heavy gratings and were curtained, but lighted windows showed above. Donald climbed from his skiff unchallenged, and rapped with his sword hilt on the heavy door. A face appeared at the lookout opening and a voice questioned him in harsh Italian. The Scot held up his letter.

Slowly the door swung open and he walked into a lofty, tapestried hall. An armed porter scrutinized him with surprise and held out his hand for the letter.

"It is for the Seigneur of the Cornaro," Donald explained, unwilling to give up the missive to a servant.

The porter shook his head at the Norman-French words, but a gentleman appeared and stared at the Scot. "There is no Seigneur," the new-comer observed, "but there is a Contessa of the Cornaro, and no doubt the letter will be for her. Will you tell me your name?"

"Aye—Donald Ban, it is, of the Clan Arran."

"*Mordie!* Well, you will wait."

He left with the letter, and Donald heard a woman's light laugh as he opened the door into an adjoining chamber. A moment of silence, and then voices exclaimed angrily. The porter dropped the candle he was holding and caught out his dagger as several men ran into the hall, tug-ging at their sword hilts.

"*A mort!*" one shouted. "Strike him down!"

"Nay," panted another. "Take the dog—bind him—let him feel the hot irons!"

It seemed to Donald that the letter had worked him mischief with these gentlemen. But it was not the first time he had faced an angry crowd. When the porter, who was nearest, struck at him, the Scot stepped back, draw-ing the round shield over his arm in time to parry the first wild slash of a sword. He drew his own straight blade and stepped back again into a niche of the wall, where two columns under a pointed arch shut him in on either side.

One of the gentlemen lunged at him viciously, and he cut down at the blade, knocking it aside and driving his assailant back with a wide cut at the head. The man stumbled, letting fall his sword, and the others drew away, seeing him helpless under Donald's blade, which swept back and forth over his head without harming him.

"Bide ye so!" the Scot cried. "I seek no quarrel here."

The men of the palace muttered, but a woman's voice shrilled at them and Donald from the corner of his eye saw the Contessa of the Cor-naro—white shoulders gleaming in the candlelight above a long blue gown. Henna-red hair she had, and eyes that blazed with wrath.

"Dog!" She lifted the letter and tore it in two. "Hound of the Lord of the Night! To come here to my house demanding gold or the death of my boy. Name of a Name—'tis no quarrel thou wilt find here, but a death that is fit for such a dog!"

Out of the flood of words Donald grasped the fact that the letter had threatened this woman of the flaming hair. "Faith," he thought, "there will be no quieting her now if she hath a child in peril—"

"Take him and bind him," the contessa urged her gentlemen. "So we can learn from him who sent him."

There were four Venetians besides the porter still on their feet; but they hesitated to rush in upon the Scot, who could slay the one stretched on the floor. Three Donald might have fought off, but he could not stop five. And he glanced sidewise at the door, which was a little open, thinking to risk a leap for it while he was still unhurt.

As he looked the heavy door swung wide. The men of the Cornaro drew back, startled, expecting, perhaps, the appearance of other creatures of the night. Into the hall walked Marie, the flower basket still on her hip, the shawl thrown back from her dark head. Slight and ragged she looked beside the very brightly clad Venetians.

An instant she caught her breath, then laughed so cheerily that a moment of astonished silence followed.

"My lady, Giulia," she cried. "You have bought my flowers at San Marco's arch, and you too, Messer Carlo." Resting the basket on the floor, she surveyed them, her brown eyes amused. "May the good saints aid us—how foolish it is to fight. At the door I heard talk of the Lord of the Night. That is stupid. Would he send a witless soldier such as this with a letter? Nay, he would burn this *palazzo*, but he would not threaten for a mere little gold."

"Back, child," muttered one of the gentlemen. "'Tis the son of the contessa they mean to take."

"Messer Vital," she retorted, "often have I seen you in the garden of the Arsenal with a young lady who was not your wife. But what do you know of the braves of the streets? Now you are all frightened, and this soldier—he does not understand why."

"Girl," exclaimed the Contessa Giulia, "he brought this letter demanding five pounds of gold to be given him wrapped in a cloth, or my boy would not live to go twice to mass. And the name—it is signed by the *Signor del Notte*." Impatiently she turned to her gentlemen.

"Vital—Carlo—how long will you let this rogue stand with drawn sword in my hall?"

"Get thee hence, little Marie," Donald grumbled. "'Tis no matter of yours, this."

"Witless!" she scoffed, and cried out at the woman in blue. "My lady, it is a great sin you would do. How easy it is to write the words 'Lord of the Night'! And to make good people into fools! The one who wrote that let-

ter is a briber and betrayer, who fears the Cornaro more than I. He found
this Signor Donal', who is an Inglisman, a stray in the streets, and offered
him payment to bear a letter to honest people. Look! He is only a thick-
skulled man of the wars."

The voice of the flower girl carried conviction—at least to the four gentlemen who were facing the Scot's long sword. But the woman was not
pacified. "Let him yield himself, then, and we will hear what he says before the Council."

Donald had no mind to do that. Instead he motioned for the prostrate
Venetian to rise, and himself stepped swiftly to Marie's side by the door.
Before the other men could prevent, he had drawn the girl back into the
entrance. "Bide where ye are, and be content that no blood is shed," he
said.

Motioning to Marie to get into one of the waiting skiffs, he backed down
the steps. Although they followed watchfully, no one ventured within
reach of his sword, and he leaped into the skiff, thrusting it off from the
landing. The other boat, at a word from Marie, followed hastily. Donald
drew a long breath.

"Faith," he muttered, "'tis content I am to be beyond reach of that
lady."

Marie, perched beside him, nodded scornfully. "Is it so you thank me for
bringing you away with a whole skin? Ah, Saint Michael, guide us—you
walked in there like a calf to the butcher's stall."

"And why did you follow?"

For an instant she hesitated, then tossed her head. "To bring you out
again on your feet, Signor Fool. Now, listen well. Those Bragoras are spoilers of little spirit. I think they sent a letter before now, threatening to
steal the contessa's child; then looked for a wight without wisdom to go
to the Cornaro for the gold.

"They used the name of the Lord of the Night to frighten that beautiful lady. If she paid the tribute, you would bring it back to them like a
mule that bears any burden put on its back. If they hacked you into pieces
the Bragoras would have no harm. And if they tortured you until you revealed their names, it would be no proof against them, for you are no man
of theirs, and anyone could write that letter. Now do you understand?"

"Aye," Donald nodded. "Something of all this was i' my mind the
while."

"And what will you do now?"

"Bid this lad row back to the steps by the church."

When they arrived at the stone embankment Donald gave the boat-man his remaining shilling and bade him wait. Marie, who had watched him with misgivings, refused to stay in the skiff. But he shook his head gravely.

"I'll not say you pilfered a shilling from me—"

"It was to pay for my boat to the Ca' Cornaro," she objected.

"Aye, that is well enough. But now I will go to parley wi' the Bragora men, and this time you will not come."

"They will throw your body into the canal," she cried.

"That is to be seen," said Donald grimly. And when he strode away she did not follow. Instead she knelt by the shrine and prayed.

Late as the hour was, Paulo Bragora was awake and clothed when Don-ald Ban knocked at the postern door. He did not seem surprised at the Scot's delay, but asked sharply, "Did they give you aught?"

"They did that," Donald nodded.

Paulo's eyes flashed, and he closed the door behind them, leading the way into the cabinet where Zorzi waited by the brazier.

"Where is it?" he demanded.

"Here," said Donald, and drew his sword. "Good sword strokes they gave me for that I carried a hangdog threat from two spoilers of honest people."

"*Par Dex*," Paulo whispered, "I see well you have kept what they gave and brought back lies to us—"

From the corner of his eye he was watching Zorzi, who suddenly sprang, straight from his chair, a long dagger gleaming in his upflung hand.

Donald caught the flicker of steel and bent to the side. He had not time to swing his long sword, but as the dagger swept past his shoulder, he smashed the heavy pommel of the sword into Zorzi's snarling face. As the Venetian staggered back, Donald thrust him down upon the glowing brazier and leaped away.

Only a second behind Zorzi, Paulo struck with a broad knife up from the hip. But Donald's quick leap brought him clear of the blade that would have slashed his bowels. Then his left fist clenched and drove into Pau-lo's eyes, and his long sword was thrust through Paulo's chest. Paulo fell heavily to the floor.

Old Zorzi was out of the brazier like a singed panther, screaming his hate. But when the point of the Scot's sword pricked his throat the fire went out of him and he let his dagger fall. Wounded or well, the Bragoras were no men to stand foot to foot in a fight.

"Stay thy hand! Look here!" Zorzi cried.

Stumbling in his haste, he drew a cloth cover from a great chest and snatched a key from his belt. Frantic with fear, he fumbled with the lock and raised the chest lid. Donald saw treasure within—leather bags and massive silver, gold crosses and women's trinkets set with jewels.

With the point of his sword he indicated a pair of scales within the chest. "Now set this up," he said.

Silently Zorzi took out the scales and placed them on the table.

"Ye'll weigh me two pounds of good silver," Donald prompted him.

Ten minutes later, with a heavy purse in his hand, he made his way alone out of the postern door into the mist. It was turning gray with the first light, and by the church door he saw Marie still kneeling.

"Ah, Seigneur Donal'," she exclaimed. "How fared ye with the Bragoras?"

"They weighed me out the two pounds of silver," he vouchsafed. "But I fear me it was none of the best."

Marie laughed under her breath. A little silver when he might, perchance, have had rare jewels from the spoilers! Hugging the basket with the wilted flowers, she lowered her eyes.

"I think," she said softly, "you are too honest to fare well in Venice. You need someone to keep you from harm."

"Aye," Donald assented, "'tis fair ungodly, this burgh. So I'll be leaving it, and seeking a ship this day for the coast of France." He held out his hand.

Marie noticed then that he had his bundle again, and something clutched at her heart. "You—you would say adieu, Seigneur Donal'?" she whispered.

He shifted the kit upon his shoulder. "Aye," he muttered, "I did think of asking you to take ship wi' me out of this ungodly place. Yet now that the day has come I see I am a fool—"

"A blind fool!" she cried eagerly. Dropping her basket, she caught his hard fist. "Now find that ship that goeth out to sea."

Passage to Cathay

He is out there now, in his black ship. They say he will not die, but he will sail that ship of his against wind and tide until doomsday comes.

You have heard his name? Nick van Straaten. You have heard that he is out there, swearing his strange oaths and striving to round that far-off cape of land—striving forever? And you do not believe?

Well, by now the Germans also have made a legend of him. They say that Nick Straaten must sail the seas for seven years, at which time he may come again to land, to find, if he can, a woman who will love him. Aye, they have begun to call him *der fliegende Hollander*, the Flying Dutchman . . .

All this happens to be true, as I well know. Since I was with him in the time of trouble, I can tell you the truth of the happening and you can believe it or not as you choose. It is all one to me, my masters.

A day of white clouds and dark shadows it was, when I watched van Straaten come ashore. No wind stirred the swell along the sea dike. I was then twelve years of age, playing with my pocket sundial, on top of the stones and beams of the dike, with one eye on old Ludowyk's dogcart, while Ludowyk sold the fishing nets he had made.

That was late in the year 1569 of grace—aye, four years before the trouble.

I could hear Ludowyk and the meesters jawing about how many groats to be paid for each net; and I longed to be off on a ship that would venture forth into the unknown seas of the world, to the far gold coasts and spiceries.

I sniffed the salt of the sea depths. The wind arms of the mills turned only slowly, sighing, in that light air. I saw only one ship come in that day, from the north to anchor off the dike. It was a bark, gray with weather and salt. And it had no sails. That is, they were tattered and ripped, lashed to the yards. One man from the bark got into a skiff and rowed himself up to the dike where I lay.

"A good day, yonker," his voice boomed at me. "Where is there a cart going to Leyden town?"

"God keep you, my master," I piped up. "Here." And I pointed out our cart, with the dog sleeping in front of it. When he climbed up the dike top and saw it, he laughed. Noticing how I was working at the sundial I had made, he sat down and pulled out a pocket compass with a needle that pointed to the north. By it, he set my dial true.

A long, stooped man this mariner was, fair as a Viking with his red beard. He stood as if leaning into the wind, his hands swollen by fisting ropes, his shoulders bent by hauling at tiller shafts. His clothing hung from him stiff as armor plate, only mended with cord. Curiously he gazed at the fishing craft and the flat land beyond.

"What port are you from, mynheer?" I asked.

"No port." He shook his head idly. "From the seas."

Now I thought that this gentle, lonely master was one of the fellowship of navigants, coming in from the waters that do lie beyond the knowledge of us townsfolk, and I forgot all about the sundial. "Have you been upon the Sea of Darkness?"

"Old vrouws' tales!" he snorted. "Do not listen to them, boy." Then he saw the disappointment in my face, and tugged at his beard. "Why, boy, I have seen fish that fly through the air off Madagascar—aye, and spouts of water drawn up to the sky."

While I was drinking in this marvel, old Ludowyk came up, counting the coins in his hand. When he saw the man from the sea he hastened his steps. "Come away, boy!" He took me by the hand.

"A good day, Ludowyk," said van Straaten.

"A bad day, when you show your face again." Ludowyk seemed to be angry. "I hear say how you have come back with an empty ship."

The stranger rubbed his big hands together. "Why, no, I have some fox and miniver skins, and whale ivory," he said.

"Pfut! And is that the treasure of Cathay?"

Whereupon Ludowyk hauled me away, walking fast. "The Devil," he muttered, "looks after his own."

When I asked how that happened, he grumbled. Nick van Straaten had tried to winter in the north, beyond Norway, beyond the North Cape, in

the floes of the Ice Sea. Half his crew had deserted at the wardhouse of
the cape, and others had sickened and died. But van Straaten had lived
through the winter. "Ya—he hath no fear of God. To go into the ice floes
with his ship. Nay, he seeks what may never be, and will not turn back.
Let it be a lesson to you, boy."

For Nick, he said, had been no older than I when he left the clam digging to gain his living on the Lofoten fishing banks. All his years he had
spent out there, until he was master of a lugger, with which he plied up
and down to Boulogne, until he had been able to buy that bark of his.
So far, good. But with that bark he had gone to seek a way to Cathay, at
the world's end. To Cathay, with its silk, and pearls, and lacquer and el-
ephants' tusks.

He thought that up beyond the North Cape there was a way by water
to Cathay, in spite of the ice. And he sought there for this northeast passage, on the top of the world.

"Pfut!" said Ludowyk, "now he is poorer than a herring fisher. He lacks
guilders to outfit his boat."

It was better, old Ludowyk said, not to think of the fantasies of the deep
seas. Here in Leyden we grew fruit and made good cordage and cloth as
our fathers had done—getting a good price at the Amsterdam market. We
were better off than any seafarer. "A penny earned is a penny got."

Truly, it seemed to be as he had said. For I saw Nick van Straaten thereafter sitting at the tavern tables to drink, and hanging around the canal to
speak with the cloth merchants, who turned a deaf ear to him.

That evening, in front of the Pieterskerk after candlelighting I heard
him roaring at our good burgomaster, Adrian van der Werf, as if he were
opzee—drunk.

"When will you lift up your eyes, my master? The Spaniards hold fast
the New World. Aye, they have seized upon the firm and continent land
of America. Already Balboa hath sighted the ocean that lies beyond."

Patiently the burgomaster listened, leaning on his staff. He was a rich
and kindly sir, and very wise. "But they have not yet found a sea passage
to the northwest," he said.

"By the three dead men of Cologne," shouted Nick, "how will we find
open water unless we seek for it?"

"In the Ice Sea?" Van der Werf tapped his staff on the cobbles. "No
human hands, shipmaster, can build a ship that will break through ice
floes."

Nick's big hands twisted in his belt and his face grew red. "There is no sea unnavigable, and no land uninhabitable!"

It was then that a lady in a dark shawl coming from the doors of the church stopped by them, looking curiously at the circle of men. I did not know her face.

"Be that as it may, shipmaster," said van der Werf, "these merchants of Leyden have no will to risk their goods in a venture to Cathay."

And Karol Bockman said that the markets of Amsterdam and Haarlem were good enough for him, God be praised. Some of them laughed, although not the burgomaster. Nick stared around at them, and swung away, biting at his beard.

He almost blundered into the lady with the shawl, because she stepped in front of him, holding up her train. She loosened the rope of pearls clasped around her throat, and held them out to the voyager.

"I would like well," she said in a clear voice, "to find a way to Cathay. Take these and seek it."

Van Straaten chewed his red beard, amazed, as were we all. Those matched pearls would outfit his ship and buy him a lading. "Faith," he blundered, "you do not know the risk—"

Her dark eyes seemed to look through him, and she smiled. So small she was, her hair jet against her white shawl, she seemed to be a slender image in the shadow of the church. "This is little indeed, my master, to risk for the treasure of the world. Besides, I have no need of them now."

The pearls would have slipped through her fingers into his, but he reached down swiftly and kissed her hand. "My lady, no."

Slipping her arm into his, she drew him away from the merchants. I heard someone name her, Lady Margaret, and someone else said that she was of Spain. But no one knew much of her.

A little way behind, I followed them—he striding along beside her, his head sunk in thought. Her voice chimed like the smallest bell of the carillon in the tower. Aye, a silver bell. At her door he bowed, and stood, cap in hand, until she had gone in. Then he drew a deep breath and looked up at the first stars, as if at something beckoning to him.

"By the three dead men," he swore, "she is a brave woman."

Then I saw that he had the string of pearls in his fist.

"Luck, yonker!" He laughed. "In spite of the Devil himself, this time I shall find the way through the ice."

Lady Margaret, Ludowyk said, was a lonely, praying woman who had been a duchess and had lost her husband in the Netherlands war.

In truth, the Lady Margaret kept to herself, with her silent maid. When I watched her in the kerk, I noticed that she wore no rings, or indeed any precious stones after she had given away the pearls. Once I did see a fine-looking officer knocking at her door, and by his cloak and the Venetian lace at his throat I judged him to be no Hollander. He had a thin, dark head and when he walked with her to church that evening he kept the center of the path as if by right, making us townspeople step aside. Yet he didn't seem to be aware of us.

After the prayers he held her back at the doors until they two were alone, except for me. His voice, swift and whispery, sounded angry.

"Nay," she drew away from him, "here, we speak Dutch."

The officer swore to himself. "Excelencia," he cried, "you cannot remain in this pesthouse."

"I have left a pesthouse for this."

"But—why?"

"Is not the man who loved me dead in Flanders? Is not my house empty except for authority?" She gathered her cape about her. "In Toledo I had to look into the eyes of men who might soon be dead. And I was afraid."

He tried to see into her face in the dim light. "Afraid? In Spain? I do not understand." He moved his shoulders as if shaking off a load. "When you are tired of this prank, send word to me. And I will get you out of here if I have to beg a tercio from the duke to do it."

"No." She held out her hand to him. "Adios."

She watched him walk away across the cobblestones. Then she beckoned to me. I thought that she was like Mynheer van Straaten, who went away to look for Cathay. Only he was not afraid. I thought she was beautiful as an angel in a painting. "You look for something," I said, "like Mynheer van Straaten."

"Perhaps I do." She smiled, pleased. "I had a writing from him."

He had been gone then a year. The Spanish lady showed me the writing on a half sheet of stained paper, where she kept it in a box by her window:

"To the Most Gracious Lady Margaret, dwelling in the painted house by the Canal, Leyden: Greeting. Know that by reason of the setting of the ice we must winter on the shore of that sea called the Ice Sea, beyond the seventieth degree of latitude, in all good hope of finding clear water to the northeast the next summer. Nicholas van Straaten, shipmaster."

It had come, she said, from a fishing craft of Norway. No other letter arrived.

After three more years had passed, Ludowyk shook his head, saying that van Straaten and his men would be frozen to death in that pagan limbo long since.

But before then the trouble had come to Leyden.

Old Ludowyk spat when he heard about the new tax. "One per centum on houses, two per centum on boats and nets, ten per centum on the price of herrings sold. Devil fly away with such thieves!"

As one man the burghers of Leyden refused to pay this new tax of Philip of Spain, whose army was advancing along the Meuse.

Then came a cavalcade of Spanish officers to talk with Adrian van der Werf, in the Pieterskerk square. They said that Hollanders would become rebels if they failed to obey an order of the throne. After that, Spanish flags were hauled down in the city, and the burghers gathered in the streets to talk of what they would do if war came.

I saw men digging out on the earth ramparts, and cannon were brought in on barges from the ships. The tavern lights showed late at night, for men waited about to talk after the day's work was done. The ramparts of Leyden, they agreed, could not be stormed—so wide was the water moat; and we had plenty of gold in the treasury at the statehouse.

Then we found that the road to Haarlem was cut off. Our goods could not go to the market there. Haarlem was besieged, and so our goods piled up in the warehouses.

The day that Haarlem surrendered we heard the big bells tolling in the statehouse tower. And Ludowyk said that no one could go by road or canal to the sea, because of the Spanish soldiers.

Hot with excitement, I ran to the door of Lady Margaret's house. The maid spoke sharply to me about taking off my shoes; then she led me out to the garden where the Spanish lady sat by the flowerbeds, listening to the tolling.

"My lady," I cried, "I will take you out of the walls in Ludowyk's cart."

"But why, yonker?" she asked.

"Because tomorrow, surely, the siege will begin. Aren't you going?"

"No," she said gently. "I would like to stay here, if I can."

Some of the burghers believed that the Spanish woman must be a spy, to stay shut up among us. Ludowyk said that spies do not go about dressed for all the world to see, and she had been a duchess somewhere or other, so she must have a whim.

That was a March day, when the first tulip shoots were showing. The next day we saw men in steel morions out on the road, and the bridges were drawn up. Then we could make out tents among the outlying farms and cannon appearing along the lines of the old dikes.

Yes, that was in March. In October when thin ice coated the water of the canals, we were still waiting in the casements along the ramparts and the flag was still over the statehouse tower. We waited by our firelocks and pikes, sitting in the places we had dug out because we could no longer stand on our feet except for a little while. We were skeletons perched like ravens on the dirt wall.

Bright shone the moon that night, gleaming on the patches of ice. Behind us rose the black ribs of houses, shattered by the great bombards of the Spaniards. But we did not look up any more at the whine and rumble of the shot. Indeed by then the Dons did not trouble themselves to work the bombards often. Like us, they waited, beyond that wide moat of water, still and clotted with the flesh and clothing of men. The glow of their campfires lay along the flat skyline, and out there in the tent lines they waited, eating their fill at night.

Broken barges lay here and there in the water. When, at first, they had tried to push bridges of boats across to us in the town, we had scattered the barges with shot or fought back the steel-covered regiments of attack with our pikes. No man of theirs had set foot in Leyden, and from the statehouse tower one could see the crosses of their cemeteries in the lowlands behind their artillery. But we did not hate now those far-off soldiers in steel. Our hatred gathered where we sat together like this, and it turned on one man, Adrian van der Werf, who came at times with some of the burghers to inspect the ramparts—for we of the watch could not go back into the houses, on account of the pestilence. When he passed by now, we turned to look the other way. Van der Werf had set his mind against ours. He would not send the message to the Dons that would surrender Leyden.

But—as we all knew—we were cut off from the world. No ships at sea could reach us, and on land there was no force able now to face the Spanish regiments. We were caught in a ring of steel weapons that could not be broken. We were starving . . .

One night we heard the thin ice snapping and something splashed in the moonlight. Then a harquebus roared from the rampart, and another. But we could see little to shoot at. Then we heard a Dutch voice bellowing:

"By the three dead men of Cologne! Open your eyes, town dogs."

I stood up then, holding to the wicker backing. And I saw a swimmer breaking through the ice beneath.

"It is the voice," someone muttered, "of the dead van Straaten."

Dripping and swearing, the swimmer climbed out of the water and up the rampart. He lay there panting and, even if he was alive, he seemed more like a water animal than a man. Skins covered him, tied together by thongs, and his hair and beard matted about his head.

"Give a man a hand, skellums," he growled, peering at us. Nay, he did not know me, after these years.

When we hauled him over the parapet, his skin felt slippery with grease, and his breath reeked of schnapps. Truly he had fortified himself against the cold and wet in swimming the canals to pass through the Spanish lines.

"What word bring ye from the fleet?" our company captain demanded.

Nick only wiped the water from his eyes. The ships, he said, were beating offshore in this west wind. It was little or nothing he knew of the siege. The only thing he wanted was to be taken to the Lady Margaret in the painted house by the canal.

I took him back to the canal, carrying the one lanthorn we had at our post.

He seemed surprised when I opened the door—for the maid had been dead since Saint Stephen's day—and carried the lanthorn straight into my lady's sleeping room. "Please, Excellency," I said, "the shipmaster van Straaten has come back from the Ice Sea."

"I am glad," her voice whispered.

He pulled at his beard and coughed, abashed at seeing her figure on the bed. "My lady," he said, "we have not yet found open water beyond the Ice Sea. Yet from the easterlings of that region I have heard of a mighty river called the Ob—"

All in a breath he was speaking to explain his return, when he saw her face fairly. Taking the light from my hand he bent over her.

The skin stretched tight across her teeth, and she did not move. Her dark eyes looked up, out of the mask of a face. Yet, her hair curled softly against her thin cheek. No doubt he had thought of her in her splendor of pearls and lace for those four years. And his long fight with the ice must have preyed upon his mind.

"You have been brave, my captain," she whispered, "and perhaps in God's good time you will find the passage."

Still he looked at her. "Have you no bread or wine in this place?"

She shook her head. "Not in Leyden. But we are not afraid, because of that."

Only then did he realize how near we were to starvation. "By the three dead men of Cologne, I will bring you some—soon."

"It will take much to feed the mouths of Leyden."

I pulled him away at that, for it is ill to promise food to the dying. His big hands pulled at his belt as he went, and he swore at each step, demanding that I take him to the burgomaster.

We found Adrian van der Werf by a fire where the canal crossed the old channel of the Rhine River. The west wind had driven the water inland, through the canals, so that the banks were flooding, and the burgomaster was working with some hand-werpen to move children out of the flooded dwellings.

Van Straaten said that food must be got into Leyden, or it would be madness to hold out. Some plan must be made—

Van der Werf stared at him. Had he not sought for a plan? "Did you find, shipmaster, the passage to Cathay? Or did you find the ice?"

"I will find open water yet," snarled the voyager.

Slowly he went back with me to the rampart. There he leaned with his head to the wind, striking his fist against the earth. "It is sick you are, men of Leyden," he growled. "There must be a way . . . ye had but open water and wind."

He was thinking of a ship, and he grew quiet. "What did my lady say? You are not afraid? Fear . . . that would do it."

All at once he became the old Nick I had known, chuckling in his beard. Taking a plank from the parapet he slid over to the water, saying to me to watch at this place when the west wind came again. I watched him swimming away and I envied him the strength that was taking him back to eat his fill.

The third night after that I slept by the warmth of the lanthorn behind the parapet. I woke hearing a faint crunch, as if a wind wheel had fallen to earth far off. The sound came again and again, until we pulled ourselves up to watch. A stirring and creaking we heard as of wagons moving, the sound carried to us on the wind. Nothing more than that happened.

But the west wind had risen to a gale.

At daybreak we saw the plain toward the sea gray with water. The water in the moat had risen and was flowing past. Watchers who climbed to the statehouse tower saw the great sea dikes had been broken through in five places.

Some of the Spanish encampments had been flooded out, and we could make out men climbing up to higher ground, crowding on knolls and embankments, pulling cannon up after them.

"Ya," said Ludowyk, who limped out to watch, "they have wet their bottoms this night."

The gale piled water into the breaks, rushing across the lowlands, tearing into cottages and trenches. Bodies began to whirl and drift through our moat—bodies of Spaniards torn out of the loose dirt in the cemeteries. Under that gray storm, the bodies turned in the water as if alive. The earth was vanishing, and clouds swept low over the water.

"It is like the judgment day," muttered Ludowyk.

Then we saw that ghost of a ship. A black bark without banner or side curtains, driving over the land itself, under a patched, gray headsail. It veered between the embankments as if driven by witchcraft, over the floodwater.

"See," I cried at Ludowyk, "it keeps to the course of the old Rhine."

In that rising flood the specter ship was feeling its way along an invisible channel, as if knowing well how the land lay beneath the floodwater.

Fear made the skin of my back cold. I thought a Dutchman must be at the tiller of that bark. Then flame flashed from its sides, and we heard the roar of cannon. This ship, steering over the land, was firing at the Spaniards clustered on higher ground.

"It is Nick van Straaten's bark," Ludowyk said.

Then I heard the great bell of the statehouse tolling, which was a signal for all living men to stand to arms. We crowded along the rampart, watching.

For, behind the bark, fishing sloops came in, over the land, firing cannon fore and aft. And behind them a great admiral ship, with the arms of Orange painted upon its sterncastle. It moved slowly, under one spritsail, its broadsides smoking and roaring. And astern of it appeared long cargo barges carrying cannon, pulled by oars.

Ludowyk wiped the tears from his eyes, watching. "The ships of the sea are coming to Leyden."

Ketches and schooners from Lofoten, sailing skiffs of the Zuyder Zee, they followed van Straaten in, on a course over the canals to the Rhine that had filled its channel again with salt water. It seemed to the good people to be a miracle.

Because a strange thing happened. The thousands of armed men of the tercios, wet and cold and hungry, caught in crowds along the embankments and punished by chain and solid shot of the ships, began to leave their cannon and to try to get away to firm land. Divided, out of reach of their commanders and half submerged, they ran from those ships that sailed over their tents of the night before. Weighted by their breastplates, they drowned where the earth beneath them gave way.

All the while the great bell tolled. Ludowyk and I could see the ships drifting toward the stone quays on the floodwater. Men pushed at poles to steer them past the wrecks of canal barges, where no ships had ever ventured before. We could see cheeses and wine kegs piled on the decks.

But we heard the bell tolling, and we of the watch understood why it was summoning us when we no longer had a duty to perform on the rampart.

Hurrying back, we joined other people along the canal walks where the water now splashed against our feet. Nay, we did not go down to the quays where the food would be landed. We hurried toward the doors of the Pieterskerk whither the voice of Adrian van der Werf was summoning us by means of the bell.

Although we hurried, we did not make much progress because we were weak, and our feet in wooden shoes slipped on cobbles. I heard men weeping for joy, and heard only faintly their voices as they tried to sing:

"We praise Thee . . . O Lord for Thy mercy everlasting. We give praise—"

We were going to make our prayer at the kerk before tasting of the food. Coming out of the doors, I thought of Lady Margaret and hurried down the canal to her house.

There I saw Nick van Straaten, alone. He limped with one leg, and his other arm hung stiff by his belt. Dried blood blackened his fingers. On his good arm he was carrying a basket. And it was strange how, sud-

denly, my belly ached at sight of the round loaf of bread and jug of wine
in it. He swayed as he walked, as if the ground was awkward to him who
had been so long at sea.

I helped him to open the door that had no latch on it. Pushing into his
lady's sleeping room, he went to the bed, looking into her face. Her eyes
moved up at him.

His good hand trembled so that he could not break the bread, until I
helped I him with my knife, first cleaning it of dirt. Then he dipped the
morsel of bread into the wine and opened her lips so that she could chew
on the soft bread. After an hour the deathly paleness was gone from her
cheeks and she could smile.

By the basket he sat, rubbing his knee, not knowing what to say. It was
a strange thing for me to see, but the lines softened in his hard face and he
also seemed more alive than before. He looked at me and sighed.

"Those skellums in our ships would not go ashore at first when the
wind came to blow up the out-dikes," he grumbled. "They said no ships
could reach Leyden. The Devil fly away with them!"

"They were Dutch," Lady Margaret smiled, "and so are you."

"Why, yes," said Nick.

Now that he had fed her, he did not think of anything else to do. Sitting
in his chair, his head dropped on his beard, and he breathed heavily. He
slept like a tired man who has come home at the hour of candlelighting.

Out of that day we had learned a lesson. The Spanish army could run
away—the armada of King Philip was not invincible. So from then we
fought back like fiends, and they melted away from our coast of Holland,
leaving us free in our land.

Now that the wars are over, we in Leyden town are building a monument to Adrian van der Werf, and our good William of Orange hath ordered
a university to be established here, to honor the defenders of Leyden.

But Nick is not here. He is sailing his ship again, up there beyond wind
tide, in the Ice Sea. He is looking for that passage he meant to find. And
he will not die, my lady says, while Dutchmen live.

The Bear's Head

Mist covered the ship. It was a mist of magic, Sir Ranulf said, because for two weeks they had not seen the sun or the stars in a clear sky.

And yet a wind drove the ship on. It was a strong sea ship with a tall mast and a square leather sail, Sir Ranulf's ship. The wind filled the leather sail and drove it beneath a cloudy sky. Sir Ranulf could not get a fair sight of the stars, so he could not know in what direction they were going.

On his fingers he counted the days—twenty-seven days since they had left the coast of the Ice Land, heading west and south in good sailing weather. But with such weather he should have sighted the coast of the Green Land in seven days.

Ranulf had put out that summer from his home on the Norway coast, with a lading of skins, beer, and timber in his trading ship. It was not a rich lading, but Ranulf was not a wealthy man. Times were hard at home and he had heard tales of seafarers who brought back profitable ladings of ivory and white bearskins from these new settlements in the western islands. He had done some trading in the Ice Land and had decided to risk sailing on to the little-visited Green Land for his profit's sake—although the summer season was nearing its end, and Ranulf himself was better skilled in faring along his own coast than in seafaring.

But for twenty and seven days they had seen no land. Ranulf wondered if they had not missed the Green Land altogether. When the twenty-eighth day dawned cloudy with white foam on the wave crests, he called to him the two other men.

"Such a wind in a mist I have never seen," he said moodily. "I know not whither to steer. Aye, I doubt not the ship is under a spell of magic. What say ye?"

Fighting Mord was the first to answer. He was a Viking, a good man with his weapons, a man of mark in Norway, who had offered to go upon this cruise with Sir Ranulf, with eight of his swordsmen—since fighting was to be expected as well as trading. A tall, dark man in the prime of his strength, who thought before he spoke. "It seems to me that we have been blown far south into a strange sea. When we can see the sun rise and set, then we will know."

"And you, Brand, what say you?" Ranulf asked.

The other man had come on board the ship an hour before sailing, saying that he had heard they were bound for the new lands. He had a way of laughing at himself, but at times he was moody. He had long red hair and clear eyes; he wore a strange, close-fitting blue traveler's cloak, with a great white bearskin about his shoulders, upon which he carried a double-headed ax with a short shaft.

"The storm maidens will drive us," he responded idly, "where they will."

"But what if we have missed our landfall upon Green Land?"

"Then," said Brand, "it will be the worse for us."

And he went away to sit on his bearskin near the penthouse built against the poop for the single woman on the ship, Sir Ranulf's younger sister.

"It seems to me," observed Ranulf in a low voice, "this far-wandering Brand hath brought trouble upon us from the sea. He lies there, singing often to himself. His like I have never known before."

But Fighting Mord, who had taken part in many Viking raids, had greater knowledge of men. "Nay, Ranulf, he is restless, hungering after new sights. He is even a land seeker. Still, he has a wild way with him."

And presently the Viking went to stand by Brand, who was running his hand through Kristi's long hair, as light and soft as silk. Brand was telling the girl a tale about a town called Paris where he had tasted wine and seen silk dresses upon the women, and Kristi was listening, although she looked up at Fighting Mord. She was sixteen, venturing for the first time away from her homeland—Ranulf, her brother, had thought that, owing to the lateness of the season, they might have to winter in the Ice Land, and he wished the girl to be under his protection.

Kristi had only cotton frocks and rough wool cloaks; until now she had only talked with other girls and priests. She did not know—because she had no mirror except a piece of polished bronze—that her gray, elfin eyes were lovely, or that men looked long at her supple arms and soft, white throat.

To Ranulf, Kristi was still the child who had stolen sugar from the storehouse and had wept over a slain kitten. When she had asked to have a board hut to herself on the ship, he thought that she was frightened. She paid long visits to the animals in the cargo deck below, especially to the goats that were to be sold to the settlers in Green Land.

Now she let Brand caress her hair because she wanted to hear about the wonderful gowns of Paris. Leaning against the rail, Fighting Mord listened also, until his temper began to irk him.

"Now, hear me," he said then. "It seems to me, Brand, that you have a hand better suited to rubbing a girl's hair than holding a sword."

"This is pleasanter," nodded Brand.

"What if I bade you try your skill with a sword?"

"I will never do it," Brand answered, but to himself he added, "again."

Kristi glanced at him scornfully, and the ship's men within hearing turned to stare. For in that age no man of mark went without a sword, or hesitated to use the weapon he wore. Brand, it is true, carried that short-handled ax which, except for its polished steel and silver inlay, might have been a woodman's or a butcher's arm.

"Well," observed Fighting Mord after a moment, "you have a pole-ax. Will you use that?"

"Nay. I bear it to frighten off quarrelers."

Fighting Mord looked at him steadily. "There's something in you not easily understood." He put his foot on the stranger's knee and trod heavily.

He was a strong and heavy man, the Viking. Still, so suddenly did Brand seize his ankle and throw him off that he struck the deck on his head and shoulders, and Kristi gave a low cry of fright. At once Fighting Mord sprang up, drawing his sword. But Kristi gripped his arm, pleading with him, and Sir Ranulf ran up to beg him to have no weapon-play on the ship. Fighting Mord yielded reluctantly. "So long as we are on this boat in peril of our lives," he cried to Brand, "I will not lift hand against you. But when we have made our landfall, then we will take to the weapons and it will go ill with one of us."

"That," assented Brand, "is easy to say."

Kristi gazed at him as if trying to see what was beneath the skin and hard bones of him. "What makes you so strange?" she asked.

"A tale," said Brand, "that I have no mind to tell you, little Kristi. Yet

I will tell how once I served the Emperor of Constantinople, where even the palace guards wore gold helmets. A magician there was—"

Kristi got up with dignity. "You are hateful to me now, and I will never let you touch my hair again."

"Not even," Brand smiled suddenly, "if I hang your mittens on a sunbeam to dry?"

"There's no sun," Kristi pointed out. Then she stamped her foot angrily. "Oh, you will not mock me!"

She went away into her hut and shut the door. Brand turned over on his back and looked at the sky, through which the pale sun gleamed for a while. Then he rolled up in his bearskin and went to sleep.

But Fighting Mord sat on the bench under the hang of the afterdeck with Sir Ranulf beside him. They were drinking beer and between his knees Fighting Mord had an open sea chest. "Do you not see," he said, "how fair your young sister has grown? If she had fitting garments and gold to deck her, she would be the match of any woman."

"That," uttered Ranulf, "I did not know."

"Well, here is a silk dress and here is an embroidered cloak, with red slippers. Give them to her, with this gold arm ring—" the Viking lifted a small band of fine red gold—"for I have a mind to her. Are you willing that it should come to a match between us?"

Ranulf felt amazed. For Fighting Mord was a man of mark in Norway, a leader in the wars, with threescore swords to follow him, and rich lands to his name. It seemed good to Ranulf, for the sake of his wealth, that Kristi should wed so strong a man. "Right gladly," he cried.

"Did you think I had come upon this cruise merely to smell the western sea? Give Kristi the presents, and when we come to a town, then you and I will lay down the terms of the match. Until then I shall look to Kristi's safety myself, and I will deal with any man who seeks to beguile her."

Well content, Ranulf called for fresh beer. But a serf came running, stopping beneath the deck. "Listen, my masters," the man cried. "The gulls!"

So it happened that Sir Ranulf had other things on his mind than Kristi for many days. When he went up to the open deck, he saw gray gulls circling and screaming about the masthead—gulls that must have come from some shore. The clouds had thinned to a light haze; the sea gleamed blue under a mild sun. And soon they saw the white surf along a coast on the starboard beam.

"Land!" cried the seafarers.

The sky cleared and they saw the new land, level and dark with forest growth. Late that day when the sea had calmed, they came abreast the mouth of a fiord. Into this Sir Ranulf steered his ship, for he could not find a better place for a landfall.

"It is like," he told Fighting Mord, "we shall find a settlement on this fiord."

When they were in it, they lowered the sail and all hands took to the oars. They rowed the ship slowly up the narrow channel, where the walls of the forest drew ever closer upon either side, while the gulls clamored overhead. The branches of the trees nearly met above the mast when, after sunset, the forest wall fell away and the ship came through into a lake red with the last sunset fires. They could smell the odor of ferns and forest mold from the shore. Then Sir Ranulf ordered the anchor stone to be dropped, and he rowed ashore in the aft-boat.

That evening they gathered wood and cooked salt meat in a pot on shore and Kristi baked hot bread. For twenty and eight days they had lived upon dried fish and hard bread, so they feasted well. After they had done that, Kristi watched the bright stars mirrored in the still lake, and she thought this place fair enough to be the home of the gods.

The next morning the men were eager to explore the surrounding country, and Kristi occupied herself with making a bower out of pine branches while the serfs brought the animals ashore. The gaunt cows and the hungry goats went at once into a meadow where golden wheat grew rank. Kristi wondered who had planted that wheat, and she wondered more when the men came back at nightfall without having found a trace of any habitation. But Fighting Mord had slain an antlered buck with an arrow, and they had fresh meat to eat.

"By Thor's thunder," he laughed, "I did not know this Green Land bred such game."

Brand had brought in a strip of strange bark as long as his arm. On the outside it was the hue of gray silver; it was all of one piece that could be bent and rolled and it smelled sweet—as did the entire forest of this lake—yet it was thin as well-woven linen.

"Now I have been in many lands of the earth," he said, "and I have never seen until now the silver tree from which this bark comes."

"What good is it?" demanded Kristi contemptuously.

Brand, the far-wandering man, shook his head. "It may be a sign." Kneeling, he scratched with a twig upon the ground as if seeking for a message out of runes. "They said in Ice Land that we would find bare rocky heights and bare fields rising from the sea's edge in Green Land. Now here we have found no fiord but a river. Aye, the lake water is fresh and sweet. Here is a lofty forest and standing grain that was never sown. Here is bark from an unknown tree. So, it seems to me that we have come to some unknown land."

"What land could it be," retorted Mord, "except Green Land, or perhaps an island?"

"It is not an island."

Ranulf nudged Mord and whispered, "Let be, the man is fey. He may have the gift of seeing what is to be."

The next day he remembered to give Kristi the presents from Fighting Mord, and the girl carried them off to her bower, to lay them on her knee and run her fingers over the fine texture. After a while she fetched a small keg of water from the lake and washed herself from head to foot, and put on the new garments reverently. The shoes were a little big, and after she had studied herself in the bronze mirror she got out her comb and combed smooth her unruly hair, plaiting it into two long tresses after the manner of the great ladies she had seen. Then she walked slowly through the camp.

All the seamen and the Vikings stared admiringly, but Kristi kept on until she found Brand. Then, when he said nothing, she felt her cheeks grow hot with a rush of blood.

"Don't—don't you think they are pretty?"

His eyes smiled at her. "The garments are pretty, little Kristi. But you are no lovelier by reason of them."

She felt hurt, and turned away from him, running back to her bower, apart from the camp. Hastily she took off the new things and put on her old dress. She was undoing her hair when a shadow fell over her and Brand came and sat by her. In his two closed hands he held something.

"This," he said, "is an ornament that was worn once by a princess in Constantinople. She was lovely as the starlit night, but you are like the dawn in the sky. Now take it."

He showed her what was in his hands—a slender necklet of linked gold in which were set square stones that gleamed with blue fire. Pushing back the mass of her hair, he placed it about her bare throat and snapped the clasp. Then he looked long at the flushed girl.

"But this is a—treasure," she whispered. "Why did you put it upon me?"

"Because," he said, and stopped, hearing the tread of feet nearby, "because you are fairer than the sapphires that were chosen among the jewels of an empire, and the beaten gold of the master smiths loses its luster upon your breast, Kristi. It is yours, because the body of me aches by reason of your beauty." And he bent over to kiss her opened hand, which trembled when he touched it.

Then he stood up to face Mord and Ranulf, who had followed him to the bower. "All this," he said, "cannot be helped. What have you to say?"

His face black with rage, Fighting Mord leaned down and clutched at the necklet on the girl's throat. But the clasp held, and the girl bit her lip to hold back an exclamation of pain. Before the Viking could wrench it away, he felt the touch of Brand's hand on his shoulder and turned.

"Now," he said between set teeth, "I will cut the life out of thee for coming in my way."

Brand took up the great ax that he had leaned against the girl's bower and he walked beside Fighting Mord out to some clear ground beyond sight of the camp. Then he stood still, leaning on his double ax head, looking at Mord's Vikings who had wind of the quarrel and had come up to see the weapon-play. "Ho," he said, "the ravens gather to the man-slaying." He walked to the nearest tree, an old oak. Swinging up his great ax, he whirled it around his head with one hand until the steel whined in the air. Then he struck it deep into the tree trunk. "Pull it away if you can, little men," he told the stalwart Vikings.

"Hark you to this," he said to Fighting Mord. "I am a Berserk of Berserker blood."

And Fighting Mord growled deep in his throat, gripping his iron sword hilt. For the Berserks were wild fighters. Before a battle they cast off their clothing except for the bearskins, and they went into the weapon-play as other men to a feast. Aye, they wooed the kiss of the Valkyrie maidens and they fed the wolf packs with blood. They did not stop until they were slain.

"Berserk, or common man," he snarled, "it is all one to me."

"In a day of the past," chanted Brand, his eyes glowing, "I followed the war bands from sea to sea in the long ships. One comrade lived to join the guard of the Emperor with me. At this time we both drank deep of wine and we looked about us for fighting. One night in the taverns we quarreled when we were out of our minds and we took to the swords. I cut his skull open, and slew this one ship's mate of mine. Then I took oath that never would I bear sword again and never would I lift weapon in brawl or quarrel. I took what I had of gold and gear and I wandered from land to land to find that one wherein I would be at peace. Now I think we have come to a new land unknown to our gods."

He looked at the high forest ruddy with autumn's gold. "This is not like other lands; and I have a fear and a foreboding. Thou or I must safeguard this maiden. If we take to the weapons we may both find our deaths, or you alone. Now it has come to this between us, that neither can abide by the other in the same place. So I will take food and a pot and fire in it. I will go off alone and seek for other men, or some sign of what this land hath in store for us. But you will not lay hand upon Kristi, or I will come to know of it." He turned on his heel and went to the oak. There the other Vikings had been trying, one after the other, to free the ax. With a crooked grin Brand watched until the last wrestled with it, the veins standing out on the man's bare arms.

When he had done and the ax was still fast in the tree, Brand walked up to it. Clasping both hands on the end of the shaft, he thrust up quickly and then pulled down. The steel squeaked shrill in the wood and the ax came away in his hands.

Going back to the camp, Brand filled a sack with salt and meal. He put embers from the fire into a small iron pot and covered them with moss and dried wood. Then he rolled the sack with his bearskin into his leather sleeping bag, took the ax on his shoulder, the pot on his arm.

"Why do you go, Brand?" Kristi asked him. The men had told her he was faring away into the forest.

He smiled down at her. "To look for a star to set in your hair, little Kristi."

Again she was angry with him, but now she felt an ache in her heart. "Will you be coming back, Brand?"

"If you will be wanting me."

He strode off into the forest then, and Sir Ranulf said after supper that surely the red giant was fey. "It is clearly to be known from his talk of stars and an unknown land where the gods have not set foot."

But the next day a serf came in to the lake shore with wine berries that he had plucked from vines in a clearing. Sir Ranulf knew that wine berries did not grow in Ice Land or Green Land.

They talked much of those wine berries. Kristi gathered many and crushed them, to make a sweet, strong drink of the juice, and the men said that while it was not like beer, it was well enough. Then Fighting Mord proposed to Sir Ranulf that he and his Vikings take the ship back to the sea and cruise south along the coast, to seek a settlement before the first great storm of the winter closed the sea to them.

When he had gone, Kristi felt more at peace. Her brother told her how Mord had said he would make an offer for her when they reached a settlement. It excited her that a man of mark should have made such a proposal; at the same time she was frightened.

She liked to wander alone in the forest, while Ranulf's seamen and serfs built a long house out of hewn logs and turf against the need of winter. The forest had clad itself in a rich mantle of fallen leaves except where the somber pine trees stood. Kristi saw many deer flitting away, but no reindeer. She watched the two cows and the sheep feeding in the last of the wild wheat, and she helped the younger men bring in grain and ferns for winter feed. She thought that this was a kindly land, although silent.

Then Fighting Mord came back with the ship. He had found no settlement or sign of living men. Yet once he had seen smoke in a clear sky and the ship had passed along wide white beaches of sand. Reluctantly he and Ranulf agreed that this could not be the coast of Green Land.

It disturbed them because they both felt near them the presence of other living beings. How else had the wild grain and the wine berries come there? And in the forest, along the animal trails, they had come upon pointed tracks shaped like human feet, yet different from the imprint of good Norse feet. And soon the presence made itself known beyond doubt.

After the first hard frost and a light fall of snow, one of the sheep disappeared. It vanished whole from the grazing flock without trace of blood, so a wolf could not have taken it off. Ranulf set an armed guard over the animals. In spite of this another sheep vanished. And one of the seamen who had gone into the forest to search for it did not come back.

That night a good ash plank disappeared from the very door of the house.

It was then that the great snow came. For three days it raged around them with a fury that amazed the Norsemen.

The men believed that Brand had worked their misfortune. The Berserk, they whispered, had laid a spell of magic upon the ship and all in it. He had led them to this country beyond the known world; he had gone off to make sacrifice to his strange gods. He alone had been able to pull out the ax that was fastened by magic in the trunk of the oak tree. And who but Brand would have use for a common ash plank?

"This much is true," assented Ranulf moodily. "While Brand abode with us fortune favored us, and since he went away these unknown gods have shown their enmity. Now it is to be seen what sacrifice they will require of us."

The snow ceased on the third day, and in the morning of the fourth day Ranulf understood how great the sacrifice would be.

During the storm Brand had worked in his bark hut, deep in a grove of giant pines near a height from which he could watch—on fair days—the distant lake with its camp. He worked by firelight, while the wind roared through the pines and fine snow drifted through the smoke hole. With his ax and knife he cut a small ash board into two lengths, pointed at one end, square at the other. He thinned these lengths of seasoned wood—each about as broad as his hand—rounded the edges, and made notches in the center to pass straps around. From time to time he stopped to cook venison steak or to bake meal cakes, or to sleep.

But it took him a long time to finish the lengths of wood, to polish them and grease them with fat so they would slide easily over the snow. It was noon of the fourth day before he was able to tie the skis to his feet and venture out into the forest, upon the deep covering of virgin snow. His skis, pressing down the soft surface, slid along bearing his weight easily and he was satisfied with them.

He crossed deer tracks and then he came to a broad trail that set the hair stirring on his scalp.

It was made by scores of feet. But these feet were as broad and as long as Brand's forearm; they left the crisscross mark of webbing in the snow. And they went toward the camp of the Norsemen. Brand sped along the packed trail, running where it was level, and shooting down the slope to the lake.

He came thus into the camp, and the first thing he saw was Ranulf and the seamen gathered about the body of Fighting Mord. The leader of the Vikings had arrows fast in his chest and another through his throat.

"Well," quoth Brand, "he did not belie his name." He caught Ranulf by the arm. "Where is Kristi?"

All the seamen were silent. They looked frightened as if they had seen spirits rise up out of the earth. Only Ranulf was able to relate what had befallen—how, after Kristi had gone out of the house before sunrise to look to the animals, a clamor as of human wolves had broken out. Running from the house he had seen in the faint light Fighting Mord struggling with strange shapes of men who yelped like fiends. These men had inhuman faces—white bones without flesh. They had long hair bristling with feathers, and they had wounded several of his companions before they had raced away on their round snowshoes. And they had borne Kristi away with them.

"Bring me an iron-ring shirt," Brand growled. "Bring me a horned helmet."

He slipped the mail shirt on beneath his cloak. It had pieces that came down over the thighs. He put the bright helmet with its two projecting horns on his red head. He wrapped the bearskin about his shoulders and took up his ax again.

"Nay," cried Ranulf, "do not follow. Thor himself could not get Kristi from the hands of the fiends in the forest. Do not give them another life."

The Vikings muttered assent. True, they had no snow skates such as Brand had made for himself and they could make no journey through the deep snow; but not one of them would willingly have faced again the warriors of this unknown land.

"I will follow," said Brand. "Do ye bide here, little men."

He said it over his shoulder. Already thrusting himself off, with the staff of his great ax, he was sliding out toward the forest on the trail left by the warband.

When the sun was down to the treetops he came to the end of the trail. First he heard the barking of dogs; then he saw a great cluster of huts with smoke rising from a fire in the midst of them, in a clear place.

The Berserk stopped to tighten his belt and to clean the snow from each of his skis. When he struck the ax shaft upon the ground, it jarred against a stone and the steel blade sang shrill.

"Aye," said Brand, "thou singest loud, for soon there will be smiting of weapons and the ravens and wolves will be fed by thee."

So saying he went forward, gliding fast. Scores of dark men came before the huts to look at him. They had bows and painted shields; white marks were painted on their faces so that they appeared to be bones. They were tall men, and they yelled with rage as their first arrows flew.

Some of the arrows struck against Brand's iron-ring shirt and bounced back, and the savages yelled in dread. They gave back when the giant Berserk swung his ax. But several arrows caught in the white bearskin and one slashed Brand's thigh.

At sight of the flowing blood the savages began to leap about him boldly. They surrounded him, throwing stone axes, and dodging the sweep of the ax.

Brand could not move swiftly because of his skis, and they were too fearful to come to grips with him as he pressed forward among the huts.

"Ho, Kristi!" he shouted.

And the girl's cry answered him.

Brand turned toward it when a net of woven vines was flung at him, falling over his head. He tore it, and lifted it off. But a dozen savages flung themselves upon him, gripping the ax fast. Brand swayed under their weight, while their clubs knocked the helmet from his head. He struck out with his fists, until more of them piled upon him, when he fell under the weight of bodies.

Then the savages yelled exultantly. They pulled the cloak and the iron shirt from his bare trunk. They cut the skis from his feet, and women ran from the huts to stare at him. They bound his wrists with withes in front of him and led him to the fire dancing about him.

Brand was bewildered by their nimbleness. He saw Kristi led out into the front of the crowd that gathered in a circle about him. The girl was pale; still, she did not weep.

"Now that was poor sport, Kristi," he said moodily, "and I have done nothing for you."

Three tall savages wrapped in deerskin robes came and stood before him with folded arms. They had eagle feathers in their hair. They looked boldly into his face, while the circle pressed inward. Then a warrior who had been at the fire came up to Brand and thrust a pointed chip of wood into the side of his chest. It was as long as a finger and the outer end of it was smoking and burning.

"Now, little Kristi," Brand said, "they have pricked me with a splinter."

Another piece of wood was thrust into his other side, and the fire began to bite at his flesh. Anger smoldered in him, and he flung up his red head to chant the song of his kind—the song of shields clashing upon the long ships and steel smiting; and the cries of the kites and wolves that fed upon bodies of the slain, who had been caught up by the winged battle maidens, speeding aloft to Valhalla's hall.

So he sang, and the chieftains of the savages grunted in admiration. But tears came into Kristi's eyes, so that she covered her head with her cloak. Because of the pain in his sides and the sight of her tears, Brand's anger grew great. Still he sang on, because it was not time to end his death song yet. And suddenly one of the chiefs gave a shout and drew a knife. He stepped behind Brand and cut through the flesh between two of his ribs.

Brand's song ceased. The anger that was in him suddenly filled his brain. The snow and the yelling crowd became red before his eyes, and with the strength of frenzy, he jerked his bound wrists against his uplifted knee.

Some of the withes cracked and slipped. With his shoulder sinews cracking, the Berserk tore his hands free from the bonds. He leaped forward through the air, knocking the savages aside. And before they could grasp him well he had caught up his ax where it lay unheeded on the ground.

Leaping away from them, he swung it about his head and the steel whined. The curved blade crashed into the face of a man, shearing away part of the skull. It split open the skull of another.

When they scrambled away from him, Brand sprang back to the fire. The fit of the Berserk was upon him, and he did not think or plan anymore. He saw only the red mist before him and the darting bodies of his foes. Snatching from the fire a small log burning at one end, he ran at them, the blazing log and the bloodied ax making circles among them. His great arms heaved and slashed.

They could not use their bows in that press, and it must have seemed to them that the Berserk was a god dealing out destruction. They ran from him, through the huts, and he leaped after them. He broke the spine of a chief with a blow, and after that fear came upon them and they fled from the village, far into the forest. But they left behind the captive girl to appease this death-dealing god.

Under a red sunset, Brand stood leaning upon his ax, panting, the steam rising from his wounded body. But when Kristi came up to him, weeping and wiping at his hurts with a coil of her long hair, the red mist faded from before his eyes, and he grinned his crooked grin.

"Now that," he said, "was but poor weapon-play, yet much good came of it."

"It is my doing, Brand," she said mournfully, "that thou art hurt. Because in my heart I prayed all this day thou wouldst come to find me."

He cleaned his hand and wiped the tears from her cheeks. "And I have found thee in such a way," he answered softly, "that nothing shall ever come between us again."

Kristi turned away so that he should not see her face; still she said nothing against it. With strips from her smock she bound fast the cut on his back, while he tied on his skis again with new thongs, and picked up his bearskin.

He lifted his ax to one shoulder, and he lifted the girl to the other. He set his foot forward and began to glide back along the trail through the twilight.

Over the treetops a star gleamed in the cold sky. Kristi looked at it and spoke suddenly: "If I asked for a star to put in my hair, could you get it for me?"

"Certainly," said Brand.

Forward!

I

My brothers, it was a bad night when the order first came to me. True, in the North all nights are bad, with the mists from the swamps and the breath of the sea that is not warm but cold—cold as the wounds of a dead man.

But that night the bells were ringing all over St. Petersburg. They clashed and muttered as if imps were dancing on the bell ropes and a fog came up the river and rolled across the bridges.

I had a lantern tied to my sash—such a fog it was—when I made the rounds of the sentry boxes by the great cathedral. Although Easter was at hand snow still lay along the fronts of the stone houses.

Ekh, you, my brothers, turn loose your horses in the tall grass at such a season. You have not visited the cities of the Muscovites, the Moskyas we Cossacks call them, where the houses are built up out of stones and the roads between the houses are called streets—streets covered with hewn logs. So it was that night of the year 1788 after the Christ. And so it is now, for all I know.

The order came in this fashion. I was standing at one of the sentry posts listening to the bells, thinking that all this ringing was like a summons, when the little bells of a troika drew nearer in the fog, and a three-span sleigh came to a halt beside me.

"Is that the *sotnik*, Ivak? —— burn you! You are hard to find as a pig's bristle."

Lifting the lantern, I made out an under-ensign of the Preobrazhensky regiment, with his dark-green coat and red facings and brass buttons. He had few hairs in his beard.

"Are you Ivak, the *sotnik*, senior under-officer of the squadron of Don Cossacks quartered at the palace?" he asked again.

It was true that I was next in command to our *ataman*, our colonel who left matters pretty much to me, as he was always riding escort to the Empress. Her Majesty liked fine tall fellows who filled their uniforms and could sit a horse. She sent for us, out of the steppe fifteen hundred versts away, to see what we were like. We Cossacks of the Don are not bad-looking chaps, and we can ride better than anyone else in the world. Until my father's time we had always been our own masters and we came to St. Petersburg to see what the Empress was like.

"At command!" I replied.

"Well then, listen." He looked at me keenly. "An order has been issued by her Majesty. Some minister or other—I forget his name—sent me out after you at this hour. How would you like, Ivak, to go back to your steppe? To the Black Sea?"

Now God could have sent nothing to warm my heart more than this. We Don Cossacks were all homesick, really sick. Now and then it had been permitted that we go out after wolves. But what are wolves? A stag is better. Aye, we had no hunting for a whole winter; all we did was to stand in the wooden boxes they made for their sentries, instead of riding a cordon as a man should.

The ensign must have seen how much this pleased me, because he went on less cautiously:

"You are detached from service with the squadron, and you alone will go of the Don ruffians. After sunrise report to one of the English officers, Lieutenant Edwards, quartered in the Admiralty street. He is going with you."

"Am I under his orders?"

At this the ensign was silent a moment. Some men never talk openly, and only a fool will share his blanket with that kind.

"Nay," he said after a while, "you are on a mission for the Empress herself. Accompany Lieutenant Edwards and act with him so far as your orders permit. You are to escort a foreigner to the Black Sea. Arrange for supplies, for post horses, and choose a route. You know the country down there, of course, and her Majesty is pleased to remember your service against the Kuban Tatars."

"Good! Who is this foreigner?" I asked. "The Englishman?"

"What a dolt you are! Don't you know a soldier never asks questions! A lashing would teach you Cossacks a thing or two."

He pulled at his clipped mustache and told me that the man who would be in my charge was a high officer.

"Pardon," I said again, "but in our service a man is a dolt if he doesn't get his orders clear in his head. Who is the high officer?"

The Preobrazhensky manling screwed up his eyes and spat. Well for him he did not spit on my boots! My rank was equal to his, but then the Muscovites held themselves above us Cossacks.

"You were hatched out of the same egg as Satan! Call him Pavel. That's enough. And don't blab about your mission to the tavern wenches, either, Ivak."

Evidently he thought, my brothers, that we men of the steppe talked about military affairs to womenfolk, every night, like the Muscovite officers at court. When we talk to the girls our words are otherwise.

He leaned over the side of the sleigh to whisper:

"Report to the Englishman, Edwards. But come to me—I am the ensign Strelsky of the Guards—for a final word before setting out. Don't fail!"

"I hear."

Wrapping his furs around him, he shouted an oath at the driver and whirled away. But my ears have listened for quail moving in thickets and wild pigs rooting by the rivers at night. I heard him mutter something that sounded like:

"Pavel—Edwards—Ivak—good riddance all three."

I wondered what final word he was saving for our setting forth—what word he could not speak to me now. And I wondered who Pavel might be, and why the order had come to me direct from the officers of the Empress, who was now monarch of all the Cossacks, instead of through our colonel, in the ordinary way.

As matters turned out, I did not see the *ataman* again, because my officer was having a fine carouse in the Winter Palace that night, and I said farewell to my brothers of the squadron a little before cock-crow. The *essaul* who assumed my duties, because he was envious of the order from the Empress and my departure for our steppe, said dark things:

"As God lives, Ivak, evil will come of this. It is a secret mission and when you dismount at the end you will step into a dungeon, like as not."

"Or they will tie your scalp lock with a riband like a Prussian pigtail," said another.

"It may chance that Pavel will be a woman," put in the other *essaul*, "and then, Ivak, you will be in worse trouble than a calf tied to a cart-tail."

I buckled my bag and saddled the Kabarda stallion that I had brought up into Muscovy. Then I took my lance from the rack, for we had been equipped with lances having long streamers, like the Polish hussars, and said farewell to the *kunaks*, my brothers.

"At least," I told them, "I will not be standing in an open coffin—" for that is how we called the sentry boxes—"saluting Moskya officers and picking my teeth. Nay, in another month I will be dancing with your girls in the Dnieper villages."

They were sorry to see old Ivak go, and so they cursed my beard until I was in saddle, then all came forward to press my hand and bid me go with God, as is our custom. Truly, though we had jested, their words and mine came close to the mark. For the journey that began that day was a race and not a journey at all. We raced with Death.

Aye, it followed close upon the heels of one of our company. And the end of the road was a strange place—where not even an order of the Empress bids a Don *sotnik* go. And here, my brothers, is the tale of the journey and the man who made it.

The quarters of the Englishman, Lieutenant Edwards, were in a fine brick house with a courtyard near the river. Even at sunrise many officers were being carried home from the festivities in sedan chairs and sleighs by their servants, *heydukes* dressed like Turks or Poles or Tatars, in turbans and pelises with silver frogs, though why the high commanders of St. Petersburg should dress their servants like their enemies I do not know. Nor why the most trusted officers of the Empress Catherine the Great should be chosen from among Prussians, who were as stiff as lancepoles, or French, who wore white wigs. But that is how it was.

I found the Englishman in the courtyard, in high boots and a fine blue coat. He had been at the festivity, but he was not drunk, because he was looking to the saddling of a big roan. The horse was dancing and quivering, and the grooms kept their distance from its heels.

Lieutenant Edwards took the reins, gaining the saddle in the same instant. As I live, there was a fiend in that roan. It circled and reared, and the officer's three-cornered hat flew off into the mud. Then he lost his whip, and the roan started to bolt.

The Englishman could ride a bit, and he pulled the beast up short. But the roan knew what to do next; it wheeled against the fence, and the man had to slip a foot from stirrup to save his leg from being crushed against a post. At once the fiend with four legs reared, and Lieutenant Edwards followed his hat, rolling over in the muck almost under the nose of my Kabarda.

Now few things are as pleasing to a Cossack as a bit of tricky riding. I was smiling, and the officer thought I was laughing at him, which was not so. But a man does not feel proud when he has tumbled out of a saddle.

"Climb down, you pig of a Moskya," he said in good Russian, "and my men will give you a whipping."

"Health to your Honor," said I, and dismounted, for his rank was higher than mine and it would have been insolence to address the officer from saddle. I, also, could speak the language of the Muscovites well—the speech of the Moskyas, which is not quite the same as our Cossack tongue.

"The *sotnik*, Ivak, reports to you by order."

He looked me over, frowning. Perhaps he had never before seen a Cossack. His cheeks were clean shaven and his eyes were clear. Probably he was not more than half my age, and certainly he lacked half a head of my height.

Perhaps my *svitza*, my long coat, was ragged at the bottom; but if the Englishman had eyes for such things, he would have seen that my sash was a fine Turkish shawl and the red morocco in my boots was good stuff. He called to his servants to bring him his hat and whip and they did so, keeping out of the way of the roan, which was ranging the courtyard, snorting.

The Englishman's chin was set and his nostrils quivered and it seemed to me that he meant to use the whip on me himself, which would have been an evil thing for both of us. Evidently he had a quick temper and was not exactly a coward.

"If your Honor permits," I spoke up, "I will ride the roan for a bit and bring him to hand."

"Five rix-dollars that you don't!"

"Agreed."

The Englishman laughed as if he thought I were jesting, but he watched while I walked over to the roan. The horse tossed its head and wheeled off. A second time and a third I approached him, talking under my breath.

Presently I had the rein, and the roan laid back its ears, but as I kept on talking without trying to gain the saddle, it fell to watching the grooms.

Then I jumped into the saddle without laying hand on the horse. It reared and then kicked out, feeling the grip of my knees. Once I lashed it with the heavy Cossack whip, and all the infernal in it was loosed.

The grooms scattered as we plunged here and there. Beyond keeping it away from the wall, there was little about the task to trouble a Cossack, since the muddy footing soon tired the roan. Many a time have my folk lassoed the wild horses on the steppe and ridden them into the villages.

"Bravo," cried the Englishman, after I had made the circuit of the place three times. "Well done!"

He himself held the rein while I dismounted, which was needless. And he had forgotten all about the whipping. The English are a strange folk, not unlike us, with a black temper and the stubbornness of an ox and a way of laughing readily. He ordered one of his men to fetch the rix-dollars for me—a thing I had not expected. A Muscovite officer would have forgotten the bet but not the punishment.

When he ordered brandy he did not forget a stoop for me. He asked who had sent me, and then who had issued the order. I drew myself up and said—"The Empress." This announcement made the Englishman thoughtful and, after he had seen that the roan was rubbed down, he looked around.

"Where are your men, *sotnik*?"

"Your Honor sees that I am alone."

At this his quick temper struck spark again, and he demanded with many oaths how he could journey to the Black Sea with Pavel, with an escort of only one man.

"True," I assured him, nodding, for it was unwonted. "Yet that man is Ivak, the galliard, the *jighit*, the outrider. I can lead you across the whole of the steppe by starlight, or you can bind up my eyes and arms, and I will race you to the camp on the Dnieper."

This was a good boast, because my Kabarda stallion would have picked its way unguided to the Cossack villages. But the Englishman was not in the mood for more wagers.

"You can't lead the way for Pavel," he growled.

And I wondered all the more who Pavel might be, and why he was not to be led. It was clear to me that many things had not been explained. My people have a saying that where there is much smoke in the air a fire is sure to be. I began to think about the fire that made all this smoke.

"Pavel will never reach St. Petersburg." The Englishman laughed as

if that were a jest. "He is beyond the sea and the ice is in the Gulf still.
Pavel wrote that he would be here, but no vessel has put in to the harbor.
By the time the ice is gone many things will have happened and Pavel
will be wiser. Better for him if he never comes!"

Ekh! My head sank lower when I heard this. My spirit was burning to
be astir and flying toward the warm sun of the steppe.

"Pardon, your Honor," I said. "But this Pavel is a high officer and among
these Muscovites the imperial one himself cannot do more things than
a high officer."

"But Pavel is not a Russian. He is—" the Englishman frowned and
tossed away a glove that was a little soiled with mud—"a pirate."

Now on our great rivers, the Volga and the Dnieper, we had many pirates,
who took a toll from the merchants. They tossed the merchants overboard
and made themselves gifts of the merchants' money boxes and goods.
That is how they took toll. So I knew what the Englishman meant, since
I had happened in among the pirate bands a few times when they were
off on a frolic. *Ai-a*, things warmed up then! Heads were bashed in, and
boxes broken open.

"On your faces, dogs!"

And the hedgehogs, the boatmen, threw themselves down.

"Kindle up on all sides, brothers! *Sarina na kitchka!* Let the merchants
drink river water."

And, splash, a pot-bellied fox-fur would go and drink himself to
death!

So, if Pavel were a pirate, I thought that we would escort him to be
hanged on a steel hook. For that is how the pirates are dealt with. Surely,
then, he would not come to St. Petersburg.

I waited in the courtyard of the Englishman's house until restlessness
came on me, and he let me exercise the roan. Every day then I rode out
to speak a word to the Don Cossacks and let them see what a fine horse
was in my charge. And everywhere I asked for news of Pavel, the great
pirate, and found that no one had heard of him; until one day, when, in
spite of the mists, I had taken the river-road down among the tribesmen
of the sea who wore little caps and huge boots and had their red jerkins
spotted with tar.

They laughed at me and pointed at another rider, who had stopped to
watch them cutting at timbers. I asked him about Pavel and he smiled.

"*Stuppai!*" he cried. "Forward!"

When he said this he spurred his horse and we raced along the bank of the Nevski, scattering the dogs and the peasants who floundered in the mud. The yellow mist rolled along with us, driven by a giant of a wind from off the sea. The cloak of the rider who had cried "Forward" whipped out like a loose shroud. I saw two long pistols in his belt and they were good ones.

In the time it takes to kindle a fire I could no longer see him, but the hoofs of his horse smacked in the mud behind the roan. At the first cross street where log houses showed up in the fog, I pulled in the Kabarda and, sure enough, the hoofs of the other nag sounded close behind.

"Evil will come out of the sea," I thought, shivering in the damp breath of the swamps and the harbor. "That is how it is—evil."

And the other rider swept up, slowing to a trot as he neared me. I put one hand on my belt, near the hilt of the saber, and he smiled. He said nothing, and the skin of his face was white—drawn tight over the bones. His plain blue coat was weatherworn and his buff boots caked with mud.

But his eyes—they were black as river stones—spoke to me as he passed, dripping water like a man who has forded a deep stream.

"*Sau bull!*" I cried, seeing that he meant no harm. "Health to you!"

He waved his hand without speaking and the mist swallowed him up.

After he had gone I took off my *kalpak* and crossed myself, muttering the names of the Father and Son. For this man had the look of the dead who rise up from the sea. And surely the bells of Petersburg had been tolling miraculously.

That night Lieutenant Edwards said to me:

"Pavel has come. He sailed across the gulf in an open boat, and when the ice was upon them he held a pistol to the head of the chief boatman. For two days they had no food, but he changed his priming and kept it dry and said, '*Stuppai!*'"

The thought came to me that I had met Pavel, the pirate, on the river-road, and surely he looked like a man who had drifted on the sea for a long time. I would rather have crossed the border on a bad horse; but the sea was his home and the steppe was mine.

Edwards was not pleased, and he said that Pavel knew only that one word of Russian. He said that Pavel was a rear admiral.

"What is that?" I asked.

"A field marshal of ships—a *hetman*, you would call him. But all the same he is a pirate and a lawless fighter. The —— take him! Not long ago he rebelled against his king and became an American."

I had not heard of that country and wondered where it was, in Russia or Poland. The officer laughed and said that it was a country of vagabonds, without money to pay for a ship-of-war or powder for soldiers. Instead of a king, it had a merchant for *hetman*, a merchant who grew tobacco.

I did not wonder then that Pavel had come to seek service in Russia, where the officers wear diamonds and silver cording, and have fine women in their houses, yet it was strange that he should have a Russian name, and I asked the Englishman why this was so.

"Pavel means Paul. His name is John Paul Jones, and he was hatched out of the same egg as Satan."

As the days passed I understood that they would not hang John Paul Jones in Petersburg. Instead he went every day to the court, and carriages drove up to his door sometimes two or three at a time. Always high officers were with him, and I grew very weary of saluting, for I was stationed at the door of his house. Every morning there was a *heyduke* with a letter from the Empress, and because *heydukes* like to lick up mead I learned many things.

The man from the sea was high in favor at court because he was to be sent down through the steppe to the far-off Black Sea, to take command of the Russian fleet and pound to pieces the fleet of the sultan who was at war with the Empress.

John Paul had pounded the English ships, and burnt them; afterward he had been given a gold sword for bravery for other deeds by the *hetman* of the French; so the Empress had called him and he had come. Time pressed, for he was needed by the Muscovites, who were expecting an attack by the ships of the Turks, down where Father Dnieper loses himself in the Black Sea.

This pleased me because it meant that we would soon show our heels to the accursed city of fogs and snow. Edwards gave orders to get together a half-dozen horses, with two Tatars to act as followers, and the necessary highway passes and order for post horses. He was to be John Paul's aide-de-camp and he told me to go to Strelsky for the passes.

I found the ensign of the Guards sitting in his quarters by a tile stove, with his fur greatcoat thrown open and a glass of brandy near his hand.

When he saw me he told me to close the door; then he took a pinch of snuff and dusted it off his silk neck-cloth.

"You start at dawn tomorrow, Ivak. This order is for *yamshiks*—the pick of the post horses."

He sharpened a quill pen and cleaned his teeth with it while I drew a wooden splinter from the stove and lighted my pipe.

"You're a golden fellow, Ivak. I warrant you've stolen Tatar horses from across the border. They tell me you can use a sword, too. Well, you're lucky."

"*Allah birdui*," I responded. God gives.

"Well, you're no skirted choir singer, blast me if you are. I like your sort, Ivak. You have a head on you as well as a sword hand. *Tch-tch!*" He shook his head admiringly. "Have you got together enough men and horses for the journey? Sometimes your Father Dnieper—that cursedly treacherous river—is a stepfather? Eh? Pirates and roving Tatars swarm like bees around a clover patch."

"We have a change of mounts and two Talmak Tatars for dragomen," I answered. "How large will the escort of soldiers be?"

Strelsky looked over at a high lacquer screen that stood in one corner of the chamber and wiped the brown dust again from his chin.

"No other escort goes with you, Ivak. Haste is imperative, and you must not spare the horses. A great number of followers would delay the march."

I bent my head as if that were most true. Instead, I was wondering why not even a vedette of hussars accompanied us. John Paul was high in favor with her Majesty, and surely the Empress would not let him ride forth without a retinue. But so it was.

Strelsky pushed the flagon of brandy toward me, and we looked at the bottom of the glasses several times, each busied with his own thoughts,

"You Cossack chaps like to go and warm up in the taverns on the road," he said after a while. "How would you like a hundred rix-dollars to weight down your wallet—eh?"

"*Allah birdui!*"

Without getting up he opened the lid of a box on the table and motioned for me to take what was inside. It was a sack of silver coins of the kind Edwards had used to pay his bet. I put it in my belt and the ensign nodded.

"Harken, Ivak," he went on in a lower voice, "we understand each

other, I think. There is more to the order, about your journey, and it is secret. You serve the Empress?"

"We have taken her bread and salt."

"And silver. Good! Well, John Paul must not reach the Black Sea."

"How—not reach the Black Sea?"

For a long moment he stared at the painting on the screen, and I noticed
the toes of a pair of boots showing underneath the screen.

"Do not our ships there wait for him to take command, aye, to show
the gunners how to point the cannon, and the sailors how to guide the
ships without running aground?" I asked.

"We have Muscovite commanders—better ones."

Strelsky scowled, because more than once the Moskyas had lost their
vessels because they could not manage the sails and because the rigging
was stiff. On the other hand the Turks were good seamen, and they were
helped by the corsairs from the Barbary Coast.

"John Paul is a hireling; he would betray us. Why do you bother your
head about such things, Ivak? When you have spent the rix-dollars and
come back to the Winter Palace, I swear that you will have the rank of
colonel and be at the head of the Don regiment. Your *ataman*, your colonel is a bad one, a wine swiller. He will lose his baton."

"Is the order about Paul Jones written and signed?" I asked, pretending to be pleased with all he said.

"Nay—deuce take you, Ivak. Are such things to be written on paper?"

I scratched my head, the way, my children, the warriors do when they
are puzzled. Now we Cossacks weigh down a horse a bit, but because a
buffalo is fat it does not mean he is a fool. Nay, the weasel is the greatest
of all fools because bloodlust crazes him and he thinks only of killing, and
the weasel is thin and sharp enough. Strelsky made me think of a weasel.
I began to smell so much smoke that the fire could not be far away.

Strelsky was a fool. He thought to please me by promising me the pro-
motion to colonel in place of our *ataman*. As God lives I would have liked
to be colonel and hold an ivory baton on my hip, but our officer was our
little father. Why should he not drink when there was nothing else to do
in this city that smelled of the sea?

"True," I nodded again. "An order is an order. God keep and reward
you, Ensign—I must look to the horses."

He stared and said farewell doubtfully, and I went out, taking pains not to close the door tight. I walked down the hall, thumping my boots, and came back again, moving gently, like a cat.

Without asking permission I pushed open the door. The screen had been moved and a man in a very fine silver coat was standing by the table, yawning. On his breast was the badge of the Order of St. Anne, and some others. He had very tight pantaloons and polished Hessian boots, the kind that Edwards wore.

Strelsky was speaking, and once he called the other *"mon Prince."* When they saw me they looked angry, and the pockmarked face of the prince grew dark.

When I took my *kalpak* in hand and bowed several times to the girdle as if greatly confused by sight of such a great noble, he swore in a language I did not know.

"Pardon, Excellencies," I muttered, "but I came back to ask again about the order. Is it the command of the Empress that Pavel—Paul Jones—is to be slain on the road to the Black Sea?"

Neither answered, and the full red lips of the prince—lips like a woman's they were—drew together as if he were biting them. Strelsky began to curse, then he laughed.

"Can't you see beyond your horse's ears, *sotnik*? Haven't you silver in your wallet? See to it that the river brigands or a band of Tatars seizes the American and rubs him out of the world. If this happens you will be colonel of the Don regiment; if not, you would better flee to the Turks, to keep from being flayed. Do you understand now, you dolt?"

But the prince seemed thoughtful, and it was clear that he was not a fool like Strelsky. Taking out a lace kerchief, scented like a woman's hair, he waved it in the air and held it to his nose as if my sheepskins annoyed him. So it was difficult to get a good sight of his face again.

"If a word of this order passes beyond your lips, Ivak," he warned in broken Russian, "you will wake up with a pistol ball in your brain."

"*Ekh!*" I lifted the bag of silver and tossed it on the table. "Then I beg your Excellency to keep the money for me. A dead man can't spend anything, even a copeck."

The smoke had cleared away enough for me to know that the Empress had not issued the order, or the Moskyas would have been bolder with their words. Someone else had a quarrel with Paul Jones, and I thought of the English officers who loved him only as dogs love wolves, and whose ships he had burned, besides taking from their grasp a high command in the Russian service. Before his coming the Empress had listened to the advice of the English colonels of the sea when she wanted to make war with her ships.

Why did I return the money? Well, it weighed on my spirit. Better if I had kept it—much better. I saw the watery eyes of the prince blink as if something had come up out of the ground under his nose. And when I went out into the hall I heard the door close, tight this time.

At John Paul's lodging all was quiet; the two Tatars were snoring in the stable, the boxes of luggage were packed in the courtyard, and John Paul was writing a letter in his room upstairs. He was always writing letters, though none were ever delivered to him. He had no body servant in Russia, and so, the door being open and unguarded, I sat down on the sill to smoke my pipe and regret that the rix-dollars were no longer mine.

Presently to the door came two women, one old and bundled up and the other straight and young. She had a thin face, pale under the paint that the Moskya women use, and her hood was thrown hack to show coils of black hair.

They wanted to ask the American for work to do—sewing. I told them to go to another door in the street because we had no need of sewing.

Then they began to argue and the younger one said they had had nothing to eat that day. Overhead, the American stirred and came down to see what was happening. The old one drew back, but the girl addressed him boldly in some kind of French, I think, and he shook his head.

The girl took his hand and put back her cloak and smiled, trying to slip past him into the house. But he would not permit it, giving her some money instead—I do not know how much. Then she jumped up on her toes and kissed him, and went away to where the crone was waiting. John Paul returned to his writing because I heard the scrape of his pen.

I was glad the women had gone because every minister of Petersburg had a regiment of spies and the foreign nobles had nearly as many, and it is an ill place where a man can be watched without knowing it. The great clocks of the towers had struck many times when wheels creaked up to the house and an equerry of the palace reported that a *tarantass* belonging to her Majesty had been brought for the American to use on his journey.

As Paul Jones was asleep by then, I went out to look at the *tarantass*, which was a long, narrow wagon with big wheels, leather bound. In front and rear were places for footmen to stand, holding on by straps. A sloping roof covered it like a house, and within was room enough for two to sit or recline but not to stand. The windows were small and heavy shutters closed them.

Two pairs of matched bays were hitched up, one pair to the shaft, the other to the traces. I was very sleepy by then, and dozed a bit until John Paul woke me up.

"*Stuppai*, Ivak," he cried with a smile. "Forward!"

I was angry that he should have found me asleep when dawn was streaking the sky, and I cursed the Tatars a bit when I found that he had been to the stables and had the horses fed before waking me. We were ready by the time Edwards rode up, yawning, with his body servant and a led horse with double packs. All the servants of the palace had gone except the equerry and the two postilions. For a while we delayed while the two officers talked, and John Paul went up to the *tarantass* and glanced inside carelessly, though he could have seen little in the faint light.

"Ivak," Edwards called to me, "here's a —— of a mess. The American will not ride in the carriage of the Empress. He wants to make the journey in a saddle. We cannot send back her Majesty's gift."

"Health to your Honor," I pointed out. "In that case we can throw the luggage in the wagon and use the pack animals as spare mounts for the servant and Tatars. Then, perhaps Pavel-Paul Jones can sleep in it when we halt."

In this way our progress would be swifter, and I was glad when the American ordered the packs thrown into the *tarantass* and we set out with three extra mounts, leaving the equerry standing at salute. *Ekh*, I was glad to ride for the last time through the muddy streets in the pale dawn and hear for the last time that clamoring, invisible ringing of the bells.

II

When the net is invisible the fish thinks the water is clear. That is how the fish is caught.

For a time that day I watched John Paul, to see how he would bear himself. *Ekh*, he was at home in the saddle, that chap, and he forced the pace faster than the Englishman, Edwards, wanted to press on. Because it was the season of the *rasputitsa*, the flood during the spring thaw, the roads were no better than fords across the treacherous swamps. The carriage would slip from the crown of the road and sink into the mire up to the hubs.

After John Paul had dismounted once and put logs under the wheels, to force the carriage back to the road, I made the postilions change places with the Tatars. I was angry because we had to drag along the *tarantass*, but if I had known what evil was stored up for us within it, I would have unhitched the horses and left it like a stranded ship in the great pools of the flooded country.

If it had not been for John Paul we should not have reached the first of the *zamoras*—the post stations along the highroad to Moscow—that night. The sun had gone down behind a cloud bank when we drew up at the inn and a score of slouching rogues came out to stare at us. They showed their teeth but nothing more when I elbowed them aside and shouted to the pig of a tavern keeper to make ready a leg of mutton and brandy spirits and bread for their excellencies, the officers, who had chosen to quarter themselves in the carriage after looking once at the inn.

They sat on the shaft and ate the dinner when it was brought, but I went to the stables before eating to make certain that the Tatars had watered the horses and given them oats. I found all as it should be, the beasts bedded down and the Tatars not yet drunk on *chirkhir*, and I was turning away to seek out my dinner when one of them touched my knee.

"Horses!" he said, and after a moment, "Nine riders on the road, Ivak Khan."

Now Tatars have ears like weasels, and it was quite a while before I heard the hoofbeats coming nearer. The Tatar who had spoken peered up at me and pulled his forefinger across his throat, then touched the hilt of my saber. He meant that men were around who would cut my throat, and warned me to be on guard.

Just as he did so a screaming began in front of the inn, a shrill screaming that was horrible to hear. I took off my *kalpak* and crossed myself, for it sounded like a woman vampire calling from the forest, but the cries were coming from the wagon.

"Aid—Aid! Who will hear the prayer of a Christian maid?"

John Paul and the Englishman were on their feet, staring at the *tarantass* in astonishment, because all the day that wagon had given out no cries and now there was either a woman or a vampire inside it.

A body of horsemen came clattering up to the fire, and the leader dismounted and strode over to the wagon. He was an ensign of the Guards with a long mustache and a long saber and a red face. The six troopers with him kept to their saddles and worked their horses around so as to hem us in.

"Let us see what is boiling in this pot!" growled the ensign, jerking open the doors.

He began to haul at something and presently pulled out—for he was a strong man—a girl who was bound with belts at the wrists and ankles. She was slender, with tangled dark hair, and she wore a silk cloak lined with hare's fur.

All the time the ensign was unbuckling the straps she leaned on his shoulder and wept, chattering like a squirrel. Servants of the American, she said, had overtaken her in the street of Petersburg and had gagged her. Then she had been carried to John Paul's house and placed in the wagon. She said—and this was quite true—that she had had nothing to eat all day, and had been shaken up and down like wheat at threshing.

The ensign, whose name was Borol, asked her if she was not Anna Mikhalovna, and she assented eagerly. Then he frowned and turned to Edwards, explaining how complaint had been made that morning at the quarters of the Guard by this girl's mother. An order had been issued that he should follow the American, find the girl, and request John Paul to return to Petersburg.

When Borol pointed at the American, John Paul spoke one word to Edwards, who turned to the ensign—

"Salute the rear admiral."

Borol chewed his mustache and clicked his lips; then drew his heels together and saluted sullenly. It was plainly to be seen that John Paul was not in such high favor now. He took Edwards's arm and the two paced up and down while the aide-de-camp explained about the accusation and the order to return.

Meanwhile Borol made a great show of warming Anna Mikhalovna at the fire and ordering brandy for her to drink, and I went closer to stare at her. She was the girl who had called at John Paul's door the evening before with the old crone.

Ekh, the whole thing was clear in my mind, all at once. The girl had not been in the *tarantass* when it was first driven up from the palace. Some time before dawn she had been placed in it, bound, most likely. Then John Paul's enemies in Petersburg had spread a story that the American had carried off the girl, and now he would be recalled to explain the matter to a court of men who hated him. It meant that he would be kept waiting at the Muscovite palace instead of joining his command, even if nothing worse happened. In my mind was the picture of the foreign prince with the Hessian boots, and I wondered how much the English had to do with the plot. They had no love for John Paul, and made no secret of it.

The story of Anna Mikhalovna could not be true. Why had she kept quiet in the wagon all day, only to cry out like a bugle when the troopers came up? And as for John Paul's servants carrying her off, he had no servants. Besides, she had tried to enter his house last evening, and when she had been turned away this new plot had been made against him.

Probably his enemies had counted on a scene in his courtyard when we started off; but he had chosen a horse instead of the carriage and the girl had not been seen, because no one had looked inside when the packs were thrust through the door.

It was a plot that men who spend their lives at court would hatch—a small and skillful plot, the kind that ties up a man as with silk cords. What could John Paul do but go back? He belonged to the world of the court, and according to his code it would be necessary to clear his name before he could accept his new mission.

Edwards looked like a man who has come to a fork in the road, puzzled, yet a little pleased. But John Paul had grown pale and his eyes were dark as coals.

Just a few words he said to the ensign, Borol—Edwards interpreting—but they were like sword pricks. The American had seen through the plot, and the wish of his enemies to disgrace him.

"I came to Russia in an open shallop, through ice on the sea, because the Empress summoned me, and when I offered my sword to her, Count Besborodko, the minister of state, was instructed to do everything possible to make the situation of the Chevalier Paul Jones pleasant and to furnish him with all possible occasions on which he might display his skill and valor. Besborodko—" the American handed back the order which was signed by the minister—"has misunderstood his instructions. He has taken pains to afford me the chance of displaying the talents of a lawyer, not a soldier."

Edwards smiled as he translated, and I thought that John Paul was a man who would not be led by others. But his pride was hurt and his muscular face was drawn. He had a hard path to follow in Russia, because he did not know the ways of the great Russian lords, who looked on all soldiers as slaves.

Borol shrugged and said it was none of his affair—such a disgraceful matter it was, carrying off a young girl. He was a *graf* of Hessia—whatever that might be—and the mission touched upon his honor—whatever that was. And he pushed up the ends of his mustache, clanking his scabbard as he did so.

Now I had been seeking for some word to say, because I would rather have lost my scalp lock than return to Petersburg. Something about the *graf* reminded me of the prince in the silver coat: they were like two cups, and if neither was an Englishman, then the English at the palace might not have hatched the plot. I smacked my thigh and whispered in Edward's ear.

"Your Honor's pardon, but that girl is the one who tried to get into John Paul's lodging last evening. An old crone was with her, and the American gave them money to go away. Somebody must have given them more money—the pretty sparrows!"

This surprised the Englishman, and he looked as if he did not know which fork of the road to take.

"The deuce!" He took snuff and added carelessly to Borol. "This Anna Mikhalovna—I think I've seen her. A friend of Besborodko's perhaps?"

"Not at all, Lieutenant. She's a farmer's daughter—lodged with a priest near the cathedral last night."

"Ah." Edwards glanced at the silk cloak. "Then she couldn't have come begging at the rear admiral's quarters late in the evening."

"Impossible."

I stepped forward.

"She was there, only dressed differently."

Borol shook his head impatiently and ordered some of his men to escort Anna to the inn. Edwards needed no more words to show whether I had told the truth.

"Ensign," he remarked, "this is not a flash in the pan, it is —— serious. The American entered the Russian service on the Empress's pledge that he would have a free hand and sole command of the Black Sea Fleet. He is a Chevalier of France and a friend of Lafayette. Who stirred up this hornets' nest at his heels?"

Now those who had sent Borol had picked a man with a good sword arm but a sluggish brain. He chewed his mustache and barked out:

"—— take it! You English have cooked up the whole thing."

Edwards started as if he had been touched with a whip.

"What a knowing fellow, egad!" he drawled. "Upon my word, Count Borol, you must know us better than we know ourselves. Deuced quaint, I swear, to fancy that because we do not count Admiral Jones among our friends we would think up a foul plot and bait it with a farmer's daughter. Unfortunate, very—that it should be necessary to prove to you by example that the English strike in the open."

And his eyes glittered, just like the time when he had caught me smiling at him. Quite happy, he was, because the ensign had given him offense. A strange folk!

"I thought—" Borol was beginning to be sorry he had talked so much, but he was in for it now.

"Indeed! It may be necessary for you to think twice. A man of your high intuition, Count Borol, must realize that by accusing the English officers of Petersburg of a blackguardly intrigue, you cast some slight aspersion upon me." He bowed, very elegant. "Of course you will give satisfaction at once, and as the challenged party, the choice of weapons is yours. Do you prefer swords or shall we say pistols. Necessity compels us to dispense with seconds."

It was clear to me that the Englishman's temper would brew trouble for us. If there was a duel, and someone was sliced, the enemies of Paul Jones would have good reason for calling him to account, since dueling was forbidden. To make matters worse, the American, when he learned what Edwards was about, insisted on meeting Borol himself. And, knowing of the plot against John Paul, I could see that Borol was well content; if he wounded the admiral, high influences in Petersburg would free him from blame; if John Paul cut him up, the American would be made to suffer for it. A plan came into my head and I stepped forward.

"Borol," I said, "God has given you a long arm but a short wit. A while ago you would not believe my word that the girl had come begging of the admiral. Now I say that you lie."

And I added other plain words for the soldiers to hear, so that their leader's ears began to burn.

"Dog of a Cossack!" Borol was beside himself with rage. "I'll have you strung up by the thumbs and your hide cut up for whips."

"Oho," I thought, "when the cock crows loud he is in his own barnyard."

Carefully this time I counted over the troopers and found there were seven with the ensign included. But my Tatars had heard nine horses, and if two others had come with the company they must be in hiding in the trees beyond the firelight—spies, without a doubt, or perhaps Strelsky, or even the prince of the silver coat.

"First," I told Borol, "I will teach you a lesson if you are not afraid to challenge a man whose arm is as long as yours."

"Draw your steel, you hedgehog!"

"Ivak!" Edwards turned on me angrily. "My affair with the ensign does not require the aid of a clown. Back to your place!"

"Pardon," I pointed out, "but my quarrel with Borol takes precedence of your Honor's affair. He made light of my word in the first place."

The American and Edwards stood about as high as my chin, but they were crossing steel with the ensign, who was a giant. Edwards began to explain impatiently that, although Borol's military rank was equal with mine, the man was a count, or some such thing.

"You do not know, Excellency," I assured him, "that in my country the Cossacks hold me to a prince. Aye, my grandsire was *hetman*, having to his order ten thousand sabers. Is not that rank enough?"

Borol, who was foaming at the mouth, tossed his cloak to a trooper and began to roll up his right sleeve, crying that I might be emperor of a million pigs, but he would have satisfaction all the same.

"One moment," I said. "You have challenged me and so I have choice of weapons. Is it not so, Lieutenant Edwards?"

He nodded, staring at me curiously. Borol grinned, knowing that a Cossack would chose sabers, which suited him very well.

"We will fight with pitchforks," I said.

So amazed were they that the crackling of the fire could be heard in the silence, when I walked to the manure heap by the inn door and picked up two forks with iron prongs. My ears were pricked and I heard the stamp of a horse close by in the darkness, where someone watched, unseen. Eh, the trap was set and ready to be sprung if the American or those with him showed fight. I yearned to take on Borol with sabers and teach him a thing or two, for among the Don Cossacks few were a match for me with the blades.

But it was not to be. I cleaned the iron prongs in the earth and held out the two forks to Borol, offering him choice of weapon. How his eyes stuck out!

"With those things!" he sneered. "A gentlemen is not a dog of a farmer."

"True, my little Count," I nodded. "A Cossack would think it disgraceful to draw steel on such a man as you. Choose!"

He glared at the prongs, at me, and at Edwards, who was beginning to be amused. Then he stepped back with an oath, and felt in his saddle holster for a firearm.

"Take them!" he shouted to his men. "Draw pistols!"

For the second time Borol had made a mistake. His men obeyed, it is true, but when they had their weapons resting on their hips, with muzzles in the air, Edwards had caught up a double-barreled horse pistol from his saddle bags and the American had in hand the two light, silver-mounted French pistols that he carried in his belt.

It was clear even to Borol that we would not be taken alive, by force; but before he could give an order to the troopers to fire, a voice came out of the darkness behind the fire—

"Withdraw!"

And they did so, taking with them the woman, lest we question her, but leaving the *tarantass*—which I regretted. The trap had been sprung, but the panthers were not caught. Aye, from that hour we were hunted like beasts, we who were men.

Then the American showed that he had had men to his command before now. I had seen that he could ride and face an adversary; now it was clear he thought of those under him. Through Edwards he reminded me that I had had no dinner and bade me to the inn to seek what I could find and to return to talk with them.

When I wiped my hands on the tavern dog and came forth again, the two officers were casting dice on a saddle cloth, laughing like boys, though there was gray in the hair of John Paul. After I saluted, Edwards asked me to sit with them and light my pipe, and they put away the dice.

"Old raven," said he, "there is more in your noodle than comes out your mouth. The rear admiral would like to ride back to Tsarkoe-seloe and clear his name before the Empress. Knowing a little of the Russian court, I advise him to ride as far from it as his horse will carry him; a victory or two will do more for his cause than a dozen petitions, which might get no farther than the servants of the minister of state. What is your word?"

They were quick of wit, those two, and they saw how old Ivak had uncovered a fine snare, all the more deadly because it was sprung by a silken cord.

"If your Honor pleases," I responded after thought, "what is in your heart toward the American? Good or ill?"

"The deuce!" Edwards frowned. "Would I have come as his aide if not honestly? Pirate he may have been, but that chapter is written. Take care what you say, Cossack!"

"Lieutenant," I made answer, "we be three men, and the road before us is fifteen hundred versts. Wolves track us, and they be two-legged wolves. If we do not speak openly together now, how shall we make a plan? Without a plan, how shall we arrive at the end of the road?"

He glanced at me, and the flush left his keen young face.

"As bad as that? I wondered why an escort was denied us, on one pretext or another." He stooped to draw a coal from the fire for his long clay pipe. "Hm. Would these two-legged wolves shed the blood of our officer?"

"Aye."

"Ha! The stakes are high, then. But I do not think the Empress would stoop to plotting."

"Nay."

"Who then?"

That was a knotty question, and I shook my head. Later I had reason to curse my stupidity, that I did not tell them about the prince of the silver coat. Yet it did not come into my mind that Edwards might know him. Besides, I was not sure of John Paul's loyalty. My orders were only to guide him to Kherson, our headquarters on the Black Sea.

Edwards explained to the American what I had said, and when he had finished I made bold to offer advice.

"By your Honor's leave, what authorization has the admiral to take command when he arrives at Kherson?"

They told me there was a letter signed by Catherine herself that he should take over the fleet at Kherson. That was good though it might have been better.

"Then," I said slowly, "if I were John Paul I should ride to the utmost, not sparing the horses, until he sets foot on his flagship."

It surprised them that a Cossack should know what a flagship was, but we fellows of the borderland have taken oars in hand and gone out in skiffs against the fleet of the Turks, and we have smelled powder mixed with salt water.

"But this plot with the wretched girl has failed," Edwards pointed out. "His enemies are behind him, and the road is clear ahead."

"His enemies, Lieutenant, are powerful, and Muscovite spies are whelped even in the forests of Muscovy. Avoid the cities, and use spur and whip. If you will trust me I can lead you safe to Kherson."

Edwards laughed.

"Even odds, for a hundred rubles, I beat you into Kherson."

"Done!" I nodded.

They gave me leave to depart and I went to the stables where the straw was cleaner than the inn beds. I was not asleep when one of the Tatars touched me, and I began to listen, for he did nothing more than to hiss warningly. The hoofbeats of a horse sounded faintly from the highway, and soon disappeared to the south without pausing at the inn.

The only Russian who would pass a tavern after dark would be carrying an urgent dispatch. Moreover, he had not halted for a change of mounts at this post station, and surely there was a reason for that. I swore at my oversight in not placing sentries on the highroad, and then I remembered that we had no men to post as sentries.

III

A raft upon the river is made of many logs fastened together; so long as the logs hold together the raft is safe. If they drift apart there is no longer a raft.

Have you, my brothers, ever slain a bear with a dirk? If you know how to go about it, the task is easy. In winter, go to a *berlog*—a winter sleeping place of a bear, down under the snow, where a round air hole shows, rimmed with yellow. Thrust a long stick into the hollow under the breathing hole until the bear springs up, *whuff*—throwing the snow all about him. Then step in and stab with the knife before his eyes grow fully accustomed to the light.

If you are a little slow, the bear will go back to sleep again with a full belly.

So it was with us. Before we had grown suspicious our enemies had their way with us; but now that we had our eyes open it was otherwise. Before long we left the swamps and the mud and passed by the last of the Muscovite water-towns, Novgorod, on the bank of a small river in flood.

Like a flash the oaks and the pine forest closed around us as we pounded south toward Moscow. Probably when Strelsky made out our permit for post horses he never thought we would go far enough to claim the *yam-shiks*, the picked horses that his paper allowed us.

But at each *zamora* I combed over the nags for the best ones, keeping only the Kabarda of mine that ran loose beside us for three days until I gave it into the keeping of an honest Armenian who would bring the horse to Kherson by slow stages. For we were covering then nearly a hundred versts, which Edwards said was eighty English miles, a day.

The postilions of the carriage complained, and finally became useless. So we were not sorry to leave them at one of the huts. The two Tatars did their work more to my liking, and the postilions may have been in the plot against us. Even the *tarantass* proved itself a friend now, because John Paul and Edwards took turns about sleeping in it, as well as they could for the jolts. *Hai*, they could not sleep as well as I in the saddle, but they made no protest and we made no stop.

Several times we heard the wolf packs howling, and once the wolves were at our heels for ten verst posts. We had to burn much powder and my horse was slashed by their teeth when we pulled up at the next post station. Still, we saw nothing of the two-legged wolf that had passed us in the first night. I scanned each rider we turned out of the narrow way between the trees, without coming upon one who might have been a Muscovite spy.

The officers cared little for the rider that was ahead of us, and looked on our ride as a new game.

"*Stuppai*, Ivak!" Paul Jones would shout.

And forward we went, Edwards jesting with me that I would taste his dust into Kherson and lose a half-year's pay thereby. Only when we sighted the domes and spires of Moscow in its great plain did we halt, for six hours, so that the American might dine with the governor of the city.

On the sixth day out we had to halt for three hours to repair a wheel of the carriage. In the stables of the post station I asked for news of a rider from Petersburg who was bearing dispatches a few hours ahead of us, knowing that any man who wished to make the utmost speed along the highway would claim that he carried dispatches. The men of the *zamora* told me that an officer had passed south at sunrise, which was twelve hours before. Dried mud was still on his boots and his permit had read from Petersburg to Kherson. Thinking of Borol, I asked if he spoke with a German accent and looked to be about my size.

They said it was not so. The officer had cursed them in good Russian for delaying him. So, after all, we had no real reason to suspect that a spy had gone ahead.

But when a man hunts wolves he does not lie down under a tree to doze because no wolves are in sight. I pushed the horses that night, keeping awake to do so, and promising the Tatars half a flask of corn brandy to stir them up a bit. We put a hundred and twenty versts behind us, from sunset to sunset, and changed horses six times, and it was my two officers who were stirred up finally.

Edwards, who was suffering from saddle sores, cursed my beard and my soul and my father's grave and other things, yet I took no offense, knowing that weariness had gripped him and there was no meaning in the curses.

"—— take you, Ivak," he promised. "I will give orders to slow down to a hand pace. You are rubbing the bones out of my buttocks."

"I hope your Honor is well," I replied, knowing how to handle him. "Because if not, I will have to wait for you in Kherson, to spend the hundred rubles."

"Blast you, Ivak—sink you for a lying rogue!"

And he leaped from the *tarantass* and ran to a horse, jumping into saddle and plying whip and spur until I was tasting his dust, as his beast was fresher.

"I'll lead you into Kherson even if your Tatars have to carry me on a door."

And his words were near to the truth, as will be seen presently. Meanwhile, however much we pressed the horses we did not gain sight of the officer who was ahead of us. If we rode like the wind, he went like a witch on a broomstick on All-Hallow's Eve—or like a man with his neck in a noose. We came out on the vast level that lies south of Moscow, where the sun was warm on the dense foliage of the trees. In the black soil the wheat stood high and rippled under the breath of the wind like a great pool of water. Dust hung behind us like a giant's plume, and the *moujiks* we met stood aside and doffed their wool caps, bowing as low as their sashes, astonished at the pace of our horses. Eh, it was good to be under a clear sky again!

Before long we knew that the rider ahead of us had sighted us, although we had not set eye on him.

At a *zamora* we were told that all the horses were out. Never before this had such a thing happened! Not a nag in the stables!

Edwards was for waiting until fresh beasts could be rounded up, but John Paul said we would press forward on the best animals to the next station. We did so, but here also the keepers of the station bowed and prayed forgiveness because all the horses were out.

I said nothing, riding instead in a circle about the hut and stables, while the two officers made use of the delay in eating dinner. Aye, there were few tracks leading away from the *zamora* along the highway, but a round dozen traces went from the stable yard into the fields, and they were fresh tracks.

Calling my Tatars, I sent them off to follow the tracks for a few versts and bring back what they found. Then I spurred my tired nag into the group of Moskyas who were watching with covert interest. I pulled out a pistol and cocked it, then primed the pan.

"What are you doing, Uncle?" asked the one who had said there were no horses. "And why did you send the Tatars away?"

"God keep you, brother," I made answer, "or the Devil will get you. I sent the Tatars for a priest."

"Why a priest?" He made shift to laugh and invite me down for a nuggin of mead. "Eh, what would a Cossack do with a priest?"

"Several things. Nay, I would have the last rites administered to you by the *batko*, the little father, so when your soul stands in the company of the holy angels you will not smell rank of a bribe."

This I said, knowing that his palm had been crossed with silver by the rider who raced us to Kherson, and that was why the horses were missing.

"But, worthy *sotnik*—noble handsome Captain—there is no priest in the village."

There were half a dozen of the Moskyas, with knives and clubs, but when they looked at the pistol they all began to praise me and say that they were my slaves.

"Then tell me where you have hidden the horses, if there is no priest."

They exchanged glances uneasily, and I added a word, for I did not know if the Tatars were on the right trail and time pressed.

"You will have a gift—" I looked at the first speaker—"worth many times the ruble the officer gave you, if the horses are brought back."

His eyes began to glisten with greed and he made great show of bravado, and after a moment another spoke up, saying that the horses had

been put out to pasture only half a verst away. I waited, keeping them under the muzzle of the pistol, until the Tatars galloped back with a score
of horses, many of them good and not all, judging by the looks of them,
from the post station.

Then the Moskyas jumped to harness a team to the *tarantass*, and I
picked out five ponies with Arab blood just as my officers came out. When I
was changing my saddle the chief keeper came up and asked for his gift.

"Your life," I said. "I give it you."

Before we were out of hearing that keeper shouted after us that the ensign who had come before us had said we were chiefs of the pirates from
the Dnieper, and that we would steal all the horses.

I told this to Edwards and he looked thoughtful.

"Why are you so eager to reach Kherson in haste, Uncle Ivak?" he
asked after a while.

"I had an order to take John Paul there, alive.

"True, but you press on like a horse that scents water."

So, seeing there was a new doubt in his mind, I sat back in the saddle
and told him the truth.

For ages the Cossacks had fought the Turks and all the Moslems who
came over the black water. Only a generation ago had the Russians built
a fleet strong enough to meet the armada of the Turks, and to navigate
these new men-of-war they had to engage foreign officers. Many great
ships with masts as tall as pines were in this fleet, which was stationed
near Kherson, in the narrow gulf called the Liman, or Port, at the mouth
of Father Dnieper. This Liman was near to the great river Danube also
and the Crimea.

But as yet our fleet had not fired a shot at the Turks, who were muster-
ing up their vessels-of-war and blocking it in, as dogs circle around the
lair of a tiger.

Aye, the Russian ships had been built hastily of green timber, which
was rotting so fast there was danger of the heavy guns falling through the
bottoms. And in all the crews were barely one full company—two hundred men—that knew how to work the sails and make the ships go forward against the wind. They did not go forward at all, but sat in one place
with anchors down, except the smaller craft, the galleys and double shallops, that ranged the coast and far back up the Dnieper.

These were commanded mainly by Greeks and Genoese and made
prizes of many merchant craft, honest Armenians, and some French and

English. These prizes were taken back to the Liman for examination, and they never sailed forth again. Perhaps they were kept to help the fleet, perhaps they were burned. Who knows?

The galleys of the flotilla, as the lighter squadron was called, even raided Cossack villages for supplies and carried off girls.

To all these misdeeds the commander of the Black Sea fleet could have put an end, if he willed. But he gave no orders, and his chief aide, a Greek by the name of Alexiano, plundered and snatched where he willed.

That was bad for my people, but worse was in store for us. The Turks were growing bolder and very soon they would strike at our fleet. How could our ships, which were unable to sail, beat off the Turks? Nay, the battle would be a disaster.

And that would cripple the army, which was acting in concert with the fleet. Protected by the Turkish ships-of-war, the Moslem army could advance on Kherson and the Crimea and march up the Dnieper, rolling over the villages of my people.

That was why I was eager to bring John Paul to Kherson to take command. If he were a leader of men—which remained to be seen—he might make an end of chaos and win the battle upon the sea.

"How do you know so much, old raven?" Edwards asked.

I told him that many Cossacks had volunteered to serve with the fleet and some had returned in anger to their people.

"A pretty mess, if you have told the truth." Edwards shook his head. "Egad, Ivak, surely there are skilled officers in the fleet—Grèvé and Ten Broek."

"True, Lieutenant, but they are navigating officers upon the ships with three rows of guns. The Russians and Greeks command, and the crews are a hard lot—fishermen, criminals, and soldiers, not at all easy to lead."

"Then Paul Jones is the chap to take them in hand, I warrant."

Edwards laughed and explained that once, I suppose when the American was still a pirate, he had commanded a great ship that was manned by the refuse of the French coast and a few Yankees. I did not know what Yankees were, but Edwards said they were people without a king, who chewed tobacco and fought like fiends.

Paul Jones had commanded the *Bon Homme Richard*—so the lieutenant named his ship—and had fought, with such a crew, until he overmastered an English ship, although his own vessel sank.

I do not know how true this was, but in the next days John Paul, who had discovered that I knew much of affairs in the Black Sea, questioned me through Edwards very patiently, and by the way he returned to the same things again I knew that he remembered all that was said, and it warmed my spirit like corn brandy, because he seemed to know much about ships and the ways of the sea.

Aye, we went forward joyfully. Were we not in the steppe at last, only two days' ride from Kherson? The tall grass was all around us, high as our horses' shoulders, with the yellow broom and the blue cornflowers making it gleam like a banner. Quail ran before us and the scent of clover and hay made the air sweet.

We sang and lashed at our horses, being perhaps intoxicated by long lack of sleep, a thing that makes the blood burn in the brain. We had come nine hundred miles in nine days, and we no longer thought of the plotters at Petersburg—aye, we were like blind fools.

One of the Tatars wakened me from a doze by thrusting his stirrup against my foot.

"Ivak Khan! Ivak Khan! Vultures have gathered together in a flock."

He did not mean that vultures were in the air. I saw at once what he had seen, and cried out to halt the *tarantass* and turn back.

We had come to the summit of a high knoll, and less than a verst ahead of us, down under the knoll, men were sitting with horses picketed near at hand. I counted twenty and seven, and the Tatar—who had eyes like a goshawk—said that they were armed, some having muskets. Their coats were of different colors.

They did not look like a detachment of Russian soldiers nor Cossacks, who would have chosen the knoll for a halting place. Even as the *tarantass* was being turned a man stepped out of a growth of tall hemp, a pistol shot away, between us and the waiting band. He shouted and the men by the horses stood up.

I took time to study the lay of the land before riding back after the carriage. It was ill luck that I had been asleep when we breasted the knoll or I should have gone ahead to look over before the carriage and the officers came upon the skyline. But it was good luck that the knoll should be where it was.

The highway here followed the left bank of the wide Dnieper, which was about two versts away. To reach the knoll we had passed through a network of gullies, where an arm of the river had stretched across the trail into the steppe. We had forded this water and pushed through great patches of rushes as high as the head of a mounted man.

From the summit of the hill where I was, the ford and the rushes could not be seen, because clumps of willows hid them. Where the estuary joined Father Dnieper a great raft of logs was floating lazily down the river.

My Tatars were already galloping the *tarantass* down toward the inlet, and I soon saw that they would be hidden by the trees before the riders, who had been waiting by the highway, could come up to the summit of the hill. The man who had been on watch was standing still, because I had kept to my place. If I had rushed away with the carriage he would have run up, no doubt. Skulkers are bold when backs are turned.

After observing all these things I wheeled my horse and clapped in the spurs, overtaking the carriage at the river and bidding it halt.

"What the —— are you about, Ivak? What has happened?"

Edwards, who was dozing in the carriage, had been wakened by the jolting.

"Bandits or foemen have happened," I explained quickly. "We cannot gain the last *zamora* ahead of them. Our beasts are tired and theirs are fresh. What is your will?"

"That we make a stand, Ivak. *Tsob-tsob, Tsoboe!* Hustle! Better to make a stand and greet them with bullets than rush into these infernal gullies that lead nowhere but out into your cursed steppe."

"And what does the admiral say?"

Edwards spoke to John Paul quickly and the American cast a glance around, apparently not in the least disturbed.

"He says to go down this inlet to the river. We might slip past the stand-and-deliver chaps along the river."

Now there was truth in Edwards's choice, to stand and face our pursuers, and there was more wisdom in John Paul's advice to take to the riverbank, but I had a better plan. Pulling Edwards out of the *tarantass* and calling to the Tatars who were riding the horses attached to it, I jerked the heads of the leaders to the right and lashed the beasts until they started off, dragging the carriage into the rushes toward the steppe. Meanwhile Edwards had climbed into my saddle and the Tatars and I each took a stirrup—the servant being the third rider. Then we waded into the water and began to trot off, around a bend toward the river. The bottom was hard here and we raised little mud, while the track of the carriage going in the other direction was clear as a cattle path.

All this had taken not two minutes and we were well out of sight when we heard the horses of the band splash into the ford. Although the two officers had left behind valuable baggage and clothing, they had not bickered for a second. For a moment I wondered if my suspicions were false—the band might have been vagabonds or deserters who would have left us alone for a little silver.

I thought to myself:

"When a plan is made and a path chosen, only a fool loiters to think of other paths. The outlaws will divide at the ford, some going after the wagon, some coming this way. It is better to deal with a dozen than with them all."

We pushed on around many turns, and finally went up to the edge of the rushes where the cover was still good and the footing firmer. Here we made better speed, the mounted men bending low, so their hats could not be seen. As we crossed the bare spaces, or climbed over rocks, our ears were pricked for musket shot, but none came.

Soon we began to splash through water again—even where trees stood, because Father Dnieper was in flood. Aye, we should not have known where the land ended, except that the raft came into view drifting past, just at the edge of the trees and brush where the current was not as swift as in midstream.

The *burlaks*, the watermen on the raft, were singing, sitting in the sun and smoking. The raft itself was made of fine long oak trunks bound together with ropes, about twenty logs in width and four tiers in length.

"To the left," I whispered, and the officers swung off through the trees, finding there a dry ridge of earth down which we ran, coming out again a little in advance of the raft.

"If we could get our hands on that raft," I explained to Edwards, "we could cross the Dnieper, at need, and land on the other side. See, it has three sweep oars. Our pursuers could not swim their horses across, and boats are few along here."

"But the rogues would see us on the raft."

"Aye, if God wills. But they would hit upon us before long on the shore, and they have muskets."

Edwards spoke to the American, who glanced at me keenly and nodded. He was no waster of time. The Englishman rode a bit from the trees to where he could speak with the *burlaks* without shouting. They stopped their song and took their pipes out of their lips to stare the better.

"Hola, little brothers! How much will you take for the raft?"

They stared all the more, until one with a beard shaded his eyes and, after looking over the officers, made answer:

"Health to you, serene great lords. This is fine oak, and we are taking it to the shipyard at Kherson to sell the timber to the shipwright."

"Sell it to us."

The stupid Moskya took several puffs at his pipe and shook his head.

"Pardon noble lord, but it is for the shipyard. Such fine oak—"

The skin prickled up my back with impatience, for any second we might be sighted by the riders behind. Edwards was growing red with rage when John Paul exchanged a word with him, and he sang another tune.

"How much are the logs worth, little brother?"

"We will be paid two hundred and forty copecks for them, Excellency."

"We will see that it is made into ships," Edwards promised, "and give you five hundred."

The *burlaks* looked at one another. They had broad, sunburned faces and moved clumsily, like cattle.

"That is too much," said the one with the yellow beard after a while. "God knows, Excellency, no one would pay more than two hundred and forty—"

"Plague take ye! Then two hundred and forty it is. Draw in closer and we'll come aboard."

After many delays and much laboring at the raft, which was unwieldy in the slow current, we climbed upon it and pushed off from shore far enough to be out of good musket shot but still hidden somewhat by the trees. There was a log lean-to on the raft, and into this I made the officers go with the servant and ordered the Tatars to off-saddle the horses, while I slid out of my long Cossack coat and placed it with my cap out of sight, the *burlaks* grunting like cows at our antics.

By degrees I had them steer and row the raft out into midstream, where we were in full sight from the bank but so distant that a watcher would not notice anything unusual about the raft. Although I scanned the shore and the Tatars watched the reeds and the flight of birds for suspicious movements, nothing more was seen of the bandits. And it was clear that they might have contented themselves with the plunder of the *tarantass*, yet I was uneasy, for a hidden foeman is like a snake unseen in the path.

At nightfall we ate what food was in the saddle bags, the *burlaks* sharing their fish and barley cakes with us, being only too pleased to have real coins in their belts instead of kicks and promises which they would probably have been given at Kherson. They kept at the sweeps because the current was powerful here and other craft were about. One raft, smaller than ours, kept us company, the men on it sitting by bright fires and licking up vodka until my throat ached.

One of them was a giant with a hawk's beak of a nose who sang like an angel out of paradise. They hitched their raft up to ours, to let our *burlaks* do the steering for them, and prepared to make a white night of it. *Ekh*, but it was a night, with the moon rising into a clear sky and the smell of the scorched steppe grass heavy in the wind!

The two officers listened to the singing, and once John Paul struck up a chant and all the *burlaks* kept silence until he had finished. I leaned my back against the hut and thought that presently we could land and take to horse again. But Edwards and his servants were very weary, sleeping like dogs, and we had only three horses, which were also weary.

So I listened to the wailing of an owl on shore, and the wash of the waves against the logs. We were in my country at last, and within a few hours I could round up a fine company of galliards, real fellows, and first-rate horses and escort my admiral into Kherson.

I was musing so when one of our *burlaks* gave a cry. A splash sounded, and I saw that the other one, at the sweeps, had fallen into the water. While I looked the one who had cried out turned around on his feet and sat down. He grunted softly and all at once bumped down on the logs.

The moon was behind the clouds just then, and the flickering fires on the raft behind us made the blackness over the water as if a veil had been drawn around us. When the flames rose, the two rafts were visible, and the three men who sang and danced about the fire, but the surface of Father Dnieper was all the darker.

My ears strained to catch the sounds of the night. Once more the owl wailed, and my Tatars snored, and the big *burlak* chanted with a full throat:

> "Over little Father Dnieper the cocks will crow;
> Row down little Father Dnieper in the dawn."

Ekh ma! A moment ago the two rivermen had been standing at the steering sweeps; now they were gone. Everyone else was asleep on our raft. Were they fools to sleep so? Nay, when one has climbed out of the saddle the first time in ten days for more than an hour or so, drowsiness is like a plague.

I started to crawl toward the *burlak* who lay still on the logs and just then—thuckk—came a long knife, burying its point deep into the timbers of the lean-to where my head had been. I dropped prone and grunted as the riverman had done. And out of the water a lance length from my eyes a head reared up.

A man swam silently to the raft, looked around, and thrust an arm over the logs to pull himself up. For the third time the owl hooted softly, yet it was this man who uttered the call. The next moment one of my pistols roared in his beard and he fell back like a stricken water fowl.

Now the night teemed with sound, although the song of the big *burlak* had ceased. Oars rattled in rowlocks and a long skiff entered the circle of firelight. My two Tatars and the last of the rivermen scrambled to their feet. The oars were weighed in the skiff and musket barrels gleamed. I had drawn my saber, and when another swimmer came to the edge of the raft I cut down at his head and needed not to look at him again, knowing well by the feel of the impact when a man's skull has been opened up.

Red fire flashed from the skiff, and a half-dozen muskets roared. One of the horses reared and screamed, and one of the Tatars leaped up and staggered to the edge of the raft, to throw himself into the water, having his death wound. The last *burlak* began to feel of his belly and presently groaned and fell on his knees.

Smoke eddied over the raft as John Paul and the Englishman ran out with drawn weapons. The servant must have skulked in the hut, and this did him no good. Because, led by the singer, the three rivermen on the raft that was tied to ours leaped over the gap and pressed on us with cutlasses that must have been hidden somewhere between the logs of their raft. And the skiff, bumping against our logs, disgorged a dozen foemen.

"Sarina na kitchka!"

The cry of the Dnieper pirates went up, and my last Tatar began to howl his death song, drawing a knife as he did so. One of the men from the skiff thrust a pistol close to his head and ended his life.

So we stood in the eddying smoke, three against fifteen.

The surprise had been cleverly planned. Men who knew that we were upon the raft had put out from shore in the great skiff, and two or three had taken to the water, swimming with throwing knives in their girdles. Probably they were Greeks, who are skillful at casting dirks. They had accounted for our two chaps at the sweeps, and the noise made by the oars of the skiff had been drowned by the loud song of the *burlak* with the hawk's nose.

Our foes had uttered the cry of the river pirates, yet I knew that no Dnieper pirates would think it worthwhile to tackle a timber raft. They sought us out and struck without thought of giving quarter. And they paid a heavy price for their boldness.

The big *burlak* from the other raft made straight toward John Paul with his great, curly head lowered and the muscles standing out on his bare right arm. But he found me in his path. His cutlass banged against my saber, and I saw that he held a dirk in his left hand.

At the third pass I twisted his blade aside and chopped short at his skull. He dodged like a Tatar and came at me with the dirk, his teeth gleaming. *T-phew*—what a fellow! He dropped to the logs with his throat sliced half through. The American's rapier had made a pass over my shoulder, when my guard was down, and well for me that John Paul was quick of hand.

I think they were Greeks, but the fellow who rushed at me with a pike from the skiff wore a regimental coat of some kind. Backing away to take stand against the lean-to, I glimpsed Edwards standing alone on the raft, his rapier flashing in and out, one arm in the air behind his head. The Moskya with the pike swerved toward the Englishman, and so gave me a chance to cut him down.

"Bless you for that, Uncle Ivak! The deuce! How things are warming up!"

Edwards was smiling, when a musket barked from the skiff and his left hand gripped his chest. Then I heard the roar of John Paul's pistol and saw him draw back from the smoke cloud. He tossed the pistol at two men who rushed at him, and plucked out his rapier, they giving back before its point.

He took a step toward Edwards, and we both saw the Englishman fall prone. Then John Paul glanced up and down the raft, stepping aside from a ruffian and slashing the man across the cheek as he did go.

"*Stuppai*, Ivak!" he cried.

How was I to know what he meant by that word? He slashed the tether of a horse and caught up the rein, swinging himself up to the beast's bare back as the horse obeyed the rein and sprang into the water.

I could not follow him. Men rushed at me from all sides, and caught my arms, after I had cut one open. Then something whistled in the air and all before my eyes was red. Nay, a chap does not know when he has been hit over the back of the skull. As if from far over the water, I heard Edwards shout:

"With the admiral, Ivak! To Kherson—or I'll win—wager!"

Then a faint popping sounded, which must have been men shooting at John Paul. But the red before my eyes had turned to black and I heard nothing more for a space.

IV

A Greek to his dagger, a Turk to his gold, and a Cossack to his horse.

A little is my life owing to my heavy sheepskin *kalpak* and a little to the desire of the murderers to loot before casting the bodies overboard, but much to the escape of John Paul. The raft had drifted close to the left bank of the Dnieper just before the fight, and the American had only a distance of a musket shot to swim his horse.

When the shooting failed to bring him down, the skiff was manned in haste, too late to overtake him. The few men left on the raft began to strip the coats, boots, and small gear from the fallen; after this they thrust knives into the bodies of our three rivermen, and the Tatars, and I saw them slay the servant because at that moment I began to see and hear again.

Knowing that presently they might remember me, and seek among the horses, I made shift to crawl a little, then a little more, and I crawled up the incline of logs that made the roof of the lean-to. The bandits were examining the garments they had plundered, by the glow of the fire on the other raft, and finding them poor enough, so that there was much grumbling and they did not think of me at the time. They had even snatched the clothing off their dead comrades, and were staring enviously at the Englishman's fine coat and buff boots.

Edwards seemed to be breathing, and his eyes moved. I heard them say that since one of the travelers had escaped it would be best to refrain from killing the Englishman. If the American should cause pursuit to be made, Edwards could be held as a hostage. In the end they waited for the return of the skiff and I waited for strength to come back into my limbs.

Meanwhile the raft drifted idly, nearing the shore. The moon came out and the half-light forced me to keep my head down, relying on my ears to tell me what was happening below. From the talk of the robbers several things became clear.

They had a leader, who had gone off in the skiff. And they had attacked the raft with the purpose of wiping us out. The fight we had made angered them, and I heard debate of how much more money they should ask of the leader when he came back; a strange thing, which made me suspect that he was unknown to them, and had hired their services.

"We could have done better at one of the Cossack *slobodas*," one remarked.

"Nay, we'll lighten the purse of the officer before we let him go. The Cossacks have patrols out, along the river, —— take me if they haven't. They bite, now, those dogs."

I wondered what officer they meant, and I would have given a dozen horses to hear the name of the man who was paying them for this night's work. By their talk, they were fugitive Moskya serfs, deserters from the army, Cherkessians and one or two Greeks. Edwards's fix was a bad one, but I could do nothing to help, and he had bade me follow the admiral, if possible.

"Where is that coat of that ox of a *sotnik*?" demanded one suddenly, and my ears pricked up, I assure you.

Another said that I must have crawled into the water, like the Tatar, and they began to argue again until someone found my saber and they cursed me for the evil I had worked among them.

"Search the raft for the dog," a voice suggested.

I heard boots cluttering over the logs, and my skin began to itch as if a thousand ants were crawling over it. Then the sound of oars came over the water, followed by a low-pitched hail.

The skiff had come near again, and the men on the raft were ordered to head in to shore and land everything from the raft. After that they were to hack loose the fastenings and set the logs adrift, loose in the current.

As the raft was worked in closer to the shore and the skiff, talk between the men of the band made it clear that John Paul had not been caught. He had reached the highway and headed south, with several in pursuit of him, one of the four being the leader of the band.

By the time the raft grounded in a shallow cove, the moon was low. Most of the men busied themselves in carrying Edwards ashore and he cursed them heartily when they jerked him, so I knew that he could not be very badly hurt. One or two of them had poked about a bit for me, but had not thought to look on the top of the hut.

The nearest searcher went to untie the remaining horse—one had been slain by a bullet—and I heard him say:

"His Excellency will be well content with this affair of ours if we bag the American. If our officer fails to run him down, bless us, we'll be flayed alive."

The threat sounded somewhat familiar to me, but just then I was sliding down the incline of the log roof. My boots struck squarely on the back of the man who was edging the horse past the lean-to, and he shot into the water so swiftly that I failed to grasp his saber. The horse reared, but being uncertain of the footing did not run.

"What are you about, Pietr?" voices demanded from the shore.

"It was the dog of a *sotnik*," I responded, growling, and waiting for the flood of pain caused by the shock to ebb out of my skull, while I gripped the rein of the horse.

"Have you his coat—had he any money? Hola, Pietr! What—"

The one called Pietr began to bellow from the water into which he had fallen and I climbed to the back of the horse, then reined it around the hut. It jumped to the shore quickly enough, and by the time the robbers, who were scattered all around, had gripped their weapons we were trotting away through the trees. They ran after for a space and several pistols barked. The balls whistled wide through the branches overhead and stirred up the pony to a smart gallop.

No one gave chase because there was no other horse on the raft.

In this fashion did I win free of the Dnieper outlaws, though Edwards remained a prisoner in their hands.

In the black murk that comes before dawn, I drew up at the first post station on the highway not far to the south of where the raft had landed. Here I changed horses and I wet my gullet with some vodka, taking likewise a saber from the keeper, who swore that no other riders had stopped at the *zamora* during the last half of the night. He said he thought horses had passed by, not far away, but had fancied them wild horses, out on the steppe.

This surprised me, until as the nag settled down to steady gallop, I remembered that John Paul was in a strange country, knowing no word of the language. How was he to explain matters to a clown of a *zamora* keeper, even if he had not been closely pressed?

Likewise the outlaws had not cared to delay to try to steal fresh mounts from the station. True, John Paul might have headed out into the steppe and avoided pursuit in the dark. I should have done so. But he did not know friend from foe, and doubtless chose to take his chances in a straight-away race along the road, aware that he was within day's ride of the Russian lines.

Behind me a line of red light spread along the horizon and a wind began to breathe over the plain. Birds chirped and the sea of grass changed from gray to red-and-gold, then to brown. It glittered with the dew as if decked out in jewels. My head pained me, but such a dawn warmed my veins more than the vodka. —— take it all, there's no country like the steppe!

My head began to buzz all of a sudden and weakness came upon me so that I, Ivak the *jighit*, the outrider, the Tatar-chaser, the *sotnik*, gripped the saddle horn to keep from falling. Such a shame!

By and by the buzzing stopped and I looked around, seeing the sun peering over the horizon, and a black-browed Cossack lass staring at me from the back of a cow.

She was taking cattle to pasture, and by a line of great stones shaped like skulls along the highway I knew that one of the villages of my people lay half a verst away. My horse, a big black Turani that knew a thing or two, had slowed to a walk and its ears were pricked back as if asking why in the fiend's name I was rocking the saddle like a cradle.

The maid was round-eyed as if I were a ghost out of one of the old burial mounds that lie on the steppe under those great stones. God knows what people sleep in those mounds, but it is quite true that of nights they rise up and slip about—ghosts sure enough. To mend my dignity I called to her smartly and bade her be off to the village to round up a band of the galliards, the bravest fellows and the *jighits*, and send them after my tracks.

"Aye, Uncle," she responded, "but your scalp lock is running blood—"

"Little sparrow," I grunted, "what are a few drops of blood to a chap who rode from Petersburg in ten days? Nothing at all! I'll fetch you a bag of candy from Kherson if you stir your legs. Hold! Did an officer ride past in a blue coat on a roan with one white foreleg?"

"Aye, Uncle. Two gentlemen, they were, riding a musket shot apart. One was a foreigner, the other a Russian with a wig and a red face, taller than I am."

She sped away toward the village, her white legs flashing under her tunic, and I spurred up the Turani, cursing my broken head. By the girl's words I recognized the officer who had been riding before us all the way.

Now he was behind John Paul, and we knew what sort of cock he was. The leader of the outlaws, the officer who had bribed the *zamora* keeper and hired the pirates. That's what!

We sped over the level trail like a hawk and presently two riders showed up, above the grass ahead. They pulled in when they heard the Turani and faced about.

Drawing their blades they took stand, stirrup to stirrup, closing the narrow way, and their horses were nearly blown. By their bearing they were outlaws of the band, and their jaws dropped when they saw my face. Afterward I remembered that they must have thought me dead, and when the big black rushed on them in the eye of the rising sun they believed a bloody specter had come up out of Father Dnieper to settle their hash.

I spurred on the Turani instead of pulling him in, and stood up in the saddle just as we came upon the two. By feinting a slash at one I made him throw up his saber to guard his head. Then, leaning down as the three ponies came together, I cut at the other's neck, getting home over his blade. His mount reared and shelled him out of the saddle like a pea out of a pod.

His mate had raked my shoulder blades with a slash that was too late to cut deep. Twisting the big black around, I crowded the outlaw as he was turning. He warded desperately with his sticker, leaning back to do so when he should have spurred his nag clear.

The shoulder of the Turani struck his pony and the man lost his stirrups, falling to earth like a clown. Such riders! I had not a moment to lose, and so kept the black dancing around the outlaw.

"Speak up, you dog!" I cried at him. "Where is your officer and the American?"

"Only a little span ahead, noble sir! Truly, it is all our officer's doing! He came to us with papers from the government, promising many things if we would rub out—*Ai-a*, spare a poor chap, noble lord!"

I hastened on, wasting no more time on the outlaw. And in no time at all I heard the music of steel kissing steel. Eh, a great fear came upon me that John Paul was being sliced by the leader of the dog company.

But when I rode up to them, only two men were to be seen where the trail dipped through a hollow. Two ponies were standing riderless, with heaving flanks and spraddled legs, foundered. And in a spot where the grass was short John Paul made play with his rapier, and his antagonist was Strelsky the ensign.

Swift hope flashed into Strelsky's red face as I trotted up, until he saw out of the corner of his eye that Ivak had come instead of his two murderers. John Paul motioned me away with his free hand and I drew rein to watch.

Strelsky was the prettier sword of the two by odds. But the American had an arm like a wrestler and an eye like a wolf. He did not seem tired in the least. His brow was placid though his black eyes darted fire. Until I looked him over I had felt that it was folly to let him risk a stab when the Turani could have ridden Strelsky down.

By then the Russian knew that his men would not come up, and his face showed strain; moreover he kept trying to watch me, trusting in his greater skill to keep John Paul's blade in play. So it happened that the point of the American's rapier pricked his cheek and drew blood. It angered the ensign and he began to attack, making many feints that pulled John Paul's guard aside, but failing to get home. A second time his cheek was raked, a piece of flesh falling out.

Then Strelsky lunged fiercely at the throat and John Paul parried just in time, making a swift ripost that caught the Russian's blade under his. The American stiffened his wrist and Strelsky tried desperately to disengage, but suffered a deep cut over the eyes. Blood ran down into his eyes and he stood helpless.

John Paul stepped back and lowered his point, while the Russian cursed and gripped his sword, expecting to be spitted at once. His face was scarred for life, if he lived. This pleased me because Strelsky was not a fellow to love. He wore the uniform of the Empress, but he had given me an order that held treachery in it.

The American was a foreigner, yet, after the fight on the raft, my heart warmed to him. He could stand his ground and take blows, and he kept his hand up even though the Russians for some reason had schemed to take his life on the journey, though this he did not know as yet.

Some words he spoke to Strelsky, and the ensign answered slowly, clearing the blood out of his eyes as he did so. I caught the name Edwards and the words "the prince." Whatever passed between them, it enlightened John Paul, because he sheathed his rapier and looked at Strelsky as if a snake had come up out of the ground. I think the ensign told much truth, being fearful of his life. Then Paul Jones pointed out over the steppe and said in French:

"Va t'en!"

And Strelsky turned away, after dropping his sword. At the edge of the hollow he began to run, and though I called a barbed word after him he did not halt again. It angered me to see him go free even in such a state. But from this time forward John Paul took advice from no man. Indeed, how was I to consult with him?

Why did I stand aside, to remain with him when Strelsky went off? An order had been given me and the order was to conduct John Paul safe into Kherson.

He looked me over and smiled approval, then said—

"Edwards?"

By signs I tried to make clear that the lieutenant was slightly wounded and in the hands of the outlaws. He seemed to understand, and thought for a while until there was a great pounding of hoofs and a dozen Cossack lads came up, reining in on top of us and staring at the admiral, who looked them over with interest.

Eh, I was glad to see them. The sight of several kites hovering over the tall grass where Strelsky had disappeared did not displease me, either. He was something like a vulture himself.

V

On land a coward can show you his heels, but on a ship even Satan himself cannot run away.

My brothers, have you ever called to you a *borzoi*, a wolfhound, keeping one hand behind your back the while? If the dog does not know you, he will not come. Not until he sees that the hand behind your back does not hold a stick.

Men are greater fools than dogs. They will go forward even when they see the stick that is going to beat their brains out. So it was with John Paul, and so it was with me.

For days after the duel I lay on my back in a hut of my village, while my head mended, the American having gone on to Kherson with my mates. Soon they came straggling back, very angry, some drunk and others bloody. Most of them did not return at all, having been impressed by the Russians, John Paul knowing nothing about it.

They talked with me, and other fellows came who had served in the fleet, bringing with them a Tatar *hakim* from over the border who brewed herbs that made a new man of me. The Russians' surgeons are good for nothing but to cut off limbs, and of what use to a man is a leg that has been cut off?

The men who returned from Kherson said that John Paul had been given a banquet by the field marshal in command of the army, but did not appear content. He had asked after old Ivak, which gratified me. My Cossacks said in the taverns of Kherson it was rumored that the admiral would never hoist his flag on the big ship-of-war that was called the flagship. This vessel was commanded by a Greek, Alexiano, who held the rank of brigadier.

Alexiano, they said, was a loud talker and a quiet doer. He held great feasts and many served him, lording it up and down the mouth of the Dnieper and carrying off whatever merchandise struck their fancy. So the Cossacks had formed patrols to check the raids of the seamen under Alexiano, and the Greek hung some of our boys for taking up arms against the Empress as he said.

The Turks, seeing the plundering and the lack of order in the fleet, were growing both covetous and bold. They had moved up the gulf to within two cannon shot of our fleet, which was unfit for battle. And rumors in the taverns said that John Paul meant to go out to the *Vladimir*, the flagship, and take command the next day, Alexiano notwithstanding.

The Greek would not kiss him on both cheeks you may be sure, because the coming of the American would mean the end of the secret pillaging and piracy of the men under Alexiano, in which pillaging he shared. My Cossacks said that John Paul had insisted on the punishment of the pirates who had attacked us, but no guard ship had gone up the Dnieper and no news of Edwards had come down.

"My children," I boasted, "when this American hoists his flag on the *Vladimir* he will make Alexiano pull at a rope, and the whole fleet will be whipped into shape. He is well fitted to command."

"Impossible, Uncle Ivak!" they said, several at once.

"How, impossible?"

"Because the man at the head of the fleet has sworn that he will not yield place to the American."

"Do you mean Alexiano, the pirate?"

"Not at all, Uncle. We mean the present commander, who is a Prussian prince and a very high officer."

I pricked up my ears as they explained how the Empress had appointed one of her favorites, the Prince of Nassau-Siegen, to command, not two years ago. Alexiano served only as chief of the *Vladimir*, but had charge of the fleet during the winter, while Nassau-Siegen was in Petersburg.

"Tell me," I demanded, "has this princeling a pock-marked face and full lips and eyes like a fish?"

"It is he! You have seen him, Uncle Ivak."

"Then saddle up the best horse in the village."

I rose up and pulled on my boots and coat, taking tobacco and a pipe from the nearest man and a sword from him who had the likeliest weapon. They protested, saying that they had never done me any ill.

"Would you have your *kunak*, your comrade, the first *jighit* of the village, ride to the fleet dressed like a Jew?"

Then they protested all the more, saying that Alexiano had heard of my deeds when I rubbed out half a dozen of the pirates, who were his men, on the Dnieper. He would string me up, they said, and they would not see their things again.

"Is this Prince Nassau-Siegen friendly with Alexiano?" I asked.

"As God lives, they are like two brothers! They share gold together, and they have not been parted since the Prussian rejoined the fleet, two days ago."

"Is Nassau-Siegen a good leader, liked by all the men?"

"Nay, Ivak. You have been away too long, wooing the Russian maids! Nassau-Siegen is a courtier, and, save for Alexiano's bands, the men of the fleet would not follow him if he had gold pieces sewn on his breeches. It is said that he pays gold to the Turks, to let the fleet sit in peace where it is. Meanwhile he crows like a cock, claiming honor for holding off the Turks."

By the time I had mounted and left the village behind, the last of the smoke that had hidden the fire I smelled in Petersburg had cleared away. I saw all things as they were. I saw a fleet that was only timber and cloth, unfit for battle; I saw two renegades at the head of it, enriching themselves by plunder and paying a part of the plunder to the accursed Moslems, while the Empress thought they were playing the part of valiant men in the face of the foe.

And I thought that such men would never let the American take over the command from them.

I meant to reach him and warn him, and perhaps take him back to the Cossack villages. Who knows?

Just a little I went out of my way to pass through the streets of Kherson, so winning my wager from Edwards, poor fellow. The horse was a good one and we left the shipyards behind us swiftly enough, coming at last to the salt-streaked shores of the gulf and the forest of masts that stood out on the gray water.

Among the soldiers and caravaneers of the alleys I asked for news of the American admiral, learning then that I was almost too late.

John Paul was on one of the jetties with another cavalier, making ready to put off in a barge to the *Vladimir*. I hurried along the waterfront, catching sight of the barge presently, and, giving my horse to the care of a Cossack who was fishing on the jetty, went out to greet my friend.

When he saw me his face lighted up and he said something to the other officer, who stared at me curiously. There we stood, with so much that should be said between us, and only one word that we both understood! I bowed several times, trying to think of some way to warn him. He ordered a valise to be carried into the barge and took farewell of the other officer, who was most polite.

My tongue burned in my throat, and I nearly tore my hair to think up some scheme. He stood with one foot on the log at the edge of the jetty and glanced at me inquiringly. How could I take an admiral by the arm and lead him to a tavern to talk? How could I make signs before the throng that his life was in danger?

John Paul spoke to the cavalier, who turned to me indifferently.

"Cossack," he said in bad Russian, "his Excellency is pleased to praise you and ask if you have a request to make. He says that he will grant it."

"I would go with him on the ship." I bowed to the girdle. "If it pleases your Honor."

The barge went out to a high ship with two rows of cannon and we climbed up the ladder to the deck, I carrying John Paul's valise, and swaggering a bit, for the deck was cluttered with groups of men who stared at us and whispered. An under-officer who wore a rapier stood by the ladder with a squad of sailors, also armed, and saluted. After that he went away quickly with his men and left the American alone. John Paul glanced up at a mast where Alexiano's flag hung idly, there being no wind. Then he gave an order to the bargemen and they made fast to the foot of the ladder a light *saick*, a skiff having one pair of oars, that we had towed behind us from the jetty. After this they rowed away in the barge and John Paul walked slowly to the afterdeck.

It needed no sailor to tell me that his reception was lacking in respect; Alexiano, who stood on the afterdeck, should have greeted him and his flag should have been hoisted instead of the Greek's. As John Paul climbed the steps at the rump of the ship, Alexiano turned his back and said something amusing to a man who leaned on a small cannon. This man, in gray and gold, was the prince, Nassau, and he had promised to flay me alive if John Paul reached Kherson.

Nassau picked up in his fingers a little round piece of glass and looked at me, then at the American, and laughed softly at the jest Alexiano had made. John Paul halted a few paces from the pair, his shoulders squared.

Calling to him the under-officer with the rapier, he drew a letter from his coat and passed it to the Russian, who bowed and gave it to Nassau. The prince bowed and handed it back without reading it. Alexiano, a bull of a man with a fine curly beard, watched Nassau as a dog watches its master. And every man of the crew watched the three on the afterdeck. Still John Paul made pretense that nothing out of the usual was happening. He talked with Nassau in French, and the prince, who had tried to buy the American's death, was most polite. That is the way of the Muscovites and the Prussian nobles.

But Nassau found time to speak aside with the under-officer, who presently whispered to a Greek with a handkerchief bound over his hair. This chap, who had some rank on the ship, called to him two others who advanced on me with scowls.

"*Hai*, dog of a Cossack," one grunted, "your *saick* waits for you. Get off the deck or we will pitch you overside!"

I grinned at him, seeing that he meant to provoke a fight, and his mate jostled me. When I reached for my sword the two drew knives and opened their mouths to shout. Instead, the under-officer on the afterdeck shouted—

"Form in ranks for inspection!"

John Paul had been watching us, and he it was who gave the order in the first place. Nassau shrugged indifferently, though Alexiano grew red with rage and kept muttering under his breath. He grew angrier when it became clear that the men did not know how to form ranks. Like cows, they trampled here and there, looking all around, until the officers who came on deck began to curse.

Finally they were drawn up in strange fashion: the Greeks crowded in with the Greeks and the Syrians and —— knows what else, besides scores of Moskya fishermen. On the other side of the ship under a Russian officer about a hundred of the true faith drew up, among them quite a few Cossacks, and I took stand behind them, up against the rampart of the ship. John Paul, accompanied by the under-officer, who translated his orders and answered his questions, went down the front of each rank, looking every man in the face. Nor did he show any disapproval.

From the men he turned to the deck, where cannonballs were in heaps and ropes in a fine tangle. Everything he pulled toward him, looking at it closely, the sails and the cannon especially. The mob on the deck saw that he knew what he was about, and fell to watching him instead of the officers on the rump of the ship, who had their heads together around Alexiano.

It was nearly dark when he ended the formation. Without taking any more notice of Nassau or Alexiano he nodded to me, and the interpreter bade me haul the skiff on deck, and select some Cossack carpenters for work. A half-dozen chaps stepped forward at once and hoisted the *saick* over the rampart of the *Vladimir*.

Then Paul Jones had some rags brought and these we wrapped around the middle of the oars as he bade us. A board was cut for a rudder, and a broken pike staff fitted to it for a tiller, the rudder being rigged to the back end of the *saick*.

When this was done he ordered us to go and get supper, which was being brought up, the men crowding around the pots without order. One of the Cossacks nudged me while I was dipping out the gruel.

"Eh, Ivak, better slip over the side before dark, if you don't want Greek steel between your ribs."

I laughed at him and began to eat.

"It's true," he went on under his breath. "They have marked you down, Uncle."

"And the admiral?" I asked. "What of him?"

"They say he is a foreigner who cannot speak our tongue, and a pirate who would sell us as slaves to the Turks."

"They say lies, little brother. Nassau would glean gold out of you and leave you for the Moslems to slit up."

He looked around fearfully and began to scratch his head, saying that such words would earn me a lashing. Was not Nassau a great officer who kept the Turks away because they feared him? Rumors had been heard that the officers of the *Vladimir* were in league with Alexiano to refuse to serve under the American. Nassau had said that he was a coward who would not make war, save on merchantmen, and Alexiano said that Nassau had a commission to share the command of the fleet with John Paul.

Now John Paul had been promised sole command, I knew, and it is an evil thing when an army has two leaders. Two oxen hauling a cart go forward swifter than one, but two leaders cannot make plans like one, and the end is disaster.

"Of the two, Nassau is the coward," I made response, judging that a man who would pay to have another slain does not love danger himself, however boldly he may bear himself.

"Then let the American prove himself," the Cossack grunted. "Each is in command at present and how do we know which to obey?"

"Before midnight little brother," I promised, "one or the other will take the leadership! Watch!"

It was safe to prophesy, knowing how little the two loved each other. But I feared for John Paul, who did not know that Nassau had conspired against him, and who could not summon up Alexiano and the Greeks to his aid. Every word he spoke must be translated, and how was he to be sure that his words were not twisted? As long as I was alive Nassau would try by every means to do away with John Paul for fear that the plot against the American would be known.

Why did I not speak out? Nay, who would listen? And it is not by threats and tale bearing that a leader's nature is made clear to all men. The crew of the *Vladimir* were restless because the Turkish fleet had drawn up to within striking distance, and no orders to make ready for battle had been issued. They grumbled at John Paul because he had made them stand long in ranks, but they became curious when the American, instead of going to the officers' table, ate dinner with the men on deck. Then he ordered a double allowance of spirits issued, when the ship's lanthorns were lighted.

While he sat among us a Cossack began one of our songs, and the American bade us all sing. It was sad, that song of our steppe, and he sat silent, chin on hand, seemingly thinking of nothing at all. Once I thought I saw his eyes glitter with tears, which was no shame in a man far from his own country.

But the men of the *Vladimir* all saw that John Paul cared nothing for what Alexiano and Nassau might be doing; and we soon perceived that the high officers had come on deck to see what John Paul was doing. Night had fallen and a thin mist hung over the water of the narrow gulf. Out at the mouth of the gulf gleamed the small lights of the Moslem fleet, off one of their forts, where they hemmed us in, since the mouth of the gulf, which was the only way to the sea, was narrow as a cannon shot.

Eh, it was a sad thing that happened on the *Vladimir*: scores of men ranged against one, who did not understand them. Two plotters against a hero of other wars who did not know how to plot. And yet, no other man was like John Paul. The proof of it was that all eyes on the ship watched him, even when Nassau took to striding up and down the deck near us.

Meanwhile the under-officer—he of the rapier—came and whispered in my ear. "When you are challenged, pretend to be bringing supplies to the enemy. Ask for the countersign. The admiral wishes to learn it. And Christ receive your spirit!" he added under his breath.

"At command," I replied promptly, not wishing him to see that the American's instructions were a perfect riddle to me.

John Paul drew out his watch, looked at it, then at the sky, and the lights of the Turkish frigates. Then he spoke to Nassau, who turned as if a bee had stung him. Long afterward I learned that John Paul had said that they would set out on a reconnoiter of the enemy's fleet!

Nassau, too surprised to be cautious, refused point blank when he learned that John Paul planned to go in among the enemy, but the American responded that neither Nassau nor Alexiano had any knowledge of the enemy's vessels at close hand, and this was necessary if a battle was to be fought.

"What a notion!" exclaimed the prince in Russian. "We can send an officer."

"I am going," said John Paul quietly to the interpreter, "and if Nassau is not afraid he will come, too."

By the light of the yellow lanthorn, Nassau's pocked face grew sallow and he bit his lips. He was trapped, and there was no way out because the American shared the risk he ran. Then his face changed and he said he would go.

In that moment I knew Nassau was a coward, and all the more dangerous because of that. Some plan had come into his head, when he agreed to go. John Paul turned to me.

"*Stuppai*, Ivak," he said. "Forward!"

How did he know I would understand his meaning? Nay, he could not have known. But God gave me eyes of the mind to see the truth and I lowered the *saick* with the help of my comrades, climbing down the ladder and taking the oars as soon as it was in the water.

Nassau swore—I could hear him—when he realized what sort of craft was waiting for him. But John Paul stood at the ladder top, and smiled, mockingly. An hour ago the American had been a man of honey; now he was a man of stone. The prince came down the ladder, and plumped down into the stern of the little skiff. John Paul made him climb over me to the prow where the Prussian sat, wedged like a fish between the sides of the boat. Then the admiral took the tiller and I the oars, so that the lights of the *Vladimir* began to grow smaller. We steered toward the fleet of the Turks, which could not be seen because the light mist hung over the surface of the water—enough to obscure the stars.

The oars made no sound except a little drip, being wrapped with rags where they rubbed on the gunwale. I rowed on, watching the outline of John Paul's head and the glitter of his eyes, until he held up one hand and I raised the oars. He stretched his head to one side and shut his eyes, listening like a horse in the steppe when a wild beast is rustling the grass near at hand.

Presently I, too, heard the rasping of oars, coming up behind us from where the *Vladimir* lay. The oars were being moved swiftly and, by the catch in his breath, I knew that Nassau had become aware of this other boat that was following us. Perhaps he had been listening for it, so quiet he was.

Motioning to me to row on, John Paul turned the tiller, sending the skiff to one side, out toward the main channel. The men in the boat behind could not hear us and we would have slipped away if Nassau had not called out clearly—

"To the left!"

As he spoke the words, John Paul swung the tiller sharp to the other side. The little skiff dodged like a flying fish, and made a circle until we were speeding in the other direction. Several long strokes I took, then lifted the oars and glided silently. Aye, we could hear the oars of the other boat pulling like mad for the place we had left.

John Paul leaned forward and whispered across my shoulder in French. I do not know what he said, but Nassau did not cry out again. We sat still until the boat from the *Vladimir* could be heard no longer. *T-phew!* We were trapped! Because now we heard other oars, coming from the Turkish side—some patrol boat making its rounds. If we went on we would run into the accursed Moslems; if we turned back, there was the *Vladimir*'s barge in waiting like a tiger.

Nassau must have ordered it to follow us. Perhaps he planned to go from the skiff into the barge and fire a volley at us—claiming afterward that a mistake had been made in the dark; perhaps he would start up a quarrel and throw us out for the fish or the Turks to find. I do not know.

But John Paul sat still, and I crossed myself, breathing a prayer to the Father and the Son. It happened that the boat from the Moslem fleet passed us by, the wash from it rocking our skiff, and went elsewhere, though for a long time I listened to the creak of its twelve pairs of oars and the American did likewise, for he often turned his head and bent down toward the water where the sound was clearest.

We rowed again and now Nassau began to protest in a low voice, without receiving an answer. By and by he stopped because the lights of the enemy's craft showed ahead of us. Still we went on, John Paul turning the tiller this way and that, making the skiff wind in and out among the vessels. They were galleys and gunboats for the most part and there were many of them.

Their masts stood up like a forest, and by the time we had reached the last one inshore the night had grown a little brighter. The mist cleared and the stars shone down on us. I heard Tatars talking together in the waist of the last galley, and someone playing upon a fiddle. They had good eyes those Tatars because presently they hailed us, asking for vodka. Nassau repeated the words to John Paul, who went closer, until the sheer of the stem was nearly over us.

He tossed up a flask that he carried and someone caught it.

"Allah reward the giver! Are you going to the captain-pasha with an order?"

I could hear Nassau breathing heavily, but John Paul made not a sound. He waited patiently and God put into my head the words of his command spoken on the *Vladimir*: *Ask for the countersign—the admiral wishes to learn it.*

"Nay," I made response boldly in their tongue, "we are taking salt to the ship of the captain-pasha."

"But do you know the countersign?"

So far I was following the right path; if I had said we were carrying dispatches they would have expected us to know the password. I began to grunt like a *burlak*.

"How could we know it? We came from the island."

If I had asked for it they would have felt suspicion. It had not come into their heads that any but friends of the Turks would be here; yet a small stone may make a man stumble.

"The Turks might send bullets through you," they said.

"The ——! Then tell us the countersign, so we will not have the bullets."

They talked among themselves, and the vodka gurgled. My throat was beginning to dry up when one flung out careless—

"*Stamboul!*"

"*Stamboul!*" I repeated, to make certain, and Paul Jones said one word, the one he always spoke—

"Forward."

I thought he meant to go back, but he steered forward and we went on, passing close, under the ramparts of the great Turkish fort so that we could see the dark patches which were embrasures for cannon. For the last time doubt of John Paul assailed me, and I thought:

"May the dogs eat me! Does he mean to turn over Nassau to the Turks? Is this American playing a double game, after all?"

Nassau's teeth were clicking together, but he dared not say a word for fear of being overheard by the sentries who were visible, when they moved, against the stars.

A great mass towered up over us. This was the Turkish flagship, the one of seventy guns, and as we rounded its prow we saw many lights in the rump of it, and small craft clustered around the ladder. Officers were passing about on the deck, and all was stir and bustle.

"What boat is that? Give the countersign!" a voice hailed us at once.

"*Stamboul!*" responded John Paul without hesitation.

"What are you about?"

"We are Tatars from the galley," I said, not daring to take time to think. "We came to look at the flagship and the officers."

"May dogs litter on your graves! Don't you skulkers know that all men who stray from their ships are to be shot? The dawn of the day after the morrow the whole fleet advances against the unbelievers."

The sentries on the ship cursed us again, and perhaps they would have loosed muskets at us but refrained for fear of bringing out the officers who were shut up in the after cabins, debating together. We rowed away then and John Paul steered the skiff for quite a while to one side until the oars caught in seaweed and the gleam of phosphorescent salt was to be seen, flickering along the shore. That is what the Russians call it, but we Cossacks know that it is the spirits of the drowned running along the edge of the waves seeking a resting place.

No fort or house was near, and after John Paul had listened a little he made me change places with him. Then he began to speak to Nassau in a low voice.

The prince sprang to his feet and answered vehemently, laughing without any merriment at all. Then he peered at the American, who had begun to take off his coat.

"*Sotnik!*" Nassau cried, at me. "This foreigner is mad—no doubt of it. After leading me though all the Turkish fleet he threatens me with a duel in a boat. Help me disarm him—seize him from behind."

I caught my breath and stared at the two officers.

"Why should his Excellency, the admiral, wish to fight with your honor?" I asked. "Nay, it is some jest."

This I said to dig out truth behind Nassau's words, for he was a skilled liar. Yet the natures of men appear unmasked in a moment of danger, and the prince was no longer the same officer who sat in Strelsky's room not long ago. His nerves were quivering after the ride through the fleet of the enemy.

"The admiral swears that I have plotted against his honor; he accuses me of hiring men to waylay him. As God is holy, *sotnik*—"

Nassau stopped, suddenly remembering who I was, and what he had wanted me to do. Strelsky must have confessed the whole affair to John Paul, to shield himself a little; but Nassau believed of course that I had told John Paul of the plot.

"This mad American," he went on while John rolled up his right sleeve, "accuses me of holding Lieutenant Edwards prisoner. What do I know about that? He demands that the Englishman be given back to him. Aid me, Cossack, and a purse of a thousand rubles is yours—nay, ask what you will!"

When he heard me laugh he knew that I would not aid him. Once he glanced at the shore, as if thinking of flight; but the Turks were all around. The soft gleam of the shining salt crust looked like the teeth of a great mouth, open to swallow a man. *Ekh,* the skin crawled up and down my back!

A little breeze made the boat rock in the scum of seaweed, as if the hands of the dead were reaching up at us. John Paul kept his balance easily, his feet wide apart, the rapier poised in his hand. As I live, not a lance length separated the two, although Nassau had drawn back far into the prow. All at once the prince cursed fiercely and whipped out his blade, thrusting up from the hip like a flash.

He gave no word and no salute, and such was a coward's stroke. Yet John Paul had good eyes and parried. The glow of the stars and the shimmering of the salt made the rapiers visible as they clashed and twisted and ground together, while Nassau panted.

Ekh! That was swordplay! Steel in the dark; blade feeling blade; eye peering into eye; arm straining against arm! The blood boiled in my veins and I was young again. For Nassau was no mean swordsman; nay, a fine hand with the weapon had he, quick and wary and merciless. Neither could draw back. Twice the hilts clashed together, as if the rapiers had been sabers.

Once, John Paul staggered and the skiff swayed. Nassau laughed grimly in triumph, until John Paul caught himself and warded a thrust at the throat, forcing the prince's blade up—up if as if it been an eagle's feather. Eye glared into eye while the blades were locked, and suddenly the American took a step forward.

A great cry came out of Nassau's strained throat and he tumbled out of the skiff into the floating seaweed. I stood up in readiness to leap after him or not—judging him badly wounded—as John Paul should command. He gave no command, but after a moment reached down and caught at something beneath the tangle of weed. It was the arm of the prince that he hauled into the skiff, and after it the body.

He let Nassau lie in the bottom of the boat and presently the injured man began to choke, writhing as if a hundred fiends were in him. He belched out salt water and soon—though it was hard to believe—I heard him whimpering and snuffling like a girl.

I have said that John Paul could be a man of stone. He made no move to staunch Nassau's wound, but sat down in the stern and took the tiller, motioning for me to row back. He steered through the ships of the Turks and found the lights of the *Vladimir* again. Still he paid no heed to Nassau, who lay between my legs, often bumped, of necessity, by the oar ends, and shivering, as I could feel.

Flares were lighted as we pulled up to the ladder. John Paul, having donned his coat again, walked up to the deck and was greeted by many officers who stared at him curiously. But they stared more at Nassau, who came up on my arm. His gray-and-gold coat was green with slime; his sword and hat were missing and his wig was somewhere back on the beach for the Turks to wonder at.

He was able to stand, and I saw no blood flowing at any place. Nay, it was long before I understood the truth. *Nassau was not hurt.* Not in the flesh, not by steel. But his spirit had suffered; something within him had given way that night. He walked to his cabin, speaking to no man.

So it happened that John Paul gave order to hoist his admiral's flag, and though Alexiano grumbled, it was done as he commanded. Then he stood before the officers and spoke, and afterward I asked one of the Russians what he had said. He had told them that the Turkish fleet would advance within hours, and that he would hold a council of the ships' officers in the fleet.

Still Nassau issued no word, and after a while it was clear even to Alexiano that John Paul was in command. He was given a cabin, and, their nature being such, the Russians thronged into it with many compliments and questions on their tongues. Nay, John Paul sent out all except old Ivak. When we were alone and the door shut he sat down in a chair, his cheeks pallid and his eyes burning. With one arm he tried to draw off his coat, until I sprang to his aid and saw for the first time that he was wounded in the upper chest near the armpit. The blood had run down under the coat where it was hidden and had not yet soaked through his breeches.

Together we bound it up, after washing out the hole where Nassau's weapon had entered. The bleeding was all outward and I saw that the American meant to conceal it, because when the bandage was in place he grinned at me and closed one eye—so!

And that, my brothers, is how old Ivak brought an admiral to the Russian fleet. Aye, he was a man, that Pavel, as I like to name him. Deuce take it, he was my *kunak*, my comrade, a galliard.

What of the battle? Nay, that tale is told by others; how John Paul scattered the Turks and burned their ships and how ill the Russians rewarded him. Am I one to read what men have written in books? I brought a leader to men who lacked a leader, and what honor had I thereby?

One gift was given me. Behold, my brothers, this Damascus dagger, with the gold inlay in the hilt and the writing in jewels. I have been told what that writing says:

Pavel to his friend, the Cossack Ivak.

Who would not be content with such a gift?

The Sword of Honor

Chapter I

For they'll harken to such a man through all the swish and the sweat,
Through rattle and rumpus and raps, and the kicks and cuffs that they get—
Through the chatter and tread, and the rudder's wash, and the dismal clank
Of the shameful chain which forever binds the slave to the bank.

Big Pierre was the last man to leave the bark, except the apprentice lad and the master. Lowering himself by the mizzen chains, he dropped to the river and struck with a resounding smack. He was all of a hundred and ninety pounds of bone and sinew, and he had landed on solid ice.

There was a ladder running from the waist of the bark, but Big Pierre was in a hurry. For one thing, three silver crowns jingled in his pouch, faintly but cheerfully—and he meant to set about the spending of them as quickly as possible. It had taken him a half hour to pry the silver coins out of the master of the bark, who was a Hollander; so the other members of the crew had gone ahead to seek out the taverns of St. Petersburg.

"—— him for a Dutch dog," muttered the sailor, "who would drink till cockcrow on copper copecks. *Bon sang*, but it is cold!" He turned his back on the wind that cut through his wool jerkin and short jacket. His greased boots and leather cap were Dutch, but Pierre Pillon was a son of Provence to the core, and he swayed across the slippery ice of the Neva as if it were the wet foredeck of a ship.

Little did he relish the cold breath of the northern seas; he had the swarthy skin and black mustache of the men of Toulon, who live under a blazing sun. His long hair, clubbed with a ribbon at the nape, was yellow as ripe wheat.

His wide, sloping shoulders and corded arms were shaped for strength.

His hands were noticeable, being scarred and hooked and swollen. The Dutch skipper had looked at those hands when he paid over the silver, thinking that with them Big Pierre might tear a man's throat out.

At Toulon six months ago Pierre Pillon had shipped on the bark that was bound for Muscovy with wines and hemp. In that autumn of 1787 the river Neva froze early and the pack of the Gulf of Finland came down, putting an end to navigation and catching the bark still at her anchorage.

The master swore in three languages, and set the crew to work, taking in the sails, boarding up the ports, and housing the deck. That morning he let them go ashore with a few coins and the promise of their wages in a week.

Pierre's wide-set brown eyes glowed with pleasant expectation. It was a feast day; perhaps there would be a procession of the saints' images; certainly there would be girls to talk to and warm wine to quaff. He meant to see everything in this big village on the northern sea.

He reached the jetties of the dockyards and cast a glance to windward. Bare hulks of ships, housed in and blanketed with snow; the gray ribbon of the river, stretching away to the forest on the horizon; a gray sky, shot with a single yellow gleam over the swaying pine tops; smoke curling up from log huts on the flat shore; dogs roaming among the deserted wharfs, but not a man to be seen.

Marking the position of the bark, he went on, with a shrug at the forbidding scene.

"Faith, 'tis a land God looks on only at night."

As soon as he turned a corner, a boy appeared around the bow of the bark and hurried after him, yet without making any attempt to catch up. It was easy to keep Big Pierre in sight because he walked down the middle of the snow-covered streets; and it was a simple matter to follow him without being seen, because he never looked back.

Swinging along at a round pace he waved his cap at the horses, three abreast, that raced up to him, drawing sleighs, and forced them to turn out. When the drivers cursed he grinned back cheerfully and shouted out his marching song:

> *"Malbrouk s'en va t'en guerre—*
> *Mironton, mironton, mirontaine!*
> *Qui sait s'il reviendra!"**

---

*Malbrouk, he's gone off to war—Who knows when he'll be back?

238 THE SWORD OF HONOR

When Big Pierre sang from an open throat, there were many who turned to listen and some who waved back. He had a weather eye out for a tavern all the while, and stared admiringly at the great doors of the churches, painted with amazingly colorful demons and angels—a sight that brought the cap from his head with a fine flourish. Then, at a side street he paused abruptly and ended his song on an unfinished note.

A gun limber was being driven along slowly, three men tied by the wrists to the cart-tail. They were naked, their skin blue with the bite of the wind. Behind them walked three grenadiers, swinging knouts—short staffs to which were attached leather thongs tipped with iron.

At a word of command from a sergeant who brought up the rear, one of the soldiers jerked down his lash with a hiss on a naked back. Blood spattered down into the snow, leaving a trail of red drops between the wheel marks of the limber.

Pierre's shoulders twitched in an involuntary shiver. The muscles in his cheeks grew rigid, and his voice was hoarse when he spoke to the sergeant of grenadiers.

"*Ho, la!* Where is the tavern of this village?"

He spoke in French and the other understood. The sergeant had long curls whitened with flour, and walked with his toes turned out, his thin back straight as the rattan cane he carried. Pierre, who had seen a bit of the world, knew the earmarks of a soldier who had served under Frederick the Great of Prussia.

"Follow your nose, take the first turning to your left, and look for the sign of the Fleur-de-Luys." The sergeant's blurred eyes ran up Pierre's powerful body and fastened on his set face. "So—a little blood makes your gorge rise, my lad?"

"What are these birds?"

"Deserters, that were caught. Thirty-one—" the Prussian resumed his count of the lashes under his breath—"thirty-four for that cock. Trying to get off in time of war, they were! You are going to the tavern, eh?"

"Aye," grunted Pierre and rolled away.

The sergeant halted to stare after him thoughtfully, until the boy who had followed Pierre from the ship came up and pulled at his sleeve.

"If it please you, sir," the apprentice whispered, "the tall rogue is one of the crew. Master Ruggewein bade me say the others be at the merchants' shops by the bridge.

"They will be drunk by candlelight."

The sergeant nodded, pursing his lips.

"Master Ruggewein did say," piped up the boy, "that this big lout is a bad one with his hands. You had best take a squad of muskets with you, if you would fetch him in."

The sergeant's face wrinkled in a noiseless laugh. He had seen the Provence sailor shiver when the knout fell and he felt sure that the man was squeamish at a little blood-letting. The Prussian was a drillmaster in the grenadier corps, and he had seldom encountered a chap he could not handle with cane and tongue.

The candles that gleamed inside the horn windows—the only sign of festival in the Fleur-de-Luys—leaped as Big Pierre came through the door with a flurry of wind-driven snow. A breath of frosty air cut into the aura of drying sheepskins and stale cabbage soup and dirty humans about the red-hot stove.

Pierre looked around and, failing to find any of the men from the bark, made for the counter where a pyramidal candle of some kind of animal fat bubbled and smoked, disclosing the butts of wine casks in the gloom behind.

"Brandy, if you please, Mignon," he smiled at the proprietress, a buxom woman who hailed from Brittany and better things. "One can't get such a thing as brandied grapes in this dogs' village, I suppose. No? Well, fry up a cod in oil and leave the bottle—isn't this a feast day? Where are the girls? Why doesn't anyone strike up a song?"

He glanced hopefully at the long benches where fat-backed Russians sat sleepily over vodka, or kvass—a fermented milk drink that the Provençal who liked good wine had christened "pig's lemonade" after a sip—and at the walls, where straw had been shaken down.

On this straw, stirred by the wind that swept through the cracks, he could make out pairs of feet in the shadows—the boots of a dragoon sleeping off the effects of the Fleur-de-Luys vintages, the rag wrappings of beggars, the bare feet of pilgrims, swollen and calloused. And one pair of broken horsehide shoes out of which thrust toes belonging to a peasant girl, whose yellow hair spread all over the straw.

The very —— of a lot, Pierre thought, and turned his attention to the opposite wall. Apart from the others, several men sat here on a carpet that had once been respectable. They had keen eyes and long, thin beards and hooked noses—Mohammedans by their turbans and voluminous *kha-lats*—traders by the packs stowed jealously behind them.

"Eh, what are these folk?" he asked the Brittany woman.

"Bashkirs, or some other tribesmen. They come from the south with rhubarb and saffron. But they will not go south again, monsieur."

"Why not, Mignon?"

"The soldiers say there is war with the Turks. I don't know; but those heathen will be clapped into jail all the same." The woman, who had once been pretty, became talkative. Pierre was good to look at, and he had given her a whole silver crown. "Folk come here from all the world—"

"*Bon sang,* and why?"

"It's a rich country. The nobles only carry gold—won't bother about silver or such-like. And I've heard tell the Muscovites have made them-selves lords of the heathen empires down in the south. The empress has her palaces full of foreign gentry, to wait on her."

"Who is the king?"

"He died. But Catherine is more of a king than he ever was. Yes, this is a feast day." She glanced at a black and gold icon banging over the stove with lighted candles beneath it. "*She* is like a pope, too. The peasants say she is an angel out of heaven. But the *boyars* will cut up something fierce this night."

Pierre, who was hungry for excitement, wanted to join them instantly. "These *boyars*, where can a chap find them?"

"*Tiens,* my good lad—they are at the winter sports or the theater; they're the grandees, the princes, certainly." She glanced at the door anxiously. "You may see them in the street—such as ain't under the tables. Only their servants come here." The woman from Brittany ran back to the kitchen, returning in a moment with the cod Pierre had ordered, smoking in bub-bling oil in a wooden dish. Wiping the perspiration from her red face, she leaned close to him to whisper—

"Go back to your ship, my man. Go, quickly!"

Pierre took the platter and looked at her inquiringly.

"This is an evil place, monsieur. Ah, pray to the good God and get away out of sight before it is too late."

Between mouthfuls of the cod, washed down with white wine, the man from Provence surveyed his surroundings. It was not like other tav-erns, but he had seen worse. True, the men were not sociable and no one laughed; still, he would hit on one of his mates from the bark presently and go the rounds of other taverns. The evening had barely begun.

"*Corbleu*—what is wrong here?" he asked.

"This land is not as others. There is a curse upon it. 'Tis a simple matter to get into it, but one does not get out again in a hurry."

Pierre thought of the bark, and the snow barrier that was rising around the town. Yes, he could believe that. He was in for a bad winter, but he never bothered his head about the future. In his thirty years of life he had been in many tight places, and enjoyed fighting his way out. He poured a glass of wine for the woman and waited for the loosening of her tongue.

"*She* is the curse of this land—that witch of an empress, monsieur. She is worse than the blind witch of Tanteval, who lives in caves and sings when the surf roars and a ship is wrecked. *She* is an old woman, but her face is young. It is quite true that she killed that poor man, her husband. And all her lovers she raises to great power, then casts them aside."

"I would like to clap eye on her," observed the sailor, his mouth full of cod.

"I have seen her, of nights!" The woman crossed herself and breathed quickly. "Ah, if it is known that I talked of these things they would burn me. Catherine rides in a gold coach without wheels, drawn by roaring beasts. And her skin shines more than the gold—perhaps witches' oil is rubbed on it, and she rides to the Devil's Sabbath. A giant with one eye always sits beside her—a prince of Muscovy."

Pierre waxed cheerful. All this would be well worth seeing. He knew the superstitions of the coast of Brittany.

"Faith," he laughed, "you will be saying that this lord is twin to the King of the Auxcriniers, who looks up from the waves. Him with the livid skin, when the lightning flashes, and the beard of shells. Whoever sees him is sure to be shipwrecked, I've heard."

The woman hesitated, and clasped her hands in her apron.

"Just the same, monsieur, I say to you that she is seeking for souls."

"The deuce!"

"Souls, or serfs—'tis all the same. *She* lures men to serve her, and then there is no escaping. They will carry off a fine, upstanding lad like you for the army—" The door was flung open, and the candles flared. An old man, his head covered with what looked like a woolen nightcap, and a pack strapped to his back, entered hurriedly. He panted as he leaned on the arm of a young girl.

Pierre forgot witches and the catching of souls in an instant. He twirled his mustache with both hands, bowed with an air, sweeping his cap over the earth that was the floor of the tavern.

He knew the man for a Jew, but the young woman was more than pretty. Even while she shook the melting snow from her dark tangle of hair and her foxskin *shuba*, she glanced around the room, her brown eyes resting longest on Pierre and the group of the Mohammedan traders.

Here was no blowsy Dutch *vrauw*, but a young thing of fire and laughter. Pierre, whose wits were not laggard, noticed that the old man was frightened and the girl amused.

"Good day, little sparrow," he cried. "Eh, it is good to come in out of the storm, is it not? Only say—shall I clear a place for you at the stove, or will you share a glass from this fine bottle?"

It seemed to him that she understood and would have answered, but changed her mind so quickly that he was not sure.

He had seen her type before: the poise of the head, the olive skin, the full eyes and the delicate lips. This was no daughter of gnomes, or child of a Muscovite ox. A Gypsy? Perhaps.

He stood in front of her, holding out a freshly filled glass, smiling. His eyes, clear as a boy's and as fearless, smiled as well as his lips. The high spirits and the vitality of this girl in the foxskin *shuba* appealed to the sailor's mood.

Although she shook her head, her lips curved and white teeth gleamed vagrantly. Pierre saw that just under her eyes the skin was lighter than above, as if her face had been veiled from the glare of a burning sun. A ring, nearly as long as her middle finger, aroused his interest at once.

It was heavy silver, set with sapphires and small emeralds that made a pattern. Apparently meaningless, this pattern was formed of an Arabic word, possibly one of the numberless talismans of the Moslems, possibly a signet. Pierre looked at the merchant on the rug.

One had risen and was fingering his scimitar hilt irresolutely. Pierre— though he watched for it—did not see the girl make a sign, but presently the Bashkir squatted among his companions again, turning his back as if indifferent to the newcomers.

But Pierre felt sure that the merchant knew this girl, and that she was an Arab; more likely, a Berber. He wondered what a woman of the southern tribes was doing in this place. Before now he had seen such, standing in the slave markets of Algiers.

The Jew kept plucking at her sleeve, scrabbling his beard with a shaking hand. She paid absolutely no attention until she had finished her scrutiny of the room. Then, she spoke to him and he went off like a well-trained dog, to sit in the darkest corner, and the girl walked around the circle of tribesmen.

They did not look up, but Pierre thought she spoke to them and they answered, before she went to sit by the Jew, as far from the glow of the candles as possible. One by one the Bashkirs got up and went out, leaving their goods. Only urgent need would take such men into a storm, and only the risk of life itself or greater plunder would induce them to leave their belongings unguarded.

Pierre shrugged and drained his glass, and being by then in high good humor, lifted his voice in song—

> "The captain of police is dead,
> Because he lost his life."

Neither the song nor the bottle was ended when the sergeant of grenadiers appeared in the Fleur-de-Luys and came to the counter, ordering rum laced with brandy.

> "A little while before he died,
> This fine chap was much alive."

"Come, my likely lad, empty a noggin with Sergeant Kehl of the Guards," the grenadier proclaimed huskily.

With a cupful of Pierre's brandy inside him, he confessed to being a veteran of the Seven Years' War, Bulow's regiment. The Russian service was a smooth thing, he said, after the pipe-clay and button-shining discipline of old Frederick. The Russian officers were easygoing—didn't know a bayonet from a ramrod—and left everything to the sergeants. And it was no hard matter to pick up money, one way or another.

"Aye," assented Pierre, "enlistment bounties."

Kehl drew the back of his hand across his lips and glanced up at the big sailor.

"No harm in saying regimentals would look well on a strong-set lad like you."

"Fifteen years," laughed the Provençal, "I've been with the colors of France. Aye, ropeman, topman, and sergeant of marines. I was with D'Estaing off Algiers."

"*Gerechter Herr Gott!* That is different." Kehl lowered his voice confidentially. "I'll tell you something. These Russians are cattle—they've only one general officer who is worth his snuff. That's old Prince Suvarof, and he rose from the ranks. They must have foreign gentry to command their ships for them. Join up, and you'll wear a sword in a year—a lively lad with a hard head like yours."

"Do they keep you for seed?" Pierre shook his head. "I've served my time."

Kehl was a man of firm convictions. He believed that any peasant could be won over with a drink and a promise. Already he had the others of Ruggewein's crew locked up in the guardhouse. To bring in a French sergeant of marines as a volunteer would mean a double bounty, whereas if the man should put up a fight and taste a musket butt, Kehl might not get anything.

He was doubly mistaken in thinking that Pierre was a peasant and would not fight a crimp's squad.

"The frontier is closed," he snarled. "The master of your bark has paid you off. Your mates have all entered the ranks—"

"Crimped, eh?" Pierre frowned and then laughed. "Name of a name! That pinch-beck Ruggewein has saved his rix-dollars. Nay, Master Kehl, I'm for the south, where a chap can set his teeth in white bread and olives."

"What then?"

"Who knows? I'll hear the bells of Avignon again, I'll drink white wine again, and sleep on the deck of a fishing tartan when the breeze comes up soft-like off the land."

Kehl had no imagination, and cared nothing for Provence or the men of that coast. But a thought struck him and he put it into words crisply.

"The empress's fleet in the Black Sea, down in the south, is at war with the Sultan of the Moslems. The Russians have sent a foreign admiral to take command. Ach, yes. One is coming from that of country of sea traders and rebels, over the ocean."

"The United States?" Pierre glanced down interested.

"So. I see you know your way around the world. At the arsenal it is said that this man who is coming was once a pirate—his excellency, Jean Paul Jean, or some such name."

"Never heard of him. But, wait—*bon sang!* Is it John Paul Jones?"

"So."

Pierre set down his glass untasted and leaned his elbows on the counter.

"Tell me of this Black Sea and this fleet."

The brandy warmed his vitals, and he threw off impatiently the hand of the woman from Brittany, who was making efforts to warn him not to listen to Kehl. He was trying to decide how much of his companion's gossip was a lie.

The Black Sea, Kehl explained with an air, was the sea of the Mohammedans in back of Constantinople. They had proclaimed a holy war against the Russians, who had built and equipped a fine fleet of some twenty large ships—two being sail of the line—in the rivers that emptied into this sea.

Prince Potemkin, the reigning favorite—now in Petersburg—was to take command in person of the greatest army ever gathered under the eagles. (Kehl, because he understood French and was on duty at headquarters, had his ear to the ground. Most of the Russian officers spoke French to one another by choice, and the foreigners by necessity.)

"A fine, upstanding chap like you," he added, "could pick up more than a dram's worth of loot. Aye, and a fat share of prize money. And why, you ask me? Because, my dear fellow, the sultan has mustered in the bashaws and such-like from the Barbary Coast."

"The corsairs? From Tripoli—Algiers?"

"So! 'Tis said they have the cabins of their ships plated with gold. They walk on silk, nothing less; aye, the very knives and spoons they eat with are full of jewels."

Pierre, who had seen well-born Berbers and Osmanlis supping off mutton stew with the aid of their fingers and a water basin, did not smile.

"Every mosque down there is chuck full of treasure—more than Potsdam palace itself, I swear. And their women—*wunderschön*—better than these here dishwater drabs." He pointed his pipestem at the owner of the Fleur-de-Luys.

But Pierre was no longer listening. Over by the wall, in the shadows, the woman of the foxskins was looking at him, without flinching. He could see the whites of her full eyes, emotionless as an animal's—cold as a basilisk. And his memory harked back fifteen years to Africa.

To a *tartan*, a fishing craft of Toulon blown offshore and dismasted and drifting until the three lads in it sighted the lateen sail of an Algerian felucca, and were picked up.

For the two others, his companions, who turned renegade and became Mohammedans, he had no blame. They disappeared into the white-walled alleys of a rich city; they had weapons at their belts, and the chance to use them—free men in the brotherhood of the coast.

Because he was massive of shoulder and heavily thewed, no choice had been offered Pierre. For two years he had lived on the rowers' benches of the Algerian galleys.

And because he lived—which few did—in the stench and the filth of those chained to the oar, with the bench for his bed, his muscles had hardened to iron. The glare of the sun and the toil of the oar had tempered him as metal is tempered by heating and thrusting into cold water.

He had been lashed by the boatswain's whip. His back, from the nape of the neck to the loins, still bore purple scars.

At the end of the two years, when he escaped from the Algerians during a lucky fight off Cape Bona with a Portuguese sloop-of-war, he made a vow to the Holy Mary of the Seas. This vow was that he would never submit to the lash again. Let a man flog him and he—Pierre Pillon—would kill that one with his hands.

That was why he had winced at the spectacle of the flogging of the deserters a while ago. It reminded him of the galley's waist and the bloodied backs of the slaves.

A rush of cold air put an end to his reverie. The tavern door had been kicked open and a pair of strapping figures swung into the room. They were men as large as Pierre, resplendent in white silk *khalats*, bound with red sashes. Both wore turbans and red morocco boots.

Yet they were not Mohammedans, and Pierre wondered if they were *boyars*—noblemen—'til he scanned their broad red faces and saw the cudgels that they carried instead of swords. One, who was puffing at a large meerschaum pipe, spoke to Kehl, and then they began to search the room, running about and jostling the drinkers, kicking benches out of their way and poking into the straw.

"Heydukes in the livery of a high official," explained Kehl. "They are looking for some Gypsy or other—a girl who was to sing at their master's house. She ran away."

Out of the corners of his eyes Pierre glanced at the Jew in the shadows. The woman who had come with him was no longer to be seen, but the Provençal fancied that the packs by the wall had changed position and that the girl was among them, crouching down with the fur cloak pulled over her.

He said nothing, because he did not relish the behavior of the heydukes.

"She came in," added Kehl. "And she did not go out. *Na*—they will run her down. Look, now, the lads are having a little fun."

The sergeant chuckled, but Pierre stood up swearing under his breath. One of the servants had halted to survey the refugees of the straw. He aimed a kick at a protruding foot, missed, and, with a foolish grin, poured the hot coals from his pipe into the broken tip of the peasant girl's shoe.

She screamed and whipped around in the straw, and the other heyduke caught a handful of her tresses, trying clumsily to thrust them into the blaze that was springing up where some of the coals had fallen.

Pierre Pillon usually acted on impulse, without bothering to think things out. Walking over to the newcomers, he kicked out the fire in the straw and stamped on the fingers of the second heyduke. He had taken the half-empty wine bottle from the counter. This he upended and thrust down the neck of the man with the pipe.

For several seconds the heyduke gaped at him over the butt of the bottle, until the white front of the uniform turned plum color. So did the man's face. He began to breathe heavily and finally found his voice.

"Put him down! Crack his skull!"

Pierre stepped back, eyes alert. But those nearest him gave way, hastening to the walls. His heel struck a stool, and as the two Russians ran at him he reached back and gripped it. A twist of his shoulders hurled it into the first man's chest, knocking the big heyduke flat on his shoulder blades.

The other struck at Pierre's head, and the sailor ducked under the cudgel, taking a kick in the stomach as he did so. His assailant, bellowing with rage, ran at him again. Pierre, standing his ground, moved his head aside as the cudgel came down on his shoulder. His knotted fist went out, catching the heyduke full in the throat.

The man spun back against a table and reeled, dropping his stick and coughing. For a moment he gasped, his hands fastened on his throat, then ran out of the door unsteadily. His companion followed as best he could.

At once with a scamper and rush the vagrants of the straw fled from the tavern, crowding to be first out of the door. Those at the tables followed, and Pierre saw the Jew and his girl slip out with them.

"*Ventre au diable!*" he swore. "Is the tavern a lazar-house? What's amiss with all these chaps?"

Kehl was studying him with professional interest, astonished at the latent power of the man, and the ease with which he had put down two formidable antagonists with cudgels.

"Those two ninepins you bowled over were servants of his Highness, the Prince-Marshal Potemkin. He's the reigning favorite, you know— emperor in all but name—and your goose is cooked, my lad. When the Prince-Marshal hears that you've helped a wench get clear of his hey-dukes, you'll swallow a bullet the wrong way."

"Hark'ee," said Pierre suddenly, more than a little disappointed at the tame end to what had promised to be a pleasant brawl. "I've had enough of Petersburg. The folk here can't sing; their liquor makes 'em doleful; and they can't fight! I'll join the service, but—" he poked a knotted finger into the Russian's midriff—"but only with the rating of sergeant of marines, and service in the Black Sea fleet. A bargain's a bargain. Is it agreed?"

"Agreed! Quick's the word, my tall buck. When you're in regimentals all Potemkin's heydukes can't smell you out."

Pierre nodded. He had thought of that, but he had changed his mind for another reason. To walk the deck of a king's ship again, to take a crack at his old enemies the Turks, and to serve Paul Jones, the American. All this tempted him greatly—Pierre knew more than a little about Paul Jones, who was a Chevalier of France.

"Remember old Schnapps and Snuff," he said dryly, when Kehl turned back to the counter for a last glass and a leer at the woman behind the counter by way of payment. "I'm for the south and the marine guard. You're for the bounty."

"Agreed."

At the guardroom by the Neva bridgehead, the sergeant brought his heels together with a click and saluted smartly. A young lieutenant who was dealing piquet against himself looked up and yawned.

"Sergeant Kehl, with a man for the ranks!"

"Well, take him away. Bed him down with the other cattle!"

"With the *Herr Leutnant's* permission—"

Kehl bent his stiff back a little and lowered his voice, explaining that this man was different; a —— of a fellow, a regular Turk, and strong as an ox. Besides, he had been sergeant of marines, claimed to be a veteran of the French service. So, would it not be better for the *Herr Leutnant* to have the recruit sign the rolls?

"The deuce! I see very well you want the rix-dollar bounty before sun-up." The young Russian shuffled the cards together, looked at his watch, and drew a long paper rolled up at both ends from a drawer of the table.

"You there—what's your name?"

"Pierre Pillon, sir."

"Ah, you speak French. Curse me, Kehl; here's a proper paragon of military virtue—Ulysses as well as Mars." He dipped a quill into ink and scrawled on the roster. "Pierre's the —— of a name—our non-coms will never get their tongues around it. You'll be Peter—Pietr, son of—who is your sire, if you know?"

"Mathurin, sir."

"Who is your master?" As the Provençal hesitated, he turned to Kehl impatiently. "Who is his owner?"

As far as Pierre's memory went he had been a vagrant of the coast, picking up a lean living among the fisher folk, who were little better off themselves. But neither he nor his father before him had been a peasant, bound to the land and a seigniorial lord.

"The sea, monsieur," he hazarded.

"Well, no matter. We'll enter you as a masterless man. Make your mark here." When the sailor had drawn something resembling a star on the rolls, he nodded. "Now, Peter, son of Little Matthew, you've pledged yourself to serve the Empress Catherine, the anointed of God. Be brave and obey orders. Dismissed!"

But Pierre glanced at Kehl, who clicked his heels again and coughed. The lieutenant called for his servant, who gave the Prussian a silver coin which he pocketed swiftly.

"Your excellency—" his dry lips parted, showing yellow teeth, in what was meant for a smile—"this Frenchman is an old hand—knows the musket drill. He requests to be sent to the Black Sea, rated sergeant of marines."

For the first time the officer glanced at Pierre, taking notice of his massive build and the eagerness in his swarthy face.

"You, Pietr—you request to be sent to that lake of the ——?"

"Aye, sir."

The lieutenant looked puzzled and pulled at his mustache.

"Oh, burn and blister me, Kehl, this is rich. A man asks for service down there where—" he checked himself and laughed with relish. The sergeant of grenadiers sniggered. "I'll see to it, Pietr, that you're rated properly."

It struck Pierre as a bit queer, this enlistment. Moreover, he did not like Kehl's amusement. But he was dealing with strangers, and entering a new service. On the king's ships he had never exchanged as many words as this with the gentlemen of the poop; yet the officers of his acquaintance had always kept promises made to the men.

"Now go to the deuce or the recruit battalion." The lieutenant was looking at his watch impatiently. "The empress and the imperial retinue will pass over this bridge, and I want you two mangy dogs out of here."

Pierre saluted and followed his companion to the door. They had barely gained the street when they heard a distant musical jangling of sleigh bells that came nearer rapidly, echoed by shouting down the street.

The sentry at the bridge called out, and in a moment the officer appeared from the guardhouse, buckling on his sword belt and fastening his tunic at the throat and snarling at a score of soldiers who tumbled out half asleep and fell into ranks beside the new recruit. Kehl watched with a covert sneer, as the young lieutenant fumed and swore at the guard for slovenly dressing and fell to beating them into better alignment with the flat of his sword.

The bells swept nearer rapidly and the lieutenant ran to the front of his men and flung up his blade.

"Pre-sent arms."

A Jew who had been bartering tobacco and sweets at the guardhouse hurried to cross the street and upset his basket in his hurry. Stooping to gather up his scattered possessions, he fumbled in the snow, his head craned over his shoulder.

Around a bend in the street a troop of hussars came at a trot, stretching the full width of the bridge. The huckster began to run out on the bridge. Pierre saw the two lines of black horses sweep past, knocking the Jew headlong. Then he heard a curious roaring and blaring of music.

A sledge, filled with horns and bagpipes and men, slid by him, a sledge drawn by a dozen bears, growling and snarling. He turned to look at the Jew, who was trying to crawl out of the way.

The bears, lashed by men who ran alongside, overtook the unfortunate trader. When Pierre saw him next he was writhing in the snow at one side of the bridge, bleeding from the throat.

Sleighs whipped past, filled with men and women in court dress, wrapped in furs, laughing, with flushed faces.

Last of all came a long sleigh, gilded, two gold eagles poised on either side of the driver. A dozen white horses drew it, and on the runners and behind stood linkboys holding blazing torches.

"*Slave bohun!*" cried a voice down the street. "Glory to God—health to your Imperial Majesty!"

Pierre had a glimpse of a swarthy and strikingly handsome nobleman whose gigantic body was clad in the white dress uniform of a cavalry colonel. Over his belt was a gold star, on his chest the ribbon of an order.

Beside him sat a woman, erect and powerful as a man, in a long ermine cloak.

"Health to your Majesty!" cried Kehl.

The sleigh sped away across the bridge, a second troop of hussars trotted by, and the lieutenant dismissed his men. Then he strode over to Pierre, the drawn sword swinging in his hand.

"So, you keep your feet when the empress passes?" he bellowed. "We must teach you a thing or two!"

For the first time, as he replaced his cap, Pierre was aware that the other civilians near him were rising from their knees with bared heads. Only the soldiers of the guard and himself had stood while Catherine passed along the street.

Before he could answer, the officer struck him twice over the head with the flat of the saber. The force of the blows half dazed him and he dropped to the snow. When his brain cleared, he checked an impulse to rush at the man with a sword. The lieutenant was his officer now, and he—Pierre Pillon—a soldier of the empress.

Blood trickled down his face as he stood up, and he wiped it away quietly. But the youngster with the sword had caught the flash in his eyes, the quick twist of anger on his lips.

"Sergeant Kehl," he ordered briskly, "take this fellow to the barracks under guard. He is a bad customer."

The officer was returning his sword to its scabbard, hoofs drummed again on the hard-beaten snow, and four riders swept down the street as blown leaves flicker in the wake of a wind gust. Coming abreast the guardhouse they quickened their pace instead of slowing down, and the sentry's startled challenge went unheeded.

As they passed the lighted windows, Pierre saw three Moslems, wrapped in flying cloaks, bending over the necks of their horses. They were gone in a second—four blurred shapes streaking across the bridge—while the sentry, running out of his box, stared after them and fingered his musket. But Pierre had seen that the other rider was the girl of the foxskins, and the three were the Bashkirs with whom she had spoken in the tavern.

By now the sentry had made up his mind that they were no heydukes, and, spurred by a shout from the officer, he fired his piece. The bark of the musket—fruitless as a pebble tossed into the darkness—was answered by a woman's laugh, shrilling over the drumming hoofs and vibrant with savage delight.

"*Na*," grunted Kehl, "that would be Kalil, the Gypsy girl of Potemkin."

He listened until he was sure that the riders had got away from the town, then he nodded to Pierre and struck off toward the barracks, being, as the lieutenant had said, in a hurry to spend his rix-dollar while wine was still to be had in the taverns.

The next day Pierre was sent to a camp on the outskirts of Petersburg and given a uniform and knapsack. The hair on the front half of his head was shaved off, and he was made to strip with the others of his detachment and enter a bath house. Here he was steamed and scalded and, following the example of his companions, rubbed himself down with a coarse towel. Then he waded through a tank and lined up to submit to the casual scrutiny of a surgeon who walked through the room holding a scented handkerchief to his nose.

At sight of Pierre's scars, the Russian paused a moment and raised his brows, saying something to the non-commissioned officer who accompanied him. Pierre could read in their faces that they thought him a refractory peasant who had tasted the knout frequently, and might give them some trouble.

And this same sergeant kept a close watch on him during the first drill, after the recruits had got into their new leg wrappings, double pantaloons, and sheepskin *shubas*.

The Provençal had expected to be sent south, and it was not pleasant to realize he had been thrust into an infantry company. But Pierre had learned a lesson from the buffet he had been given that first evening. He had been gulled by Kehl, and he was not going to whine about it. Instead of a berth as sergeant of marines, he had been put into the ranks. This was Kehl's doing.

Pierre set about making the best of a temporarily bad bargain. The first thing to be done was to familiarize himself with the Russian words of command, and this was not difficult because his companions were green men who had to have everything dinned into them.

They were strange men, slow-moving, voiceless—cheerful enough after dinner. Pierre thought the food—gruel and bread with vodka at times—poor enough, but these shaggy, blue-eyed men gorged themselves on it with muttered delight. Among them were short, slant-eyed beings who never spoke and who looked like old men—Finns—and others with long, oily hair and blunt faces—Tatars as he came to know later.

Pierre discovered that the muskets issued them were of French make, and he showed those of his squad how to clean theirs—as well as the mysteries of the ramrod and priming pan. He could think and move three times as quickly as any of them, and carry the weight of knapsack, musket, and heavy coat without feeling it during a day's drill.

When the sergeant found out that Pierre knew the drill and gave no trouble—being rather helpful in coaching the other *moujiks*—he left the Provençal to his own devices.

And Pierre was satisfied when he overheard his captain say to a staff officer who came through on inspection that the company would be sent to Kherson on the Black Sea while the snow made transport easy.

"They are not good for much, it's true," assented the other, "but down there they'll learn to use the bayonet and that's all Suvarof cares about."

"Well, they're not the White hussars," the captain pointed out. "But they won't turn their backs when the first cannon goes off—I'll answer for that."

Pierre wondered how these peasants could be expected to stand against the veteran armies of the sultan. The next day the sergeant was replaced by a foreign drillmaster, and at the end of the week Sergeant Kehl appeared with his rattan cane and his thin smile.

For the first time the recruit battalion was put through musketry drill, without powder or balls. Kehl's method was simple: he showed by example what he wanted done with each command, loading, ramming home the charge and wadding, dropping in the bullet, priming the pan, and then aiming and firing. He alone had powder horn and bullet sack. Months later Pierre learned that the recruits were never trusted with these until they were in the field, confronted by the enemy.

Then Kehl called out men from the ranks and made them go through the motions. When they made mistakes he would order them to present arms, and lash their backs with his supple rattan. This he could use with telling effect, and Pierre saw one tow-headed Russian sway on his feet, tears wetting his face. For not standing rigid he was given a beating over the head that finally stretched him unconscious in the snow.

The company, muskets grounded, was kept at attention all the time, until Kehl's sharp eye picked out Pierre. Then the sergeant was pleased to bark an order to stand at ease and to call out the Provençal.

Pierre shouldered his musket and stepped forward. For a quarter of an hour without a moment's letup Kehl put him through the manual, and the musketry drill. The big recruit handled his weapon, which weighed close to twenty pounds, with its bayonet, as easily as a pike. Kehl seemed surprised and ill pleased when he discovered that his victim of the tavern had mastered the Russian commands, and Pierre's mustache twitched in a grin.

"*Shagom marsh!*" snapped the sergeant.

Pierre did not move. This was something new.

"What's that?" he asked.

"Ah, you are sullen! You give a bit of lip to an under-officer? Good! *Pre-sent arms!*"

Instead Pierre executed an about-face as Kehl stepped behind him, with the rattan raised to strike. It was unprovoked, deliberate—Kehl's way of dealing with a man in the ranks who stood up to him.

"Listen, sergeant," said the Provençal, "if you lay that stick over my shoulders I'll make a new buttonhole in your vest with this bayonet."

Kehl checked the downward swish of the cane and glared at Pierre, who was still smiling, ominously. It took a full moment for the meaning of the recruit's words to dawn upon his understanding. Then his teeth clicked together and his eyes narrowed.

"Many years ago," went on Pierre, "I vowed to the Holy Mary of the Seas that I would let the life out of the next chap who tried to flog me. Glad it's going to be you."

Amazement gave place to cunning in the Prussian's thin features. He looked around and saw no officers near. Visibly, he reflected. Pierre waited, sure of his man.

"Good!" said Kehl ponderously. "You have threatened a sergeant. To-morrow it shall be reported. Tomorrow—" he hesitated, and his wrinkled face cracked in a smile—"well, the orders are out, and you may as well know. Your battalion goes into a wagon train, to Moscow and the Black Sea."

Pierre, leaning on his musket, looked at him inquiringly.

"I will not report you, and you will march with your regiment. *Tfu!* My bold lad, you'll never see a town again. Of those who go to the Black Sea not one in a hundred comes back. If the Turks do not rip you up, the tribesmen will do the business for you."

"Tell me," inquired the Provençal, "is it true that *Monsieur le Chevalier* Jones is going with us, to the fleet?"

"Aye, he landed at Riga a week ago. What is it to you?" he added curiously.

"Ah, you do not understand. Ten years ago, I served on Paul Jones's ship, the old *Richard*. But you have never fought on the deck of a ship—you cannot understand. No other commander is like that chap. When I heard that he was to take over a fleet of the empress, I said, 'Pierre my lad, you also must serve this empress; then you will see *Monsieur le Chevalier* again, and tell your mates in Toulon all about it.'"

"But you are in the infantry!"

Pierre shrugged and spread out both hands, hinting at his indifference to such a slight obstacle to his plans. He had the light heart of the southern Gaul, who weeps when most happy, and laughs in the face of black calamity—who fights like a wounded tiger when it is least expected of him.

And in one thing he prophesied truly. Few lived to tell the story of what happened in the Black Sea in that year 1788, but Pierre Pillon was one of them.

Chapter II
The Eyes of Kalil

Clouds banked low over the line of the forest on the horizon. The spires and windmills of Petersburg faded into the shroud of mist and windrift of snow, tossed up by the gale that swayed the treetops. Black masses moved over the snow, following the ribbon of road, cut through the forest—sledges filled with great bales covered with tarpaulins. The center of each sledge had been left empty and here were crowded twenty or thirty men, protected a little from the bite of the wind.

Behind the sledges came a supply train, behind this flat sledges, bearing caissons and artillery, behind this a scattering of sutlers' outfits, a few Gypsies, and packs of wild dogs.

Two thousand men, a battery of field guns, and a consignment of stores were on their way to the Black Sea.

Pierre Pillon had never seen such a land. Earth and sky met in a long line in the distance. The forests had been left behind. Always the sun rose on the left and set on the right, red in the mist. And at all hours the howling of wolves was heard.

They camped every night at the watch post stations—log huts scattered around the stables—shrouded by dancing wraiths when the wind whipped up the dry snow. Truly, Pierre thought, this land was akin to the sea. But he had never crossed a sea so vast as this plain that was with him when he rolled out of his blankets before dawn and when he went to sleep.

In the heart of the frozen sea they halted for a week, with the domes and cupolas and the white walls of a glittering city in the distance.

"Is this Constantinople, brother?" a man of his squad asked, after gazing a long time at the city.

"Nay," Pierre laughed.

He had the ability of some veterans of picking up a strange language quickly, and he could make himself understood in Russian eked out with lingua franca after a fashion. "Constantinople has minarets like spears. It is on the sea, like Toulon. Besides, here is too much snow."

He noticed that while the infantry remained in camp, the officers spent most of their time in the city, and after a while he learned that it was Moscow.

It was a month after leaving Moscow that they began to see in the distance a river that was not frozen over. The snow was gray instead of white, and patches of reddish earth showed here and there. The sun was higher in the sky, and its warmth struck through their greatcoats.

"Surely Pierre," said his squad mate, a stoop-shouldered man with wistful eyes—a fur hunter, Feodor by name—"this is early for the spring thaw. The priests have not yet held the Easter procession."

"We have been journeying south. The heat of the sun is greater. If we kept on long enough, little brother, we would reach a land where there is no snow."

The fur hunter shook his head incredulously. But Pierre's prophecy came true. In a few days the caravan was halted while they fitted to the sledges the wheels that had been strapped in the loads. The highway was no more than a line of muddy ruts, and the number of horses to each wagon was doubled. Pierre's battalion was chosen to push ahead of the caravan with some twenty wagons loaded with grain and ammunition. The infantry no longer rode in the vehicles; they marched beside the road and helped haul the wagons that bogged down, and pull the horses out by the tails.

He worked with a will, feeling sure that now they would come to the end of this empty land and find vineyards and orchards, and perhaps olives and muscat wine. Were they not going to the southland, on the sea? *Tiens!* There would be taverns and girls to chaff and fresh fish. All this he told to Feodor.

"But there is a maiden, who wears her hair down," exclaimed Feodor after listening, sorely puzzled, to the Provençal's prophecy of good things to come. "She must belong to a *boyar*. Only the nobles have fetched women along this weary way." Pierre looked around and shaded his eyes. Sure enough, an officer's carriage was moving past the files of foot soldiers, and in it was no officer but an olive-faced girl wrapped in a colored *khalat*.

"Why it's Kalil," he muttered, "that singing girl of the tavern."

For a moment he cudgeled his brains as to why the woman who had been keen to fly from Petersburg should have lingered with the column; and why her friends had deserted her—then gave up puzzling as a bad job. As the carriage passed he took a sprig of jasmine that he had picked to carry in his musket, and tossed it into her lap.

She glanced back, searching the faces of Pierre's squad until she picked him out. Then she flashed him a smile, whether for the incident in the tavern or the flowers, he did not know. He watched the carriage out of sight, humming under his breath, and grimaced at a new thought.

"We're in Asia now—captain said so. Perhaps we'll see some Turks before long. They have curved swords—cut off heads like grass with a sickle. What will you chaps do then?"

"The *batyushna* will watch over us."

"The little mother? Who the deuce—oh, you mean the empress. Nonsense; she's a thousand leagues off by now."

"Our officers will look out for everything."

"Feodor," said Pierre out of the depths of his experience, "those officers of yours will hang back when the *pas de charge* is beaten; they'll stay in a safe place until it's all over. When you come back all cut up, maybe with prisoners, maybe with just wounds, they'll fall you in and march off at your head. Then they'll be given a cross or a ribbon or a sword of honor, and you bullies will have an extra tot of rum—those of you that haven't turned up your toes."

"As God wills." Feodor frowned, trying to understand. "Nay, Pietr, we have heard there is a *batko* waiting for us down yonder."

"A little father?"

The fur hunter nodded cheerfully.

"Little Father Suvarof. When it is time to charge he only says—'Come ahead!' Then he marches with us and God gives a victory. That is the way of it."

Pierre assented without being convinced. He was wondering how Feodor and his mates would act when things warmed up, when they smelled powder. They were as green as sprouts; and Pierre had seen the Moslems fight.

It was one night after the battalion had crossed the river that the girl of the *khalat* came and sat at Pierre's fire. For the first time the men noticed that they had found no post station to halt at; they were in the open steppe, and fuel was scanty.

Near the brush shelter that had been built for the captain they had seen a kind of stone monument. It was a woman's figure, more than life size, the face turned to the east. Feodor was troubled by it.

"The Tatars in the company know what it means, but we do not know. All over the steppe these stone women sit—like that. It is not good."

"How, not good?" demanded Pierre, who was filling his clay pipe.

He had been singing, because his companions liked it. They had an ear for a tune, though the Provençal considered their chants both cheerless and endless.

Feodor shook his head.

"When one of the stone women are moved to a village it takes ten strong oxen to pull them to the west, although one can draw them to the east. They were made by men who came out of the east a long time ago and who will come back again someday to where these women are."

"What of it?"

"It is not good to see one at night. *Ekh*, and here we are sleeping under the feet of that one."

Pierre made himself as comfortable as he could on his blanket. He sniffed the odor of grass, warmed by the sun. The bivouac that evening was on dry ground. Before then they had slept in mud, chilled and restless. He had no fault to find.

"Eh, didn't I tell you! Look at that."

Feodor crossed himself and pointed to where a slim form was moving toward them from the direction of the stone woman and the captain's hut.

The girl of the *khalat* stepped out of the shadows, and Pierre sprang up to offer her his seat. She knelt, holding out her hands to the fire, masses of black hair about a white throat. The Russians drew away from her but Pierre lifted an elbow and twirled his mustache. Her brown eyes flicked up at him; and she made room for him on the blanket.

"*Tiens,*" muttered the Provençal, sitting, "if this is a new trick, it is at least entertaining."

"I can speak a little French, monsieur," she said suddenly. "But that pig of a sergeant does not know it. He is asleep in the cart."

"Good," smiled Pierre. "You are no Tsigani. A Gypsy sits on the ground, a Berber kneels."

For a moment she searched the faces of the other soldiers, until she was satisfied that they did not understand.

"True, monsieur, my mother was a Berber of Fez, my father a Levantine, a Jew. With my father I have been to many cities and army camps, because he is a trader. But at Petersburg he disappeared and I am on my way back to my own place. At Otchakof on the Black Sea," she went on, "there is a Turkish army and *serais* where I will have silver for my songs." Again the Provençal nodded. He had seen such *serais*—heard the monotonous note of *rabeb* and *gosba,* beloved of the Arabs. Once or twice in the alleys of Algiers he had seen women of Fez who were slaves of the Turks. But this was no ordinary woman, who could speak French, whose hands were tapering and delicate. Moreover, she was beautiful.

"Your name," he asked, "is Kalil?"

"Kalil, daughter of Mokador. I am frightened." She glanced at the big Provençal beseechingly. "This battalion has lost its way. It will never reach Kherson, where the Russian army is."

"The deuce! And why not?"

She leaned her chin on her hands to gaze into the fire for a while without answering.

"Today," she replied at last, "I saw a rider on the skyline, who turned his horse back into the tall grass. The officers of the Roumis, the white men, did not see him. But he will come back with others."

"Tribesmen?"

"Aye, this is their steppe!"

"Well, they'll get a few bullets to crack their teeth on."

Pierre was rather amused at the thought of undisciplined riders attacking a strong column well supplied with powder.

"Go!" She smiled curiously. "Go, and tell your captains that they are being spied upon. They will not listen."

"You are a Mohammedan, Kalil." He had noticed that the arch of her brows was darkened with *kohl* and the tips of her fingers tinted with henna stain.

She flung up her head, startled but not afraid.

"Then go, O brother of the ravens, you who are so shrewd, tell your captain that I am of the Moslem. Why not?"

But Pierre had no liking for that.

"It is written in the Book-To-Be-Read, O Kalil, that a daughter of Islam should go unveiled before men?"

She turned on him suddenly, making no effort to conceal her surprise and curiosity.

"Nay, in the *khaysamah* it is written in going before eunuchs and Jews and Christians there is no shame. You have been among my folk, Monsieur Pierre, you know our laws. You are a follower of al-Islam!"

"Nay," Pierre laughed. "I bear scars that your folk put upon me at Algiers. I know that there is a holy war proclaimed and I go to send as many of your warriors to the prophet's paradise as I may."

"It is well for you," she assented. "If you had been a follower of the true prophet, one who had turned back to the *giaours*, I would have left my knife in your liver when I ride away this night."

As Pierre was silent, she went on in a lower voice.

"In the tavern at Petersburg you did not betray me when the dogs came to nose me out. You overcame them with your bare hands. So, in return, I will take you with me to safety."

"How?"

"I have said this column will not be permitted to find its way back to the others. I know where two horses can be stolen from the lines. We can ride to Otchakof."

"Why, to Otchakof?"

Kalil glanced at him, a world of flattery in her tawny eyes. In truth, she had seen few men like this one, with the bones of a giant, the yellow hair of a *giaour*, and the dark skin of her own people. The flattery was art but the admiration was sincere, and it irked her that Pierre took no account of either.

"It is a great city, held by the Moslems, and the Roumis will never take its forts. The galley of Hassan Pasha is there, and the pigs of Roumis will never take that, either."

Pierre took his pipe from his lips and thumbed it thoughtfully. "Hassan of Algiers?"

"Aye." There was pride in her voice. "You have heard of the galley." She pointed to his boots caked with dry mud, and his stained coat. "You did not come hither to serve with these oxen. I know that you would like to be on a ship again. Many *giaours* aid Hassan Pasha, and their reward is a just share in the spoils."

"And—"

"In the cabin of the pasha are chests of gold and fine silks and rubies from Badakshan and strings of pearls that you could wind around both arms. I have seen them. Come to Otchakof and see for yourself. Hassan of Algiers is a just man."

In silence Pierre listened; the soft gutturals of the woman's voice mingled with the hissing of the fire. Her long hair gave out a scent that was not musk or aloes, but more like jasmine when the sun is warm upon it. Why not go with her? She must know her way out of this infernal steppe. Aye, she could lead him down to the sea.

And then, a few mumbled words, a shaving of the head, other garments and he could turn Moslem—renegade. Life would be easier than this.

"Fly away, little Kalil," he said slowly, "I'll bide here."

Anger darkened her cheeks and narrowed the full line of her lips. When she realized that he meant what he said, she rose and went away, her slender back and the poise of her head expressive of utter scorn. When she had disappeared into the shadows he listened until he heard the tramp of the squads going the rounds to change guard.

"Eh?" he muttered, bending down.

Blue-eyed Feodor stared up at him anxiously.

"Did she put a spell on you, brother? I saw her stop and look at that stone woman, just like a sister—"

Pierre nudged him and held up a hand for silence. They could hear a bustle in the horse lines, a trampling and shouted questions that no one answered. Then hoofs thudded off into the darkness and lanterns winked into being, wandering around aimlessly. Before long he saw his captain, who had gone to investigate the disturbance, walking back to the hut and went to intercept him.

"Tribesmen around? Danger of attack?"

The officer, who had a liking for the Provençal, was more than a little irritated. The guides had wandered off the trail that day and now horses had broken loose from the picket lines. His quarters were highly unsatisfactory and he was sleepy. One of the horse tenders had sworn that he saw a witch ride off on a pony, as if it were a broomstick. He wondered what had got into the men. He was new to field service, but the *moujiks* of his estate had been just as prone to restlessness on a warm spring night.

"Back to your place! And stay away from vodka if you can't keep your tongue between your teeth."

The next day Pierre was sure that they had lost their way. Men were sent to a hillock to study the lie of the land, and they changed direction more than once before noon. All around them the stiff grass, brilliant with poppies and the purple cornflowers, swelled over dunes that were like waves.

And over one of these ridges rode a thousand horsemen in skullcaps and fluttering caftans, brandishing long muskets and scimitars.

They charged down on the column, firing as they came. Only one company of Russians was in time to loose a volley before the horsemen were on them, slashing with the deadly curved swords.

Pierre was in his squad with the advance—half a company under his captain. They had pushed on ahead and three hundred yards separated them from the wagons and the main body. In the brilliant sunlight Pierre could see clearly all that took place. The raiders got home with the first charge, something that should never have happened if the infantry had been properly drilled, and accustomed to their muskets.

As it was, with the bayonets they beat off the horsemen, who circled around the rear, wiping out the detachment in that place.

"What are those fellows, your excellency?"

Pierre's deep voice, addressing his officer, was the only one heard in the advance guard, where the men had turned and were staring blankly at the scene behind them.

The captain, who had grown red in the face, fingered his sword and his reins irresolutely. It was his first engagement and he was wondering what was expected of him.

"Bashkirs," he muttered. "Tribesmen from over the border. Listen—"

As if satisfied with the damage they had inflicted, and the few horses they had driven off, the raiders had formed in a solid mass on the slope across from where they had waited in ambush. Now a shrill yell broke from the mass, high-pitched, exulting.

"Allah il akbar—ya Allah!"

It was the ululation of the Moslems, and Pierre had heard it before, when the Algerian corsairs sailed out to meet their prey. An answering growl rose in Pierre's throat as he watched the dust settle around the wagon train. He expected to see the carts close up, the infantry form to face the raiders, the front rank kneeling, the rear standing. Then a few volleys, and the tribesmen would scatter. Such chaps as they would never charge massed infantry.

"Only look, little brother," exclaimed Feodor, nudging him. "Christ aid us!"

Pierre now saw why the Bashkirs had shouted. Between his half company and the main body one powder wagon had been moving in advance of the others. Beside this solitary wagon the major in command had been riding when the attack came. The driver of the wagon was whipping his horses toward the knoll on which Pierre and his comrades stood.

The major, after hesitating a long time, was spurring in the other direction, to the battalion. And a Bashkir in a crimson cloak with heron's feathers in his cap was racing down to cut off the officer.

The infantry by the wagons could not fire on this rider, who was now between them and their major. The Russian had drawn his saber, holding it high over his head. The Moslem, riding like a fiend, swept down on him. For a second the two blades flashed together, and dust swirled up.

Reining his pony about, almost in its tracks, the Moslem slashed at the back of the officer, who was slower in recovering. Then, when the wounded man swayed in the saddle, the Bashkir killed him with a second stroke. The major's orderly, spurring a big cob desperately, fired a pistol at the Bashkir and missed. Again the scimitar lashed out. The orderly swayed and slid to the ground over his horse's rump.

Standing high in his short stirrups, his cloak fluttering like a flag in a stiff breeze, the Bashkir swordsman darted back to his companions, who greeted him with strident acclaim.

"Ya kutb—ya kutb—Allah il Allah!"

The major's horse, with an empty saddle, trotted up to the main body and took its place among the officers. The wagon reached Pierre's half company, which scattered to let it draw up its center.

Pierre looked around impatiently, expecting an order to double back

to the battalion. The Bashkirs, emboldened as tribesmen always are by a
first success, were showing signs of attacking again. But his captain was
talking in a strained voice to the company sergeant, who was a veteran
of several campaigns.

"Bashkirs across the border—probably the Tatar tribes are out as well—
communication between the army and Moscow must be cut off—bad
business."

It became clear to Pierre all at once the Russian captain did not know
what order to give. The men were watching him, the sergeant was waiting for an order, and nothing was done.

Meanwhile, although the tribesmen were getting ready to charge, the
battalion began to break formation. The death of the major had left it lead-
erless. No one appeared to take his place. Instead, officers shouted con-
tradictory orders, and wagons at the end of the line were moving away
from the raiders. One company of infantry shouldered arms and wheeled
off beside the wagons.

Another company seemed to be in disorder. Pierre stared, too amazed
to swear. He saw that the Russians were trying to form a square with the
carts, although there was no need of it, and just at that moment it was
suicidal.

The Bashkirs loosed their horses. A ragged volley, fired too soon by the
infantry, brought down only three or four men. Only a single line, some
two hundred bayonets, faced the tribesmen, who were now gripped by the
bloodlust. Yelling they crashed into the bayonets, or swept over the two
companies that stood their ground stolidly.

What had been a few moments ago a disciplined battalion became now
a mass of men without formation. Groups here and there stood back to
back. Other groups gathered around the carts, which were motionless, the
Tatar drivers having freed horses from the traces and fled. It was like a
pantomime in miniature—puffs of smoke darting up, the glitter of scimitars in the sun, horses rearing.

Only a dull murmur reached the advance detachment on the knoll, a
murmur that was made up of the thudding of hoofs, the booming of firelocks, the neighing of horses, and the hoarse voices of men.

Pierre saw a familiar figure in claw-hammer coat and gaiters—the sergeant who had broken in the raw recruits—with a squad of men at bay
near one of the wagons.

He had abandoned his cane and picked up a musket. With the bayonet he skewered a leaping Moslem, clubbed another with the butt. His movements were as unhurried as on the parade ground at Petersburg.

Before he could get back to his men a rider lanced him, and turned, to drive the spear again into the body that threshed on the ground.

Pierre leaned his musket against his shoulder and spat on his hands. It would be their turn next.

Two hundred or more Bashkirs detached themselves from the throng that was slaughtering and plundering the remnant of the battalion, and rode toward them at a hand pace. The sergeant dared not wait any longer for an order from the bewildered captain. Hastily forming his squads into a rough triangle, with its point toward the tribesmen—three squads to every side—he called to the outer rank to kneel. This done, the pans of the muskets were primed and the men waited.

"Hold your fire," growled the sergeant.

Feodor, kneeling by Pierre, was muttering a prayer. He was as calm as if waiting for the evening pot of gruel, gazing at the oncoming riders with childish curiosity.

The tribesmen began to trot, lashing their horses up the slope. Some of their long firelocks bellowed, the smoke swirling almost into Pierre's eyes. He heard the whine of the small bullets and his captain's voice.

"Fire, my children!" The muskets flashed and men began to cough as the fumes of the black powder got down their lungs. Pierre made out horses passing, and with his bayonet turned aside a spear aimed at his head. Then the smoke cleared away and he saw nothing but the green slope with a dozen wounded tribesmen crawling away or lying still.

His officer still sat in the saddle of a big bay horse, saber at his shoulder. Pierre heard him muttering:

"Valuable wagon—major's orders are to look after it."

Then he began to sway from side to side, and his orderly ran up, catching him as he clutched at the mane of his charger. He had been shot in the head.

The Bashkirs attacked the rear of the detachment and this time plunged in among the bayonets. Taking the second rank from the other two sides, the sergeant cleared the triangle with the bayonet and gave them a volley as they rode off.

They had lost a large percentage of their men in the two charges and contented themselves with firing on the wagon from a distance. The Russians, most of whom had never handled muskets before, answered as best they could. Pierre, drenched with sweat, worked swiftly with ramrod and powder horn, making the most of what time was left him.

Meanwhile the Bashkirs had been forming for another charge, and surged up the knoll again with their lances. They struck full upon the dwindling knot of men by the wagon, and Pierre was driven back against a wheel. Half blinded by sweat, he thrust with the bayonet and felt it bend against a man's chest: then he jerked it free, took the barrel in his hands, and cleared a space around him.

By degrees the pressure around him grew less, and he wiped his eyes with his sleeve to clear away the sweat. Then he looked around.

A yard in front of him lay Feodor, thin arms clutching the breast of his coat, which was slashed open. The blue eyes of the fur hunter stared straight up into the sun without blinking. Only his ruddy cheeks had been drained of all color. Pierre leaned on his musket, panting, blood running from the bent bayonet down over his fingers. The Bashkirs were riding away, toward their main body which was withdrawing over the steppe with the wagons of the Russian battalion.

"The deuce—it's all over!"

The battalion itself was visible again—scattered white bodies, stripped of all clothing, half hidden in the trampled grass. But around the powder wagon with Pierre some twenty men still stood, weapons in hand. Evidently the tribesmen sent to wipe them out had found the game too costly, and had gone off to claim their share of the booty taken by the others.

A soldier beckoned to Pierre and pointed to the ground beneath the cart. Here, beside the shivering driver, the captain lay, his head turned toward them. Pierre dropped to his hands and knees to try to hear what the officer was saying.

"Powder—wagon. Major's orders—drive to Kherson." The wounded man stabbed the air with his finger. "South—south!"

Nodding, Pierre regained his feet and looked around for the sergeant. He found him lying under a dead horse.

"Stiff," he ruminated. "Captain going, too. Those balls in the skull always end a chap—wonder that he said anything at all. Well, we're alive, after a bit of warm work, too."

Not only was he alive, but Pierre perceived that the Russians were all looking to him for a word to what they were going to do next. They had heard the dead sergeant praise him and had seen the captain give him instructions. They were incapable of thinking for themselves, and the big Provençal became their leader without a word spoken.

Pierre threw back his head and laughed into a blazing sky. *"Sacré nom d'un cochon*—Sergeant Pillon, it is. Epaulets at the first skirmish and the command of a battalion, with its wagon train. Kehl told more truth than he thought. Well, what's to be done now?"

He thought for a moment and decided they must count noses, take stock of their supplies, and get away from the scene of the fight.

Little indeed he knew of the Russian tongue, but he could give the routine orders, and they expected no more than that. After the dying captain was lifted on top of the load and screened from the sun by a thatch of sedge branches, Pierre ordered the injured horses removed from the harness. Two of the Tatar ponies, overlooked by the pillagers, were rounded up, making six fit enough to draw the cart.

Meanwhile a trench was dug and the dead of the half company were given shallow burial. After a glance at the vultures and wolves thronging to the bodies of the battalion, Pierre abandoned thought of doing anything for *them*.

Bullet pouches and the rations in the knapsacks of the slain were taken, and Pierre looked grave when he found only three or four jugs of water in the cart. They had powder enough for a lifetime.

After every man had been given one cup of water Pierre signed to them to pile their knapsacks on the load. Then he blew down the muzzle of every musket to see if the touchhole were clear. When the pieces were loaded again, and twenty others, taken from the field, he walked to a ridge to make a survey of the country.

The last of the Bashkirs had disappeared toward the east, and the green sea of the steppe was empty of human life. Pierre signed to the driver to start his horses, and walked to the head of his little column. He did not know how far they were from the sea or what lay in front of them, but he believed that he could steer a course due south as his officer had directed. He would take his bearings by the stars.

"Come along, my heroes," he called out. *"Shagom marsh!"*

The trace chains rattled, the wagon axles creaked, and the injured groaned in unison, but the sailor rolled along in front of his detachment—"To keep a lookout for'ard," he assured himself—and lifted a mellow voice in song:

> *"Malbrouk's gone off to war;*
> *Nobody knows when he'll be back!"*

Chapter III
The Galley

Kalil, a dun-colored pony between her knees, and two Bashkir swordsmen to attend her, rode like a gray shadow over the green dunes, halting only to rest the horses and to sleep. She had coaxed the warriors from the chief of the raiding party, and when they would have sat down to argue for hours concerning suitable rewards, she silenced them with a word—

"Hassan!"

She could ride as well as they, and from somewhere she had conjured up a veil that covered her breast and face to the eyes. It was she who, when they entered a barren region of clay gullies topped by sage and tamarisk, pointed out the glint of water to the south and east.

But the eyes of the three were drawn to dense columns of smoke that rose from a grove of olive trees beneath them. Here should have been a Cossack village, and, since it was burning, here they would find Turks.

The Bashkirs rode down the hill at a gallop, reckless of rocks and hidden gullies, fearful only of being too late for the looting. They sped over a level patch of tilled land, where the grain had been trampled before their coming. And they swore in their beards when they found a regiment of cavalry dismounted and ransacking the last of the burning huts—a regiment of *spahis*, the crack cavalry from Constantinople. Where the *spahis* had looted the tribesmen knew that not so much as a belt or a woman's shirt would be left for latecomers.

With Kalil they were brought before the *aga* of the regiment, a Turk bearded to the eyes, with a jeweled crest to his turban.

"*Ohai*," cried the girl, "Hassan hath kindled a torch on this side of the river. Have the Russians fled before his wrath, O captain of a thousand—slayer of unbelievers?"

Beneath the flattery was a note of keen anxiety, and she held her breath until the *aga* made response.

"Nay, daughter of Islam. The dogs sit in their camps yonder and their ships sit at anchor. The time is not yet." Suspicion, lulled by her instant admiration, assailed him. "Who art thou and what are these jackals?"

The Bashkirs snarled but knew better than to make response to a colonel of the Turks. They looked at Kalil uneasily, having no doubt as to what punishment would be theirs if she failed to give satisfactory account of herself.

By way of answer she held out a hand, drawing back the loose sleeve of the cloak. The officer reined his horse nearer, stared at the ring set with sapphires that covered two joints of a slender finger, and salaamed respectfully.

"The signet of Ghazi Hassan, the unconquerable, the chosen of Allah—the ring that sets a seal upon all hearts, unlocks all doors. And yet—why dost thou ride from the direction of the *giaours*?"

"And yet quoth the dog when the wolf was at hand!"

Kalil laughed, and the Turk tugged at his beard irresolutely, for his men were looking on and had seen a woman laugh in his face.

"Because thou hast burned a village of peasants, hast thou grown to be equal in honor to the lord of Cairo, the conqueror of Syria, the scourge of Allah upon the sea?"

Kalil looked around with some interest, at the bodies that lay strewn in the street—bodies stripped even of socks and shirts, and marked with a crimson cross made by two slashes of a scimitar upon the breast.

"Nay," she added in a whisper, "even Hassan must have eyes to serve him among the *giaours*, and a tongue to tell him a certain thing he would know. Make haste and set me across the river, then give us fresh horses and an escort, and Hassan himself will thank thee."

The Turk, who had been more than a little doubtful, was won over by boldness. It was not well to detain a messenger of Hassan of Algiers.

Before midnight they had passed through the bivouac of a Turkish army division, and had entered the redoubts of Otchakof. While the tribesmen stared with all their eyes at more cannon than they imagined ever existed, and the lanterns of pickets, at the mounds of earth over powder cellars, and the riding lights of the squadron anchored in the roads, Kalil disappeared.

When they beheld her again they did not know her. She was sitting in an open palanquin, and in the light of the stars and crescent moon they caught the sheen of silk garments. They were aware of fresh perfume, aloes, and attar of rose.

From the city the Moslems who now accompanied Kalil led them down through a line of water batteries to the shore. Here they dismounted and entered a skiff, rowing out to a galley at anchor near the jetties—a long vessel with a high poop and the towering, slanting yards of lateen sails—apart from the other men-of-war.

A voice from the head of the gangway hailed them.

"Who art thou?"

The Berber laughed softly.

"Have I grown to be other than I am, O Jaimir? Knowest not Kalil of Fez, the slave of Hassan—the eyes of Hassan?"

"*Ma'shallah!* The pasha awaits thee with impatience this long time."

Although two officers of his staff, wide awake and armed, sat in his cabin; although Kalil had taken off her slippers and walked lightly as thistle blown over the desert floor, Hassan started up from his quilt, out of a sound sleep. One hand gripped the butt of a pistol in the sash at his waist.

"Ha!"

A glance at the girl and he dismissed his companions, and Kalil salaamed. Detaching the veil, she tossed back the mass of her dark hair with both hands, knowing that the pasha ever took pleasure in contemplation of her beauty. Knowing, too, that she had served him well, as had happened many times in the past.

Before coming to him she had touched her eyelids with kohl and her lips and fingertips with dark red henna.

"What word do you bring, daughter of Mokador?"

"The way is open for thee to strike."

"The praise to Allah!"

In Hassan's full cheeks the muscles tightened, and his black eyes gleamed.

Years ago Hassan, too, had been a slave. A boatman, then a corsair, he had risen by his strength, his dominant will, and shrewdness to be pasha of Algiers. He had served the sultan by sea—his men were fond of relating how he had put his ship beside the flagship of Orioff, yardarm to yardarm until both had blown up. Scarred and undaunted, he had rallied the scum of Constantinople to follow him to victory on the island of Lemnos.

They called him Ghazi, the Conqueror, when for fifteen years he fought the Christians in the Levant and Egypt. They said of him that he had never met defeat. In this *jehad*, this holy war, against the Russians, Hassan's name was a rallying note for the fanatical.

And his eyes were coldly shrewd.

"Who is he—this new admiral of the *giaours* on the Black Sea?"

"O lion-heart of Islam, harken to my tale, which is of the weakness of thy foes. I have seen the first blow struck."

"Bah—the village was taken as sport for my men, to blood them a trifle."

"Nay, before that the Bashkir tribesmen set upon a full battalion of the Russians and slew all but a score. A wagon train was taken."

Hassan considered her, fingers twined in his beard.

"What lie is this? Hast thou proof?"

"Two of the tribesmen wait upon the upper deck. They will tell thee that the Bashkirs of the plain and that Tatars of the Krim* are in arms and will move against the Russians."

"By the head of Othman, by the veil of the Ka'aba, does a woman make plans for me? I know that well enough. When the panther brings down the stag, the jackals will rush in. Thy tale?"

Kalil hastened to remedy her mistake, and the pasha weighed every word.

"Know then, O favored of Allah, that I went to Tsargrad.† There, in accordance with thy wish, I went from one place to another, singing and making sport for the officers, who sometimes talked of their plans, not knowing that I understood. The Russian soldiers are like sheep—they will follow where they are led, but without a leader they can do nothing. They call their pasha One Eye, and he is a great lord, ambitious and covetous, but knowing naught of warfare and caring naught for his men."

Again Hassan nodded. He had heard similar reports of Prince Potemkin, who was blind in one eye.

"But what of the fleet?"

Kalil wriggled with delight.

"In the journey out of the snow country to the steppe, I sang to the officers, heard other things. The fleet is now under command of two men—a Greek, who is a coward, whose name is Alexiano, and a Prussian, Prince Nassau-Siegen. The Greek is the very father of deceit, and the other is little better."

"Words! I sent you to Kherson to discover what kind of man comes from the Russian cities to take command over these two."

"True, and yet this pair, the Greek and the Prussian, will not readily yield their command. Even jackals will snarl when a dog comes to their kill. So, Allah hath made ill blood between the *giaours*." Her delicate lips curved in a smile. "The new admiral is an American."

"A what?"

---

*The Crimea.

†The Emperor's City—Petersburg.

"A man from over the great ocean where the sun sets."

Hassan puzzled over this impatiently until his brow cleared. Understanding came to him and he swept both muscular hands down his beard with an exclamation of triumph.

An American, he reasoned, would be a man from the United States—the new nation that had cast itself off from England's protection. All Hassan knew of these people was that American merchantmen had been taken at will by the corsairs of Algiers and Tunis. Until tribute had been paid, and Tripoli, eager to have a hand in the game, declared war on the United States, and the Mediterranean was scoured for shipping under the American flag.

No men-of-war bearing the new flag had been seen by Hassan, and he had the contempt of a good Moslem for a people that paid tribute to avoid battle. It struck him as the greatest of good fortune that the vice-admiral who was to take command of the Christian fleet in the Black Sea—who would be pitted against Hassan of Algiers—was an officer of this nation of merchants and weaklings.

"Ha!" As suddenly as a panther strikes, his hand closed over the girl's throat and he tensed with sudden suspicion. "That is a lie. My men have heard that this new admiral is a *bahadur*—a very father of battles. So he must be English."

Kalil made no move to free herself. Her eyes shone with adoration for this man who could have crushed her throat by tightening his fingers. When he drew back at last she seized his hand and pressed her lips upon it.

"Lord of my life, have not my words been truth before this? The empress summoned this officer to serve her from Paris."

"But why—why did he come?"

All of her twenty years had been passed in the bazaars where the rumors of the world are bruited and tasted and passed on. She had the rare gift of picking out the grain of truth from a whole harvest of falsehoods.

"He is a man who is like to a chained hawk, when on land. He is restless until he stands on the deck of a ship. Besides, he wishes to draw his sword against the Turks, with whom his people have some quarrel."

Hassan nodded. This was possible. "What is his name?"

Kalil essayed it. "The Russians call him Pavel—Paul. The French, *Monsieur le Chevalier Jean-Paul-Jean*. The English officers swear that he is a pirate."

Bowing his head, Hassan made no effort to conceal his pleasure.

"All things are possible with Allah! But when does he take command?"

"In Moscow it was said that he would start from Tsargrad within a month. He must be here now."

"*Inshallah!* As God wills. When the wind serves, coming from the sea, I will hoist the sails and give battle to the infidels. I will send fireships against them."

"To hear is to obey." She threw her arms around the pasha's knees and rested her dark head against them. "O my master, it is thus that I joy to see thee, a conqueror, protector of the faithful—" she murmured praises, calling him another Othman, a second Dragut, the wrath of the seas.

Putting her aside, Hassan rose and entered the adjoining compartment where a turbaned janizary stood guard by an iron lantern. Around the bulkheads here were ranged sandalwood chests and rattan boxes piled one upon the other. A heap of weapons lay in one corner, although the hilts of the scimitars and *tulwars* were set with precious stones, and the scabbards inlaid with gold and silver.

This was the treasure of Hassan—fruit of the Algiers *pashalik* and years of plundering. Wiser than most in his day, Hassan had gathered together the personal fortune of a *wazir* of the throne, and had concealed his wealth from the jealous eyes of the officials in Constantinople. Thus he could be open-handed with his followers who worshiped him the more for it, and he could sleep easily of nights, for his gold was in the cabin beside him. So it happened that he passed most of his time on the swift-sailing galley.

Now, while the janizary knelt, face to the deck—not to see the unveiled face of the slave girl who had followed Hassan into the cabin—the pasha unlocked a chest and drew out at random a sandalwood casket. This he gave to Kalil, who pressed it to her forehead before opening it.

With a murmur of delight she lifted to the light a chain of flawless, matched rubies.

"Behold, Kalil," Hassan complimented her, "the gift is fitting; for thou art a precious thing, without flaw. Abide then on the galley till thou art rested."

"Nay, my lord," she laughed, eyes aglow at his praise. "I will betake me to Kherson and spread the tidings of thine attack.

"See, my lord," she cried, knowing another way to please him. "This chain is an omen. Red as the fire in these stones will be the infidel decks, when thou hast set foot upon them."

The following day, the shrewd Algerian did not neglect to give to the Bashkirs presents twice as costly as they had hoped for.

And when they turned their horses toward the steppe, they rode with news for the tribes. They had heard of the first victory of Hassan, over the Russian flotilla commanded by a Prussian prince, when the Turks drove Nassau's ships into the estuary.

They had seen picked companies of janizaries and musketeers from the forts going aboard the vessels of the Moslem squadron, giving them double strength in men.

They had seen a hundred *agas* and as many *reis* assemble in council under the awning on Hassan's great three-decker, to which he towed with them in a barge from the galley. A thousand throats had greeted them:

"Salaam, el ghazi—Hassan, bahadur, salaam!"

Three others of the squadron were as large as the flagship, and the tribesmen had counted sixteen frigates, and more than a hundred smaller craft. These, mounting heavy guns, were to take the Russians in flank while the fireships were sent into the enemy, and Hassan's squadron with its reinforcements from the fort was to close with the Russians and board them.

As soon as the wind came astern, Hassan had sworn that he would advance. And the Bashkirs knew that he would keep his word.

Chapter IV

The piece of gold that will buy a bale of silk in the bazaar will not buy a bullet outside the walls.
                                                                    —Arab Proverb

It is the way of men in the ranks the world over to give nicknames to their commanding officers. The Don Cossacks and the Zaporoghians had christened the general of their division *Batko* Suvarof—Little Father Suvarof.

Whereas Prince Potemkin, commander of the forces of the empire, was known to them as "One Eye."

After a dozen victorious campaigns in Asia the Cossacks had no illusions about their leaders. They knew that Suvarof had won the victories and Potemkin had taken credit for them; so they said, one to another, that Potemkin was blind in his soul. And they were quite ready to follow Suvarof into the seven gates of a Mohammedan hell.

Potemkin, whatever the folk in Petersburg a thousand miles away might think, was not a soldier. He was a gigantic child of fortune, favorite of the beautiful empress; for through Catherine he ruled Russia and its millions of souls. His was the privilege of life and death, the thumb of a Caesar, the whispered word of a Mogul.

Yet, withal, he was jealous of praise. He had conquered the old empire of the Tatar khans, the Crimea and the steppe of Asia, the Caucasus Mountains, and the uplands of Persia. Now that the sultan of the Turks had proclaimed a holy war against the Christians, he devised a particularly bold move.

With the army he would strike south and east, take Otchakof—the naval base of the Turks—and move on Constantinople. In the last years the empress had ordered construction of some twenty frigates in Dnieper. With these he would destroy Hassan's fleet, and blockade the Bosporus.

He saw himself another crusader, marching on the walls of Constantinople. He would be master of the Black Sea, stronghold of Islam for more than a thousand years.

So that spring, fifty thousand men moved south and east, following the course of the great Dnieper.

Through the Cossack country they went, and that of the Tatar tribes. From the steppe they entered a desert country.

Potemkin had to leave strong detachments to guard his communications. The stores of food were beginning to dwindle, and they had none too much powder. He had not foreseen all this.

They pushed on, down a narrowing strip of land between the river Boug and the Dnieper, and came to a halt, perforce. Here the Dnieper ran into a long estuary, called the Liman, and ahead of them was the Boug curving into the Liman.

Otchakof lay at the narrow mouth of the Liman across the Boug, and Hassan's flotilla of smaller vessels patrolled the two-mile stretch of water.

Meanwhile came rumors of the invasion of Hungary on their flank by another Turkish army, and stories of unrest among the Mohammedan tribes in their rear.

Potemkin had not made allowance for the spread of the *jehad*—the holy war—to the tribes. The position of his army was critical and no reinforcements were arriving from the north. He was indifferent to the lack of meat, because wild duck and partridges were shot for his table;

his wines were cooled in ice brought from five hundred miles away at the cost of men's lives.

"If the men growl for meat," he said irritably to Colonel Popoff, his chief of staff, "let them take fish out of the Dnieper."

Nevertheless, he decided to hold a conference with his officers. He had just completed a rambling wooden palace in Kherson, seventy miles from the front. A dozen regiments had worked in shifts to build it in the waste of sand overlooking the river. In this, his headquarters, he gave a fete. Women had been brought from Kid to make it lively, and Potemkin ordered that they be attired as natives of the races he had conquered: Poles, Circassians, Georgians, and Tatars.

When the crowds around the faro tables and the musicians were greatest, Potemkin appeared for the first time. He entered the brilliant assemblage of his court, dressed to gratify a new whim—in a monk's coarse robe and sandals. At midnight Popoff announced that the council would be held, and ushered the general officers into a room where breakfast was spread—a breakfast of game and hot, spiced wines—and in the center of the table a map of the Liman was held in place by gold candlesticks.

Potemkin, with the lives of fifty thousand men hanging in the balance, could not resist playing the actor-harlequin on a stage set for death.

He listened moodily to the debate among his officers, who were not agreed. Benningsen was for abandoning their position on the Liman as too dangerous. Kutusof—who twenty years later halted Napoleon and the Grand Army at Borodino—maintained that it would be disastrous to retreat before the Moslems.

The Prince de Ligne, a noted diplomat, was all for holding fast where they were until the fleet, now under command of Vice-Admiral John Paul Jones, could drive Hassan out of the Liman and blockade the city from the sea.

Potemkin asked his favorite, the Prussian Prince Nassau-Siegen, for an opinion, since he was the only officer present from the fleet. The other officers looked at him curiously, for Nassau had expected to be given the command of the fleet instead of Jones. He had the rank of rear admiral, and the flotilla of gunboats was under his orders, while Jones led the battle squadron.

"With your Highness's gracious permission," observed Nassau, "I beg to point out that the masterly and far-sighted instructions given by your Highness to Monsieur le Chevalier Jones should be carried out."

Potemkin's one eye closed and opened expectantly. He had given no orders to the new admiral, but he had an ear for flattery.

"The squadron should proceed at once to engage Hassan's fleet, as you desire," Nassau went on, weighing the effect of his words on the man in the monk's robe. "At once! The Mohammedan fleet is the radical of the operations. As soon as it is removed—"

He went on to propose various stratagems while the Prince de Ligne took snuff and Potemkin listened, frowning. The Prince-Marshal disliked giving open-and-shut orders. For one thing, he did not know how. When things went well he could take the credit, when mishaps occurred the blame was fastened on some subordinate.

"By your leave gentlemen—" de Ligne raised two slender fingers and brushed daintily at the lace of his wristband—"may a man of letters who is not of either service inquire how our admiral can be expected to defeat the Turkish squadron, which is half again more powerful than his? I understand that frigates have been brought to Otchakof from the Barbary bashaws."

"If I were in sole command—" began Nassau, his voice rising.

"Unfortunately," murmured de Ligne, "the situation is otherwise. Monsieur le Chevalier is admiral. May I ask, Nassau, what he is doing to help matters?"

The full lips of the Prussian smiled.

"*Foi d'un gentilehomme*, the merchant reverts to his trade. Paul Jones, my lord, is laboring like a peasant fitting new rigging and drilling his crews at battery practice."

"But why?" De Ligne knew even less than Nassau or Potemkin of ships.

"He was once a merchant, and he was born a Scottish fisherman's—"

"If you will permit me, his birth does not at present engage our attention, but his actions. Is he preparing to attack Hassan?"

"No!" Nassau almost shouted, his full face, pitted by smallpox, flushing. "He has no heart for that. He complains that he finds the squadron unseaworthy—impossible to sail against the wind—and that no charts have been made of the Liman, which is full of shoals. He said the —— himself must have been in command of that squadron."

Potemkin frowned, annoyed. A certain officer of his, the Brigadier Alexiano, a Greek, had been in charge of the new squadron, and was now flag captain.

"Gentlemen," observed stout Kutusof in his slow, heavy voice, "I have studied the defenses of Otchakof from the far bank of the estuary. The old line of water batteries has been strengthened. Hassan has built a strong fortress on the hill. Its guns command the channel entrance and the anchorage of Hassan's fleet."

He glanced around inquiringly.

"How is it possible for the admiral to give battle to a stronger fleet under the guns of a fort?"

Potemkin drained his glass and leaned forward.

"We have not heard the opinion of Suvarof."

At the far end of the table a slender, stoop-shouldered Russian had been sitting, hands clasped over the hilt of a sword that was shaped like a scimitar. The hilt was gold, set with diamonds and sapphires, and chased in the blade was the legend: *For the conquest of Asia.* This was old Suvarof's sword of honor, bestowed years since by Catherine, and he always wore it.

His chin had been rested on his hands, and in the dim light the others had not seen that he was asleep. Suvarof had led Cossacks against some Turkish *spahis* two days ago, and that day he had come seventy miles on horseback. He was tired and he disliked councils of war.

"Your Highness," he replied, aroused by mention of his name, and alert at once, "was pleased to ask—"

"A plan—*mordieu*, we must agree on a plan!"

Suvarof glanced at the clock against the wall and sighed. His pleasant and rather plain face, lined and weather-beaten, was notable for a pair of clear brown eyes.

"Plans don't amount to anything," he said after a while. "Things happen differently in a battle."

De Ligne passed his snuffbox under his nostrils with a half smile. Nassau, who had been talking for an hour, chewed his lip, remembering that Suvarof was not one of the grandees of the empire, having risen from the ranks nearly half a century ago.

"Then do you desire a retreat?" asked Potemkin, knowing that this would strike fire.

One of Suvarof's maxims was that it was better always to go after the enemy than to retire.

The old general was a man of few words. He laid his sword in its scabbard on the table in front of him, shoving the map away impatiently.

Then he clasped his hands, placing one on each side of the sword. Then he looked at Potemkin.

Everyone was watching him, knowing that Suvarof's word would decide the matter.

"Your Highness, we can't go back. So we must go forward. The Boug estuary holds us." With a nod he indicated the scabbard and lifted one fist, placing it on the other. "Clear away Hassan's vessels for ten hours and my Cossacks will be across. Enough said for a soldier who knows nothing of seamanship."

"But how will Hassan's fleet be disposed of?"

"That is Jones's affair. Ask him."

Argument followed, voices were raised, and Potemkin, falling into one of his black rages, struck an officer in the face. Champagne was brought in and then vodka, and more than a few were drunk. Suvarof said nothing more, but listened without going to sleep again.

Popoff had drawn his rapier, to beat on the table, and began to make passes at the frightened servants who approached the table to pour the wine.

"A hit—a hit!" he cried triumphantly as he thrust a lackey in the calf.

Nassau, swaying in his chair, applauded.

"Go you one better, Colonel—curse me if I won't. Have in a girl to dance on the table."

"Lay you odds, Popoff," put in another, "you can't pink her in the legs."

"Done with you, *kunak*! Ten crowns!"

De Ligne, his lined face colorless as his powdered wig, rose from his place and stepped behind Potemkin's chair to whisper to the prince. Potemkin, who had been brooding over his glass, nodded and waved the diplomat away.

Signing to Suvarof to follow, de Ligne went to one of the doors where they could talk without being overheard.

"Permit me to ask, *mon general*; is our situation dangerous?"

Suvarof nodded.

"Ah. His Highness is pleased to give you full discretion. Act as you see fit but have an understanding with the American at once. He must work with you. Can you reach him tomorrow—"

"I am going to his ship now."

The heavy eyes of the diplomat studied the old general with some curiosity. "I make you my congratulation, Prince. Between ourselves, you
came with the purpose of gaining a free hand, without disclosing your
plan of operations. Pray, did not you desire this conference with the admiral?"

Suvarof's brown eyes met his stare without surprise or amusement.

"My dear de Ligne, would it not be better if Jones also had an undi-
vided command?"

The diplomat raised his brows, and did not reflect until afterward that
he had not been answered.

"How do you mean?"

"He was promised full authority, but he must act with Nassau and
Alexiano, it seems."

"But you have not known this American a week. How—"

"I know Nassau and Alexiano," said the general dryly. "And Paul Jones
is my friend."

De Ligne smiled and shook his head.

"Impossible!" He hesitated a moment. "Nassau is favored in a high
quarter—in Tsarkoe-seloe." His lips formed the words, "The empress."

A shout of laughter from the table interrupted them. A Circassian girl
was dancing unveiled on the map spread between the candles, her bare
toes touching in turn the goblets of the officers without upsetting them.
Popoff's sword glinted as it thrust at her clumsily.

Suvarof's face was grave when he left Paul Jones that evening and rode
without sparing himself or his horse to his quarters on the Boug. But he
had time to watch the Cossacks rub down the Arab that had carried him
on the last leg of his journey. When he was satisfied that they would not
give the mare water too quickly, he turned to confront a tall man who
lounged in the stable door, hands thrust in his belt.

"Ivak, you scoundrel, you are growing fat. I have work to do that will
make you lean." From long experience with his men, he was aware that
the giant had something to say to him. "What is it?"

The Don Cossack straightened, towering over the slender general. He
wore the long black coat and red sash of a cavalry regiment, both more
than a little ragged.

His saber would have cost a year's pay if he had not plundered it. When
he pulled off his sheepskin hat a long scalplock fell over one shoulder.

"Evil tidings, Little Father," he grumbled. "I was riding with the river patrol and we hit upon a village of our folk, with only vultures in it. It must have been a week since the Turks left it."

Ivak had braid on his collar—the mark of a *sotnik*, or captain of a hundred. He was past middle age, and in the widest black eyes and thin, downcurving nose there was a trace of the Eastern blood of the men from the river Don.

"We are collecting all the skiffs and flatboats along the Boug," he went on moodily, "and others are being built out of the forests as you ordered. The Turks are all on the other side and they keep watch fires going at night."

"Are the gunboats there?"

"Aye. Give me twenty men, and I will cut out—"

"Nay, I have other work for you."

"But the *kunaks*, the brothers are uneasy, Little Father. They are restless because the Turks who laid waste the village have not been followed up. *Ekh*—" he slapped the side of his head—"I was forgetting! The patrol brought in a powder wagon, from the steppe."

"How, from the steppe?"

"It was as I say. They heard a man singing in the darkness and at first they thought it was a trick, and then a wandering ghost. But it was a man named Pietr, a fine fellow, really. I took him to my hut."

"And the wagon?" demanded Suvarof patiently, knowing that the *sotnik* must tell his tale in his own way.

"They heard wheels creaking, and they rode down the party, twelve men from a Petersburg regiment and half as many wounded in the wagon. They were all that were left of a battalion and a supply train. Bashkirs attacked the train and the twelve had been fighting off other riders armed with bows slung over their left shoulders—"

"Tatars from the Kuban?"

Ivak considered a moment and nodded.

"Aye, Tatars from the Kuban; bad customers. I saw one of their arrows, fixed in the wagon."

"Do you think the tribes have mounted for war?"

"Aye, they have tasted blood. Out on the steppe the wolves are hunting in packs and the vultures are dropping lower. Yesterday I saw a rider from the Krim, down in the rushes of the river, looking at our outposts. I fired at him with my musket, but he was off like a flash—the weasel!"

The lines in the general's forehead deepened, and he stepped to the horse, picking up each hoof in turn to inspect it. The Arab thrust its lean, veined head against his shoulder, and he rubbed his fingers behind its ears absently. He moved stiffly because the ride had been a hard one, and old wounds irked him.

"Do you think the tribes are moving from the Krim?" he asked.

The *sotnik* shook his head.

"No, Father. This was a spy."

Suvarof understood that Ivak meant the Tatars of the Crimea were sending out scouts to find out how matters stood on the Liman. If the Krim Tatars took the field, the Russians would have small chance of fighting their way back along the Dnieper.

They were cut off. They must cross the estuary of the Boug, smash Hassan's army, take Otchakof. With the river between them and the tribes, who would hang back if Hassan was defeated, they would have breathing space. They could open up the Dnieper again, and bring in grain, meat and powder by sea from Sebastopol.

"Now," he said, "I will tell you what you must do to help your poor little father, Suvarof."

Chapter V
The Black Frigates

The crackling of a fire awakened Pierre Pillon, and he sniffed at frying fish. Then he groaned, being all one ache from head to heels, and thirsty beyond imagining.

Instead of arriving upon a smiling coast fringed with villages—villages with taverns, olive groves, and grape vines—he was still in the desert. The very earth on which he slept was sand streaked with gray salt.

He grunted, yawned, and rose to limp to the water jug. The fire smoldered in a ring of stones under a hole in the roof of the wattle and clay hut. Ivak knelt beside it watching the fish that sizzled in the pan.

A falcon screamed from his perch, and the Cossack took down a half-plucked crow from a mass of marmot skins and ermine that hung from a Circassian dagger driven into a post. He tied the claws of the crow over the perch, and the falcon proceeded to eat breakfast.

Pierre stared, because in his country hawking was a sport for the nobles. Ivak's hut had other treasures—a pair of soft shagreen boots and a high-peaked Kirghiz saddle covered with silk.

"Sit," growled the Cossack, indicating the saddle, and hacking the salt fish into equal halves. "God has given us bread and salt to eat."

He went to a shelf out of the hawk's reach and drew a plate of barley cakes out of a pile of odds and ends of silver, powder horns, spare flints, and finely made fish nets. Whatever the state of the army's commissary, the Cossacks usually managed to fare well.

When Pierre had satisfied his hunger, he looked up.

"*Bien merci*—my thanks to you, Cossack. Now point out the road that leads to the fleet anchored off this coast."

He had turned over the powder wagon with its burden of wounded to an officer of the advance; he had told his story to Ivak. His battalion was wiped out and he did not know where his regiment was. His one thought was to reach Paul Jones's ship, and join the marine guard.

Ivak was studying the big Provençal as a man might eye a promising horse he meant to buy. Going to the pile of sheepskins that were his bed—he had given it to Pierre last night—he put them aside and dug with his hands in the yielding sand, unearthing a stone jug tightly corked.

This he held out to Pierre, who had the cork drawn in a twinkling. The Provençal raised the jug in both hands and let cool red wine run down into his open throat. Ivak watched with interest.

"Allah, you pour out a man's measure!"

He took the jug and duplicated Pierre's drink. Then he produced two short clay pipes and filled them from his tobacco sack. Lighting a twist of hemp in the embers, he began to smoke in silence.

"An empty belly and a dry throat lead to short words," the Cossack remarked. "But now we can talk. You say you served under Paul, the American. Would you aid him, if the chance offered?"

"Only tell me how."

They were talking in the lingua franca that both understood, eked out with some Russian. Ivak had more than a little respect for a man who could bring a wagon in safely from the open steppe when the Tatars were raiding. He saw that Pierre did not know that he was an officer; but among the free Cossacks a trooper considered himself as good as his colonel, although discipline was strict.

Thoughtfully he patted the earth between his knees.

"Eh, this is my place; I have never served in the floating batteries. But Father Suvarof has sent me on a mission to the water. I need a *kunak*, a comrade, who understands the trails about a ship. Will you come with me?"

"To the flagship?"

"Aye, so."

Nothing could have suited Pierre better. He cracked his thumbs and grinned in huge delight.

"Come, *allons*! Let us go."

"You may have your skin slit open. Have you ever hunted from a *lo-pazik*, Pietr?"

The Provençal shook his head; only the gentry followed the hounds or coursed hares with dogs in his country; a peasant caught poaching would be glad to escape with the loss of his right hand.

"A *lopazik*," Ivak explained, "is a platform built in a tree. You sit in it to watch for game. A calf or goat is staked out beneath the tree at evening and you squat up in the platform until perhaps a tiger comes along in the darkness. Then you keep very quiet and make sure it's really a tiger and not a witch or something evil before letting off your piece. *Okh!* If you're a real huntsman you've sighted between the eyes and that skin is yours; if not the tiger goes off—*fut!*—frightening the wild geese and stirring up all the forest. Geese always cry out at midnight, but they sound different. I know all about it."

"Once geese saved a big city," nodded Pierre, to be polite, "by their squawking. That would have been Rouen, or Paris. That was before my time and besides I've never hunted."

Ivak shook his head in astonishment.

"Well, Pietr, it is hard to understand. Anyway, you are no green lad with a musket. Now you must go and build a *lopazik*—" he pointed through the door—"out yonder on the fleet. There are men on the *Vladimir*, Paul Jones's flagship, who would do him a bad turn if they get the chance."

Pierre pricked up his ears at this.

"Aye," went on the Cossack slowly, "I rode with Paul Jones from Peters-burg, the city of the empress. Eh, he is a *jighil*, not a *moujik*,* he thinks only of whipping the Turks, as a man should. The Turks have made the red cock crow in our Cossack villages, they have burned our hamlets and driven off our young women for slaves; they have cut off the hands and feet of our priests. Only God knows what they haven't done.

---

*An outrider—a daring fellow, not a farmer.

"Before the American came to the fleet, Pietr, there were two in command. A Greek named Alexiano, who has a pouch like a Polish landowner, and a Prussian named Nassau-Siegen, who has no belly at all. Once the Greek was a Moslem and men say that he tried his hand with the brethren of the Coast. I do not know. But between them they took many prizes near the Liman, and gained rewards for themselves, beside keeping the plunder. The prizes they took were merchant ships, and of all that loot they gave their crews not a copeck."

Pierre threw out a hand, palm up.

"Namé of a sacred dog! I have served in three seas and as many wars. But never have I seen the gun-deck hearties go without their share of prize money when a prize was taken. What kind of birds are these officers?"

"You will see." Ivak spat into the glowing embers. "In their looting they did not find time to sound the Liman, which is full of shoals as a dog of fleas."

"What kind of a sea is this?"

"You will see. Paul made soundings with me, in a skiff at night. We were fired on, but he did not give the word to go back."

"He is a man, that one." With a wave of his pipe Pierre expressed at once his knowledge of Jones's daring and his experience of the risks of navigating hostile waters.

Ivak fell into one of his sudden silences, wherein he seemed not to think as much as to dream, like the child of the steppe that he was.

"*Ekh*, a leader of men is Paul," he muttered at last. "Yet—would you turn your back on a tiger, Pietr? Not if you had seen one or smelled it at night. Paul has eyes only for the enemy in front.

"When we rode from the north to the Black Sea," he added slowly, "many times we found all the horses gone from the post stations. River bandits jumped into our path and we beat them off with cold steel. Someone would have kept Paul from his command. Perhaps it was Nassau, perhaps Alexiano; perhaps the Turk, or the —— himself. Who knows? *He* is cunning as a woman and full of hate as a trodden adder, and *he* will strike again on the ship.

"So little Father Suvarof, who knew that I came from Petersburg with Paul, sent for me and bade me seek out the traitor."

"Good!" The big Provençal struck his chest. "*C'est la guerre!* I'll smell out the rogue—I'll open up his hide."

"Nay, if you go about it like that, you will wake up some night with a knife in your liver. The men of the *Vladimir*, the flagship, are wolves; their fangs are long."

His eyes hardened.

"You must play the part of a masterless man; don't let them know you are the American's man. Say that you are a deserter, and don't stop at a brawl."

"Then," Pierre's face fell, "I am not to speak to the admiral if chance serves?"

"Not to him. Keep your ears sharp and tell me what you hear down under the deck where the men are camped. Every evening I will walk by the biggest mast. But don't speak to me unless you have learned something. All the ship knows that Paul and I are *kunaks*."

Pierre felt a twinge of jealousy, but saw the wisdom in the Cossack's plan. Ivak announced that they would set out at once, and proceeded to break camp by burying the jug and taking the hawk to the hut of a fellow officer. He led Pierre to the stables and ordered his horse and two others, picking out a trooper to ride with them to bring the beasts back.

He did not hurry, until his own horse, a black Kirghiz stallion, fresh from a long rest, broke away from the Cossack that held it. Ivak saw it rear and was at its side in a half-dozen swift strides. The stallion tossed its head and wheeled away, but the *sotnik* had a hand on the saddle horn. Running beside the horse, he leaped into the saddle.

Finding his stirrups and taking up the reins, he raced the stallion in a wide circle bringing up in front of the stables, reining in so sharply that its hind hoofs scattered gravel and sand over the onlookers. The Cossacks gave the performance no more than a casual glance, but Pierre looked glum.

"*Bon sang!* I cannot sit on a beast like that."

Ivak was utterly astonished when he learned that the Provençal had never ridden a horse. He asked how men got about in France, and learned that the gentry rode in coaches, while the peasants sat on donkeys, if they had them. He thought for a moment and ordered blankets girded to Pierre's mount instead of a saddle.

"Hold on by the mane," he directed, "and wrap your legs around its barrel so! Give him a hand up, one of you."

Cossacks strolled over from the barracks to stare at the unusual performance. To them a man who could not ride an artillery cast-off was a marvel.

"*Ekh*, here's a fellow who doesn't like stirrups—see his saddle."

"Nay, it's a new way to carry your bed around."

"Wrong, you simpletons. He's been to Constantinople and raided the sultan's stables. What are you going to do with him, Uncle Ivak?"

Pierre gritted his teeth and held fast. He saw that those troopers who swaggered in weather-stained uniforms, who wore weapons as if born to them, were veterans who knew their own worth, quite different from the recruits of Petersburg.

"Don't cackle before you lay an egg," Ivak remarked at large, not mindful to have his own dignity slighted through his companion. "This *kunak* of mine laid out more Tatars in the steppe than you would put to grass in a lifetime."

"Well, luck to him," shouted a trooper. "*S'Bogun*—go with God."

Some hours later they passed the last of the pickets and came out on the shore, where Ivak searched for and found a skiff hidden in the rushes. And Pierre had his first glimpse of the Liman.

They were halfway between the Boug estuary and the upper end of the Liman, where the Russian fleet was anchored in a half circle across the wide mouth of the Dnieper.

"Name of a dog," shouted the seaman, "this Liman—it is not the sea! 'Tis a bay!"

He could see the opposite shore, five miles away, a long line of sandy spits. To his right, nearly hidden in the heat haze, the masts of the Moslem fleet were visible. A single glance told him that they had blockaded Jones's squadron in the Liman.

When they came within hailing distance of the Russian line, Pierre rested on his oars, brushing the sweat and the gnats from his eyes. He saw two three-deckers, and counted the guns in the tiers—seventy-two. They were in the center of the line. The others were frigates, with a few sloops, eighteen in all.

Black hulls, encrusted with gray salt at the waterline, squat bows and lofty poops set with rows of stern windows that reflected the sun, stumpy masts and short spars, small sails—he did not like the look of all that.

"Dutch belly boats," he muttered, "crank and dull before the wind. They would make no way in the teeth of the wind."

He could see, however, that they carried heavy batteries. Behind the line, at the jetties by the Dnieper mouth, were half a hundred smaller craft, bomb ketches, double shallops, and great scows mounting a single long twenty-four or a mortar.

"The flotilla," nodded Ivak, "Nassau's flotilla."

Behind these, a barren shore, nearly white with salt, under the clear sky, as blue as the skies of Provence. He pulled slowly for the *Vladimir*, which he made out by the ensign at the staff over the stern lanterns. Passing under the towering stern with its gilded carving, he looked at the small gallery. This was called the Admiral's Walk, being sacred from immortal custom to that personage. No one was there.

Pierre waited until Ivak had gone over the rail. Then he kicked the skiff away and went up eagerly.

By shouted orders and the creak of block and tackle he knew that the gun-deck crews were at battery drill, but on the spar deck men were overhauling rigging, and he halted by the booms to stare around him, filling his nostrils with familiar smells.

A bearded Greek boatswain, wearing green pantaloons spotted with tar and a crimson scarf bound over his head, jostled against him and turned around to curse. Then, surprised by Pierre's bulk and long yellow hair, he growled a question.

"What are you about?"

Pierre began to explain that he had come from the Kherson dockyard, and wanted service with the marines on the *Vladimir*, but the other cut him short with a bellowing laugh.

"Oho-ho! Marines! Do you think this is Toulon? We have no marines and few men who have seen blue water. Have you? Then go below, my bully. You are big enough to pull a rope, and Number Four gun of the port battery lacks a ropeman. Bear a hand my fine lad and you'll have vodka to wet your whistle, before the Turks hack you."

He gave Pierre a push toward the fore skuttle, adding under his breath:

"I know your kind—deserter from the army, looking for a soft berth. No duffel, and a poor account of yourself."

Going below, Pierre reported to the gun captain and fell to work with a will.

An hour later he was laughing. It was hotter than the slave benches of a Turkish galley, and the men who flung themselves down beside him when the drill was ended reeked of stale sweat; the tackle of the eighteen-pounder that he had been handling was stiff and caught in the blocks. A

Syrian boy, half naked, wearing an amulet around his thin throat, had curled up like a dog, falling asleep as if worn out by toil.

Near the gun carriage a group of Tatars squatted without a word, only their eyes moving—fishermen by the smell of them. From the deck above came the shrill pipe of whistles and the patter of naked feet, but around Pierre welled the murmur of polyglot tongues.

A Cossack, who had been leaning against a stanchion picking his teeth, swaggered off, kicking the Syrian out of his way and grinning down when the yellow face snarled up at him. Pushing a Greek swabber from the water butt, he drank in long gulps, paying no attention to the sailor who fingered at his dirk, cursing venomously.

Somewhere a Portuguese was singing. Pierre chuckled, drinking it all in. So these were Ivak's sea wolves! Ten years ago he had been one of such a crew. Except that no Americans were to be seen, the gun deck of the *Vladimir* might be that of the *Bon Homme Richard* with its motley crew. And, unless Pierre was mistaken, there was a fight in these men.

Chapter VI
Pierre Makes an Enemy

"Those chaps will stand to their guns," he told Ivak after quarters that evening, standing by the bole of the mainmast.

There was a new gleam in the Provençal's eyes, a new swing to his shoulders. He had discarded the infantry coat, and the clumsy boots. His garments differed from the rest, because the bulk of the *Vladimir's* crew were drafted from the infantry regiments.

"But on the spar deck," he went on, "they are Greeks—"

Ivak nudged him in the ribs, and a man who had been passing forward stopped, to come closer. Dusk was falling—the long twilight of the southern sea—and the newcomer leered into his face.

"Oho, our little cockerel crows! Aye, 'tis our deserter from Kherson. Harken to Dmitri—you've made a bad bargain, you have."

It was the big boatswain of the green pantaloons, who turned to Ivak with something resembling respect.

"Where is his illustriousness, the admiral? He gave orders that men who could handle firelocks were to be told off, and the best of the lot picked for sharpshooters. They are to go to the tops—"

"Where?" asked the Cossack.

Dmitri pointed over his head, to the square platform that was the fighting top, above the main yard. Ivak surveyed with interest the shadowy antennae of the shrouds.

"He ain't aft, where the gentry sit at table," grumbled the Greek.

"Yonder is monsieur, the admiral," broke in Pierre. "Only listen, bosun, and you'll hear him."

Men who had come up from the stifling 'tween decks were grouped around the foremast. From the group rang out a voice that the Provençal knew well.

> "The King sits in Dunfermline town,
> Drinking the blude-red wine;
> O whaur will I get a skeely skipper
> To sail this gude ship of mine?"

It was an old ballad that Paul Jones must have got by heart from the mariners of Solway Firth when he was a lad, and he watched ships put in to Kircudbright from the American colonies. The men who listened recked not of the words, but the plaintive drift of the ballad appealed to them.

The songs of the steppe, like those of the sea, held a burden of sorrow, and Cossacks, who had an ear for harmony, soon caught the air. Rich voices joined the American's deep tenor.

> "I saw the new moon late yesterdeen
> Wi' the auld moon in her arm;
> And I fear, I fear, my master dear,
> That we shall come to harm!"

Jones was sitting on the breech of a twelve-pounder, hatless. Unlike the other officers he wore his hair unpowdered. Ten years had left lines in his swarthy face; his hands were thin, and the flesh had fallen away from his high cheekbones. But the quick brown eyes and the lift of the chin had not altered.

"Oh, he's a pretty fellow," grunted the Greek, "and very free with his songs and his double tots of rum and his airs about discipline. But what will he do when the time comes, and it's 'boarders away'?"

Pierre's temper flared instantly.

"When that time comes, you won't be treading on his heels, by —— you—"

He checked himself, remembering where he was, and why he had come to the ship. Dmitri put a hand to his hip where a knife was sheathed in his belt. But, glancing at the *sotnik* who was watching them, he stepped back with an oath.

"I'll pay you out! I'll send you to your account!"
Still muttering he hastened forward.

> "Half-owre, half-owre to Aberdour,
> 'Tis fifty fathoms deep,
> And there lies gude Sir Patrick Spens
> Wi' the Scots lords at his feet."

Lieutenant Edwards, the English aide and interpreter who had come
from Petersburg with Jones, joined in the last verse with a ringing bari-
tone. Then someone produced a *balalaika*.

Ivak grinned at Pierre.

"Watch out for Dmitri; he's a bad one with a knife. Now get down below and keep your tongue between your teeth, if you can."

When the Provençal had gone, Ivak inclined his head critically, listening to the *khorovod*, thrummed by the guitar and roared out by the deep
voices of the Don Cossacks. One youngster sprang into the center of the
circle, outlined against the after-gleam of the sunset. Arms akimbo, bare
feet striking the deck planks, he began the wild *cosachka*, the dance of
the southern steppe.

Squatting on his heels, he leaped up, his coat swirling, and Ivak began to pat the deck in time, thinking of other days when he had danced
in the villages on feast days and had broken into the ring of girls, to kiss
first one then another.

The riding lights of the squadron gleamed brighter as the red streaks faded
from the sky. Overhead the yards creaked. For the first time in a week a
fresh breeze was coming out of the south, blowing from Otchakof toward
the anchored squadron.

Jones, who had been watching the men, with Edwards, rose and went
aft to select the new topmen. Whether taking a Russian artilleryman aside
to explain by example the mysteries of side tackle and crowbar or showing the gun captains how to quicken their work by stacking round shot in
the stands near the gun muzzles, the American was in every drill.

The men grumbled, yet their food had been better since Jones arrived,
and they did not grumble overmuch when they saw that he shared in the
hard work. He was in everybody's mess and everybody's watch, tying a
Turk's-head knot for a clumsy apprentice and making a jest of it to the
boatswain's mate, who would otherwise have kicked the boy around the

mast. Or trying out a cutlass with a bearded giant of the Urals who had never been out of his depth in water before except on a horse's back.

Not knowing Russian, he could not talk to the men, except through Edwards. But they became accustomed to him and in the end they listened for his voice and took to following him around, only leaving him when he retired to the quarterdeck ladder.

Once alone in his cabin or on the admiral's gallery, he looked worried. He knew that the crew of the *Vladimir* was incapable of handling a vessel at sea. And daily advice came from Potemkin's staff, urging a movement on Otchakof.

Paul Jones answered that such a course would not be for the good of the service, and when opportunity offered he would act.

Potemkin replied—

"You are expected to do your duty courageously or to take the consequences."

Only Edwards knew what it had cost Jones to take this in tight-lipped silence and to go on cheerfully with the work of preparation, refraining from moving at once on the Turks and throwing away the lives of his men and officers.

Just now he was inspecting the muskets and hand grenades before issuing them to a gunner's mate, to stow in the tops. And he explained to the men who had been told off for duty aloft, the work of topmen, how musketry was to be directed on the gun crews of the enemy's upper deck. Ivak listened attentively and peered up at the shadowy bole of the mast. Finally he became restless and spoke to Edwards.

"Will Paul give permission for me to go to that platform, if there is a battle?"

"Can you handle a musket?"

"I can drop a wild pig in a thicket a hundred paces away."

Edwards smiled and turned to the American, who had a warm regard for the old Cossack.

"Eh, Ivak," Paul Jones asked, "why do you want to go aloft?"

"That up there is a *lopazik*." Ivak pointed to the fighting top. "'Tis a hunter's rest in a tree, and it should be easy to see game from such a high place." When this was interpreted to him, Jones laughed.

"Very well, Ivak. But you will find that tree more hazardous than the ground down here."

"Will the admiral allow me to take also a *kunak* who was once a sergeant of marines on French ships?"

"Faith; if there is a marine sergeant on the *Vladimir* he belongs in the
maintop."

That night the wind freshened, whining in the stays of the anchored vessels, and Pierre had the second watch on deck. He leaned on the preven-
ter tackle of an eighteen-pounder, staring out of the open port, listening
to the wash against the ship's side.

It was becoming clear to him that neither he nor Ivak was cut out for
scouts. If there was plotting on the *Vladimir* they could not hit on a trace
of it.

He turned his head just a little, eyeing the shadows cast by the lantern
at the mast. Then he swung around, his back against the bulwarks. Dmitri had been walking past the booms, and had stepped toward the eighteen-pounder, his bare feet noiseless on the deck.

For a moment they faced each other, the Greek grinning in his beard,
Pierre watchful, his arms folded on his chest.

"*Sant' Nicolo!*" grunted the boatswain. "You have good ears even for
a spy."

Pierre, remembering Ivak's advice, kept silent. He could see that Alexiano was on the poop, in talk with another officer. Most of the men of the
watch were asleep, out of sight; no one paid any attention to the boatswain and his victim.

Dmitri brushed a hand across his throat, under his oiled beard. He had
puffy, good-natured eyes and smelled of scent and wine.

"You are looking for your friends of the after-guard, eh? They won't
trouble about you, after you're down with the fish."

By now Pierre had seen enough of the Russian service to be aware that
if he answered the Greek back or struck him, Dmitri would knife him
and go free, if the man was in favor with an officer.

"You come," went on the boatswain, "you ask questions, you whisper
to that *sotnik*. You are to be topman, by the —— horns! Aye, Kherson is
lousy with spies and *they* picked you off to keep an eye on us."

Pierre let his hands rest on his belt, and leaned forward a little.

"With your fine ways and your French gab," hissed Dmitri, "the grandees thought you would fool us bullies. But I have been to Kherson, with
his excellency Alexiano. In the bazaar I heard talk. *When the wind is off*

the sea the Russians will be torn to pieces by Hassan's sea wolves. And that is true talk. Some of the men did not come back to the ships."

"Who said that?" Pierre was beginning to be puzzled.

"Who sent the wind? *Sukita fi adhimin*—bite your thumbs for woe, you dog! Nay, Kalil, that wench out of Otchakof had visited the bazaar. But it is truth. I came back, yet we be as good as dead men."

Dmitri stepped nearer, his breath hot on the Provençal's throat.

"The Turks will be upon us with this wind. What chance have these ships against them?"

"Don't stir up your bile," Pierre growled. "Hold hard. Who do you think I serve?"

"The *boyars* who sent us here, to have our throats cut."

"——'s thunder! I'm Paul Jones's man."

"A lie!" Dmitri threw back his head, and glanced at the poop. Down the Liman a cannon had rumbled.

The Greek hesitated, then crouched suddenly, whipping out his dirk. Pierre swung his fist into the other's face, sending him back half a dozen paces. Dmitri snarled into his beard and shifted the knife in his hand, to throw it. Then he looked up and lowered his arm slowly.

Alexiano, flag captain of the fleet, was running along the poop railing, shouting that the Turks were bearing down on them. Pierre did not understand what he said, but it was evident that the man was thoroughly scared. Dmitri was staring at his countryman in astonished contempt of such behavior.

There came a long hail from the masthead, and a second shot down the estuary. After a moment drums beat to quarters and the boatswain thrust his knife back in its sheath. Alexiano was still vociferating, and Russian officers in every sort of uniform ran out of the wardroom to the quarterdeck, some still worse for wine.

"*Moujiks*—that's what they are, gentry and all!" Dmitri spat on the deck and jumped to the wheel. "Here, you dog—bear a hand."

Pierre joined him and helped with lashings, listening the while to the muttering groups that surged around the mainmast and the skuttles. Here and there he heard petty officers swearing and the impact of a blow. A half-naked Syrian stumbled over a lantern on the deck and howled when he fell headlong.

"Fools!" said Pierre from the depths of his heart.

Taken by surprise, with the ship at anchor—aroused from the deep sleep of the hours after midnight, and startled by Alexiano's mad bellow—speaking no common tongue, and the most of them landsmen, it was natural enough that the men of the *Vladimir* should be out of hand.

Hassan of Algiers had closed the jaws of the trap upon them.

From under the poop lantern Ivak emerged completely clad and looking pleased with events. He grinned when he saw Pierre with one eye on Dmitri, who had had worse chances and less provocation than this to use a knife on an enemy.

"Come along, Pietr, show me the way to the *lopazik*. I have leave to go there. I'll take you."

"Well, in an hour we'll all be eating breakfast in purgatory, off the leaving of the saints' table above."

Dmitri grinned and rolled off to launch himself into the noisiest group in the waist, sending men to right and left, calling them unmentionable names.

While they waited for the topmen who had gathered at the after companion, Ivak explained that Dmitri was a former pirate of the Dnieper, a first-class pilot who would fight for his bread and salt and was worth a dozen men.

Pierre jumped to the bulwarks, running up the ratlines, and deriving some satisfaction from watching Ivak, who wore boots, laboring in the shrouds with a musket and powder horn.

When they stood in the maintop, under the clewed-up topsail, he heard a voice give an order through a trumpet from the poop rail.

"The admiral will pistol any man not found at his place."

By degrees quiet was restored, and Pierre saw—now that the battle lanterns were lighted—boys bringing up powder, and the crews gathering around the guns on the spar deck. Looking over the rail he could make out Jones at intervals, going quietly around the ship, exchanging a word or two with the gun captains.

Meanwhile Ivak had sighted the Turks. The keen eyes of the Cossack, accustomed to the murk of starlight, had picked out the blur of sails that showed well down the Liman. No more shots were fired, and after an hour Pierre wondered why the Turks had come no nearer. The wind had hauled steadily to the northeast, so that the Turks no longer had it over the stern.

Dawn revealed the reason why the Turks had held back. The largest ship, that of Hassan himself, which was headed for the Vladimir, had run aground on a shoal. Several feluccas were endeavoring to get the three-decker off, and the rest of the fleet was standing by.

Chapter VII

When the fat grow lean, the lean must die; when the leaders of the herd falter and look to right and left, the weakest fall by the wayside.

—Kirghiz Proverb

The efforts of the Turks to work the flagship off the shoal were hindered by the wind. An hour after sunrise it had hauled to the north-northeast.

Jones waited, watching through his glass the confused movements of the Moslems and paying no attention to the advice of Alexiano to draw his ships back into the river behind them while the wind still permitted.

The mishap to Hassan was a bit of luck; the change in the wind was another. Paul Jones made the most of both, unexpectedly. He ordered two signals set. One was for his squadron to advance line abreast and engage the enemy. The other was for Nassau's flotilla to follow.

The *Vladimir* raised its anchor and made sail, after a fashion. Under top- and foresails, the line of black vessels stood down the Liman, white water showing under the clumsy bows. Because the foreign ship captains knew their business, because Jones himself had charted the course of the channel, and mainly because even untried Russian seamen cannot go far wrong with a fair wind dead astern, none of the vessels fouled and none grounded, although at times muddy water was to be seen around the hulls. The line was ragged, as seen from the poop of the *Vladimir*; but the Moslems on their hundred-and-twenty-odd vessels could not know the weakness of the Russian squadron.

A puff of smoke showed on the bows of Hassan's ship-of-the-line, and rolled to leeward. White smoke, pierced by the orange flashes of the guns, poured over the water in front of the accompanying frigates.

Jones set a course that would take him between the stranded vessel and the second largest of the Turks and held his fire, Alexiano arguing fiercely against both courses.

Something whined overhead—clattered—and white splinters dropped on the poop deck. A block and tackle thumped down by the quartermaster at the wheel, who glanced at it and up at the sails. Then he spat on the deck and planted his feet.

A rumble as of a laden cart going over a bridge came from somewhere in front of the *Vladimir*. The first broadside struck them. White fragments whirred from the bole of the foremast, splinters that rose and fell like spray. A gun carriage slewed around, dismounted. Those who remained standing among the gun crew turned to stare at their mates who sat and writhed on the deck.

A red-cheeked infantryman held out his right arm as if it were something he had never seen before. Blood from veins slashed open spattered on his feet. Dmitri ordered the survivors to carry the wounded below, and bellowed for a lad to empty a box of sand over the growing wetness on the white deck.

The man with the slashed forearm did not seem to know what to do.

"Down with ye to the pit, little brother," grinned Dmitri. "Others will see a deeper pit before this sun sets."

He glanced up at the sunlight, full on the bellying sails, and a man laughed. Others swore, fidgeting in their places. Another broadside whined and rattled overhead and they ducked falling gear.

"Too high!" called out Dmitri. "We aren't up with the angels yet."

Then the roar of the maindeck guns, which made the planks leap under their bare feet, snapped the inertia of the men. Smoke swirled up and around them, and the side tackle men who were nearest the ports peered out to see the result. They began to shout hoarsely because they could see where hits had been made. Jones had waited until even unskilled gunners could do execution.

This was necessary, too, because among the numerous shoals he could not wear ship—to bring first one broadside then the other to bear. So he headed in between the largest of the Turks, more slowly now because the wind began to fail.

For a few moments his ships were targets for a destructive fire. The Turks served their guns rapidly. Many of the Moslems had dropped anchor to keep from running aground, and were in a position to rake the Russians as the latter came up, sluggish in the light wind. And now the flotilla of Hassan—a hundred-odd feluccas and xebecs in the shallows of the far bank—opened up with heavy forty-two-pounders and mortars.

Being out of range of the lighter guns of the Russian squadron, they could fire at leisure, and the effect of their fire was visible.

Through the cloud of rolling smoke that hemmed in the lower decks of the *Vladimir* the masts of the frigate alongside were seen to list sharply.

This vessel, the *Little Alexander*, had been hit several times between wind and water, and was sinking. Another bark near the end of the line had been dismasted and was drifting down on the Turks. Above the growl of the guns the men on the *Vladimir* could hear a roaring that was like the muttering sigh of surf on a rocky shore. This was the ululation of the Moslems.

"*Allah akbar—allah, il-allah!*"

To Pierre Pillon and Ivak, who were leaning on the rail of the maintop, waiting the time when they could use their muskets, this sound was familiar. They looked at each other gravely, and Ivak bent his head to Pierre's ear.

"The decks of those ships are crowded with men. I can see the coats of Osmanli infantry. They have more than we—twice as many. Will Paul try to board them, do you think?"

"We will see."

The Provençal turned away to caution the others not to fire until they could bring down a man with a bullet.

Although a boatswain's mate had been placed in charge of the half dozen in the fighting top, no one except Pierre knew what was expected of them, and as men will when life is at stake and decisions must be made, they began to listen to Pierre, those who understood his lingua franca explaining to the others.

He wrapped the netting they found lying on the platform about the rail, to check flying splinters. He stacked the grenades near the mast and told off the quietest of the lot to hold the lighted linstock, waving it gently so the flame would not go out, against the time when the fuses of the grenades were to be ignited.

A faint hail from the quarterdeck reached their ears, and was repeated, while the Russians stared blankly at Pierre, who had not understood.

"Ahoy the maintop!" Dmitri's stentorian voice clove through the uproar. "By the eyes of ——, are ye all dead in the tops? The admiral asks whether ye can see our flotilla, and tell him its position."

The pall of smoke below them hid their surroundings, but Pierre climbed over the rail and dropped to the mainyard.

"Aye, aye!" He went out to the end and came back to shout down at the boatswain.

"The flotilla lags behind, half a league."

Nassau's boats, instead of following up and engaging the Turk's flotilla, were making little way, obviously hanging back. For a moment Pierre stared down at the deck. Paul Jones was standing at the break of the poop, watching the *Little Alexander* through his glass. For a while Pierre searched for Alexiano in vain.

Then he saw him run out from the main cabin to the wheel. Cupping his hands, the Greek gave a command that Pierre did not catch. It was obviously in Russian because the sailors on the foredeck shouted a response and in a moment Pierre saw the anchor, loosed from the cat-heads, drop into the water.

"Bon sang!"

It was quite clear to the Provençal that Alexiano had given the order to let go the anchor on his own initiative. Equally clear that Jones could not have understood the order.

But in another second the American turned his head and ran to the side. He had seen or heard the cable going out. Striding to the break of the poop he shouted a question at Alexiano, who shrugged bulky shoulders as if absolving himself from all blame.

What Paul Jones said then no one else heard, but Alexiano flinched as if hit by a bullet and the admiral shouted through the trumpet to man the braces, Edwards interpreting as soon as the words were out of his mouth.

"What is happening?" asked Ivak, who was fiddling with the flint in his musket.

Pierre's answering gesture took in the whole ship.

"Hold fast and watch out aloft," he answered.

The *Vladimir*'s snub bow was coming around more and more quickly. The men below braced the maintopsail back in time. The whole mast swayed, and the mizzen-topyard came down with a splintering crash. There was a ripping of planks on the foredeck as the cable ran to its end, snapping off a cat-head and part of the rail.

The great ship swung to her anchor within pistol shot of two Turkish vessels.

For a moment there was a lull as the guns on all three ships were trained anew.

"That *sacré enfant du* ——, Alexiano has put us in irons!" cried the Provençal. "And the good God knows we will never get way on us again."

With the sandbar on which the three-decker of Hassan was stranded and the two ships hemming them in, with the wind now light and baffling, with their anchor down, they were as good as dismasted. The sailing qualities of the *Vladimir* were poor under the best conditions.

"Nay," the Cossack grunted, "the man is no more than a coward. He has arranged matters so we will not board the Moslems. *Ekh*, what now?"

Anew, the diapason of the guns roared below them. A shrill whining filled the air. Pierre coughed as the powder fumes got into his lungs, and leveled his weapon at the throngs of men that swarmed on the deck of Hassan's ship.

Smoke formed a swirling pall around them, out of which thrust the masts and sails. The firing quickened into a steady roar.

Whatever their failings, the ships that had followed the *Vladimir* into action stood to their guns. It was Pierre who first noticed that the starboard battery had ceased firing. After peering down a moment, he pulled his men away from that side of the fighting top.

"The big ship has struck its flag!" he shouted gleefully.

The guns of Hassan's three-decker no longer flashed and smoked. Its foremast had fallen, bringing with it the mainyard, and its hull was scarred and rent open. The other three-decker, anchored off the *Vladimir*'s larboard quarter, was now confronted by two Russian vessels, and, seeing that Hassan had surrendered, slipped its cable.

Slowly its head came around, as the wind filled its sails.

"What now?" asked Ivak, ramming home a charge in his musket.

"Pick off the men at that wheel!" exclaimed Pierre.

Taking careful aim he fired, and saw the half-naked seaman who had been turning over the great wheel stagger and raise a hand to his shoulder. Another ran to take his place, and the three-decker slid away from them.

The sharpshooters in the mizzen top of the *Vladimir* were following Pierre's example, but without his success. Ivak, who had finished loading, thrust the men away from in front of him and raised his piece slowly, lowered it as smoke drifted in front of him, and sighted again, without taking a rest on the rail.

He pressed the trigger, and Pierre saw the Moslem helmsman drop to the planks. Confusion reigned on the crowded deck, and for a moment no one came to take the wheel. The great ship drifted away from them, until the *Vladimir*'s guns no longer could be brought to bear on it.

Then it stopped suddenly, spars quivering. The masts listed, until the tiers of guns pointed skyward and at the surface of the water. Pierre, watching, saw its flag come down, and knew that it was fast aground on one of the shoals that fringed the channel of the Liman.

"What now?" asked Ivak, who had loaded again, and was looking around for something to shoot at.

For several moments Pierre did not answer. The firing was dwindling near the *Vladimir* and the smoke had cleared away.

The main squadron of the Turks, disheartened by the surrender of the flagship, had lost all formation. At least three frigates, trying to flee, had run aground. Two others were sinking, and the rest were making all efforts to escape down the Liman.

Jones had taken instant advantage of the turn in the tide of affairs, and signaled Fanshawe, who was in command of four frigates on the left of his line, to head down the Liman and head off the Turks at the narrow entrance.

Fearing now that they would be cut off, the remaining Turks were in utter disorder. Only the strong flotilla, in the shallows where Jones's ships could not penetrate, were keeping up a steady fire.

"Good!" exclaimed Pierre, grinning at Ivak. "You see what you have done. Behold, that three-decker has surrendered."

He spoke lightly, but Ivak was palpably astonished, glancing from his musket to the great ship. Then he set down his gun, and took out pipe and tobacco sack from his girdle. Filling the bowl, he seized the still-burning linstock and got a light from it.

"By the horns of the uncrowned one!" he muttered. "We had some sport from our *lopazik* after all. But to my mind a tiger has a lot more fight in him than that thing yonder."

After pondering this a while he went back to the bole of the mast and sat down, spreading his legs out at a comfortable angle and looking up at Pierre speculatively.

"If this is a battle of ships," he observed, "it is no more than a dogfight. The dogs snarl and yelp and the fur flies. Then they go off and lick their rips, and that's the end of it."

But Ivak had not yet seen the end of this.

Chapter VIII
Nassau Bears a Hand

A haze of powder smoke and heat overhung the Liman. Through this murk the cyclopean eye of the sun glared on battered ships, and men that toiled unceasingly. In the weed- and wreckage-strewn water, this eye of the sun marked a glowing path as it sank to rest.

And through the haze slipped a white winged thing, as a gull, circling among clouds, flashes into a ray of light.

It came up swiftly on a long slant toward the smoking deck of the stranded Turkish flagship. The men in the maintop of the *Vladimir* identified it as an Algerian sailing galley; its rake and shear, twin lateen sails, and high poop with gilded and carved woodwork were unmistakable, even if it had not carried the green flag with a silver crescent at the masthead.

"The galley of the captain-pasha," Ivak pronounced. "Hassan keeps his sea wolves aboard it."

They watched it pass under the far rail of the Turkish three-decker, losing way as its sails were blanketed by the mass of the line-of-battle ship. Then they saw several men jump from the waist of the larger vessel to the high poop of the galley. At once the Algerians headed away, keeping the three-decker between them and the guns of the *Vladimir*.

"Smartly done," assented Pierre. "There's a sting in those hornets yet." He could make out men in white and red cloaks who wore turbans different from the peaked headgear of the Turks. They crowded around one powerful figure in yellow. A scimitar was drawn and waved defiantly at the Russians, who were beyond musket shot.

"Aye," nodded Ivak, puckering his brows. "It is in my mind that Hassan escaped on that vessel. I will climb down from this tree and tell Paul what we have seen."

It was no easy matter to go down the damaged ratlines, but he made the deck. He stepped over a great rent in the planking, and, circling a group at work getting a gun back on its carriage with crowbars and tackle, bumped into Dmitri, who was swinging an ax at the wreckage of the mizzen top-yard.

In its fall this had smashed the wheel, putting the *Vladimir* out of commission for at least a few hours.

Dmitri turned with a barbed oath that changed to a grin when he saw the Cossack.

"Out of the way, Uncle. This is not your place."

"Where is Little Father Paul? What is Alexiano doing?"

By way of answer Dmitri pointed with the ax. The Greek flag-captain was standing by the gangway head, waiting until a boat could take him off to a felucca that had come up when the firing stopped. Ivak watched until he saw Alexiano go over the rail of the little vessel and the felucca stood off to the other side of the Liman. Then he touched Dmitri's shoulder.

"Tell me, Pantaloons, is that big buffalo in the boat with one sail going to give chase to Hassan's galley?"

"Not he! His excellency—" and he smiled scornfully—"was sent by Paul to bring up the flotilla. By the holy name-days, was Hassan's galley about here?"

Ivak explained what they had seen from the maintop.

"Rare prize money escaped us then," Dmitri muttered. "'Tis said the cabins of the pasha are plated with gold. Paul is below in the steerage, fitting a spare tiller to the rudder stem."

As he made his way below Ivak reflected that Alexiano was where he could do no more harm for the time being. He found Jones with his coat off, helping some sailors rigging give-and-take tackle, to steer by hand. Through the interpreter, the Cossack made his report, and Jones looked up with a smile—in good spirits as always when there was action in view.

"Gentlemen, we have not done with the captain-pasha. Ivak, did you have good hunting from your *lopazik*?"

Near at hand heavy guns boomed, and the sailors glanced at the American questioningly. Motioning them to continue their work, Paul Jones started for the upper deck without waiting to put on his coat. When Ivak and the Englishman gained the poop ladder, they found him standing at the rail, his swarthy face tense.

All around them barges and squat sloops were pressing forward slowly, firing on the stranded Turks. Ivak saw the mortar on a bomb ketch flare, and watched a flaming shell describe an arc crashing into the waist of the dismasted three-decker.

He heard a faint outcry following the explosion of the bomb, but the Turks made no effort to answer this new attack, being unable to bring what guns remained serviceable to bear on the gunboats, or perhaps accepting with the resignation of their race the kismet that was in store for them. Ivak had heard it said that the Russian flotilla under Nassau-Siegen had come up at last, and instead of engaging the Turkish gunboats, was destroying the ships that had already surrendered.

"If they had arrived an hour earlier," grumbled the Englishman, Edwards, "we would have accounted for all Hassan's squadron, instead of half. Nine frigates got by Fanshawe and put to sea."

Rowed by fifty sweeps, a long barge was approaching the *Vladimir*. Its prow bore an enormous bronze eagle; its stern was roofed over with tim-

bers carved and gilded. Under this was a space where a half-dozen men
sat. At one time this barge had carried the empress upon an inspection of
the new fleet. Now it was devoted to the use of Nassau, who sat on a divan, nursing a sword between his knees.

"*Monsieur le Prince*," Jones hailed in his clear voice as soon as the barge
was within hearing, "those ships have struck. They are our prizes."

Nassau stood up to watch the firing.

"Is it to me you are speaking?" he shouted. "Did you think that quarter was to be given to the Moslems?"

"Aye—why not?"

"The orders of his Highness, Prince Potemkin, were that no quarter
should be given and no prizes taken," responded Nassau at last.

"No such orders reached me. These vessels can be floated off, with a
change of wind. They would be invaluable to the fleet."

"My dear Chevalier, I am no merchant to figure the profit of salvage."

Nassau smiled at his own quip—for it was generally believed among
the Russians that Paul Jones had been a merchant.

Though he kept his voice under control, Jones was growing angrier.
"*Monsieur le Prince*, this is a wanton waste of human life and property.
If you will—"

"Death of my life! Once again I remind you that I have secret orders
from his Highness himself. *He* does not wish this *canaille*—" Nassau
waved his hand at the men peering from gun port and bulwarks on the
flagship—"these mongrels to get the foolish notion of prize money into
their heads."

He was speaking French, and only a handful of officers understood.
But Jones instantly resented the slight to his men.

"The men and officers of my command have been under a hot fire for
six hours and they have borne themselves well—a circumstance, *Monsieur le Prince*, that you have not been in a position to observe."

Nassau's full face turned a shade darker, and the Englishman, Edwards,
nearly choked in the effort to suppress a chuckle.

But Jones was intent on the need for action while the daylight lasted.

"Nassau," he continued, "we are wasting time. Will you order a division of your gunboats to engage the remaining vessels of the Turks'
flotilla?"

"It is too late, my dear Chevalier, to make good the mistake of the squadron. Yon have let Hassan escape. He and his galley, which is moored under the Otchakof batteries by now, are worth half the Turkish fleet."

Jones listened in frank astonishment. The *Vladimir* had done everything possible under the circumstances to close with Hassan's ship. It was the first time that he had encountered the ignorance and undisguised insolence of those who were close to the throne of the empress.

"You, my Admiral," went on Nassau, as if weighing his words, "will be called to account for failure to act courageously."

For a full moment Paul Jones was silent, the muscles tightening on his jaw, his fingers fastened on the rail. Edwards glanced at him and laid a hand on his arm, whispering that the prince must be trying to trick the man who held the post he desired into a statement that could be turned to account later.

"It is not so," Jones said under his breath, and then clearly. "*Monsieur le Prince*, my men will cut out the galley of the pasha before dawn. It will then be for his Highness to judge if we have acted courageously."

Nassau shrugged. He knew as well as Edwards and the other listeners that the surviving vessels of the Turks were gathering at Otchakof, under the guns of the strong water batteries, and within range of the new fort on the hill. To his mind, to attempt to cut out the galley of Hassan would be simple madness. The Moslems would be swarming around it like angry bees.

"A promise—" he began.

"I have given you my word."

By degrees it became clear to the listeners that the American meant what he said. Nassau started to speak, thought better of it, and took snuff instead. The pause that followed was broken by a shattering roar.

The *Vladimir* quivered and rolled, and men who had been flung to the deck got to their feet and ducked a rain of debris. The Turkish flagship with all on board had blown up when one of the shells from the gunboats reached its magazine. Only its lower ribs blazed in a rolling cloud of smoke.

At once the barge bearing Nassau and his staff pulled away, dipping over the swells.

"Egad," murmured Edwards, "they go back faster than they came."

Moslem seamen were jumping from the rail into the water; others who could cram themselves into one of the boats were pulling away for Otchakof.

"Good!" barked Ivak when he heard of Jones's purpose. "Hassan's men will have their blood warmed up. They will fight like hemp eaters after this. But will Paul go with us?"

"He ought not to. No admiral has seen fit to lead a cutting-out party in person before. So—I'll lay you dollars against rubles that he goes."

It was midnight before Jones returned from the flotilla. He had rallied Korsakof's division of gunboats and dislodged the remainder of Hassan's small craft, driving them within range of the Moslem batteries. Scattered about the shoals the hulks of nine Turkish ships still smoldered and flickered, like the embers of gigantic watch fires.

Before he left, Jones had given instructions to the second in command to pick out a hundred and forty men and issue them small arms—cutlasses and boarding pikes, and pistols for every other man. The Russian, who had had no dinner that afternoon, was pleased when Ivak offered to select the detachment for him.

"But they must be volunteers. His excellency said so."

"Aye, they will be," Ivak assured him gravely.

Whereupon, after assuring himself that Lieutenant Edwards would supervise the selection, the Russian retired to the wardroom and dinner. Cossacks, he reflected, knew the business of boarding—they were half pirates anyway.

They began to pick out men, choosing first the veterans from the army, then the Don Cossacks, and sailors selected by Dmitri.

To Edwards it seemed as if they picked out the greatest rogues of the lot, but Ivak was satisfied and so was Pierre. Those who were chosen began to make fun of the rest until Ivak ordered them below for gruel and vodka and a little sleep, naming Pierre and Dmitri to watch for the return of the admiral, while he and Edwards went aft to see to the small arms.

Paul Jones ordered the boarding party mustered in the waist for inspection. He had brought back with him three long shallops—riverboats captured from the Turks—and he set some of the Cossacks to work at once wrapping rags around the oars.

They were all watching him, as he examined their pistols and greeted some that he knew by name. They noticed the square set to his shoulders, and the way he wore his three-cornered hat a little aslant. They tried to listen when he called the lieutenant from the *Vladimir* and Ivak together for a few words.

When he took his seat at the tiller of the shallop they nudged one another and whispered. He was going with them. No doubt of that now.

Edwards was with Jones in the first boat; Ivak and Dmitri had the second, and the lieutenant took the last, in which Pierre found himself.

"*S'bogun!*" a voice called after them.

The dark mass of the three-decker fell away as the oars bit into the water and started down the channel almost silently because the thumping of the tholepins was muffled by the rags. Jones's shallop was in the lead, the others following close enough to keep it in sight.

Out of the maw of the boat eyeballs flickered at the man who sat in his shirtsleeves by the tiller. The dull gleam of bared steel or teeth that flashed in a smile gave him assurance that they were ready for what was to come.

"He is like a man of stone," one whispered under his breath. "Aye, like the stone figures—the *kurgans* on the steppe."

They sensed his cheerfulness, and it made them light-hearted, so that they turned to stare at the burned framework of a stranded ship, still licked by little flames, or at the campfires along the shore, which were like red eyes winking at them. They had never seen so many fires before, and Paul Jones studied the shore thoughtfully.

These were not watch fires. The Turks must have moved back several regiments and bivouacked near the line of the Otchakof fortifications. He headed inshore until they were skirting the outer fringe of the rushes. By doing so he avoided whatever patrol boats were out in the channel. If the shallops were seen by pickets on the land, they were taken for Tatar fishing craft. Cutters might have aroused suspicion, but certainly the Moslems were not looking for a raid by the Russians that night.

Jones followed out his plan, which was to work along shore under the very guns of the water batteries, until he came to the jetties. That evening he had noted carefully the position of the galley, anchored in the center of Hassan's flotilla.

"Here's the corner bastion," whispered Edwards. "Yonder lantern is on the palisade. What's all the stir about?"

Far off in the darkness horses neighed and wagons creaked and armed men marched, or so it seemed. The shore was rife with movement, but nothing could be seen and the murmur of the wind in the rushes and the lap and gurgle of the water made it impossible to judge what was happening.

"On my soul and honor, some mischief is brewing," added the Englishman, bending closer to the water to listen.

Jones laid a hand on his knee warningly as they passed under the stern of a small xebec and heard men talking on the deck.

Evidently they were noticed, because the murmur of voices ceased and someone hailed them in Turki.

"*Ma'uzbillah!* Even the dogs take refuge behind walls. Are ye from the river Boug?"

"From the river," a Syrian in front of the officers made response promptly.

Edwards wondered what had happened at the river; but they were not challenged again, although they made out the loom of the two water batteries and the muzzles of cannon a stone's throw away. When they heard the clattering tholepins of a guardship approaching, Jones gave command to cease rowing, and they drifted until the other boat pulled past. He steered around anchored vessels, penetrating into the mass of shipping from which Edwards for once wondered whether they would escape again. But in the early hours of the morning the Moslem crews slept like the weary men they were, until the long hull and the raking yards of Hassan's galley loomed up before the shallops.

Then came a sharp challenge and the flash and bellow of a musket, proof that the Algerians were awake. Edwards swore under his breath, finding time to wonder again why the watchers on this particular vessel should fire at small boats so casually, not knowing that the Algerians were accustomed to keep all other craft away from the galley for a good and sufficient reason.

"Mr. Edwards," observed Jones, "be pleased to order the men to pull with a will for that galley."

Chapter IX
The Horseman in the Mist

And with a will the men in the shallops bent to their oars, closing in like hawks on a heron. Delay would have brought a discharge of slotted carronades. Jones, rising to his feet, steered under the counter of the galley and let go the tiller as the sailors dropped the oars. Some tossed grappling hooks with lines attached over the rail; others pulled themselves up to the sills of the open ports, actually gaining footing on the muzzles of the cannon.

Over their heads a shouting arose—a pattering of bare feet on the deck boards—the angry mutter of a drum. Muskets flashed along the bulwarks; and bullets slapped into the water behind them. Since firearms were invented the children of Othman have usually overshot their mark.

Edwards saw Jones catch a line and go up it, his feet braced against the galley's side. Turning to a bearded giant at his side, the Englishman offered him a shilling to lift him to his shoulders. Promptly the sailor dropped his pike and gripped the officer about the knees, heaving him up easily as if Edwards had been a man of straw.

Someone gave him a hand and swung him to the rail, in time to see Jones standing on the bulwark.

"Up with ye, lads," he called down to those in the shallop. "Don't fire till ye can singe their beards!"

Drawing his own pistol, he thrust it into the face of an Algerian who was running at the admiral with a drawn scimitar. The man crashed down into the scuppers and Edwards jumped over his body. A dozen sailors had gained footing on the deck beside him, and those who came up from the shallop discharged their pistols as they straddled the rail.

But now a flare at the break of the poop scattered the darkness and showed turbaned figures thronging from forecastle and poop. They stared in amazement at the Christians climbing into the waist, then rushed, scimitars in one hand, knives in the other, and a shout ululating in their throats.

They hewed at the pike heads thrust toward them and leaped forward, stabbing with their curved daggers. Cutlass clanged against scimitar, and the shouting grew to a hoarse roar, wordless and menacing as men came to grips and blood spattered on the deck.

Sailors were coming up from the third shallop, and Pierre, cutlass in hand, plunged into the fight. Throwing his smoking pistol into the face of a Moslem, he slashed the man through the ribs and stooped to pick up a half pike that lay by a dead Russian. With this in his left hand, he cleared a space for others to follow.

The big Provençal, stripped to the waist, shining with sweat, teeth gleaming through the tangle of his beard, roared from an open throat. The mighty thews and the height of him made even blood-crazed Moslems pause, and the sailors rallied to him as the Algerians thronged forward in greater numbers.

Paul Jones, leaving the bulwark, thrust to Pierre's side, his slender rapier making play under the whirling arm of the giant.

The boarders were being pressed back and harassed by musketry from the galley's poop when a shout went up from the other rail.

"*Hourra!*"

The second shallop had passed to the far side of the galley, and Ivak and the Cossacks—who were old hands at this sort of thing—swarmed up the side almost without opposition. Their rush took the Algerians aback and broke up the crowd of Moslems in the waist into little knots. The Cossacks had the advantage of pistols, and held their fire until they could bring down a man.

Raging like trapped wolves, Hassan's men were beaten back to the quarterdeck. Many, cut off from their fellows, jumped over the rail. No one cried for quarter and no quarter was given.

Around the poop ladders a bitter struggle began, almost in silence. Good swordsmen and dour fighters, the Algerians held the ladders against the pikes and cutlasses of the borders, while the muskets of the *reis* and his officers picked off the Russians.

"Mr. Edwards!" Paul Jones's voice rang out. "We must dislodge those fellows on the poop. Order the boatswain to whip up that bucket of hand grenades from his shallop. He can light his slow match from the lantern at the mainm'st."

At the moment Dmitri was occupied in a self-appointed task. He had armed himself with an ax and was hacking at the door of the poop cabin, which had been fastened from within. The overhang of the deck protected him from the muskets of the Algerians, and he was making the splinters fly. When Edwards shouted at him he had chopped a hole in the door and smashed the bar that held it in place.

Either he did not hear, or he refused to obey the order. Edwards started toward him, when a shout went up simultaneously from Algerians and Cossacks.

"Hassan!"

A stocky form thrust through the men on one of the ladders, and the sailors below scattered. The pasha, the sea rover of Algeria, stood on his own quarterdeck for the last time, his beard bristling as his lips lathered in animal-like rage. His cloth-of-gold coat was stained and spotted on the side where a bullet had raked his ribs.

He held up his left hand and spoke, panting between the words.

"'Tis quarter he offers you, sir," explained Edwards in the lull that followed the appearance of the Moslem leader. "He says that you and your men will never win free from here."

Paul Jones smiled.

"On the contrary, Mr. Edwards, I will offer him quarter. The galley is my prize."

The first words had barely passed the Englishman's lip when the Moslem swung up his heavy scimitar and leaped, not at the officers but at Dmitri, who was peering into the dark entrance of the cabin.

The Greek saw him coming and hurled the ax, drawing his knife at the same time. Hassan, quick on his feet as a wrestler, dodged the missile and struck. The curved blade of the scimitar swept across Dmitri's torso and came away dripping. And the big boatswain moaned, falling heavily on his face, the soft muscles under his ribs severed and his stomach cut open.

Hassan spared him not a second glance, but rushed at Paul Jones, who took the sweep of the scimitar on his rapier and turned it aside with a twist of the wrist. Before Hassan could strike again, or the American could recover his guard, Ivak came back between them and engaged the pasha's blade with his saber.

For a full moment those on the quarterdeck stepped back, to give room to the swordsmen. The two blades clashed and slithered together and sparks flew under the waning glow of the flare overhead. Ivak, the taller, was also the calmer of the two; but Hassan's strength and cat-like swiftness evened the balance.

Jones and Edwards, resting the tips of their rapiers on the deck, followed with fascinated eyes the progress of this duel; for here was no riposte, no thrust in tierce, but the savage onset of giants, both swordsmen of a race of swordsmen. So might Sohrab have fought with Rustam on the plains of Iran, slashing with a full-armed sweep and leaping clear, the two blades making a ring of light over their heads.

They passed over the groaning Dmitri, smashed against the quarterdeck rail, and jumped clear. This gave the Cossack the chance he had been looking for. He tossed his saber from his right to his left hand and struck over Hassan's guard.

The pounding of their feet on the deck boards ceased, and those who watched saw that Ivak's blade had cut to the Moslem's shoulder on the right side and was caught in the neck muscles. Hassan's scimitar clattered on the deck. Then, with a wrench that must have meant sheer agony, he twisted free and leaped to the rail, springing into the water.

A wail like the cry of a seagull stilled the shout of the sailors. Out of the black cabin entrance emerged a shape half hidden in swirling silk and a veil that concealed everything but a woman's eyes. A woman's eyes that blazed with fury, and wild grief.

Her bare arms, gleaming with bracelets, were raised over her head and her anklets clinked as she sprang over the prostrate Greek and climbed to the rail. The superstitious sailors drew back and crossed themselves as if an apparition had come up out of the underworld.

Ivak, who stood nearest, peered at her and gave tongue—

"Kalil! The she —— of Hassan."

Poised on the rail she stared down at the men as if summoning Allah's thunderbolts out of the sky to blast them.

"Aye, Kalil," she screamed, "the beloved of Hassan. Hear, O Hassan, for I come to thee . . ."

With that she was gone, disappearing into the void of blackness so silently that men were found thereafter who swore that she had vanished into the air itself. But the Russian lieutenant who had been reloading his pistols methodically stepped to the rail and leveled his weapons at the two streams of phosphorescence that moved away from the galley's side where the Moslems were swimming.

Edwards however struck up his pistols with the flat of his rapier.

"Would you fire on a woman? Let them have their chance, man! Faith," he laughed, "this night is out of the very pages of the Thousand and One Nights. Look yonder!"

The Moslems on the poop had lost heart at the downfall of their leader, and the *reis* himself, cloaked and hooded and striding with the pride that is greater than defeat and disgrace, had descended the ladder and thrown down his weapons in front of Paul Jones. The others followed his example, hearing that the American had offered them their lives. Some fifty surrendered and were astonished past belief when they were not slain out of hand in spite of promises.

Jones issued strict orders that none of the prisoners should be harmed, and they were herded in the waist of the galley. Edwards, cupping his eyes in his hands, could no longer make out Hassan and Kalil swimming toward the shore. But he thought he could see two shadows moving away into the mists.

He wondered—for Edwards was always cool and meditative of the why and wherefore of things that happened in the Black Sea—whether Hassan had come down because he had understood the order to bring the grenades, or whether he had tried to reach Kalil.

Pierre bent over Dmitri, who lay curled up, one arm gripping his slashed abdomen. The other hand stabbed the air in the direction of the cabin entrance. The Greek seemed to want him to go in there.

"I'm counted out, Pierre," he muttered through set teeth. "Search the poop. Hassan keeps treasure—on galley. Loot, for all."

Pierre's memory was stirred by half-forgotten words; Kalil—she had talked of the riches on this galley. And Dmitri had hazarded his life to break down the door.

The two were unnoticed in the corner by the wheel, while the Russians were gathering the prisoners together and combing out the forecastle and lower deck, and the Cossacks under Jones and Edwards were endeavoring to make sail. The flare had gone out, leaving the deck in gloom. But across the Liman the sky was growing less opaque, and the outlines of the shore and fortifications were taking shape.

The Greek gripped Pierre's knee convulsively.

"*Sant' Nicolo!* Alexiano will follow me—with short shrift. We—both— *renegados* in Algiers. Moslems we were, by ——! And the Moslems will seek him out and put an end to him. The followers of the prophet have marked their bullets for those who go over to the *giaours*."

"Aye, aye," said Pierre, and Dmitri's torrent of words went on.

"Kalil talked with Alexiano after he took command. He is afraid. He promised that he would do what he could to hamstring the Russians if Hassan would spare his life. Now he is more afraid, because the Russians have flayed Hassan. He knows the Moslems will find him." A gulping groan choked the words in his throat. "The dogs! The sons of swine—I did not fear them."

Inarticulate curses bubbled the blood on his lips, and Pierre hastened away to seek Ivak. He found the Cossack inspecting Hassan's sword by the lantern, and after a glance around to see that there was no fighting and nothing to be done except by sailors, the Provençal led the way into the poop cabin, cutlass in hand.

The passage was empty and most of the compartments dark. They stumbled over a pile of quilts left by someone roused from a sound sleep, perhaps Hassan himself. At the end of the passage was a glow of ruddy light, and Ivak halted to listen and make sure that no one was breathing near at hand.

Then he strode through the opening and kicked against a solid teak door to make certain no one lurked behind it. The compartment had no other opening and the air was heavy with the smell of sandalwood and aloes.

"Allah!" he said feelingly, as he caught sight of the scimitars and *tulwars* piled in the corner and the round shields hung on the bulkheads. "*Hai*, here is a blade made in Damascus; here is the saber of a mameluke—*aga*—mark the crescent of emeralds—and here—may the —— fly away with me else is the sticker that belonged to Gherai Khan. He used to be master of the Crimea."

While Ivak was turning over the trophies, Pierre opened one or two of the sandalwood boxes and poked a speculative finger into the rolls of silk so delicate in texture that he could see through it. A rattan chest pleased him better, being filled with gold plate of every description. Ivak joined him and picked up some of the pieces eagerly.

"This is from the table of a Roman duke. See the crest! And this noggin was fashioned in Stamboul. Yonder's a Persian thing with writing on it. *Ekh*, Hassan took plunder from all places. What a fellow! He—"

They stared in mute amazement at the glowing jewels in an ivory casket that Pierre opened. Even in the dull light of the lantern, precious stones gleamed with a life of their own. Pierre had never seen such things, but Ivak knew the value of plunder like this.

"You could match stones with the caliph of grand Cairo," he muttered, "and have enough left over to buy Egypt."

His eyes yearned toward the weapons while Pierre's fingers itched to bear off and hide some of the gold.

"In other years I heard of this," he whispered. "In the galleys of Algiers they told me of this ship of Hassan's. *Bon sang!* What will become of all this?"

Ivak scratched his head with the hilt of his saber.

"'Twill go into the breeches of the grandees—Potemkin and his monkey Nassau and the rest. May they pare the ——'s hoofs!"

For a moment temptation seized them and they did not look at each other. "Nay, 'tis Jean Paul's prize," swore Pierre suddenly. "We will tell him—"

"After locking it up," assented the Cossack—who had been examining the door, which had a serviceable iron lock with a key in place. Evidently Hassan or Kalil had been sleeping in the cabin when the galley was boarded. "I promised the lads they would find loot—"

A sudden lurch of the ship made him lose his footing and stagger against the chests.

By mutual consent they turned to the door, and Ivak locked it carefully, thrusting the key into his pocket. In the dark passage he stopped abruptly, pulling Pierre to his side. They could hear a man moving toward them cautiously, and others breathing near at hand. Ivak's blade slithered from his scabbard and he crouched, motioning for Pierre to do the same. They could not tell who the others were in the poop, and if they had been seen handling the riches in the stern cabin. Ivak was ready for a knife thrust at his throat, if they had been spied upon by a Greek or Syrian who would most certainly expect that they had carried off on their persons the pick of the loot.

His keen ears caught the click of a pistol hammer pulled back and then a man's knees blundered against his shoulder, and a hoarse voice muttered feelingly—

"—— your eyes!"

Pierre seized the Cossack's sword-arm, and stood up. He had heard that expression in the past, though he did not know what it meant, and invariably it was used by men of one nation.

"That is an Englishman," he whispered, adding, "Is that Lieutenant Edwards? 'Tis Pierre Pillon who speaks, and the *sotnik* Ivak is here."

"What the —— are you two about?" grumbled Edwards. "Are the cabins cleared? Well, bear a hand then, at these nine-pounders in the poop. Pillon, you can lay a gun. Come with me—'ware my left arm. There's a bit of shrapnel in it."

Sailors were trying to bring one of the small guns to bear on the shadowy outline of a felucca that had opened fire on them with grape. The other vessels were closing in on the galley. Matters could not very well be worse for them.

Some of the Russians on the foredeck, while fighting was still going on at the poop, had slipped the cable without waiting for orders. The result,

not at first perceptible, was that the galley had drifted with the wind until it brought up in the mud. Edwards thought that they were now within
musket shot of one of the shore batteries.

Owing to the confusion among the Turks, this battery had not opened
on them; but the nearest feluccas were aware by now that a small party
had boarded the galley and captured it. Their escape was cut off and in
another hour it would be full daylight, when they would be blown out of
the water if they did not surrender.

One of the shallops was still beside the galley, lashed fast by a sailor.
Edwards had offered to fight the galley, if Jones would take to the shallop and make off with a boat's crew. In the smoke and the dense mist that
hung like a veil over the Liman he could still escape. But Jones had refused to leave his men behind.

The American had ransacked the vessel for another anchor and cable
on the chance of working the galley off—without finding anything that
would serve his purpose.

Now he was throwing overside everything movable, to lighten ship.

"'Tis the end of our luck," groaned Pierre.

He thought ruefully of the treasure he had had in his hands a moment
ago, and searched the uttermost limits of a vocabulary enriched by years
in a slave galley to express his opinion of Russian seamanship, while Ivak
listened in approving silence.

"*Allons, mes camerades,*" he said grimly, seizing the first of the powder sacks that were fetched up from below, "stand by to show these ——
how honest Christian mariners say their prayers."

For half an hour the dozen cannon of the galley roared defiantly at the
growing array of Moslem small craft which took position around Hassan's
ship. Hampered by the dense mist and the danger of firing on their comrades, the Turks held off—content to wait for daylight when they could
see their target clearly. Pierre worked at the nine-pounder until the first
shots from the shore battery smashed into the galley, and a chain shot
struck the gun, dismounting it and killing three of its crew. He was hit
by flying splinters in the chest and thigh, and, after a glance at the useless piece, made his way to the quarterdeck with difficulty.

He limped to the wheel where a man stood motionless, leaning on the
spokes. Pierre looked around.

They were still aground. The mist, like a gray curtain, shut them in.

The deck was stained and slippery, and the men who labored on it stumbled over the wreckage of gear and the bodies of their mates. At first Pierre thought that the prisoners had been wiped out by the Moslem fire. Then he saw that they had been set to work in the foredeck, where the glow of flames showed through the companion.

Another burst of the heavy guns of the battery swept over the galley, too high to do much damage. The red flashes seemed to Pierre to come from almost over the bow.

Jones came aft and halted by the men at the wheel. He was hatless and in the dim light his face showed, lined and haggard; his eyes, probing into the mist, were steady.

In the walk of the man, in the poise of the head was the indomitable courage of ten years ago. It was part of his nature, this stubbornness.

To cease firing and call for quarter would mean the slaughter of all his men except the officers by the Moslems, who were half mad with rage, in any case, after the burning of the ships the day before.

Of this, however, Pierre did not think. He spoke to the admiral, shyly, looking up from bandaging his thigh.

"*Tout va bien, monsieur.* All goes well—eh?"

The American glanced around with a quick smile and responded in French.

"What is your name, my lad? Pierre? Well, Pierre, so you don't want to strike our colors?"

"But no—no!" Pierre mustered up his courage, and quivering with delight, said the words that had been on the tip of his tongue for days. "Ah, monsieur, it was warmer than this on the old *Richard*, was it not? *Sacré nom d'un chien*, but it was an affair, that. Me, I was there."

Jones walked to the rail and came back, glancing from the sails to the dark patch that was the battery.

"I was in the marine guard on the poop, monsieur," went on Pierre anxiously, "and you—you said, '*All goes well, Pierre.*' You remember, perhaps?"

"Aye," said Paul Jones, smiling again at the eagerness of the sailor. "I think you handed me a musket—"

"*Tiens!* It was so. You remember everything." The big Provençal grinned and looked around to see if others had heard what the admiral said, forgetting that they could not understand. It occurred to him to tell the American what they had found in the cabin, but he thought that it did not matter, when they might be blown out of their skins in another moment.

So he waited, nerves strained, for the next discharge from the battery. No doubt the Turks were lowering the muzzles of the cannon.

The firing grew heavier all around them, and he heard the rattle of musketry. A confused shouting arose on shore. Edwards came up and remarked that the fort on the hill was firing.

The two officers stared into the thinning mist with growing curiosity. In the direction of the battery the tumult increased and they could hear shouted commands and the tramp of marching battalions.

After a while Edwards looked at his watch. It was nearly five o'clock and somewhere the sun was rising. No feluccas were within sight and the men at the galley's remaining guns had ceased firing for want of a target. All Otchakof seemed to be in motion around the battery, but only stray bullets whined around the galley. Unable to make out what was on foot, they went forward to the bow, where the flames were now under control.

"Here they come, sir," called out Edwards suddenly, "to board the galley."

Out of the mist a horseman splashed through the rushes, turning toward the stranded vessel as soon as he saw it. When the water was up to his knees he stood up in the stirrups and howled like a wolf. A dozen Cossacks who had been looking on with interest gave tongue immediately.

Straining his eyes, Pierre made out that the rider wore a black sheepskin hat and a red sash. Unless he was mad this must be a Cossack *sotnik*, riding out of the Turkish fortifications. Doubtless a trick.

"I have it, sir," chuckled Edwards. "Faith, we're all dead, and this is Charon's blood brother, come to usher us across the Styx."

But Jones motioned impatiently for silence and Ivak came running up. He hailed the rider, who roared back a response.

"That is a *sotnik* of the Don regiment, your honor," Ivak informed Edwards. "He presents Little Father Suvarof's compliments to his excellency, Admiral Jones, with the request that his excellency cease firing on the bastions, which are now in the hands of the Russians."

It was long afterward that Pierre understood what had happened. Suvarof had crossed the Boug when the fleet engagement was at its hottest. He had attacked the advanced posts of the Turks with the regiment of cavalry that had crossed with him, and had driven them back into the trenches before Otchakof by evening: by then his full division was on the peninsula, taking position in front of the trenches. A firm believer in opportunity, Suvarof had attacked the trenches at dawn when Jones's raid had drawn the attention of Hassan and his men to the flotilla. Suvarof himself had led the bayonet charge that took the water batteries in flank and drove the garrison up into the Otchakof wall and the fort on the hill.

It was the Moslems in retreat that Jones had heard when he was rowing down the Liman, and the campfires he had noticed were those of Suvarof's division.

The courier in the mist shouted again, and Ivak began to chew his mustache and swear under his breath.

"That dog brother says, sir," he explained to the officers, "that the cavalry is in the field now, and the navy can go home and sleep—if we can sail that far without running aground."

Jones and Edwards glanced at each other with understanding. Ivak was from a cavalry regiment.

"Tell him," instructed the American gravely, "that we will land men to show them how to turn the guns in the batteries to bear on the town."

Ivak brightened perceptibly and the Cossack splashed away with a wave of the hand. Tired as he was, Paul Jones called for volunteers to go with him into the bastions, and, wearied beyond belief, all those who heard tumbled into the shallop when he took the tiller again.

Chapter X

Matched pearls for a woman's throat—gold dinars for the fingers of the aged men—a robe of honor, of samite and silk for the councilor. When the city was taken many were found to plunder the bazaar. Yet, one there was who rode on to another place saying, "What is profit without honor!"

It was many days before Pierre Pillon saw Paul Jones again. And it was more than a few hours before the least wounded of those on the galley could sleep. Jones had left Edwards in command of the prize, and when the Turkish flotilla withdrew to the protection of the fort and the open sea, the Russian lieutenant was sent to the *Vladimir* for a spare anchor, cable, food, and a surgeon.

Edwards had been told by the American to let no other officer take over the galley, and under no circumstances to permit it to be burned as Nassau had burned the frigates. After the decks had been cleared, and the seriously wounded attended to, and the rest had a meal of sorts, Edwards worked the galley off the mud and made sail as best he could to the anchorage of the Russian fleet.

When the wounded had been sent ashore, and the prisoners with a guard, only a half-dozen Cossacks were left on the galley.

All available anchorages around the jetties and the warehouses being taken, Edwards sailed up the river Dnieper. The slender galley that had been the delight of Hassan of Algiers now lay at anchor beside the barren steppe.

Ivak and Pierre did not let the Englishman sleep until they had admitted him into the secret. Unlocking the door and leaving Pierre there to keep watch, Ivak displayed the weapons and the chests with the pride of a discoverer.

"It is all for the admiral," he explained. "We have kept it hidden."

Edwards inspected the plate curiously and lingered over the jewels with a soft whistle of amazement. Reluctantly he put them back in their places, for he was human and under his fingers lay surety of a life of ease.

"By right," he observed, "the half of this should go to Admiral Jones and his men, and half to the Crown. But Potemkin will get his paws on it, and then—" He shrugged. "He may take it on the plea that he is sending it to Tsarkoe-seloe, but her Majesty will never see these trinkets."

The Cossack glanced at him thoughtfully, and when he locked the door of the cabin he put the key back into his pocket. He and Pierre had expected that Edwards might suggest some way of hiding the treasure, which was beginning to loom large now that the fighting was at an end.

When the Englishman and Pierre had made themselves beds in the adjoining cabins and had fallen into the utter oblivion of their first sleep in forty-four hours, Ivak sat down in the passageway to smoke and rub his saber clean with a cloth that he always carried in his girdle. In spite of the heat, the strain of the fighting, and a day of hard labor that he did not relish, the big Cossack was alert and to all appearances untired.

Certainly he polished the saber until it shone, and then put a new edge on it with a small whetstone. When he was satisfied with it, he laid it aside and after sitting for a long time, listening to the measured breathing of his companions, he rose and unlocked the teak door, making little noise for all his bulk.

When he came out again darkness had fallen. Pierre found him a little after dawn, sitting by the *kasha* pot of the Cossacks, who had built a fire and were breakfasting off a pair of rabbits and a cask of vodka which they had managed to forage for themselves.

"Pietr," announced Ivak, "I am going to find Paul. I will take the shallop and two men, and go and see that he does not get himself killed. You and the Englishman watch that." He jerked his thumb over his shoulder at the poop. "Here is the key."

He had been gone for hours before Edwards was aroused. A courier boat came up from the flagship with an order from Jones for the interpreter to join him, if Edwards's wound permitted.

The Englishman's arm pained him a good deal, but he waited only long enough to bolt some rabbit and vodka.

"Where is Ivak?" he asked in French, and when Pierre explained he swore doubtfully.

There was no wind, and they lacked men to handle the heavy sails; he could not take the galley, and the order did not admit of delay. There was no alternative but to leave the Frenchman in charge of Hassan's ship and treasure until he could find the admiral.

He took the key and glanced inside the door, satisfying himself that the chests were all in their places. Calling for a candle, he smeared wax over the crack of the door after he had closed it, and pressed his watch fob into service for a seal.

"Ivak says you are to be trusted," he remarked. "Consider that you are now rated acting sergeant of marines. Can you make these four chaps understand you? Good! Take charge of the galley and remember that the order is to give it up to no one except the admiral himself."

"Monsieur," said Pierre, "I will not let any pig of a Muscovite set foot on this deck."

"Hum!" Edwards took snuff with a wry grin. "I see that you have not been long on the Black Sea. It may be some time before you are relieved. I'll offer odds that the admiral is bombarding Otchakof, or outfitting the squadron for a raid on Constantinople."

Edwards's surmise was close to the truth. At intervals during the three days that he waited on the galley, Pierre heard the far-off booming guns, and noticed that couriers came and went along the Kherson trail that was within sight of their anchorage. After he had found the place where the Cossacks had stowed the odds and ends that they had looted from the decks, and had picked out a brace of serviceable pistols, he was more than a little content with his berth.

His men never lacked for rations—trading melons and grapes with the native skiffs that passed up and down the river, and catching small sturgeon on lines of their own making. He was stiff from the healing of his wounds, and enjoyed to the full the luxury of the poop cabins. But he did not disturb the wax seal, telling himself that before long he would sail the galley down to the fleet and disclose to Paul Jones what a valuable prize they had taken. He was indulging in such pleasant speculation when one of the Cossacks came to the quarterdeck and called to him to look up the river.

Approaching the galley he saw Nassau's great barge, rowed by twenty pairs of sweeps. The barge, instead of continuing on toward the fleet, turned and headed for the galley.

"St. Anne of Auray!" he muttered. "This high-well-born is coming to burn this vessel, like the others."

He ran to the ladder-head as the rowers on one side of the barge lifted their oars and the boat drifted down to the galley's side. Two men with boat-hooks held fast while an aide stepped from the stern to the ropes, and halted when his head came above the deck.

"Pardon, monsieur," observed Pierre, "but the orders of his excellency the admiral are that no one is to be allowed on this galley." As he had come out of the fighting clad only in a tattered pair of breeches, Pierre had borrowed some garments from the gleanings of the Cossacks and now stood arrayed in a loose white shirt, a green sash, and a pair of pantaloons that rivaled those of the dead Dmitri. In fact Pierre had a suspicion that they were Dmitri's; but then the man was dead. Over his head, to keep off the midges, the Provençal had bound the turban cloth of a slain Moslem.

So he looked like a blood-stained giant, bearded and smiling, with the butts of two long pistols sticking out of his sash.

"What ——'s leavings are you?" demanded the aide in bad French.

"Sergeant Pierre Pillon, your nobility, at present in command of this vessel."

"In command—" The officer spluttered, and realized that he was being kept waiting. "Out of the way, dog!"

"The order was the admiral's," objected Pierre. "This galley is one prize you will not burn."

A burst of laughter from below showed that he had been overheard, and the officer grew red. Presently his head disappeared, and when it came up again he waved a sheet of paper like a flag of truce. Pierre could not read his own name, fairly printed, but he knew a document signed by a general officer when he saw one. This had a scrawl, and under it a broad seal hung by a silk ribbon.

"It is you who will burn, you dolt!" snapped the officer. "This is an order signed by his illustriousness, Prince Potemkin, commander-in-chief in the Black Sea. We are not going to burn the galley. His Highness desires it to be brought up to Kherson, so that he can sail down in it to review the fleet."

"Well, he didn't bother his noddle about the fleet when the Turks were around all the same," the Provençal muttered to himself, bitterly regretting the absence of Ivak and Edwards.

What they would have done, he did not know, but Ivak was a resourceful person. The aide pushed past him and turned to assist the prince to the deck. A half-dozen others followed and stared at the empty poop and the Cossacks curiously.

"You lied, rogue, when you said you were in command here," said the aide.

"No, monsieur, it is true. The officers were summoned away."

The aide spoke to Nassau, who barely glanced at Pierre and turned into the passage. They passed by the side cabins, and stopped to inspect the seal on the end door. Then Nassau called out and one of the sailors came up from the barge with an ax.

"Messieurs," cried the Provençal angrily, "an officer has sealed up his personal belongings in that cabin."

"Who told you that?" demanded the aide.

"Lieutenant Edwards, if it please you." Nassau merely signed to the sailor and the ax began to splinter the teak. Pierre ground his teeth, well aware that he was helpless. He had risked his life in speaking, and it would need only a word of any of the *boyars*, much less an order from the Prince-Marshal, to have him shot down where he stood.

The door crashed in, and Nassau and his aide entered with more than a little eagerness. Pierre approached until he stood by the sailor and listened with all his ears. The officers were ransacking the chests—he caught the clink of plate—and talking excitedly.

After a long pause Nassau swore angrily.

"By the eyes of ——! Alexiano said there would be more than this. Those pearls are worth no more than a wench or two."

"*Mordieu*—the Greek is not to be believed."

"He was afraid to come. It's vastly quaint; he was knifed after all in Kherson by a native woman."

Nassau seemed to be in no mood for amusement, and there was more rummaging while Pierre did some rapid thinking. Alexiano had fled from the fleet to Kherson, where he must have heard of the capture of the galley. He had hinted to the Prussian that the prize was a rich one.

There would have been time, and no more for Nassau to get the order from Potemkin and travel back to the fleet to investigate the matter for himself.

"My dear count," the prince spoke again. "This casket is empty. Burn me, but that whippersnapper Edwards has had his finger in this. Have in the surly rogue, and question him."

Pierre put in appearance promptly, and a glance showed him that the suspicions of the *boyars* were well founded. Most of the swords that had lain in the corner were missing, and the chest that had held the gold plate had no more than a layer on the top, the rest being filled up with quilts.

Also the casket in which he had seen the best of the precious stones was quite empty.

He was sure that the seal Edwards had left on the door had been unbroken until now. Assuredly the lieutenant took nothing away; he had been asleep until Pierre wakened him. The Cossacks would not have known how to replace the seal, and he was morally certain that they had no loot stored on the galley that he had not unearthed.

A river thief might have entered one of the ports of the other cabins while he was out on deck, or asleep. But there was the seal again. He thought of Ivak. Had the Cossack stolen the better half of the loot? But how? Ivak had carried nothing out of the galley.

"Search the galley," snarled Nassau.

"And flog these *duraks* at the mast until they tell anything they know. Begin with this one." He turned back to his examination of the chests, turning over the ivory and silk in his fingers impatiently until an exclamation from his companion made him look up.

The aide was moving slowly back toward the bulkhead, his lace jabot and carefully dressed peruke fairly quivering with indignation. The sailor had dropped the ax and was staring, slack jawed, as if a water fiend had invaded the cabin of a sudden.

Pierre had drawn his pistols and leveled them at the noblemen. His hands quivered and his brown eyes blazed with rage.

"Messieurs," he said hoarsely, "I have sworn an oath to the good Mary of the Seas. With these hands I will let out the life of the man who lays a lash on my back. Give the order, and these barkers will do for you."

Sheer incredulity held the Prince of Nassau-Siegen voiceless. A Russian peasant would have fallen on his knees to thank the *boyars* for not taking his life. He lifted the eyeglass at the end of a silk cord and tried to focus it on Pierre, to study his face and to observe if the pans of the pistols were primed. But his fingers were not steady enough.

"Let me leave the ship," went on Pierre. "Consider, messieurs, I am a sergeant acting under orders from the admiral. I will take my men with me."

Nassau's skin had whitened, and a small patch under one eye stood out distinctly.

"Do not pull the trigger," he muttered. "You will not be harmed. Only go quickly—you and your men." And he added, remembering that his aide was present, "Since you have orders."

"Then remain where you are, gentlemen." When Pierre had backed out, the Prussian waited until his hand was steady again, and took snuff liberally.

"That is all the doing of this —— of an American," he remarked to his companion, "who has made wolves out of these dogs of mariners. You noticed, my dear Count, how the sailor swore he had orders from the admiral to admit *no one* upon the galley?"

"Assuredly, *mon prince*." The aide, who hoped for much from Nassau's influence at court, nodded repeatedly. "His Highness, the Prince-Marshal Potemkin, should hear of this."

"It is not necessary. Yesterday that *bavard* Jones haltered his own neck. Burn and blister me, if he did not play the wrong card. Potemkin will never forgive him."

"But how?"

"Tomorrow you will know." Nassau brushed the snuff from the lace at his throat. "It only remains for us to see how he will take his disgrace."

They lingered on one pretext or another until Pierre was well away from the galley with his men in one of the fishing skiffs that came up to

hover around the barge. They understood each other perfectly, each thinking what a coward the other was.

Chapter XI
The Admiral's Walk

That evening Suvarof sat in the admiral's cabin of the *Vladimir*, having
come twenty miles by horse litter and boat to talk with Paul Jones, who
was then with the frigates that blockaded the peninsula. He was propped
up on an ottoman, one leg stretched out, playing a game of chess against
himself.

Ivak came and went, passing from wardroom to the admiral's gallery,
outside the stern windows, his sheepskin *shuba* smelling to high heaven
and his damp boots creaking as he tried to walk on his toes. It had rained
all that day.

The Cossack had entree to Jones's quarters, unannounced, but this evening he seemed to be on a self-appointed sentry-go on the gallery. Osten-
sibly he was watching for Jones. Actually he eyed Suvarof uneasily, like a
gigantic urchin who both fears and hopes to be noticed.

Even privileged *sotniks* of a crack cavalry regiment do not interrupt the
meditation of a general who has conquered an empire and opened up a new
sea; Ivak probably was unaware that the man who sat hunched over the
chessboard nursing a reed pipe had once stalemated Frederick the Great
of Prussia, but he understood the significance of the sword that lay on
the table—the blade of a Damascus scimitar, the gold-inlaid hilt agleam
with sapphires and diamonds.

Suvarof, however, was more sparing of speech than usual, and only when
Ivak had paused to stare admiringly at the sword of honor did he look up,
frowning. From long experience with the Don Cossacks he knew that Ivak
had a troubled conscience and wanted badly to tell about it.

"Are you hatching eggs on the gallery, *sotnik*? Brandy or plundering—
which?"

Ivak started and took off his cap.

"As God lives, Little Father, I haven't tasted brandy since the crops
were put in the ground this season. And I haven't taken a copeck's worth
of loot from a single Turk." When Suvarof went on with his maneuvering
of the chessmen, he mustered up his courage. "It happened, Little Father,
that I've hidden some gold and fine swords and precious stones."

"Ah."

"It happened that way. We found a cabin full of such things in the pasha's galley; fine things, truly, better than you could get by raiding a hundred Turkish villages." And he told the story of Hassan's treasure and its discovery.

"That Frenchman, Pietr, is a galliard, a splendid chap. But he cannot see around a turn in the trail. I knew that somebody would hear of the treasure and loot it, so I took away the best of the things. When he and the Englishman slept the first night I went through everything and filled one chest with the best of the plate and the jewels. I made one bundle of the finest weapons. Then I lowered the chest and the bundle out of the port of the next cabin, into the shallop that was alongside us."

He glanced at Suvarof, trying to make out how his confession would be received.

"*Ekh*, no one suspected. We threw some skins over the things and watched like hawks, without telling Pietr, because whatever a chap says in this place is known to the spies. The *boyars* have their eyes and ears everywhere.

"We rowed around the Liman until dark; then we pulled up to the rump of this big ship and I climbed to the little gallery, and drew up the chest and the bundle with ropes. I covered them with the skins again, and watched. But no one ever comes out on the gallery, because only the admiral walks there, and he was away. I thought he would be on the *Vladimir*; but he was flying around after the Turks, far out at sea. He is a —— at that sort of thing."

"Do his men obey?"

"Obey? They would die with Paul, as they call him."

Suvarof nodded, moving out a pawn to make good a line of defense.

"You have stolen horses in your day, Ivak. I did not send you to the fleet to steal."

"But this is different. The gold and the other things belong to Paul."

"You think he will distribute them among his men, and you and the Frenchman will share in it?"

"Aye—" Ivak checked himself. "But, look here, Little Father Suvarof—we pray that you will take charge of the treasure now—"

"And explain things to the American, to get you off," grumbled the old officer. "What has the French fire-eater done?"

"He fought on the galley like a wounded tiger. Cut—slash—he ripped right through them. That was what he did. But he drew a pistol on the

Prussian prince, and the *boyar*'s men will flay him alive if they can catch him."

"Devil take both of you! What else have you done? Well, send him in—if he is on the ship."

"Aye, *balko*," nodded Ivak, "a few hours ago he came up." The Cossack hastened out, well content. He had told everything to Suvarof and had not been degraded and not much sworn at. Now that his general was on the ship, Ivak felt that his responsibilities were at an end. He returned with Pierre, who was less sure that they would escape unpunished, but gave a truthful account of what happened on the galley.

Suvarof sighed and filled his pipe slowly, wincing when he moved, for his leg pained him.

"Little Father," the Cossack observed after a moment's reflection, "when you sent us to this ship we built a *lopazik* and watched all that went on. When the Turks were hacking at Paul we were able, by God's mercy, to do a little to help; but when the *boyars* fell away from him and plotted, we could do no more than a dog outside a fox's burrow. The *boyars* were worse than the Turks—"

"Enough said," grumbled Suvarof. "Go, you and the Frenchman, and sit on that chest until I summon you."

"Well, God be with you, Father!" Ivak nudged Pierre and they went out to sit in the rain and speculate as to what would happen to their trove.

Suvarof's quick ear had heard footsteps in the passage, and when the door opened he was bending over the chessboard again. Then his dark eyes gleamed with pleasure and he swept the miniature silver warriors off the board.

"Ah, Jones, my friend; I cannot stand to greet you. A ball through the hip, so I came to your flagship to get well."

Flinging off his wet cloak, Paul Jones stepped to the table. He smiled, but there were fresh lines around his eyes that told of a sleepless night, and the hollows under the cheekbones were deeper.

"It is I who must apologize, *mon general*, that none of my staff were here to receive you. Faith, every officer appointed to me seems to be absent at Kherson."

Suvarof glanced around the spacious cabin with its walnut wainscoting, its gold candelabra, and the portrait of the Empress Catherine hanging opposite the stern windows. "Humph! I have been well entertained." He had noticed the empty cabins and the absence of servants and had guessed at the reason. "Sit, *mon camerade*. Do you play chess? No? Then we will talk—see I have had a bottle of Madeira heated, in that basin. Fill your glass—fill your pipe, and tell me why the —— you sent a report to his Highness before you showed it to me."

Mechanically Jones did as the older man suggested, but without tasting the wine or lighting his pipe.

"My report gave Potemkin the details of the engagement in the Liman."

"Well?"

"His Highness was pleased to return me his revision of it. He forwarded it by the Chevalier de Ribas, who came out to me this afternoon." Paul Jones's hand on the wineglass tightened convulsively so that the slender stem snapped and the wine spilled upon the table, dripping unheeded on his knee. "By ——, sir, 'tis not to be believed!" Without comment Suvarof held out his hand, and the American drew from his coat pocket several crumpled sheets of paper, the outer one bearing fragments of the prince's seal.

When the general had finished reading, he folded the sheets carefully and sighed. The report in his hand stated that the battle had been fought under Potemkin's personal direction, in accordance with the orders the Prince-Marshal had given. Nassau was given credit for the disabling of nine of Hassan's ships, and breaking up the Turkish flotilla. The loss of the Moslems was given as four thousand and the Russians eight hundred. Only once was Jones's squadron mentioned, when it was stated that owing to their deep draught the line-of-battle ships were obliged to remain spectators of the action.

"Well?" he said again.

"That is not my report. It is a version written in Kherson, omitting everything of the truth, except the number of killed. *Mon cher camerade*—" Jones flushed and sprang to his feet—"the loss of life in my squadron was nearly eight hundred; my men, uncovered in open boats, towed the vessels of the flotilla into action. Nassau's loss was five men."

Suvarof nodded. He had the details from Ivak and the officers of the *Vladimir*.

"His Highness," he remarked, "was in Kherson, sixty miles from the scene of the battle; but you must understand, Jones, my friend, that he desires to have the Court and the empress believe that all the credit is due to him and Nassau."

"The Chevalier Ribas informed me that his Highness was pleased to *order* me to sign this report and return it to headquarters. It is utterly false."

One by one the old Russian took up the silver chessmen and put them back in the box.

"Jones, you do not understand the Court. Wounds are not the only hardship; injustice and malice can cut as deep. A soldier must bear everything."

As the American was silent, he went on quizzically:

"Twenty-four gold swords of honor were given the Prince-Marshal by the empress at the beginning of the campaign. He has bestowed one on himself, one on Nassau, and twenty-two to the officers of the flotilla."

Suddenly Jones laughed heartily, seeing the absurdity of a commander-in-chief receiving a distinction for services in a battle that he did not know had taken place until long afterward, for orders that he had never given.

"Undoubtedly," went on Suvarof, "Potemkin will be granted the high honor of the Order St. George, of the first grade—Nassau has already been recommended for the second—as well as a gift of valuable estates in White Russia with several thousand souls—serfs."

He pointed to the sheets of paper.

"Sign this, Jones, and you also will be decorated. You will be given the estates of a grandee of the empire."

"And my men—my officers?"

"Ah." Suvarof was silent.

"My men, who were exposed at all times," Jones's voice broke. "*Mes amis—mes braves!*"

His finely cut lips twisted in sudden distress, and anyone watching the two, as Ivak and Pierre were, with all their eyes through the wide stern windows, would have thought that he and not the old Russian had been wounded that day.

"Ah." Suvarof closed the lid upon his chessmen and picked up a candle to light his pipe, which had gone out. "My friend, we in Russia are of the old world, half Asia in our blood. You are of the new, and perhaps the old must learn of honor from the new. I would rather lose this leg than have you leave us. Consider, Jones: Otchakof will fall to us in a month, and we will advance on Constantinople; we will march across Moldavia and drive the Moslems from the Adriatic. Potemkin will not always hold the reins of power. You would not refuse to serve with old father Suvarof—eh?"

"Would to God I could go with you!"

"If you refuse your signature to the report, it means the end of your career on the Black Sea. "

"Aye, the end!"

Jones picked up the folded sheets, and tore the pieces across, and tore the pieces again, tossing them to the deck.

Before the American could move to prevent him, Suvarof gripped the table and limped erect on one leg, holding fast to the hand of his companion. Eye to eye they stood for a full moment, the swarthy seaman supporting the wound-scarred soldier.

"Sir," cried Paul Jones, a little hoarsely owing to the lump in his throat, "surely I have had honor, since I have had Alexander Suvarof for a friend."

After the manner of men who know their own minds, and the luxury of an hour's ease after hard days, they talked henceforth of anything but their parting—of horses, the rigging of ships, the campaigns of other days, and comrades who were dead. Suvarof, remembering the two men on the gallery, called them in, bidding them to their blankets and saying that he would look after the chest and the bundle.

What the two friends said after that no one heard, although orderlies who were in the service of Potemkin tried their best to listen at keyhole and casement.

The Prince of Nassau-Siegen was in high good humor when a month later, his barge rowed down the Dnieper to the flagship. He was surrounded by officers who sought his favor; he wore the ribbon of the George, and the flag of a vice-admiral was on the ensign staff.

He had come to the *Vladimir* to see how the American would take his *cogée*—his dismissal. An imperial courier had arrived the day before from Petersburg with an order for Jones:

> *According to our imperial desire, based upon necessity, the sphere of service for our Vice-Admiral, the Chevalier Paul Jones, is now fixed in the northern seas. His Excellency the Vice-Admiral will at once proceed on the journey to our capital. His Excellency the Vice-Admiral will without ceremony present himself at our Palace of the Hermitage, where he will be acquainted with our further wishes.*
>
> *Catherine.*

Nassau was a little surprised that Jones should have invited Potemkin and the staff of his Highness as well as the captains of the fleet to a banquet on the flagship the day of his departure. He found a distinguished gathering on the afterdeck where an awning had been spread.

In full court attire and dress swords he found the Prince de Repin and de Ligne, the diplomat. Ribas and Popoff, the chief of staff, waited on Potemkin, who had gratified his whim of sailing down in the galley of Hassan of Algiers. In attendance were Grevé Fanshawe and the other captains.

And the courtiers who had come from Kherson were more than a little surprised when they noticed the dress swords of the officers of Jones's squadron. Edwards wore jauntily thrust through a silk sash an almost priceless scimitar of Yemen with an inscription worked in gold, the weapon of a shah.

Fanshawe had a *tulwar* of blue steel, and Korsakof—the Russian lieutenant who had boarded the galley with Jones—a sword with a hilt set with matched sapphires and diamonds. These blades aroused the instant envy of those who lacked such trophies from the Moslems, and questions were asked the owners, who replied that Admiral Jones had taken from Hassan Pasha his sidearms and given them away.

Jones himself wore only the plain rapier he had brought to the Black Sea.

And Nassau, who was familiar with the quarters of the *Vladimir*, noticed that the dinner was served on massive plate, fashioned after the Venetian and Spanish manner, plate that he had never laid eyes on before and superior even to Potemkin's almost royal service. He learned by dint of questioning that the admiral had made a gift to the various ship captains of certain jewels that were to be sold and the proceeds divided among the crews.

"Some say that Suvarof gave the things to Jones," whispered one of the flotilla officers. "He has no notion of values—that little grandfather—always gives everything away."

A search of the faces around the tables disclosed that Suvarof was not there, and Nassau, although he had a suspicion as to the source of the splendor that had appeared on the flagship, had no opportunity to mention it.

Jones stood up to give the first toast, and not a man there but expected that he would compliment the Prince-Marshal by mentioning his name.

"Your Highness, my lords, *messieurs*, I give you a name that will stand in the pages of history. When we are forgotten—one who is fortunate in being served by courageous men—" he glanced fleetingly at Nassau, his dark eyes mocking—"one who has achieved what other centuries failed to bring to pass, the downfall of the Turk in Europe; but who, gentlemen, is worthy of the homage placed at the feet of—"

He lifted his glass, bowing to Potemkin.

"The empress! *Messieurs*, I give you Catherine the Great." Potemkin started in surprise and displeasure, but the Russians tossed down their wine and dropped the glasses over their shoulders, to shatter on the deck.

The innate courtesy that had inspired this toast to the woman who had shown not the least gratitude for his services stirred the approval of the officers. They braved Potemkin's growing dissatisfaction by accompanying Jones to the side of the *Vladimir* when it was time for him to enter his barge to go ashore.

They waited at the rail and then glanced at one another curiously. Nassau had given orders that no salute was to be fired when the American left his flagship.

Jones swept a glance along the deck, dwelt on the massed crew for a moment, and turned to the ladder, a smile at the edges of his lips. Edwards and Pierre were already in the boat.

A Cossack advanced from the waist of the ship, and it was a moment before Jones recognized Ivak, in his dress uniform, a red coat, trimmed with fur, polished black boots, and a white ermine cap.

The *sotnik* pushed past the other officers and stood at salute. Then he brought his other arm in front of him and held out in both hands a sword. There was no mistaking the weapon, shaped like a scimitar, with the diamonds flashing in the hilt, Suvarof's sword.

Not an officer present but would have given an arm to be its possessor— not Potemkin himself.

"The General Prince Alexander Suvarof presents his compliments and bids adieu to his friend, Paul Jones," Ivak said in Russian, raising his voice.

A murmur arose in the waist of the *Vladimir* and grew to a roar that was echoed by the crews of other ships who heard it. No one ordered, and no one could have suppressed it.

"Little Father Jones!"

The Corsair's Raid

An Arab's dhow lowered its sail and drifted into the bay. When it grounded on the beach the old man at the steering oar looked around with keen eyes at the drowsy fishing huts and the empty hills rising to a solitary gray tower. "O my *Rais*," he said softly, "here at last thou art safe."

At the sound of his voice the tall man who had been sleeping by the mast sat up. As the old Arab had done, he glanced about him. Then he yawned. "What is it?"

"This," the Arab explained, "is the very small island I told thee of. It is verily a place of peace, being ruled by an honorable Christian lord. A man like to thee, except that he never quarrels and hath no enemies. Yonder, up there is his tower. Now, God being willing, have I done all that I promised thee."

"Aye, Khalil," assented the tall man, "and, God being willing, some-day thou wilt be paid."

Stepping over the prow of the slender dhow, he drew it farther up the beach with a powerful lunge of his long body. Although the old seaman addressed him as *Rais*—Commander—he was not an Arab. Blue eyes gleamed from his sun-darkened face.

"Wait, Khalil," he added over his shoulder, "until I come again."

"If it be written, my *Rais*, thou wilt come, but not otherwise."

The tall man smiled. He walked up the shore, planting his feet wide, because he had not felt solid earth beneath him for many months. Now at last he was free. He would taste Christian food and wine, and hear the voice of friends: best of all, he would sleep under a roof where the sound of a foot's tread would not mean death.

As he passed the huts, children ran out to stare at him. He wore no hat, and his fine gray mantle was ripped and stained with salt and blood.

Few strangers landed upon this miniature island, between Christian Sicily and Moslem Africa. Fewer still were sea-battered giants who smiled. Yet this tall stranger with the head of a dark god walked alone up the road to the castle.

Once he stopped, seeing another sail heading in to the bay. Then he made it out to be a small trading galley—a Venetian, no doubt, putting in for water. Here, he told himself, he was safe from his enemies and he need not watch every sail.

Impatiently—for he was very hungry—he turned off the winding road into a path that seemed to lead direct to the castle. He wanted to cool his throat with wine and hear a Christian voice give him welcome. Through deep brush he passed into a narrow ravine and stopped abruptly.

A stream ran by his feet, and on a rock a spear's length away sat a young girl. She held a hawk on her gloved wrist, and she was feeding it bits of meat from a pouch, smiling the while at a big black hound who rested his head on her other knee and gulped enviously whenever the falcon caught a tidbit from its mistress's fingers.

"Nay, Dominic," she said gravely, "all food does not belong to you."

Then she caught her breath and cried out. The dog had heard the man behind them, and whirled with a growl to leap at the stranger.

The man carried no weapon or stick, and as the dog sprang he stepped aside. Swinging down his arm, he caught the hound by the scruff of the neck and held him for a second, kicking and snarling. "It seems," he observed, "this Dominic needs cooling." And he swung the hound into the pool by the rock.

As he did so, the hawk screamed and flew off. The hound, Dominic, emerged from the water, surprised but still intent upon the stranger. This time the girl caught him and held him firmly by the collar. Whereupon Dominic did what any other dog would do—he growled heartily, and being still held passive, he shook himself vigorously from one end to the other. And this wet the girl's white-linen garments.

"I grieve," said the stranger, "for your dress, Damsel. You should not have held the hound."

"If I did not," she cried indignantly, "he would tear your flesh, for that is his way with vagabonds."

"Does he so with the guests of the castle?"

The girl had been startled and spattered with water, and now she felt angered by the calm voice of this wayfarer, who wore nothing but tatters streaked with salt and dark with more ominous stains.

"Dominic," she responded, "knows well, as I do, that you are no guest of Rocafort."

"Still," he smiled, "I shall be welcomed in the hall."

"By whom?"

"By the lord of the island. I know not his name."

"Well, he is Sir John Rocafort, and I am his daughter. It seems to me you are too sure of yourself. What man are you?"

The stranger hesitated briefly. "I am Andrea Doria."

"The *Rais* Doria—the great corsair?"

The girl looked at him, amazed. All her years she had lived on this island, seeing no other men than the Arabs and soldiers, and the few seamen who visited the port at need. From them all she had heard tales of *Rais* Doria, and he had become the hero of her dreams.

"Are you the knight who turned sea rover and harried the Turks from these waters—aye, and took the treasure ship of the Sultan of Cairo?"

"I am Doria."

She flushed, rising to her feet to look into his eyes. They were quiet as the sea itself, and there was a fire in them she could not endure. She did not know how fair she seemed to this man. Because she scorned him she wished to hurt him.

"Oh, we are honored in Rocafort." She bent her head before him. "Only tell me, Messer Andrea, pray, why did you not name yourself the Duke of Austria or even the Emperor?"

At this mockery the wanderer stiffened. Andrea Doria had a great pride in him, and now this pride was touched.

"Because," she cried, "you chose a dead man's name. I have heard how Doria was caught in his ship by the Turkish galleys and cut into pieces and thrown into the sea."

"They did that to my men," said the corsair grimly. "But they were taking me to the Sultan when I escaped in an Arab's boat."

To the girl, who knew so little of the world, this seemed a stupid lie. This tall wayfarer, who had not even a sword, sought the welcome due to a matchless champion.

Her eyes brightened mischievously. Here was something to atone for a wetting. "Have you a token upon you, Messer Andrea?" she asked blithely. "A seal ring?"

"They left me naught but—" he saw the glint of laughter in her eyes and closed his lips. "If you would have a token, loose the hound. The brute knows by now I am no runagate rogue—if you do not."

She let go the dog's collar, and Dominic advanced stiffly at first, but after sniffing round Doria's legs he wagged his tail idly and sat down.

"How well, *Messer Andrea*," she said demurely, "you know dogs! Now, what is to be the next test, sir?"

"Sir John—you take me to your father?"

Aye, dogs he knew, and men and the handling of ships, but not women. Moodily he watched her going before him up the path. How lightly her red slippers moved, and how the sun shone upon the tangle of her fair hair! He had not seen a gentle girl of his own kind for years.

The maid of Rocafort was merry in her mind. She no longer thought of the great corsair. Here was a stubborn, frowning giant who tried so clumsily to deceive her. She meditated a second test, and when they entered the castle yard she clapped her hands, summoning a passing steward. After speaking to him briefly, she turned to Doria.

"Now, I must change my dress, Messer Andrea. But this man will set meat and wine before you, bidding you welcome to Rocafort."

She tripped away, and Doria, standing in the sun, was aware that heads appeared in the embrasures of the shadowed wall to stare at him. After a moment the steward emerged, bowing low. He ushered the stranger through a passage into a stone chamber, where a plate of food had been set on a table, and Doria, glancing at the smoke-blackened walls and the smiling Arab women working among the pots and pans, stopped short. This was the kitchen, and the solitary plate on the table held only broken bread and stew.

"By the hide of the sacred boar," he muttered, "would you have me break a week's hunger on scullery fare?"

And he thrust the plate to Dominic, who had followed them in.

"Where's Sir John," he demanded, "who welcomes his guests in this fashion?"

"He—he is not to be seen," the steward answered uncertainly.

Doria rubbed his chin. A strange household, but even so he must sleep. After his ordeal at sea, drowsiness beset him like the torment. Paying no heed to the cup that stood upon the table, he seized the great flood of wine and drank, tilting it higher and higher, while the servants stared. When it was empty he set it down with a crash.

"Now take me to a bed," he said briefly.

This the steward hesitated to do. He was imagining vividly the effect of so much wine at a draft upon a man of the stranger's size, and so he almost ran up the steps of a tower to throw open a narrow door. Doria found himself in a clean, sunlit chamber, and he flung himself down on the canopy bed. With his arm across his eyes, he was breathing deep in a moment. The servant tiptoed from the chamber, closing the heavy door carefully.

Then he sought out an iron bar and fitted it into holes in the solid stone-work outside the door.

"And so," the girl said, "he would not sup or sip in the kitchen?"

"I made it ready, Mistress Marguerite," explained the steward, "as you bade me. Aye, he threw the food to the dog, but he did more than sip, for he downed a flagon of Cyprian at a breath, and now he lies on his back drunk as Fulk the Bowman at Candlemas."

This the steward imagined to be the case, and he did not add that he had barred the tall stranger in the tower room.

"What say you, Master Ricard?" Marguerite turned to the massive old swordsman, who was captain of the men-at-arms, and so had the castle in his charge during the absence of its lord, Sir John.

"Let him sleep off the wine," responded the soldier bluntly; "then will I talk with him. By the saints, Messer Andrea Doria was a woundy rover of the sea, serving no king or lord as I have heard, but still he was a bold and cunning gentleman. Nay, now that he lies in pieces at the sea's bottom—severed in such fashion by an infidel sword—'tis a shameful thing that a wandering boaster should take his name."

"'Tis a sinful thing," echoed the steward. "Look 'ee, Mistress Marguerite, there is a Venetian galley putting in. Let Master Ricard take this lying knave in hand and put him aboard the galley. Yonder men of Saint Mark are ever greedy of rowers for the benches. They will take him without ado, and so the matter will be at an end."

Marguerite looked thoughtful. Her two advisers having disparaged the stranger, she began to consider him more kindly. Ungainly he might be, yet he was no fool. She looked upon him as her prize, and wondered what he might prove to be.

"Nay," she answered, "my father would not wish us to hand a castaway to the galleys. Give him proper garments, Pietro, and when the wine is out of his head bring him down to supper with us."

She had greeted this tall man as a vagabond; now she would try him as a gentleman. "What," she wondered aloud, "if he is Andrea Doria after all?"

Master Ricard crossed himself. "May the *Sieur Diett* forbid! 'Tis true the sea gives up its dead at times—"

"Blessed Mary, aid us!" Pietro's jaw dropped. "He—he dripped water at first, and he had stains of blood upon him, and he had a look as—as of one walking in his sleep!"

"Now out upon it, Pietro!" The girl laughed. "Would a spirit heave Dominic through the air or drink a flagon down? Do as I bid thee." And she ran off to her chamber, clapping her hands for the tiring maid. She would put on the red-damask dress and headband with the embroidered silk girdle.

Pietro, however, did not go up to the tower. Dusk was falling, and he lingered in the hall, lighting the candles and chattering, until Ricard, who was growing hungry, growled at him.

"Cease thy mouthing and go up! If he be indeed the ghost of Doria thou canst make certain by looking under his garments. He will bear red lines upon his skin where he was hacked into quarters."

Vigorously Pietro shook his head. "I have seen enough as it is. He would touch no food, and bears neither headgear nor sword nor pouch—which humans are wont to have."

"Wilt disobey thy lady?"

"It is no part of my duty," the steward said with dignity, "to tend a ghost."

"He is naught but a vagabond."

"Then 'tis your duty to handle him, Master Ricard. I've heard tell that if you take a sword with a cross upon its hilt and thrust it into the floor by a sleeping spirit, the fiend will slide down it and vanish."

"Well, that may be." The soldier rubbed his shaven head. "But look 'ee, Pietro. I'll need a light, so thou must bear me up a candle."

"Listen!" cried the steward. The candle in his hand began to shake and scatter its grease. "Did you hear—"

Ricard heard. Through the twilight came a windy shout. *"Doria! Doria! Yield to the steel!"*

"'Tis his cry!" Peering at each other, they breathed heavily. A dog howled suddenly. Feet pattered across the yard. Near them in the darkness steel clashed.

"Ho!" roared Ricard. "Arms! We are beset."

Andrea Doria slept the sleep of exhaustion—he who would waken otherwise at a whisper. When the clamor pierced his tower room he sat up to stare into darkness. He heard his name shouted and his war cry. Then the unmistakable clash of weapons brought him stumbling to his feet.

For a moment he racked his brains. Then he felt for the wall and swept it with his hands to find the door. Lifting the latch, he thrust at it, then heaved his shoulder against it. When he heard iron grate against stone and knew it to be heavily barred, he crashed his foot against it, his deep voice roaring.

"Open, ye louts!"

No one heeded him. After searching in vain for another door, he shrugged in resignation and went to the embrasure to listen. Men were running below him, and at times he caught the flare of a torch against walls. Some women began wailing. In a few moments the tumult died down, except for the cries of the women.

Doria returned to the door, pounding upon it methodically. After a while he saw light against the crack, and the bar was taken down. An Arab serving woman stood in the hall with a lantern.

"What hath come upon this place?" he asked in her speech.

"*Y'allah!* Calamity!" She tore at her hair fiercely. "The anger of God—"

He took the lantern from her and went down the winding stair cautiously. At the foot a man crouched, coiled up like a dog. Doria surveyed him and recognized Pietro's jacket. "What is the fighting?" he asked.

Pietro glanced up with agonized eyes and howled. Leaping to his feet, he vanished into the darkness. Doria thought that he conducted himself like a man who saw a ghost.

Going into the hall, the corsair glanced warily to right and left. Candles flickered on the long table, set with silver dishes. Against the table leaned old Ricard, his head clasped in his hands. Through his fingers blood trickled.

"They have taken Mistress Marguerite," he muttered. "Look!"

He seemed dazed as he clutched Doria's arm and crossed the hall unsteadily to a dark corridor. Here he stumbled over a carcass and bent down to feel of it. The hound Dominic lay dead of a dozen wounds. "Ah, *Sieur Dieu!*" Ricard muttered. "This hound hath fallen in his duty—and I live."

Pushing forward into a lighted chamber, the two men saw it to be empty, except for an Arab serving maid who lay moaning on the floor bleeding from a cut across the face. Ricard clutched her shoulder. "Speak thou," he urged. "What befell thy lady?"

"Like the wind they came," she screamed. "Pietro, the dog, brought them with a knife held at his throat. They snatched her up and like the wind they went."

Doria saw that the embroidered covers of the chests had not been disturbed. The girl's gold headband lay on the bed, beside her white-linen dress that Dominic had soiled. So, the raiders had not lingered to plunder. They had sought only the girl. "What men were they?" he demanded of the wounded captain.

But Ricard only muttered brokenly. Sir John, the lord of Rocafort, had no enemies who would strike at him thus. Sir John was away on a journey with the best of the men-at-arms. The raiders had rushed the courtyard, knocking down all who stood in their way. "'Twas Andrea Doria," he said, "and his devils. Now they are clear of the castle with Mistress—"

"Man," cried the corsair, "Doria's men are fish bait beneath the sea. They are dead, or chained to galley oars. Would Doria use steel on serving wenches or ravish a girl like yours?"

"Living or dead, I heard their war shout. And—and I mind that one calling himself Andrea Doria came spying upon my lady this day."

"The devil!" Doria stared at the soldier blankly. Himself, he knew no more of this raid than dead Dominic. He had been asleep, locked in the tower room. But he was Andrea Doria, and Pietro at least knew it—and now he was loose, prowling about the castle. So they might well think he had a hand in this spoiling.

A sound of distant shouting came through the wide window, and Doria strode over to it. Beyond an outer wall a band of men some two dozen strong were making toward the road that led down to the bay, far below. They looked like seamen, well armed. They had torches to light the way, and Doria caught a glimpse of a girl's red dress between two of them.

A few men and boys had followed from the castle. The raiders halted suddenly and turned, to shoot a volley of bolts from the crossbows. Two of the pursuers dropped, and the rest scattered, running to cover.

Doria shook his head. These raiders knew their way about, and hit hard. They were more than a match for the men of Rocafort. The only chance to make another stand against them would be upon the road, before they reached the open beach. If he could rally these fellows of the castle with a few bows, and lead them—

Below him a torch appeared, lighting a small garden under the window. Pietro bore the torch, running, with three armed men beside him. They paused to look under the cypress trees that lined the walls, and Pietro exclaimed angrily, "Blessed Mary, I saw him coming down. He made his way through a barred door."

One of the soldiers said something Doria could not hear, and the steward shouted, "He named himself Doria, and pretended to be cast away. Aye, he made as if he were cup-shot. If we can hold him we can drive a bargain with those friends of his—or else strip the skin off him."

When they had hastened from the garden, Doria swung his legs over the window ledge. It was clear enough that he could not argue with these men, and he had no mind to leave his skin to dry on Rocafort's gate.

"Hark, ye with the broken head," he called over his shoulder, "and remember this. Doria had no hand in this onset until now, but he will bear a hand in it before sunup."

Ricard did not even look up, and Doria let himself drop into the top of a cypress. His weight tore through the thick mesh, which rasped his garments and skin. He fell out of it, rolling upon the ground, and got to his feet without other harm.

Then he went through the door by which the searchers had entered, and, finding the ground clear of men, began to seek for the path up which Marguerite had led him that afternoon. When he found it he broke into a run, leaping and sliding down the slope, dim in the starlight.

The worse for more than one tumble, Doria limped out on the beach. A glance over his shoulder told him that he had cut across the path of the raiders, who were not more than halfway down the hill.

Ahead of him, two fishing skiffs were drawn up on the beach, with three armed seamen standing guard over them. He thought that the raiders had got possession of these skiffs, and had rowed themselves in from the galley, which was anchored off the entrance of the bay—some half mile out.

A steady breeze was blowing across the bay—a night breeze that would not die away—and Doria sniffed it with relish. "It will do," he assured himself as he circled the skiffs to his own dhow.

"*Wallahi*," cried Khalil, "it is good that thou hast come, O my *Rais*. This is no place of peace."

"What men are they who have come from the galley?"

"Ziani's."

"And what is he?"

"A merchant. A slave merchant of Venice." Khalil lowered his voice. "I have seen him often in the market at Tunis, selling Christian girls to the pashas. He sells only a few, but he gets good prices."

"The devil!" Doria thought of Marguerite standing by the pillar of the *souk*, under the eyes of the rich pashas who were connoisseurs in women. So this Ziani raided the islands to carry off young girls who had few swords to defend them. And he used Doria's name to cloak him. "Khalil," he said grimly, "I will drive a bargain with this Messer Ziani, and I will take the girl from him."

The Arab shook his head indulgently, "Now thou art hot with anger, my lord. What can we do? Let us put off from the shore."

"Aye," said the corsair slowly, "thou shalt lift the sail and go, but I will not. Listen."

And he bent close to the old seaman, talking eagerly. Khalil listened intently. Once he lifted his hand to try the wind. Then he shook his head. "Nay, my *Rais*, they are armed—"

"And there is one place where weapons and armor avail not." Doria laughed, and thrust the slender forty-foot dhow out into the water. Khalil gave up argument, and hoisted the long yard. The triangular sail filled, and the boat slipped away into the darkness. Doria watched it until he saw it beat up against the wind; then he strolled down the beach.

The raiders were just leaving the road and crossing the sand, with two or three torches still alight. Beside Marguerite, holding her by the wrist, walked a man with the shoulders of a wrestler and the close-clipped beard and curled hair of a dandy. He stopped to peer at Doria's tall figure advancing into the torchlight.

"A good evening to you, Messer Ziani," Doria greeted him. "You use my war cry in a bad business, and I like it not."

One of the swordsmen took a torch and stepped up to the corsair, staring into his gaunt face. "The devil," the man cried. "This is Andrea Doria, who was taken by the Turks."

"Aye, I am Doria," acknowledged the corsair, "who was awakened by your clamor at the castle. Now I warn you that the Demoiselle of Rocafort is no merchandise for the slave market."

Marguerite checked the sudden cry that rose in her throat; but Ziani did not loose his grip of her wrist. He had planned her capture with some care, and saw a good profit in it, for the great pashas would pay high for a maid like this. On the other hand, he hoped to keep his share in it a secret.

While many merchants reaped a harvest from the secret sale of Christian Greeks and Georgians to the Moslems, he did not wish it known that he carried girls by force from the islands of Sicily. And he was startled by the appearance of the man he believed out of the way. "What do you want?"

"Will you set this girl free?"

Ziani glanced up and down the beach. No men were behind Doria, and his own skiffs were within reach. At the mouth of the bay his galley rode at anchor, and certainly no other vessel had come in. "What I will do," he parried, "is my affair."

"Then I will buy her."

The merchant scanned the seaman's torn garments. "With what?" he asked pointedly. He had heard tales of this man's daring, but he saw no reason to fear Doria now.

"With eight hundred gold sequins, to be paid in any Moslem port."

"Eh!" Ziani's brows went up. "It seems you do not care much for money."

Four to five hundred would have been a good price for the girl in Tunis. He might get more, of course, but he would have to pay certain bribes, and the cost of the run and back with his ship and crew.

"Nay," Doria laughed, "as I have none. Make it a thousand, if you wish—and get it if you can."

"I have no interest in either promises or threats."

Doria folded his arms, still smiling. "Nor do I deal in promises, Ziani. I have a slight something in me which it seems you lack. 'Tis called honor. Since I was a guest at Rocafort and since you have beset it in my name, I must buy this demoiselle from you and set her free. Having no gold here, I will exchange myself for her."

"You—what?"

"I will surrender myself to you here. The Sultan will give you not only gold but precious stones for Andrea Doria—and you know it well. But you must release this girl at once."

Shaking his head in pretended amazement, Ziani calculated quickly. He could find envoys of the great Sultan at Tunis, and if he managed the bargain well, he could clear fourteen hundred profit—enough to buy three ships. More, he would have near two thousand gain.

He did not believe Doria—the corsair had meant to trick him—and he *could* not believe Doria had approached him without having aid within call. But in a moment he saw his way to make certain of everything.

"Done!" he cried.

"Nay!" exclaimed Marguerite suddenly. "Nay, he must not sell himself!"

But Doria walked into the group of staring men-at-arms with his hands lifted to show that he had no weapon. "Demoiselle, you see now that I am Doria."

She looked up at him, tears gleaming in her eyes. "And I—I thought to put shame upon you. Oh, why will you do this?"

He smiled slightly. "Set her free," he said to the merchant.

Again Ziani scanned the shore. "In a moment," he muttered, making a sign to the men nearest the corsair. Two of them stepped to Doria, caught his arms, and searched his mantle and shirt for weapons. They found nothing, and Ziani's brow cleared. The way was open now, the profit clear. After all, Doria was a fool—or else captivity had weakened his brain. "To the boats," he ordered.

Strong hands hustled Doria forward, and thrust him into one of the skiffs. Men handed in their weapons and jumped in. He felt the boat shoved clear, and turned to look anxiously for Marguerite when she was placed in the seat beside him.

"Ziani!" he cried. "Set her ashore! You agreed!"

But Ziani, seated in the stem behind him, with a drawn knife in his hand, roared with merriment. The men in the bow sneered.

He clasped his head in his hands, listening the while to the wash of water as the skiff drew farther from the shore, and the other boat, crowded with men-at-arms, followed slowly. And soft hands rested upon Doria's arm. "Why did you do it?" she whispered. "They have tricked you."

"They have," he said, "but now you are here at my side, I will not let you go."

He put his arm about her, and looked up at the bright stars over the bay.

"Eh, lads," Ziani grinned, "the mighty Doria courts his girl before us! We have a pair of lovers here."

Her cheek pressed against Doria's shoulder, the girl was weeping silently.

"Aye, Ziani," Doria answered, "'tis a rare sight this, for never before hath Andrea Doria wooed a woman." He gathered Marguerite into his arms and stood up, facing the merchant, balancing in the swaying boat. "So greatly do I love this girl that I will have none other, nor will I let you lay hand upon her again—"

Someone shouted in the bow, and Ziani, frowning, clutched his dagger—glanced quickly to right and left. As he did so Doria set his foot upon the stem and leaped past the merchant. With the girl in his arms he went down into the water.

"'Ware, Messer Ziani!" cried the oarsman.

A shadow was rising against the stars. White water rippled nearer, and a dark prow entered the circle of torchlight. Men cried out and leaped from the skiff. The speeding dhow crashed into the skiff, crunching down its side and overturning it.

Doria had taken a long leap. He came to the surface, swimming with one arm, while he held the girl fast with the other. Someone blundered against him, and he kicked himself free as the boats crashed.

"Khalil!" he called.

He listened for the splash of a thrown rope, and swept his free arm across the water. But Marguerite, half choked, was in her wet gown. It needed all his strength to keep her head above the water. He had missed the rope, and now, with the torch gone, he could see nothing.

The dhow, staggering off the skiff, was gaining speed again. Doria forced his way toward it. The black side was over his head, and then it was past him. But he grasped for the steering oar and caught it.

Putting forth all his strength, he held the girl against the oar as they were jerked through the water. His fingers slipped down the wet wood slowly as Khalil, feeling the weight upon the oar, sought to free it.

"*Yak ahmak!*" Doria choked out. "Oh, fool—pull us in!"

A moment later Khalil had drawn them over the side. "The praise to Allah—surely it was a miracle."

Doria sat on the rail, getting his breath looking at the second skiff that had come to the rescue of the men clinging to the overturned boat. He laughed as he pulled himself in. "Aye," he cried to the Arab, "a miracle that this Ziani snatched the girl I meant to carry off!"

But he did not laugh as he carried her in his arms, silently through the darkness up the road to her home. Once he bent down and pressed his lips against the tangle of her damp hair.

"Tell me," she whispered, "what you said at the boat—it was to trick that Messer Ziani!"

"Certainly," said Doria gravely. "I wanted to be put beside you in the skiff without waking his suspicions. I bade Khalil sail past us, close by, and throw me a rope end. But the old man was excited. He ran down the skiff and forgot the rope."

"I know," she assented. Then, after a moment she said faintly, "But when you told them that you—I—"

"Ah!" Doria looked down into her face, dim in the starlight. "Then I was mad. I would have carried you to Sicily and made you a seaman's bride—I who love you so. Ever since we quarreled at the stream I have thought of that."

With a lift of his shoulders he trudged on up the hill road toward the lights of Rocafort. "Nay, little Marguerite! Doria is no more the great *Rais* Doria—he hath neither ship nor men nor gold. And he is afraid."

"Then you will let me go?"

"Aye, so."

"I would like a dry dress." The girl stirred in his arms, and smiled. "But, *Rais* Doria, I do not want you to be afraid."

Elf Woman

First of all, the coming of the foot-loose girl:

That morning, Rang the Icelander picked clean the bones of an eider duck. He drank clean the barley soup from his bowl. He put the bones in his bowl and gave all that to the dog.

"Now," he decided, "will we need another duck."

The dog, wagging its tail, and Rang, knowing by the flash of sunlight on the silver ring that the winter sun was up over the sea, stepped into the *stofa* of his strong stone house. Bending over the stone-pit, he washed head and hands in the steaming water from the spring. Drying his hands on a sheepskin, he overlooked his hunting weapons—a throwing stick, a weighted line for casting at birds, a stone-sling for small game, a looped rope for wild ponies, an ax for bear, and a three-tined spear for fish. Rang took the bird line and went out to see what might be.

He went through the haystacks, covered tight with sealskins that shielded his stone house from the winds, and he overlooked his claim, in that mild winter light.

Among the thin birches his ponies grazed—four tens and three of them, as they should be. Over the river, eider ducks winged down toward the sea marsh, at the river's end. All was as it should be.

Even the smoke came lazily from the mountain high up there where the Sleeper breathed. A puff of smoke. Rang began to count to ten and on to seven. Another breath of smoke. That was as it should be.

"He sleeps," Rang told the dog. "And the snow is white over the glaciers."

Now Rang spoke to that dog because the two of them lived alone in the valley, which Rang would not leave. On that day he was seventeen years of age—by count of the years on the time-stick over the hearth—and his father being dead, he was master of his claim. All that valley from the glacier ice to the sands at the sea belonged to Rang, with the living things in it.

Then the dog barked and Rang saw the sheep. They were strange sheep cropping the grass across the stream. Surprised, Rang counted them. Five sheep would not wander across the claim unless driven. And the neighboring men, here and there beyond his valley, had all gone off to the Althing, by the town, to sit in judgment on a manslayer. Rang had not gone to that judging, because he would not leave his stud of ponies and his valley.

This, Rang thought, was by way of being something strange. Thrusting the bird line into his belt he hurried down through his shaggy ponies. He hurried by leaping the slope in ten-foot drops, for that boy was long in the limb and sure in the jump. Heading toward the narrow gut in the stream, he hurried out on a rock and leaped the waterfall where spray swirled up in the wind. He hurried on to the sheep, and stopped by two stones.

There was the foot-loose girl between the stones on a bed of moss with an eider-down cape tucked around her knees. Her hands wound wool thread from a skein on a staff. She pushed away the loose hair blown over her face by the wind, and she looked up at him—dark eyes shining in her thin face.

"Well," Rang demanded, "what?"

Her bare arms trembled over the tangle of wool; the sleeves of her smock were torn. She seemed to be hiding between her rocks, by the twigs of a burned-out fire.

"Are you foot-loose, to be driving sheep over hill and dale?"

She whispered yes, trying to draw down the tangle of her hair. "And I am afraid," she added, seeing him frown.

"Of what, girl?"

But she would not say of what. She only worked at her skein of wool, and the Icelander rubbed his yellow head, not satisfied. "This is Rang Dale," he explained, nodding at the valley. "And that is Rang River."

"And what man are you?"

"Rang."

At that she laughed.

"I am Caill—I would like well," her voice chimed like a bell, "to be in Rang's house up there." She nodded, wistfully. "Then perhaps I would not be frightened."

Considering this carefully as he did all such matters, Rang frowned.

This seemed to frighten her again. "I can turn mare's milk into good sour cream," she whispered. "I can weave—wool into cloth."

Now that Rang had considered, he announced his judgment. "Food you may have, foot-loose girl, in my house, and shelter against this night's cold. But this claim of mine I will not share."

She flung up her head, trembling. "Bright you may be, and full of wealth, and proud by good right. Dark though I am, and without a claim—yet I will never set my foot in your house."

"Suit yourself, Caill," Rang agreed.

And he went away angry, wondering what could make the girl over there afraid in this valley. No harm could be hidden here where his ancestors had lived by the stud of horses.

His father had found death in the sea, coming back on the west voyage with sheep from the Green Land, when there had been famine on Iceland. His grandfather had come to a peaceful end when he had broken his back in a wrestling bout—for the Icelander folk were mighty wrestlers—at the Althing bullfeast. Yea, and his sire had never come back from venturing on the uplands too close to the Sleeper.

For that Sleeper who lay outstretched beneath the island stirred at times in his sleep. When he turned over, the earth shook. The mutter of his waking ran along the land—the steam of his breath filled the sky and came down in ashes around the mountain. Those ashes choked to death men who were caught on the mountain.

And then the Sleeper spat out molten rock and steam from his mouth. The fire of his spittle ran down the glaciers, turning ice into steam. Rang knew the signs of the Sleeper's waking. *Black lines upon the snow of the mountainside.*

It was in the mist of the next morning that he heard the wailing. His ponies broke and ran uphill. And Rang, who had not heard the like before, traced it down to the water.

On the far side walked a dark man. Under his arm he pressed a skin—he blew his breath into one end of a pipe, and moved his fingers over another pipe.

Rang hurried and leaped the waterfall. The stranger stopped, staring: "Now that was something to do!" he shouted. "But I can liken it easy."

He sounded a blast on the pipes. Then putting aside the pipes, he faced

Rang and leaped in his tracks, cracking his heels high in the air where his head had been.

Rang reached angrily for the pipes, but this stranger moved quickly before him, pulling a knife from his belt. Steel flashed under Rang's chin, and the Icelander stepped back, surprised.

"You frighten the beasts!" he exclaimed.

The man of the mist nodded.

"I frighten more than beasts," he said softly, "when the mood is on me. For I am a ready man at slaying or marauding or thieving. Yea, I will match you, Icelander, at what you will."

He grinned crookedly, and nodded. "It is easy to see that you are a sleepy and simple man—very tender in what you do." Sheathing his knife, he took up his pipes carefully. "But now I am making the pipes sing to bring a smile to the lips of this elf-maid."

Then Rang saw that the girl Caill was perched on a rock with her staff of wool, watching them.

"You are quick to boast," he remarked. "Honeywords."

He thought of that name because the dark man had a soft, throaty voice.

"Yea—quicker than you will ever be," said Honeywords. "For I have fared forth over the seven seas, and my eyes have seen all the wonders of the world itself. I have seen the dragon that swims this sea of yours with ten legs creeping on one side, and ten on the other. Can you match that, Icelander?"

The girl Caill was coming closer, listening.

"Well, hear this," growled Rang, who was no hand at words. "In the dark of a night my eyes can see. Yea, every stone of this valley I can see."

Honeywords grinned. "Easy to do, when that volcano of yours spits out fire. Now, hear this, horse-herder! Through wind and wave and mist have I come hither. Yea, from Saint Patrick's isle have I come in a skiff without a sail. Can you match that?"

His eyes gleamed and snapped, while Rang thought slowly as usual.

Then Rang's dog barked, far off.

"What may that be?" Caill asked.

Up the river scores of men were climbing, feeling their way around the quicksands. They had round shields slung to their backs, and they carried spears that were not fish spears.

"Raiders," quoth Honeywords. "Now there will be a gathering of spoil and a shedding of blood, and a great rapine in Iceland." Rang had far-seeing eyes, and he made out a ship drawn up on the shore. Its prow reared up, shaped like a dragon's head. From its stern hung two steering oars, like legs.

"There sits your dragon," he said, "on the beach."

Some of the ship's crew were letting themselves down over the side.

"Who are the raiders?" he asked Honeywords, who seemed to know all that went on at sea.

"I am not so curious," Honeywords shook his head, "as to want to look at them closer to find out. Nay, I will hie me the other way." Tucking his pipes under his arm, he caught at the Icelander. "Man, are ye beside yourself?"

For Rang had seen some of those raiders spreading themselves out toward his ponies, grazing down by the river, and he jerked away from the piper.

"You run quickly," Honeywords shouted, "to find your death. Turn away!"

With empty hands Rang was hurrying down to the river. "He had his warning," Honeywords muttered. "Now I must be hiding you, Caill."

"The sheep!" cried the girl. And she was off, scrambling through the rocks looking for her animals.

Honeywords looked thoughtfully. With no one to see him, he crossed the stream to the Icelander's hut. Thrusting his shaggy head through the door curtain he blinked at something that hung from the roof, gleaming in the late sun. A heavy silver ring, lopsided. When the men of Rang's family gained a bit of silver, they had heated it, and molded it to this ring. They had kept this treasure of silver carefully. Honeywords felt its weight curiously.

Rang hurried down his land to the leader of the shipmen, where they had caught his ponies. They had their legs bandaged, they had iron shirts on their bodies, they carried wallets and axes and short swords. Silently they watched him. Two of them stepped around behind him.

And Rang felt the chill of fear in his blood. This leader, this tall man who leaned on a spear, had the half of a boar's head over his own. The snout and the bristles were gleaming gold.

"Why do you make a landfall here, Swinehead?" Rang asked.

The tall man looked at Rang's empty hands. "We saw the skiff." Softly he spoke, with a twang to his words that was not Icelandic. "Men call me Hjor."

His curling beard twitched in a smile as Rang looked over him. A dragon's head on a boat's prow—a swine's head on a man. Long iron weapons in the hands of a hundred shipmen. Never had such things as these appeared on his beach before.

"Then, Hjor, turn loose my ponies."

Gently Hjor shook his head, and the jeweled eyes of the boar gleamed. "Why, no. Some of us can ride them to town, youngling." He stared at Rang's skin jacket and uncut hair. "Are the Icelander-folk all as dumb as you?"

Now Rang was beginning to understand that these were no guests or settlers making a landfall.

"Yea, they are dumb as their cattle, Hjor," Honeywords shouted, running up. "They tend horses and catch the fish of the sea. Now they herd themselves in the Town, to make laws. There they listen to the law-talk of their chieftain, Gizur the Old."

It seemed to Rang that Honeywords must have discovered all this from the foot-loose girl.

"By Freya's boar where is this Town?" Hjor scanned the empty ridges that closed in Rang's valley. "I see it not."

"Two hours over hill and dale," chanted Honeywords. "Ochune, good are the signs. The menfolk of this coast will be sitting at their Hill of Laws. Wait, Hjor—abide here until night falls, lord of the Kattegat and Skagerrak—spoiler of ships. There will be a moon to light the path to the slaying and spoiling. There will be a wailing of women, when your seafarers run in with their swords. Yea, good are the signs, Hjor." Shuffling his feet and fingering his pipes, he grinned up at the raider. "Only wait until dark. And I will be after spying and peering before you, along the way. I will be your forerunner to the destruction, even as I found this landing place, marking it with the skiff. I will go on ahead—"

Gently Hjor shook his head. "You will stay by me, piper."

"Nay, this horse-herder knoweth the way. Let him lead you, Hjor."

"He will lead and you will follow."

For the first time Rang realized that the words he had heard meant that these two would seize the herds and the silver of all the Icelanders they found, and would slaughter the men, like cattle. No one in the Town could have noticed their arrival in this valley.

This much being clear to him, Rang reasoned that he must forewarn the folk in the Town. Edging toward a pony, as Hjor's men drove the herd up toward his hut, Rang jumped to it. Swinging himself up, he kicked at the animal's ribs.

Something whisked through the air, as the pony sprang forward. It fell away beneath him. Rolling over, the Icelander saw a spear-shaft thumping the ground, and the point of it was through the pony's loins. The horse cried out. Hot anger came over Rang when he saw this. Tears ran from his eyes, and he threw himself at the nearest of those raiders, to grapple him. The man laughed and stepped back, bringing the flat of his ax down over Rang's ear.

"He sheds tears," the raider gibed, "before he is hurt."

Blood ran from the Icelander's head. Fingers of pain tore beneath his skull as he tried to raise himself. He heard Caill's voice cry, shrill with fear.

Hjor looked around sharply. "Find me his woman."

The weapon-men were starting to beat through the dwarf birches when Honeywords pranced out in front of them. "Yonder she hides."

Up the river he pointed, at a grassy mound, where there was no sign of a living being. "Yonder in the elf-mound. An elf-maid, she, dwelling beneath the grass until the rising of the moon. Yea, that is the hour of her coming forth upon the earth."

Hjor grunted, but some of his men came closer to hear.

"When the moon is full upon this maid," Honeywords explained, "she sings, and she combs her hair with a shining comb. Some of you, mayhap have seen the mermaids of the waters. Fairer indeed is this elf woman. White as wands, her arms. Like fruit blossoms her breasts. With her distaff she weaves a mist of magic about her, and if you can enter that, you will find her dearer than mortal women."

"No such lorelei lives," Hjor snarled. He and his men thought no more of looking for a woman. Instead, pulling Rang with him, he pushed into the hut. The sunset was fading, and Hjor peered at the Icelander's hunting weapons. "Sticks and cords!" The tined fishing spear he tossed away contemptuously. And with the throwing stick, he poked into the chest where the Icelander kept his precious things—the green cloak of silk that had been his mother's and that jewelry he had made her out of pearl shell. These Hjor tossed aside indifferently. Spitting into the steaming water pool, he called for Honeywords.

Rang noticed that the silver ring, his treasure, had vanished from its cord. And the raiders discovered that the piper of Erin was not to be found. In the twilight, he had slipped away while Hjor was inspecting the hut. Hjor breathed deep. "By Freya's boar!"

Taking up Rang's roping pole, he broke the shaft away from the cord and jerked the noose over Rang's head, tightening it about his throat until his injured head ached.

"You feel that?" he asked softly, "We will cut the skin from your head and pull it off and leave you for the wolves to find, Icelander, if you do not lead us by the shortest way to the Town. Do you understand that?"

"Yes," said Rang.

Knotting the free end of it about his own left wrist, Hjor went outside, pulling Rang with him. He peered into the dense mist over the river. "Can you see your way through this?"

"Yes," said Rang. "Soon the moon will be clear on the hills."

For a while, until the moon showed, Hjor inspected the foot of the trail that led to Town. Tracks cut up the ground, and it was broad enough for his men to ride two abreast.

When the moon's glow showed through the mist above them he peered into Rang's eyes from beneath the boar's head. "You," he advised, "go first, and go quietly." Rang felt a cold iron point sear the flesh under his shoulder. "And keep to the path or you will have the whole of this blade in your guts."

Silently Rang started up the path by the river. He did not think he would come down again into that valley.

Then he heard a voice singing, clearer than the rush of the stream. After a step or two he saw the moonlight full upon the top of the grass mound, and a woman singing there, bending over, combing at her hair.

Soft she sang, heedless of the men, the silk of her green cloak shining on her slender body, with a necklace gleaming on her bare throat.

For a moment Rang hardly thought it to be Caill, so different she seemed.

"The lorelei!" said someone, and by her bare feet lay the distaff, and around her the mist thinned away. The lines of men edged toward her, staring. They came around the mound hungrily.

"Fetch her along," Hjor said. "We have no time to play with the young witch now."

So the moon was higher when they started up the path again, with Caill among the men. And Rang pondered, each step sending pain shooting into his head. He wished that he had some of Honeywords's cunning. For in that night light he could see; still that did not help him to make a plan.

He saw where the path forked ahead of him, and that showed him something he could do. He stopped. "On the right hand," he said to Hjor, "goes the path to the dales, easy to follow but long. On the left goes the hill path—"

"Up or down, take the short way. Stir yourself, animal."

Rang turned left, climbing. Here he did not know the landmarks, for this path led up to the white glaciers of the Sleeper, not to the Town, and Rang had never explored it. Out of the birch clumps he climbed, past the face of black rocks shining with wet, out along a ridge crowning one of the glaciers. White and cold lay the ice.

Above him he could see the breath of the Sleeper puffing out, after he counted ten and seven each time. He was thinking about Caill, who seemed so beautiful now in the moonlight in her fine cloak, and what might happen to her presently.

They were passing under bare rocks, skirting the edge of the glacier when Hjor jerked the rope hard. "I see no roofs about here. Where sits this Town?"

Rang did not answer, because he was holding his breath. A cloud of smoke billowed down over them, and the men began to cough, choking. Edging closer to Caill, he whispered, "Hold your breath." Some of the ponies neighed and plunged.

A squealing and a wailing broke out above them, in the smoke, as if fiends danced there. The ponies reared, clattering on the loose stones along the path above the glacier. One of the raiders yelled in fear.

"'Tis that mad piper of Erie," Hjor shouted, "who swore by his soul he would deliver Iceland to us."

His eyes aflame with suspicion, he whirled on Rang. A stick whistled through the air and clanged against his headgear. A throwing stick, Rang saw it to be. A long fish spear followed, out of the smoke, sticking in a man's thigh.

Lifting his shield, Hjor stopped. A stone smashed against the shield.

"The mountain lives!" a man shouted, staring. Along that path bedlam was breaking loose; with the whistle of the wind, the billowing of smoke, the hurling of weapons, and men tumbling from frightened ponies.

Above them, in the rocks, shapes in fishskins and seal pelts jumping. Rang saw them to be the fishers and hunters of the Iceland folk. A

net sailing down upon the heads of the nearest raiders, and the while the
pipes of Erin wailing—

Rang jumped among his ponies, shouting at them, and they headed
back, rushing down the path, spilling men. Then the rope tore at Rang's
throat, hauling him back.

Light arrows rattled against the iron shirts of the raiders, and sling-stones
slashed their faces. From between the rocks a seal hunter slipped, to make
a cast with his roping-pole, and catch a warrior in the noose, throwing him.
Amazed, the weapon-men were ducking and scrambling for shelter.

Then Hjor's voice boomed out: "Sticks and stones and smoke, messmates! You are hiding your heads from fishing folk. Up with you!"

Climbing to a rock, he called those raiders together: "Shield wall! Shield
wall!"

Obedient to his voice, the war band gathered, shields overlapping. Limping and uncertain, they rallied toward Hjor's voice: "Fight down to the
ship, lads!"

Unnoticed for that instant, Rang pulled the noose from his neck. "I
will show you a way down," he shouted, forgetting the pain in his head,
running toward Hjor's rock. Up to the rock he leaped with empty hands.
Before Hjor could strike at him, his legs and arms caught around the warrior in a wrestler's grip. The blow knocked Hjor off balance, and Rang
locked his arms.

The two of them rolled off the rock, and Rang shoved Hjor out upon
the glacier ice. As he did so, he felt himself shoot downward. Sliding, he
let his body go limp, and curled his arms about his head.

Over the gray ice he slid faster, scraping against rocks. He whirled
around, and brought up in soft, wet snow. He got to his feet, finding no
bones broken. A stone's throw away lay Hjor without his sword, but with
his shield arm twisted under him. The heavy shield had caught fast beneath the snow, and Hjor groaned. Rang jumped on him with his knees.
He caught Hjor's beard and twisted it one way, while he knelt on the man's
broken shoulder. And Hjor yelped at the pain.

Sliding and scrambling, Honeywords appeared beside them, pulling
out his sheath knife.

"Let me stick it in his throat," he panted.

Rang shoved the piper away, and Honeywords gibed at him: "Horse-
herder. Slay him now, or he will feed you to the birds!"

But Rang was thinking about that. He felt anger rise in him, because Hjor's men had killed the pony. Still, he thought how they would obey Hjor's voice. So thinking, he ground his knee again into Hjor, and the warrior yelled, tears running from his eyes.

"Call to your war band up there," Rang said, "to throw down their shields and weapons, or you will weep more than that."

"What then?" gasped Hjor, sweating.

Rang considered. "The Iceland folk will summon you to trial for making a landfall with weapons."

Hjor's eyes gleamed when he heard this. He nodded his head, and Rang got up from his knee. Swallowing hard, Hjor shouted up at the path, "Down shields, Hjor's men. Throw away your swords. The power of magic on this mountain is too much for us!"

Faces peered down at them through the drifting smoke, and they heard iron clatter upon stones. Rang felt with his feet in the snow, and took up Hjor's sword, while Honeywords stared at him as if he had changed his shape.

"By the powers!" the man of Erin cried. "You shall not be saying at the court that I was forerunner of these seasnakes, Rang. Look ye! I ran fast to the town, and summoned forth the folk, to keep you from being cut out of your skin. So you owe your life to me. Do you understand, Rang?"

"Yes," said Rang.

On the beach, when the moon was high, the Iceland court held inquest upon the raiders. The court sat by the dragon-ship.

Gizur the Old sat by the fire they had lighted, with good men and true from the Thing to consider the judgment after witness had been taken. On one hand sat hundreds of the hunters and fishers, with the weapons, the iron shirts and the shields of the raiders close by them. On the other side, away from the ship, sat Hjor and his raiders with empty hands.

Gizur pulled at his white mustache, and spoke each word carefully. For the law of Iceland, made by the first comers to the land, was older than Britain or the Angle and Saxon folk, and it was the duty of the old men like Gizur to see that the law suffered no change.

The witnesses, Gizur said, had established that these raiders summoned before the court had suffered some flesh wounds but no body or bone or death wounds. So he took no account of those flesh wounds. The Icelander Rang, however, had suffered a head wound, and the raider Hjor a broken shoulder. These he set against each other and took no more account of them.

Hjor breathed easier when he heard this.

"The death of the pony is to be atoned for," Gizur continued. "And for that I will let Rang name his award."

Standing up before all that court, Rang considered carefully what the true value of the pony might be. "Hjor's sword I shall take," he announced, "in full atonement." He thought a good ax could be forged out of the blade.

And Hjor almost laughed, seeing how carefully the Icelanders dealt with little things. Not so Honeywords. "What a simple folk you are," he gibed, "and tender in what you do! Will you be after letting these man-slayers go off scot-free in their ship? They will come back to take the hides off you. Whatever!"

Now in this, Honeywords was thinking about his own hide. But Gizur the Old was not pleased.

"A word more," Gizur said, "and you will be in contempt of this court, man of Erin. The law may not please you, but in this land men must have equal right, by law." Hjor sprang up, to run with his men to the ship and push off, when Gizur bade him wait, as there was one more point to be judged. "It is evident, Hjor, that you and your shipmates made a landfall at this spot with intent to do bodily harm."

Hjor stopped as if struck, and Gizur added that he could plead his own cause.

"True enough, we made a landfall," muttered Hjor, looking about him cunningly. "But where is the witness who says we came with any malice aforethought? I do not see him."

"There are the witnesses." Gizur said. "They are those killing weapons of yours." Gizur nodded. "Nay, those swords and battle axes and spears were made for manslaughter. And by carrying them you are guilty of intent to kill. For that, atonement must be made."

Chewing his beard, Hjor waited.

"I award," said Gizur slowly, "to those who were to be killed but are not—to the Iceland folk—all goods and gear that are movable upon your dragon-ship."

"And the ship itself?" demanded Hjor.

"That is yours." And Gizur ordered him sharply with his men into it—to the stern. Those raiders hurried to obey, hiding their exultation. They watched the Icelanders, armed with the killing weapons, haul fur

cloaks and beer kegs and dried fish and a chest of gold from the dragon-
ship. Every bit of cloth and loose rope and every sea chest, the Icelanders
passed down to the beach. They even pulled the long steering oars from
the stem and heaved out the rowing benches. When Hjor shouted protest,
Gizur reminded him that the oars were movable gear. And he bade the
Icelanders throw out the rowing oars.

At this, Hjor stormed forward. Then Gizur with his own knife cut the
yard sheets, and the yard came down. Iceland fishermen slashed loose the
one great sail of the dragon-ship and tossed it to the sand.

"Robbers!" yelled Hjor, in a fury. "How will we sail—"

The dragon-ship began to move out into the swell. Scores of fishermen
shoved at its sides, running it out into deep water. The ship slid past the
break in the swell, and turned slowly, caught by the offshore wind.

"This is murder," roared Hjor, his hands groping for a stick or a pole
in vain.

"No," Gizur shouted back, where the armed fishermen waited in the
swell, "it is what you had in mind, intent to do manslaughter. You will
judge for yourself how it turns out."

The dragon-ship drifted farther out, into the moonlight.

Rang did not see it. He went to where Caill sat, and she held out the fine
silk cloak and the pearl shell trinkets to him. "Those are yours, Rang."

Instead of taking them, Rang shook his head.

"Why did you make yourself into an elf-maid," he demanded, "sitting
on that mound?"

"I thought I could beguile them into looking at me," she whispered,
"so you could escape." A shadow of the old fear touched her eyes. "Why
did you leap upon Hjor up on the mountain?"

"I could not have them fighting where you might be harmed."

"You are foolish," she said, laughing. "You were not like that at first."

Bending over, he picked her up in his arms, and began to carry her. Along
his river, up his land he carried her, to his hut. And he would have carried
her across the threshold if Honeywords words had not jumped out into the
moonlight close by it. He peered at those two and he grumbled.

"Ochune! Too tenderhearted and simple am I."

"You!" cried Caill. "Indeed you are, a fine, scheming man."

Honeywords looked into her face, and shook his head. "I could have
had gold and gear as the forerunner of the sea raiders. Yet for the sight of

a girl and the sake of a boy, I saved Iceland. 'Tis the heart of a poet I have and nothing else."

Listening, they heard the wail of his pipes as he walked away, the sound of it soft and mournful as he pressed the bag under his arm. But they did not see over his other arm Rang's ring of silver.

/

The Night Bird Flies

You will be thinking that this strange story is a lie; but it is all true, and many men have sworn to it. It befell on the Côte d'Or, within those drowsy hills of Burgundy, on a clear midsummer day when the good Charles was Duke—may God grant him everlasting rest! It came about, men say, because Bryn Briogan had eyes to see in the dark. Others say that he brought trouble with him, as a dog brings fleas. But you will hear the first and the last of it, and you will judge for yourself.

Now the first of it was the ferryman, snoring in his barge on the river, when someone clapped him on the breech and he awoke to ferry Bryn Briogan across to the island. Him and his horse.

"It will be a silver denier," said the ferryman when Bryn was for leading his horse out of the barge to the land. "A denier, messire."

Bryn shook his head then. "A pity," he said. "For I have a copper farthing in my wallet, but no silver. So you will have nothing."

The ferryman scratched his big head. He looked carefully at this man and his horse. For the man, he saw, was long and lean—ragged and sundarkened, with a wide, hard mouth and a look of laughter about his eyes. And the horse was fine and high—black with a white blaze in the forehead. He had a saddle of red leather, strange to the eye.

"I'll take the farthing," he said.

"Tell me," remarked Bryn, "if there is a place hereabouts where a man with a sword may find service."

"Aye, the Castle Ferrand up yonder."

"And what manner of master has this Castle Ferrand?"

"The Lord Renault de Ferrand of this island is a just and high lord, and rich as a bishop."

Then Bryn tossed him the coin, and mounted the charger walking up the road. The ferryman pushed off the barge and rubbed the farthing, which was clipped and bent. "And more," he shouted after the rider, "he hath a great gallows upon which to swing off such a tripe-gutted bottle-whacker as thou art!"

Over his shoulder the rider looked back. "Have a care, little man, for this horse and I can overpass that water without a boat to serve us."

And at this the ferryman felt the chill of fear creeping up his back; his knees shook, and he thrust at the sweep with trembling hands. A sudden dread had come upon him, so that—when the stranger had disappeared from the hillside—he rowed his barge back across the stream and went on foot by roundabout paths to the village of Ferrand that lies beyond the castle, to tell of these words. "He and his horse," the ferryman repeated when he had emptied a cup or two, "have no need of a boat. Nay, they can ride over a river."

While the ferryman was doing this, Bryn Briogan was riding down below the road in a little valley girdled by a wood of live oaks. He might have gone on, but a thought came to him.

"Malik," he said to the horse, "we have not filled our bellies for a night and a day, and here is some good grazing."

He turned the black charger into the field and dismounted, slipping off the bit and the straps of the headstall. The horse thrust down its long neck eagerly, and the man went to sit in the shadow of the oaks. It was not good in that age of men to let a charger graze unwatched, or to sit oneself where enemies might come up behind. Bryn knew this well, for he had many enemies and his skin bore the scars of wounds.

He took the empty purse out of his wallet, tossed it away, and lay back in the tall dry grass, drawing his belt a notch tighter and chewing on a stalk. He had need of food and some good wine. But before he could have that he must hire him out again as swordsman in a lord's service. Service and war he had known for years—and the waking under a burning roof, and the watching the stars go down, and the waiting for death to pass by . . .

Bryn sat up in the grass, looking out into the field. Soon a smile touched his dark face.

Two fellows in long shirts had come down the road. Seeing the horse Malik grazing in the field, they had thought him to be astray without master. A fine beast, they thought, and went into the field to take him in hand for themselves.

Now Bryn watched them as they went up to the charger, who tossed his head and moved away. The rogues followed after, and again Malik walked off. Bryn chewed on his stalk, at ease in the shade. And then the fellows separated, one going up to Malik's head and the other behind him. Malik lifted his head and screamed—he wheeled and reared, striking down at the man behind him with his forefoot. And that man yelled, rolling in the grass with a broken shoulder bone. Malik wheeled again, catching the arm of the other in his teeth.

He was angry now, the charger. And the rogue would have had a broken arm if Bryn had not whistled. Malik pricked his ears and loosed the thief, to canter off to where his master sat. So the two fellows picked themselves up and ran for the road with flying legs.

"A fine fighter he surely is," said a clear voice behind the soldier. In a second Bryn was on his feet, his hand on his sword hilt.

Then he laughed at himself. For the voice was young, and smooth as running water—a girl's voice. She stood there in the flecked sunlight between two trees, within a pebble's toss of him.

"Aye," agreed Bryn, "a champion of fighters he is—he has no match beyond the sea."

He forgot his hunger and shaded his eyes with his sword hand to see the better. He forgot the two rogues, and took a step forward. For the girl was looking eagerly at Malik. Slim and straight she stood, a bare arm lifted against the heavy mass of her hair. The hood of her gray cloak was thrown back upon her shoulders. She had a broad smooth forehead and full bright lips, ripe for kissing.

"Stay your step, messire," she said.

Then he saw that she held in one hand a bow already strung—no plaything, but a longbow that—and an arrow with an iron point in the fingers of the hand. Into her eyes came a flash of anger. Bryn wanted much to see the color of those eyes, and to lay his hand upon the heavy tresses that overhung her slight breast. A fire that was more than the sun's heat burned in him.

"A bargain I will make with you, Demoiselle Diana," he said gravely. "I will not put hand or slight upon you—fair though you are—but you shall sit and speak with me a while. Soon or late it will come to that between us—"

It was a long speech for Bryn Briogan, and the sight of her tangled his tongue like wine. But the maid's answer came clear as a bell's note:

"Think not to beguile me—I will not have it. Keep your distance, Messire the Uncouth, or this arrow will pass between us and you will find your death upon it."

Bryn was not minded to stay his step for this war gear in a maid's hand.

"Let fly the arrow then," he said, "if you must."

And he walked forward, smiling. No word of warning did she give him, except the flame of anger in her eyes. Her body tensed, the bow came up, and the slim white arm swept back. Bryn bent his knees and flung himself to one side. Even as he did so, the shaft whistled by his shoulder, ripping through a fold of his mantle.

He rolled over and sprang up warily. But the sun-flecked space between the trees stood empty, and the maid had vanished.

Only Malik remained by him, looking at him, startled. Whereupon Bryn laughed aloud, jerking back the headstall upon the horse. "By heaven, Malik, we were worsted—she rolled me in the grass like a cup-shot rogue!"

Nearby stood a ruined gray tower, covered with ivy. Bryn would have searched it, but he fancied that the girl was in there, and he could not dodge a shaft sped from cover.

He was musing upon her as he rode up the highway and heard horses trotting toward him. Four men came into sight—the leader a noble in fur-tipped mantle. A heavy man, with a roving eye and long, curled ringlets. He stared at Bryn, who drew rein and saluted him without moving aside.

"Eh," the stout Burgundian said, "what is your name, and whom do you serve?"

"Seigneur, I am Bryn Briogan, once of Ireland, and lately knight of the city of Jerusalem."

"Another starveling from over the sea," muttered my lord, glancing at Bryn's spurs, from which the gilt had long since worn off. "What would you have?"

"Faith, decent service and a seat at table."

The stout nobleman ran his eye down the stained leather jacket and worn scabbard of the Irish crusader and frowned. "An empty purse and belly, hein? Well, I am governor of this island, by the Duke's grace, and I am weary of begging crusaders and their tales. Why should I pay for an idle sword?" He looked shrewdly at Bryn's black charger. "Yet have I need of a horse like this. I'll give you thirty ducats for him."

Bryn shook his head and smiled.

"Forty, then—silver ducats of Paris weight." The Seigneur de Ferrand slapped his stout wallet, which jangled cheerily. "Forty-five? With the saddle, fifty? Come now, what's your price?"

"'Tis more than your purse holds."

"By the Devil, his horns—"

"Because," said Bryn gravely, "I will not sell this horse."

De Ferrand's brow darkened, then cleared. "Sir Bryn, you are a right stubborn man. If you will not sell the charger, you will not. Then come you to the chateau." When the crusader was silent, the Burgundian added jovially, "At the least, sit and sup with us. I will not have a man ride hungry from my land."

"Then I will do it," said Bryn, but he was thinking of the girl who lived in the broken tower beneath them. And De Ferrand, trotting at his side, glanced covertly at black Malik, knowing that the poverty-ridden crusader bestrode a better horse than his own.

Bryn had a great hunger in him, and that evening he plied dagger and fist in the cold veal pie and the dish of pigeon and boar's steak, and washed down his throat with wine.

Still, he had the feeling that the men were looking at him stealthily. Some of them whispered in a dialect he did not know. The biggest of them, Hugo, the Genoese captain of the garrison, lifted his goblet and hailed Bryn:

"*Par Dex*, Sir Wanderer, will you drink with me?"

He leaned across the board, and they clicked goblets. Hugo had an arm that could break a bull's ribs.

Out of the corner of his eye Bryn saw that the monk at the table made the sign of the cross as they did this. Nor did De Ferrand join them in drinking. Instead the lord of the chateau leaned back in his high chair, plump white fingers plucking at his beard.

Hugo, however, sprawled at ease, his restless eyes moist with wine. "Cup for cup, Sir Bryn—and tale for tale. Now they tell me this charger of yours is a great fighting beast, and a king's ransom will not buy him."

Bryn nodded.

"Well, that may be," grunted Hugo, "but I have a young Spanish devil will carry me twenty leagues between sundown and sun-up."

"That is good," Bryn assented, "but my black beast Malik hath not his match for speed in the East. And the colts here are plow horses beside him. He will not let anything go past his head." Bryn's voice dropped into a soft chanting. "Sure, it was at the rising of the moon the power came on him. It was out of Damascus where the winds whisk through the hills. The wind came strong behind us, and it put a slight upon the horse, to feel it passing him.

"He stretched out, speeding faster and faster, but still the wind passed him. Then he took longer leaps and the power came upon him. He leaped high, over the trees without touching hoof to ground. Faster he went, until he left behind him the clouds of the sky, and he felt the wind on his nose. Then he was satisfied and drew himself in and came down gently."

Silence fell upon the table, and Bryn waited in vain for a man to laugh or cap his tale with another.

De Ferrand sighed, and smote his fist on the board. "Enough!" His small eyes glared at the wanderer. "Will ye tell of those other night rides of yours?"

"Nay," said Bryn, "for I have another thing in my mind to do this night."

Then Hugo laughed under his breath, but De Ferrand spoke hoarsely: "Art weary of life? Then give ear to this true recital of what took place on this island within the year—although you know it well.

"First," said De Ferrand, "there was the death of Viterbo, the merchant riding toward Venice. He came to his end upon the road within sight of the ferry. He was alone, going in haste at night, bearing, it seems, some moneys. The blow that slew him came out of the air, and he fell from the saddle with his skull shattered."

"A pity," said Bryn.

"Sancta Maria! 'Twas more a pity when the young Seigneur d'Estampes met his fate. He also was crossing the road of the island alone after sunset. Some woodcutters heard him chanting a love lay as he passed by their cabin. Deep in the shadow of the forest he went, when it came upon him. The louts heard his song end, and then a scream and a beating of hoofs that went away. After that they heard, far off, the scream of a horse. It was a day before we found the body of D'Estampes, and his nag. They had fallen from the high cliff and they lay there on the stones with their bones a-broken."

Leaning back in his chair, De Ferrand faced the crusader. "Now this Seigneur d'Estampes had a hardy soul in him. He was riding to seek a woman that night, and what could have driven him mad with terror within a moment, so that he drove his charger from the cliff?"

"As to this lord—God rest him—I know not," responded Bryn. "But no man could make a horse take such a leap."

"True!" cried the Burgundian. "To my thinking the youth did not lose his head. It was the horse, crazed with fear, that rushed over the cliff before the rider could see what was there and throw himself from the saddle. And the proof of this we found. In the sand of the road where it passed through the wood we found the tracks where D'Estampes's charger plunged into a gallop. A spear's cast behind this place we found fresh tracks of a beast shod with iron that came from no road. It had come down from the air. And these tracks did pursue the other, to the cliff's edge, where all ended."

Fingering the gold chain at his throat, De Ferrand sighed. "The third death was the worst. A fair wanton from the village was found in the spot where the merchant Viterbo met his doom. She was lying alone in the road, her skull crushed."

"Nay," rumbled Hugo, "the worst of it was the mark. Upon the foreheads of the merchant and the girl lay the prints of the iron hoofs that struck them down."

The pallid monk laid down his quill and got to his feet. "It is clear to us all," he said, "that the island of Ferrand hath been visited by the powers of darkness."

"Brother Jehan," muttered the master of the chateau, hath rare knowledge of Satan's brood. He is a very skilled witch finder."

"A foul fiend," resumed the monk, "a messmate of such vampires, infests this poor island. At certain times he has been seen. Once he appeared in the shape of a black, winged thing, flying over the tops of the trees."

Bryn felt a chill run up his back. He had a healthy dread of the powers of darkness. Nonetheless, he wanted to go down the road to seek for the girl of the tower.

"Have you naught to say?" demanded Brother Jehan.

"Messires," Bryn yawned, "such things may be, but they do not keep me abed o' nights."

"*Par Dex*," exclaimed De Ferrand. "'Tis you who are charged in these slayings. Read, Brother Jehan."

Taking up his parchment sheets, the monk repeated in his high voice, "Item—Rigolt the ferryman hath testified that, after bringing the man known as Bryn across the river, the aforesaid man shouted that he and his horse could fly over any river without need of a boat. Item—Jacques and

Picard, being serving men of the castle, testify that they were walking in peace along the highroad when the aforesaid man, who had hidden himself from sight, whistled in a diabolical manner, and thereupon the black horse rushed at them. The said horse did strike the worthy Jacques with his hoof, breaking his bones sorely, and seizing Picard in his teeth to his great hurt. Item—As they fled to save their lives, upon this very spot where the merchant Viterbo and the wanton died, they saw the aforesaid man in talk with the forest girl Alaine, suspected of being a witch."

Brother Jehan took up a fresh sheet of parchment and read his fourth item. This was Bryn's tale of his night ride near Damascus.

"Upon this testimony," the monk cried, "is this man calling himself Bryn Briogan charged of night flying and commerce with Satan, and murder, and now is he and the black horse subject to the mercy or punishment of my lord Renault de Ferrand, govern—"

A shout of laughter drowned his words. "Rare and good, Brother Jehan," cried Bryn. "'Tis a grand hocus this of yours—'twould shame a Gascon jester!"

He laughed alone. The monk's eyes blazed with wrath, and in a moment Bryn understood that this was no jest.

Putting his hands before him on the table, the crusader thought quickly. He read only fear and curiosity and hatred in the faces about the table. Witchburners, these Burgundians were; and he knew that his doom was at hand. They would put him to the question soon, under the water sack or upon the rack. And he would not have that.

So he kicked his chair behind him, hearing it strike against the legs of a man. He leaped away from the table to the wall where he had set his sword and belt. Seeing a shield, he caught this up, smashing it into the face of a servant who sought to grapple with him. Turning with his back to the wall and his sword bare in his hand, he shouted above the tumult, "Come on, ye hearth cats—will ye taste good steel?"

"Have done!" De Ferrand commanded. "I will speak with this man alone, and do ye leave the hall."

When the last of them had vanished through the hangings—Bryn heard them muttering and arming themselves outside—the Burgundian came close to the crusader. He had not unsheathed his sword. "I grant you a truce," he said softly. "You were mad to draw weapon like this."

"Say what you will," Bryn answered, leaning on his sword, "I will not yield me to the rack and question. If I am to meet my death, I will have it here."

"Fool! A crossbow bolt in the ribs will put you down. Mark you, I am governor i' the Duke's name, with the right of hanging miscreants. You have set your head nicely i' the noose—"

"Lies and weird tales have done for me."

De Ferrand pulled at his ringlets thoughtfully. "I am not sure. For I may pardon you."

Bryn waited in silence.

"You are a bold fellow, Bryn—a nimble fellow with a good sword hand. I do not think you are the night rider that hath ravaged the roads. Nay, I suspect another."

He glanced over his shoulder, lowering his voice to a whisper: "These slayings do not bear the mark of a bold fellow like you. But a young witch haunts the wood by the ferry. Aye, she flits about in these bright nights. Now who would slay a village wanton but another woman? And who could beguile D'Estampes like a fair woman? This wild thing they call Alaine is a witch, who serves Satan."

"Nay," growled Bryn, "is it like that a girl's arm could shatter a skull?"

"She hath unholy weapons to her hand."

"What bargain will you make?"

Again the seigneur looked up and down the hall. "You were seen in talk with Alaine. She will be afoot a night like this, and I doubt not you could find her by the wood. Your horse will be given you. Bring her with her limbs bound to the tower postern—it leads to my chamber—before sunrise, and you shall go free. I swear it, by the saints."

"And if I do not?"

"All boats on the island are locked and guarded until sunrise. And after that I will make sure that you do not gain a ferry. If you do not bring yourself to the chateau by high noon, Bryn, you will be hunted down by dogs and bows."

Bryn mused a while, and nodded. "Fetch Malik to me, saddled."

They left the hall by a small door that led into an empty passage. Bryn strode close behind his host, wishing to keep him within sword's reach.

But they met no one at the foot of the tower stair, and De Ferrand opened a postern with a key. Bryn peered out into the darkness beneath the trees and saw the white blaze upon Malik's forehead. He heard the other's voice at his shoulder: "Remember you have sworn—"

"To seek for the girl Alaine," murmured Bryn, "and to find her if I may."

Carefully the crusader set his trap. Near the tower, he loosed Malik, then settled himself to watch.

Slowly the moon settled toward the castle ridge behind him. Then a whistle sounded.

Keeping out of the patches of moonlight, he made his way through the trees.

Ahead of him the horse stamped restlessly. He could make out the loom of the black body and the gray form of a girl, motionless and listening. In two long leaps Bryn was upon her, even as she sprang away.

She twisted and strained like a wildcat in a net.

"Faith," he said, "methought you had changed into a troll. Now will you be still and listen to a Christian word?"

Steadily she looked at him, as a child looks at a strange thing.

"Is your name Alaine?"

She nodded, without speaking.

"And they do tell in the hall how you are a witch—"

"May God shrivel their tongues! 'Tis a black lie."

Her soft voice rose angrily, and Bryn grunted assent. "They are a loutish lot, these Burgundians. They have written down that I am a foul fiend—" he laughed, and told the attentive girl of the scene in the castle hall, and his bargain with De Ferrand. "Faith, he awaits us in his tower. Now, Alaine, I hold you and I can bind you within my mantle and carry you—"

"Try! I will get away."

"Well, that is to be seen. I think it likely you are an elf-child and be-like a witch who can vanish from mortal sight."

"Then," cried Alaine, "why did you come after me this noon?"

Bryn rubbed his chin and glanced at the lowering moon. "For the reason I have caught you this night—sure it is, Alaine, my eyes have never seen so fair a maid. If I cannot take you with me to my homeland, I will be forever alone and sorrowing."

"Sir Bryn, how could you leave the island? They have guards at the ferries."

He laughed, running his fingers through the coils of her hair. "Oh, I can find my way over the water, but you could not without me. Now let us be making a bargain between us. Not for gold or salvation would I take you to the castle—and, faith, I doubt if De Ferrand would hold to his word if I did—but you must bide and talk with me until the first of the sunrise. Will you do that?"

Quickly she looked up at him. "Aye, I will do it. But first, your horse—where is he?"

Springing to his feet, the crusader whistled, and heard a faint stamp of hoofs under the shadow of the ridge. Putting on his mantle and steel cap, he hastened forward with the girl running at his side, entered the gloom of the ridge, and stepped out upon the highroad. Here Malik stood, docile enough.

Then the breath caught in his throat and he stared, voiceless, at the black line of the ridge above him, where the summits of the trees stood stark against the moon's glow. Above the trees, across the sky, leaped a phantom.

Clear against the silvered clouds Bryn saw the great black horse, and the rider with wings beating behind him, swooping toward him! Bryn flung himself into his saddle, while Malik stamped and reared and a girl's scream pierced the night.

Malik, mad with excitement, danced and reared. Bryn turned him to face the thing that leaped out from under the trees and crashed upon the road. He had no shield, but he leaned forward and struck at the onrushing shape. The steel blade clanged against metal, and as it did so something struck Bryn's head. A roaring filled his ears, and yellow flames sprang before his eyes. He rolled from the saddle and fell. Blood filled his nostrils, and he felt earth under his hands.

Hoofs thudded near him, and Malik's battle scream rang in his ears. His sword was under his knee and he caught it up as his head cleared and he was aware of monstrous shapes rearing over him. His helmet had been knocked off and warm blood trickled down his face.

Something lashed down toward him and he moved aside, springing to his feet and gripping the black form of the rider of the sky about the waist. The rider twisted, lifting his right arm for another blow, when his horse swerved and he came down.

Again Bryn was struck, and again a glancing blow on his shoulder; but the impact of heavy iron sickened him. The panting breath of the other through the slits of his closed helmet beat against his wet face. "If he is a devil," Bryn thought, "he is mortal, and one of us will have his death here."

As they strained on staggering feet, Bryn felt the huge strength of the man in mail. He saw a long arm rise against the sky, holding a weapon that seemed to be a war club or smith's hammer. But swiftly Bryn released his grip—flung up his right hand and caught the handle of the weapon.

Putting forth all the strength of shoulder and arm, Bryn bent back the weapon. With a curse, the man in mail let go his grasp and clutched at something in his belt.

As he did so, Bryn set his feet and swung the massive weapon. It crashed against the steel of the helmet, and the steel crackled and snapped. Again Bryn lashed out, and the face of the helmet shattered as the man reeled back. And Bryn struck a third blow that crunched upon bone and flesh. The dark figure fell prone in the road, stirring a little, and became a still shadow against the white dust.

Then a light flamed before Bryn, a voice cried out: "He is slain!" and Alaine knelt beside him.

"'Tis the devil is dead, not me," muttered Bryn. "For love of God, bring me water."

Catching up his battered helmet from the road, the girl darted away, and Bryn limped over to look at his enemy. The great body in black and bloodstreaked mail lay sprawled on its face. To the broad shoulders a pair of long swan's wings had been attached by straps. Now the wings were crumpled and broken. Bryn turned him over with his foot and bent to look into what had been his face.

Bryn pondered the broken countenance. "'Twas Hugo," he said at last. "Aye, the Genoese captain."

He heard Alaine returning, and he drank deep of the cool water she brought in his helmet.

"That, there, was Hugo," he said, "but what is this?" Upon his light steel cap was the mark of a massive hoof.

"Look at the weapon in your hand, Sir Bryn," she responded.

The head of it flared out, into the shape of an iron hoof, with even the marks of nails upon it. Bryn let it fall beside the body.

"Why did he do this?" Alaine whispered.

Sure, Bryn thought, the Genoese had robbed upon the highroad in the guise of a fiend, and sure he had slain here his own light o' love who had left him for De Ferrand. But what of tonight? Hugo had tricked him at the table into boasting about Malik—had not known that he, Bryn, would be here upon the road this night. Then why had the night rider come?

Suddenly Bryn laughed. Why, Hugo had sought the girl for himself, spying down from that ridge behind the trees. And he had seen her come to the road with another man . . .

Bryn picked up his sword from the road and sheathed it. Then he bent down and lifted the girl in his arms. She lay quiet against his shoulder, and a slim arm encircled his neck. He pressed his cheek against the heavy mass of hair, and lifted his head to whistle to Malik.

"Faith, Alaine," he whispered, "ye have had wooers a-many, among lords and devils. But now, girl, ye'll have only one, a poor churl of a soldier without service who'll carry you to his own land."

After that day the tongues of the good people of the island wagged long and loud. For, they said, the captive crusader had vanished like mist from his cell, and the witch girl Alaine was no longer to be seen.

But two tongues said nothing. The seigneur, De Ferrand, brooding in his tower, looked at times down upon the gibbet where hung the long body of Hugo with the hammer-hoof tied to its neck, after a just trial that had proved the corpse guilty of theft and murder and black magic and treason to its merciful and noble liege lord, the Seigneur Renault de Ferrand.

The Drub-Devil March

Chapter One

When the small boat grated on the beach, he jumped over. In the wash he felt the sands of Africa under his feet. Forgetting that he should not do so, he ran the boat's bow up three paces to the edge of dry sand. There was almost no tide.

Then, remembering why he had come, he let go the boat and straightened his long body. Curiously he looked at the gray mainland, with its tufted greenery showing over garden walls. A flat country he thought it to be, and dismal enough—this shore of the enemy.

On his thin freckled face he felt the hot shore breeze. He was overlarge for his age—eighteen the first day of that month of March in the year 1805. Silently he took his jacket, book, and moleskin valise, handed out by the boatswain. "Thank you," he said, and handed back a shilling extracted awkwardly from his pocket.

Fingering the shilling, the seaman stared grudgingly at his solitary passenger—at this odd young Yankee, embarked at Syracuse on the Neapolitan packet, and the only one to go ashore at the port of Alexandria in Egypt. At a time, moreover, when the *gentry* were all for leaving Alexandria, bag and baggage. Not that the slow-spoken Yankee belonged to the proper gentry. "Lad," warned the English seaman, with a vague idea of repaying the shilling with advice, "look well about you for cutpurses; and cutthroats—among the pygan savages here, and pay no girl more'n twenty piastres, which is a shilling more'r less. And by the same—"

"I'll bear it in mind, bo'sun," acknowledged the Yank quickly.

"And by the same token, when and as in trouble, take yourself, young Yankee, to yon brig that flies your colors," added the Englishman, his heavy voice edged with faint contempt.

He pointed out at the black hull of an armed brig anchored in the road among the passing raking sails of feluccas. "Not as A-merican colors be safeguard along the Barbary way, where as I have 'eard tell at the port Tripoli an A-merican fraygate was surrendered, full armed and manned—"

"At Tripoli, yes," agreed the young Yankee. He hoped the sailor would still his tongue. Instinctively he held out a hand calloused by the chafing of salt-encrusted rope.

"At Tripoli her captain 'auled down his colors. Captain Bainbridge he was."

The young Yankee folded his jacket over his arm, his somber eyes lowered to the prints of his feet in the sand. The contempt in the English seaman's voice was impersonal, stubborn—something that had to be said because it was true. "And not a man wounded among all of them. Nah, not a fight in the lot of them." He spat into the water. "Surrendered with whole skins to the pygan corsairs of Tripoli!"

Gripping his book, the lanky boy answered under his breath: "She grounded on an uncharted reef."

"Ah."

The Yankee lifted his eyes, tense with fear. "They went in and burned her afterward—the Americans did."

He prayed inwardly that the boatswain would cease his loud abuse of the Americans at Tripoli. Already people were glancing their way, and a young woman appeared at his elbow, a silk kerchief gripped over her head, her slippered feet sinking into the sand. She was asking questions in good French and labored English, of which the boatswain seemed to understand little. Eyeing her, the man said: "Nah, then."

"She is asking," said the Yankee, who caught the drift of her French speech, "the price of a passage to Syracuse on your packet vessel."

"Yes," assented the girl, "please. To Syracuse or anywhere."

She held her head turned from the Yankee, who saw the fall of dark hair against a young cheek, and the bright peacocks embroidered on the scarf.

"To Syracuse?" The boatswain pondered, trying to get a sight of the girl's slim breast in the V of the shawl. "Fifty-two sov'reigns, or Venaytian sequins."

The girl let out her breath in a sigh. Her head turned slowly toward the quay jutting from the beach, where carriages waited among eddies of servants—where wealthy would-be passengers waited for a chance to

board one of the few vessels leaving the port of Alexandria. Her dark eyes
half closed, her small shoulders lifted defiantly, she began to walk toward the quay.

The Yankee's gaze followed the bright blue of the peacock scarf, and it
seemed to him strange that this young woman should be alone and afoot
on the beach. The thought only touched his mind, while he repeated silently the words he should not have spoken: *They went in and burned her
afterward . . .* He remembered how the fire had sprung from the sacks piled
against the polished oak of the wardroom, crackling and burning ame-
thyst color from the tar and charcoal in the sacks—whirling up the masts
and the tarred shrouds in a hot dry night wind, mirrored in the still water,
until the heat began to explode the charges in the shotted guns, and they
fired their requiem for the doomed frigate, the *Philadelphia* . . .

Clamping shut his lips, he walked away from the landing boat, not toward the crowd on the quay but toward the nearest alley of the town.

He walked, the boatswain noticed, planting his feet wide like a man
who had been long at sea. Not like a proper gentleman! Such a traveling
gentleman, in the boatswain's opinion, would have fondled the neck of
the trim wench who had come by to catch his eye. Aye, a proper gentleman would have hallo'ed for a chaise to convey him into town, instead
of trudging off carrying his own bag.

"Nah," said the seaman, pocketing his shilling. He was certain only
that this young Yankee was like others of his kind, a man with an eye for
trade who would pay down good money to escape a fight.

The Yankee walked hastily into the shade of the first alley and looked
around him there, hoping that he was not followed from the beach. Beside
him veiled women dozed in the shadow of a half-ruined kiosk. Bells jangled
past him as dusty donkeys trotted by, their loads bumping against him.
The dust hung in the air, and the stench of the ground choked him.

Against the wall a long human body smelled sickly sweet. Peering
down at it, the Yankee made out a ragged dolman over shoulders where
the flies had not clustered. The unburied body, then, must have been a
French soldier, a relic of the French army of occupation, abandoned in
Egypt like the charred skeletons of Napoleon's fleet off one of the mouths
of the Nile . . .

Wings flapped over his head. A tawny-white buzzard came to rest on
the clay wall above the body.

The Yankee thought it a pity that no one troubled to give the body, even though it was a foreigner's, a grave. Frowning, he reminded himself of his two mistakes at the beach. First, he had lent a hand in beaching the boat; second, he had shown temper at the taunt of the English seaman, who was probably no more than a deserter, keeping his hide whole and his purse full under the Neapolitan flag.

Carefully the youth repeated the identification he had made up for himself: "My name is Paul Davies. I am a graduate of the King's College in the city of New York, now seeking lucrative employment as teacher of the French language—or ciphering—in some Christian family. My purpose in venturing to Egypt is to improve my mind by sight of the temples and pyramids of the ancient world."

The only book he had was the one he carried so ostentatiously, being *The Pilgrim's Progress* by a certain John Bunyan—an account of a journey which Paul had found only mildly interesting.

And his education, he knew, hardly qualified him to teach anyone, because it was that of a midshipman, recently promoted to lieutenant in the United States Navy.

Down the center of the alley limped a tall man leaning on a long staff, crying out *"Ya hu-ya hak!"* His shaggy head bent back, he would have blundered into Paul, if the Yankee had not stepped aside quickly. The crier, a blind beggar, was followed by two armed men, who stopped Paul, asking questions he could not understand.

By their tufted red skullcaps, he knew they were police.

"Giaur Inglisi!" exclaimed one impatiently, and jerked open Paul's valise, pulling out the few linen shirts and the pair of slippers it held. An English foreigner, they thought him to be.

He had no weapon. He could not resist. The one thing he should not do under any circumstances was to start a fight. So he smiled helplessly while the police ransacked his small bag, finding little.

Then they looked attentively at his narrow civilian trousers and white shirt, and the bigger of the two thrust his hand against the bulge in the shirt over the belt, where Paul's wallet lay.

Before they could extract the wallet, they heard the heavy tread of feet approaching, swiftly in quickstep. Around the corner behind them swung a platoon of stocky figures clad in uniforms green with age. The figures carried muskets brightly polished, and their sun-darkened heads turned quickly and silently toward the pair of police. At once the police stepped back to the wall, gripping their long staves warily, leaving the narrow street clear for the marchers.

Greeks, thought Paul, noticing their baggy pantaloons cut off above the knees. Barely he had time to scoop his belonging back into his valise and step aside. The Greeks swung by like a pack of mastiffs passing stray wolves. The Turkish police hugged their wall. And the Yankee seized this chance to stride off into the dust after the marching detachment.

He kept close to it, observing how the throngs in the alley scattered at the sight of their muskets.

In this spring of 1805 the flotsam and jetsam of the wars jammed the port of Alexandria. After the remnant of Menou's French army had surrendered, the redcoats had come and gone in their quest after Napoleon. On the heels of the departing English the letting of blood went on with bands of the Egyptian Mamelukes raiding the garrisons of the Turkish sultan—nominal ruler of the land—while deserters herded together to pillage and Bedouin tribes swarmed in to raid impartially, the flames of burning villages made beacons at night from Grand Cairo to the sea.

In the kaleidoscope of lawlessness, Paul Davies had been assured that the only safeguards were a British passport or a strong armed escort. Having neither of these, he was well content to follow after the marching Greeks, who might guide him to some place safe for Christians. When the sergeants at the rear of the small column began to stare back at him curiously, he slowed his pace to drop farther behind.

Somewhere on this African shore he had to find a man. The person he sought might be in the streets of Alexandria or up the Nile at Grand Cairo, or out in the desert. If Paul could cross his track, he should not be hard to find. But Paul could not let it be known that he was seeking for him. Nor could he waste time in his search. He had to ransack the town for a trace of his quarry, and having found the trace, to follow it to his man. And to contrive a meeting as if by happenchance. So much he had reasoned out in his slow fashion while still at sea on the deck of the Neapolitan packet.

But here, afoot in the streets, his task seemed to be hopeless, unless luck gave him a hand. And he had the ill luck to lose the Greeks. Climbing a flight of steps to a wide sun-drenched street, he saw no trace of them except dust drifting away. Nor could he catch an echo of their footsteps. On either side the buildings seemed to be empty ruins.

In one of these—where massive red stones bore carved inscriptions—Paul sighted a slender man stretched at ease beneath a broken statue of Hercules.

"Well?" observed this foreigner, brushing away the flies indolently. Unshaved, in worn smart clothing, he had an air of being at home in the ruin, and the clipped voice of an Englishman of breeding. Silver gleamed on the butt of the pistol in his sash. Seeing it, the Yankee felt a surge of familiar fear. With his sleeve he wiped at the sweat above his eyes.

"Where," he asked cautiously, "can I find a quiet lodging-place?"

"There, sir." The Englishman's fan pointed at a bare rise set with tiny slabs of stone. "It has no equal."

Studying the distant slope, Paul nodded, his gray eyes amused. "Besides the cemetery, sir, is there any decent lodging in this port?"

The Englishman, who had been contemplating him through half-closed eyes, moved his head from side to side. "Decent, sir, there is none. I have quartered myself upon these gods of Greece. If you still have money, try the Devil's Coffee-House across the way. It may still be there. Ask for Eugene, but on no account make a wager with him. Especially—" he added bitterly—"upon the physical momentum of a knife-blade against a playing card in the air. It cost me eight pounds to discover that Eugene can stick the blade through the card. Mind you, he can accomplish the seemingly impossible in other ways. But he will not steal from you."

Paul nodded, amused—and fancied that he had hit upon the explanation of the missing men. "The armed platoon—the Greeks—turned into this coffee-house?"

The other's haggard, handsome face went blank. "Armed Greeks? I've seen only Hercules." His fan pointed indolently at the headless statue grasping a club above him. "And I vow he'd not leave his post for coffee."

Chapter Two

Seeking the street again, Paul observed that the spot chosen for a siesta by the drowsy Englishman afforded a clear view of all who passed by. The watcher had lied to him.

Squinting against the sun's glare, he made out a painted sign suspended over a dilapidated gateway: "*The Devil's Coffee-House.*" By it squatted a peasant, haggling over pomegranates in his basket with a young Eurasian resplendent in a zebra-striped cloak. The two paid no apparent attention to Paul as he entered the gate and crossed a courtyard littered with wagon wheels and broken jars.

As soon as the Yankee had passed into the ancient stone dwelling beyond, the Eurasian buyer of fruit tossed a piastre to the peasant and walked off briskly, swinging a gold-tipped cane. Passing the Greek ruin, he slid his eyes toward the lounger but did not turn his head.

Paul stepped into cool shadow reeking of fish and rancid oil. At once he felt that he was observed. Against the wall in front of him, a giant sat polishing the copper bowl of a saddle-drum. From an embroidered jacket the man's bare arms projected like massive vines; from his girdle gleamed the hilts of knives. One hand dropped on the drum, and the sound echoed deep along the walls.

A glance showed Paul only bare benches and a table set with clay jars and drinking bowls. Beside him a curtain moved, and a broad man stepped close to him. *"Tiens!"* ordered a staccato voice. "Face to the door. You understand English?"

Instead of turning his back on the pair, Paul studied the speaker, aware of a plump moon face bisected by black waxed mustachios above a military dolman and a body as round as a wine tun.

"Eugene?" he asked.

"Johann Eugene Leitensdorfer, Military Engineer. And you?" Black eyes probed shrewdly from the pallid round flesh. "A moment, and I will tell you. *Un homme du monde nouveau.* You are from the New World, certainly. Quebec, the Federal City, New York? Proud, perhaps stupid, perhaps merely—*das Junge.*" A powerful hand plucked Paul's book from him. "*Gerechter Herr Gott*, a pilgrim. In Alexandria." The eyes gleamed reflectively. "Why? One moment. You make the search for someone. For who? Two gold crowns that you make the search for another American—I wager!"

Eugene's voice, making play among languages, had the quality of music. It compelled attention.

"I am searching for a lodging."

"In Alexandria?" The keeper of the Devil's Coffee-House shook his head. "No, an American younker would come only for another of his kind. In trouble, certainly. Here there is immense trouble. I know." He rapped out the words. "Two gold crowns down on the table for a month's lodging all found, and the woman to cook."

Drawing his wallet from his shirt, Paul laid two gold pieces on the table. Eugene hastily pocketed them. "So. Now tell me your name, and what you really want! Will you drink wine or *arack*? Wine for you better is."

With a single motion the giant at the drum rose and took the heavy jar that Eugene picked up. Lifting it high in one hand, he let a stream fall into his wide mouth.

"Selim," said Eugene after a moment.

The big man lowered the jar deftly, without spilling the wine, and handed it back, smiling.

"Drunk," explained Eugene Leitensdorfer. "From the *janizaris*; Selim is a deserter. He is sick in his heart for his own Dalmatian mountains. I am from the Tyrol—the Alps, certainly. Now, you?"

Having had a moment to size up Eugene, Paul did not venture to say that he was seeking employment as a teacher. He felt instinctively that the Tyrolese would ridicule any such tale. "I risked landing here," he said carefully, "to see something of the ancient monuments of Egypt, like the Pyramids. Few Americans have seen them."

"Only one—" Eugene paused, to tip his bowl of wine beneath his mustache. "I guided him."

Paul waited silently for more tidings of the other American, and then asked anxiously: "Who was he?" This might be the first trace of the man he sought.

"Now, I do not believe that you are stupid, Monsieur Davies. You pretend to be stupid. You cannot see the Pyramids at Cairo and come away alive. Even he, your countryman, had to leave from Cairo, although I had him in my care. So. If you wish a monument to see, go up to the *cimetiere arabe*—the graveyard—on the hill and look at the marble column which is Pompey's, the Roman."

Paul smiled, realizing how deftly the stout Tyrolese had parried his question. "And if I do that?" he asked. Twice these strangers had told him to seek the cemetery.

Eugene shrugged. "Thieves will sight you, and perhaps they will take the rest of your gold crowns. But they will not kill you, because the place of the dead is here a sanctuary—"

"Will I find the other American there?"

Barely could the boy keep from crying out: "Isn't he William Eaton, the American Agent, engaged upon a secret mission? Isn't he here in this place where I can reach him within an hour, before he starts on his journey?"

But no more than a half-dozen men knew why William Eaton had landed on the African coast with an escort of a few Marines. On the brig *Argus*,

anchored in the road, Isaac Hull knew, and so did Paul. That knowledge
he must keep to himself.

"No." Eugene's dark eyes probed the boy's face curiously. "He is in a
safe place. A most safe place." White teeth flashed under the waxed mustache. "He has been arrested by the Turkish army, at an order from the
governor of Alexandria, and at my advice."

Startled, Paul exclaimed: "Arrested—where? For how long?"

Reflectively Eugene pulled at his mustache. "*Ahh!* His Excellency the
Minister of the Spanish Crown would have paid a purse of gold to inform himself of that. I, Eugene, refused his Spanish gold. So, I have spies
quartered at my door." Suddenly he gripped Paul's arm with iron fingers. "Young sir, I like you, and by Salbal and Bathbal and the seven en-
throned kings of Purgatory, I will help you to keep alive, except that you
lie to me. You lie that you wish to see the ancient monuments of Egypt!
Other Yankees hide—or they are taken captive into the bagnios of Tripoli. What do you seek?"

Hot blood throbbed in the boy's head. He could not answer. Suddenly
Eugene cracked his thumbs, snapping them like pistol hammers. "Loot!
Perhaps you ran away to sea—perhaps you then deserted your ship, to seek
a dream—fortune? Look!"

Magically, his knot of a hand unfolded under Paul's eyes, revealing
a shining gold coin, delicately inlaid with a head that might have been
a Roman Caesar's. "The golden drachma of Cleopatra Selene, Princess
of Africa—daughter of Cleopatra and stupid Mark Antony. And who is
this handsome soldier? Who knows? The drachma bears only her name.
It came, I have been told, from her tomb, *Kbour Roumyah*—tomb of the
Outlander." The voice of the Tyrolese softened as a violin mutes, ten-
derly. "She ruled the Roman who ruled Africa. She ordered that her body
be carried to Egypt's edge, to the height overlooking the sea and the desert. Never have we found her tomb—like those tombs broken and looted
in the King's Valley. Think you how Cleopatra Selene would lie, splendid, in death. In walls of soft, pure gold—"

Close to Paul's eyes the ancient coin shone in the half-light. "I have
seen the door of her tomb," the man's voice went on, "and I have marked
its site on the mountain, in the map of my mind. Soon I shall find my way
back to it. Will such loot tempt you—"

He broke off to listen. Paul thought: *He is making a test of me, and he is
boasting of himself.* Then the drum sounded under Selim's hand. A shadow

cut across the sun's glare in the doorway. The Englishman who had been taking a siesta sauntered in and poured himself a bowl of wine.

Over the wine Eugene questioned the stranger swiftly in a language unknown to Paul. Then, as if touched by a spur, the tavern-keeper threw off his military cloak, kicking off his boots, and slipping his brown feet into sandals. He wrapped himself in a clean white burnoose, drawing a fold of it over his head, until only his eyes showed. With the change, his manner changed, and his very eyes looked different as he stared at the boy on his way out.

"You!" he exclaimed. "As to you, I have not made up my mind. Sleep here, certainly, but remember that Eugene Leitensdorfer has not bestowed his protection upon you."

"And don't wander," added the Englishman sharply, "from this door after dark."

Stung by the casual contempt, Paul started to retort, then closed his lips tight upon the words.

Left in the coffee-house with the drunken Selim and the native woman, who stared anxiously from the kitchen, Paul reflected that even a hanger-on like the owner of the fan had the broadsides of Nelson's line-of-battle-ships to protect him; a French beachcomber had the magic of the Emperor's name for safeguard. Americans, however, were looked on as defenseless men who paid tribute—

Years before, his older brother had written him from the Mediterranean: "I hope I may never again be sent to this coast with tribute unless I am authorized to deliver it from the mouths of our cannon." Paul remembered every word clearly, because after reading them he had put aside his books—being then full fifteen years of age—to join the Navy in which his brother, William Bainbridge, served.

Slowly he paced the dirty sand of the coffee-house floor, his thin body aching with the shame that had come upon his brother and himself . . .

William had never been a coward. Paul knew that as surely as he took the two steps forward in the sand and turned, seeing only the impassive Selim. Twice William had been wounded, defending his ship from seizure. In his veneration of the older man, Paul visioned him as laboring man-fully against the curse of ill luck—forced to strike his flag to two French frigates of greater force; forced by civilian officials to hoist the Turkish colors when he delivered a year's tribute from America to Algiers.

Ill luck had driven the forty-four-gun frigate *Philadelphia* on the reef off Tripoli. But Captain William Bainbridge on his own responsibility had surrendered his crew and his ship. *He gambled, taking a chance as he always did,* Paul told himself savagely. *He tried to float his vessel off by throwing over the guns; he had no luck.*

Then, with William Bainbridge captive in Tripoli, the ill luck had turned against Midshipman Bainbridge . . . In the crowded lobby of the theater at Malta, Paul had heard words he thought meant for him: "Those Yankees will never stand the smell of powder." Blindly, when the speaker jostled him, he had struck out . . . Stephen Decatur had drilled him at firing a dueling pistol, which he had never handled before. Through the smoke he had seen the Englishman fall dead. Sir Alexander Ball, governor of Malta, had demanded a Court of Inquiry. But Midshipman Bainbridge's fellow officers had contrived to get him out of the port.

Now he had to be Paul Davies . . . Midshipman Bainbridge was hiding out to escape Sir Alexander Ball's Court of Inquiry. And Captain Bainbridge, in prison at Tripoli, faced a Court of Inquiry on the loss of the frigate. Ill luck had shamed them both.

Paul had determined to reach his brother, to attempt, however futilely, to release him.

Twice before now he had failed to reach Tripoli.

Eugene and the Englishman did not return. The glare of the doorway softened to shadow. A distant call to prayer stabbed the twilight silence.

As if that had been a signal, men stirred and coughed out in the courtyard. Going to the door, the boy saw them, squatting against the walls, whispering with their heads together, looking like thieves in hiding, armed with every kind of weapon. When he would have gone out to examine them closer, he felt Selim's hand on his shoulder. "*La!*" said the janizary, drawing him back.

Unable to answer the deserter, Paul obeyed. But from the courtyard he had sighted a squat white figure calling to prayer from the base of the Roman column on the cemetery rise. A ray of the setting sun struck it, and the figure very much resembled Eugene.

Turned back from the courtyard, Paul crossed the sanded floor to the kitchen. He had no mind to wait longer in the coffee-house, losing precious hours. The kitchen was half dark, except for the glow from the mouth of the oven, where the native woman was pulling out slabs of bread.

Beyond the oven loose stacks of wheat lay against the wall; and above them Paul noticed the barrels of muskets projecting. Sacks by the rear door looked much like soldiers' packs. And at the door itself, chewing bread and garlic, he found a Greek sergeant.

Once past the Greek, Paul reflected that the marching detachment had stored its gear in the Devil's Coffee-House, and that a new band seemed to be gathering from the street.

The sun had left the cemetery height, and Paul thought he saw shapes rising up from the graves and moving toward the pillar. Whatever Eugene was doing, in whatever guise, he was surely collecting men and weapons about him, in the dusk of evening. And the boy quickened his pace through the narrow alley, determined to risk making an offer of a bribe to the Tyrolese to guide him to the man he wanted to meet.

Paul did not heed the carriage hurrying toward him. The other occupants of the alley shrank against the wall to escape the wheels. Paul was aware of a woman in the open seat, and of a man in a zebra-striped cloak who stood up to shout at him angrily. Then he grasped at the reins of the horses, feeling himself borne back, and gaining a footing, jerked the team to a stop.

Instantly a horseman pushed past the carriage, a turbaned rider swinging up a staff. Paul was struck over the eyes and would have lost his footing except for his grip on the reins. Blood dripped into his eyes, and he turned blindly to grapple with the outrider who had struck him.

Then the woman's voice cried out. Hands pulled at Paul's shoulders, half lifting him into the seat of the carriage. When he could wipe his eyes clear with his sleeve, the chaise was in motion again, away from the cemetery. The man who had shouted at him had vanished, and the woman beside him was exclaiming in rapid French, her fingers touching his injured head anxiously.

She was scolding him prettily for venturing into the street afoot after sunset—instead of in a carriage, or at the least on horseback. Her servants had not realized that he was an American gentleman.

Paul, with his scarred forehead throbbing, wondered fleetingly how she had realized he was an American. Strangely, he sensed that he had encountered the twain in the carriage before. The vanished escort had looked like the elegant Eurasian who loitered outside the gate of the coffee-house, while the voice of the contrite lady seemed to be that of the girl who had wandered the beach.

When he stared at her, she pulled the dark mantle back from her head.

Close to him, her eyes looked full into his. Graceful she was, poised alertly like the girl of the peacock-embroidered scarf; yet her throat was rounder and she seemed somehow older—smiling at him like one who had smiled often at men. Her fingertips falling from his head, brushed his hand. "Permit me, I pray," she said softly, "to repair the damage my servants have done."

Even the words were a caress, as she gave her name, Hortense D'Aliermont. The carriage, she explained, was that of the legation of Spain. "When you are bandaged, and you have forgiven us," Hortense added swiftly, "it will take you wherever you wish to go."

That might prove to be an aid to Paul. Moreover he might possibly gain information from the Spaniards, who, as allies of Napoleon, had an ear to all that passed on the Mediterranean. And he had dire need of help, from any source.

Chapter Three

A candle guttered on a dusty iron table, lighting the stained shield of arms over the gaping door. A black man draped in white salaamed to the lady. "Pray rest here," she bade, formally. "I will send you wine, Monsieur Davies, and a better nurse than I."

Draped again in the mantle, Hortense D'Aliermont showed none of the familiarity of the carriage on the terrace of her house. That house, behind blind barred windows, was astir with sound. Darkness closed in on the candle's gleam.

A light step quickened in the doorway. A tray with wine decanter, glasses, and a roll of linen cloth was laid on the table beside Paul. He recognized the younger woman who brought it more by her silence and the quick turn of her head toward him than the peacocks on the shawl, or her worn slippers.

"My sister Marie Anne," Hortense called down from the gallery overhead. "If you will pardon me—" that same cool courtesy of voice—"for a quarter-hour, the little Marie will attend you."

The little Marie glanced impersonally at Paul's forehead. Quickly her slim hands gathered up the linen. She wore only one bit of jewelry, a ring set with moonstone, carved into the semblance of a flying bird. "It has stopped bleeding," she said, "and I have no boiled water. This cloth—" She shrugged a shoulder. "What about your arm?"

"Forget my arm," Paul assured her, rolling up his stained sleeve. "Did you find passage on a vessel?"

Blood flushed the girl's skin beneath the eyes. Her fingers tightened on the clumsy bandage, as if she would gladly have gagged him. "No," she said softly, her lips shaping the word.

Although obviously attended by a bevy of servants here, Marie Anne had been alone on the beach. She stood by the table silent, as if longing to run from it.

She seemed to be listening. From the door stepped a man clad in fashionable black, a set smile on his full face, his glance roving from Paul's sleeve to the girl's head.

"Platina," her low, husky voice explained, "secretary to His Excellency the imperial envoy. Monsieur Davies."

The secretary made much of pouring the wine affably, his manner a reproof to the girl. "You are from the American brig—the *Argus*, is it not?"

Paul let the question go unanswered, having no desire to explain his arrival to a stranger. Then he remembered quickly that Marie Anne had seen him debark from the Neapolitan craft. But the girl, sitting passive between them, kept silent.

The secretary, Platina, made no secret of his curiosity about Paul. As he eyed the boy's stained shirt, his questions grew sharper. Was it true that the heavy American frigates, the *Constitution* and *Constellation*, had arrived at Syracuse? What was the feeling in the American Republic as to a possible war with the Barbary States—with Algiers, Tunis, Tripoli? Was it not true that Monsieur Jefferson, the President now elected for a second *régime*, had no mind toward war of any kind?

Platina pronounced the strange names badly and indifferently. His questions might have been only casual politeness—the inevitable questions of Europeans regarding the inexplicable happenings in the barbaric young republic that had rebelled against the authority and the protection of England. But Paul's guarded answers provoked a gesture of impatience. "Satan and all the saints, your American business in the Mediterranean will soon be settled, Monsieur Davies! Have you not heard that His Majesty the Bey of Tripoli will agree to a peace, and release all your captive seamen for half a million of your American dollars?"

Paul had not heard it. It was like a lash across the head. A half *million* dollars. Before he thought, he echoed the words of his brother's letter: "We'll give the Barbary powers nothing more, except the fire of our frigates!"

His boast had a brittle sound. Platina cocked his oiled head, as if at an unexpected sound. "I seem to recall that your new vessels of war have already fired their guns twice against Tripoli, without effect."

Silently Paul acknowledged the truth of that . . . *The guns had not broken down the massive stone walls . . . His own gunboat had drifted dismasted, yet continuing to fire with the twelve-pounder . . .* He set his teeth, determined to say nothing more. Platina, pleased, savored the boy's uneasiness and asked gently: "Will those same frigates fire on Tripoli again, where more than three hundred of your seamen are captive? The Bey has good hostages against attack. Will your frigates endeavor to run themselves up on the coast, again? I think not, Monsieur Davies."

When Paul made no answer, the secretary regarded him thoughtfully. "I believe His Excellency will wish to talk with you at supper. I shall provide you with a suitable coat and neckcloth." And with a word to Marie Anne, he retired past the bowing doorman.

"You are very ignorant," Paul heard the girl say, "but you could be more courteous to those who might aid you."

Hortense had been solicitous about him; her brat of a sister seemed bent on tormenting him.

"When empires are at stake—" she mimicked the slurring rapid French of Platina—"and Egypt is a prize to be won, you expect us to be concerned about a handful of tobacco-growing Yankees and the trade of their sea captains!"

Paul exploded: "Your Platina was concerned enough!"

"To gain information, yes. He earns his *pilaf* and wine efficiently." She prodded the word at Paul. "Moreover, Monsieur Davies, tonight Hortense complains that lawless soldiery is astir in the Arab quarter. Naturally, we wish to be informed about that."

From the doorway sauntered a half-dozen servants, heavily armed as the *bashi-bazouk* who had struck down Paul. Below the steps they separated, moving out into the darkness of the garden.

As Paul watched them, the girl taunted him again. *"Alors*, have you not heard that in France before the beginning of the spring campaign, Napoleon's *jeunes braves* have all assembled at the Channel resorts, such as Boulogne?"

"Napoleon's—daring young men?"

"Ah, you take interest! Yes." Marie Anne counted on her fingers demurely. "The marshals, Murad, Berthier, Massena, Ney—and I forget the others. But where they go, the Grand Army will follow. Do you perceive the meaning of that?"

Napoleon's army assembling on the Channel! Would even the Emperor dare invade England? Surprised, he stared at her, and she nodded as if to a child who had mastered a lesson. "Now you perceive that the life of one foolish stray Yankee is worth less than one tiny bit of information—in His Excellency's garden."

If she had wanted to anger him, she had succeeded in doing so. "In this same garden, Mademoiselle D'Aliermont, do they habitually post an armed night guard?"

It was her turn to be surprised. Her fingers tensed on the wineglass no one had thought to fill for her. "No," she said at last, softly.

"Thank you for that."

This terrace, then, was a trap, baited by the comely elder sister, who seemed to serve as the eyes of the Spaniards. Under the bare pretense of hospitality, his hosts meant to use him as suited them best. So Paul reasoned—not thinking that the taunts of the odd girl had led him to reason so. When he stood up, measuring the distance to the nearest guards, she watched him curiously and shook her head.

Twisting the ring on her finger, as if chatting intimately with him, Marie Anne warned him: "Do you want your head broken again? These blacks have their orders, and even in the street they would track you down. I do not think Platina has made up his mind about you. Perhaps they will let you go. Perhaps they will keep you and entertain you with hashish in the wine you drink, so your stupid head will be filled with fine fancies, and your stubborn tongue will be loosed. Platina suspects you are no chance traveler." Amused, she laughed up at him. "So do I. Paul, you know best what you are."

She waited judging him silently.

"You have relieved your conscience," he assured her. "Good-bye."

Before he could step from the table, Marie was up with her hand on his arm. "If you want to leave, I will show you a way. I promise."

Again she waited, not urging him. Thinking that she, at least, had been honest, Paul nodded. "If you will."

Walking a little before him to guide him, yet holding to his arm, Marie Anne seemed to move unwillingly as if carrying out a duty imposed on her—past the servitor at the door, past the others who carried candelabra and dishes in the long hall, up the winding stair, from one dim cor-

ridor to another above. They were observed, Paul knew, but no one inter-
fered with the girl.

Somewhere near in the dimness a woman snickered. Pushing open a
door, Marie Anne drew him after her and closed the door. A heavy bolt
rasped. "Platina wanted me," she whispered, "to coax and flatter you into
a better mood. They will think I am very successful."

There was a lilt of gladness in her voice. Under a cross on the bare
wall a small candle glimmered in red glass. Picking up something bulky
from the clothing hanging behind a curtain, Marie stopped abruptly before the candle.

"Holy Mary of the Seas, give aid to me," she whispered, and put out
the candle. Then in the darkness she pulled at his hand.

He found that in truth she had a way of leaving, unseen. Across the
matting of a veranda, over the railing, and down the twisted tentacles of
an aged bougainvillea—not so difficult a descent as the swaying shrouds
of a brig—through a narrow door in the mud-brick wall of the garden that
she locked after them, tossing the key back over the wall.

Out in the crowded alley she no longer led Paul; dropping behind, she
directed him where the robed figures and veiled women moved, into a
covered way where fires burned and voices clamored in argument, stray
soldiers elbowing Moslems. Sighting stalls on either hand where the folk
knelt on clean rugs to inspect lengths of cloth or bits of jewelry, Paul
thought this labyrinth to be the *souk*, the market. A good place to hide
his tracks . . . At a stand where meat sizzled on spits over glowing coal,
he felt the ache of hunger.

For the first time in the crowd Marie stepped to his side. She had turned
her shawl, with the dark side out, covering her head and face. On her
shoulder she bore a small bundle. In that fashion she had followed him,
as women followed their men, attracting no attention.

"If you are hungry," she cried, "we can eat here. Wait."

Still gripping her bundle, she selected a loose slab of bread from a stand,
taking a handful of rice from another, adding bits of smoking meat to
the pile, tossing back copper coin in payment. They had an hour, she explained, before His Excellency would descend to the dining-room, and
Platina and Hortense would go look for them. After that, it would be hard
for them, because the Spaniards might send searchers into every alley and
mosque of Alexandria.

It seemed to Paul that she was arguing against her own anxiety. Although she took some rice and sugared fruit, she only pretended to eat. By now he appreciated how skilled she was at pretending.

"Paul," she said in a breath, "I am not going back. If I have helped you, then do one thing for me."

Munching his laden bread, he nodded. "A passage on a ship, Marie Anne?"

Her head went back, and he felt her eyes searching his face. "That was clever. Yes. I cannot pay the fortune they ask—even if there were a place left. But—"

"How old are you?"

"Eighteen, truly—"

"Say fifteen. You are young to be running away from your sister."

"Not from Hortense. She says a roof is a roof, and there are worse. But I will not spend another night under that roof."

Marie Anne must have packed her bundle of belongings days before. And she must have tested carefully the escape route from the veranda. She meant what she said.

"Have you any place to go, mademoiselle?"

Impatiently she shook her head, throwing away the fruit at which she had been nibbling. "Have you ever waited like a beggar for your place at somebody's table, set with silver plate? On my veranda I would think about a ship coming in with a white clean deck and seagulls swooping over the filled sails. The men who worked the sails had kind eyes." Her own eyes brightened, and her supple lips parted as she coaxed Paul. "Then today at noon for the first time I saw a strange ship anchored far out, an American ship, and you—"

"The *Argus* is a vessel of war," he began to explain, "and cannot take passengers."

"I know. But English officers are embarking their wives and families. Have you a sister, Paul?"

"Only brothers."

"I thought so. Paul, the thing I would like you to do is not too difficult. Please listen, and think how it might easily be done."

He listened, knowing at once that it could not be done. How carefully she had planned it! For him to take her out to the *Argus*, pretending that she was betrothed to marry him. To request passage for her to a safe port.

Reading his face even as she begged, she whispered: "It will be so easily done. I have a ring, and I would be no trouble on shipboard. I promise.

Paul, what have you to do except to say a few words? You do not even have to pretend to like me. And then you can forget it—as you say—because we will not see each other again, ever! And the American officers—they would find a place for the betrothed of a countryman."

Ironically, Marie had made her request to the one man who could not carry it out. Paul almost laughed, thinking of shrewd, cautious Isaac Hull, newly in command of the brig, faced by a Lieutenant Bainbridge who was presumed to be in Sicily on sick leave—with a request for accommodation for a mysterious French bride-to-be.

"The commandant of the brig," he said carefully, "would not do it. I know him."

"Well, then we will go to the man who can order him to do it."

Staring at her, Paul wondered if she were not even then trying to get information from him. "Who?" he demanded.

"Your agent who is here—Eaton."

He could not believe she had spoken the name of the person he had to find and meet. In a flash he realized that in her he had a guide to Eaton; and a pretext for approaching him.

Sensing a new mood in him, Marie was explaining all in a breath: "The one the Arabs call Drub-Devil, because he would beat even a devil—"

"How far away is he?"

"A half-hour's ride." Marie no longer coaxed. Some dread in the depth of her hardened and hurried her words. "All our spies, and those of Tripoli, swear that he is in the city with money to spend to raise an armed force to go against Tripoli. And do not tell me that your ships will not obey him. They must."

As Paul pondered, he was aware of something familiar in the throng that pushed past them, going from stall to stall. The towering doorkeeper of the Spaniards stood still, a biscuit's toss away. Apparently the black had not sighted the two fugitives from His Excellency's table; but as Paul watched him, he turned back quickly into the dimness of the *souk*. When Paul nudged the girl and nodded at the retreating figure she exclaimed: "He saw us!"

Gathering up her bundle, whispering to Paul to follow, she slipped into the crowd, almost running from the arcade into an alley. There she called: "*Arabaji—arabaji!*"

Out of the darkness a shabby chaise rattled up, the native driver hauling in two thin horses, who required no urging to stop.

"I lied to you," Marie told him unexpectedly when the vehicle started off with them at a sluggish canter. "My friends of the legation no doubt were looking for us long since. But I wanted those few minutes to talk to you."

She had contrived to feed him and put her case to him quickly enough. Soon, she assured him, they would be safe enough, with William Eaton.

"You seem very sure you can find him."

"Why not?" She laughed a little. "Even your Drub-Devil cannot walk away from his villa through a battalion of Turkish infantry with orders to keep him jailed."

To Paul it was fantastic that this child should know so much of the doings of a great town—as fantastic as that he should be riding with her in this hired rig—or that Marie should be holding out a ring to him, pressing it into his hand. Saying: "Now is your chance to plight your troth to Marie Anne D'Aliermont. I assure you that my family was honorable, once. And my heart has not been touched by the fine eyes of any other man." Excitement edged her voice; she seemed to beg him to be merry with her. "So will you pledge marriage with me? Say it! It is not as hard taking sulphur and salts, sir."

"It's not true."

"What I am telling you is true."

"About any betrothal. I'm—I can't lie to Eaton." Her head turned as if he had struck her. "Marie, I'll do my best to get you a passage on some vessel. I promise that."

Her hand withdrew, and she seemed to draw away from him. After a moment she asked quietly, "Do you wish me to request entrance here?"

Their rig had slowed to a walk where trees loomed over a courtyard wall. At the open gateway Marie slipped down, and following her, he found her questioning an officer whose epaulets shone faintly in the starlight. Not a word of their speech did he understand. But when Marie put something that clinked faintly into the hand of the officer, his answers became more fluent.

No light showed within the gate. When Marie turned back to their carriage she seemed puzzled.

"Gone," she said. And: "Your Drub-Devil got away after all. The *Akinpasha*—the major swears that your clever Eaton went out only for a walk, with all eight of his Marine escort, who presented their muskets when the *Akinpasha* stopped them. But I think they bribed him, and told him a good story."

"We could wait for him inside."

Dubiously Marie shook her head. "The Turks have been waiting all day and part of this night. Where could they have gone, that no one saw them?"

Not out to the *Argus*, Paul reflected. And certainly nine Americans in uniform could not have wandered the streets without being observed. His own experience had shown—he remembered the omniscient Eugene Leitensdorfer, who had been in touch with Eaton.

"The people at my lodging," he told Marie, "might help us."

Chapter Four

Yet the coffee-house was as deserted as the villa. When they had steered toward Pompey's pillar above the cemetery, and thence into his street, he found Selim and even the drum gone from the public room. He saw that the muskets had disappeared from the kitchen, the sergeant from the back door, the bread from the stove. Only the native woman remained, setting a place for him at the table. She moved sluggishly, her face swollen as if she had been weeping.

Clumsily he tried to question her about Eugene. Out of her answers he caught only a phrase she repeated, something about Arabs, he thought.

Returning to the carriage, he found Marie waiting inside the empty courtyard. There, he noticed, she could see into the inn. She had not trusted him beyond her sight.

Putting his valise and book beneath the seat of the chaise, he said irritably: "My companions have absconded like Eaton. And Eugene's native wench says only one word, like a parakeet—"

With a flash of temper, Marie whirled on him.

"She is *not* a wench or a parakeet, but Eugene's wife, in Alexandria. I do not know how many other wives he has in what places. But she is a better Christian than I am, and I think he has left her again. What was the word she tried to tell you?"

"It sounded like *boorja arab*."

"Burj al Arab. That means the Arab's Tower. It is the place, Monsieur, where the caravans come in from the desert." Her anger made the words echo clearly. "It is also far out of the city, near the sea, perhaps five leagues from here . . . Well, what is your pleasure now?"

The silence of the street weighed on him. He heard only the broken sound of the woman's sobbing. Evidently Eugene had taken with him after nightfall all the skulkers who had kept hidden during the day—and William Eaton had departed somewhere out of sight with his Marine escort. It might be only coincidence, but Paul had no other trace of the man he sought.

Frowning, he tried to guess the actions of the naval agent—a quick-tempered sergeant in the Revolutionary War, who had taught school in Connecticut to educate himself—usually in trouble with his superiors, calling them "abject chameleons" when he had been obliged as Consul in Tunis to make the yearly payments of tribute to the corsair Beys, whom he called "insatiable as death." Now that war had come at last, he was straining to raise an armed force in Egypt with the aid of a friendly Arab prince, and with that force to strike those same Beys by land . . . Yes, Eaton might well have enlisted even Leitensdorfer's batch of irregulars, who had set out for the Arab's Tower . . .

"Hadjali," Marie told him, "saw you enter this place. He is what we call a renegade, because he protects himself by serving the Barbary powers—as Hortense and I earn our keep by being useful and pleasant to the Spaniards. Both Hortense and Hadjali saw you leave here, while they were observing the antics of the talented Eugene. In consequence, at any moment a search may arrive to find you communing with the stars—"

"Can you tell our driver to take me out the Arab's Tower?"

It exasperated Paul that he had to call upon this brat of a girl to help him at every turn. He had not thought she would take her seat beside him again, as she did, reminding him that she had no other place to go, and that he had made her a promise.

When the gleam of water opened before the chaise, and the lantern of a sentry was lifted to light the carriage, Marie covered her face against the light, and the guard waved them on. "He took us for an English milord, and a girl of the streets," she explained. "And at least, Hadjali will not be *certain* we went this way."

Yet as the wheels rumbled over the planks of a bridge, she laughed, saying that here in this canal she had come to Africa years before, a spoiled child, in a barge with music playing and the Tricolor flying . . . Her father, a division commander on Menou's staff, had sent for his two motherless daughters, from France—to live like princesses in Africa, until Napoleon

vanished in a courier vessel, and the remnant of the army was left to destruction, her father dying in the plague.

"Hortense was brave, Monsieur; she protected me even as she made
dresses for me out of our treasure of Oriental stuffs. You know so little
of women, you would not understand the difference that comes between
them when a younger sister grows up.

"When you are not voyaging in Egypt," Marie asked unexpectedly,
"what do you do?"

He hesitated. "I want to be a teacher, Mademoiselle D'Aliermont."

At that she was silent, drawing into her corner of the seat, aware that
he had lied, telling herself that she could not trust this young American,
in spite of his honest eyes. Something within him was merciless—some
secret thing. Marie Anne did not understand how that could be. Yet instinctively she understood that it was both foolish and dangerous to be
so pleased when his head turned toward her, and to feel protected merely
because he was within reach of her hand.

No, she told herself, he would not keep the promise he had made her.
But she had nothing else to hold to.

When Orion's square shone clear overhead, she slept, her weary head
hidden in its hair turned toward him. The cold of the desert night struck
into his limbs. Carefully he drew off his jacket and laid it around her.

This slight girl had courage; she did not speak of the danger to herself
in aiding him. And he felt that he had always been a coward.

The glare of sunrise lay upon the cracked stone walls of the Burj al
Arab, and the sounds of pandemonium echoed within it, out to the tran-
quil blue of the sea. The Tower, once a citadel of the vanished Greeks, gave
shelter to those who sought trade or loot in Alexandria.

At the well beside the Tower, Arabs were striking their pavilions, and
leading out their slender nervous horses; a throng of black-tent Bedouins
labored at loading strings of kneeling grunting camels. Over the uproar
presided the man they called Drub-Devil.

With his red hair lifted by the wind, and the chin jutting from his
florid face, he tongue-lashed the camel drivers in broken Arabic. "God!
This hour is the hour for going upon the road—not for smoking pipes and
milking goats."

William Eaton had the bulk of middle age, and the enthusiasm of a
dreamer who wastes no time in reasoning. For all his scolding, he was
happy as a child about to start a journey. He had spent his past years in

the Mediterranean: and to Paul, who had not met him before, he seemed unlike any other officer—especially one with the rank of general.

"Elijah took the bread the ravens dropped," Eaton assured him, "and I have no mind to refuse a recruit who would join my force without pay." Curiously his blue eyes took stock of the tall boy. "Your appearance has indeed something miraculous about it. You understand that rations are problematical, while hardships are certain? Why do you wish to go with us?"

Paul, who had nerved himself against interrogation, warmed to the New Englander's good humor. "To help, sir, if I can to strike a blow that may free William Bainbridge and his crew."

"Hm! And it may not. How, Master Davies, did you find my encampment?"

"Through the kindness of Mademoiselle D'Aliermont."

Quizzically the adventurer glanced at the girl, who had hung back in the shadow of the wall. "A charming guide. I have no doubt my secret is known to all Alexandria, and Cairo as well."

He even bowed to her, and Marie Anne made a graceful curtsy. After the strain of the night, she almost sang with gladness to find the American Drub-Devil so amiable, even if uncouth. Apparently he did not hesitate to accept a civilian, untrained like Paul, among his soldiers.

Despite all that he had on his mind that morning and the worries he did not confess to, William Eaton noticed the grace of the young girl, and fancied Paul Davies to be fortunate in her. When he had made a hasty inspection of the loads that passed on the camels set into awkward motion, he said laughing: "At your age, Master Davies, I carried a musket for a week, to a recruiting station. In '79, it was. I do not know what use we can make of your knowledge of Plato and John Bunyan; but if my adjutant will pass you—why, be one of us, in God's name."

But when Paul asked for passage for Marie Anne, he shook his head decisively. "No, that can't be done."

When the boy urged that it was vital for her to get transport out of Alexandria, Eaton swung back to her impatiently. "It will be known in two hours. I can tell you now. We are not proceeding by sea."

"Not—" Paul bit off the words. He had seen the instructions drawn up at Syracuse for William Eaton, naval agent. They were: to embark whatever force he had raised at Alexandria in American vessels, to proceed by sea to make a landing at the nearest Barbary stronghold, which happened to be the port of Derna. "The *Argus* was to await you, sir."

His voice lowered, Eaton said: "By now the brig will have put to sea."

Suddenly he laughed, nodding at the medley of horsemen and caravaneers. "Faith, we'd need an ark of Noah to embark this outfit. Moreover, my friends the Turks are quite justifiably suspicious of our presence in the city. They'll be glad to see me depart harmlessly by land. Aye, with my allies."

From the cool shadow of the Tower the long line of camels was starting west. Beside the line moved a Bedouin woman, sturdy as an animal, a bundle on her head. Behind her a half-grown girl drove a herd of black goats.

Incredulously Paul watched this advance guard of an armed expedition. He thought: *Eaton must have known he could not take such a train on shipboard—he is disregarding his orders.*

"General Eaton," cried Marie Anne, "there is no passage to Derna by land."

The ruddy New Englander smiled down at her. "Even Mademoiselle D'Aliermont is informed of our destination which we have endeavored to keep secret."

Nodding at the baggage train already entering the haze of dust that hid the skyline, he added: "The desert can be crossed, child. What do the poets say, Master Davies—from the river Nile to the Pillars of Hercules? Aye, my expedition may look but ill on a parade ground, but its members are all hardened to desert marches."

"Then take me, General Eaton," exclaimed the girl.

While he was silent in surprise, she urged swiftly that she could speak the languages of the native peoples, she could interpret for him, she knew army routine. "And I have need—" her glance sought Paul desperately—"to leave Alexandria by any means."

For an instant Eaton hesitated. Every trace of good humor left his florid face, and his voice roughened as if with inner tension. "Mine is a difficult undertaking. To make a desert march of five hundred miles—"

"But you will rendezvous somewhere with the ships!"

"We must be prepared to meet an enemy force of Tripolitans of unknown strength, well fortified; and, I doubt not," he added bleakly, "well advised of my movements and strength. I am sorry, mademoiselle. I wish that every member of my force had your spirit."

Before Marie could speak again, they heard the swift beat of a drum.

Dark against the morning sun, two compact groups of men were marching in from the direction of Alexandria. Two horsemen led them, and the first rider was Selim, pounding the shining drum slung at his knee. Eaton shouted, and almost ran to meet the cavalcade.

Marie went back and picked up her bundle. "Paul," she said quietly, "you did not speak for me."

"Faith, I did."

She shook her head, looking up at him fleetingly. "Perhaps you think you did. If you had been willing to say we were betrothed—" Her supple lips quivered, and pressed together firmly. "Good-bye, Paul."

When he stretched out his hand to stop her, she stepped away, fumbling in her girdle. Into his hand she dropped a small silk purse with the weight of a few coins in it. "Arabaji!" she called. And to Paul: "Pay him, please. I do not want to trouble you more."

She went away as she had walked down the beach, with a defiant lift of her slight shoulders. Their driver of the night must have been following them, because he hurried up at her call, begging for money. Pocketing Marie's purse, Paul extracted a gold sequin of his own and tossed it to the man, who snatched it and pressed it to his forehead.

When Paul freed himself from the Arab and looked for the girl, she had disappeared into the shifting throng. Cloaked horsemen, magnificently mounted, were racing out to greet the incoming detachment. When he rounded one of the towers of the *caravanserai*, searching for the small figure under the blue scarf, he almost bumped into Eaton, who was taking the salute of the officer of the infantry detachment.

This officer was Eugene, resplendent now in bottle-green tunic and black boots with the ribbon of a medal gleaming on his shoulder. "Colonel Leitensdorfer reporting, sir," he was saying crisply, "with the Greek regiment, two *sous-officiers*, thirty-eight men, and cannoneers, twenty-six."

The cannoneers were the motley rapscallions Paul had observed in the courtyard of the coffee-house.

"Only give them cannon, General," said Eugene in a lower tone, "and you will see how old hands they are. Where do you have the guns?"

"Over there."

Glancing where Eaton pointed, Paul sighted a half-dozen figures in the blue-faced-with-buff of American Marines, engaged tranquilly in roping a pair of yoked bullocks to the trail of a single brass nine-pounder.

For a second Eugene's expressive face went blank. Evidently he had expected more than that. "So," he grunted.

"There will be more—in time," Eaton assured him. "Fall out your men. Let them eat. Tell Mr. Farquhar to see that they have transport for their belongings."

In another moment the quick eye of the Tyrolese had picked out Paul. "By Salbal and Bathbal—the schoolteacher! Is it that my lodging was not good enough? How did you find the rendezvous?"

Paul explained, and Eugene muttered irritably in German: "Like a lord, in a carriage! After I hide my command by gravestones and Roman baths, and bring them here at night, far from the road. And what then do you do, Herr Davies? Here, in a carriage, you bring a woman who is a Spanish spy."

"She's not that—now."

"*Das Junge!*"

As if speechless at such Yankee credulity, the Tyrolese strode off, leaving Paul to pursue his stubborn search. In half an hour he had found no trace of Marie Anne, but he felt that he had stumbled into a stage set for an insane play.

Accustomed to the orderly movement of shipboard, to the shelter of his own narrow quarters, and the quick give-and-take of familiar commands, the uproar of the Tower bewildered him. The seedy Englishman, the admirer of Hercules, accosted him with a smile—introducing himself as Percival Farquhar, and asking if he had a bag to be loaded. A lanky lieutenant of Marines, watching the stowing of the loads on the camels, observed in the slurring drawl of Kentuckians: "They-uns will steal the buckles from your belts."

In the corridor that ran through the massive walls of the ancient fort, Paul glimpsed another familiar face. The man who passed him aimlessly had an animal's ease of stride, and no more than the slits of eyes showing under a striped headcloth. But as he passed, there was a flicker of recognition in the eyes, a quick turn of the head away. After a moment Paul remembered him—Hadjali, the renegade. Yet when he swung back, hurrying to catch up with the man, Hadjali was not to be seen. The teeming Tower seemed to have the power to render fugitives invisible.

Then he realized that Hadjali, who drew pay from Spanish agents, would also be looking for Marie Anne. With her purse in his pocket, he feared that she had no more money, and certainly she had no friend to aid her in the Tower. She had not driven back in the chaise, which departed heavily loaded with portly Moslems.

At noon he made his way out of the gate, convinced that Marie could not possibly be within the *serai* walls. Glancing at the faint trail that led straight to the west, he stopped short.

Far out on that track gleamed the brass cannon, followed by the squad of Marines, with four riders coming after. This tiny nucleus of a military force was followed in turn by all the hundred-odd armed Arabs who had appeared to greet Leitensdorfer. Behind them trailed the two detachments of infantry, with a queue of natives driving cattle, and women bearing loads, and a few children.

This line of tiny human forms moving out over the gray plain danced oddly in the heat haze.

"*Eh bien*," observed a harsh voice, "you see your American expedition has started without you."

In the last patch of shadow Eugene sat at ease against the wall, his tunic unbuttoned, a porcelain pipe smoking in his hand. Behind him two horses were tethered—one a powerful gray with silver-worked saddle, the other a thin sorrel with a quilt roped on him.

"Or you, Colonel." Paul was too weary to endure more of the Tyrolese's jeering.

Drawing a measured puff from his pipe, Eugene nodded. "I make *das Rechnen*. I count nine Americans, and you, younker. Three hundred and eighty-one outlanders, and mineself, Eugene Leitensdorfer. What total does that make, of good men? Ten. The nine Americans and mineself." His summing up seemed to please him, because he went on mildly: "Also, an adjutant has many duties, such as watching for deserters and picking out the spies."

"An hour ago," observed Paul, "I sighted Hadjali here."

This stirred the placid Eugene more than Paul had hoped. Hastily he started to pull on a boot he had been rubbing with a candle-end. "Hadjali, that viper—where?"

But when Paul explained, the big Tyrolese sat back, swearing. "If you see a stag, younker, when you are hunting, do you then run after him? No. Hadjali, like your mademoiselle, is not stupid. Yah! By now he is very damned safe."

"How?"

Leisurely Eugene rose and stretched his arms, his thumbs cracking.

Seemingly he turned to inspect the horses. His glance swept the ring of watching natives, probed the haze of the plain, and passed to the edge of the sea below. His knotty hand stabbed out and down. "By now—he goes there."

Close in to the white ripple of the wash, a slender xebec loafed, her lateen yard lowered. Paul had seen scores like her—fleet and able as gulls—off the shore of Tripoli. Lying as she was, a man could have waded out to her in a moment's time.

"Yes." Eugene nodded thoughtfully. "He will have an easier voyage than we—"

Abruptly Paul caught his hand. On the little finger a ring had been wedged, an opalescent moonstone cut into the shape of a flying bird—the one piece of jewelry Marie had worn. "How did you get that?" he cried.

"From the blind witch of Tanteval, a gift, certainly." Freeing his hand, Eugene slipped off the ring and pocketed it. "In the full of the moon it brings good fortune—"

"Good fortune like the gems and the gold of Cleopatra Selene!" The tale the glib Eugene had told him, to beguile him in the coffeehouse! The man had a magpie's eye for loot. Marie must have given him the ring as a bribe; and if she had—

He stared out at the thin column of marchers, sinking deeper into the great plain. If the elusive Hadjali had managed to slip away in the xebec, Marie might have gone with the column somehow, with Eugene's connivance.

He went to the sorrel horse—having no least doubt which of the two mounts was meant for him—and swung himself up by grip of the mane, starting after the marchers at the best pace of the reluctant horse.

In a moment Eugene was beside him, riding like a centaur. The Tyrolese did everything with ease, from calling to prayer to play-acting as adjutant of a skeleton army. "Younker," he said, "I do not think you are stupid. No. Only, you are not accustomed. Perhaps it is that you live still within the walls of your honorable home where nobody starves and thieves do not break in . . . No, listen to me. I have still two minds about you, but about Mademoiselle I am certain if she comes with us she will not report back as a spy to Alexandria."

"General Eaton would not allow her to make this journey."

"No? If she makes one march with us, can General Eaton send her away? Where?" Putting spur to his horse, Eugene said over his shoulder: "Inform the officers about her now, and she will be sent away."

As he passed the group of women at the rear of the column, Eugene turned in the saddle and pulled at his waxed mustache, his elbow lifted high.

Paul reined in his horse as he came abreast of them, searching among the blue-wrapped figures until he found one in the lead that carried a familiar bundle. The Arab woman, unveiled, stared at him with frank curiosity. Marie had her head covered, but she had recognized him.

She said softly: "If you stop, they will see you. I ask you not to speak to me, ever."

In some way she had got herself a pair of native sandals. Her feet slipped in them at each step, already cut by the particles of stone in the sand. After a moment he rode on, feeling for the first time the impact of heat rising from the baked ground.

With sunset the earth changed, magically. Their campfires touched with flame the high ridge of the coast, the ridge of stones between the motionless sea and the tawny uplifted waves of the sand. Ahead of them the sun flamed and sank.

At Eaton's fire the sheiks of the camelmen quarreled with him, grasping at him, demanding pay for the journey before they would make another march. He shouted scorn at them and drove them away, until they came back, quieted, to claim their portion of the bread and the coffee of the Americans. In return the Arab women brought dates and baked bread to the Marines. Among those who carried the woven trays of food Paul made out Marie. Silent as the others, she slipped away into the shadows.

Lieutenant Presley O'Bannon of the Marines, observing them, parted with frugal words: "These savages have not read the Articles of War."

When he was free of his guests, Eaton came to throw himself down by Paul. Wiping his face with his sleeve, he said bluntly as was his manner: "When my pockets are empty, I wonder how many followers I shall have. I meant to tell you, Mr. Davies—my adjutant doubts if you will stand this journey. Frankly, he argues that our inexperience may cause us difficulty." He hesitated. "Some of the escort will be turning back tomorrow; and you could accompany them safely, I think, to Alexandria. If you—"

"I can help with stowing the loads, sir. I can handle ropes and tackle." The other's doubt quickened the boy's pulse. "I mean to go all the way with you."

After a glance at him, Eaton nodded. "I see you do. Although I'm eter-
nally blessed if I know why a civilian wishes to make a camel driver of
himself."

In rising, he added casually: "It would be better for you to comply
with the discipline of the force you accompany. Colonel Leitensdorfer
has served under varied flags in rather strange capacities, but—he gets
things done."

Lying on his borrowed blanket, Paul reflected that Eugene plainly meant
to get rid of him, while he could not count on Eaton backing him.

For forty hours he had not slept. Against his aching shoulders pressed
the stones of the hard earth; against his tired eyes stood the wraiths of
thorn-bush. He breathed in the smoke of smoldering dung fires, thinking
how weary Marie would be, who had helped him to start this journey.

Chapter Five

Across the arid wasteland the stubbornness of Eaton drove his vestige
of an army. Due west he led them as Paul saw by the bearing of Orion's
square rising at night. By day the lash of his tongue drove them, until they
had advanced most of the twenty-five miles that he set for a stage—then
at the evening halts he blarneyed them, and sang over his wineglass. His
eagerness was like a fever that in turn affected the others.

By the end of the second march, Farquhar had observed Marie and reported to the commander: "We have a beauty stowed away among the
native allies."

Yet Eaton, recognizing her, accepted her presence almost eagerly.

"Child, your courage will be an example to us."

Marie curtsied to him quietly, saying she would be careful not to trouble the General. "By your kindness then, I will go with you to the American ships."

"Such as they are." He laughed, pleased by her demure respect. "A brig,
a schooner, and a sloop will await our coming at Bomba Bay."

He spoke as if he had no doubt of reaching the rendezvous with the
vessels. And Paul thought that then the Americans would have no alternative to embarking Marie on one of the ships.

Stared at curiously by the men, Marie kept herself among the native
women. To Paul she spoke only with cool politeness, refusing to ride his
sorrel, managing to get a donkey for herself from the Arabs. She had a
ready smile for Farquhar, even when she refused his urging to sup with
the officers.

"Why should I?" she asked. "The women are kind here, sir, it is the fashion for the ladies to dine apart from the gentlemen!"

She could jest easily with the Englishman, who was of her caste. She picked blossoms of wild jasmine to set in her hair. It seemed as if she played upon Eaton's good nature, and Farquhar's open admiration, while she greeted Paul only with silence. Although she plied the silent O'Bannon with questions about America, and even rode beside the Pasha—the shy Hamet Pasha, leader of what Eaton called his cavalry, who wore a jeweled headband with a woman's grace.

"The poor Hamet," she assured O'Bannon, "has cause to be heartsick. His wife and children are held captive in Tripoli."

Alone in the expedition, Hamet had not been hired to fight for Eaton. He was, Farquhar explained, of the princely Karamanli family, with a claim to the rule of the Barbary ports—to which Eaton had sworn to restore him.

Yet Hamet in the last days had wanted to turn back to the Delta of Egypt, complaining that Eaton's force was not capable of crossing the desert. His fear was shared by the remaining European, the Italian physician Mendrici, who had made a fortune in Cairo and had lent much of it to Eaton, who had used up all of his own funds with the four thousand dollars advanced him by Hull of the *Argus*. "Our worthy physician," Farquhar summed him up, "is a coward. He flinches at sight of a knife in Selim's hand. Yet he left a hotel suite on the Nile for this. Now, why on earth?"

Silently Paul wondered why the Englishman had come, and Eugene. The Tyrolese had his head together with Mendrici often, over the Italian's wine. Once Paul noticed the physician examining a coin under a candle with a magnifying glass. When he turned the gold piece in his thin fingers, Paul recognized it as Eugene's specimen from the tomb of Cleopatra Selene—the tomb that Eugene insisted he had sighted on the mountain height beyond Egypt.

Toward those mountains the expedition was making its way. In the column itself Selim's cannoneers and the band of Greeks held the balance of force—with Eugene, if he should ever decide to part from Eaton. The loot of a royal tomb would be a prize Paul could not imagine Eugene passing by. It might draw even the timid Mendrici into the desert.

But of Mendrici their commander had as little doubt as of Eugene.

"He accompanies us in spite of the danger," Eaton declared, "aware that we lacked a physician."

By degrees Paul realized that Eaton was shutting his eyes deliberately to the weakness of the members of his force. And he began to wonder how Eaton had obtained the rank of general, and whether in a clash he could stand up to the adroit Leitensdorfer.

The older man was driven by a craving for action. "After eight years," he would say, "we are opening our gun ports instead of our purses to them."

They were always the Barbary beys. "I'll do no more groveling to them." No more haggling over terms to keep a peace. He would succeed in striking his blow against them by land. No more bargaining as consul for the release of American slaves. "We paid them timber and tar for ships, with small arms and cannon—the worth of forty thousand dollars a year and more demanded, because we paid so much. Always the threat of war, and the Barbary cruisers loosed against our commerce, and Congress fearful of any act of war."

His ruddy face darkened with the anger that was like a fever. "We paid. The English lion showed his teeth, and the Barbary beys spoke softly. But we sent them jewels of the finest, bought in London. They asked for a frigate of thirty-six guns. I answered that the timber for such a frigate had not grown along our rivers. Paul, there are no trees in Barbary."

Eaton glowered at the boy, his mind miles away.

"When the *Philadelphia* arrived at last in pursuit of a xebec like the one that dogs us, Paul, I felt as if the dirt of the Barbary ports had been cleansed. Then the Bey of Tripoli was given his frigate—with forty-four guns, and her crew for slaves. Bainbridge surrendered her."

Familiar fear gripped Paul. "She listed on the reef," he said evenly. "Sir, those guns could not be served."

"She had muskets. In forty hours, when the wind changed, she floated free."

Paul was silent, knowing that William Eaton had sent the fullest report of the loss of the frigate from Tunis. His report had been barely fair to the captain, and outspoken in its regret for the loss of the vessel.

"The matter of seamanship," Eaton mused, "I cannot judge. But because of the tribute paid so many years by Congress, under threat, Bainbridge should have fought his ship. Because reports of American slaves had been made out too long, he should never have hauled down his flag. Now, with officers and crew captive, the Bey raised his demand to a half-million dollars."

Eaton had been drinking late that night. In his cups, he had a way of dwelling on the last war. "Time was—" he would say, and tell of happenings before Paul's time. When much excited, he would read an ode he had written upon the death of the Patriarch. Although he apologized for his lack of learning he loved to repeat the lines: "*On the fields of fair Elysium, ranged in open order, with arms presented, stood the host of heaven.*"

Paul thought the words about Washington reviewing the host of heaven were puzzling. But William Eaton said them like a hymn.

The desert took their strength from them gently as the days crept into the first weeks. Because they lacked a map, they had to keep the sea within sight, climbing down into the wadis that channeled the coast ridge. When they made camp in one of the dry ravines, a storm broke over the heights. Before this march was over, not only Eaton but all his men would deserve the name of Drub-Devil.

The surge of muddy water that swept down the wadi carried away much of their hoarded stores, with the tents and cattle of the natives. Eaton swore that at the desert's end, at Bomba, the ships would be waiting with food, money, arms, and men.

"Aye," nodded O'Bannon, "and water."

They had parted with the last money they carried, the officers and Paul, to pay the insatiable camel drivers, who deserted notwithstanding after the storm. Eaton persuaded a Bedouin tribe that had joined them to load the remaining sacks of rice on their camels.

Because the animals of the tribe had to graze wherever green growth showed, the marchers must needs wait for the beasts. Because the stages grew shorter, in this fashion, the sacks of rice, biscuit, and flour hoarded by the Americans dwindled alarmingly each day.

Daily they sighted the orange sail of the xebec that followed them by sea.

And as if to tantalize them, a dark ridge appeared above the line of the plain far ahead of them at sunset.

"*Salalum!*" cried the Arabs, pointing at it. Eugene identified the black hump as the mountains, rising from the Libyan plain they had been crossing. There the desert ended, and the plateau of Cyrenaica began. On that plateau, where the Romans had raised wheat and built palaces, there should be grazing and water and perhaps game to be killed, and ripe dates to be gathered. So Eugene prophesied.

But by the next halt the mountains, standing bare as stone walls, still lay far off. Not so much as a pool of stagnant water was to be found.

It was not hunger and thirst that broke down the march. The Europeans had strength enough to keep on to the heights. The nomad tribes hung back complaining that their animals were beginning to die. Moreover, since their camels and sheep could not graze, milk was failing in the animals.

And the nomads had grown daily in numbers, since half-starved tribes, sighting the column, had hurried in to beg for food. Unruly as a mob, they pressed around the marchers, their children scurrying underfoot to snatch up out of the dirt the hard ends of biscuits thrown away by the soldiers.

Then, rounding the point of a cape, they sighted the columns and tawny shapes of buildings. In the furnace heat of mid-afternoon they stumbled into a city of ruins, where marble porticos reared drunkenly over a rubble of broken stone. The huge cistern, half caved in, held yellow water. It stank of sulphur, and the horses would not drink of it. Eugene shrugged his heavy shoulders. "Dead for a thousand years."

Eaton was for rushing on, but the Tyrolese advised a halt in this skeleton of a Roman seaport. Immediately the column broke up, the nomads searching the hollows for water that might lie under wet sand, Hamet's Arabs quartering themselves in a withered palm grove, the Greeks stretching out in the shade of the ruins, scraping the sand away to gaze curiously at the mosaic paving beneath, while the striped jerseys of the few Marines paired off, to quest around in their never-ending search for old coins. Eugene shook his head. "It is not good." Wiping his eyes, he stared out to sea. "The Tripolitan's sail, where is it?"

"Hauling to nor'west," muttered Paul, without thinking. He had kept close watch on the triangular orange sail of the xebec that escorted them along the coast as an albatross follows a ship.

Eugene scowled at him, in a bad temper. "So a seaman speaks. Be so kind, Monsieur Davies, to explain to me in English—where *is it*?"

Pointing out a speck in the haze to the westward, Paul said: "There." The vessel had hauled to windward fast after they halted, as if to hurry ahead of them. He had an impulse to explain as much to the truculent Eugene, but anger kept him silent.

Apparently the Tyrolese drew his own conclusions from the xebec's departure because he lifted his gaze to the shoulder of the mountain now overhanging them. The lines deepened about his eyes, and he rumbled, dissatisfied, "*Herr Gott und*—General Eaton, will you allow your ranks to lie in the sand and kill flies? This is no place to kill flies. Give them duties. Where is firewood? Where is food?"

Out of his explosive complaining, Paul gathered that Eugene wanted a feast prepared for all the Europeans, as a distraction. They had no water to cook rice. When Eugene demanded that the Yankee buy sheep from the Arabs, Eaton grimaced and pulled a slim sack from his pocket. Out of it he shook three Venetian sequins—all that remained of his money.

He seemed to act upon the advice of the Tyrolese as if it were Bible writ.

"But the nomads will not slaughter their animals for food," he objected. "Now that they are near starvation themselves, will they sell a sheep for three sequins?"

Marie's soft voice broke into the tense argument of the men. "I think their women will sell some sheep, General, for no money at all."

Her donkey had drawn close to the fetid water of the cistern. The women, she explained, had been fascinated by the ornamented brass buttons on the blue coats of the Marines. The buttons would add splendor to their bracelets and throat chains. For a handful they might give up a sheep.

Marie proved to be right. Eaton fed his command that evening with portions of roast mutton and a cup of sour wine, around fires made from driftwood and dead palm branches. But the tribal folk gathered beyond the firelight, patiently watching the strange Christians who gorged themselves on meat and smoked fuming tobacco afterward.

Paul noticed that Eugene made an excuse to go off afterward with Mendrici to the Italian's tent. The physician had some good wine left in the casks that were his private property. Yet Paul had overheard Eugene and Percival Farquhar discussing whether the tombs hidden away in the heights before them might be intact, with their riches. Farquhar must have need of more money than the small pay he had drawn from Eaton—

A loud whoop sounded from the sprawling figures of the Marines. "Cain't no wolf take our victuals from us!"

Whether some Arab had filched a slice of meat, or whether the man was merely letting out his voice, Paul never knew. Close to him Farquhar was bending over Marie, saying in rapid French: "I'll never believe the Yankees were descended from Englishmen."

He was whispering into her ear, fondling her hand. And the girl sat pas-

sive as if enjoying it. Paul felt his body stiffen. Awkwardly he started to
his feet. Those two, the thought shaped in his mind, were whispering so
he would not hear. And she was not the Marie Anne who had slept with
her head on his arm, in the carriage—

He found himself standing with his hand gripping Farquhar's shoulder, saying: "It is ill doing, sir, to speak so of a man."

Farquhar's head jerked up, over his high collar. His thin nostrils twitched
as if he were trying not to smile. "Lad, it was not of you I spoke." Then his
voice altered. "But if you conceive that my words did reflect upon you, I
am at your service, sir, with whatever weapon you select. Egad," he added
ruefully, "we'll find no suitable seconds among our fellows."

Paul stared at him. He had blurted out a stupid thing. The older man
had answered with a patrician's courtesy. Marie still held fast to his hand,
her eyes searching Paul's face as if discovering something new in it. "Paul
Davies," she said quickly, "did anyone tell you why Monsieur Farquhar
joined your Yankees?"

"No," cried Farquhar, "and I'm damned if he'll hear."

"He will, because I am going to tell him."

To Paul's surprise, the handsome Englishman freed his hand from the
girl's clinging fingers and sprang up. Something like fear flashed into his
set face. He said, "Mr. Davies, I will wait for your word," and turned to
stride off alone.

Marie sat for a moment chin on hand. "A woman likes attention from
a man, if he is nice to her. Don't you know that?"

Kneeling beside her, stirring the fire mechanically, Paul heard her explain that Eaton had told her how he had engaged Richard Farquhar, Percival's brother, to manage his accounts in Cairo, and how Richard had
taken out thirteen hundred dollars to pay his own native debts—she did
not know what. But the day after he had been dismissed, Percival had
driven up to Eaton's villa to offer his apology, and to serve without payment in his brother's place. "He said not to pay him anything, because
he was not worth it, and that in time he would make up a portion of the
debt. The General took him at his word."

The gentleness in her voice was something apart from the sounds of
the camp and the uncertainty of the night. "He is not like you, Paul, who
are so serious and somber. He makes a jest of everything."

Suddenly she put her hand into the Yankee's. "Paul, he lived once in a
manor house and had his own stable of racing horses. I think he was an

officer then. Now—he laughs at what he calls the Once-Honorable Percival. He did not mean to harm you. Would you hurt him?"

In the smoke of the fire Paul saw the smoke drifting from the pistol he had fired in the duel at Malta. "No, Marie," he cried.

"Then you must tell him so."

Not until he had lain awake long in his blanket did Paul realize how inexorably the girl had pressed him to make his peace with the Englishman. Her gentleness had been stronger than their anger.

Chapter Six

Even drugged by sleep, he sensed a change in the encampment. The nomads, astir as always before sunrise, were moving near him. O'Bannon called out. When he got up to go to the embers of the fire he almost fell over Marie, curled up on a sheepskin near the ashes. She was awake, and she explained the Arab women had warned her to stay away from their tents. "They said," she repeated drowsily, "for me to stay with my own men—"

In the half light of dawn the tribesmen were collecting around the tent that held the stores. O'Bannon complained that three horses had disappeared under the eyes of his sentry.

More than that. Within the guarded tent Paul found the precious sacks in disorder; one at least was missing by his count. While he was trying to strike a light to a tallow dip, Mendrici scurried in, shivering with cold or fear, and stammering that they were being attacked. But at the tent entrance Paul could make out only the mass of tribesmen faced by the eight Marines in their jerseys with their muskets held on the noisy crowd. Eugene appeared to inspect the stores, snarling at Mendrici and swearing that if they had been attacked by Tripolitans most of them would be dead in their blankets already. The Bedouins had demanded an issue of the Americans' rice; Eaton had refused as usual and had gone to argue with Hamet . . .

The clamor outside the tent was cut by a musket volley. Paul ran to the entrance, to be elbowed aside by Eugene. He learned afterward that the Marine lieutenant had ordered the volley fired over the heads of the throng. It drove the excited nomads into a frenzy, as they caught up spears and knives, crowding together to rush the line of Europeans in front of the tent.

There Selim faced his fellow Moslems with scimitars in both his hands. Farquhar stood quietly by him, with pistol poised.

Before another shot was fired, Eaton's stocky figure stepped out between the groups, walking into the frantic Moslems. He had no weapon, and he did not raise his voice as he walked among them.

Spears and muskets were leveled at him. Hamet raced into the crowd, wildly slashing with his sword, wounding a man in front of Eaton. The American caught the rein of the horse, and shouted over the outcry. For a moment his voice held them, and heads turned to listen.

Beside Paul, Farquhar lowered his pistol with a sigh. "Touch and go," he observed critically.

At mid-morning the Englishman traced for the line of the shadow on the sand with his finger, and said; "At least we will have the finest marble monuments for our graves."

Lazily he nodded at the pillars still standing in the ruins. It gave him a certain satisfaction to think of death. And he was well aware that the mad expedition of the Yankee had come to a full stop.

Marie in her own way sensed the change in Eaton. The ebullition of the dawn clash had drained away from him, and he sat among them complaining morosely. The Arabs could not be moved forward again—they were preparing to search inland for grazing and water, Hamet with them. "I promised them that a hundred Marines would land from our vessels at Bomba, to join them. The fickle chameleons asked for proof that our ships would be still waiting in the bay of Bomba."

"*Ja!*" Eugene assented quickly. "For them you should have a sign."

"Am I Moses, to draw water from the rocks?"

Eaton's fatigue lay on him like a blanket, and his body yearned for a cup of Mendrici's wine, which stifled thirst without staying it. He had cajoled his semblance of an army across the Libyan desert. He had not blamed O'Bannon for the luckless volley that morning. The trouble lay deeper than that, and for once William Eaton saw no way to remedy it.

Through his tired mind crowded the impossible difficulties that beset him: food would suffice, at half rations for the Europeans alone for about three days; the surviving horses, without water for two days, would barely serve to draw the fieldpiece up the heights. Already he was two weeks late at the rendezvous where the *Argus* waited—if the ship had not given him up and sailed away from the hazardous coast.

"The Devil," Eugene persisted, "has given a sign."

When they looked at him curiously, he explained. He had been investigating tracks around the ruins with the Bedouins who were curious about the missing horses. During the night their enemy had appeared for the first time, to play a trick on them—to steal mounts and rations under the noses of the Yankee sentries. Such a trick alarmed the Arabs more than an attack. No one knew where the Tripolitans had dropped from.

"From the xebec," put in Farquhar promptly. "Xebec lands three spies to bedevil us. Then—presto—flies off to Derna to report us. Two to one, I have it solved. Done with you in shillings, Eugene?"

The Tyrolese shook his head with a rumble of agreement. Almost, the Tripolitans had managed to set Eaton's exhausted command to fighting itself.

In the silence that followed Paul looked up. "If Isaac Hull is in the *Argus*, sir, he will be waiting at his station."

He knew that stocky, careful Hull would stick to the rendezvous until new orders reached him.

Eugene grunted. "Our Arabs will believe only their eyes. Show them the ship!"

"Then give me your gray charger," cried Farquhar, "and an Arab, and I'll race him to the spot."

Ninety miles it would be, Paul reckoned from what Eaton had let drop. Two days in the saddle would get a messenger there. It was vital for Eaton to gain communication with the ships.

"General Eaton," he called anxiously. "You—"

"I have done it once," Eugene proclaimed. "Yes, I Eugene Leitensdorfer walked the way from Tripoli to Grand Cairo. *Isso*—you would not have known me. A dervish, a begging dervish—*ahmak*, mad, making prophecies, curing sick eyes by touching with my finger. Also, I lived."

When he had made his boast, Paul said: "Let me try, sir."

The Tyrolese shook his heavy head indulgently. "Younker, here you are blind and dumb. How can you speak? How easily you would be killed!" His glance roved from the silent O'Bannon, to Mendrici, who had feared to leave the tent. "Perhaps Selim," he suggested doubtfully.

Not Selim, Paul thought. The swaggering janizary, leader of Eugene's bravos who called themselves cannoneers, had no loyalty to Eaton. The whole crew recruited in Alexandria would be more apt to hunt loot than to give intelligent advice to the American vessels.

Getting up to face Eaton, the boy ignored Eugene: "Sir, I request permission to ride to Bomba immediately. I am able to perform no useful duty here, while these gentlemen have all important duties—"

"The young cock crows!" snapped Eugene.

"I have seen the pinnacle headlands of Bomba. I can identify them, as well as the rig of the *Argus* and the *Hornet*."

His desperation held the attention of the older men. Paul felt that he was the one to make the try, and that Farquhar had volunteered only as a sportsman, to race a horse against odds.

Eaton merely turned his head. He seemed stricken by his exertions in the numbing heat. As usual he let Leitensdorfer have the word.

Truculently the adventurer heaved up his broad body. "If this younker came back—if he swore by Salbal and Bathbal and *Authierotabal* he had sighted the ships—would our nomadic allies believe it? He cannot speak their speech! They do not doubt your word, General Eaton. No! They merely behold you beaten by your enemies. So, they become afraid. You must break their fear. Show them a sign, a vision to stir their hearts—trick them, like the Tripolitans. Do not reason—"

"*Le coeur a ses raisons*," Marie broke in, smiling, "*que le raison ne connais pas.*"

The Tyrolese whirled, surprised: "*Hein?*"

"The heart has its reasons, which reason does not know."

He stared at her; then his harsh voice boomed out. "True, as the little mademoiselle says. Do not argue. Touch their hearts. General Eaton—pardon me, but you must get your command into motion. Sound the *pas de charge. Now!*"

Eaton wiped his flushed forehead. "Gentlemen! Mr. Davies, I'll ask you to come with me."

Through the furnace of the sunlight, he led the way to his tent, stared at by the drowsy Greeks who hugged the shade. Letting the entrance flap drop behind them, he poured himself a cup of wine, gulping it down.

"You'll not have one, Paul?" He hesitated, putting the cup down. "Two weeks ago Hamet Pasha detached two riders, to make all speed to the Bomba rendezvous. I think he was losing confidence even then. They did not rejoin. By now we must allow that they were captured or killed. I did not want it reported in the camp. You are a civilian, and unacquainted with the country. Someone must make another try. As the colonel suggests, Selim would have the best chance of success."

Eaton's stupor of weariness, Eugene's dislike of him, Farquhar's indifference, all linked together against Paul. The boy's sandy head went up in challenge and his lean brown hand clenched against his sides.

"I have the best reason for going."

"May I ask what that is?"

"My brother is one of the prisoners in Tripoli. He is—" he forced the words through his clenched teeth—"William Bainbridge."

"Captain Bainbridge? Of the *Philadelphia*?" At first Eaton was puzzled, then sharply skeptical. "Why, his brother must be the lieutenant, in Syracuse, or Malta. Much younger, I believe. Yes, he was with Decatur when they burned the frigate. And—"

He paused, remembering that Lt. Bainbridge had fought the notorious duel at Malta. "And in the bombardment of Tripoli," he said instead, "the gunboats—"

Paul's fists knotted, and his lips stiffened. "I had gunboat Number Five."

Eaton's tired eyes narrowed in thought. Number Five had failed to close with the enemy, for some reason.

In Paul's mind the picture was clear, of the line of small improvised bombardment vessels moving through with the reefs toward the gray fortifications rising above harbor—of the yard stripped from the mast of his vessel by a chance shot from the forts. He had made every effort to steer the drifting boat, until it struck on a submerged reef within range of the forts. He had fallen behind the battle line that Decatur handled so brilliantly, and had almost lost his ship.

"Young Decatur mentioned you in his report," Eaton observed, still uncertain that the boy before him was Bainbridge the naval officer.

"Aye, sir. He stated, '*I regret that Lt. Bainbridge's boat, being disabled, prevented him being equally successful.*'"

Macdonough, Tripp, and the others had been successful. They had won that first futile engagement of an American fleet in the Old World. Even with their miniature unhandy craft, they had an instinct for doing the right thing under fire.

His brother had surrendered, in that same trap of a harbor. And his own name had become a byword from Malta to Gibraltar.

When Eaton, convinced of his identity, asked him sharply how he managed to appear in civilian dress on the African shore, he explained mechanically that he had taken advantage of a month's leave to hurry to join the land venture being fitted out at Alexandria. The name he had taken, Paul Davies, was a family name.

"Your month's leave will have expired."

"Aye, sir."

Eaton studied the boy, curiously. "Lieutenant, you've had two tries at the Barbary coast, and you want to go on with a third? I understand about your brother. If we fail this time, you'll be in hot water with Commodore Barron. If we succeed—"

Instinctively the older man reached for the wine. His long jaw thrust out. "Barron's lying up in hospital. Some dysentery. God knows where our ships are."

Paul did not explain that he himself was supposed to be on sick leave. Older men, veterans of the last war, would give consent easier after they had said their say.

"In their offices," exclaimed Eaton, "they can't know what we face along the Barbary coast. If only we had not lost the Patriarch, in his tomb."

"Aye, sir," nodded Paul hopefully, wondering who *they* might be.

"Time was, a year ago, I tried to tell them in Washington that we must meet the aggressions of the Barbary savages and pirates by retaliation." The New Englander raised his voice as if defying his political opponents. "The Secretary held that we'd better pay tribute. We should not commit an outward act of war. Even Mr. Madison predicted, instead, a political millennium in the United States—arising from the goodness and integrity of mind of Mr. Jefferson, who was to move all nations by his persuasive virtue and mastery skill in diplomacy." His hot blue eyes focused again on the boy. "To hell with diplomacy! If I succeed, and William Bainbridge is freed, I do not know what will happen to me. If I fail, I haven't a doubt the blame will be mine alone."

When he paused, Paul put in quickly: "Aye, sir. May I have a horse to start at once for the rendezvous with Hull?"

Eaton nodded, and looked at his watch. With shrewd caution he added: "Lieutenant, you'd better keep your—family name."

On returning to the council, Eaton explained that Paul, who was actually a lieutenant in the American Navy, would be the one to go ahead to the ships. To Paul's surprise, Eugene accepted this after a second's thought. "*Bien*," he said.

He was more surprised when, after a musket and powder-flask, with a bag of dry meat and rice, had been handed over to him, Eugene appeared, leading his powerful gray, saddled. A good horse.

When he mounted the gray, Marie was not to be seen. Selim, who had been deep in talk with the Tyrolese, also swung himself into a saddle, flinging his cloak behind it. The janizary had a musket slung over his broad back. "Your eyes, younker," explained Eugene, his mustache lifting in a grin. "I have told him of the landmarks."

Eaton nodded. "It's a task for more than one."

A moment later Eugene said: "Your tongue—to communicate with Selim." By the rein he led a wiry Arab pony on which Marie Anne perched sidewise. She had her scarf over her head, her bundle roped behind her.

To Paul, Eugene whispered: "Now you will take care, younker. Do not separate. Do not let your woman out of your sight." For an instant he stared up at them. *"Kinder!"* he exclaimed. "Children!"

And he led them through the camp, shouting out something in a language unknown to Paul. Farquhar waved his hat to Marie, calling out: *"Bonne chance!"*

"Marie," Paul said, "you're a fool."

Apparently she had not heard him. She was humming, *"Mironton, mironton. Malbrouk s'en va t'en guerre*—You think, Lieutenant, that the camp is safer for me? Have you forgotten that I once asked to go on a ship?"

He thought about that, while she hummed softly.

Chapter Seven

Early in the afternoon when they were climbing the shallow ravine that opened up the heights, he thought about something else. In the shadow, keeping out of the glare of the sun, Selim reined in and held up his hand. Paul had been following where the broad back of the janizary led.

"He wants you to listen," Marie interpreted, "to his drum."

With the horses quiet, Paul could catch the faint tapping of the saddle drum. Going to where he had a sight of the half-moon bay and the rubble of ruins far below, he saw something that made him whistle.

Sunlight flickered on the brass of the field gun in motion. A dark queue of human beings strung out behind the gun, and tawny camels brought up the rear. A tiny animated spot on the gray sweep of the coast below him. Something had started Eaton's force forward again.

After a while he asked Marie: "What was he calling out when he led you through the camp?"

She squirmed in the saddle before answering. "'Maggots get up from your dungheaps and look. This—this girl child is riding ahead of you to Derna.' And then he told me to sing something gay."

Paul grinned. Eugene, after all, had produced a sign of his own, to get the column going again. He had played a trick. He had shamed the men by the sight of the girl riding off ahead of them.

On the bare shoulders of the mountain, Selim the janizary took command without a word. Out of sight of the sea, he forced the horses cruelly, heading into the glare of sunset, squinting at landmarks Paul could not make out: stagnant water lying in a pit of a red rock gorge; a dark ridge where wild fennel grew, to stay the hunger of the beasts.

He served as their eyes. When gray wisps floated away on the skyline beside them, Selim's sun-darkened head turned to inspect the running gazelles. A moment, and they had vanished in a fold of the earth. But when something tawny stirred against gray rocks ahead of them, the soldier slid from his saddle. Throwing his rein to Marie, he ran on crouching, priming the pan of the musket he took from its sling.

When Paul joined him, thinking that he had sighted enemies, the janizary gripped the boy's arm, scowling. Dropping to his knees, he laid his musket across a standing stone and sighted carefully. At the shot, wings threshed in the nest of boulders beyond them. Drawing his long curved knife Selim dashed forward and threw himself on a great bird, slashing off its head.

It was a bustard. They managed to eat some of its flesh—Selim chewing avidly at his portion. Then for the first time he lingered, allowing the horses to breathe. Going away a few steps, he spread out the cloak that also served him for a blanket.

On his cloak the giant of a man acted strangely. Facing away from the sun, he laid down his short sword and knife. From his belly he unwrapped a length of white felt which he folded and set upon his shaven head, to hang down behind like an empty bag. Making a motion as if washing his hands, he raised his voice in a cry that Paul had heard often: "God the merciful, the all-powerful—"

With his evening prayer finished to his satisfaction, the janizary swaggered over to talk cheerfully to Marie.

"His heart is good now," she explained, "because he has on his *kalpak*, which is his hat. He could not wear it until now, because the Turks might have seen it and beaten him to death as a deserter. Now, when the

Tripolitans see it, they will know he is a janizary, which is an old infantry soldier, like the Guards."

"Has he seen any sign of a Barbary force?"

Laughing, Selim shook his head.

"He says no. If they saw him now, ten Tripolitans would run away from him. He called them dog-born dogs."

She translated dutifully, word for word. Silent, she rode beside Paul under the half-moon that gave only a fitful light. When the exhausted horses stopped to crop at green growth, Marie's head dropped in a stupor of sleep. As long as the janizary wanted to push on, Paul could not halt to sleep.

At need, he reflected, he could not force obedience from the soldier. At most, he might persuade Selim, by Marie's help, to carry out an order. And he began to understand that Selim was careless of danger. The man, Marie made clear, was trying to find a way to his home somewhere in the Serbian mountains across the sea. "He has not seen it for six years."

It was strange to think that the janizary with the scarred animal-like head actually had a home. Marie managed to find out things like that . . .

Paul had his first sight of an enemy the next noon, when they halted on a headland, and he searched the horizon for any sign of the American ships.

Pointing down beneath them, Selim said: "Tobruk."

A strip of the coast showed, where a mud-walled village circled a tiny harbor. Among the smacks moored there Paul recognized the lines of a slender vessel with its yard lowered to the deck—the xebec that had followed Eaton's command.

"Lieutenant, you are seeing ghosts," Marie retorted. "I see only harmless fishermen."

Paul shook his head, wondering if the scout vessel had cut in to escape observation by the *Argus*. From this haven of Tobruk to the very rock of Gibraltar, the Barbary powers lay sheltered by their landlocked ports, hidden and insatiable, drawing sustenance from Africa behind them, and levying tribute on the commerce of the sea. The xebec, which looked to the casual eye like a fishing craft, could strike like a serpent.

"Well, it can do us no harm now," said Marie.

By sunset it seemed as if they had escaped any harm. Ahead of them rose the pyramid peak that Paul remembered as towering over the gulf of Bomba. Selim, too, picked out his last landmark—a miracle of green, an island of foliage in the waste. He chanted its name, the Well of the Gazelles. He described its water, bubbling up from the rocks and flowing in a stream.

The stumbling horses scented moisture on the wind and thrust out sweat-flecked heads. Not for six weeks had beast or man come upon a flowing spring. The ache and fever of thirst sharpened in them, as they rode into a stand of poplars, with high grass underfoot.

The Well of the Gazelles lay in a natural cistern of eroded rock, flecked by shade. Selim, urging his mount ahead, started to swing down to the pool. Then he paused, motionless.

"*Ahai!*" he shouted, and turned in the saddle to strike at the head of Marie's pony and turn it back.

In the clear water floated two bodies. Their limbs spread out, their heads bent down as if trying to peer under them. They had been stripped of clothing.

When Marie had drawn away, the janizary pulled out the nearest body, finding it cold to the touch, but not long dead. Attentively he examined the mottled face from which the eyeballs projected. With difficulty he pulled loose a thin silk cord that, knotted under the chin, had strangled the man.

"*Pashalik,*" he growled, pointing from the body back toward the east. The two had been the riders of Hamet Pasha, who had failed to rejoin the command. They had been killed not long since, and left where Eaton would find them, if he got that far.

They drank heavily of the cold water, after piling loose stones on the dead Arabs. As they climbed from the oasis up to the headland overlooking the coast, they saw no signs of human beings near them. The flame of sunset crept higher, lighting the natural towers of rock along their way.

Coming out on the far slope several hundred feet above the sea, Paul examined the line of the horizon slowly. The sea was turning dark as the glow faded to an amber hue on the higher clouds. No ship was visible.

Until the first stars showed, southerly, Paul waited, reckoning that Hull might have taken the *Argus* far off the shore, with a stiff breeze blowing. The sea had looked choppy. The cautious Hull might not have cared to anchor for the night.

When he set about gathering what wood he could find, Selim came close to peer at him, and then to stand in his way exclaiming.

"He will have no fire lighted," the girl explained wearily. "It will show

up and down the coast, and draw the Tripolitans to us. He thinks they
are not far away."

Paul knew that to be true. But it was necessary to light a beacon at once,
so long as it might possibly be noticed by a lookout at sea.

The beacon also must be clear and bright. When he had struck sparks
from the flint and pan of his musket into a sprinkling of powder, and the
flames ate into his pile of combustibles, Selim snarled and picked up his
musket to strike out the blaze. He had been sullen since he had seen no
American vessel awaiting them.

Paul did not try to hold the janizary back. Instead, he stepped between
him and the fire, with his musket across his knees. The big man hesitated, and the blaze caught, whirling up from the brittle thorn-bush. In a
moment they were framed against its glow.

Shots flashed at them, from near at hand. Sparks flew up as a bullet
struck the burning wood. Paul thought the shots came from three or four
weapons, from the side behind the screen of darkness.

A glance showed him that the ground around the fire offered no cover.
"Uphill!" he called and motioned to Selim.

Keeping Marie between them, they ran from the circle of light, into
masses of boulders and rubble. Above them the glow revealed the face
of a cliff.

No more shots came out of the night. Paul imagined their unseen ad-
versaries reloading calmly, watching their scrambling climb up the treacherous broken rock. He halted Selim to listen, and heard nothing.

"We can't climb much farther," whispered Marie.

Paul nodded. Below them their beacon flared bright. He thought: *They
came from the well and waited to close in on us; now they must be waiting for darkness again, to attack here.*

Already they had led off the horses, or the beasts had run off, frightened by the shots. While Paul tried to renew the priming of his musket,
his hand shaking with excitement, the light began to fade. The fire was
burning out.

Selim crouched listening, trusting to his ears, not his eyes. Although
the three of them had made a great clatter in their dash up the slope, their
enemies had made no sound to disclose their position.

Paul realized that his own position was bad as could be, and that he
had only a few moments to remedy it. Marie was sitting passive by him,
her face a white blur turned up to him. She had found a long flat stone to

sit on. And he noticed the edges of other flat stones ascending like steps behind her.

Instinctively he glanced up. Above the peculiar stones a dark patch showed in the sheer wall of rock. A cleft or cavern it must be—except that it seemed to be square.

When the fire below them dimmed to embers, he touched Selim's arm. Pulling the girl to her feet, he led her up the course of stones, feeling his way around loose rocks. After a moment his foot came down on a level space of stone, and he could make out nothing in front of him, although his shoulder brushed against smooth rock. The cliff seemed to open here in front of them.

Before the boy could investigate further, the janizary gripped him in sudden warning. Paul could see nothing beyond the muzzle of his musket. But he heard movement outside in the darkness below him.

On either side a faint rasping of stones drew closer. Aiming blindly at the sounds, Paul fired his musket—glimpsing by the flash the shapes of crouching men and the gleam of metal below.

Selim did otherwise. With an ear-splitting yell he swung his musket at the climbers and leaped after it, his scimitar rasping out of its sheath. His war cry resounded again, and loose stones slid away beneath him. A man yelped, and another voice barked a command. The racket diminished into silence.

Presently the janizary climbed back, panting and carrying his musket again. He rumbled excitedly.

"He says," Marie interpreted, faintly, "he killed one or two, but the others ran away."

Whatever the janizary had done, he had startled and driven back their invisible assailants. The slope below them remained quiet.

Paul availed himself of the respite to examine their niche in the cliff, finding it to be a dozen feet deep and oddly square. Since the opening was no wider than the stretch of his arms, he started piling the loose stones into a barricade at the edge. Selim helped him silently, and it pleased Paul that the janizary accepted his leadership, in even a small thing like that. But it puzzled him that some of the stones should be square, obviously shaped by man-made tools.

At the same time Marie discovered that the center of their crypt was occupied by something massive and hollow made of smooth marble.

It felt like a long chest, as high as the boy's waist. The top of the chest lay broken in several parts on the floor, which was littered with debris of tiles and bricks. Paul had never encountered anything like the vast marble chest. He tried to jest about it. "We will put you in it, mademoiselle, if our fort is attacked again."

Her low laugh echoed in the darkness. "Be careful! You might put me in my grave."

This space around them that he had walled in so carefully she thought to be an empty tomb, one of the many that honeycombed the heights in Africa. The marble chest she called a sarcophagus.

It made the strange girl merry, that he should not have guessed how he had got them into a tomb, which might hold them forever.

"Have you no fear?" he demanded.

She became quiet. "I am sick with fear," she admitted, her voice taut. "But you and Selim are doing what you can. There is nothing more we can do." After a moment she said as if to herself: "If the help of God comes to us, then we will not be harmed."

When he thought she had gone to sleep, he heard her whispering and went closer to hear.

"*Holy Mary of the Seas,*" Marie was praying, "*give aid. Thou who dwellest in the stars, hear me . . .*"

Quietly he moved back to the entrance of the tomb. Marie had her religion, and she seemed to believe that prayer would aid them in some way—when they had nothing to eat but shreds of dry meat tucked away in Selim's girdle, and no water to suffer their aching throats to get down the hard meat. They were cut off from the sea, cornered where the Tripolitans could be reinforced from the countryside.

Two days must pass, Paul reckoned, before Eaton's column could reach the gulf of Bomba.

Although he stared out into the haze of moonlight until it danced like mist before his tortured eyes, he could perceive no movement on the slope beyond the tomb. As the moon swung westward, the stone lintel over the entrance took shape, with a pattern cut into it. The pattern formed into Greek letters, Paul thought.

He felt then as if he had visited the site before, although he had never been ashore at Bomba. Something about the tomb on the mountainside facing the sea was familiar . . . Eugene's words—the treasure trove, the gold-plated walls, and the jewel-inlaid sarcophagus of the African princess, Cleopatra. There was little left of such a treasure because it had been broken into, ages before.

Then he remembered that Eugene had passed this spot on the coast, and must have noticed the entrance of the ravaged tomb. Why, then, had the Tyrolese hinted at loot to be found here? It was another riddle that Paul was too weary to solve.

Beneath him Selim lay on his cherished cloak, breathing evenly, sleeping as calmly as if the three of them were not pinned on a cliff under the watch of the outposts of Derna . . . Eugene had called the place the Tomb of the Outlander.

At a touch on his shoulder, Paul lifted his head with an effort to look out into morning mist that cleared slowly to reveal no vessel standing in to the white line of the heavy swell.

Beyond the low wall of stones Selim and Marie were motioning to him, kneeling over a flat slab of marble.

"A gift of water," she called to him.

The marble was a portion of the lid of the sarcophagus, lying in the vine-covered rubble outside. A shallow trough had been incised in its surface, and the trough still held a little rainwater. This had been meant for the birds, Marie said. Sometimes those who planned their stone caskets ordered such hollows made so that the birds might find water there for ages.

It cheered her to find what she called a gift. Paul thought of the clear spring within a mile of them that they could not attempt to reach. They could only sit in their crypt and wait for the Tripolitans to appear in force. Then they would have no alternative but surrender.

When the sun burned away the mist, he looked for a long time at one point in the haze along the skyline. Out of the haze a ship appeared with tops'ls set in what he took to be a light breeze. When he was certain, he said: "There is the brig *Argus*, standing in."

Leisurely and gracefully the dark vessel with the crowded white canvas ran the length of the gulf and back, keeping her offing. By her actions Paul knew that Isaac Hull was searching for the men who had made the signal the night before. A masthead lookout could have observed no more than a splinter of light on the horizon. Probably officers who had telescopes on the afterdeck were patiently studying the bare escarpment of the coast, puzzled because the signal had not been repeated.

All morning the shore below the tomb had been deserted. If the Tripolitans had remained, after the appearance of the ship, they were careful to keep out sight.

Just before noon the *Argus* came into the wind and swayed up a boat. Pulling away, the boat headed for the shore at a point near the Well of the Gazelles. The oars moved leisurely, as if the cutter were performing some routine duty. Evidently that duty was not to replenish water casks, because the cutter turned to follow the shore without approaching it.

Selim watched it with impassive curiosity, while Marie, lying against the barricade, questioned Paul impulsively. Were not the Americans coming to shore? Couldn't some signal be made to bring them in?

To all the questions he shook his head. One cutter's crew would not be apt to risk a landing. He imagined Hull, puzzled by the silence of the shore, warning the officer at the tiller not to venture within musket shot. Hull handled his ship and crew with efficiency.

Nor could the men in the cutter distinguish any waving of clothes on the face of the cliff, almost a mile distant. They would be watching the beaches—

As the cutter neared him, Paul made his decision. It seemed impossible that any of their antagonists could be hidden still in the boulders below their vantage point. He had been marking the course of a brush-strewn gully that led down to the water. In five minutes, that could bring him out within sight of the boat, which would be passing it.

When he explained that to the girl, she pointed to the slab of marble, saying: "We have water. Can't we wait?"

He had only a few moments to act. Unreasoning hope buoyed him. She lay without moving, whimpering a little as if in distress, and he did not think until afterward that she had grown too weak to stand up.

As he crawled down from the ledge, his musket slung over his shoulder, a fever of eagerness gripped him. Although his feet slipped on the smooth rocks and he had to catch at the brush to keep from falling, he heard nothing else stirring near him.

The gully proved to be the dry bed of a stream. When he thought he was close to the shore, he began to run. Scrambling through boulders, he dropped heavily into a sandy hollow. He heard the wash of the sea.

Then he saw the man lying in his way. A lean body, face down without any weapon—wounded or asleep.

Taking his musket in his hand, Paul walked to the prone figure and bent over it, tensed to swing down the butt of the gun if the man moved.

As he did so, he heard the swift impact of feet behind him. Instantly the figure beneath him twisted over. A brown arm lashed up at him with a knife. Paul warded the sweep of the blade with his gun.

Then he was struck between the shoulders, the blow sickening him. Arms grappled him, and sharp metal thrust deep under his ribs. He found himself on his knees in the sand, and he heard voices arguing above him.

He strained to pull himself up. Then to his surprise he found he could not move. A foot thrust against his shoulder, turning him over.

Against the glare of the sky four heads wrapped in gleaming cloths bent over him. Hadjali's foot stirred him curiously, as if he had been a trapped animal.

Chapter Eight

One of the oarsmen in the cutter sighted movement in the shallow ravine as they passed. He told the officer at the tiller that it looked like a gray horse loaded with a pack. But when the officer, Midshipman George Washington Mann, observed the mouth of the ravine, he could make out nothing moving. He held the cutter on its course, carrying out his orders to observe the shore for a recognition signal.

His orders carried out, Midshipman Mann rejoined his vessel and reported in a voice that he tried to keep deep and sonorous that he had made out no sign of friend or enemy within the African wilderness. Flushed with excitement, he held himself stiff in his short jacket and flowing tie before the commander, who at the mature age of twenty-two had been at sea for eight years, and in action against the enemy.

For a chance at such action Midshipman Mann would have offered up his right hand cheerfully. Instead, he had been kept on the *Argus* for six weeks, everlastingly holding within sight the landmark of a solitary pyramid peak.

The next morning, in fair sailing weather, they sighted movement on shore far to the east. The telescope picked up scattered men approaching like grazing animals, stooping to pick at the ground. Except for tiny specks that were blue coats among them, and the glint of metal from a field gun, there was nothing to identify them as General Eaton's force.

When the cutter was beached at the east point of the gulf, Midshipman Mann went ashore, to be greeted by wildly shouting Arabs and an officer of Marines who had lost the buttons from his coat.

Holding out his hand, the officer said: "Trade you this for salt pig, beans, barley, and brandy." His hand held wisps of dusty fennel. "Two days' rations, George."

The voice issuing from the clay-stained figure with the scrub of a beard on its sun-blackened head was that of Lt. Presley N. O'Bannon, detailed at Alexandria to escort General Eaton.

"Aye-aye, sir," piped the midshipman worshipfully.

Marie was conscious that friendly Arabs swarmed over the barricade of stones and ransacked the tomb noisily, churning among broken bricks and pottery as if searching for something. They besieged Selim with their cries, who swore by the ninety and nine holy names of Allah that he had driven a hundred Tripolitans from the tomb.

Then the unwearied janizary was carrying her down the slope where Paul had ventured out to the ship, and had disappeared. Selim edged around a nest of boulders and set her down in a sandy hollow where two of their Bedouins squatted to peer at a crisscross of tracks.

These desert men explained that their herds had been left to graze near the dead city, and that they had followed the Drub-Devil for nearly three days without food. But the tracks of the valuable horses held their eyes. One horse of the six, they declared, had been shod. And one man of the five who entered the hollow had worn shoes instead of slippers.

Taking up sand from a dark patch on the ground, the Bedouins sniffed it and swore that blood had run into the sand here. Selim and Marie recognized Paul's tracks, knowing that he had been taken off by the riders—still alive, Selim thought, or his body would have been stripped and left for the vultures.

The Bedouins hurried off after the horse tracks, looking like a pair of vultures themselves, hoping to come upon some discarded article or a stray beast. Marie did not want to look at the stains in the trampled sand where ants swarmed. When Selim brought her fresh water and grapes in two new shining cups, she felt better. He said there were two ships now instead of one, and piles of stones on the beach, and she should go and eat more. Himself, he thirsted for a taste of the wine in the Americans' kegs.

"Selim," she asked, "these watchers of Tripoli—will they take him with them to Derna?"

Impatiently the janizary nodded. "*Aiwah!* They will question him, a prisoner, and then perhaps they will sell him. Eh, they caught him like a sheep."

On the beach where excited throngs gathered around the clean-look-ing sailors and the boats, Marie searched until she found Eugene argu-ing with a knot of Arabs. He waved to her and freed himself to rush over and hug her. "The little Marie!" he exclaimed. "Out of the tomb, you are safe!" His mustache twitched, and he laughed. "By Salbal and Bathbal, half of our army has been scratching at the *Kbour Roumyah* for gold and gems, and finding nothing. Did I tell them the tomb would be lined with gold? Well, they marched faster because of it. Loot! It is the best hope. *Enfin*, now we can pay them Spanish silver dollars from the American sea captains."

Gorging themselves with food and good wine, the wearied men thought of nothing else. No one asked her where Paul was. She found Eaton apart, talking gravely with young officers from the ships, and he did not heed her until she explained how Paul was missing. "Ah! Master Comman-dant Hull sighted his fire." Eaton's jaw thrust out stubbornly. "Marie, the Lieutenant—Paul—undertook this mission against my advice. He claimed it, by right."

"What right?"

"He felt—" the New Englander hesitated, glancing at the other offi-cers—"an obligation to do it. I cannot reveal the nature of the obligation, except that Paul wished to render aid to his brother, an officer unfortu-nately captive in Tripoli, and facing a Court of Inquiry."

Out of his hurried words she grasped that *something* had drawn Paul along the coast, not thinking of her or of himself, to the blood-stained ravine.

"He reminded me," Eaton went on quickly, "before leaving, of a certain promise he had made you, mademoiselle—of a passage on one of our ves-sels. And I am sure that Master Commandant Hull will be able to afford you shelter on the *Argus*." To the elder officer he said briefly. "Mademoi-selle D'Aliermont, who has been a material help to us on the march."

The American commandant had nice eyes and an assured manner.

"If we can be of service to Mademoiselle—" He left it at that. If he was surprised at meeting a waif of a woman, he did not show it. Yet he waited for Eaton to give him a direct instruction.

"You can, Hull. She'll be safer on the brig, whatever happens."

Marie recognized the ship, anchored beyond the schooner, as the one on which she had longed to embark at Alexandria. And here, on a beach of Barbary, they offered to take her out to the brig.

With half a curtsy, she smiled up at them. "Thank you, General Eaton—and you, Commandant." Then, hesitating, she asked: "The army—it will go on to Derna?"

Eaton's head, shaggy with uncut hair, thrust forward. "I shall endeavor to do so, mademoiselle."

Stubbornly he spoke, more to the naval officers than to her. Listening to the low talk of the three, Marie realized that Eaton's plans had been shattered.

The *Argus* had brought him the stores of food and some money, but not the reinforcement of the hundred American Marines he counted on, or the field guns he had promised to Selim's cannoneers. Not a musket or a cannonball or one bullet to be landed at Bomba.

Nothing of the kind had been issued to Hull at the Syracuse base. Even O'Bannon and his squad were expected to rejoin the ship.

Hull could not act against his orders. In issuing those orders, his superiors at Syracuse and Washington evidently believed that the hot-headed New Englander had gone too far and would fail.

"They sleep in their beds," Eaton stammered; "they sit at desks, hear gossip, read scandal in their daily journals . . . How can they know what it means to be a human being in Africa—"

His mutterings were silenced by news that sent a stab of fear into the girl. Leitensdorfer and Selim appeared with the pair of Bedouins who had followed the trail of the horses. They had taken a prisoner—one of the Tripolitans who had remained behind to observe the movements of the strange American force.

The prisoner had revealed—Eugene did not explain how he had been persuaded to talk—that the Bey of Tripoli had sent an army to Derna. "Its strength might be five hundred or a thousand. It was hurrying to reach the Derna seaport before the Americans could appear. Perhaps in two days, the prisoner believed, this relief army would reach the city.

"Do you believe that?" Eaton demanded.

"Selim believes," Eugene nodded heavily. "*Ja*, it is so."

Sensing the New Englander's incredulity, he hesitated. "I tell you why, messieurs. By the mountain Eisch we had a tale about a *Lindwurm*—a dragon that came out of its cave to seize and devour sheep and good people. So! No one pursued this dragon into its cave. All the people certainly were afraid of the dragon, because it roared and made fire in the entrance of the cave. Now there was one younker, a boy with a small spear. Alone of the people, he thought about the dragon, and once when it was away, this younker ran into the cave and waited for it there with his spear." Rubbing the polished bowl of his pipe, he added: "In the cave the dragon was afraid of the boy."

The Tyrolese nodded thoughtfully. "That dragon of the tale is like the Barbary corsairs. So long as it hid in the cave and made flame, it was safe—is it not so? These Barbary-*volk* shelter themselves in their ports, deep in the land. Now if you also come into the land and into the port of Derna, then Tripoli will be afraid—also Tunis and Algiers. *Ja*, I think they have sent the army to drive you away, into the sea."

Yet Eugene did not chuckle as usual at his own story. He seemed unwilling to say what was in his mind.

Isaac Hull asked quietly, "Will Hamet and his Arabs go on with you, General Eaton?"

Instead of answering, Eaton moved away, walking with an effort. Passing Marie, he looked at her and asked her to come with him to interpret what he had to say—he knew so little Arabic, except for swearing at camelmen. They had to go around the knots of men lying asleep, their bodies cooled with water. For two months they had not had their clothes off, and now that they could rest safely under the guns of the brig and schooner they slept where they lay. Eaton muttered: "What was the name of Eugene's mountain? The *Eisch*? Well, Marie, the Connecticut River runs over its rapids, in verdant foliage. Aye, between elm trees."

At Hamet's shelter, he pulled himself together with his old jauntiness. The Arab chieftain lay on a robe of black felt, hot with fever. His officers sat by him without rising, their thin faces impassive. Like judges, Marie thought, in ragged robes. Eaton seated himself on a stone, heedless of the sun's glare.

"Hamet Karamanli, Pasha," he said, "I am only one man, a sentinel of an outpost."

Marie, anxious, could give his words easily, because they were simple. The Arabs did not look at her, a woman.

And Eaton astonished her. Instead of arguing, he told them of that outpost of his country as he dreamed it might be. Perhaps a fort would be built, perhaps even a haven of a port for ships to come in under the American flag.

"That flag would provide a refuge," he said. "Under its protection, refugees would be immune from arrest or capture."

Across from the island of Malta and the ancient ports of Sicily, this outpost of the New World might serve to keep commerce free from raids of the corsairs or the exactions of the Spaniards and the demands of the Emperor. Hamet, as ruler, would have the protection of the United States, as a most favored nation. If that single outpost could stand here, people would come in for its protection. In time the old evil order of the Mediterranean would change, like a plague-stricken lazarhouse, when clean air is let in from a single window.

"That is what I am fighting for," Eaton said. "Not to win a battle at Derna. I am going on, with what force I have. Will Hamet, who is my friend, accompany me?"

The sick Arab glanced at his officers and lay back in silence. As minutes passed, Eaton's words that described his dream seemed boastful; they merged into the silence of the limestone cliffs.

"Have I not come as far as this place?" Hamet asked at last, twisting the beads of his rosary in his fingers. "The American vessels are here. But the aid you expected from them is not. Without that aid it would be useless to go on against the fortifications of Derna and the army of Tripoli. Without it, I will not go on."

Eaton understood before Marie could translate. Evidently the two leaders had spoken often together of the matter. He said, "Wait," and went back to his officers.

Except for the boat crews they were the only ones awake. When Eaton had reported Hamet's decision to Hull, he turned to Eugene. "What is your advice, Colonel?"

Eugene brushed at his mustache and wagged his head.

"As military engineer, dervish, or honest Tyrolese-coffeehouse-keeper?"

Eaton's bloodshot eyes smoldered.

"This may be life or death. I asked the question of Colonel Leitensdorfer."

"*Bien.* As I have seen Derna, General Eaton, you also have seen it: a battery on the shore, walls with loopholes. In the *Bilad*—the castle, more cannon. The governor, the Bey of Derna, commands perhaps six hundred men. The rest of the population will take no part for him or for us. Make the reckoning yourself. We have lost one of seventy men. So. We have sixty-nine souls to rely upon."

Irritably Eugene shook his head. "Even if we can march the seventy miles to Derna before the other army can arrive, we must have a battery of guns to use against the walls." His plump finger stabbed at the solitary brass nine-pounder, surrounded by sleeping men. "One toy only we have. A battery we must have."

Eaton asked: "O'Bannon?"

The Kentuckian eyed the end of the cheroot he had borrowed from Hull. "Can't manage to haul anymore guns. No way. Not if we are lightin' out smart for Derna."

In the silence that followed, Isaac Hull stirred restlessly. "Forty cannon, ranging from nine to twenty-four pounders, might serve to support your advance, Colonel Leitensdorfer?" he asked.

"*Gerechter Herr Gott!* Is it that you do not English understand? One battery! Four guns. Not forty."

"I said forty."

While Eaton had been absent, Isaac Hull had been studying the remnant of an expedition, strewn along the beach. At Syracuse he had been instructed to use his efforts to protect the lives of the Americans on shore, but not to risk his three small vessels in Eaton's mad enterprise. To keep safely within his orders, he should evacuate Eaton and the Marines here at the rendezvous, leaving the unknown missing man to his fate.

But under Hull's dour caution there lurked a devil of impulse. He had to strain to keep the devil properly under hatches.

"From Mantua to the Pyramids," the Tyrolese was declaiming, "I have waged war against the Emperor, and for him, but never have I seen the angels of Heaven bring up ten batteries of guns."

Hull's temper surged. "The brig *Argus* mounts eighteen guns, the schooner *Nautilus* fourteen, and the sloop *Hornet* eight. I think all of them can be brought into an action upon the shore."

Eugene puffed deep at his pipe, struck by the young officer's tone more than by his offer. A ship's broadside, he knew, might pound another vessel at short range but was not meant for distant targets on shore.

Looking up quickly, Eaton asked: "Can you get three or even two of those guns ashore?"

"*Nautilus* has a pair of wheeled carriages for two long twelves." Hull thought for a moment. "They might be got off in the cutters."

Marie could not understand what the Yankee officers meant about moving guns. The lieutenant of the schooner, with the face of a handsome schoolboy, put in his word about molding bullets for the expedition, and

sewing bags into cartridges on the way to Derna. The child in the neat blue
jacket, who had edged closer, listened as if to the whisper of a prayer.

But she knew they were going on with their march. In some way the
ships were going to join the marcher.

His face flushed, Midshipman Mann ventured to break in on the discussion of the senior officers. "I beg leave to volunteer for this expedition."

Carefully Isaac Hull tore two blank pages from his notebook, handing
one to O'Bannon and one to the boy. When a quill and ink had been produced, the two wrote out their formal requests on the pages.

"*Camp 21st April 1805*," the Marine scrawled, spelling out words pain-
fully. "*Sir, Unwilling to abandon an expedition, this far conducted, I have
to request your permission to continue with Mr. Eaton during his stay on
land.*" Then he added "*Or, at least until we arrive at Derna.*"

The midshipman penned eager phrases to explain that he was not trying to leave his service in the ship, but to contribute his services: "*In general to the Interest of my Country . . . I am aware that objections may
be made from sentiments generally entertained as to the issue of the
expedition.*"

With her bundle opened and a hand mirror propped beneath her, Marie
Anne forced a comb through the tangle of her hair, while she scrutinized
her reflection intently. She beheld peeling skin and thin chapped lips, and
she wondered how she could restore even a trace of prettiness for the officers on the brig.

She tried not to look at the book that lay on the valise at her knees, because it had been Paul's. The picture in it was of a forlorn pilgrim, bending under a heavy bundle—and Paul carried a secret of sadness with him.
He was injured, besides, and she knew he might die. To think about that
was like pressing pain into her—foolishly.

"We have a babe in arms with us now," Farquhar's amused voice proclaimed. "A mighty midshipmite. Are all Americans under age?"

Comb in hand, she smiled up at him instinctively. Even if not as assured as Hull, the Englishman was gay.

"I'm sorry about Paul," he said. Then he noticed the comb and mirror.
"How old are you, mademoiselle?"

"As old as Cleopatra."

"As lovely as Cleopatra."

Deftly he aided her in her rude toilet. Eaton was getting his command into motion again, bidding them push on to a well of good water ten miles on. Eugene was handing out rolls of silver Spanish dollars to the Arab chieftains and the Greeks—dollars borrowed from Hull—and proclaiming that the first men to reach Derna would find loot in the governor's palace.

"Faith," laughed Farquhar, "I've heard Eugene promise that before."

Slowly the girl gathered her belongings together, her head bent over them. When Farquhar bade her good-bye, explaining that he must see to the loads, she caught his hand quickly. "You have been kind. Will you let me ride your horse, for only the two days?"

Then she slipped Paul's book into her bundle, knotting it fast, telling herself that if she did not take it, it would be left behind.

"I think," said Farquhar, "we have all gone mad. Alexander the Great was the only chap who managed to lead an army across Asia. Now I know why he drank himself to death."

And he lifted his fine voice in a quick beat of a song.

> *"Some talk of Alexander,*
> *And some of Hercules,*
> *Of Hector and Lysander—"*

Beating time with his arms, he shouted, "Selim!"

From a knot of sleepers the big janizary arose, clutching his drum. Pulling out the sticks, he began to beat the drum for assembly.

Chapter Nine

In the early morning watch of the second night, John Dent, commanding the *Nautilus*, altered his course to stand in toward the invisible African coast. At the same time he ordered lights doused along the deck where the watch still worked at running lead into the bullet molds and tying up the hot bullets into small handy bags.

The orderly waist of the schooner was encumbered by some strange gear, two of her guns being mounted on clumsy wheeled carriages, beside nine kegs of powder, sacks of cannon balls, and the chests containing the bullet bags.

The schooner heeled only slightly in the light offshore breeze. When the sky showed clear above the sunrise on his port quarter, John Dent let out a silent breath of relief. Just off his starboard bow twin fragments of islands showed; beyond them, against the monotonous gray of the coast escarpment, a spate of green became visible. That green was the valley of

Derna, fertile because a river ran through it. Near the outfall of that river, hidden in the recess of the bay, the city of Derna would lie.

"Steady as you are," he told the helmsman.

John Dent was nineteen years old and newly in command of the schooner. As he counted the powder kegs again to verify their number, it crossed his mind that the two officers who had had the *Nautilus* before him had been killed off Tripoli—one of them, Richard Somers, by an explosion of powder.

It worried Dent that he had no suitable tackle to horse to the improvised fieldpieces, when he gained touch with Eaton's force on shore.

Promptly after sunup a morning ration of rice and a few dates was laid beside Paul. A veiled girl, who had filled a jar with water at the river's edge, offered him some. He cupped his hands and leaned out from his carpeted niche to drink.

The water was still cold, and when he had sipped it, he rubbed his wet hands over his inflamed eyes and rubbed back his hair. When he had finished, the girl lifted the jar to her head, steadying it gracefully with one hand, merging into the throng passing through the city gate where the Yankee prisoner had been placed in the recess usually occupied by idle members of the guard.

He had been put there, he knew, for all these common folk to see. Women carrying out infants, and clothing to rinse in the river, donkey drivers and turbaned mullahs, peasants driving in carts of grain and fruit—they could hardly escape seeing that the American brought in by their masters the corsairs was helpless and injured, craving water like any poor soul of the fellahin.

Hadjali had cared for him well enough after his capture, giving him the gray charger to ride from the Well of the Gazelles to the cedars and date palms of Derna. There the slash under his ribs had been dressed by an Italian physician, plumper and better clad than Mendrici.

But his trousers were fouled with the blood that drew flies ceaselessly after sunrise warmed the air. Only with an effort that set him to sweating could he get to his feet and move along the shadow of the wall, stared at by his curious guards.

They gave him a blanket to pull over him when the night chill came in from the bay. By their speech he identified Sardinians, Neapolitans, French, and even some Germans among the soldiers—fugitives, renegades,

or adventurers from war-torn Europe. Some of them were undoubtedly captives like himself who had elected to do armed service for the Beys. Others, like Hadjali, had been drawn to the wealth of the Barbary ports.

While the *corvos*—the guards—carried Spanish muskets and Amer-
ican-made pistols, the townspeople were not allowed arms. They went
about their tasks lashed like animals, and as callous of hurt as animals.
They stepped out of the way when *corvos* marched down the street which
seemed to be the great street of the town leading back to the gardens and
the white walls of the governor's palace.

From the wall above Paul's niche, giant hooks projected. His guards
pointed these out, explaining that offenders were pushed from the summit
of the wall, to fall upon the hooks and die there, sometimes very slowly.
"Like fish strung up."

And like fishhooks, the points of heavy steel were barbed and clotted with
remnants of flesh. They were old and evil as the resplendent castle.

"*Douceur,*" the *corvos* begged of Paul. A sweetening, a gift. In Spanish
silver, or Venetian gold—they knew the value of all the coins, and they tried
to get him to pay for wine, or a water pipe. But he had left only the francs
and carubs in Marie's purse, and he did not want to give those away.

His inflamed body craved water.

Lying on his blanket under the eyes of the crowds, turning to ease the
throbbing ache in his side, he realized that fever was burning away his
strength. When he closed his eyes against the swarming flies, the street
around him had the sounds of his own street.

In his home at this hour he had walked out so often, careless of anything except the scent of the lilacs and the salt breath of the river where
vessels passed carrying people on casual errands or long journeys, wherever they willed to go . . . Whatever might come of it, he would find his
way out to a boat—to go home . . .

That morning, when he had given away the rice he could not eat to
one of the beggars that haunted the guard post, he found that the gate itself was being cleared. A detachment of infantry wearing fezzes aslant
arrived at the double, and formed up with bayonets fixed. Mounted spahis drove the huddles of peasants aside into alley mouths.

After them trotted grandees from the palace, splendidly horsed. Officers of the Bey, Paul guessed. Hadjali accompanied a foreigner in black
with the glint of a gold chain at his throat, who held a lace handkerchief

to his nose against the stench of the alleys. They drew rein just outside the great gate, and after a moment Hadjali called back at Paul.

"Yankee—what vessel is that?"

In his wall niche Paul could see nothing except the masts of polaccas drawn up on the shore a quarter-mile out. "Which vessel?" he asked.

Impatiently the renegade swung down from his saddle, coming over to haul the prisoner to his feet and hurry him limping out to the cavalcade. There Hadjali pointed to the east.

A mile away, off the headland that topped the valley, lay the *Nautilus*. Under the glare of the early morning sun, Paul made out a boat pulling away to shore, with the measured stroke of naval oarsmen. The boat seemed to be heavily loaded.

"*Goëlette*," he said briefly.

Hadjali snarled. "A schooner! We know it is an armed schooner. But which one, and what is its mission near Derna?"

Paul was silent. Around one of the islands he observed square tops'ls heading into the bay, and a tiny wisp of a sail escorting them. That would be the *Argus* following a sloop in.

The next moment the riders had sighted the other vessels. The foreigner spoke sharply in Spanish. Deferentially Hadjali answered. Paul caught the word "Excellency" and wondered if the stranger were an envoy from Madrid. Then he winced at the sting of a whiplash across his mouth.

"You have a tongue," Hadjali gibed. "Use it, Yankee. What armament have these vessels? And why are they so interested in entering our port? Do they wish, then, to pay a ransom for you?"

The officers, who had understood him, looked curiously at the prisoner, who merely wiped uncertainly at his mouth. Paul was blessing his stars that they did not realize they held the brother of Captain Bainbridge, who was in Tripoli.

"Our frigates," he said, "carry forty-four guns."

The renegade's dark eyes gleamed. "That also we know, my friend. We counted those we took from your flagship in Tripoli. These are no frigates—"

The cavalcade started into the street, and Hadjali hastened to mount to follow them. Passing his prisoner, he called down: "Your price is two thousand dollars, Yankee, and I have no wish to lose it. Back to your cubby with you."

Something in Paul's face amused him. "Since you understand so lit-

tle, I will inform you. Your general who marched from Alexandria so secretly has at last arrived. That schooner has been trying to land guns, and
failing to hoist them up the cliff to him. If he will have the kindness to
wait until tonight, he will surely join you with his command, after Hassan Agha arrives from Tripoli to greet him."

With a word to the nearest guard, Hadjali cantered off after his superiors. The soldier jerked his head toward Paul's niche. Stepping back,
the prisoner limped and caught the corsair's arm, as if in pain. While he
rested, he slipped the silk purse from his pocket into the man's fingers,
which closed on it swiftly, feeling the coins within it. An eye glanced
down inquiringly.

"Hassan Agha," said Paul. "Who is he?"

Fortunately the man understood a little French. He answered in mono-
syllables, while he slid the purse into his girdle. "Commandant. Army
of Tripoli. Officers of the advance." He nodded at the dust stirred up by
the horsemen.

"How great is the army of Tripoli?"

But the guard, his money safely stowed, only shook his shaven head
topped by the smart fez.

Sitting down on a stone by the water fountain, Paul cupped some water in his hand and washed his lacerated mouth. From his seat he could
watch carts hurrying out to the shore battery with powder cartridges.
Beyond the battery gleamed the blue surface of the bay, empty now of
all the corsair shipping which had crowded into the river mouth and the
line of wharfs.

Eaton must be on the height to the east. Between that and the city lay
a hollow sprinkled with fruit orchards and houses. The houses nearest
the town were being occupied by troops, who deployed among the ditches
and brush heaps, where fire from the wall would cover them.

From all around him the inhabitants were being herded back into the
streets or across the river. Paul did not like the looks of such a methodical
defense. If heavy guns were brought down the eastern slope, they might
do damage. But he thought of the single nine-pounder the Marines had
hauled across the desert . . .

The sun was almost overhead when he heard the bark of the gun and
sighted a wreath of smoke in one of the orchards halfway down the slope.
Except for the drifting smoke, the dark gardens seemed deserted and at

peace. The sound of the gun was like a faint handclap, followed by a spatter of musketry.

The single gun kept on popping stubbornly, aimed ridiculously at the side of the city.

Paul had been watching every motion of the ships. They followed a strange course—the dainty sloop, the *Hornet*, heading in to the eastward, and then coming about. The little craft drew closer to shore, as if intending to try a landing.

She came on toward the shore battery, closing in. Behind her the schooner and brig came to anchor.

The sloop kept on. The eight guns of the battery flashed, and smoke drifted back, eddying over Paul.

When he could see her again through the smoke, the *Hornet* was closing within two hundred yards of the battery. Her sail rose over the rampart where the guns flashed and slid back. At a hundred yards she let go the anchor, and her four guns went into action. The whirr of grapeshot came into the air.

At the gate the infantry scattered to take cover, and the prisoner slid to the ground. He began to crawl toward the battery as soon as he was left to himself. Small particles of shot lashed against the old walls above him.

Then he heard the guns of the *Nautilus* and the deeper note of the carronades on the *Argus*. The ships had closed in to the shore itself. Their fire was sweeping the stone bulk of the battery, the gardens, and the walls of Derna. Moving a little at a time and listening, he could interpret the reverberation of sound.

The sun slanted from the west when he caught the first change in the sounds. The battery was silenced. Its garrison was streaming back into the hollow, away from the *Hornet*.

Almost within reach of the platform of the battery, he edged himself to the right, to see across the hollow. There was nothing to see. No smoke puffed from the orchard where Eaton's cannon had taken position.

Beyond the wash of the surf the *Nautilus* lay at anchor, her sails reefed down, her guns searching the buildings wherever musketry sounded. Blue figures moved about her afterdeck, and once a telescope flashed in the sun.

Paul had a strange impression that only the three small vessels were alive in the sweep of the bay.

Up along the summits behind the city bodies of horsemen moved, coming toward the city. He could not make out what they were. He crawled up into the battery, finding the guns secure on their carriages, the powder intact in the pits, and not a man visible. The garrison had carried off their injured.

From one gun to the other he went, trying their elevator screws and touchholes. Then the sounds altered ominously. Along the west of the city the musketry fire quickened. He did not hear the broadsides of the ships. Something like a low cheer came from the sea.

Raising himself to an embrasure, he stared out at the black sloop, lying out from him like a crippled bird, her sail flapping in shreds.

Her men were clustering aft and cheering. Across the hollow other men were visible coming down from the orchard, keeping a rude line. They disappeared among the trees, under the lash of bullets from the houses.

Then they emerged in the bottom of the hollow, running down to the beach. Their dusty gray changed into the blue of the Marines and the drab coats of the Greeks. The stocky figure of Eaton, and lanky awkward O'Bannon. They ran slowly, stumbling among the rocks.

They were circling the buildings, heading for the silent battery on the shore, and Paul counted forty of them before they began to fall to the ground.

Two of them climbed to the rear of the battery, their muskets poised, the breath rasping in their bodies. Behind them panted a boy in midshipman's garb. They stared down the emplacement, and sighted Paul.

"The first and the fifth and sixth piece are charged and primed," he said. "All of them are serviceable."

The Marine let out a yip. "Jerusalem! Eight guns." With his sleeve he wiped the blood from his cheek. "Shot away the rammer out of our'n," he explained, and gripped Paul's arm. "Them cannoneers did," he insisted. "Them flummydiddlin' cannoneers shot away the rammer—"

"Easy," Paul told him. The other was a boy named Dave, from Tarrytown. "Bear a hand, Dave," Paul directed. "This trail—"

He was pulling futilely at the heavy trail, and Dave laid aside his musket to heave at the trail, swinging it. Others bent in to help, and the gun came around. Dave never stopped talking. "Hit was too hot up there. So we-uns took an' come down here."

Paul groped in the pail for a burning match, feeling the priming on the gun's breech. It pointed at the wide gate where he had sat that morning, where garrison troops moved in disorder, throwing together a barricade or gathering for a counter-attack. One part of his mind assured him of this, while he kept on counting the men who climbed into the battery from the beach. Twenty-four—and O'Bannon's hoarse voice. "Stand back there—"

Beside him a gun of the battery exploded. Paul stepped aside and laid his match on the priming of his gun. The hot smoke swirled up at him.

The blast of his gun was almost drowned by a half-dozen heavier reports behind him, and the hiss of solid shot passing near his head. Dave ducked and said "Jerusalem!"

The *Hornet*, lying so close in, had not fired that broadside. The smoke eddied up from the *Nautilus*. The schooner was warping in abaft the battered sloop.

"Those sailors," called O'Bannon, "will shuck us out of here next. Mr. Mann, will you break out that ensign you are carrying."

The flushed midshipman gaped and tugged at the small flag he had stowed under his jacket. Then, remembering, he called back, "Aye-aye, sir," and ran to lay the ensign on the stone parapet, spreading it carefully so it could be seen clearly from the ships. Then he climbed up beside it and waved his cap.

But the *Nautilus* and *Argus* were firing over the battery into the town.

Into the battery Percy Farquhar climbed, laughing. "Five bob you owe me, Eugene." He was only a step ahead of the Tyrolese, who puffed under the weight of a musket. "Won by two paces. You'll bear me out, Paul?"

In the stress of the moment the Englishman had not thought that Paul had not been with them, in the race. After them pushed Selim the janizary and his men, noisy with excitement. Their familiar voices and the pressure of their bodies around him as they all worked to turn the battery on the entrance of the street made Paul feel as if he had never been away from them. Eaton gripped his shoulder, exclaiming like Dave: "Bainbridge! Thank God! I thought I sent you to Bomba, and here you are safe in Derna."

When Eaton moved his left arm, blood spattered from it. "This morning I prayed God that I would not be the failure that all my life I have been."

The man called Drub-Devil, who had thought himself a failure! . . . Something stirred in Paul's memory. At the gate the news Hadjali had let out and—the soldier had confirmed—that a relief force might be approaching from Tripoli.

Before he could speak of it, O'Bannon strode up, his coat flapping open. "The *Hornet's* boats are coming in at last, sir."

It seemed to them as if they had been in the battery an hour, whereas only a few moments had passed. The two boats from the sloop were grounding on the beach below the battery, men climbing out of them.

"I think we can go into the town," added the lieutenant thoughtfully. "If you will give the order, sir."

Wiping the sweat from his eyes, Eaton called: "Come on, you fellows."

O'Bannon called down at the boats: "What say, sailors? Rise and shine upon the battery. We are going to take the town."

Thirty of them ran on with Eaton over the ground where Paul had crawled that morning. His mind kept counting them as he tried to follow, walking slowly, weakly, into the empty gate, past the recess from which the guard had disappeared.

All the inhabitants had disappeared from the street. Paul walked on, finding himself alone, toward the sound of scattered firing. He felt the surge of an old fear.

Thirty men could not advance against the hundreds of disciplined soldiery he had seen staring at him when he was penned up. The firing seemed to be going away into the side streets.

When he made his way into the open square, he found a crowd clustered around the door of the mosque, and horsemen coming and going like hounds questing after game. They were Hamet's Arabs. He learned afterward that they had broken in from the hills when Eaton's force had taken the battery and turned it on the town.

The enemy had disappeared from sight. Paul climbed after the Americans up the street through palm gardens to the castle enclosure. When he saw Eaton and Hamet standing talking on the terrace above him, he went to the pool where water lilies floated, in bloom. Kneeling, he drank from his hand, and washed his aching burning head. In the shade beside him a fine carpet stretched empty. He crawled over to it and sat down.

Chapter Ten

The old Moslems who stood before him with their hands crossed and their heads bowed had come up from the sanctuary of the mosque. Some of them had offered him water when he was held in the niche. Their plea he could not understand, except that they called him Pasha and Akinpasha. When he took them up to Eaton, he learned that the old men were sheiks of the town who offered themselves as hostages for the payment to be exacted from the people by the conquerors who had come in from the sea. They asked only that the victorious soldiery should not take their girl children and animals in the looting. And they wanted to know how much tribute would content the Yankee pashas.

"The poor devils have had to deal with Spanish and Tripolitan masters," Eaton muttered. "They can't realize we're any different. God, I'm glad my children are growing up at home—"

By showing the old men a gold piece from his pocket, the New Englander tried to demonstrate that the Americans would not loot; instead they would pay for food and materials. The committee of hostages murmured assent, but looked forlorn as before.

"Tarnation take 'em!" complained Eaton. "They think we're after Italian gold, like this. Here!" He flung words at the despairing men. "*Yah rafik*—"

Their eyes quickened and the nearest of them tried to catch Paul's hand. Their voices babbled excitedly. Eaton, pallid, his injured arm slung by a neckcloth, explained, "I've named you as our surety against looting, Lieutenant Bainbridge. The poor beggars seem to understand you're not like the *corvos*." He winced with pain. "I must get this wrist dressed—the bones are shattered, I think. While I'm on the brig, you will assume command by seniority. O'Bannon's asleep, and I don't trust Leitensdorfer with these rich villas deserted. Keep Selim out of mischief if you can. I'll send Mademoiselle to you to interpret—and get Hull to put patrols ashore. We must maintain a show of force—God knows it will have to be a show. Hamet thinks the Tripolitans have drawn back to the heights. I've put the three Marines at the doors here—"

"Where are the others, sir?"

Eaton's eyes shifted. Too many men had been hit during the charge on the battery. "One is only slightly hurt." The ebullition of the action was draining out of him. "You are in bad case yourself, my boy. Hull's surgeon should have a look at you."

"Turn about, sir, I've had two days' rest."

When Eaton went down the garden steps, the old men crowded after him, shouting to the housetops. From the mosque door women edged cautiously to listen, and human heads appeared along the parapets of the flat roofs. The shouting went out into the streets—something about peace and mercy.

At sunset, making the rounds of the disordered rooms of the palace, Paul found servants emerging from dark corners to stand submissively with hands crossed. They seemed frightened. Lanky Dave put down a gilt incense burner he had been inspecting. "Seems like the harem should be somewhere about," he murmured.

"It isn't," Paul assured him. "And all this property belongs to Hamet Pasha now."

Passing through chambers fantastically rich in carpets on the floor, and hangings of cloth of gold, he came upon Marie Anne waiting at the head of a stair. Her hair was drawn back neat with combs, and her blue scarf was tucked about her throat. He only noticed the beauty of her small head, and the remembered sound of her voice.

"Lieutenant, criers are going through the streets saying that by command of Hamet Pasha, ruler of Derna, no man shall take property, or he shall lose his right hand."

She had meant to appear at her best, and to be cool and efficient before Paul. She had told herself that this silent officer was less honest than Isaac Hull, and less of a *compagnon* than Farquhar. But in a moment this stranger became Paul, haggard as a skeleton, the blood not washed from his coat. "How long," she demanded angrily, "have you had fever?"

"Have I? I don't know."

"Then how long since you have eaten something?"

"Last night."

When Selim appeared, reeking with wine and news of how the Bey and his officers had taken refuge in the mosque and then had smuggled themselves out of the town, Marie got the servants to make a fire in the brazier, which heated the state reception room. They fetched a pot for her and water which she boiled with bits of meat, to make a thin soup.

Selim kept pulling at his sleeve, asking a question. Marie said the janizary wanted to know why Paul did not post sentries around the city.

Going to the balcony outside the window, he stared into the haze of dusk vibrating with faint sounds. He had no men available to watch this haze dissolving into night. "Tell Selim to go and find sentries," he ordered at last. "Tell him to find the sheiks and their boys to watch until sunup. I trust him with this responsibility."

At moonrise they took the soup out on the balcony to drink. The balcony had cushions strewn for his late highness the Bey, who liked to sit there and observe the city. Down below torches flared and lanterns bobbed. The people had come out to offer fruit and bread to the strange sailors who marched back and forth, keeping together, without breaking into any houses.

The sight of the patrols, the splendor of the gardens under the night sky, exhilarated Paul. Marie belonged to it.

But she had known the balconies of Cairo and the hopelessness of the foreign officers, who could never change or understand the multitudes of Orientals in the streets below them.

"The hills are dark," she whispered, showing him the slopes dim under the moon beyond the lights.

The fever in him kept him talking, about his brother and the loss of the great frigate. She listened intently, because this was Paul's secret that he had kept to himself. It frightened her, and she was barely able to hide her fear from him.

"But if you cannot get to Tripoli?" she asked cautiously.

That morning he had felt hopeless enough. The change of the day and the nearness of Marie intoxicated him. "We will. We won today."

Did they? His injury and the battering of the great guns, the dread of the people who had whispered to her that the coming of the Americans would only increase the wrath of Tripoli—all that had passed through the girl's consciousness. She wanted to urge him to protect himself.

"Perhaps there are things we are not meant to do. But Paul, we must never lose what we are, ourselves. What you are."

"A prince of Asia, just now." He laughed excitedly.

She decided quickly to humor him. "A pasha, certainly—as Eugene would say."

Because she was so gay, laughing softly with him, he took her hand, and slept, with her beside him.

They started for the fort the next day when the danger of their situation became apparent.

Mounted forces of Tripolitans appeared along the heights in strength. The army that had come too late to defend the town now threatened it, concealed in the dense verdure of the valley. The Bey and the greater part of his garrison had escaped after the confusion of the attack, and had of course joined the column from Tripoli. Their movements could not be observed.

The rambling circuit of Derna ran for some two miles, and the whole of it could not be defended. The presence of the ships secured the shore, and the Arab horsemen formed a small mobile reserve. But the weak side of the town, cut in two by the ravine of the Derna River, lay toward the hills.

On that side Eaton and Eugene picked out a half-demolished *caravanserai*, to make over into a fort. On the edge of the ravine, it commanded the southern slopes—when cannon could be moved up to it from the ships.

Daily the stone walls of the new fort rose higher. Peasants hauled the stones up from the ravine, being paid a little each day with money Eaton borrowed from the naval officers.

When the walls were breast-high and the embrasures began to take shape, Eaton had the American flag hoisted on a staff. Whereupon the people called it the Kalah Amrica, the American Castle.

It looked across the city toward the palace vacated by the Bey. The walls of the fort began to take on significance in Derna. Never before in that part of the world had there been a Kalah Amrica, with a strange flag like this one.

The people, profoundly distrustful of their old masters the Tripolitans, hoped for much from their new fort. It was sturdy, with a ditch around it. And they gained a few rials from it—something hitherto unknown.

Naturally they knew nothing of the argument between Eaton and Isaac Hull about it. To Eaton, the fort was a necessity, a first step toward his hoped-for occupation of a point of the African coast. Hull had parted with all his money and most of his stores readily enough, but he did not want to lose any of his cannon.

"Before you're satisfied," he grumbled, "you'll have the *Argus* dredged up the river."

"Faith," Eaton laughed, "if I could move the *Argus* to the mountain, the vessel would be of real service."

Chapter Eleven

The attack came as a complete surprise. That morning some cavalry had been observed moving above the fort. Leitensdorfer had gone up with a detachment of sailors to strengthen the working party there. Eaton was on the shore, where the guns of the battery had been placed to bear on the town. The Tripolitans must have filtered down into the hollow from the point where Eaton had first approached Derna. Their rush carried them past the outer buildings into the streets. Only handfuls of Arabs and Greeks were in that quarter to resist them, and these were driven to the housetops.

Gaining force as infantry pressed after the horsemen into the streets, the attack reached the main square of the city.

The fort and the battery both held out, but their garrisons were too weak to counter-attack. Around the mosque Selim had rallied a mixed group, without anything to support him.

From the terrace of the palace Paul heard the roar of the attack rising and nearing him. It had the terrifying force of an insensate thing. It swept across the square. Around him, he had a half-dozen muskets firing. Popguns against the rush of a thousand men already tasting victory.

Then something inexplicable happened. Heavy, measured reports sounded from the bay where the *Argus* had raised her anchor to drift close to the jetties. Her bow guns had come into action, trained over the housetops. After one reverberation from the bay, there was a flurry among the horsemen leading the attack.

An eighteen-pound cannonball had stripped a row of them from their saddles. Frightened horses plunged. Sudden panic seized the Tripolitans at the death that had struck from the sky. The mass of them dissolved into fugitives running away from the square.

As they ran, musketry from the roofs harassed them. Cannonballs followed them out of the fruit orchards up the bare hills, where Arab horsemen lashed them with savage pursuit. For once the Tripolitans did not contrive to carry off their dead.

Stripping a body beneath the steps of the mosque, Selim the janizary recognized it by its cloth-of-gold girdle and red morocco boots as that of the renegade officer Hadjali.

"*Yah muslimin,*" he proclaimed to the inhabitants who had gathered around him, awestruck. "O Moslems, it is written that for every man the place of his death is appointed. Verily, God appointed that the leaders of these dogs should taste death here. Your eyes have seen it. Who will give silver for these boots of a pasha?"

"*Aiwah!*" the listeners agreed. Beyond any doubt the Tripolitans had been driven away by an act of God. They knew nothing of the skill of a gun-layer on a ship.

"If you'd moved the *Argus* up the mountain," Isaac Hull observed to Eaton with satisfaction, "the vessel would have been carried by boarding; and where would you be now?"

Eaton said nothing more about guns for his fort. He kept on raising the walls of his fort, trying to forget that they had not a rial left in their pockets, that the Tripolitans still cut them off from the inland food supplies, and that no aid had reached him from the sea. Long since, he had sent the *Hornet* over to Syracuse, and now he dispatched the *Nautilus* with urgent appeal for stores, guns, and the reinforcement of a hundred Marines—which would make Derna secure.

Over there the port of Syracuse was packed with gunboats, bomb ketches, a squadron of frigates. A whole treasury of money, hospitals, and theaters where the sick could be treated with medicine, and officers amused. Politicians dined there, he knew, on silver plate!

No answer came to his appeals. The breath of the desert wind, scorching with midsummer heat, inflamed his crippled arm.

One morning Leitensdorfer emerged from the ditch of the Kalah Amrica spluttering. Hugging a broken clay jar crusted with earth, he bellowed: "By Salbal and Bathbal—the drachms of Selene! The gold of the ancients!"

The jar that the diggers had turned up was heavy with gold coins bearing the head of a king. Forty-six, they counted, and they found no more buried money, although Leitensdorfer heaved up the earth in his search. Eaton decided that the only fair thing was to divide the coins among the whole force, from diggers to commanders.

That gave one gold piece to each man. Farquhar flipped up his and laughed. "We hold the gorgeous East in fee. Doubles or quits, Eugene? Toss you for the five bob you owe me."

But Leitensdorfer turned away sullenly, pocketing his single coin. He seemed aggrieved that the expedition had come upon no more wealth than that. Paul followed him and offered to swap. "Trade you mine for that moonstone ring of Marie's?"

The ring could not have any value except to him, because Marie had once held it out to him as a betrothal ring. Now, as he anticipated, Eugene fished among the oddments in a pocket and handed over the ring with the flying bird carved on it. With a quick glance around, he pocketed the heavy coin. Somehow in spite of his brilliant play-acting, he could not change himself from a Tyrolese innkeeper. He had gone hungry for too long.

The stores of the *Argus* had been exhausted. The crew gleaned what they could by trading in the market of the town, fetching in rolls of silk and weapons, prize goods taken from the Tripolitan corsairs at sea. Marie helped them exchange their trophies for Spanish dollars, to buy eggs and milk and meat from the peasants. The Marines gave up the last of their brass buttons, and the trove of gold pieces.

Only once did a sail head in from the horizon of the sea. A polacca from Naples stopped for an hour to take on fresh water, and to part with fresh fish to the men of the New World who offered pocketknives and tin chests for it. The polacca also had news from the outer world.

Hearing it, Mendrici fell into a fever of excitement. Napoleon's army was leaving the English Channel. It was moving east, toward Italy or Austria—possibly against Russia. To the others at Derna the news had no meaning. An emperor was marching somewhere with his army. But Mendrici left on the polacca, which would take him to an Italian port.

The *Argus* could not leave. When Eaton talked stubbornly of a fleet to invade the port of Tripoli, and of a column to be started overland against their arch-enemy the Bey, Isaac Hull shook his head silently. Along the bare hills of the coast they could not go beyond the range of his guns.

In the marketplace, women from the farms offered food without payment to the Americans. They wanted to share with the hungry men.

When Paul went through the streets, families came out to stand in his way and beg him to settle disputes. They tried to leave dates and milk with him.

"I'm not my brother's keeper," he assured Marie. "Why do they follow me and what do they keep calling me? Judge?"

"No." She hesitated. "They think up names for people."

"Then what is mine?"

"I think you *are* your brother's keeper."

"You haven't told me."

"They call you *A Maut*, which is the Dead."

She looked up into his thin brown face. The fever had left him, after the infection of his wound. "When they saw you first at the gate, you were covered with blood and dying. You were crawling out under the horses of the Tripolitans toward the battery—"

"The safest place."

"They say no man could be so brave as to do that. It must have been appointed for you to do. Now that you are alive, they like to touch you and have you decide their troubles for them."

Paul opened his lips to laugh. Then he had the odd feeling that these people pressing about him and Marie herself saw something in him that did not exist. He had been afraid of death. Now he was glad to be well, and to have a pomegranate in his hand to share with Marie when they could get away from the people . . . In two months he had got no nearer to Tripoli.

"I wish they could decide my troubles for me."

She shook her dark head quickly at that. "When I saw you, that first evening, I prayed to the Holy Mary of the Seas. For both of us." Then, without thinking of it, she took his hand. "Now we can come and sit by the well. We have some fruit, and we can pretend that the cactus thorns are the lilac trees of your home."

That morning he had been out with thirty men, beating off raiders who sneaked up in a dust-storm against the fort. Suddenly he realized that it would be something to sit by running water and chew the seeds of a pomegranate.

Chapter Twelve

When she first sighted the ship Marie did not believe her eyes. The sails showed above the island. She closed her eyes and waited. The ship was standing in, not heeling like the *Argus* in the light breeze. It moved steadily, over spurts of spray. Four courses of sails towered above the raking bowsprit of the frigate.

Unbelieving, the girl watched until the great ship turned, the sails flapped and came aback, and the anchor chain rumbled out. The frigate was anchoring beyond the slanting masts of the *Argus*.

Then the familiar rub-a-dub of Selim's drum sounded in staccato excitement—*rrrub-aaa-dub*. By it, Marie was convinced that the frigate had actually come, sending a launch smartly out to shore . . .

Captain John Rodgers of the thirty-six-gun frigate *Constellation* had difficulty in making out the ranks and ratings of the wretchedly clad figures surrounding him on the shore under the stone rampart of a battery that had all its guns trained inward, not properly out to sea. The Marine officer with a beard over his unbuttoned ragged coat—the so-called colonel of engineers wrapped in a flaming Turkish robe—the equally grotesque captain of cannoneers, gripping a copper drum of outlandish shape under his bare arm.

And Captain Rodgers had equal difficulty in making them understand his instructions in regard to them. So he repeated his message carefully.

Peace had already been concluded with the Bey of Tripoli, terminating the action against the Barbary powers. That treaty of peace had been drawn up and signed by the Commissioner of the United States Government, and signed by Rodgers himself among others.

It terminated the payment of tribute by the United States to the Barbary States forever. Although the sum of sixty thousand dollars was to be paid the Bey in the exchange of prisoners, because there were more Americans than Tripolitans to be released—

"Sixty thousand dollars!" The flamboyant colonel thrust up his massive fists. "Sixty—with ten thousand dollars and one hundred men, certainly, we had marched to Tripoli!"

"The treaty," replied Rodgers, making allowance for the excitement of irregular officers obviously in a state of semi-exhaustion, "was the most favorable ever to be gained by the United States from Barbary."

The officers confronting him did not seem to realize that.

"Captain Bainbridge and all the personnel of the *Philadelphia* have been released from captivity already," he added.

Paul, hearing that repeated, told himself that his brother was free and out of Tripoli, on shipboard again. Isaac Hull glanced at him and stepped over to his side.

"Bainbridge," he said, "they tell me that while the—the Court of Inquiry must be held, upon the loss of the frigate, the officers of the vessel have all signed a declaration, approving your brother's action. It is irregular, but—"

Something tight within Paul dissolved. He looked at the prints in the sand. "Thanks for telling me that."

In his mind passed swiftly the vision of a heavy frigate grounding under full sail in pursuit of a swift corsair, in dangerous waters. Then the image of the ship went away.

Rodgers was facing Eaton, explaining that he had orders to evacuate all the latter's command on the *Constellation*. How many should he be prepared to receive on deck?

"They are all here, Captain."

Startled, the seaman swung to survey the ragged groups waiting by a brass nine-pounder on the beach. "I thought you had a regiment!"

"The regiment is here. All of us are here except Hamet, and the two Marines up at the fort. There!" With his good arm Eaton pointed up at a gray enclosure of stones mounting no guns, on the bare hillside. He repeated slowly, "The fort," and stopped.

Those two words held the friendship of Hamet and the Arabs, and a dream that had become his life.

"How much gear?" asked Rodgers. "Baggage?"

Eaton turned away from his fort and roused himself. "That gun," he said.

"I see." Curiously Rodgers glanced at the stooped tired man—a notional civilian, he had heard. Obviously Eaton's expedition had been the cause of the advantageous peace terms gained from the Bey.

Rodgers had expected to find much greater strength in the Derna detachment. He wanted to say something in appreciation of that, but it lay outside his instructions to do so. "We all understand, General Eaton—" he began, and hesitated. "I may say it is generally realized how the peace project postdated your achievement in capturing Derna, and the actual signing came after your repulse of—"

"The dragon," prompted an amused voice from the parapet.

"The dragon was frightened by the small boy in his cave."

Perplexed, Rodgers stared up at a dirty gentleman sprawled on the parapet.

"The evacuation had better be after dark," said Eaton, squaring his shoulders. "We are under observation by the enemy—"

Along the line of the hills the commander could discern no sign of an enemy, but he agreed readily. The operation would be simpler than anticipated. He wondered briefly if ever again an American expeditionary force would be landed upon the North African coast.

After Paul picked her up and stepped into the water to lower her carefully into the boat, Marie Anne felt again that she was dreaming, and that the great ship could not be waiting in the darkness.

Holding her bundle tight, she was lifted to a deck faintly white in the starlight, and as firm as the floor of a house under her feet. Above her the network of shrouds soared against the stars.

Lanterns moved around her and quiet voices sounded. The smell of steaming tea from a pot, the silence of the Arab officers by Hamet on a carpet, the brown faces of the Greeks over a lantern, the voice of Dave droning "Turoo-li-ay-ay," Farquhar begging O'Bannon to get him a commission as lieutenant in the Marines—all this closed around her as if in a dream.

Paul was helping her up on the boom where she could see. He had forgotten about the ring he said he had for her. They sat on the boom staring at the familiar shore beyond the glint of open water. On the shore the Bedouins had taken down all the tents and had taken the horses to start back to the desert whence they had come.

A bell chimed sharply, musically. Someone called down from the afterdeck, and voices answered promptly, dying away toward the bow, far off.

"Now Selim is really going home," she whispered.

"We're going home," said Paul. "Somehow. If you will come with me."

She would go with him, anywhere. Even if the great ship had not come in— Suddenly she realized, with a sense of wonder, that she was going home.

Berzerk

That day Brana heard oars in the firth. She dropped her rake and ran barelegged across the clover fields to her lookout. Here was the place, high up, where she liked to lie and dream and watch the gulls circling over the mist that often hid the bleak coast of Norway.

In this high seat of her own the girl Brana could not easily be found by the people of the homestead. Hiding out here, she could look down at the women of the homestead working among the cattle pens or picking wool, she could listen to the sound of the axes where the men chopped interminably at the timbers in the forest.

For the forest Brana had no love. It was dark, and bears snuffled through it, and in the dimness of the northern nights werewolves might be heard howling there.

She was a Viking's girl, with the colors of gold and fire in her long hair, and the blue of deep water in her eyes. Moreover, she was now fifteen winters of age, and many girls of the coast had gone to their bride bowers after fourteen winters. But she thought that the youths who came in to Orn's Firth had thin beards and a small way of doing things. They brought hewn timbers down from the forest to the water of the inlet, or they fetched in fish from Lofoten.

It pleased her better when warfarers came in from the long ways of the sea, to shelter themselves at the homestead and drink beer with her uncle Orn. These warfarers often gave her bits of bright silk for her garments, and carved ivory, and they had tales to tell, while she poured their beer, of raiding and burning. Although her uncle Orn would shake his head in his stubborn way, saying that she would not be so pleased when she knew more of war or the men who went forth to it. Wait and learn, he would say to her, blinking wisely. Orn, being old, did not know that Brana was waiting for the day when a tall man might come into their gray inlet, to refit his longship, and would look upon her and demand her for his bride to carry off to his homestead, wherever that might be . . .

That morning she saw a dragon ship coming out of the mist, into Orn's Firth.

No ordinary Viking longship this. Painted war shields lined its rails. The dragon's head above its prow gleamed with silver. A good ship, she thought, and it must have on it a man of mark. The blood throbbed in her body when she ran to tell Orn.

"Ho, redhead," he laughed at her, "you have been dreaming again."

"It is you who sleep, Orn," she cried, "here in the hay when you have a great guest to greet."

She ran by the cattle pens to the women's sleeping room of the homestead. She put on the blue cape that matched her eyes, in such a way that the mends did not show. Clasping it with the silver clasp, she wished that she had at least one gold ring for her slender arms. And she persuaded Ingiald the maid to comb her hair smooth, without braiding it. After this, in her excitement, Brana forgot to put on her shoes and ran barelegged down to the landing place.

There she saw that the strangers had come for trading.

The homestead men were carrying down piles of wool, and casks of honey, and bearskins for trading. Brana had eyes only for the man from the dragon ship. Tall he was, with a bold swing to his shoulders, and laughing eyes. Edging closer, she heard his name spoken, Hrolf the Gautlander, the earl's man, who had made the voyage over from Gothland. His weapon men looked hard as broken ice, coming down the landing plank in their gray iron shirts and wolfskins. Yet their landfall had been friendly enough, with the peace flag flying over them.

Now Hrolf stood on the shore examining the trade goods Orn set before him. "Have you no wine?" he asked, looking for more than he saw.

"We make only beer," said Orn placidly, as his homesteaders set down more goods—wood carvings and piles of dried Lofoten fish.

"My followers are thirsty for wine," Hrolf smiled. Then he looked at Brana, and looked at her again. When she lowered her head modestly, she discovered that she had not put on her shoes—she, a woman of fifteen winters stood before a mighty seafarer like a barelegged child. Her face felt hot with shame.

"We make only beer," he said, proudly. "And it is good enough."

Brana thought otherwise. Beer and bearskins, honey and wool, these of the homestead did not seem to her good enough to lay before seafarers.

The smile went out of Hrolf's face. He stared at Orn.

"If you do not like it, Gautlander," Orn rubbed his beard, "I cannot help that. You can drink with me or not, as seems best to you."

"Do you think yourself," Hrolf demanded quickly, "as good a man as me, homesteader?"

"Certainly," said Orn, who was stubborn about such matters.

Hrolf grew pale in the face, and the gold rune ring moved on his arm. "That is bad to hear," he said.

His arm pulled the sword from the sheath at his hip, and he stepped toward Orn. His arm thrust hard, and the point came through the shirt at Orn's back. Orn laid hold of the sword in front of him, and dropped down to his knees. A man howled like a wolf.

The homesteader nearest dropped the wool he was carrying. "*Berserksgang!*" he cried.

Berserk rage. Brana saw Hrolf's followers leap high in their wolfskins. They caught at their weapons and struck at the startled men in front of them. They howled and they struck. Brana could not stop looking, nor could she move her legs.

Running forward, the gray men from the ship grasped at the homesteaders with their hands. They panted like animals in fury. Some of Orn's followers swung up their weapons, and iron crashed hard. Those who fought were killed; the others, seeing Orn fall, ran up toward the forest.

Brana found that she was running back into the house. Now she knew that the gray men were Berserks, who went wild with rage when anything angered them.

Inside the house Ingiald was not to be seen. The serving women who ordinarily obeyed Brana were running out, past the cattle pens. Looking for Ingiald, the girl went to her sleeping alcove. But it was empty. When she ran back to the hall, Hrolf stood there, without his sword. Brana pulled a skinning knife from the wall, and threw it at him, trying to slip past him.

Catching the knife in the air, he gripped the girl's loose hair with his other hand, and held her, turning her face up to him. Now he seemed to be quiet.

"Girl," he said, "do not take iron in your hand. Do not anger me."

With her throat choking, Brana stood still. His blue eyes shone down at her. "I searched far for gold," he chanted, "and now I find red gold in my hand." He nodded his head. "It is lovely you are, girl."

His hand stroked down her hair, and he smiled. "Red have I made the ground where I stepped," he chanted, making a song, "and rain have I drawn from women's eyes. Far have I followed the paths of the sea, to find this gold that holds me fast."

Brana thought, too, that she was held fast by the blue fire in his eyes, and the music of his voice. "Soft as your words are," she said, her voice trembling, "you shall not put your hand on my hair. You have shed Orn's blood, and for that you shall soon make atonement."

"Was his name Orn?" The fit seemed to have left him. "He angered me. As for atonement, you are more beautiful than any maid of these firths. I shall let no harm come to you. Ask for what you wish, and you shall have it."

"Until this hour," Brana cried, "I wanted a bride's bower, with flowers."

Hrolf laughed, taking his hand from her. "A bower, or the jewels of a queen, it is all one to me. But you shall stay with me."

He seemed sure of his words and of himself. That day he kept her close to him, while his men killed an ox and prepared to feast on the fresh meat. Carefully they gathered up the trade goods of the homestead, carrying them into the ship. Seeing this, Brana wondered that Berserks should be so careful of small things. Hrolf understood that she was beginning to be perplexed.

"These matters that you find strange now," he said, "you will understand later." He told her this much: he was the earl's man, and the earl had given command that the unruly Vikings along this Norse coast must be disciplined with fire and sword. And Brana remembered that there had been many outlaws among the Vikings of her coast.

She could not get away while the ox meat was cooking because the Berserks were all about the homestead. When she heard oars in the firth, she went to look at the landing, but saw only a dragon ship, deeply laden, coming in.

This new ship had no shield wall. Its timbers were gray with salt, and the few men in it wore animals hides. Sighting the smoke from the cook fire, they turned in to the shore above the landing, flying no peace flag or flag of any kind.

"What have you come for, seafarers?" the Berserks hailed them.

"For meat," answered one from the weathered ship. For two summers and winters, he added, they had tasted no cattle meat.

"I find that hard to believe," said Hrolf, "but come you in anyway."

When these newcomers walked along the shore toward the cook fire, Brana saw that their hair had not been cut; their faces were dark and thin. The one of them who carried an ax gripped in his hand bent over the blood-stains on the ground and sniffed like a dog. "More than an ox," he said, "has been slain here."

And when he stepped inside the hall of the homestead, he trod care-fully, staring up at the beams overhead. Lank and restless, he was, with scars on his thin hands.

"You act," observed Hrolf, watching him, "as if a house was some-thing strange to you."

"Strange indeed it seems," the dark seafarer agreed, "since I have not entered one for four years."

Hrolf sat down beside him in the high seat, while their followers scat-tered along the long table below, and he called to Brana to fetch beer in horns for them. As the girl set down the drinking horn by the stranger, he put his fingers on her arm, smiling at her.

"I suppose," said Hrolf, who missed nothing of this, "you have not seen a woman, either, for four years."

"Five." The dark man drank greedily, and coughed. He made Brana sit beside him, and he looked at her slender arms and long hair with great satisfaction, while he tore and swallowed the half-cooked beef hungrily. Sweat came out on his bony face, and muscles worked in his temples as he chewed. But he kept looking at Brana, or down at the long table where his few men were gorging among the Berserks. The girl was surprised to see by his eyes and teeth that this guzzler could not be as old as she thought. His skin seemed lined as an older man's, but something within him was fresh and youthful.

Voiceless she sat, not daring to speak, for fear of Hrolf's anger. The stranger kept his ax between his knees even while he ate.

"All that you say," observed Hrolf, watching out of the corner of his eye, "sounds like a lie to me. I do not believe that man lives who has not seen a woman for five years."

"Well, I live," said the owner of the ax calmly. "It was because of the new land," he explained.

"What new land?"

"I call it Vine-land, and it lies beyond the West voyage."

"Ice-land we know," Brana put in, "and Vikings tell of the Green-land beyond, where the glaciers are. Beyond that, the sea runs over the edge of this world into *Hel*."

Although she made her voice sharp with disdain, the stranger did not appear to be disturbed. Stretching his long arms, he smiled up at the carved heads of Wotan and Thor on the pillars of the high seat. "So most people think," he said, "and I can't help that. But you two have set good beer and meat before me, so I shall tell you a marvelous thing."

His dark eyes shone with a boy's happiness. "From that same Green-land my father, Eric, was once driven by a northeast wind, and instead of going over the edge of the world he sighted a new land, covered with mist."

"A mist of magic, no doubt," quoth Hrolf, "Eric's son."

"Leif is my name. I was young in Ice-land, and I begged my father Eric to take me to this new land of his, that the eyes of common men had not seen. And now I tell you of a strange happening. My father says well enough, but when he rides his horse down to the sea to take ship his horse stumbles and he stops, saying that evidently he is not meant to go farther. So I fare on alone with these shipmates, until a northeast wind carries us on beyond the end of the voyages."

At the long table the Berserks were listening now, with Leif's men.

"First we sight a coast," went on Leif, his mind going away from the hall, out somewhere beyond, "dark with forests, no island at all, but a mighty land, and this I name Mark-land. On we go then with the wind, and make our landfall on a coast sloping gently to the sea, with wide beaches and sand. Up a firth sail we, to fresh water. Yet, we find dew heavy on the long grass, and this dew tastes sweeter than other water."

"A marvelous thing," grunted Hrolf.

"So it is. Yea, no frosts kill that grass—strong it stays through the winter, and cattle would need no fodder there. Deer and fur beasts run free in the woods. And of wine casks we have no need, for wine berries grow on the vines there. So I name it Vine-land. If I live I am going back."

Hrolf emptied his drinking horn. "It is easy to tell of great deeds you have done, out of everyone's sight."

Leif's mind came back from beyond the sea and he looked at Hrolf. "My messmates tasted those grapes," he said. "And the hewn trees of Vine-land we have brought in our ship's lading, to sell on this coast."

"If you are indeed Leif, Eric's son," said Hrolf, "you will have trouble selling anything on the coast of Norway. Because you are outlaws, whom no man has seen for long years."

"True." Leif nodded indifferently. He seemed to care less about this than about his voyage back. "As you inlaws say, my father was outlawed for manslaughter here. That is why we looked for a new country. We had no other."

"Then why have you ventured back?"

"To trade for a better ship."

Hrolf got up quietly, stepping down to his men at the long table. Brana, watching him, caught Leif's hand impulsively. "Open your eyes, fool," she whispered, "and take care for yourself. These men here are Berserks who kill when their anger is touched."

Leif looked at her with his head to one side. "I have seen Berserks before now, girl. Are you not with them?"

"No," she cried angrily. "Oh, you are simple in mind! This morning they killed Orn, my uncle, because he spoke a quick word to them. Do not cross them, but get you out of here."

Now Leif seemed to wake to his danger. Glancing down at where his score of followers sat among the greater number of weapon men, he called out: "Leif's men, get you to the longship. I hear the wind rising and you must take the oars and row up to a safer landing."

Without argument, his shipmates picked up their weapons and began to go out the door. Brana waited for Leif to follow, but he sat still, looking at her. Tears of helpless anger wet her eyes, and she tried to hide her face. Leif bent over to see her better.

"Don't cry, girl," he muttered.

Brana tried to get up from the high seat. His arm held her shoulders, and he frowned as if puzzling over something strange.

Hearing Hrolf's step, she tried to pull away.

"What a mighty thing—" his eyes shone at a new thought—"if you would come with me on the voyage."

Suddenly his arm went away from her, and Brana gasped. Hrolf's hand had caught him and thrust him back against the high seat. Hrolf was scowling at Leif, who looked down the hall. The last of his men had gone out.

"So you think yourself," Hrolf muttered, "to be as good a man as I am."

Hearing these words that had been spoken to Orn, Brana shrank back. Leif shook his head slowly.

"No," he said, "I am a better man."

From the table a tall man with one eye tramped up to his chief—Starkad, the foredeck leader of the Berserks, growling and pulling at his sword. Leif sat still over the empty horn.

"I hear you," Hrolf said between his teeth. "That is easy to say. Look at this!"

Drawing his sword, he tossed it into the air, and reached for Leif's ax. But the seafarer pulled it close to him. When he did not get the ax, Hrolf snatched Starkad's blade and hand ax and tossed them up with his own sword, so that he had three blades going in the air over his head. Fast and well he handled them, saying, "See how I am weapon-fast. Iron obeys me and will do me no harm."

Stopping the weapons, he offered them to Leif. With a shake of his head, the shaggy man refused them. "That was a small trick. I will do a greater one."

Starkad's teeth clashed. "Can you not see we grow strong with *Berserksgang*? At such times we pull trees from the earth."

Leif did not seem disturbed. "It would be a more remarkable feat to pull down this house. Aye, that would be something to boast of."

Hrolf snorted. "Eleven men lie out in the cattle pens because one said a hard, quick word to me."

"Eleven is a small number."

Hrolf stared, voiceless. Around him, the gray men pushed close to Leif and the girl, and still Leif did nothing but watch them, while she waited for the first to howl.

"I will tell you," Leif observed, "something worth hearing. My nature is more than berserk, for I am a *hamrammir* man. My guardian spirit is a bear, and in the time of darkness this bear's spirit is apt to enter my body."

He shook his head, glancing at the scars on his hands, and the eyes of the Berserks went to those scars. They listened, breathing heavily.

"So I rise up in the darkness with the bear's strength in me, but I crawl like a beast, seeking something to devour. Aye, at such a time my shape is changed to a beast. After the fit leaves me," Leif went on, "I am in my own shape again, but feeling weak."

While he spoke the light failed in the hall. Outside, the pale night of the north had begun, and some of the Berserks noticed this, whispering to Hrolf, who stared at the shaggy Leif silently. Around the high seat the shadows were closing in, and, wrapped in his bearskin, Leif's outline grew dimmer.

"Easy to say," replied Hrolf slowly, "but I would like well to see this happen."

Crouching on his seat, Leif said nothing.

"Starlight begins," went on Hrolf, "and so now we will go outside the house. We will know that you are indeed a *hamrammir* man if we hear after darkness the growling of a beast and see the shape of a bear come forth. That would be something to see."

He touched the quiet girl on the arm. "Come, Brana. No woman should see a *hamrammir* change his shape."

Some of the Berserks were moving toward the back door of the house, and some out of the front of the hall. They went readily enough, gripping their weapons and looking back.

Brana did not stir.

"Come you on," said Hrolf again.

"Aye," growled Leif. "Better for you to go, girl. I feel strength coming into me."

Stepping away from them, Hrolf looked back once. When Brana did not run after him, he went out the door, closing it behind him.

The two of them sat together in the empty hall, with the bones scattered along the ground, and the fresh oxhide flung into a corner. Leif sighed, drawing the drinking horn to him and looking into it. She saw his face change in the twilight. He looked thin and tired.

"Well?" she said softly.

"Not well." Leif shook himself restlessly. "Why didn't you go with the warfarers, Brana?"

She could not say why. She wanted to stay here at Leif's side, to feel him near her. Pouring beer from the jug, she offered it to him, but he pushed it away moodily.

"Perhaps a *hamrammir* man may not drink beer," she whispered.

Leif looked at her and went to the opening in the wall by the door. Already the glow of the cooking fire outside picked out the figures of the armed men in mail grouped in a half circle beyond the door, waiting. At the back he saw the same thing, only not so clearly.

"I thought so," he muttered. There was no other way out of the house. He stopped in front of the quiet girl. "Get out," he told her.

"No," Brana whispered. "While I am here, they will not slay you."

"If you are sure of that, it is more than I am," Leif grumbled. "Are you afraid of me, here in the dark?"

Brana shook her head. She came closer, to touch his arm, and felt his lips against her hair. "Outside there," he whispered, "they are no Berserks. Well do I know the Berserk rage. They go about in wolfskins spreading the tale of their anger, and plundering and slay as if they were true Berserks. Aye, Hrolf has hit upon a good plan. If everyone on this coast is afraid of his anger, he can get together a great treasure. He will go far."

"I know," Brana nodded, "but I cannot bear for him to touch me."

"He will do better than I."

"I know." Suddenly Brana laughed. "Much do you know of the spirit lore, Leif. But Ingiald told me years ago that a *hamrammir* never is conscious of changing his shape."

Leif sighed. "I thought I told a good lie. I wanted to get my crew away from these manslaughterers. It was the only way I could think to do it." He chuckled, remembering. "I think well that half Hrolf's men believed the tale."

Before long he stopped chuckling. A dull thumping sounded against both the doors—a thumping and a creaking. Listening to it, Leif went and pushed the narrow front door. Hard as he pushed, he could not move it. He stepped to the opening.

"Hrolf," he called. "Will you let the woman out of this hall?"

Although Brana could make out the gleam of Hrolf's arm ring where he stood among his weapon men, she heard no answer to this. The noise at the doors stopped but a faint stirring and crackling began.

The faces of Hrolf's men stood out more clearly in the half light of the sky, and they seemed to be growing red. Their mouths hung open, their hands moved restlessly, holding shields and weapons. Suddenly Hrolf's sword struck his shield with a clang of iron.

"*Loud growls the man-bear,*" he chanted, making a song, "*caught in the trap. Now feels the man-bear the sting of his death.*"

The red glow shone brighter on the men waiting expectantly outside.

"He sings well enough," Leif muttered, as the clanging of iron grew louder, "but it is a sham and a counterfeit song. Your inlaws yonder have no wish to hear what we may say. They have it in their minds to do more than manslaughter."

"What?" Brana asked, her throat choking. Something bitter caught at her nostrils.

"Something that will be hard for you to endure, girl." Leif thought about it and nodded. "Hrolf has murdered your uncle Orn. Now have you the right to speak against him and demand atonement. So he will slay the two of us, and my shipmates will not be here to bear witness against him. Yea, he will say that he killed only a *hamrammir* man. He has thought out more clearly than I have what he must do."

Leif sniffed the air, and looked up carefully at the thatch of the roof on the great crossbeam over their heads. The sound of crackling and snapping came from up there, at the front. Then red sparks dropped down, and Brana knew that the men outside had set fire to the thatch on that side.

Her house was burning over her head, while those men in wolfskins waited, and she thought that after the burning there would be no evidence against Hrolf, and no voice to speak against him. She caught Leif's hand, holding it tight.

"You do not weep now," Leif said.

She gripped his hand tighter, for comfort. He was shivering, sweat shining on his face. An ember stung her bare arm and she pressed herself against him.

All at once Leif cried out, as if his body had been wrenched. His shaggy head thrust down between his shoulders, and the wood of his ax haft creaked when he picked it up. Smoke rolled down on them, and Leif hacked with his ax at the window opening. At the second blow of the ax a spear clanged through the opening, past Leif's shoulder.

Then he stopped working at the wall. Crouching, he glared up through the smoke. It seemed to the girl that this was not the flesh-and-blood Leif of a moment ago, but a man gripped by some other strength. Tears flowed out of his staring eyes down his cheeks, and quick groans came from inside his body. He did not seem to know that he was crying.

Embers dropped with black soot along the front of the hall, and the flames hissed overhead. Leif was staring up at the great center beam when he leaped back. Straining, he shoved the long table back against the far wall.

Here, in the smoke, he jumped up on the table and began to chop at the end of the heavy beam where it met the wall. Fast and skillfully, his ax edge bit into the wood, and long chips fell.

"Come here," he croaked, and Brana stepped close behind him.

His ax smashed up into the shaking beam. Bits of burning thatch dropped down around him. The beam cracked loud, and Leif smashed at it with the butt of his ax.

With a splintering sound the end of the beam came down, breaking the table. Leif jumped clear, moving with frantic haste. Catching up the wet oxhide from the ground, he threw it over Brana's head, gripping it close around her.

The roof was falling in now.

Flaming thatch rattled down, and hot air seared Leif's throat. He kept moving. Over one shoulder he swung the roll that was Brana in the bloody oxhide. Holding fast to his ax, he stepped up on the beam's end where it lay in the wreck of the table.

The beam sloped up to the front wall where fire smoldered. Above that upper end, he could see a dark patch of the sky. At that point the burning thatch had fallen down to the floor of the hall. And up the sloping beam Leif was hurrying, balancing with the ax and Brana, his chest straining not to breathe in the air that would strangle him.

Stepping on the top of the beam, he gave a yell and leaped out.

Now Hrolf and his men, watching with satisfaction, beheld this shaggy figure leaping down in the smoke and the fire glare, with a mass of oxhide upon him. And for a second astonishment held them still. They heard a faint echo of the yell.

The figure landed on its feet and rolled, and the oxhide rolled away from it. They saw then it was Leif, with Brana in the hide.

Starkad, the one-eyed, stepped toward him, swinging high his sword. Leif saw the iron coming down, and whacked with his ax at Starkad's knee joint. The ax blade cut away half Starkad's leg, and Leif rolled to his feet, pulling up his ax.

His face was twisted out of human semblance. Tears streaked his cheeks.

"*Berserksgang!*" a weapon man shouted, watching him.

"Fools!" Hrolf shouted.

With his shield before him, and his sword point out, Hrolf ran at Leif. And the ax swung low at his knee, as it had done with Starkad. Jumping aside, Hrolf kept clear of it. And the shining ax swung wide.

Gripping it with both hands, Leif let it swing and hurled it at Hrolf. It flashed over the shield into Hrolf's face. It smashed the bones in his head, and he dropped there, where he stood.

Leif did not wait for him to fall. He caught up his ax and rushed at the weapon men, smoking as he was. Beating down their swords, he leaped among them, and they closed their shields together, crouching, afraid of the anger of this lank man. They had seen Starkad and Hrolf smashed down, and they were afraid. So they pushed close their shields, trying to crush him.

Then they heard running feet. Spears and axes struck their backs, while voices shouted Leif's name. Twenty Leifs seemed to have come out of the darkness, in the smoke. Here the weapon men had caught Leif, and he had multiplied himself into twenty maddened fighters. The glare of the flames made it hard for the weapon men to see these new Leifs.

"Peace!" they yelled—those who lived—throwing down weapons and shields.

So they begged for their lives before they realized that Leif's men had come back to the burning homestead. Those shipmates had heard Leif's yell, and they had run to him fast, out of the darkness . . .

A week later Leif himself was fitting a new steering oar on the aft deck of Hrolf's dragon ship, which he had appropriated because it was better than his own vessel.

Now that he had washed in fresh water, cutting his hair, and putting on new wool garments, Brana, who sat with him, knew that he looked like any other boy of the quiet Viking coast. Yet he was making ready to go on the West voyage toward that unknown land of his as if it were no more than a jaunt down to Gothland.

"Leif," she said, helping to hold the pole he was shaping with his ax, "you have a fine new ship, with plenty of gold and silk and precious things in it. Stay here, then, in my place and we will build a new homestead."

On the shore by the landing, the people who had survived in Orn's Firth were tending the cattle again, around the black ruin of the hall. Troubled, Leif leaned on his ax, looking at them.

"No," he said, "I must get to the Green-land before the winter storms."

Brana took his hand, with the scars of work on it. "Then tell me—do you remember nothing at all of how you killed Hrolf?"

"Nothing." Leif frowned, trying to think.

"The men say you went berserk."

Leif shook his head. "I remember a spear that flew by me. And then I felt anger."

"Why, Leif?" she breathed softly.

"They were hurting you."

Gripping tight his hand, Brana closed her eyes. When she did that she felt safe. And she knew she had found what she had been searching for. No matter upon what unknown seas Leif chose to steer, Brana would be there with him.

Among the Missing

The first thing I noticed was her red hat in the crowd when the ship came in. It was a red beret, pushed back from a slim, pale face that seemed to be made for laughter. The beret had a feather stuck in it, and the girl wore a jaunty karakul jacket. But her young face was tense with a kind of hunger, and her gray eyes, slanting a little, never left the transport coming in to the Haidarpasha landing by the bridge—the place of honor, you know—horns playing somewhere because the Turkish brigade was coming home. The survivors had been relieved, after heavy losses in Korea. The thing that struck my mind about the girl in the beret was that she had been starving for a long time until that transport docked.

Fantastic? Well, it might be. Man does not live by bread alone. Tell me a man's dream, and I'll tell you what kind of person he is. Soldiers of any nation can usually get themselves food enough—after two World Wars I can testify to that—yet most of them carry some pin-up pictures, or letters, or even a card with a Hail Mary. Why?

By coincidence I ran into the girl in the red beret again the next day. Having made a hobby of legends and what people call antiquities, I'd managed to be stationed at Istanbul, the old city, whereas most of the Army group of AMAT—American Mission for Aid to Turkey—had duties at the new capital of Ankara. And usually after lunch I walked down the boulevard with the trams to the Aya Sufia, which is what they call the oldest standing church on earth. It's in the parkway where the palace used to be, and it has been made into a museum, so I would find only a stray tourist or a class of schoolkids there. Well, as I reached the gate a polished limousine pulled up at the curb, the driver slid around to open the door, and out stepped the girl who had been waiting at the dock. She went straight into the courtyard of the church.

She had not been alone in the car. In the back sat a solid youth in a camel's-hair coat. I knew him—Masur Aridag, the son of a member of Parliament, and the successful head of one of the new motion-picture studios. We exchanged the usual bows and how-are-you's, but Aridag stayed put in his car and I went on in. The girl was no longer visible. That surprised me, because she had been only some thirty paces ahead of me. And the carpeted floor, bright with sunlight, stretched clear without partitions or furnishings to those incredible marble walls, fourteen centuries old.

The next day it rained. When I took my walk past the Aya Sufia, there was the black limousine parked again at the curb with the driver dozing and young Aridag reading a newspaper. Did you ever stop to think how we take for granted that the strangers we meet are doing the most ordinary things, like catching trains or going to the movies? They might be on their way to rob a museum or to hear a doctor's diagnosis that meant life or death. Well, here was matter-of-fact Aridag waiting like a businessman on Fifth Avenue for a very attractive girl who might be his fiancée to come out of St. Patrick's doors. I told myself that, and then remembered the strange hunger in her face when she watched the transport coming to its moorings.

I would have bet dollars against piasters that she was inside—but where? People don't usually vanish when they step into St. Patrick's. Even Cinderella had to go away somewhere. This time I wandered around the dim walls, passing an attendant who tried to keep warm in his overcoat, and a stocky Turkish infantryman who got up to salute me, or rather my lieutenant colonel's insignia. Turkish soldiers are not allowed to wear service ribbons or bright metal insignia of rank.

I heard the faint tapping of small heels on stone, not far off, but evidently not from the carpeted floor within sight. It took me a moment to place the sound overhead and to realize that there must be a narrow gallery above the massive pillars of the ground level. Going back to the entrance I found a stone stair, almost dark, leading up. Then I remembered Byzantine ladies had used the galleries to be secluded from the men below.

Perhaps I should not have gone up—a middle-aged American officer, merely curious about what seemed odd. The girl was waiting by one of the narrow windows close to the stairhead. Almost she ran at me, holding out her arms, her face a white blur. Before she touched me she stopped, rigid, saying something I didn't understand, and then in English, "Will you please excuse me? I did think you were somebody else."

Probably I had been the only person to climb that obscure stair after her, and Cinderella had sighted my uniform in the dim light. The way her eyes strained up at me showed she had had a shock. She kept on talking in her careful, learned-at-school English, "We always did come here before. In his letter Karal wrote how, if I did not find him at the *gumi*—the ship—come here or he would send me a message."

I broke off a stupid apology, realizing what was back of her words. The girl had not expected to see Karal at the ship. Still, she came to this gallery to wait, as his last letter had asked. To hold on to a last link with her soldier, who was probably reported missing. "Did they report him missing, Miss . . ."

"My name is Lailee Baibars . . . No, sir. They said he must be killed: but they did not recover his body."

After that, I didn't try to go away. This Turkish girl, lightweight, dark hair, and gray eyes, had taken two beatings already—one watching troops at the dock, the other when I blundered up the dark stair, an idiot more than twice her age. Her lips quivered over those last words, tension in her was near to breaking. I knew the symptoms, and also that there was a mighty slim chance of a combatant missing in action in Korea turning up again.

As we walked that corridor, she kept telling me that Karal was no ordinary man; he had a way of doing things like climbing the Karadagh above their town, and getting money to send her, Lailee, to medical school at the University, and waiting outside the door of her room one morning for her to wake up and dress an arm he had torn. I gathered that the Lailee part of the twosome kept all the rules, while the boy Karal made his own rules; he got his commission without benefit of the military academy, and they were to be married after his return. When two kids grow up together that way, the tie between them doesn't break easily.

She had depended on this boy who had chosen to do the crazier kind of things, like volunteering to fight a battle halfway around the world. Somehow she would have to get over him, and the best way to do that seemed to be to go down where Masur Aridag waited in a warm car. Aridag, it appeared, was kind; he drove her around in the car and telephoned every morning; I gathered he would wait patiently until Lailee was ready to marry him. Probably some part of her woman's mind told her she ought to get out of that silent gallery, with its memories.

So I held out my hand to help her down the steps. Turkish women, even of Lailee's age, were homebodies; they went from the family home to the husband's. It wasn't a question of a medical career or marriage with Lailee; it was only a question of which man she would marry—Aridag, waiting alive and rich, or the other, no more than a memory. So I made a mistake.

Instantly she backed away to the wall, saying, "Please. Aridag is jealous and he did not want me to come back to this place."

How can you size up a strange woman's mind? After long strain, little things could hit her with the impact of bullets. Probably she felt that if she took the first step down from the gallery she would be leaving this Karal.

"He said he would send a message. He always kept a promise to me."

I couldn't leave her in that state of quiet hysteria. The chances of any word from Karal reaching Lailee now across thousands of miles of winter in Asia were practically nil. *Don't argue about that*, instinct warned me. *Talk to her someway, to quiet her.*

Right then I saw an odd thing. The girl pressed back against the wall, beside the life-size figure of a man in a jeweled coat with a plump, satisfied face—a Byzantine emperor of fourteen centuries ago, preserved in mosaics. I knew him and his portraits.

"Who is that?" I asked sharply.

Justinian the Great, she answered mechanically, who built the great church and made the famous Code of Law, and preserved civilization in this city after Rome fell to the barbarians.

Yes, it was Justinian all right, the great politician who built so many memorials to himself. And they say he did a lot for civilization as well—collecting its books and churches and people here during those dark ages. But did he?

Beside the gorgeous Justinian, in my mind, appeared the dim outline of another man, who never had his portrait made because the emperor wanted no memory of him to survive. "No," I said, "the other man did that. The one who isn't here."

At that, watching my face, she listened.

He was a big man (I told her in my cocktail-table talk, not knowing the historical lingo) with a beard like a yellow flame until it turned gray. Because he limped, he used to ride a white horse up the avenue here almost every day in the lunch hour. When he had any money, he'd detour around the Strategion Square and give it away to the war vets sunning themselves there. You see, he had a screw loose in his head.

Well, he was the one they called for that day. That morning was worse than the air strike at Pearl. Until then the citizens of Constantinople, as it was called in the time of these emperors, believed themselves safe from any danger, behind their triple walls. Then all at once disaster came racing on them, hell-bent, and this church filled up in no time with civilians praying and carrying on, and calling for this forgotten man, Count Belisarius.

When they yelled to Justinian bring out Belisarius, he pretended not to hear. The great emperor was jealous of this veteran who had been the general of the army. For Belisarius had once licked the Vandals, who had taken Africa for themselves, and after that he had outfoxed the Goths who had settled down around Rome in Italy. He was a soldier's soldier, by which I mean he never understood the politics of war, only the fighting part. There was never his match for finding a way to win a battle.

Now of course Justinian had to work nights, to keep his Roman-Byzantine empire out of the hands of the barbarians. If these barbarians got Constantinople, they got the jackpot and the game was over. So Justinian, the emperor, used Belisarius, the general, like something expendable, sending him from one front to another. No sooner had Belisarius paraded in down the avenue to the palace, the Gothic king and all the German commanders as POW's, than Justinian told him he was needed on the east front, to put a stop to the Persian King of Kings.

At that point Theodora, the empress, spoke up and said Belisarius hadn't had time to unpack his bags, and Belisarius, who had the screw loose in his head, said that was all right—he'd send his kit east without unpacking. Theodora had a gleam in her eye and Justinian noticed it.

"Why did she?" demanded Lailee.

Well, she was about Belisarius's age and she had played in the streets when he played hooky from military school. When she went on the stage—which means the circus here—Theodora did a strip-tease act that was something to see, with her impish eyes and mane of dark hair. Belisarius, who was landing in Sicily then, didn't see it, but Justinian did, and married her. He was only a senator then.

After Justinian was elected and Theodora became empress she had a whole troop of pompadoured ladies to help her bathe, and Russian minks for her wraps. She loved this being empress, but she still had her circus temper, and it broke at times.

Belisarius, who had loved her as a kid in the streets, worshiped her as empress from afar. She was beautiful.

When he had finished with the Persian King of Kings on the east front—and they say it took a miracle to do it—Belisarius had been through twenty-four years with the troops, and he had picked up that limp, along with a twitch to his nerves. He'd spent his pay for bread for his own division, when the commissary biscuits were bad. Still his eyes lighted up when he bowed in his scarlet campaign cloak before his two sovereigns on their gold thrones and emerald-jade footstools.

"Noble Belisarius," cried Theodora, "you have grown quite gray. But it's very becoming," she added quickly.

Now the real reason for Justinian's jealousy of the soldier was Theodora. Also, he didn't relish the popular ovation given his victorious general.

So Justinian declared that Constantinople had never had such a hero as Belisarius, and on the spot he named him First Citizen. Then he took steps to ensure that his Master of the Armed Forces wouldn't stay hero. First he sent away all the biscuit eaters—the veterans of spearhead division—to duty on distant frontiers, which were all at peace after the winning of the last Persian war. Then he promoted the soldier to a desk upstairs by making him Commander of City Militia. The militia had nothing to do in peacetime but hold field days in the Hippodrome.

For a while the crowds in the Hippodrome would cheer the retired Belisarius when he showed up, but soon the citizens went back to their favorite chariots. It seemed as if everyone had forgotten Belisarius in peacetime, except Theodora.

Driving out on the avenue each day, she would halt her imperial carriage, drawn by white mules, and her escort of household guards, to stand up and wave at him, and he would take off his civilian hat to bow to her. It was like an act she put on. Until the day of doom—

It came because of the peace and prosperity Constantinople had within its triple walls. Why, every citizen had a cart in his stable, with the Hippodrome and government bread for the unemployed. The gold reserve of the world was locked up in the palace treasury.

Out in the steppes above the Black Sea, the Khan of the Utigur Huns heard about all this wealth behind the walls of Constantinople. Without bothering to declare a war, the Huns started moving in on it, and, being mounted on steppe mustangs, they came fast.

They rode across the River Danube on the ice. When the news was flashed by blinkers to Justinian, he told his cabinet in the palace not to be alarmed. They had the army of the Danube and the new Master of the

Armed Forces—a general named Sergius—and the wealth and fortifica-
tion of their city to stop the Huns. What Justinian heard next was that
Sergius had been captured by the Huns after his army had been scattered
over the countryside.

That started the panic. Some senators began to figure how there was
no longer an army between them and the oncoming Huns. "August emperor," they begged Justinian, "let Belisarius restore the situation."

And that was the one thing Justinian wouldn't do. Instead he called out
the city militia and the cadets himself to defend the Long Wall up in the
mountains. But those Huns went through the Long Wall like paper.

Then panic really got loose in the city. Suburban commuters tried to
cart their belongings into the city gates, while Constantinopolitan families mobbed the boat landings, and the biggest crowds screamed under
Justinian's windows, "Mightiest of Emperors, do something quick! Give
us Belisarius to defend us!"

In their fear they imagined that the soldier who had won all his battles might save them now from the Utigur Huns.

Justinian had to give in to the mob. Summoning Belisarius before his
empress, he said, in effect, "Now listen. You are my Commander of City
Militia. It's high time you took command and defended my city."

Being a soldier, the First Citizen was accustomed to getting orders like
that. "As of when?" he asked, without batting an eye.

"As of this minute," directed the emperor with sour triumph. "Take
over. And that is all."

But what was left for Belisarius to take over with? His own regiments
had been sent off to distant frontiers, and even the militia was gone. Justinian had called him in just in time to take the blame for disaster.

"No," spoke up Theodora suddenly, "that is not so. Belisarius, tell me
what is the one thing you need the most?"

Standing up there in her purple and gold, she made an eyeful for the ad-
miring Belisarius. "Most merciful glory," he responded, "that these citizens forget about Huns for a few hours."

"I think that can be managed, most noble Belisarius," she told him
thoughtfully.

Belisarius did his best, considering that he had little time and no trained
regiment left. In his faded scarlet campaign cloak he rode his white horse
up the avenue from the palace, telling everyone, "Pass the word for the

biscuit eaters. Say Belisarius wants those who have served under him to come to the Strategion Square."

They came up from the speakeasies and down from the tenements. The veterans of Tricameron and the Salarian Gate came running, with flasks on their hips and the best swords they could pick up on the way. From behind counters and gaming tables, they came running. They were all overage and overweight. One, who was blind, asked, "What is this, fellows?"

"It's the old army," they told the blind man, "going out again with Belisarius and the standards."

"We have some Huns to chase," Belisarius told them, at the assembly point. "They'll be hard to catch."

By making a joke of it, he quieted down the panic, some. By sending out for spears from the theaters, armor from the museum, nets and boat hooks from the fishermen, and even silver platters to serve as shields, he armed his mob after a fashion. He took horses from the peasants' carts, and he took the peasants, with planks from the lumberyard and trumpets from the civic orchestra. He even took the prized chariot horses from the Hippodrome stalls with their chariots.

By noon he had three hundred war veterans mounted and pretty well armed. He had two retired brigadier generals, one of them sober, and about five hundred more riders who could swing a spear and obey a trumpet call. More than that, he had a mob of hunters with bows, boatmen with boat hooks, and peasants with the planks. Just about then, all the churchbells began ringing, because smoke showed on the northern skyline, where the Huns were burning villages as they came in.

"Let's look into this. Why should we wait?" Belisarius shouted. "Fall in! . . . Guide right on the standards! First lancers, ma-arch!"

The city orchestra played them up the avenue and out the towers of the Golden Gate. Belisarius went out of the walls because he had no trained force to hold seventeen miles of fortifications. A showoff, with a screw loose, he kept on going up the road, to the village of Chettus, toward twenty thousand triumphant and dangerous Huns determined to crack the treasure vault of the city he left behind.

Where the lights of Chettus village straddled the road, with the dark forest beyond, he halted his motley command. It was not an army, and it had no visible means of standing against the oncoming Asiatics. It simply followed where Belisarius led and he kept up the pretense of a great joke they were playing, getting all units to light large fires and keep in motion around them. Because he knew the Huns would have scouts at the edge of the forest fronting them and he wanted the encampment to look bigger and better than it was.

Perhaps, like Hannibal and the other great commanders of men, he had only that one thing—the ability to keep men following him trusting in him until luck gave him a break.

"I wish we had the band here," he told one of his brigadiers. "I'd like fine to have the enemy scouts report we're having a good time in this village tonight."

"You're crazy," replied the brigadier who was not the sober one. "So am I. I've seen the circus following on."

"How much of the circus, general? And where is it?"

They searched through the campfires until they found it, and Belisarius said something profane when he pushed through the spectators to the vehicle of ivory and gold plate hitched to four white-tasseled mules with a slender pin-up of a woman doing a song routine in it.

"That's all of it," explained the brigadier.

Now, the several thousand males of that forlorn hope in Chettus village had seen Theodora, if at all, robed toe to chin on the throne of an empress. The actress behind the mule team had little enough on.

Getting close to the apparently oblivious Theodora, Belisarius said forcibly, "Most divinely noble—"

"To whom," she rapped at him, "are you speaking, soldier?"

And she went on with the song about how the Vandals ran at Tricameron. That silenced Belisarius, who dared not speak her name, and could not eject her against her will and the inclination of her audience. Her act was a good one—pulling Belisarius up to her cart stage, after the song of how he held the Salarian Gate against the Goths. After she held him in both arms and kissed him, the watching fishermen and veterans shouted, and there was nothing Belisarius could do about it. "It's good for the morale of the troops, darling," she whispered to him.

After she went into the strip-tease routine, over in the lines of the lancers and charioteers, Belisarius had to go out and make a personal check-up of the sentries, to see they hadn't been drawn in to the show. He blessed his star of luck that the Huns never went into an action after dark.

Of course the word got around. Some of the old-timers remembered watching Theodora in her circus days. Perhaps no one quite believed that The Glory of the Purple and The Joy of the World was performing for them in person, but they passed the word along the fires, "It's Theodora, like in the old days." And their morale zoomed in Chettus.

"Don't you think, darling," observed Theodora, putting on her wraps because of the chill in the early-morning air, "that your soldiers have stopped worrying about the Huns?"

"I do," admitted Belisarius, who had braced her to see she took off for the palace. "Now the show's over, Theodora. I want you to go home."

"The show isn't over by any means. I've always wanted to see how you win a victory, Belisarius, and I'll watch this one. The stage is yours now, dearest."

What could Belisarius do with her? If he called over a squad to put her under arrest, all she had to do was pull her rank on him, and there would be a scandal to rock the empire.

"Then for gosh sake stay in the village," he told her.

It jangled the screw looser than ever in his head, to have her sitting out the battle. Not that he could offer any legitimate battle. By experience he knew the one thing Asiatic Huns feared was a trap. But with his fake army he could set up only a phony kind of trap. Until then he hadn't really expected it to work. Now it had to work.

Desperately he tried to imagine what the Huns would be doing. He had to guess right at every point. Well, by then he thought the horsemen of the steppes would be contemptuous of any Christian armies. Their scouts would report the presence of a defensive force maybe several thousand in strength, holding the village of Chettus on the road to the city. So what would their khan decide to do? Why, to advance in column of march along the road, sending perhaps one brigade ahead to strike the village at sunrise and clear out the defensive force so the main body could advance on the city.

Belisarius couldn't waste any more time. Trying to forget about Theodora, he led all his missile throwers—the archers, peasants with javelins, fishermen with hooks and nets—out of Chettus, a mile or so, to the thick forest. There he posted them under cover on either side above the strip of roadway. He left one brigadier there with one trumpet, and told the officer, when the head of the Hun cavalry column came up, to sound off the trumpet and throw everything he had at the road.

"And after that?" observed the brigadier. "Well, we had a good life, Belisarius."

As it happened, Belisarius had guessed right at every point. In the dawn's early light, with the sun breaking through the forest mesh, the dark mass of the Huns flowed silently along the road; the trumpet blared and the varied missiles whammed down, bothering the flanking horsemen. What happened next took the entire galloping column by surprise.

Trumpets sounded off ahead as if signaling masses of troops. Before they even sighted Chettus, the leading Huns found Roman cavalry coming hell-bent for them along the road, on a half-troop front. These were Belisarius's three hundred veterans. Behind them charged other horsemen—the five hundred who could stick in the saddle.

Behind the cavalry, strange vehicles started dust flying. These were circus chariots. Behind the chariot screen the mob on foot flashed silver-plate shields and whacked boards together to simulate great forces in motion.

The horses from the Hippodrome really did it. Those big racers nearly went mad, what with the racket and the novelty of their race. They came on as if rounding the Spina for the homestretch, and they had been trained to rough any other horses on the track.

Belisarius and his three hundred and all the rest of the circus poured into the forest road with unbelievable momentum, with dust and uproar following.

The Huns, who had expected to do their own charging at the village, acted with the instinct of animals sensing a trap. The leading units started to circle away and got tangled in the brush, with the sun in their eyes and things like fishnets and hooks dragging them out of their saddles. Belisarius's flying wedge went deep into the column and kept moving.

He lost a lot of the three hundred veterans along the way, but with such momentum behind he kept on going and the whole column of Huns started to get out of the trap, as they supposed it to be. They started back. Even a column of Huns could not reverse direction without confusion. Once it started back out of the forest belt, it kept going . . .

Of course the main body of Huns was intact, waiting on the road. But the khan figured it would be silly to storm the triple wall of Constantinople city if the Christians were to rout his advance column in the open. So the khan announced they assemble next at the River Danube, cross it, and go home before the ice went out.

So Belisarius won his battle, and Theodora watched him do it.

"What did she do then?" demanded Lailee Baibars, who seemed to have forgotten her own trouble for a while.

That not being military history, I couldn't tell her much. "I think Theodora went back to her throne. After all, she was a great empress. Did she go out to help Belisarius, or to save the empire for her and Justinian to rule?"

The slight dark girl took my question literally. "I think she went out to live or to die with Belisarius."

We weren't alone by then. Aridag's driver had come up to the gallery to wait at the stair, and Lailee said that Mr. Aridag thought she had delayed too long. I flicked on my lighter, to be sure it was the chauffeur behind me in the dimness; then I waited to see what the girl would do, there by the mosaic portrait of Justinian.

An odd thing happened. Steps sounded quickly on the stone stair. A stocky soldier appeared beside the driver. When he saluted me I recognized the Turkish private who had been sitting below in the church. Going straight to Lailee Baibars, he spoke to her, and her face changed as if she had heard a voice out of the air itself.

"Why, he has been waiting to give me a message!" she whispered. "When you made a light, he saw me here."

Yes, it was odd to hear that message from the other side of Asia just then. Karal had told him to wait here for the girl, but he had not known about the gallery. The missing officer had given the man the message when they met behind the enemy lines after the engagement that had inflicted such loss on the first Turkish brigade in Korea. This Karal had told the private how to work his way back to our lines, and had then gone off to look for others of the platoon.

The message? No more than he was well, but would be delayed getting home.

It did something to the girl. All the strain went out of her slim face. "He's alive, certainly!" she cried, actually hugging me, and thanking me for telling her what to do.

It didn't follow at all that he was alive, unreported, behind the Chinese lines all those weeks. "Sure," I said, "sure." But what had I told her?

Gathering up her handbag, Lailee peered and dabbed at her face like any girl getting ready to step out. Then she called the driver and went down to Aridag and the waiting car.

I didn't see that car again parked outside the Aya Sufia. Sometimes I turned in from my luncheon walk and went up to the empty gallery without seeing a sign of Lailee Baibars. Of course, the Turkish soldier never showed up again.

After a month I'd have bet dollars against piasters that Lailee had married Aridag. She had not come back to wait at the gallery message center. And I was sorry, because the girl in the red hat had been a bright spot, a touch of a dream, in my routine of desk work and meals in a strange city.

When I went down, as protocol required, with a Turkish major to be at the sailing of the transport, I thought of her. The crowd around me wasn't doing any waving or weeping on the Haidarpasha landing. The same music of flutes and horns sounded somewhere, and the whistles of all the Bosporus steamers sounded when the moorings were cast off, because the big ship was taking a replacement brigade to Korea.

I looked around for her red beret—yes, she was a lovely girl—and I wondered, rather fantastically, if she had managed to send an answer by anyone to the message. Then I saw her face, but not in the crowd. She was bending over the rail of the ship above me, with a small group of women in khaki-gray, hugging their kits. She didn't look hungry, only excited and young.

"A nurse!" I exclaimed.

My friend, the major, thought I was speaking to him. Conscientiously, he explained that a few volunteer nurses were going this time, as an aid to the morale of the troops.

I must have looked queer then, remembering how the Empress Theodora had followed her soldier out. Because he added quickly, as if excusing it, that one of them, a young medical graduate, wanted to go to join an officer missing and believed dead in action.

"She called him a soldier's soldier," said my friend, with the curious reticence of a Turk hiding his pride in something. "We made an exception for her," he added, "because the lieutenant had just rejoined United Nations forces after carrying out his duty under conditions of extreme difficulty. We had only recently had the report. You see, sir," he apologized, "it was an exceptional case."

"By glory," I said, "it was."

To his surprise, I yanked off my cap and waved after the transport turning past the old wall of the city at peace, starting its voyage to the frontier that was so much farther than the village of Chettus.

The Lady and the Pirate

As soon as the elderly admiral stepped ashore from his launch at Istanbul, the pretty dark girl showed him the tomb. Since he was senior naval officer of the American Mission for Aid to Turkey, she had been chosen to show him the sights on his arrival to become technical renovator of the very small Turkish navy. She did not realize, and Terence McGowan had no chance to warn her, that she was making a mistake in introducing the admiral to anything as old as the gray tomb smack against the blue water of the Bosporus.

When the dapper and slightly deaf admiral peered obligingly through the window of the tomb, he noticed something unusual, a pair of lanterns of massive wood gilded over, the sort of things that had been stern lights on corsair craft or galleons of Spain long ago. He said so.

"Sir, they are old as you say," explained the brunette, Miss Mary Hisarbey, brushing back her shoulder-length bob; "four centuries old. But they are not Spanish. They are the lanterns of the Captain of the Sea."

Now the admiral had a fetish for exactitude and a chronic dislike for anything out of date—after being present in the engagement of the Coral Sea. Until then, his observation of Istanbul had revealed only old minarets and a coal-burning flagship, a battle cruiser christened *Yavuz Sultan Selim*, that, in his opinion, might as well have been Noah's ark.

"Never heard of the rank," he grumbled.

"It was Barbarossa's," prompted his aide, Lieutenant Commander Terence McGowan, who had been a year at the Istanbul station and had grown very fond of Mary Hisarbey.

The name sounded familiar. But the admiral, unlike Terence McGowan, had read few books about the East except the *Arabian Nights*. Hearing the name mentioned, the crowd behind him craned forward eagerly, as if expecting him to lay a wreath. McGowan had warned him that these Turks had a great deal of pride.

"Why, he was the pirate!" cried Mary Hisarbey.

A pirate laid to rest in a tomb under galleon lanterns made no kind of sense to the admiral. Unless—"H'm—unh." He cleared his throat. "Somebody out of the *Arabian Nights*, eh?"

The dark girl looked as if she were going to cry, in spite of the flower spray on her shoulder lapel, and the crowd acted as if something they'd been looking for hadn't happened. Hastily, McGowan suggested they proceed up the Bosporus.

At the end of the afternoon, when the launch was returning down the Bosporus, the name of Barbarossa still bothered the admiral. A name had to be more than a name. It had to have rank and identification.

"They made him admiral of their first fleet," explained McGowan, who had had a tough day.

The admiral lighted a cigarette and stared at the ancient fishing ketches, brightly painted with eyes at the hawseholes, to see their way over the sea. So he had been told.

"I know we make pirates of our admirals, McGowan," he stated, "but I've never heard of it happening the other way around. Exactly how did it happen here?"

"To be exact, it happened here because a girl was snappy-looking enough to be rated Miss Mediterranean."

"McGowan," said the admiral, "it still sounds like the *Arabian Nights* to me. Can you give the identification of this Barbarossa and the girl you call Miss Mediterranean?"

Taking the girl first (explained Terence McGowan, getting on the side of the admiral's good ear and using verbiage he knew his senior officer would understand) she was Julia Gonzaga. Call her Julie, age sixteen, and a pin-up if there ever was one, from shins to hairline. The Gonzagas? They were tops in the four hundred of the sixteenth century, residing in Rome, Venice, or Capri, along with the d'Estes and the de' Medicis. So Julie had a home environment of Italian villas—and cocktail parties where the drinks were sometimes mixed with poison. She was a lady.

It started when Julie took a passenger vessel, one of your Venetian galleons, out to a family villa on an island and the ship grounded in the Messina currents. A redheaded fisherman came alongside to sell—so he said—his catch of fresh swordfish to the noble first-class passengers. When he had his first good observation of Julie, the fisherman forgot about selling anything. Instead, he braced her, asking if he couldn't take her anywhere.

Julie didn't object or try to bargain; she was tired of sitting in the deck chair looking at Stromboli, which wasn't erupting that year. She said certainly he could take her and her cabin luggage and servants and the nuns, too, out to her island in the archipelago. You see, at that age she was accustomed to having everyone roll out red carpets for her.

The redheaded fisher guy said fine, he knew the island because he came from one near it. He spread a clean carpet for her on the stern of his shallop, and put all Julie's traveling companions for'ard of the mains'l, so he could admire her better while he answered her questions, which she asked freely, since he was much older, about twenty-five, and acted different from anyone she'd known. He told her that he looked like a wrestler, broad in the beam, because he'd been a wrestler, and his name was Red Beard, Barbarossa in her lingo, because his beard was red, and he let it grow to make it hard for another guy to strangle him. Also, he was a Turk because he wanted to be one.

When Julie had finished with her questions, the red fisherman asked one himself: Would Julie change course and head off the wind to his island, and be his wife?

That did not surprise Julie. (Terence McGowan got this part from Mary, who understood more about women and Turks.) Many grandees had been calling on her family with wedding rings for her already. She did not make the mistake of telling Red Beard—Barbarossa—she would only be a sister to him, because, young as she was, she sensed how he wanted more than that. She said her family thought her too young to marry, and anyway Barbarossa was too poor.

"So will you first make a great name for yourself, Barbarossa," she countered, smiling up at him, "and when you have done so, come and ask me again, please?"

He looked down into her matchless eyes. "Julie," said he, "that's a deal between us."

And when he beached on her island, Barbarossa picked her up like a bouquet of flowers and walked her ashore, sniffing the nice smell of her hair. Before Julie could tell him good-bye, he kissed her gently and jumped back into his shallop. She was surprised as well as mad, because he'd kissed her and run off without a last word from her.

Anyway, she told herself, he was only an island boatman who smelled of swordfish. But her family told her—when they had quieted down a little—how the red fisherman was little better than a pirate and woman snatcher, because he owned his island and a whole fleet, since nobody else seemed to be able to take it away from Barbarossa, and Julie had only the saints to thank that she hadn't lost her innocence and cost them ten thousand Venetian gold ducats in ransom besides.

Julie had not realized how much of a name Barbarossa had made for himself already. Nor did she know then that the ex-heavyweight wrestler had room in his head for only one idea at a time, and that one idea was Julia Gonzaga.

The red fisherman lost little time in making more of a name for himself. He exchanged his best shallop for a Venetian eighteen-oared galley by boarding her, and he picked up two papal royal galleys by lying in their course where they never looked to be engaged by such a small craft.

By the time Julie's family had betrothed her to marry a count, Barbarossa had a task force, and from Gib to the peak of Samothrace he had the name of a pirate. Yet Julie still thought of him as the awkward and kindly fisherman who wanted to do things for her. Just about then she heard from him. A pilgrim, calling at her garden in the Reggio villa near Rome, put a slip of paper into her hand, and the scrawl on the paper said:

> *My Lady*:
> I have made little of a great name for myself yet, still I ask you again to be my wife.

Julie tore up the paper, thinking, *The very idea*. And forgetting to ask the pilgrim where he'd got it, until he was gone. That was a mistake. When Barbarossa heard the pilgrim's story, he was sure she'd double-crossed him merely to get a ride in his boat. When he got angry, he stayed that way.

The week before her wedding, Barbarossa called. He and his raiders came in from the shore so fast by night that her servants could only rush Julie out of her bed to the back of an unsaddled horse. Some said she had a nightgown on, some said she had none, but all agreed she was worth seeing. When she got over being scared to her very bloodstream, Julie felt mad, besides being disgraced.

What with getting her wardrobe together after the raiders had finished with the villa, and being married in a cathedral, she was in a state of mind. In those days girls learned the facts of life after the wedding, period. No divorce. And Julie was proud. She had the title of *contessa* and no children, and what she learned she kept to herself.

Until her next sea voyage, that is. Long after she thought the pirate Barbarossa had forgotten about her, the count, her husband, had to make a business trip to the Knights at Malta, and told Julie to accompany him. She did, and their galley arrived there, under the guns of the Valetta forts, with the rowing slaves fainting, and Barbarossa's fine flagship with the scarlet pennon and gilt stern lanterns sheering off just out of range.

"May Saint Michael the Archangel drown him where the sea is deepest!" Julie cried.

After that no one wanted to embark with the *contessa*. Isabella d'Este hinted that the lovely but pallid Julie was a *femme fatale*. When she wintered at the Spanish court the Duke of Alva himself whispered that bathing at the beaches might be dangerous for the *bella contessa*, and she'd be safer in his hunting lodge. But Julie would have none of that. "If your high excellency desires truly to protect me, why does he not catch the unspeakable Barbarossa?" she asked.

They caught him. Andrea Doria, the great admiral and politician of Genoa the Proud, trapped him caulking and oiling his vessels in the Djerba lagoon, where our air patrols used to watch for Rommel's oil tankers. Djerba, that flat, swampy island.

Doria was a cautious man. And war galleys then were like destroyers now, hard-hitting with their bronzed prows and heavy foredeck cannon, and powered by oar sweeps pulled by galley slaves; dangerous when they closed and loosed a rush of boarders, yet fragile and unhandy in heavy weather. They had to run before the wind in a storm. When Doria finally maneuvered his fleet into the lagoon, the lagoon was empty. Barbarossa had dredged his vessels clear across the island.

Doria passed the word along that Barbarossa hid himself away. And Barbarossa answered that he never sailed without his broad pennon on his masthead by day and his beacon light showing by night.

They fitted out a great fleet to watch for him off Cape Matapan, and he was running down the Balearics instead ferrying D. P. Moors across to Africa. Moors that the most Christian king had purged out of Spain, without any other place to go.

Then Barbarossa stopped the show in Venice. Every year the most illustrious, the doge of the serene republic used to stage a show, putting out to sea with a good-looking girl sitting by him and him throwing a bridal ring into the water. "You can have done," Barbarossa wrote the doge, "with marrying the sea henceforth, because the sea is my girl now, and no one but me shall wed Miss Mediterranean."

People laughed, but that year the doge's wedding of the sea was called off. They said because of weather.

"Stupid," declared Julie's husband. "Afraid of a shadow. What has Barbarossa got but a name?"

And Julie thought, *My husband would never carry me away to an island of the sea. I haven't seen an island for years.*

Barbarossa was a seaman. Perhaps his forefathers had been Vikings of the long ways of the sea. Certainly as fisher he'd known the feel of the currents and the signs of a storm in the sky. Those who tried to catch him were soldiers and officials, carrying out a mission. There's a difference.

For one thing, he wouldn't have galley slaves on his ships. He said he wanted all hands to be fighting men. For another, he had madness in him. To go after things like Julie, as no levelheaded man would have done. Once when his officers pulled him out of the wreckage of a Portuguese galley they had rammed, he cursed them. He was still alive. "Lubbers," he said, "if God doesn't slay a man, how is anyone else going to do him in?"

They said he had luck. But in all the Mediterranean he had no place of his own to shelter in. Until a place was made for him. At the far end of the sea, Sultan Suleiman the Magnificent of the Turks had been keeping himself posted about Barbarossa, and now he sent for the pirate to come on his carpet.

The sultan expected to see a small-time pirate. Instead he saw a giant with eighteen ship captains following, ushering in gifts, including some remarkably fine-looking women.

When Suleiman had accepted the gifts, he asked, as if casually, had his visitor any strategy to defeat the Europeans?

Thinking that over, Barbarossa shook his head and said no, he had no plan except to close with them and fight them.

Suleiman was not one to hesitate. "Do it then."

He gave Barbarossa the rank of Captain of the Sea and a blank check to draw on, with the arsenal to build a new Turkish fleet for the sultan. "Build what you like . . . with sails of satin and spars of gold if you want," he specified. "But do not put to sea with less than one hundred and eighty ships. I do not want you taking any more long chances. That's an order."

So the redheaded fisherman had a jeweled sword to wear and all Constantinople to set up shop in. He wondered if Julie might think Captain of the Sea was something of a great name. On the whole, he did not think so, because he had to take orders from another man.

You see, he still visualized her as the proud teenager he'd held, light as flowers, in his arms. It was like a beacon on his course. When he heard her husband had been promoted and Julie was now a *marchesa*, he sent her a present of the best family table service he could find.

This complete gold service arrived in time for Julie's gala party with royalty present. Only it turned out to be the d'Este gold plate, which had been missing for years, and Isabella made no bones about claiming it. But Julie kept track of the Sardinian wine merchant who'd been released from jail in Istanbul to bring it, and she stopped him outside the crowd to ask if there wasn't a message this time with the gift. Yes, the Sardinian said, there was a message, if she asked for one.

He gave her a fine gossamer scarf, with directions, "If you are unhappy, go anywhere to the sea and wave this, and a fisherman will see it."

Observing her, Catherine de' Medici, who was no prize beauty, told the scuttlebutt it was too bad the lovely Julie had such dealings with the underworld.

Although she looked like a perfect hostess, Julie really felt confused. To go and wave at the empty sea! Like a child! When she wasn't happy. Only the inward part of her that nobody saw knew that. Anyway, what would happen if she did . . . or if she didn't?

Anyway, Julie argued with herself, she was only holding on to a memory of her lost youth. She had to argue like that when she caught a glimpse of the far-off blue sea.

In no time at all, Barbarossa was called back on the sultan's carpet. He tried to guess what Suleiman might have on him now; he'd been careful to have one hundred and eighty sail following in line when he headed out for the Gallipoli light, because he knew Suleiman would count them off from the sun garden where he kept the best-looking girls.

On his part, Suleiman noticed the dents in his captain's skull under the gray-red hair.

"Now hear me," said he. "You're doing a fair job as my Captain of the Sea. But you're still using command tactics when you should be planning operations like an admiral. Stop leading with your head; you're going to need it now," barked the sultan, and let the cat out of the bag. "Listen, Barbarossa. I have a terribly big empire to manage. Figuratively speaking, it's a big as one of those superbattleships Andrea Doria is building."

"Galleasses. No better than junks in a calm."

"Be that as it may be," continued Suleiman, who was not accustomed to interruptions, "my empire being so big, I have to leave the European area and go off to Africa and Asia to put down the Mamelukes and give a hand to my cousins the Moguls, out India way. Now, while I'm gone, I don't want any of my European enemies to knife me in the back. And would you," said he, passing the wine, "see to that?"

When Barbarossa didn't answer right off, Suleiman hastened to explain, "This isn't an order; I'm only asking. I figure the odds against you to be about seven to one. So take those new heavyweight mortars and ten thousand janizary shock troops—"

"I can't use soldiers on my sea. Keep the marines. No," explained Barbarossa, doing some figuring of his own, "I was only trying to count up your enemies here. Six I know of, but . . ."

"The Knights of Malta are the seventh. What do you say, Red?"

Barbarossa didn't say, quick off. Always he and the sultan dealt the cards face up between them; how they played their cards was each man's affair. And Suleiman would sell out nobody; he was a good chief—even his enemies called him "the Magnificent," as well as "the Terrible Turk."

"Chief," answered Barbarossa, "chief. I know you love your wife Roxelana faithfully. But you are taking off on a long business trip and you will be tired, with all these affairs of state—"

"If you happen on a Venetian red-head," said Suleiman, keeping his voice low, "with broad hips and a narrow waist."

"There's a brunette," said Barbarossa, without batting an eye, "the pick of the Mediterranean, and no Venetian babe could open the door to her."

Suleiman piped down even more. "Red, I don't think you'd lie to me. I know you keep most of my hundred and eighty warships for decoys while you work with your own eighteen, but you never said different. Tell me now, is this a fact?"

"Chief, you hold her in your arms, it's fire and silk, and her lips, rose petals."

"Get her."

"Give me the order in writing."

Suleiman did that, but slowly.

"Go your way now," said Barbarossa happily, taking the order. "And think no more of being knifed in the back by any concert of Europe."

"I am going a long way. And I am beginning to think I've ordered you to take the long chance that I just warned you against. Damn your punch-drunk head, I don't want you killed!"

"If God doesn't rub a man out, how is anyone else going to do it?"
Suleiman couldn't answer that.

Julie was sunning herself on the bathing beach at Nice when it began to
change along the Mediterranean. So long she had been staring out at the
empty sea she was sure Barbarossa had forgotten her. When the fleet wore
in against the land breeze she hardly noticed it, thinking it was Doria's or
the French Toulon, until Barbarossa's scarlet pennant was sighted. Immediately all the royal set evacuated the Riviera. This time Julie had time to
put on her riding dress and take her jewel box, and she looked like a girl
again, at the excitement.

Her husband, the marquis, however, told her it was no laughing matter,
and she must be more mindful of the good name of his family.

Anyway, the raid on Nice brought in the big shot himself, the emperor
of the Holy Roman Empire, to bring Barbarossa's situation in hand; the
emperor calling in his German veterans from his other wars and sending Hernando Cortés, the conquistador, who was killing Mexicans by the
millions in the New World.

"This time," announced the marquis, "they will take Barbarossa's base:
Algiers." He had the low-down at court. "It is all set up because that old
friend of yours is selling out the Turks."

It confused Julie to hear Cortés called a noble conquistador and Barbarossa a pirate. Before she thought, she spoke. "Then they're making a
terrible mistake. Barbarossa wouldn't sell out Suleiman."

How did she know that the redheaded fisherman who had tried to carry
her wouldn't sell anybody out? Women have hunches like that.

But when the emperor came back from Algiers without Algiers and
most of his Germans, and Cortés with only a few of his *caballeros* of
Spain, and all of them without the armor they'd ditched to swim better,
the marquis said it had been due to an unforeseen storm, and how had Julie got her information in advance?

This time Julie didn't answer him. This thing was bound to break,
and probably she sensed how it would break. For one thing, the marquis only told her politely how worried he was by her being pale and no-
account. For her health, so he said, he took her to Venice by coach, assuring her the gondolas and the canals would be perfectly safe. When he took
her to see the Ducal palace, he led her straight to the conference room.
And there, waiting for her, sat seven of the greatest sea lords, including
the doge himself in his red cap of office. They all stood up to compliment
her on her looks.

Andrea Doria explained the idea to her, with maps—how they could only win the war one way, by everybody ganging up. But Julie understood in a flash what they were after, and said so.

"You call yourselves Christian soldiers, and you gang up against a man who fought you fair," she said.

The marshal of the Holy Roman Empire said a woman couldn't judge very well what was fair in war. The lord admiral—that being Doria—would decide the strategy.

"To use a woman to bait a trap!" said Julia.

The vice-commander of the Knights of Malta stood up and swore by his honor that she would be safe this time on the flagship. Especially, he added—not liking Doria—on the lord admiral's flagship.

"I wasn't thinking of myself," she told the commander.

"Evidently not." The thin face of the marquis flushed dark. "I had thought you hated this renegade pirate, but I am led to believe you love him. Speak up," he insisted, when Julie held her tongue.

The tightness within her gave way at the word. "My lord husband, it is true hatred can turn into love," she spoke up all in a breath, "and love can also become hatred. I know nothing about Barbarossa except one thing. He will never shame me as you have done this minute."

Then she curtsied to Doria. "Will you kindly have a chair put for me on the deck of your ship, admiral? I will go with you gladly on your cruise to meet Barbarossa."

When she did, everyone who saw Julie remarked how she seemed to be enjoying it—the doge himself handing her into the admiral's barge at the quay, and the flagship decked with streamers, while salutes were fired all around. Julie had on her newest blue dress with the gossamer silk scarf at her throat. She couldn't help enjoying it, although she knew it was staged like this so Barbarossa would be certain to hear about her.

She hadn't been to sea for so long. And all the sea was covered with sails, from the gun barges to the five great new galleasses, like castles filled with tiers of guns. Seven fleets she counted with seven flags—the arms of Genoa above her, the lion of St. Mark, the Maltese cross, the shield of Spain, the eagles of the great emperor, the crossed keys of the Papal Curia, and another she didn't know that Doria said was Portuguese.

She almost felt like waving her scarf, until Doria gave her the totals—two hundred ships, two thousand guns, sixty thousand armed men. And more than all that, the five new dreadnoughts.

"And what," asked Julie anxiously, "does Barbarossa have with him? By the way, where is he?"

At Preveza, said Doria, refitting his fleet of perhaps eighty sail. At the landlocked port of Preveza, watched by a screening force of light galleys. This screening force, Doria explained, would withdraw to decoy Barbarossa out to where the five galleasses waited. When Barbarossa had broken his strength against the five dreadnoughts, Doria's main fleet of two hundred galleys would encircle the battle to sink every unit of the pirate's Turkish fleet. It would all happen like that, barring bad weather, which, being an act of God, Doria could not control.

This strategy Julie didn't understand very well. But realization came to her like a blinding flash of lightning. Barbarossa was trapped. If he tried to save his crews by landing, he lost his fleet. If he fled away from the armada and from her, the name of Barbarossa would cease to be a legend in the Mediterranean. If he came out to fight against such power as this, and against her, he was lost. And so, very likely, was she. There was no other possibility.

"I understand," she said quietly in her deck chair, "everything now."

Barbarossa came out to fight.

It happened just as Admiral Doria and Julie had anticipated. Except that Barbarossa's vessels got under way at night, surprising the screening force and scattering it before it could draw him seaward. Yet he came on.

The wind being against him, he had to work out with the oars. His lookouts sighted the forest of masts lying in wait off the island of Santa Maura, yet he kept his course to close his enemy.

After dawn the wind died. The five galleasses, becalmed, lay in his way, their great firepower blasting his galleys back. He sent his galleys in singly to fire their bow guns and draw clear. What with that, and the mighty sea castles fouling each other in the calm, one of them caught in flames. After that the small galleys worked in through the smoke to board the great ships. It was mid-afternoon, and the weather thickening, before the fifth galleass hauled down her colors.

If only Barbarossa had kept all of Suleiman's armada with him, and the heavy mortars and janizaries, he might have had more of a chance. As it was, he had taken too much punishment. When he made signal to close the enemy at Santa Maura, his flotilla had thinned behind him. His own galley limped forward with half its oars gone.

Past the stern of Doria's flagship the galley of Malta rounded and the commander hailed, "Lord admiral, do you not see that the enemy will close us? Bear down, bear down!"

"Back to your station!" shouted Doria. "Obey your orders! We will have every sail of his by sundown!"

"Admiral," cried Julie from her chair, "I find the conversation on my cruise most entertaining! What with so many commanders all running up different signals, and squadrons rushing by in the heavy swell," she added. "And the spectacle is really magnificent."

Then through the circling squadrons the dark wedge of Barbarossa's ships came on, with the roar of the guns like the swift roll of drums. When a flying squadron struck against this wedge there was a vast splintering sound.

With each lift of the swell, the wedge was closer. Like an injured wrestler, it felt for a grip on its enemy. And there happened at Preveza what sometimes happens at sea—the great fleet maneuvering, colliding, and changing course could not break up or check the small fleet bearing in.

Under the darkening sky, Barbarossa's scarlet pennon showed clearer. Julie recognized the gilt stern lanterns bearing down on her. So few oars moved the battered galley toward her. Julie's mind told her, *He knows I am waiting here, yet he will not turn away. Nothing now can keep his ship from crashing into mine.*

She didn't feel as if she were going to die. She felt excited and tense, as if at her wedding. What was really happening she couldn't understand because of the loud drumbeat and the darkness over her head.

Then lightning glared. In the flash, Andrea Doria's nerves snapped. He cried, "Give way!" And unsteadily he ordered a signal flag bent—all ships to shelter from a storm. So the mighty armada turned and ran from Barbarossa. The long oars churned, the steering sweeps were thrust hard over, and their galley turned from Barbarossa's boat. Their armada followed, running before the wind rising to hurricane force.

Rain squalls swept the deck. The galley, with oars inboard and only a patch of foresail spread, ran north. Braced with the sweep of the rain, seeing an inlet in the coast as night closed in, Julie wondered why they didn't light the stern lanterns that served as guide beacons for the fleet.

She did not know that Barbarossa was following until the other galley drew alongside with its lanterns glowing aft. It hung to windward, accompanying them. No guns could be worked on her galley in that lash of rain. A shaft of lightning showed Barbarossa standing by the steering sweep across from her as the red fisherman had stood at his tiller, and she thought, *How much heavier he's grown.*

Then she felt warm and protected with Barbarossa between her and the flying spray. She waited for each flashing beacon of the sky to see him again until he drew ahead with beacon lighted, guiding her toward a break in the dark coast.

When her galley reeled and swept into the gut of an inlet, Barbarossa sheered off, heading out toward his scattered fleet. Watching the two lanterns turning away, she remembered and laughed, hurrying to pull the scarf from her throat and wave it.

"*Marchesa*," said Andrea Doria. He looked aged and sick. "What do you wish for?"

Julie hardly heard him, watching into the darkness. "I almost forgot. I was so very happy."

Barbarossa kept the sea until the last of his ships found shelter. Perhaps because of that, he died soon after. From Gib to Gallipoli light, his name was a great name. And when Sultan Suleiman came back from Asia he built that tomb close to the water, with the two stern lanterns hung inside it.

When Terence McGowan finished with his identification of Barbarossa, the admiral flipped his cigarette into the water.

"McGowan," he said, "I was a swab this morning."

The admiral squinted shoreward at the Golden Horn with sunset lighting the minarets of the mosque of Suleiman the Magnificent, and at the small tomb dark by the water. He cleared his throat. "H'm—umh. I'll give you five to one in dollars that Barbarossa wanted Suleiman to keep those stern lights going, and Suleiman did it. But after four hundred years, people forget a detail like that. Furthermore, I think I owe these Turks something. It would be a good thing if I went back tomorrow morning with electricians and got those lanterns going again. Will you break out some flowers and et ceteras, and Miss—Miss Mediterranean to attend again?"

"You mean Miss Hisarbey?"

"I mean Miss Mediterranean." The admiral looked at his aide. "Do you know any reason why the American Mission for et cetera can't have a good-looking Miss Mediterranean?"

"No, sir," said McGowan promptly.

St. Olaf's Day

The first of it was Ernst Salza's waking in the morning. Straight to the window opening he went, and saw a sea mist coming in. Then he felt sure that this would be his great day. Mist and a light breeze—they were sheer good luck.

To check his excitement, he smoothed out the blanket on his wall pallet; he cut himself a slice of black bread and spread cheese sparingly upon it with his knife. Drinking a little water, he gave himself the pleasure of eating a few Syrian dates that had come in on his last ship. For Ernst Salza was a careful man.

As he broke his fast there in his sleeping cell, his thin body towering in its black gown, he lifted his eyes to the whip on the wall, the whip that had lashed raw the flesh of his back when he had become an apprentice, forty-eight years before. An apprentice of the Hansa that outsiders called the Hanseatic League, which he now served as agent.

Beside the whip hung the motto he had picked: *"Success comes only with the last farthing."*

Once Klas Stortebecker had seen that motto and laughed. "Never try for the last farthing, Ernst," he had gibed. "'Tis bad luck, that."

Klas was superstitious. Klas buried the men he killed, and had a Mass said for them, with candle and bell. But Ernst Salza had shed the blood of no man.

But Klas would come as he promised, and the mist would hide his coming.

At the window, Salza could barely make out the masts of his own cogs moored to the bridge that divided his Kontor, or warehouse, from the rest of Bergen-town. He could not see the fishing fleet clustered in the half-moon harbor, or the quays of his competitors, the Norwegians and foreign merchants on the opposite side.

He had closed, by virtue of the Power of the League, all the Norwegian coast to those foreigners except the Bergen port of arrival. He had fixed a high duty on the goods they imported, while the Hansa goods came in to the Kontor free. Still the strangers flocked in, to gnaw at his monopoly of the fisheries and the lumber . . .

With a key from his chain he unlocked the clasps of his record book. Carefully selecting a quill and touching up its point with his knife, he dipped it in ink, and wrote:

"Declaration. I, Ernst of Salza, Achtzehuer of the Bergen Kontor of the Hansa League do avouch and affirm on this day of St. Olaf in the Year of Our Lord 1428, the harbor of Bergen was attacked during the fourth hour—"

He hesitated, thinking whether he should write more.

"—by the masterless men and outlaws of Visby," his pen traced out the words crisply. *"Wherefore, I do accuse these men of Visby commanded by one Klas Stortebecker, of piracy. I demand that all Christian ports be closed to them, and victuals kept from them, and that they be hunted down and harried to their deaths."*

This he read through carefully, and signed his name beneath. Now, whatever happened to Ernst of Salza this day, there would be evidence in writing that the Hansa had neither part nor parcel in the raid. And who would know the hour in which he had written it?

Out in the mist he thought he saw the tracery of a ship's mast moving in. With a tingle of excitement he closed and locked the book. Quickly he carried it out to his desk in the meeting hall. Over that desk hung his new map of the Northern Sea marked boldly *Mare Germanicum* and in smaller letters beneath, *oder, Nord-See.* For forty and eight years Ernst Salza had driven himself unsparingly to make that inscription a fact.

A glance at the dripping water clock showed him that it lacked a quarter of the third hour of the morning. The time was close.

When he strode out of the hall, the journeymen on the stairs bowed to their belts. At the gate, the Kontor guards clashed their halberds in salute. Ernst Salza kept military discipline within this warehouse that he had built like a fortress. Glancing to right and left as he crossed the courtyard, he noted mechanically that the pack of mastiff dogs were loose, the men-at-arms cleaning their crossbows, as he had ordered.

But out on the quay, where apprentices trundled barrels of pitch and soap ashes, the half-dozen men of the bridge watch were gathered around something, and that something wore a skirt.

No women were allowed upon the bridge, not that Salza cared what might go on between the Kontor's men and Norwegian wenches, but he was jealous of the trade secrets of the Kontor. So his men slept in their cells of nights, like monks, and the women were kept out.

"A redhead, my sir," Bode of the guardsmen explained. "With a trifle to sell."

Red indeed was her hair, hanging long upon her shoulders—so she could not be married. White and clean her small linen slippers, so she could not have walked far. No broad-cheeked peasant lass, but a girl with impudent eyes.

"What to sell, woman?" Salza asked. She curtsied gracefully, smiling, showed him a blue cape, bright with embroidery that she held. "My name, sir, is Kari, and will not the merchants of the great Hansi give me a price for this that I made?"

"No," said the agent, without a second glance at it. The girl Kari drew back the mass of her henna-red hair, and the lustful eyes of the halberdiers went up and down her body. Her long eyes had the color of the sea in them. "We have cloth narrow and broad to sell, not to buy," Salza added mechanically, wondering what had brought her here.

Bode touched his arm, and he saw the square leather sail of a longboat turn in to the quay, with one man at the steering sweep. This stranger let down the yard with a crash, and let go an anchor stone. "Ho—good is the landfall," he called, "on St. Olaf's Day i' the morning."

Jumping up to them, he swayed with the feel of the sea in his legs. Leather covered his long body; a pair of horns projected from a dinted and polished iron cap. "I rode the long ways," his voice chanted, "on this steed of the sea."

A gold ring gleamed on his arm, and Salza saw that it had Icelandic runes upon it. He thought that this man might have stepped out of the mist of a century before now.

Suddenly Kari laughed. "By the saints 'e hath the look of a Viking. Do ghosts, coming out of the mist, have a way of speaking, my sir?"

Vikings, Salza thought, no longer sailed in their dragon ships to raid out of Norway's coast. No, they had lived in a darker age of barbarians. The seafarer looked at Kari's hair, and the scar along his chin made it seem as if he grinned. "Aye, woman," he said, "they come back at times from the isles of the sea to the old country."

Reaching down, under the aft deck of the boat, he pulled up a hoop, with a great brown bird, perched upon it, hooded. Its wings lifted restlessly as it sensed the men near it.

"An eagle, that," cried Bode.

"Nay, a falcon of the Green Land that gathers meat for me."

"At sea?" demanded Salza, noticing the white marking on the bird's throat, the grip of its talons. Not for many years had a trading ship touched at Greenland, to fetch back one of these giant falcons, the rarest of their species, and seldom trained.

"The sea or the land—it is all the same to this sky-soarer," the Viking said. Over the water a crane was winging lazily. "Now watch," he said, "for this bird is fast."

Pulling loose the thongs, he drew the hood clear of the restless head. Taking the falcon's talons on his arm, he tossed it up. The brown wings threshed over Salza's head, and the hawk was soaring.

"Hungry it is indeed," cried the Viking.

So swiftly did the brown falcon circle up that it was over the crane before it passed. The wide-winged creature sighted the falcon and swerved, its long beak pointing up. The falcon circled higher, and the crane headed for shore.

Suddenly the brown bird swooped, driving down at its prey. Cutting in from the side, it struck the crane, and feathers sprang into the air. Hawk and quarry shot down, until the brown wings threshed, and the falcon reached the ground tearing at its victim.

"Savage it seems," Salza said coldly, "yet I'll pay thirty nobles in hand for it."

The Viking, watching the bird shook his head. "Elijah ne'er sold his raven."

"Forty then," Salza nodded. "Coin of Lübeck."

"Not for forty, or a hundred."

The Viking, it seemed, was quick at bargaining. And Salza wanted that falcon the more. His mind quested along its possibilities. The falcon could go with the Baltic convoy, from Lübeck the headquarters of the League, on to Muscovy, or even down the rivers and over the Brenner Pass to Venice, where he could get Eastern jewels for the bird. And those jewels might be cleared in the Amsterdam market for more than a thousand nobles.

"We can give the highest price," he conceded, "because we have a market. Agreed at a hundred."

The Viking only shook his head.

Unreasonably—for he was watching the haze over the harbor intently for a sign of the ships coming in—Ernst Salza craved the brown falcon, as he had never craved liquor. He could see the picture of it so clearly now; himself appearing with the royal Greenland bird, before the council at Lübeck to announce the triumph of this St. Olaf's Day, and the full mastery of the Norwegian coast. "Have it your way," he cried, "and name your price for the falcon. Almighty! Have you no need of monies?"

"That have I," the Viking laughed, "for this is the day of my namesake, Olaf. And I shall be opening up the ale kegs in Bergen-town."

"Well, so—"

"So the falcon is mine, and will be mine, merchant." Olaf the Viking rubbed the scar on his chin. "For I doubt much if the bird can be held by any hand than mine, devil that he is. Here!" He pulled off the gold arm ring. "Lend me a fistful of farthings on this surety."

Checking an exclamation of anger, Salza turned the heavy ring in his fingers, pondering. "There are runes written on it," he murmured.

"Aye."

Salza glanced into Olaf's gray eyes, level with his own, and made his decision. This seafarer, who kept a rare falcon for hunting mate, who knew so little of the power of money, who thirsted after ale from a keg, would not have the skill to read. He handed back the arm ring to Olaf. "As you will, outlander," he said indifferently. "Keep the ring. The Hansa does not deal in pawn. If it is coppers you want, my men will bring you out two score, and a quittance to sign against their repayment."

He called out in German to a passing clerk, and strode away from them into the Kontor gate. Across the harbor he had seen four sailing barges coming in from the fiord, and he had made out the wolf's-head crest of Klas Stortebecker on the leading sail. Olaf was watching his falcon, which had taken to the air again and was coming down in lazy circles to the longboat. Carefully Olaf coaxed the bird to its perch and tied the hood upon his head. He gave the bird water.

When a journeyman approached with a fistful of copper coins, Olaf pouched the farthings without counting them. He took the pen the other gave him and made a cross where the man's finger pointed, beneath some lines of fine writing on a scrap of parchment.

"Dunderhead!" cried Kari involuntarily, when the man had gone with his receipt. "Did you read what you put your name to?"

"Not I," Olaf stretched his long arms, and picked up an ax with a bone handle and shining steel head from the boat. "I know what was said and agreed between us. And who says dunderhead?"

Taking the girl's chin in his great fist, he tipped up her face. "Red hair dye from Venice," he muttered, "and a lady's slippers on your hoofs."

Crimson flooded Kari's throat and surged up to her cheeks. She had tried to dye her hair for this morning as she had heard the famous ladies did in Venice—who were the loveliest in the world.

"Are you light of love?" demanded Olaf. "I think not."

Kari choked with rage upon a word. Yet the harshness of the Viking frightened her.

"Word maker!" she gasped. "Duck stealer!"

"The falcon steals the ducks, Kari. I think well you have stolen away from the farm for this holyday."

It was true enough. Kari had become weary with tending the cattle up in the mountain saeter of her father; she had got together this splendor—as she thought—of garments and appearance, to come to Bergen-town.

"Still, you are lovely enough underneath, girl," Olaf admitted. "And as this is my day for wine and women, you can come with me to the feasting."

"If you are thinking that I will sit on your knee and pour your farthing's worth of beer—"

"Ale," said Olaf, shouldering his ax. After consideration, he drew the cape she had brought over her shoulders and pulled the hood over her head, hiding the hair. "You will do well enough," he said, taking her hand, "young as you are."

Kari was nearly sixteen years old. Tears of rage filled her eyes, and she pulled away her hand.

She hoped that this boaster who had wounded her tenderest feelings would choke on his ale and lose his wild hawk. And she wanted to run away from him quickly.

But at the end of the bridge, the Kontor apprentices were ranging barrels in a row across the way, and behind the barrels loitered Bode and his men-at-arms, leering at her now that they were clear of the Achtzehuer's eye. Olaf had to push through the apprentices.

"No weapons on this holyday," shouted Bode, noticing Olaf's long ax. "Put away that woodchopper."

Olaf stopped, turning this way and that. He saw that the Kontor's men carried no arms here, but crossbows and halberds were stacked out of sight back of the heavy casks which made a fair breast-high barricade.

He looked at Bode, and his voice chanted slowly, "Messmate, when I make use of this ax, wolves and ravens are fed, and strife starts, and a war is waged, for I am a fast-fighting man. Now what do you say?"

Kari felt a thrill of excitement, seeing Bode's hands grip hard on his belt. But he hesitated, glancing at the Kontor. "Well, take it off the bridge," he growled, "you and your light o' love."

When they walked through the Street of the Shoemakers, Kari tossed her head. "What war have you seen, seafarer?"

Looking into the open shops, Olaf answered thoughtfully, "In Tsargrad, in Hispania where the Moors are. In Granada and the Isle of Crete, and across the western sea. But this is a day of homecoming and peace."

He headed after the townspeople in festive cloaks, where a merrymaker walked on stilts, and a trained bear danced. Down in the square by the docks, tables had been set and kegs opened. Olaf sniffed the odor of steaming cod and hot punch, and something else.

"Reindeer steak!" he muttered happily. Kari shivered.

Finding a place by the dancing bear, where they could hear the fiddle music, Olaf called for cheese and a horn of ale, and berries and cake for the maiden. At first Kari would not touch the dainties. Then, because she was hungry, she began to eat.

Pushing back his sleeves, Olaf leaned his elbows on the table. "Eh," he said contentedly, "they are singing 'Come All Ye Faithful.'"

When the singing stopped, Kari noticed that the best-dressed burghers and Norwegian shopkeepers went from the tables toward the quays, and a buzz of whispered talk ran around her. Visitors were landing from a convoy—sailors who had lost their way in the mist, and put in for the feasting: Klas Stortebecker and the mariners of Visby Island.

The first group of strangers rolled up to the tables, talking with the meisters of Bergen. They wore sea capes and some had on mail, but their scabbards were empty of swords.

"Stortebecker and his lads fly the peace flag," called out a Flemish trader. "They come to drink. They bring honey mead."

Klas Stortebecker came up, broad as a bear with half his head bald, and white scars showing on the bare skin. "Fire the pots," he bellowed, "fill the tankards, ye Bergen folk. Kindle up for Stortebecker."

Behind him more men staggered up from the boats, with hogsheads on their shoulders. These they set down by the great open bed of coals where an ox had been roasted.

"They stint not their drink," said Olaf, watching.

Some of the women around them were fearful of the Visby sea rovers, who had put the torch to more than one town. Still, they seemed peaceful enough on this St. Olaf's Day, and across the harbor stood the walls of the German Kontor, with a strong garrison. Kari looked at the fine wolf's head embroidered on Stortebecker's tunic.

Olaf had not put his arm around her, or tried to pull her to his knee, and for that she was glad. The shouting rose loud about her, as the seamen gulped meat and swallowed beer.

"Bergen beer," said Olaf. "They do not open their own hogsheads."

A giant from Visby kicked away the dancing bear and called for a champion to tug at war with him. The stout Flemish merchant came forward at the challenge.

"The bull's hide, Lefard," roared Stortebecker. "Pull the hide, man."

The Visby gamester took one end of the rawhide stripped from the bull's carcass, and showed the Fleming how to hold to the other end by the legs. Lefard took his stand at one side of the smoldering bed of coals, and, at a word from Stortebecker, heaved at the hide, while the Fleming strained back, across the fire. The taut hide moved back and forth as the giants tugged. Suddenly the man Lefard threw himself back on his heels. Jerked off balance, the merchant plunged into the embers, the hide falling across him.

He writhed up, and fell again and dragged himself clear of the fire, smoking and blackened. A whimpering came from his mouth.

"The goat bleats," said Stortebecker, looking around. The Bergen men were silent, startled. "Let the goats bleat!" Stortebecker roared.

Olaf grinned and drank more ale.

Kari shivered, feeling for the hurt of the burned man. And Lefard, striding back to their table, took the nearest ale horn, which was Olaf's, and emptied it.

The big Visby man looked at Olaf, who said nothing. Then he bent

over Kari, pulling the hood back from her head. At sight of the flaming
red hair, he crowed.

Two heavy hands gripped the girl's waist and lifted her high. She felt
the blood rush through her body. And then she jolted down on Lefard's
knee, as he seated himself on the bench.

"Pour out the ale, girl," Lefard said in her ear.

Kari felt cold with fright. She made no move to touch the ale horn. Now
she felt ashamed of her red hair. "For wine or for a woman," laughed Lefard, "I wait not."

His shaven head turned toward her, and his hand smelled of the wet
bull's hide. Beside her, Olaf watched curiously, saying nothing. And Kari
closed her eyes as she felt her throat choking.

She heard Olaf's chanting voice: "Messmate, you play hard. Let this
child go, and pour your own drink."

While the Visby man stared at him, Olaf reached down to the ground
between them. His hand came up gripping the ax under the head. The head
of the ax caught Lefard under jaw and ear, knocking him aside.

"Blood!" Stortebecker bellowed. "Beware and yare, lads. Out with the
steel."

Getting to his feet, his ax arm swinging, the Viking called, "You find
a quarrel easily."

Kari, gasping at the bellow of voices, saw twenty men of Visby run
to the unopened hogsheads. Ripping off the tops, they began to pull out
swords, shields, battle-axes. Some of these weapons they tossed to their
mates at the tables. A wailing rose among the women, and the unarmed
Bergen men surged up like cattle startled by a wolf's coming.

"Steel it is," sang out Olaf, vaulting the table, and making for the hogs-
head.

The nearest swordsman stepped out to him, slashing at his head. Olaf
checked his run, poised, braced on his feet. His ax flashed in front of him
as the sword came down. This sword and the hand gripping it flew up into
the air, cut off by the ax blade.

Stortebecker caught an ax from a man near him. His eyes gleamed red
and he snarled as he ran at Olaf, who turned to meet him. Neither man
had a shield.

Swinging his hands over one shoulder, Klas Stortebecker slashed wide
with all the reach of his arms. As he did so the Viking leaped forward, inside the stroke.

His hands gripped the ax haft short and the head of the ax smashed at Stortebecker's face. The Visby chieftain bent his head, taking the blow on his skull, falling to the ground.

As he did so, his hands clutched at Olaf's legs. But the Viking, quicker than he, was away from him. A glance to right and left showed Olaf that the swordsmen were closing around him, and he leaped clear of them, back to the table.

He came running to Kari, his ax in one hand. Catching her about the knees in his right arm, he heaved her up over his shoulder, and ran on.

Behind him the bearlike Klas hauled himself up, shaking his head. "Leave the goats," he bawled. "Fetch back that strife starter."

As he ran through the Street of the Shoemakers, Olaf heard them coming after him. He headed for the barricade at the bridge, for the wall of kegs and the men-at-arms. Without slowing his pace, he thrust his ax hand on the top of the kegs and slid over. "There is a hue and cry," he called to Bode, "coming this way."

The Kontor's men stared at him bewildered, when he raced down the bridge toward his longboat. Kari's breath was squeezed out of her, and she hung fast to his swaying shoulders, until she felt him jump down into the boat. Then he lowered her to the aft deck and reached for the rope of the anchor stone.

Abruptly he stopped, staring beyond her. The brown falcon with its hoop had gone from the boat.

"Hide and hair of the Horned One!" Olaf swore. For the first time anger twisted his face, and he swung round to search the quay with his eyes. Down at the barricade voices clamored and metal crashed. Two apprentices ran out the Kontor gate with a pack of mastiff dogs. All this seemed to Olaf to have the making of a brawl, but he saw no sign of his falcon.

Taking his ax he ran into the unguarded gate of the Kontor. When he came upon stairs leading up, he took them three at a time, and so he found himself in the great meeting hall of the Kontor. And he found himself not alone—men in uniform lined the wall, waiting leaning upon staves and halberds.

Behind the table Ernst Salza sat in his high seat calmly, with a massive book before him. Behind him the hooded falcon perched on its hoop in a clerk's hand.

It seemed to Olaf that these silent men were waiting and listening. Through the window opening he could hear the disturbance on the bridge.

Pushing through the attendants, he went up to take his hawk, and he spoke to it. At his voice the bird spread its wings.

But the clerk would not give up the hoop. "Achtzehuer," the man exclaimed, troubled.

Salza was listening intently—to the brawling below that had passed from the streets of the town to the quay, against his instructions. It was coming closer now, and he wanted to go to the opening to look out, but thought that he should remain at the desk, taking no notice of it. Impatiently, he turned on Olaf, snapping out words: "The Greenland falcon? The Kontor owns it."

Olaf shook his head, startled. "No—"

"Here!" Salza flung open the huge book, taking a parchment slip from between the pages. "The quittance for it." And he read swiftly: "*For the value of forty farthings, more or less, paid into my hand, I, Olaf, an outlander, do sell and devise unto the Bergen Kontor of the Hansa League, a brown falcon marked with white, weighing—*"

"That was never said between us—"

"Never? You signed to it." Salza nodded at the clerk. "He witnessed."

Before Olaf could answer, a rush of feet came upon the stair, and Klas Stortebecker plunged into the meeting hall with his Visby weapon men wedged behind him. When he sighted the Kontor guards along the walls, and Olaf at the desk, his broad face darkened, and he came forward slowly.

Salza, motionless, watched him without expression. "Well, Klas?"

"Ho!" the sea raider snarled. "'Tis not well, Ernst. Not with the bridge held against me, and this woodchopper holed up here."

He glared his suspicion, breathing heavily. Salza glanced from one weapon man to the other. "If you want him, Klas, take him." And quietly he drew the record book toward him.

It happened then so quickly that only Olaf saw it all. The falcon at Salza's side moved its wings, restless at the voices. And Salza thrust it away with his hand, unheeding. The hawk's beak flashed down, and Salza, with a cry of pain, struck at the falcon. The threshing hooded bird rose into the air, clawing at the man.

The talons struck into the man's head, and the falcon's beak ripped across his forehead. Jumping for them, Olaf caught the hawk beneath one wing, and pulled him clear, loosening the hood on the brown head and tossing him up. The falcon threshed and headed out the opening toward the light.

Salza screamed, throwing himself down on the table. Even Stortebecker swore at the sight, for the iron dignity of the Achtzehuer had been stripped from him. Hurt, with blood running into his eyes, he groped about the table. But he had no thought of his own pain. His fingers searched frantically for the book.

"Wait, Klas!" he cried. "I will explain—"

One hand struck the book and he caught the pages to close them. Stortebecker looked at the written page, and planted one fist on it. He had seen his own name.

The Viking backed against the wall, feeling behind him, not taking his eyes from the two at the table.

"It says St. Olaf's Day," Stortebecker muttered, and pulled the book around to him suddenly. "It says—"

"Wait!" cried Salza again, reaching for the book.

Tracing out the words with his finger, Stortebecker was reading slowly, chewing at his lip, "'And that they be hunted down and harried to their deaths,'" he repeated at the end. And he ripped out the page, dropping the book. "Sold out by the Kontor, lads!" he roared. "Aye, invited hither by this Kontor head, to frolic with the Bergen folk over the bay, and help ourselves with free hands to gear and goods of the merchants' stalls—"

Olaf spoke from the wall, "Well, here are gear and goods."

Stortebecker glared around at the rich tapestries on the walls, at the silver lanterns hanging over the desk, at the open door leading to the warehouse beyond. "Turn to, lads!" he shouted. He stuffed the parchment page into his belt. "Great liars these merchants be, for we have lifted no hand against the honest Bergen folk. Let them buy back their own goods in Lübeck."

And the sea raiders leaped for the walls.

Hidden under the aft deck of the boat, Kari heard the uproar of battle inside the Kontor. Frightened, and not knowing what to do without Olaf, she lay quiet on a robe of eider-duck feathers. First the brown falcon came down to its perch by her. Then Olaf leaped in.

Without a word he hauled up the anchor stone and shoved off with an oar. Hoisting the yard, he knotted taut the sheets. Throwing himself down beside her, he fastened a hood on the restless falcon. Then he wiped the sweat from his eyes, and shook his head. "It seems that I do not understand trading in the old country," he said.

Kari laughed a little. Now she did not feel frightened. "No," she said, "you do not, Olaf."

Settling down on the feather robe she felt warm and comfortable, between Olaf and the hawk. It was as if this place had been made for her. When she felt the sea breath from the fiord's mouth, she pulled the hood over her red hair, and under its cover her eyes searched the troubled face of the seafarer. "Nor do I," she admitted.

She was thinking, watching the line of the sea, when Olaf asked where he should set her ashore.

"On the isles," she said softly, "of the western sea."

The Golden Empress

The dust of the last chariot race settled slowly. One side of the Hippodrome became a tumult of waving green and exultant shouting. The favorite green had won.

Slaves ran beside the sweating, rearing horses as the slender chariots were led past the *kathisma*, the imperial box at the north end of the great arena. But Zoë, the Empress, did not glance at them. She was disappointed because all that afternoon there had been no spill.

She felt aggrieved by the tame ending of the last race. Listless, she lay on a couch scented with oil of poppies, beneath the heavy purple canopy that kept the harsh light of day from her face. Only her handmaidens, who labored in her attiring-rooms that were veritable laboratories of perfumes and unguents, knew the pains by which that face preserved its beauty. Her court and the world of Constantinople believed that Zoë had discovered the secret of everlasting youth; her maidens knew better.

Vain she was, and amorous. The lovers of her youth had grown gray and paunchy by now. These days it pleased Zoë to select mighty men from among the officers of the palace guard and the gladiators, to take them to the deserted throne room. There she clothed them in the Emperor's jeweled mantle and seated them beside her on the throne.

Her city of Constantinople was the queen city of the world, the ghost of the Rome that had been overrun by barbarians seven centuries before. The people liked her because she was magnificent and careless and generous. She gave away islands to her courtiers and golden shields to the barbarian Goths who pleased her. In amusing herself she entertained all Constantinople, with water festivals on the Bosporus, and especially the games in the Hippodrome. Secretly, she longed for the vaster amusements of the Caesars of Rome who had matched war galleys in mimic sea fights, and had armed women with swords and spears to struggle for their lives in the arena. That, Zoë thought, would be stimulating.

"What is that?" she demanded.

Below her, at the entrance of the royal box, a group of men had pushed past the guards. These men towered above the guards; they had long hair and wore uncouth mantles. Fair, grim men they were, who walked with long strides toward some empty seats.

Their leader was young. The skin of his throat gleamed white against the fiery red of his hair, and he laughed as he came forward.

The black boys swinging the peacock feather fans behind the Empress ceased their motion. The eunuch who sat at her feet veiled his eyes as he turned toward her, as if dazed by looking into the sun.

"Radiant Magnificence," the eunuch sucked in his breath respectfully, "they are some new barbarians. I will have them driven out—"

He was rising to hasten down to do this when Zoë cried to him impatiently: "Nay, fool, summon them here."

But the eunuch, surprisingly, hesitated. "They are war-wagers from the sea. They have not set foot in Constantinople before. Their leader is called the Unruly, and if it please Your Magnificence—"

"Then bring the chieftain alone." All that the eunuch said only made Zoë more determined to meet the red-haired giant who had pushed past her guards.

The man called the Unruly uttered an exclamation in his deep voice. Zoë wondered what he might be. She knew the yellow-maned Goths who served in the army, the fierce Alans and the Bulgars and the silent Tatars, but she had never encountered a barbarian so masterful as this flaming-eyed youth who stood poised upon her platform as if it were the afterdeck of a ship at sea—he the master of the ship.

"By Sergius and Bacchus," she said, "what is he? Fetch me someone who knows his speech."

The eunuch vanished, leaving the red chieftain and the Empress contemplating one the other in silence. He returned with an English officer of the cataphracts, the mailed cavalry of Constantinople. The officer wore a gilded breastplate and a helmet with scarlet plumes, and he raised the back of his hand to his eyes as he bowed before Zoë's couch. The barbarian looked at him in surprise.

"Ask him what man he is, whence he cometh, and why he thrusts aside my guards to seek me," she demanded.

The English mercenary spoke to the stranger, who considered a moment. Then, raising his head, he began to chant:

> *"On the long ways of the sea,*
> *On a steed of the sea,*
> *Harald the Unruly*
> *Rode the dark billows*
> *To the city of gold.*
> *No man could stand in the sea king's path—"*

"He sings," the officer lied discreetly to Zoë, "his amazement at the beauty of the Most Imperial. He hath sailed many seas and looked upon the faces of the women of a dozen cities, yet never hath he beheld so fair a face."

"Who is he?" Zoë asked, pleased.

"The younger brother of a Norse king, driven from his own land to seek his fortune upon the sea." The officer had heard of the exploits of this dour Harald, who had raised havoc along the shores of the Mediterranean.

Zoë glanced up at the Norseman. "How crude and how daring! Truly he must have a gift for his song. Maria, give the royal barbarian something from the table—that enameled cup."

From the obscurity behind the couch a quiet girl rose, picking up a goblet.

"Witless!" exclaimed Zoë. "Fill it with wine of Chios for him!"

Harald the Unruly took the goblet readily enough. "Hail!" he cried, and quaffed it down. When he handed it back to the girl, she shook her head. Perhaps because all the people were looking at her, and she dreaded the anger of the Empress, her aunt, a flush spread from her throat into her cheeks. Harald considered her in silence.

"Stupid!" whispered Zoë. "Did I say to make eyes at this great brute? Go back to thy place."

The girl turned away quickly, and the English officer explained to the stranger.

"Nay, Lord Harald, the cup is thine gift from the Empress."

Harald smiled. It was a rare and goodly cup. When he smiled, his bleak eyes softened. From his bare arm he pulled the gold ring inscribed with runes and offered it to Zoë.

"Say, thou with the feathers," he demanded, "where sits the Emperor who is overlord of all this?"

"There is no overlord. She, the Empress, rules alone."

"A woman!" Harald could not understand how a woman without a husband could keep order in a city so vast that all the men of Norway would not people it. The army of the Norse king would not fill a single side of this arena.

"It is clear," he remarked, "that the man who could win this Empress for a bride would sit in honor."

"Aye," the Englishman admitted, "if he could rule this Empress."

That, Harald thought, would be simple to do. Women could manage about a homestead well enough, and rear children, but no woman could be mightier than a man.

Zoë knew that they were talking about her. She no longer felt listless; in fact, she was conscious of a thrill of interest as she tried the great ring of the Norse chieftain on her slender arm. "Ask him," she demanded, "what he thinks of my sports?"

Both men turned to look down at the arena. Small figures were struggling, in couples, upon the raked-over sand. Some were striking with lead-bound fists, others were wrestling. Down the straightaway, athletes hurled javelins high into the air while clowns dressed in the skins of beasts ran away in pretended fear.

The Englishman knew that this Harald could cast a spear sixty paces with either hand. He could go round a ship on the oars when the men were rowing.

"He says," the Englishman informed Zoë, "that all this is sport for slaves."

Zoë pouted. She rather agreed with the strange warrior, but it piqued her that the Norse chieftain should be contemptuous of her athletes.

"Let Antiochus appear—at once!" she commanded, sitting up.

Presently the crowd also stirred, and a shout went up. The fist-fighters withdrew from the arena before the imperial box, and a strange figure walked into the cleared space. A heavy, round helmet covered his head and the nape of his neck. His right arm and shoulder were encased in scale mail, held in place by leather bands. A kilt of silvered scales covered his hips. His left arm bore a small, round shield, and his right hand held a short, straight sword.

Coming below the Empress, he sheathed his sword and extended his right arm toward her, as he called out something in a deep voice.

"He says," the Englishman whispered to Harald, "that he, who is about to die, salutes the Empress."

"What is he?" Harald asked in surprise.

"A gladiator. A swordsman."

Silence settled down upon the arena when Antiochus the gladiator faced his opponent, an Ethiopian, naked to the waist, armed with a longer sword but without a shield. The big black soon worked himself into a frenzy, leaping in and out with the swiftness of a panther

Zoë, biting hard upon her lip, leaned forward, her eyes glued to the bodies of the two men. But Harald, after the first moment, understood that the Ethiopian was doomed. In spite of his physical strength and quickness, he handled his weapon clumsily. Antiochus, although he kept his sword and shield close to his body and hardly seemed to move, was the faster fighter, and at home with steel . . . Suddenly the gladiator's short sword licked out and thrust deep into the heaving chest of the black. Antiochus stepped back and looked up at the imperial box.

As Zoë extended her hand, thumb down, she felt a pleasant, irresistible thrill. In spite of the stupid priests who protested every time she did this, she could not resist the final thrill that her ancestors, the Caesars of Rome, had enjoyed without restraint.

The crowd rose to its feet, jostling to see down into the arena. Women bit at their clenched hands, their faces flushed.

The tall Ethiopian was sitting down, as if tired. Antiochus sheathed his sword and drew a slender dagger. Going to the wounded black he cut the man's throat with a deft slash and blood spurted out upon the sand.

"Ah," Zoë whispered. "Antiochus!"

Then the imperial box below her surged violently. The Norse chieftain was leaping down from bench to bench, thrusting nobles and servants aside. He vaulted the arena rail and strode toward Antiochus, who was wiping the dagger clean.

"It was a foul stroke," Harald said, "to slit the gullet of a stricken man."

Antiochus merely looked at him. The gladiator did not understand the Norseman's speech. So Harald dealt him a buffet against the jaw and he fell heavily. With startling swiftness he got to his feet, his sword out, his heavy face a mask of rage. Standing before him, Harald saw how broad he was in the shoulders, and how the muscles knotted when he moved his arm.

One after the other the ten Norsemen leaped the rail, to run to their chieftain. They drew their swords and lifted their shields and they formed a ring about Harald. Greek guards and officers had rushed into the arena, to come between the fighters. Above the tumult Zoë's high voice was heard, and presently the Englishman thrust his way through to Harald.

"Art mad, lordling?" he grunted, "To strike the gladiator! Now, the Empress bids thee to her box."

By then the guards hemmed in the Norsemen, separating them from the fighters of the arena. Harald accompanied the Englishman back to Zoë, who stared at him with new interest. The afternoon had proved a delightful surprise to her.

She explained that Antiochus had challenged to a death combat the barbarian who had struck him.

"It seems to me," Harald answered, "that he goes about it with much bother. He struck a foul blow before me, and that will be his bane. Call off these gilt lads, thy guardsmen, and we will fight easily enough."

"Knowest thou," she retorted, "that Antiochus hath fought more than three score? Some escaped with wounds and some he maimed, but eight and twenty he hath slain."

"Then it is time he met his match."

"If you must—" Zoë thought how entrancing it would be to see two such men in a death struggle. To see this violent youth cut down by the invincible gladiator, or to watch Antiochus meet his end there below her in the sand where he had always prevailed. "Let it be tomorrow after the gladiator hath rested. Tomorrow at this hour."

A sudden impulse seized her. "And the reward will be the favor of the fairest woman of Constantinople of the victor's choosing."

If the two champions fought for her favor, Zoë could relish the combat to the full.

A sigh and a stir went through the stands of the Hippodrome after the last chariot had been led out. Two men stood beneath the royal box, their shadows stretching over the hard-packed sand.

"Hail, Empress," chanted Antiochus, "I who am about to die salute thee!"

The crowd had heard that salutation often. All eyes were on the red-haired youth beside the gladiator. The Norseman wore no armor except for a steel cap; on his left arm he carried a shield, and his right hand held a long, straight sword. Although he had towered above the nobles in the royal box, he looked slight beside the heavy gladiator.

Beneath the purple canopy Zoë feasted her eyes on the two fighters, and gave a signal to the master of the games. Silver trumpets blared and the Norseman and the gladiator faced each other. They did not move. They stood like stone figures.

The Norseman took the first step forward, clashing his sword against his shield. Then Antiochus sprang.

Through the air he hurled his weight, to smite shield against shield and overthrow the Norseman. But Harald leaped back and the shields only clashed lightly. Antiochus thrust low with his short sword, and Harald brought his own blade down, driving the point of the gladiator's into the sand. He stamped his foot against the gladiator's sword, to pin it there.

The gladiator was too wary. He freed his blade and lunged back in time.

Harald pressed him, slashing to get home on that bare throat or to hew into the ribs on the unguarded right side. The skill of the Norseman lay only in attack . . . Crouched by the arena rail, Ulf the Strong, Harald's lieutenant, quivered and grunted as he watched the smashing blows. Ulf knew the force of those blows. He could see the sinews standing out on the legs of the straining men. He saw more than that. He saw that Antiochus was not tiring. He saw that from time to time the gladiator's short sword licked at Harald's bare right arm. Twice, thrice, cuts appeared on the Norseman's forearm. Blood began to drip from the cuts. And Ulf's fingers clenched in the sand. For with that blood the strength was draining from Harald's sword arm. Muscles had been severed and Harald's blows were growing weaker.

Antiochus crouched lower. He thrust his blade strongly against the Norseman's sword, to test the strength of the failing arm.

The Norseman gave way. His useless sword arm quivered and suddenly the crowd behind Ulf began to roar, sensing the moment of the kill. Harald leaped away and slipped his shield down to his left hand. Swiftly he flung the great shield at the gladiator's head. Antiochus dodged and came on again.

Now the Norseman had no defense. He tossed his sword up into the air just as the gladiator came within reach. Then Harald leaped high to one side, catching the upflung sword in his good left hand. As his feet touched the ground his sword swept down. It bit deep into the right side of the gladiator above the belt.

Antiochus fell to his knees. He tried to thrust once with his short sword; then the Norseman wrenched his own blade clear and the gladiator fell limp on the sand.

Just as the mob had roared when Harald had staggered, it bellowed now at the downfall of the sword-slayer. Zoë, who had been tearing a silk scarf into shreds as she watched the combat, leaned forward with a shrill cry of delight, holding out her hand with the thumb down.

But Harald, if he saw the signal to put Antiochus to death, did not heed it. Already Antiochus had had his death blow.

"He was a mighty man," Harald panted as Ulf ran up to him, "with his weapons."

Ulf nodded, watching the gladiator. "Well for you, Harald, that he did not know you could cast spear or wield sword with either hand." And he began to tie up his chieftain's injured right arm with strips of cloth.

Slaves ran from the royal box and lifted the Norseman to their shoulders.

While he was carried up toward the canopy, men maddened with the lust of slaying clutched at his limbs; women struggled to get close to him, to catch a drop of the blood that dripped from him.

Zoë sprang up, her body yearning toward him. She caught his head between her hands.

"My strong one! O mightiest of men—my champion—Thou art sore hurt! But come, the reward is thine. Choose thou the woman who will favor thee—" and her eyes smiled upon him.

The Norseman had not forgotten. It seemed great good fortune to him. "That black-eyed maid yonder," he said, pointing.

When the Englishman translated this, utter silence fell beneath the canopy. All heads turned where he had pointed, where behind the imperial couch a frightened girl knelt. She had been weeping during the fight.

Zoë's face changed. It became hard and lines appeared about the eyes.

"Witless fool!" she hissed in a cold rage. Then she drew herself up. "Thinkest thou to have at thy call a woman of the purple? That is Maria, my kinswoman. And thou art no more than a barbarian!"

Even while the Englishman was saying this to the surprised Norseman, Zoë whispered a command to the eunuch who was ever at her side. In another moment the imperial guards had closed in upon the dozen Norsemen and had gripped them before they could lay hand to weapon.

"It should be clear to you now," Ulf grumbled, "that this queen they call Zoë is mightier than you."

They were sitting on the grass at the bottom of a hollow tower. The tower was high as a ship's masthead and it had no roof. Nor did it have a stair on the inside. The one iron-bound door was locked from without. At times a guard appeared at the summit of the wall to look down at the captive Norsemen, who had been stripped of their weapons and hurried into this tower to await Zoë's decision as to their fate. Not one had been able to escape to the dragon ship, where the rest of Harald's crew waited.

Harald looked at his bruised messmates.

"She did not hold to her word," he said, "and she overthrew us by treachery." He thought for a moment. "It comes into my mind that this Empress thought herself the fairest of all women, and belike she was angered. These are not simple-minded women."

Ulf grunted. "If that is clear to you now," he said, "it is a pity that it did not come into your head yonder in the bear-pit. Now it seems to me that the Icelander foresaw this ill luck, and that many of us will lose our home-coming."

"That may well be," Harald agreed. Presently a youth appeared at the tower's rim—he must have climbed an outer stair that served the guards. He was shedding tears, and crying words in Norman-French that Harald and some of the messmates understood. Harald sat up to listen, When the youth went away, a guard came and spat down at the Norsemen.

"That youngling was saying," Harald said to Ulf, "that he was brother to the dark-eyed Maria the Porfr—whatever it is. He was saying that this Empress in anger hath given command to make Maria captive and put out her eyes with hot irons."

After that afternoon in the Hippodrome, it did not surprise the Norsemen that Zoë should command this.

"If they will do that to the girl," Ulf pondered, "what will they do to us?"

"We are warfarers," said Harald, "and soon or late we will find our deaths otherwise than in a bed. But Maria is no more than a tender girl, and it is a shameful thing they will do to her."

"What led you to ask for her, of all the women of Constantinople?"

Harald pulled at the grass between his knees. "I know not. But I will not sit by while they put out her eyes."

"It is hard to see," Ulf pointed out, "how you can do anything else."

By then it was the end of dusk, with only a red glow in the sky. Ulf could hear the guards eating by their fire. From the summit of the tower a hooded woman peered down at them, making mocking sounds. At times she spat, or she threw stones taken from her dress, at Ulf. Suddenly Ulf became greatly interested in what the woman was doing. He touched Harald gently.

"A rope is coming down," he whispered.

The two of then went to the tower's side and searched with their hands until they found the rope dangling. It was stout and strong and the woman had made it fast above because two men could swing on it.

"Now how are we to know," whispered Ulf, "What *this* woman hath in store for us?"

"We will find out," quoth Harald, taking hold of the rope with his good arm. But Ulf, who had two sound arms, climbed the rope first, bracing himself against the wall with his feet while the Norsemen below held the end of the rope taut.

When Ulf put his shaggy head over the top, he saw that the tall cloaked woman was standing alone at the head of the outer stair. He wondered then how he would speak to her. "Hi, Olga, Gretchen, damzelle—"

"Hi, blood-drawn butcher's calf," croaked the woman in a deep voice. "Shut your lip and come over."

"The Icelander," whispered Ulf joyfully, as he hauled himself over the edge. "How come ye here?"

"By the sense that fools lack. Bid Lord Harald tie himself in this rope's end, and we will haul him up."

While they worked, the Icelander explained that he had been in the crowd at the Hippodrome, but high up among the commoners. He had gone out of a gate and had hidden himself until he could speak with his friend the Englishman, who was angered by the treachery of the Byzantines. So the Englishman had got him this dress with a stout rope to coil beneath his cloak.

Before the guards understood what was happening, the messmates swarmed down and cast them to the ground. The struggle lasted only a moment, but some women who had been hanging about the soldiers' fire screamed and ran away.

"This place," the Icelander complained "hath too many women in it. Now we must make our way quickly down to the ship."

"Wait," said Harald suddenly. "Strip these five of their armor. Take their shields and spears—five of you. Nay, the cloaks as well. Put them on."

Ulf and the Icelander saw the cunning of this, and in another minute five Norsemen stood dressed like Constantinople guards—looking enough like the Byzantines to pass for them in that dim light.

"Now," said Harald, "we will find Maria's house, and take her away so that her eyes will not be put out. Come with me, for I shall find that girl, and Constantinople will not soon forget this night."

His saying came true. At that hour Zoë was at supper with the Caesar and advisers of the empire. She was still in a fury, which did not mend when a slave brought word that the Norsemen had got out of their tower.

The second message, a half-hour later, startled all the Sacred Palace. The Norsemen, Harald and seven others including a strange woman, had been brought into the courtyard of the palace of Maria the Porphyrogenita, by five guards. At least, everyone had taken the five for guards—until Harald made his way up the stairs and found Maria lying on her bed. He wrapped her up in a coverlet and carried her down, and went forth in the center of his men, who had got new arms from the house. They vanished into the network of dark alleys leading to the waterfront.

"Draw up the chain across the harbor," Zoë commanded. "Summon the captains of the war vessels. Light up all the harbor front!"

She called for her litter and a cohort of the palace guard. Surrounded by torches, in the midst of her Goths and Tatars, she was carried down through the gardens and the markets to the marble docks of the Golden Horn.

There she drew a deep breath of anticipation. Her commands had been carried out. Beacons lighted on both sides the harbor cast a gleam over all the dark water. The great chain at the narrow harbor mouth was clanking up—already its ends appeared, dripping, out of the water. In a tumult of hurrying slaves and shouting seamen, several lofty war galleys were preparing to put out from the docks, to where the slender dragon ship of the Norsemen lay waiting in the deserted middle of the harbor—having rowed out from its jetty as soon as Harald had boarded it.

It seemed to Zoë that at last she would behold a spectacle worthy of the Caesars of ancient Rome—a battle of gladiators upon ships, before her eyes.

"Sound the trumpets!" she cried.

Over the water resounded the melodious blast of the horns that signified the Empress was ready to watch the spectacle.

Maria, standing on the aft deck of the long dragon ship, heard that blast. She arranged the coverlet about her shoulders and she faced Lord Harald with pride.

"Do ye make war upon a woman? Set me back on the shore, or men will name you coward until the day of your death."

Harald laughed. "A coward? Tell me where it will please you to be landed and I will set you there."

Maria clenched her hands. "You dare not!"

For answer Harald took up one of the steering sweeps, motioning Ulf to the other. "Out oars, lads," he called. "Pull back to the jetty!"

And he thrust over the sweep he held. The men pulled in grim silence; they had little desire to go back among the war vessels that would spout Greek fire and stones at them. They were trapped by the chain, but at least they were better off in open water.

Maria clasped her hands together as if she were praying. Quickly she glanced up at Harald as if to read his eyes. "Stop!" Her cry was so sudden that he echoed it:

"Weigh oars, lads." And he looked down at her. "What now?"

Maria's face was flushed, her head bent. All at once she felt afraid of him, and her lips quivered. "I—you must not risk your life again. These men—" she pointed out into the darkness. "My brother and I, we rowed over the Golden Horn and there, in the middle, the great chain sags—and perhaps—" her voice trailed into silence.

Harald bent toward her eagerly. "How far below the surface lies the bight of the chain?"

A little more than a yard she measured with her hands, and Harald looked at Ulf, who shook his head moodily.

"Nay, Harald, the boat will break her back on that. Then we would find our end in the water."

But Harald touched the girl on the shoulder. "Then you do not wish to go back?"

"Oh, I have told you—besides, I do not want to be blinded."

Strangely Maria did not add that her aunt had often condemned her to such a fate, in a jealous rage. After all, who knew what Zoë would really do?

"Now, lads," Harald called to them, "we will get away. Pull for life. And the others come aft. Each man with a bit of gear. Fetch away the anchor stone."

As the dragon ship turned its carved prow toward the harbor mouth and the long oars churned the water into foam, a mocking shout resounded from the shore. The dragon ship, gaining speed swiftly, headed toward the dim gap where the chain was covered with water. All the Norsemen who were not at the oars staggered aft along the runway with bags and chests in their arms. Two of them lugged the great anchor stone.

Harald did not take his eyes from the dark gap as the dragon ship rushed upon the chain. The keel grated and the narrow craft swayed, jarring suddenly to a stop. The fore part, suspended in the air, creaked ominously.

"She will not clear," shouted Ulf, looking over the side.

"Forward, all!" Harold roared. "Forward with the gear!" He watched the lifted prow as the men ran forward with their burdens. Slowly the prow sank, while the stern rose a little beneath his feet.

"Pull, lads!" he barked at the rowers. "Pull her over—"

The oar blades thrashed the water white. The chain rasped along the keel and the prow sank gently. The Norsemen yelled as the dragon ship rocked and slid clear of the chain, gliding into open water.

Harald looked over his shoulder at the lights already vanishing behind the point of the city. "Now," he laughed, "that Empress cannot say she is mightier than the Norsemen; for I take away with me the greatest treasure of her city!"

And he summoned the Icelander to the steering sweep. He picked up Maria gently in his arms and carried her down to the cabin space below the aft deck.

The Icelander looked after them, and then he said to Ulf:

"It is clear to me that Lord Harald carries in his arms the one who is mightier than he."

His Excellency the Vulture

The testimony of Master Thomas Moone, of the ship Golden Hind, *as to the mutinous bearing of Sir James Falconer, leader of her Majesty's gentlemen, in the Great South Sea, in the year 1578. Which explains how the general came to visit the port of Lima, to the great gain of her Majesty, the Queen of England.*

Master Thomas Moone finished reading the day's entry in the log of the *Golden Hind*, written in the hand of the general commanding the expedition to the South Sea. Since Master Moone, although a navigator of rare skill, knew naught of letters and words, he interpreted the entry in the log in his own fashion to the helmsman who was his companion on the quarterdeck of the ship.

"A fair wind, an' a fair sea. The coast of the Spanish New World on our quarter. A goodly cargo o' Spanish silver i' the hold. There, I reckon that be all for today."

Moone closed the book carefully.

"Lookee, lad; you bear too far to sea. Has Spanish silver dazzled you, that you cannot see the shore?"

The man addressed, a full-muscled, bronzed seaman, gave over the helm a ways, with a glance at the compass in front of him, then jerked his thumb over his shoulder at a brass culverin that poked its nose from an embrasure on the poop.

"I did naught, Master Thomas Moone," he said stoutly, "but follow the general's command, which being inspired by book science and the secret arts of navigation, did seem to me more rightly trusted than my eyes, when the shore began to fall away to leeward. For by the chart it does seem true that the land be to nor'west, when by my eyes it be to nor'east."

Thomas Moone planted his stocky form beside the cannon and scanned the two hemispheres of the Old and New World which were engraved thereon. Scanty and rude as the details were, they formed the only charts available for the mariners who directed the course of the *Golden Hind,* and by the outline of the chart inscribed on the cannon, Moone saw that the coastline ran slightly to the west, whereas he could plainly see that it tended to the east.

"A fair wind makes a fair sea, 'tis said," went on the helmsman, moodily, "yet here we be with a fair wind as ever blessed the channel, and foul danger lurking nigh us. Have we not come through the cursed Straits of Magellan, where a thousand devils send a wind no ship can stand against, when the return trip is to be made? Here we be, a bare hundred men, in one ship in the Great South Sea, with the Spanish men-at-arms watching for us on land, and not a friend to turn to afloat. For food there is but salt penguin meat, and for drink—"

"Good *botijas* of Chili wine, lad," roared Moone, "with silks from Cathay, taken from the galleons, for cloth, and bars of silver for ballast."

"What good avail these, when the charts are evil, and we know not the lay of the rocks along the coast? How may we return to England?"

"By the Devil's back door, if needful," retorted Moone. "Our good general will discover some path, 'tis safe to venture. That is, if the tender-skinned and silken-clothed gentlemen in the cabin beneath us will cease their mutterings against him, for the reason that he, a sailor, is in command over them. Where should a sailor command, if not on the deck of his ship?"

A sound from the waist of the ship caught Moone's quick ear, and he thrust his red face into that of the helmsman.

"Hold your tongue, lad," he whispered hoarsely, "concerning what we've said, an ye fear my fist, for here comes the general himself, and the leader of the queen's gentlemen, Sir James Falconer."

Whereupon, with a poke of a knotty finger in the helmsman's ribs to enforce his words, Master Moone betook himself to the rail of the poop, and, leaning on the brass cannon, pretended to be interested in the coat-of-arms painted on the stern which bore the insignia of Elizabeth, Queen of England, although really his ear was cocked to what went on behind him.

Two men stepped from the ladder to the poop, one tall and yellow of hair, the other stocky and ruddy of cheeks. Both were bearded in the fashion of the day, and elegantly clad, with plumes in their hats, and satin cloaks over their shoulders, and silver ornaments on belt and shoes.

The tall man, more carefully dressed than his companion, was Sir James Falconer, the other was the general of the expedition, Mr. Francis Drake. His short figure was alert and powerful, and his eyes flickered rapidly over the poop, while he played carelessly with the sword at his belt—the arm as finely tempered as the steel blade.

While Sir James leaned indolently against the rail and watched, the general produced a telescope and scanned the shore ahead of them for several moments.

"Beyond the next headland, Sir James," he observed after a pause, "must lie the port of Arica for which we search. Then we shall see whether our hosts, the Spaniards, have prepared more treasure craft for us to have the spoiling of! How like you the thought of more silver bars?"

"More like they have carried off all the riches of the town to the woods," objected the soldier, with a shrug. "Word of our coming has outspeeded the *Golden Hind* up the coast, and robbed us of our booty. If this be truly the port of Arica, we had best land and search the town, for the shipping will be bare of silver."

"Not so, Sir James," replied Drake, putting down the telescope, "if you venture ashore 'twill be short shrift the Dons will give you. At sea, we are safe; ashore our enemies outnumber us, an' they are plagued treacherous."

"Bah! One Englishman can fight twenty Spaniards. And as for trickery, I am not the man to be caught asleep. A sailor's heart clings to his ship and ordnance, but a soldier has a love for battle—a smoking pistol and a flashing blade."

There was more than a little contempt in the voice of the leader of the queen's gentlemen. Drake he considered to be an excellent pilot, and a worthy handler of sails and cordage, but Sir James had never admitted that Drake held rank over himself. All sailors were upstarts, a breed scarce better than laborers.

The general cast a keen glance at his second-in-command. It might have been seen that there were lines of weariness on the brow over the sharp eyes and sunburnt cheeks. The months since leaving Plymouth had been full of trouble—losses among the men at the hands of Indians, a vessel lost to sight in Magellan Straits, another gone down with all hands at the same spot, and lack of good provisions beyond what they could take from the Spanish towns. Greater than all these in the general's mind was the mutinous spirit of Sir James and his gentlemen.

Alone in the Great South Sea, surrounded by Spanish craft, with the way of return by the straits well-nigh cut off by the enemy, and the way to China an unknown path, the plight of the *Golden Hind* was little short of desperate. And now the band of men on the ship was divided, the mariners in one faction, in the other the soft-handed gentlemen who had sailed to cross swords with the cavaliers of Spain for the glory of God and to win gold ducats for themselves.

Patiently, Drake had made every effort to mend the breach, only to see it grow until the two factions were on the point of drawing sword to settle the question of leadership.

"Several years agone," said Drake calmly, "my adventure, in attacking Nombre de Dios, in Panama, and carrying off a rich treasure in silver aroused the anger of his Excellency, the Viceroy of Mexico, who swore that if I showed myself within Spanish waters again I should be taken and dealt with as a pirate. Which meant that my head would hang in one of his Excellency's ropes.

"When word of this oath was brought to my ears, I swore likewise that I should return, and make my way to the South Sea where I should exact toll from his Excellency. I have carried out my vow, in the name of our sovereign lady, the queen, but I intend to give his Excellency no chance to make good his oath. Unless there is need, neither I nor my men shall set foot ashore."

"If our general," purred the smooth voice of the yellow-haired Falconer, "would fain be pent aship for fear of the Spániard, I will lead my men ashore and give the Dons a taste of English steel and powder. After all, it is the good blood that wields the blade; the mongrel ever snaps and snarls but flees the combat."

The general's bronzed cheeks flushed. He made no movement, but shot a warning glance at Thomas Moone, whose mottled face was black with anger.

"Not so, Sir James," he corrected, "for fighting blood knows no coat-of-arms."

"Aye, in men-at-arms. It is the leaders who own the mark of nobility, such as—" Falconer bowed ceremoniously—"your pardon, General, I remembered not you lacked a coat-of-arms."

"Your memory mistakes, Sir James," said Drake quickly, "for I have a coat-of-arms."

"Of honorable name? The crest is ancient?"

"As the world, Sir James. It is here."

Drake placed his hand on the breech of the brass culverin wherein was engraved the twin hemispheres of the world, not unlike armorial bearings. Thomas Moone grinned broadly and shot a glance at the soldier.

"And your commission as general?"

A smile twisted the soft mustache of Falconer. He knew the queen had given Drake no written commission, owing to fear of the Spanish monarch.

"Here!"

Drake drew his sword.

"This is my commission, blessed by the queen herself, who declared the man accursed who should betray it. She gave it me with her own hand."

Sir James smiled and drew his blade with a flourish.

"A worthy commission!" he cried, "in the hand of a man who is not worthy. Would it not be better to surrender it to one who could use it?"

"God's life!" swore Drake, who had reached the limit of his patience.

At that instant the burly figure of Thomas Moone stepped between them.

"Lookee, masters," he growled, "an ill time to quarrel when a rich port lies open to our hand, and the Spaniards are making away with all their silver. It lies there, on the starboard bow."

"Arica!" cried Drake.

Both men wheeled and scanned the harbor. The *Golden Hind* had already been seen, and the crews of the vessels anchored in the bay were pulling ashore in small boats. Few people were to be seen in the town itself, which consisted of no more than a score or more buildings grouped together a little ways from the shore.

If the *Golden Hind* was not to lose all the advantage of surprise in appearing suddenly before the town, the English would need to act at once. Falconer knew this as well as Drake, and both sheathed their swords. The soldier laughed light-heartedly, but the general's ruddy countenance was aflame with anger.

"Think not, Sir James," he said, "that you escape settlement because you lead a party ashore to take the silver from the Spanish vessels. The moment you set foot on this ship you shall be tried in the name of her

Majesty, on charges of treason and mutiny, for you drew sword against me. Go, now, and lose no time about your business!"

Already a boatswain, several sailors, and a score of musketeers, with a dozen gentlemen, thronged the waist of the ship, while the great boat was dragged up from its position astern of the ship. At a signal from Drake the helmsman prepared to bring her head to the wind. Sir James, with a glance ashore at the deserted shipping and town, leaped from the poop to the waist of the ship, to be greeted by a shout of acclaim from his men.

There was cause for the eagerness of the English to set foot in Arica. Inland from the port were the great mines of Potosi, and from Arica the treasure ships bearing silver to Panama set out. They had heard from Spanish captives that it was time for the *Santa María*, a ship carrying the annual tax of silver of King Philip of Spain, to leave Arica, and they hoped to catch it in the act of loading.

Such a vessel would be a prize richer than any they had taken. Its value would be inestimable in poverty-stricken England. To capture the treasure ship of the king of Spain was a feat that warmed the hearts of the men on the *Golden Hind*, and those who had not gone ashore with Falconer sought points of vantage along the deck of the vessel to watch what passed in the town.

On the quarterdeck Master Moone stood alone with the helmsman, the telescope glued to his eye. Drake had gone below to his cabin, troubled by the scene with his second-in-command. As the day was clear and the telescope of good quality, Moone could make out plainly what his companions in the great boat were doing.

They had landed where the half-dozen ships were moored, and the soldiers swarmed over the craft. Shortly, they appeared on deck again and Moone swore his disgust, for he could guess that no silver was to be had from the galleons in the harbor of Arica.

Again, thought Moone, the Spaniards, warned of their coming, had managed to make away with their riches in time. Probably the *Santa María* had sailed some time before, leaving the port barren of silver.

Suddenly Moone gave a whistle of surprise, and gripped the telescope tightly to his eye. Disappointed in finding nothing on the ships, the English boat had pulled to shore, where the soldiers, with Sir James Falconer at their head, entered the town.

At first everything was quiet in the streets of Arica, without a trace of living Spaniard. In landing, Falconer had broken Drake's command. The general had ordered that no one was to go ashore when he himself was not with the expedition. But his superior's caution chafed on the leader of the soldiers, and this was heightened by the quarrel on the poop of the *Golden Hind*, and by disappointment at losing the *Santa María*. The town appeared to be deserted, and this confirmed Falconer in his determination to land and wrest some spoil from the buildings.

What had attracted Moone's attention was a movement in a wood at one side of the town, near the shore. He caught the glint of steel through the trees, and in a moment the cause was plain to view. A troop of Spanish cavalry, ambushed in the wood, trotted out into the open and started at a rapid pace for the town.

So intent were the party in Arica on searching the houses that they did not see the advancing line of horsemen until the latter were halfway to the town. Then it was too late to gain the boat in safety. Moone cursed under his breath as he saw this, then gave vent to a grunt of approval. The soldiers under the orders of Falconer greeted the cavalry with a hot fire from their harquebuses, so hot that the wave of horsemen split in two and rolled around the town, giving the little body of Englishmen a wide berth.

But meanwhile other bodies of Spaniards appeared on the hills above the town, while tiny puffs of white showed Moone where their harquebuses were searching the streets of Arica. Several Englishmen dropped under the fire, and more were lost in the retreat back to the boat.

Not all escaped from the town. Sir James with three companions were quitting the place after their companions by one of the side streets, when they were pursued and cut off by a troop of horsemen. For a moment Moone saw the blade of Sir James flashing in his long arm, until a blow from a pike disarmed him and he and his men were made prisoners by the Spaniards.

No ill place was the cabin of Mr. Francis Drake. The panes in the square portholes were of good English stained glass, the beams that supported the deck overhead were curiously carved, and Flemish tapestries hung from the walls. A ladder in one corner led to the poop, while a small door at one side gave into the general's sleeping quarters.

Following the ill-omened landing of his men, Drake was seated in his shirtsleeves on a bench that ran beneath the ports, stroking a violin softly. His sword was thrown carelessly on the small table by his side. Idle and light-hearted as he appeared, Thomas Moone, who had sailed with him on many voyages, noted the line of care drawn across the brown forehead, and the pain back of the searching eyes. Moone was seated by his leader, without formality, as was their custom.

Wrinkling his nose in disgust, the sailing master spat out of an open port.

"Good riddance it be, sir," he growled, "for Sir James was ever of mutinous mind. If the Spanish dogs hang him to yardarm, 'twill be but cheating us of the pleasure. Pah! Silk-coated vermin!"

"The man is brave, Tom," mused the general, "and he was outspoken. Nevertheless he did breed mutiny and treason among our people, and if he lives, he shall answer for it. Tell me again the words of the Spanish leader at Arica."

"I heard them not," explained the sailor. "Those who came off in the great boat say that one of the Dons on horseback came within earshot on the shore as they were pulling away. He cried to them in Spanish, which several of the company knew—

"'Tell your corsair chief that his men shall be tried and hung at Lima, and his Excellency bids him come and attend the trial.'"

Drake threw back his head and laughed long.

"So the Vulture invites us to come to his lair, Tom. What think you, man—shall we do as he bids?"

"Ar't not serious, sir? No doubt but his Excellency would gladly welcome us, ha! He'll see little of us save good cannon shot. Yet why put in at Lima when the treasure ship sails north to escape us? We may overtake it, for we have the legs of the Spanish craft."

"How long since did the *Santa María* put to sea, Tom?"

"Three days agone, sir. It would be a simple matter to make up the time."

"Too simple, for the Spanish trust cunning where they fear sails."

Drake plucked at the violin strings thoughtfully.

"Nay, the *Santa María* will not be found where we look for it. But we will find it, by my faith, Tom. The Spaniards shall pay for their treatment of Sir James Falconer. He is an Englishman. Since when have Englishmen been taken at sight as pirates? The man offended but with his sword—a good blade."

"He is foul with mutiny."

"Then shall he be tried on the *Golden Hind* in the queen's name. Nay, no other than his general will try him. His Excellency, the Vulture, will find his prisoners slipped through his claws, and the black lepers of the Inquisition will lose their prey."

The honest mariner scratched his head thoughtfully and sighed.

"How may that be, sir? Sir James travels overland in the hands of many armed caballeros of Spain, who take him to the presence of the viceroy at the great town of Lima, where are no less than three thousand soldiers, as I have heard, and many cannon. Were the viceroy afloat we might lay him aboard with a good heart. Ashore, we be a scant ninety men against three thousand. How could we land, in the face of such odds?"

"The task is beyond us, Tom," smiled the general. "Our boats could never put ashore in the town held by such number of soldiers."

"'Twere madness to think on't sir. Besides, there is the treasure ship that flees us. We cannot squander time in trying to barter for the lives of the mutineers at Lima."

"No silver shall buy the lives of Sir James Falconer and his men," declared the general. "Yet they shall stand free—"

"But how, in God's name—"

The general ran the fiddle bow caressingly over the strings.

"When Sir James went to the port of Arica he carried in a pocket of his cloak a letter to the viceroy, written in an excellent conceit, in goodly Spanish—"

"The traitor!"

"Nay, you wrong him. The letter was from my hand. Perchance your Spanish caballero on horseback opened it when Sir James was made prisoner, and made answer as he did. For my letter was word that I was coming to pay the viceroy a call in person at his palace. Now that he bids me, by his caballero, to come to the trial, I shall pay my respects—"

"With good cannon shot and powder!"

Drake put down his violin and smiled at Moone.

"At the court of justice," he amended.

II

The testimony of one Fray Raymundo of Lima, as to the events connected with the visit of the notorious corsair El Francisco Andreque to that town, as forwarded to his Majesty, King Philip the Second of Spain, upon occasion of the inquiry into the most strange circumstances that did there befall his Excellency the Governor of Peru.

When the shadows lengthened along the plaza of El Callao de Lima, a certain Fray Raymundo emerged from the doors of his church. On the threshold he paused to gaze at the unwonted activity of the plaza.

Silk banners hung from the windows facing the square. Along the streets leading to it trotted mounted caballeros, their accouterments bright with silver and jewels. From the windows and balconies veiled women did not scorn to show their pretty heads, and their dresses, which were of the costliest material and workmanship. By the side of the women, often mestizos, or half-breeds, loitered Spaniards who had been poorer than the soldiers in the streets a year ago, and now owned silver enough to buy them a dukedom in Spain.

The soldiers themselves had pockets filled with gold and silver which they squandered in the shops for a *botija* of wine or a throw at the dice. Shouts, songs, and laughter echoed from wine shop to wine shop through the streets. Money was theirs to spend as they wished, for more was to be had from the mines worked by the enslaved natives, and the occasion was gala.

As he saw the holiday throng, Fray Raymundo remembered that it was the last day of the trial of the four Lutheran dogs who had been taken by the caballeros of Arica. Moreover the English corsair was somewhere off the coast, and rumor said that the corsair captain, El Francisco Andreque, had boasted that he would land and meet his Excellency the Governor face to face. Nothing had been seen of the devil ship, as it was called, but every preparation had been made to welcome it fittingly if it should have the insolence to come to the port of El Callao de Lima.

Into the crowd that had moved along the plaza to the Royal Audencia where the trial was taking place pressed Fray Raymundo, while the soldiers, adventurers, and women made way respectfully before his gray robe and pale face. It was his purpose to reach the Royal Audencia in time to see the arrival of the viceroy, and in this he was successful.

Just as the last rays of the sun were touching the silk hangings in the windows, and glittering on the silver trees and ornaments that stood in front of the houses, there was a stir in the throng that filled the plaza, and the governor was seen advancing to the Audencia where the court waited his presence, in company with several of his captains and advisors.

The Most Excellent Lord, Don Francisco de Toledo, Viceroy, Governor, and Captain-General of the Spanish realms in the New World, was no less a monarch in America than was King Phillip II, ruler of Spain,

Portugal, and Flanders, in the Old World. The gold cloth and velvet of his attire, the emerald clasp that held in place his black cloak, made the appearance of his Excellency no less splendid than that of the Incas who had fallen under his rule.

With the power of the Inquisition which knew no laws at his command, a conquered race enchained to do his bidding, and the mines of the New World at hand to yield enormous riches, there was little wonder that his Excellency's pride matched that of the only man who could call him servant.

As he pushed through the crowd his Excellency's dark eyes held recognition for few he met—a distinguished captain of cavalry, a wealthy owner of one of the Potosi mines, a brilliantly dressed woman of his court. The native chiefs who, catching the spirit of the celebration, appeared in the streets in the splendor of their state garments, the governor ignored completely. Fray Raymundo, who had reached a point quite near the path of his Excellency, was about to bow, in company with others around him, when something arrested him.

An Indian, who had entered the plaza from one of the streets leading directly to the hills behind the town, ran to the governor and prostrated himself.

"A message, oh, chief of chiefs," he cried, in Quichua.

Those who were watching the scene saw the governor, before the Indian could speak again, place a foot on the brown, muscled back lying before him. Then his Excellency, well content, wiped his shoes on the Indian and passed on to the Audencia.

A shout of laughter greeted this display of amiability on the part of the governor, and a few curious glances were cast at the native, who picked himself up with a scowl and vanished in the crowd, but not before Fray Raymundo had recognized him as a friendly Indian from a tribe which was hostile to the Spanish rule. Anxious to learn the cause of the man's act, the priest pushed after him.

The Indian did not linger in the plaza which had been the scene of his disgrace, but entered one of the side streets. The priest was close enough to see him disappear into one of the wine shops. When he stepped into the place, which was filled with half-caste mine workers, drunken sailors, and Peruvians, he found the native he sought in company with several of his tribe, drinking heavily.

To the priest's civil question about his message, the man would make

no answer beyond a sullen stare and a gesture that revealed the mark of
his Excellency's feet on his back. Troubled by the occurrence—for he knew
the native to be friendly to the Spaniards—Fray Raymundo was leaving
the wine shop when a half-caste nudged his elbow and whispered hurriedly in his ear.

"I can tell you the man's message, Fray," muttered the other, rum thick
on his breath. "He says he has seen the devil ship along the coast. There
is more that he knows, but the man is angered and will not spit it out until good wine loosens his tongue."

"The corsair!" exclaimed the fray. "That is news for his Excellency."

"His Excellency is too ready with his feet, Fray," retorted the half-
caste.

"That is a pity. Still, he should know. I will go to the Audencia. Do
you stay by the Indian until he speaks further, and then seek me out at
the trial."

With a gesture of benediction the priest gathered up his robe and turned
away. He reflected that the Indian might have been mistaken, and determined to proceed cautiously in relating what he had heard to the authorities. Once more the priest made his way across the plaza, now shrouded
in dusk.

Torches in every street scattered the gloom in Lima, and especially
along the waterfront every detail of the moving groups of mail-clad soldiers, the whispering Indians in their holiday purple and gold could be
seen. Fray Raymundo breathed deep of the fresh night air, and noted with
approval that armed forces were guarding the town on each of the roads
leading to it, and at the shore, where cannon had been stationed to await
the expected coming of the corsair that had visited Arica.

The priest was no believer in steel and cannon to inflict pain on men,
but he briefly blessed the hardy soldiers with the gallant captains who
made safe the port of Lima from the Lutheran pirate who had stripped the
altar cloth from the church of Arica, to give, so the prisoners had declared
at the trial, a suitable cloth to their own outlaw priest.

So great was the crowd at the doors of the Audencia that the good fray
was able only by persistent effort and frequent requests to allow him to pass,
to make his way to where he could command a view of the interior.

At the end of the room farthest from the door sat his Excellency, wearing his customary black cloak, and black velvet cap, with a white ruffle
at the throat. On one side stood several of his captains, bronzed, swag-

gering caballeros who were veterans of jungle warfare. At the other side were grouped the servants of the Inquisition, black-robed slaves of his Excellency. At a long table near these priests sat several scribes who were making note of the proceedings, for the records were to be sent to Spain with the tax of silver in the *Santa María*.

In the cleared space before the governor stood the prisoners, stripped of their arms and accouterments, under guard of halberdiers. They had been brought forth to listen to the conclusion of the trial. Even now, Fray Raymundo heard one of the clerks of the court reading the indictment against the prisoners.

"Whereby it does appear," the high voice of the clerk reached his ears, "that these four men be servants of this Francisco Andreque who is no other than a heretic, offending against the grace of his Majesty and his Excellency, the Viceroy of Peru and Mexico. And it is not less certain that they did land at Arica, despoiling the town and defiling the church of most fair vestments, according to their custom, when taken by our brave soldiers of Arica. And this is but one of their insolences whereby it does appear that the English dogs are pirates of the lowest order."

A buzz of excitement circulated in the crowd. The pallid faces of the followers of the Inquisition gleamed, and beautiful mestizos raised inquiring glances to their attendant caballeros. Only the governor made no sign.

"It is the just opinion of the court," Fray Raymundo heard the clerk conclude, "that the English prisoners be chastised in the way most fitting to their crime, by order of his Excellency, Don Francisco de Toledo, Governor of Peru."

Before the governor could speak a tall figure stepped before him, and the priest recognized the man who had been pointed out to him as the leader of the English.

"Would you condemn a soldier to the fate of a villain, señor?" said this man in halting Spanish. "My faith, that were a crime greater than aught we are charged with. Did you not take us prisoner in fair fight?"

The black head of the governor bent slightly, while a smile curled his thin mouth.

"I will hear what you have to say, Señor Falconer. Yet it does not bear the ring of truth to me that you claim to be honorable prisoners of war, when you were taken in act of plunder and lawless despite."

Fray Raymundo was swept nearer the governor's seat by the eager crowd which pushed and jostled to catch what was said. Seldom had such an attraction offered, for in one day there was rumor of the presence of the corsair off the coast who had promised in writing to pay a visit to no less a person than his Excellency himself, and four of the English dogs were to be executed. Surely, the Englishman was foolhardy who dared to match words with the governor.

"It is true that I did take some silver vessels and altar cloth from the church," admitted Falconer bluffly, "but they were for the use of Master Fletcher, our minister, who lacked such things. As for plunder, we took nothing from the coast but silver bars and the cargoes of certain ships. No vessel did we sink with men aboard."

"Señor," said the governor, and the priests of the Inquisition nodded assent, "that were a greater offense than to rob the church for gain. Do you pretend that you came not here of your own will, being pirates in the truest sense, since our countries are not at war?"

"We came," replied Falconer quickly, "in the service of the queen, our sovereign lady, who bade us find a passage to the South Sea, an' we could. Our orders were to take toll of the silver that flows from here to Spain and enriches our enemies."

"Yet, señor," repeated the governor with a hard smile, "you came to Spanish waters and took toll of Spanish ships, a dishonorable voyage—"

"An honorable voyage, señor," retorted Falconer, shaking his yellow head, "at her Highness's command. The silver we take is not for us, but for our country. Spanish silver, forsooth! Wrested, rather, from the people of the New World by despite. Show me the will of Adam which gave the world to Spain, and I will say that we are pirates!"

"You grow scurrilous, señor," answered the governor coldly. "And you blaspheme without shame in speaking thus of holy matters. An' you desire proof of your crimes, I have it here, taken from your person the day you were made prisoner at Arica."

He produced a roll of parchment from under his cloak and tapped it against his knee.

"This was given me by a worthy captain who found it in your belt. It is in the hand of your master, the corsair chief, who declares that he is coming to Lima to pull my beard for me, and to take what jewels he may. Call you that the letter of a gentleman?"

"My faith," muttered Falconer, "I knew not the contents of the letter. I was told to leave it in the town where it would be found. 'Tis like my general, in truth—"

"Enough of this," commanded the governor. "Is there aught to be said relating to the trial?"

Fray Raymundo considered the opportunity good to tell what he had heard about the English ship being sighted near the port. He edged forward to the front of the crowd. As he did so, he was conscious of another pushing in his tracks, and as he raised his hand for attention, this other stepped past him to the clear space before the governor. And Fray Raymundo saw a strange thing.

The newcomer, in spite of the purple robe tucked about him, was the native who had prostrated himself before the governor in the plaza and endured the humiliation of his Excellency's foot. The priest thought he caught a gleam of hate in the Indian's eyes, and a brown hand slipped from a fold in the robe.

But the Indian held out nothing more than a slip of parchment to his Excellency, who recognized him not, as he had not seen his face before. All eyes were on the governor as he tore open the parchment and scanned the contents of the letter. As he did so his pale face flushed and the blue veins showed in his forehead.

"What deviltry is this!" he snapped, glaring at the Indian. "A letter, señors, from the pirate chief who says that he is coming to the trial in person this night, and that if a finger of his men be touched before he comes, two thousand Spaniards shall die!"

A silence of amazement fell on the crowd. A laugh rose from a few throats, then stifled. Who was this corsair, to say he would come to Lima through two thousand soldiers and a score of cannon, and to the presence of his Excellency, who, as was well known, had vowed the death of El Francisco Andreque should the latter ever come within reach? Fray Raymundo crossed himself as he thought of the captured towns further down the coast and the ravaged shipping. Surely El Andreque had concourse with the Devil, no less!

He caught a few words of the governor, as the latter spoke in a low tone to his captains.

"Where got you the letter?" demanded one of the soldiers of the Indian.

"Chief, I found it upon a table at an inn in the town," muttered the native.

The captain shrugged his shoulders, and the Indian seized the chance to slip out through the crowd. As he did so, Fray Raymundo saw him shoot a venomous glance over his shoulder at the governor.

". . . lights the entire water-front," one of the soldiers was saying. "No one could land from a vessel without being seen. To make doubly sure, we have ordered all the crews ashore, but some watchmen, from the sixteen vessels at anchor. Another is expected tonight, from Panama. The harbor is quiet, and patrols of the custom-house are out in small boats. Nothing is reported."

"The roads leading to Lima?" inquired the governor sharply.

"All guarded by men with torches, your Excellency."

"The streets?"

"Are patrolled and quiet, your Excellency. Two thousand men bear arms tonight in your service, and were El Andreque the Devil himself he could not invade Lima now. His ship would be seen entering the harbor."

"Yet he sends me this missive," mused the governor. "It is, in truth, in the same hand as the other."

"A bit of bravado, your Excellency. The English dog barks out of fear, not bravery."

Without warning the governor tore the parchment in two and stamped the pieces underfoot. His face twisted into a pale mask of rage.

"Fools, idiots!" he snarled, "the man is here in town. Look," he held up one hand, which was stained with black spots, "the ink upon the parchment is not yet dry!"

The thick ink was in truth still wet upon the parchment—the Indian could have received it but a short time before.

What came to pass within the next hour occurred with such swiftness that the good fray scarce had time to cross himself and mutter a prayer as protection against the black art which brought the letter to the hand of his Excellency.

Stooping over, he picked up one of the pieces of parchment, and found that the governor had spoken truly when he said the ink was still wet. The parchment had not been sanded, and when the fray rubbed one of his fingers against it, it made a dark smear. The writing must have been done, thought the priest, within the quarter hour. If so, and if it was truly by the hand of the corsair, El Andreque must be now within the limits of the town.

There was little doubt that the soldiers, dispatched by the governor on the instant, would take their quarry prisoner, in a search of the town.

All trace of the Indian in the purple robe who had brought the letter had disappeared.

Swift questions by his Excellency of the captains and custom-house officials made clear the following facts. No man had landed from the shipping in the harbor—seventeen vessels, now that the ship from Panama had been seen to enter the port. No one save some natives from the mines had passed the guards on the roads since nightfall. The soldiers had not observed any strangers in the streets. If El Andreque was in hiding in the town, he must be in the residence of one of the inhabitants.

The priest thought otherwise. To him, a man who accomplished the deeds of the corsair was without doubt in league with Satan. What followed upon the words of the governor convinced him of the truth of his belief. For a miracle, to the mind of the fray, was reported by the custom-house officer who burst into the Audencia with a drawn sword and eyes wide with amazement of what he had to tell.

"The harbor!" snapped the governor. "What is toward?"

"The ships are drifting out to sea, your Excellency," cried the man. "They have slipped their cables! Name of the Devil, it is witchcraft. In spite of the watchers we left on the galleons, they are loose from their moorings and drifting away from the town like frightened sheep."

"Send out small boats and work them back to anchorage," commanded the governor. "Has a wind sprung up of a sudden?"

"No, your Excellency, there is little air stirring. The ships seem to be moving out of their own accord. All the seventeen are in motion. It is clear starlight, and we can see them passing well from the shore."

The governor gestured angrily for silence and whispered to one of his captains, who started and clapped hand to his sword. Slowly at first the buzz of whispered tidings spread around the hall. To Fray Raymundo the rumor came as he was repeating his prayer against heretic black arts. The corsair was in the harbor! What the guards had taken to be the vessel from Panama was no other than the devil ship of El Andreque. It had slipped in among the other vessels and begun its work of evil unnoticed.

It was now too late for the priest to tell his tidings, and he stepped back from his position before the governor to seek the harbor and learn the truth of what was happening. He had scarce taken a step when the buzz of whispers in the hall was broken by the sound of a cannon in the harbor. And when the echo had died away, no one spoke. The priest went no further toward the door.

For he saw, quite clearly by the torches held by the halberdiers at the entrance, three Englishmen walk into the Audencia, and advance through the crowd toward the governor. The leader of the trio was a stocky man with red checks and a fair beard, and eyes that seemed to take in everything in the hall with a single glance. Behind him came two tall gentlemen who curled their beards and cast sidelong glances at the mestizos.

The unexpectedness of their entrance cleared the way for the Englishmen, when the halberdiers stopped them in the open space before the governor. The leader of the English prisoners, Falconer, gave a cry of surprise which was drowned in the uproar of the crowd.

Soldiers, officials, and populace, once they were sure that no more of the English dogs were in the street, gazed open-mouthed at the trio who stood calmly in the midst of the Audencia. Although armed, their weapons were sheathed, and they showed no disposition to use them. Above the confusion the voice of the English leader reached the ears of Fray Raymundo.

"I have come, señor," he began, in very fair Spanish, "to pay you a promised visit, and to see that my men whom you hold prisoners are released without ado."

Not until then did Fray Raymundo realize that before him stood the notorious El Andreque, corsair and heretic. Surely, he thought, the man was stricken with madness to come to the trial as he had done, with two companions and swords sheathed.

Only by a slight lift of the eyebrows did that astute personage, his Excellency Don Francisco de Toledo, show his astonishment and gratification.

"You come at an excellent time, Señor Andreque," he responded, his mouth twitching into a smile, "for we were sitting in judgment upon other pirates and robbers of your breed. Now it will be possible to hang seven instead of four. You remember the vow that I made after your sack of Nombre de Dios? Tomorrow it will cease to be a vow, because its purpose will be fulfilled."

El Andreque swept off his hat in a bow which would not have discredited a Spanish courtier.

"I also made a vow, señor," he said in his hearty voice, "that goads me to fulfillment. I have sworn that I would make my way to the waters of the South Sea, if I lived, and I have done so. Even have I come to your court, which, I am told, is the second richest in the world."

"As you may see," the governor swept his hand gracefully around the room, while a slight frown crossed his brow as he considered the English captain. "Yet tomorrow, I regret, señor, that you will not see it, for vultures will be pecking at your eyes, and your body will hang upon our gibbet."

Whereupon Fray Raymundo saw Falconer start forward as if to speak, being checked by a quick word from El Andreque. The two spoke together in English briefly, while his Excellency's glance wandered from one to the other and darkened when Falconer threw back his yellow head in a hearty laugh.

"You will not laugh," he said harshly, "when your bones crack in the grip of the rack tomorrow. Enough of this play, my men will see that you have good entertainment in irons and shackles. How came you here?"

"Through the courtesy of an Indian, señor," returned the visitor calmly, "who met us when we landed on the shore further south, where we learned from a tribe hostile to you that the trial was to be ended tonight, with other things. We encountered this same Indian at the outskirts of Lima, and he consented to smuggle us into an inn where the patrons were so deep in wine, they would not have noticed had we been Neptune himself. It was there I wrote my letter, a few minutes ago to advise you of my coming."

Fray Raymundo's thoughts flew to the native who had been insulted by the governor. He might well have come to the town to inform the Spaniards of the arrival of the English, being friendly to them before his encounter with the governor. After that, with a Peruvian's deep hatred of injury, he had lent his aid to El Andreque. If the priest had been able to make friends with the Indian in the tavern, different events might have followed. But God, he considered, had willed otherwise.

Meanwhile El Andreque had stepped to the side of Falconer, and drawn his sword to cut the cords which bound him, when two Spanish soldiers grasped him. At once he turned to the governor.

"Release me, señor," he cried, "and my companions, including the prisoners. God's truth, they are worthless mutineers, but they are Englishmen, and such shall not hang from a gibbet. Give us a guard of safe conduct down to the waterfront, with a pinnace to leave the shore, in order to reach our ship."

"Rather a safe conduct to the Devil and a pinnace to sail in purgatory, señor," retorted the governor. "I have no mind to release you here hence, save in that fashion."

"An' you do that," warned El Andreque, "all Lima will grieve, and your life as governor will have short shrift."

"How mean you?" questioned his Excellency, biting his beard, for he saw that there was something held back in the words of the Englishman. Yet he was surrounded by two thousand men with swords in their hands, and the corsair was distant from the town by the length of the harbor. Surely, there could be no danger from the English. The man's words were bred of madness.

El Andreque waved his hand good-naturedly. "An' you would know how matters stand," he said, "conceive that my ship has cut your craft from their moorings, and now sixteen sail are in our hands, drifted by the wind, out of the harbor. Not a vessel of size remains on the waterfront of Lima. An' you see not what this means, conceive that without ships you cannot reach another port, nor will other craft come to you, for we shall take and sink those that we meet up the coast. Lima will be barred from the rest of the world by the loss of sixteen sail, if we are not returned unharmed to my ship by dawn."

There was a stir at these words, and Fray Raymundo saw the governor's hands writhe together in anger.

"Dog!" shouted his Excellency. "Think you to deceive me with a threat? Your life will need a greater price than that. What if Lima is cut off from the outside for months? We can live. Better that than to surrender to you on such terms."

"A higher price?" smiled El Andreque. "Well, I will be generous, and give it you. The *Santa María*, with the king's treasure, is with the other ships in port, as I learned from the Indians. She is, in truth, in our hands. How like you the thought of losing the king's tax?"

The priest saw how heavy these tidings lay on his Excellency, for the *Santa María* was loaded with thousands of bars of silver. For a moment there was silence in the Audencia while the governor stared at the Englishman, and the hands of the Spanish captains itched to the swords they feared to use.

"The gun you heard," went on El Andreque, "was a signal to me that *my* ship had done what I planned. The guards of your vessels—too few, forsooth—were crowded into one galleon, and all the cables were cut. The forts on shore are helpless. They cannot see one ship from another in the darkness. In the hands of my men there is a ransom for a dozen dukes, the price of a kingdom."

His Excellency winced and shot a black look at the unfortunate customs guards.

"Our ransom, the sixteen ships, including the *Santa María*," resumed El Andreque carelessly, "will be paid, on my word, when we reach our ship. Otherwise, you will not see the ships again, and the *Santa María* will make the trip to England as a present to our sovereign lady, the queen. By my faith, King Philip will reward you well when he hears how his tax slipped through your fingers, señor."

There was a murmur of agreement from the crowd, who knew the value of the cargo of the galleon, but his Excellency bared his teeth in rage.

"Your word!" he snarled. "The word of a pirate and thief—how can I know it will be kept?"

"My faith," answered the Englishman, and Fray Raymundo marveled to see him smile, as at a good jest. "I have kept the vow I swore at Nombre de Dios, while yours has slight chance of honor. Am I not a man of my word?"

"Your life lies in my hand."

"Slight avail would it be to you, señor, if you lose all your shipping. Ships are uneasy to make from the trees on this coast, and none come from Spain."

"I could send a thousand men out in small boats to take your ship under cover of darkness. What is to prevent?"

"Naught save that there are no small boats. Pinnace and cockboat alike have been stove in by my men, save a half dozen that lay on the shore."

"The forts can fire on all the shipping in the harbor. Perchance—"

"The first ship to be sunk would be the *Santa María*, señor,"

And Fray Raymundo knew that the governor could do naught but yield his prisoners safe conduct. There were some words between the caballeros, who found the remedy not to their liking, but his Excellency waved them to silence and ordered the guards to take the English to the shore and put them in a small boat. When the tall Falconer bowed before his Excellency and said—

"I warrant your Excellency's beard is chaffed to a turn, and as for your jewels, you will know more presently."

Whereupon the English left the Audencia, making courteous farewells to the governor, and swaggering from the door. Fray Raymundo said a prayer of thanksgiving that no man had been hurt on either side, and blessed the happy chance that rid the shores of the English, and especially El Andreque.

Which ends his testimony, except for the remark that when the *Santa María* was returned to port with the other ships, when the English ship sailed the next morning, she floated strangely high in the water. Officials of his Excellency who boarded her found, pinned to the mast in the hold a receipt for two hundred and fifty thousand pounds in silver, paid by his Majesty, King Philip II of Spain, to Elizabeth, Queen of England.

Appendix

As with all Harold Lamb story collections published by Bison Books, this volume concludes with a selection of essays originally published in a letter column titled "The Camp-Fire" in *Adventure* magazine. As I have said before, Harold Lamb and other contributors frequently wrote lengthy letters that further explained some of the historical details that appeared in their stories. The relevant letters for this volume follow.

As usual, the prefatory comments of *Adventure* editor Arthur Sullivan Hoffman are also printed here, although they are slight. Prior to these letters, however, is an essay written by Hoffman himself about one of his very favorite authors, Harold Lamb. Scholar Brian Taves located this during his own researches and sent it my way some years ago. It provides us with a behind-the-scenes look at Lamb's writing process, and some of the issues he faced in selling his stories. Hoffman is often praised as an editor, and in this essay we get a glimpse of how influential he was upon Lamb's fiction.

Harold Lamb and Historical Romance*
The Career of the Author of
"The Crusades" as Seen by His Discoverer

Though of course he didn't in the least realize it himself, Harold Lamb began writing *The Crusades: Iron Men and Saints* nearly fourteen years ago. Ancient Asia had cast its spell upon him and there were already a dozen years of work and study behind him when we discussed the question of making the Crusades the subject of the book to follow *Tamerlane*.

One of his ancestors had been of the Washington Irving literary circle

---

*Reprinted from *The Bookman*, March 1930, vol. 71, no. 1.

and others had been naval men. Heredity was so strong in him that at the age of six he definitely decided to write naval stories, and when the eyesight test at Annapolis barred the Navy at first hand his resolution became the stronger. But there were Asian germs at work in him.

Back in 1917, when he was but two years out of college, there came to me, following a sea story (historical, by the way), a fiction tale about Khlit, an old Cossack of the sixteenth and seventeenth centuries, and I published it in *Adventure*. That magazine during my years as editor ran strongly to reliable historical settings for its fiction; the readers followed it with interest and they at once took Khlit to their bosoms.

For nearly eleven years there was a steady flow of stories, novelettes, and serials—fifty-two of them—all dealing with Asia of the past. There were only four laid elsewhere, and none after 1920. Asia had him. There was a dearth of sources to draw on in the English language; in addition to several European languages, he learned to read Arabic, Chinese, and a third that I've forgotten, besides something of various other Asiatic tongues, for European sources, too, were scarce and secondhand and he wanted the ultimate facts.

Khlit wandered far and wide over Asia. Later there appeared Abdul Dost, one of the Moghuls (Mongols) who conquered India, and Khlit joined him in his adventures. Genghis Khan and Tamerlane themselves stalked, living, through the pages of his stories. Later there came a Cossack, Ayub, under Boris Godunov, with his grandfather Khlit riding sturdily alongside. John Paul Jones leaped into the procession—did you, good American, know that he died serving Catherine the Great as admiral on the Black Sea against the Turks? Harold Lamb was the first to bring this episode into English fiction. Prester John and Stenka Razin, Persian, Arab, Rajput, Lap, Buriat, Tibetan, Armenian, Georgian, Mongol, and scores of others from all parts and many centuries of Asia brought each his share of Asia's history into Mr. Lamb's stories.

In 1926 he took the rather inchoate mass of the *Babar Nameh* (The Book of the Tiger), and condensed its 160,000 words into a smooth-flowing narrative of 22,000. It is the actual autobiography of Babar, Moghul (Turco-Mongol) conqueror of India, a great-great-grandson of Tamerlane, acknowledged by European scholars as deserving a place beside the confessions of Rousseau and Cellini, yet practically unknown in this country. Mr. Lamb was the first to make it available as a continuous, unified narrative.

For eleven years before he wrote *Genghis Khan* he lived with these people, saturated himself with their histories and civilizations, the homely details of their daily lives. Always he was the scholar first, the good fictionist second. Rarely did a story appear without his historian's letter of comment for the magazine's department in which the authors chatted with the readers—letters meticulous as to every least variation from established historical fact, carefully balanced, ripe, fairly bursting with intimate knowledge of the broad and only partially explored field that had become his specialty. And very human letters—it was not dry bones and dusty records that interested him; he wanted to find out what kind of men these had been and what manner of life they led. In the beginning he couldn't. Nobody else had; there was no one to whom he could turn. He must pioneer. So he pioneered. And when Harold Lamb sets himself to a task it gets done. Concentration? Thoroughness? Gentle persistence? Irresistible driving power? Harold Lamb. The task, while a stupendous labor, was in this case only a joyful obsession. He writes me from Rome, busily at work on the second volume of *The Crusades*:

> The work here is devilish—the Crusades loom up like a sea that drowns a chap—the mass of evidence buried in hundreds of old Latin records is appalling, and the controversies are frightful. I'm having a bully time.

But during the eleven years of the fifty-two pieces of fiction he was accomplishing much more than the building of broad, strong foundations as a historian. He was learning, through fiction, to make the ancient peoples as living, breathing, and human to readers as they were to him.

The road was not easy going. Aside from the one magazine there was no market for these stories—one of those curious editorial stone walls standing across his path. "Mongols and such? Nobody writes about them; therefore nobody wants to read about them. Historical stuff, anyhow, and costume fiction is out of fashion now." The dictum was the harder to bear because he knew that people did like to read about "Mongols and such" if they were the right kind of Mongols and such. The popularity of his stories with the magazine's readers had been proving that to him for years and, later, the longer ones of these same stories, like *White Falcon* and *The House of the Falcon*, were to prove it still further in book form—not to mention the three books that have swept him into his place as a historian who is an acknowledged authority on both sides of the Atlantic and who can make his history as interesting as the most colorful fiction.

But through those eleven years that stone wall stood, and there came a time when he questioned the sense of going on with the only kind of writing into which he could put his whole heart—questioned even his right to do so. He sent me the outline of a purely conventional story of the type that most magazines will buy and I sent it back to him saying that thousands could do this kind of thing but that his own particular kind of work had never been done before, urging him to go ahead. I think his dogged fighting spirit needed no more than the reassurance of a single person in the "writing game" who saw things as he did. There was nothing from then on but steady plugging at his chosen work.

But there *had* been no mention of the Crusades. That idea, too, had been building up in him for a dozen years. In his stories there appeared with increasing frequency some "Krit," some Christian, based on the historical and much earlier but unsung Marco Polos who, by adventure more tremendous than can exist today, found themselves alone among peoples no more than myths to Europeans, their very names perhaps unknown. Several of these were Crusaders. The Mongols swept through Armenia, Georgia, and past Constantinople, crushed back the Mameluke foes of the Franks in the Holy Land, established themselves east of the Crusader strongholds, and of course Mr. Lamb went with them. The world-smashing of Genghis Khan brought about an intercourse between Europe and the East that had never before existed, so more and more Mr. Lamb met Europeans as he lived the centuries among his Asiatics. And a forefront of that Europe was Palestine, with the Crusaders finally entrenched there. More and more his interest drifted toward these European contacts on the west.

The notable fact, of course, is that he came to the subject of the Crusades from the Asiatic instead of the European point of view, one from the Western world looking with the eyes of one living for generations among those of the world to the East, and chiefly from the point of view of the Mongols, to whom both Christian and Moslem were foreigners in race and religion. An enviable approach for the historian.

When I talked to him just before he sailed for the libraries in Rome and elsewhere and for a personal examination of the scenes most involved in Crusade activity, he was keenly alive to the advantages of his position and to the opportunity it offered, but at least two years before *Genghis Khan* appeared that opportunity was beckoning him on. In a letter to readers he wrote:

> Our existing stock of histories of the Crusades is unfortunate. The
> early stock was taken from the main Church chronicles and consisted

of a lot of silence and a great deal of fanfare exaggerating the deeds of the Croises. *Then appeared the cynical history, making much hay of the fact that the Crusaders usually fought a losing fight and were sometimes the very opposite of saints. Lastly the ultra-modern history has cropped up, making much of the superstition and ignorance of the Crusaders and tracing out with great pains the "advantages" of the Crusades in establishing contact between the East and West, introducing Asia's inventions into Europe, etc.*

In decrying the exaltation of the Crusaders and in hunting out the mercantile gains from their efforts and deaths, we have somehow rather lost sight of the intimate personal story of the Crusaders—which a reading of the Arab chronicles serves to bring back to us.

So much of our history and biography and fiction, too, has been written out of prejudice or a preconceived bias. "Catherine the Great was one of the most gifted women of all time" vs. "Catherine the Great was one of the greatest wantons of all time." "Alexander of Macedonia was a superman" vs. "Alexander was mad." You know how these things shape up.

Nowadays one cannot enter a bookshop without seeing on all sides "The Truth About This" or "Outlines of That." The desire of readers to learn is real enough. The fault is with the writers, who lack both scholarship and inclination to devote months or years to finding out the truth as nearly as possible. The result is that the very modern histories are usually "outlines" right enough.

Scholarship seems to have died in the last century. Anyway, I'll wager you can't name a better story of the Crusades than Scott's The Talisman. *Sir Walter admitted that he wrote from meager information—there was little to be had in his day—but he was a scholar and a conscientious student of his epoch.*

History, our dictionaries say, is "a narrative devoted to the exposition of the unfolding of events." Discarding this husk of Latin phrasing the dictionary says that history is the story of what actually happened. By the way, it's interesting to notice that the dictionary ranks fiction equally with chronicle. And "unfolding" is just the word. What is history but the uncovering or unfolding of the past? The story of what certain men did—their adventures—because it's more interesting to read about what they did than what they were. And easier to get at the truth that way.

It's so absurd to sit down and start in to whitewash some individual or people and call it history. And equally absurd to assemble a few facts and draw personal conclusions from them without taking the trouble to get at all *the facts.*

This is beginning to wander. But it's so tiresome to look for history in many modern publications and find only personal opinions, deductions, vilification or deification, and references to faulty authorities. And so many modern "historical" novels, written by hasty

> *Americans, are enough to make Sienkiewicz and Tolstoy walk the*
> *earth again.*
>
> *Getting back to our Arab again—it's been awfully refreshing to*
> *read about the Crusaders from Arabic sources. But "The Shield" is*
> *not a story of the Crusades—the* Croises *figure only in the taking of*
> *Constantinople. . . . Also an Arab story to the effect that the sword*
> *of Roland—Durandal—was taken by the* saracins, *after the death of*
> *the hero, and hidden away in Asia Minor. So I'm thinking of a second*
> *tale, dealing with the search for the sword by a Crusader.*

It is the scholar speaking, the very human but very scholarly scholar to whom anything less than the utmost nicety in accuracy, thoroughness, and everlasting allegiance to the real truth of the facts is anathema. He can be satisfied only when he has ferreted out the last attainable fact and, with scrupulous justice and unprejudiced mind, weighed it out to its last atom of significance. Upon the road to the truth Harold Lamb is a juggernaut to all that stands in his way or crosses his path.

But the hands on the controls of the juggernaut car are very kindly and human hands and the truth he insists upon finding is the human truth, not the mere dry clatter of statistics and facts of record. He wants to know "what kind of people they were," to meet them as humans. And, when he has learned to know them as living beings, his long fiction training enables him to pass them on to us, colorful, alive, real. The years of work have borne their fruit.

A recent letter from Rome throws a good deal of light:

> *I'm more than one-half drunk with color and memory of the long trips*
> *through the Constantinople region, and—just back from there—Rho-*
> *des, Cyprus, Syria, Palestine. Camped among the Arabs for weeks,*
> *going from one Crusader's castle to another, and I've never known*
> *an experience quite like that. In the interior the country and people*
> *are little changed since the medieval days, and the great citadels are*
> *finer than anything in France. It does grip the imagination.*

Imagination and enthusiasm. Add these to the other qualities and we understand why *The Crusades* is such wholly enjoyable reading as well as being a distinguished contribution to authoritative history.

October 10, 1924: "Forward!"

Something from Harold Lamb in connection with his novelette in this issue:

> I have followed the military and naval ranking as it was in Russia,
> 1788. The naval branch of the service was new, comparatively, and

under the despotism of Catherine the Great queer grades were bestowed. The shipwrights on the Black Sea—the leaders, at least—were given commissions in some regiment of hussars. And wore the uniforms of hussars!

John Paul Jones was originally offered the rating of captain-commandant, which meant very little. He stipulated that he should have the rank of rear-admiral and got it.

He ranked every Russian and foreign officer in the Black Sea except the field Marshal, in command of all operations, and possibly Admiral Mordvinoff, who had the Crimea Fleet.

But, secretly, equal authority was given Nassau-Siegen; and the Prussian ultimately claimed credit for everything that Jones did.

Every principal character in the story is historical. The conspiracy is fact. Nassau's plot is fact. It ultimately did much to discredit Jones with Catherine. Actually, this took place after Jones's return from the Black Sea, and at his quarters in Petersburg. I have used it to show the kind of opposition Jones faced.

I have colored up the actual conspiracy against him, and the events of his journey from Petersburg to Kherson are imaginary. Nassau never came to drawn swords with Jones, but his cowardly and bitter enmity is quite in keeping with the incident in the story.

Jones's daring reconnaissance of the Turkish fleet is fact. Nassau figured in a second trip. I have put them together in the first venture. Ivak's account of the strange and unheard-of method of scouting used by Jones follows the story pretty closely. It is given in the Bibliotekia dlia Tchtenia, and written by a Captain K. A translation can be found in De Koven's *Life and Letters of John Paul Jones.*

Captain K. relates that he came across an old Cossack living near the Danube who related this story, and showed him the dagger, the gift of Paul Jones. The story struck my fancy and "Forward!" is the result.

As a matter of fact, the actual events—even to the *tarantass* and Paul Jones's position toward it—and the personalities of the people are followed very closely.

Ivak's habit of alluding to Jones as John Paul may strike you as curious, but the Russians habitually called people by their first names, and usually affixed some Cossack term of liking or disliking. Instead of General Suvarof, Ivak would have said "Little father Michael."

Jones incidentally, never shirked a duel.

November 20, 1924: "The Sword of Honor"

Something from Harold Lamb about his story in this issue:

Berkeley, California.

So far as the undersigned knows, the yarn of Paul Jones's last sea fight has never been spun—in fiction in this country. There were reasons.

The events of the story follow history closely; with the exception of Pierre Pillon, Kalil, and one or two minor characters, these people all lived and took part in the events in the Black Sea. The characters of Prince Potemkin, Nassau, and Alexiano are not overdrawn.

Paul Jones's service in Russia and the Black Sea is significant. It represents the first experience of an American—a citizen of the United States—in the old world. Paul Jones was the first of the brood of our youngsters to adventure "East." Before this the tide had set the other way; men from the old world tackling the unknown in the new.

About the Author

Harold Lamb (1892–1962) was born in Alpine, New Jersey, the son of Eliza Rollinson and Frederick Lamb, a renowned stained-glass designer, painter, and writer. Lamb later described himself as having been born with damaged eyes, ears, and speech, adding that by adulthood these problems had mostly righted themselves. He was never very comfortable in crowds or cities, and found school "a torment." He had two main refuges when growing up—his grandfather's library and the outdoors. Lamb loved tennis and played the game well into his later years.

Lamb attended Columbia, where he first dug into the histories of Eastern civilizations, ever after his lifelong fascination. He served briefly in World War I as an infantryman but saw no action. In 1917 he married Ruth Barbour, and by all accounts their marriage was a long and happy one. They had two children, Frederick and Cary. Arthur Sullivan Hoffman, the chief editor of *Adventure* magazine, recognized Lamb's storytelling skills and encouraged him to write about the subjects he most loved. For the next twenty years or so, historical fiction set in the remote East flowed from Lamb's pen, and he quickly became one of *Adventure*'s most popular writers. Lamb did not stop with fiction, however, and soon began to draft biographies and screenplays. By the time the pulp magazine market dried up, Lamb was an established and recognized historian, and for the rest of his life he produced respected biographies and histories, earning numerous awards, including one from the Persian government for his two-volume history of the Crusades.

Lamb knew many languages: by his own account, French, Latin, ancient Persian, some Arabic, a smattering of Turkish, a bit of Manchu-Tatar, and medieval Ukrainian. He traveled throughout Asia, visiting most of the places he wrote about, and during World War II he was on covert assignment overseas for the U.S. government. He is remembered today both for his scholarly histories and for his swashbuckling tales of daring Cossacks and crusaders. "Life is good, after all," Lamb once wrote, "when a man can go where he wants to, and write about what he likes best."